CAMP SPIRIT

AXELLE LENOIR

+

COLORS BY
CAB

CAMP SPIRIT © 2020 AXELLE LENOIR

Published by Top Shelf Productions, PO Box 1282, Marietta, GA 30061-1282,
USA. Top Shelf Productions is an imprint of IDW Publishing, a division of Idea
and Design Works, LLC. Offices: 2765 Truxtun Road, San Diego, CA 92106. Top
Shelf Productions®, the Top Shelf logo, Idea and Design Works®, and the
IDW logo are registered trademarks of Idea and Design Works, LLC. All Rights
Reserved. With the exception of small excerpts of artwork used for review
purposes, none of the contents of this publication may be reprinted without
the permission of IDW Publishing. IDW Publishing does not read or accept
unsolicited submissions of ideas, stories or artwork. Printed in Korea.

Editor-in-Chief: Chris Staros.
Edited by Chris Staros and Leigh Walton.
Design by Gilberto Lazcano.
Colors by Cab.
Originally published by Studio Lounak as *L'Esprit du camp*.
Translation by Pablo Strauss and Aleshia Jensen.
Special thanks to Mike Pfeiffer for lyrical assistance.

ISBN: 978-1-60309-465-8   23 22 21 20   4 3 2 1

Visit our online catalog at topshelfcomix.com.

CAMP SPIRIT

AXELLE LENOIR

+

COLORS BY CAB

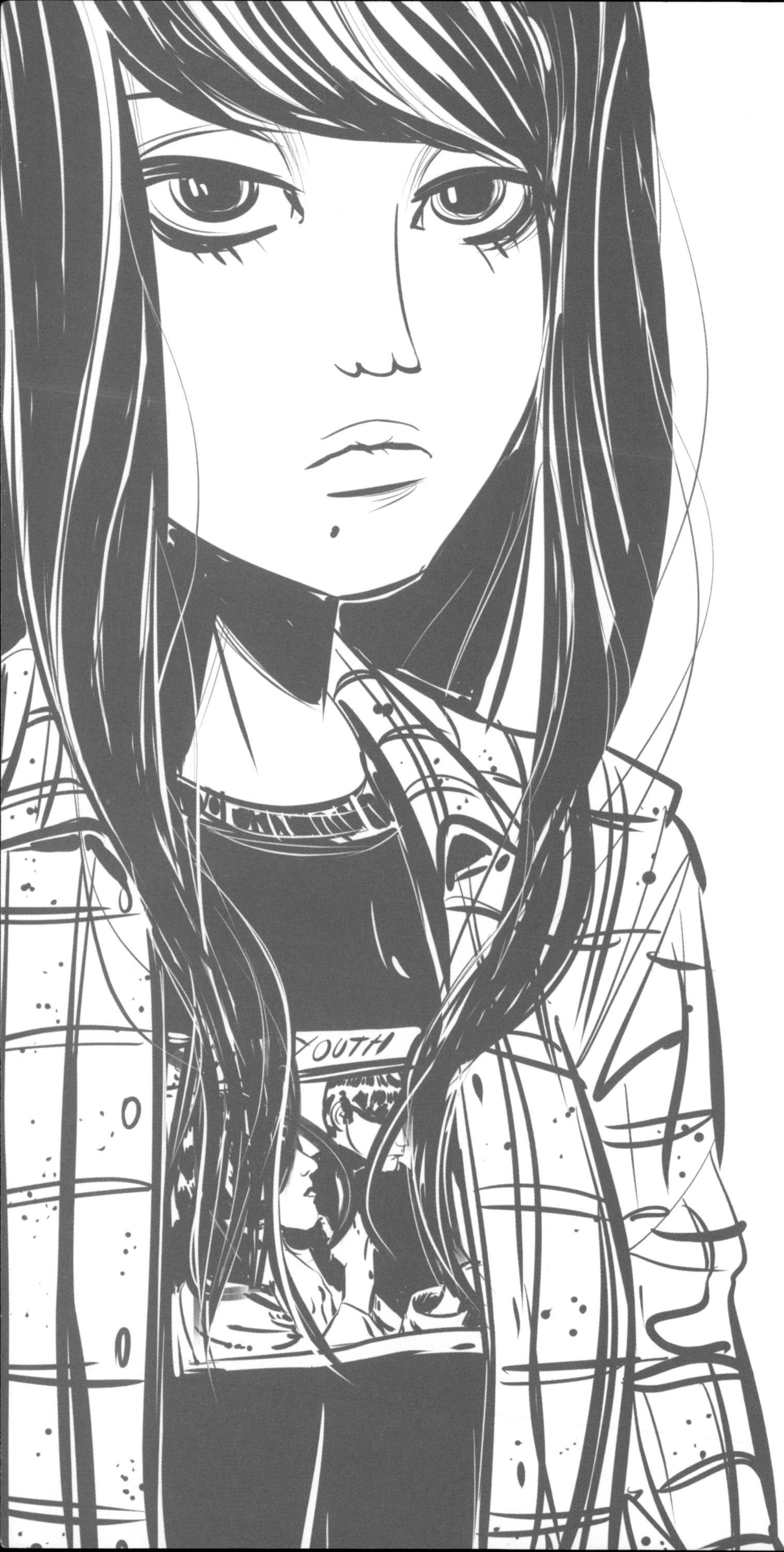
YOUTH

1

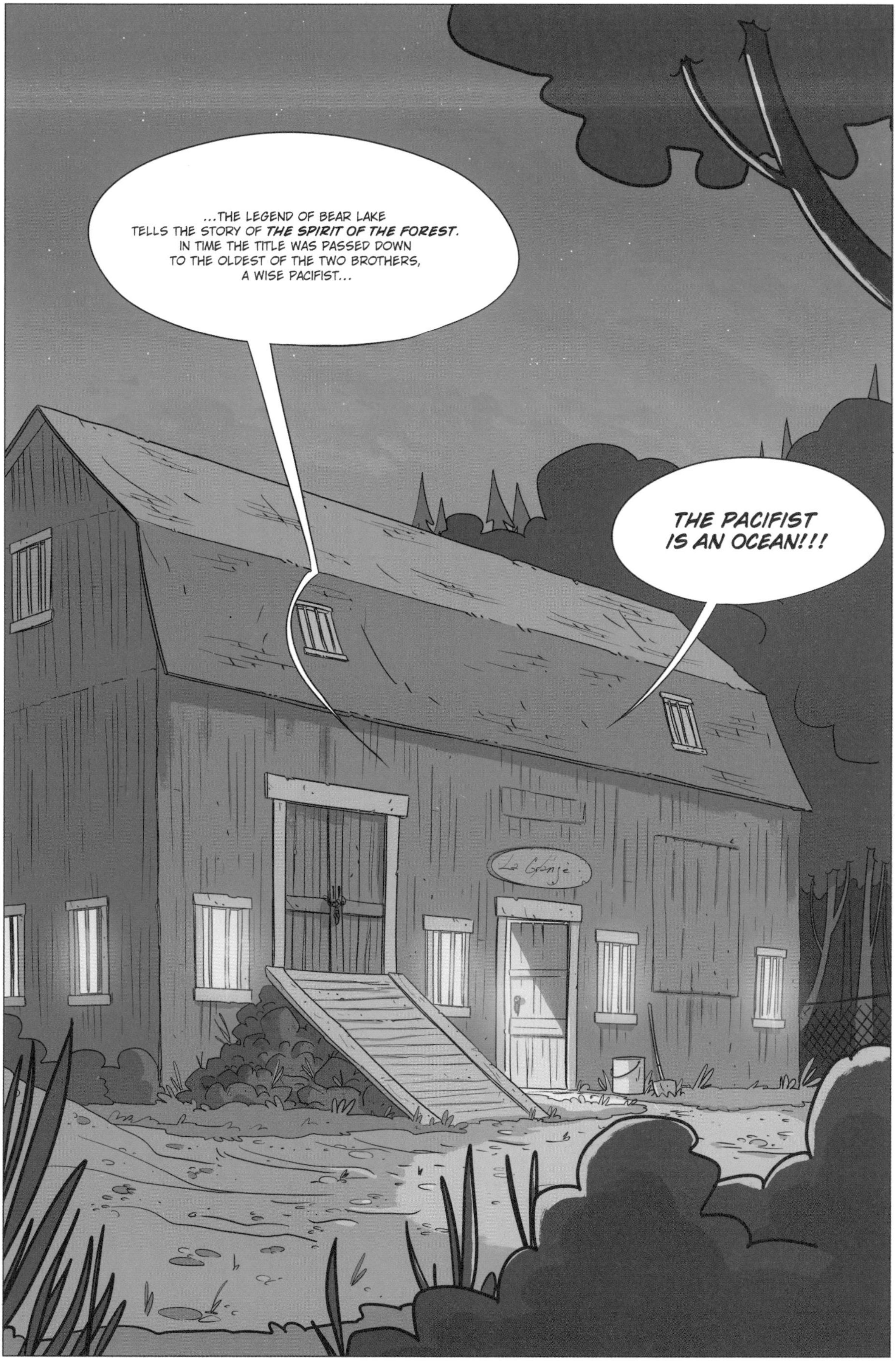
...THE LEGEND OF BEAR LAKE TELLS THE STORY OF *THE SPIRIT OF THE FOREST*. IN TIME THE TITLE WAS PASSED DOWN TO THE OLDEST OF THE TWO BROTHERS, A WISE PACIFIST...
THE PACIFIST IS AN OCEAN!!!

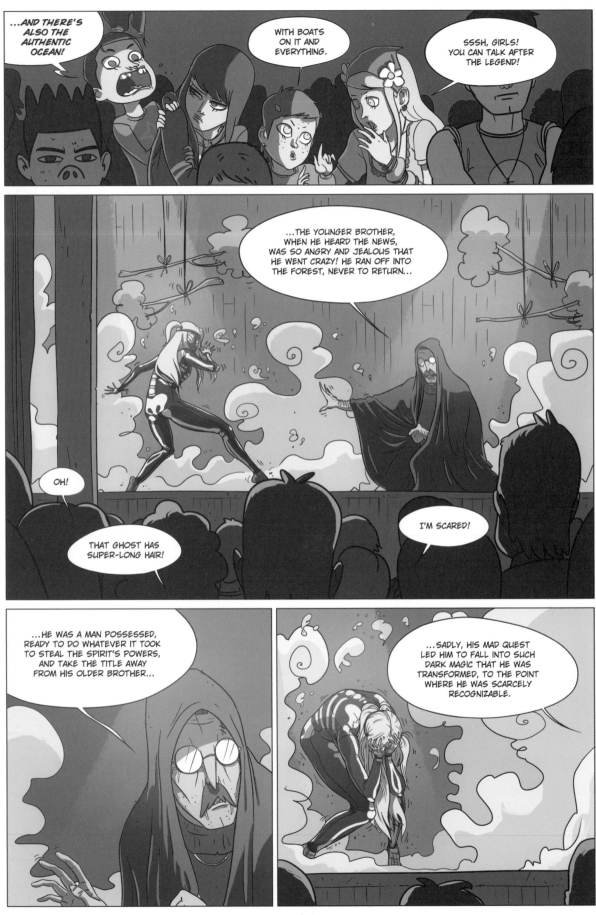

...AND THERE'S ALSO THE AUTHENTIC OCEAN!

WITH BOATS ON IT AND EVERYTHING.

SSSH, GIRLS! YOU CAN TALK AFTER THE LEGEND!

...THE YOUNGER BROTHER, WHEN HE HEARD THE NEWS, WAS SO ANGRY AND JEALOUS THAT HE WENT CRAZY! HE RAN OFF INTO THE FOREST, NEVER TO RETURN...

OH!

THAT GHOST HAS SUPER-LONG HAIR!

I'M SCARED!

...HE WAS A MAN POSSESSED, READY TO DO WHATEVER IT TOOK TO STEAL THE SPIRIT'S POWERS, AND TAKE THE TITLE AWAY FROM HIS OLDER BROTHER...

...SADLY, HIS MAD QUEST LED HIM TO FALL INTO SUCH DARK MAGIC THAT HE WAS TRANSFORMED, TO THE POINT WHERE HE WAS SCARCELY RECOGNIZABLE.

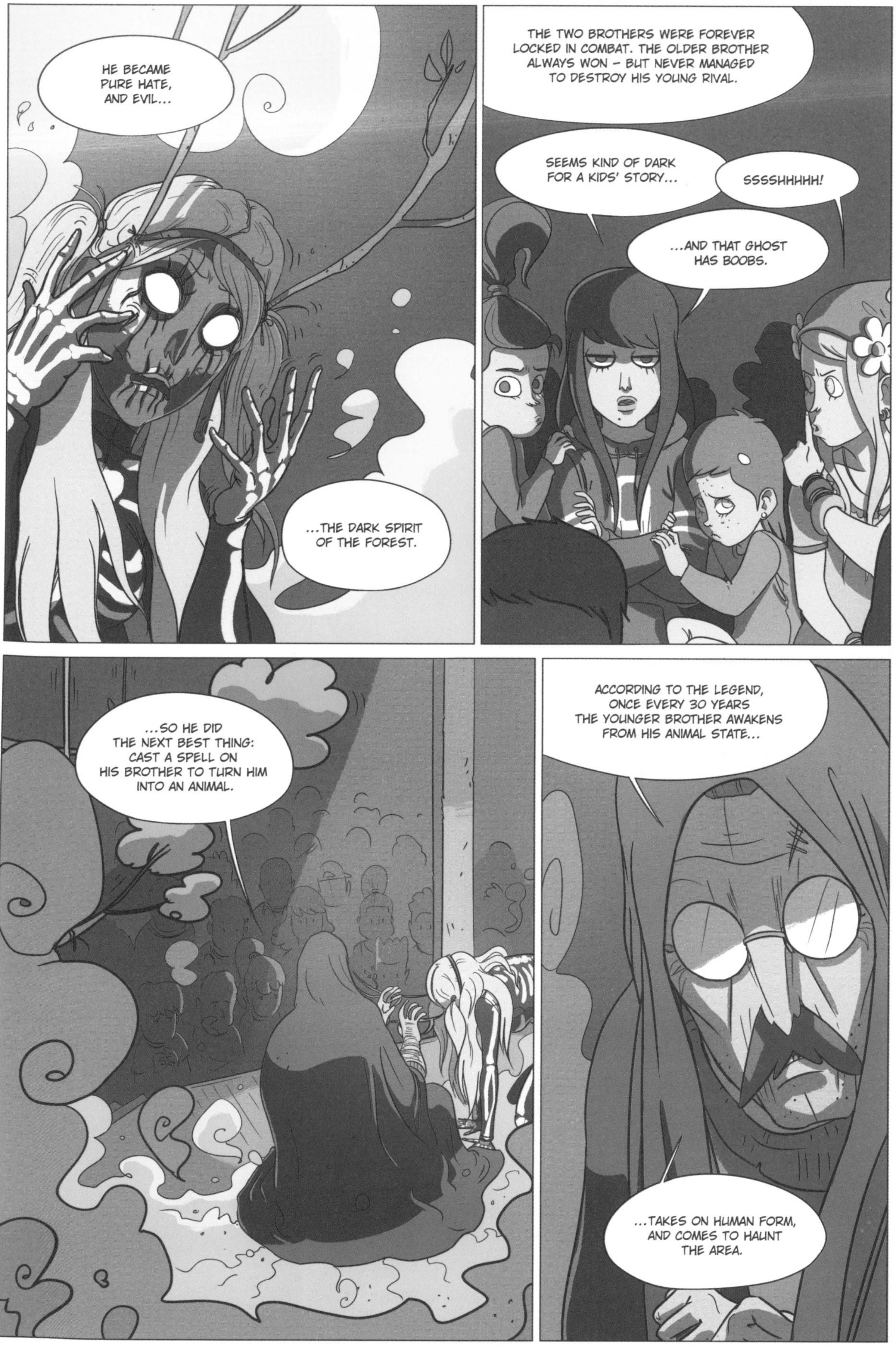
HE BECAME PURE HATE, AND EVIL...
...THE DARK SPIRIT OF THE FOREST.
THE TWO BROTHERS WERE FOREVER LOCKED IN COMBAT. THE OLDER BROTHER ALWAYS WON – BUT NEVER MANAGED TO DESTROY HIS YOUNG RIVAL.
SEEMS KIND OF DARK FOR A KIDS' STORY...
SSSSHHHHH!
...AND THAT GHOST HAS BOOBS.
...SO HE DID THE NEXT BEST THING: CAST A SPELL ON HIS BROTHER TO TURN HIM INTO AN ANIMAL.
ACCORDING TO THE LEGEND, ONCE EVERY 30 YEARS THE YOUNGER BROTHER AWAKENS FROM HIS ANIMAL STATE...
...TAKES ON HUMAN FORM, AND COMES TO HAUNT THE AREA.

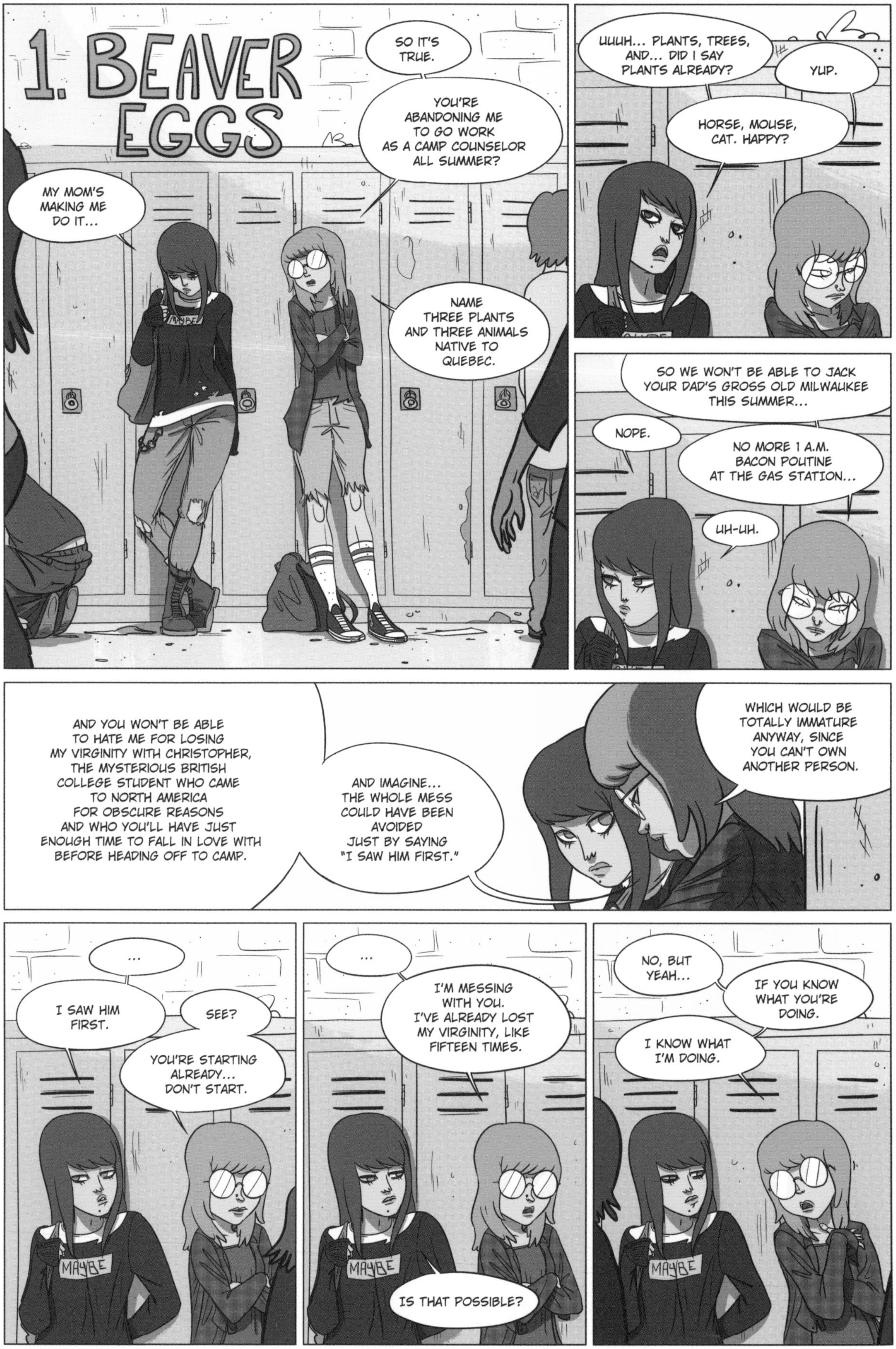
1. BEAVER EGGS
SO IT'S TRUE.
YOU'RE ABANDONING ME TO GO WORK AS A CAMP COUNSELOR ALL SUMMER?
MY MOM'S MAKING ME DO IT...
NAME THREE PLANTS AND THREE ANIMALS NATIVE TO QUEBEC.
MAYBE
UUUH... PLANTS, TREES, AND... DID I SAY PLANTS ALREADY?
YUP.
HORSE, MOUSE, CAT. HAPPY?
SO WE WON'T BE ABLE TO JACK YOUR DAD'S GROSS OLD MILWAUKEE THIS SUMMER...
NOPE.
NO MORE 1 A.M. BACON POUTINE AT THE GAS STATION...
UH-UH.
AND YOU WON'T BE ABLE TO HATE ME FOR LOSING MY VIRGINITY WITH CHRISTOPHER, THE MYSTERIOUS BRITISH COLLEGE STUDENT WHO CAME TO NORTH AMERICA FOR OBSCURE REASONS AND WHO YOU'LL HAVE JUST ENOUGH TIME TO FALL IN LOVE WITH BEFORE HEADING OFF TO CAMP.
AND IMAGINE... THE WHOLE MESS COULD HAVE BEEN AVOIDED JUST BY SAYING "I SAW HIM FIRST."
WHICH WOULD BE TOTALLY IMMATURE ANYWAY, SINCE YOU CAN'T OWN ANOTHER PERSON.
...
I SAW HIM FIRST.
SEE?
YOU'RE STARTING ALREADY... DON'T START.
MAYBE
...
I'M MESSING WITH YOU. I'VE ALREADY LOST MY VIRGINITY, LIKE FIFTEEN TIMES.
MAYBE
IS THAT POSSIBLE?
NO, BUT YEAH...
IF YOU KNOW WHAT YOU'RE DOING.
I KNOW WHAT I'M DOING.
MAYBE

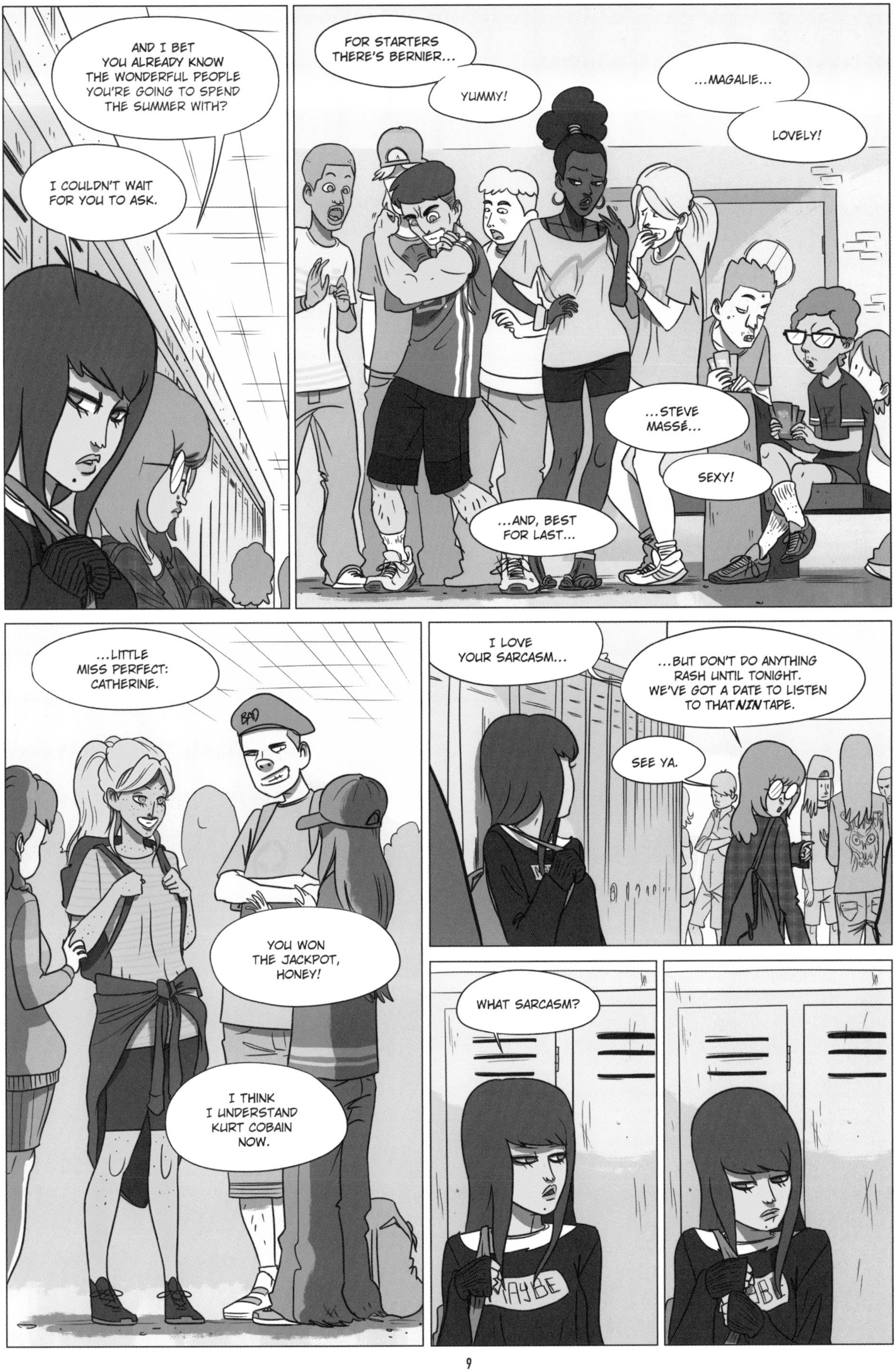
AND I BET YOU ALREADY KNOW THE WONDERFUL PEOPLE YOU'RE GOING TO SPEND THE SUMMER WITH?
I COULDN'T WAIT FOR YOU TO ASK.
FOR STARTERS THERE'S BERNIER...
YUMMY!
...MAGALIE...
LOVELY!
...STEVE MASSÉ...
SEXY!
...AND, BEST FOR LAST...
...LITTLE MISS PERFECT: CATHERINE.
BAD
YOU WON THE JACKPOT, HONEY!
I THINK I UNDERSTAND KURT COBAIN NOW.
I LOVE YOUR SARCASM...
...BUT DON'T DO ANYTHING RASH UNTIL TONIGHT. WE'VE GOT A DATE TO LISTEN TO THAT ***NIN*** TAPE.
SEE YA.
WHAT SARCASM?
MAYBE

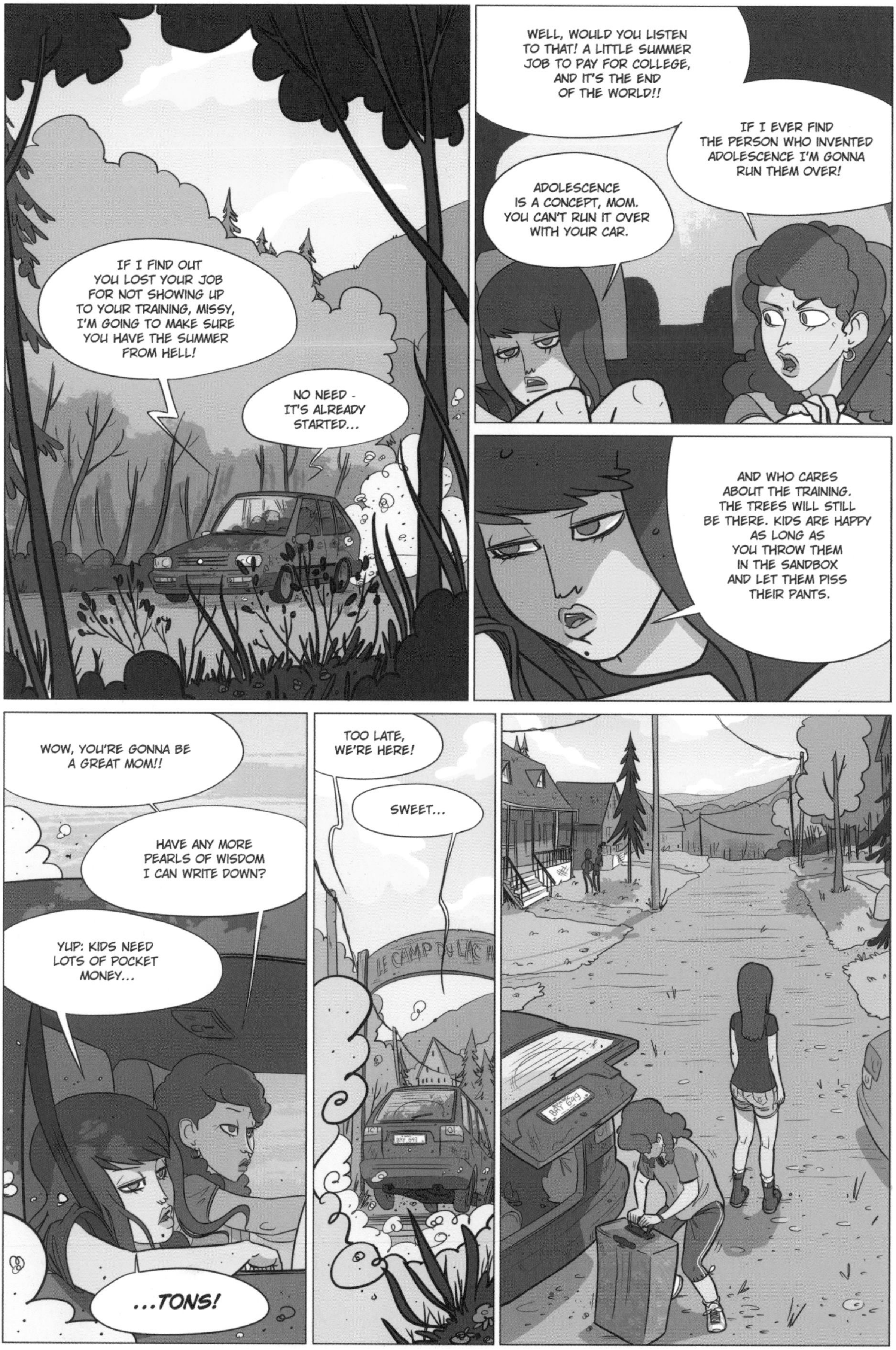
IF I FIND OUT YOU LOST YOUR JOB FOR NOT SHOWING UP TO YOUR TRAINING, MISSY, I'M GOING TO MAKE SURE YOU HAVE THE SUMMER FROM HELL!
NO NEED - IT'S ALREADY STARTED...
WELL, WOULD YOU LISTEN TO THAT! A LITTLE SUMMER JOB TO PAY FOR COLLEGE, AND IT'S THE END OF THE WORLD!!
ADOLESCENCE IS A CONCEPT, MOM. YOU CAN'T RUN IT OVER WITH YOUR CAR.
IF I EVER FIND THE PERSON WHO INVENTED ADOLESCENCE I'M GONNA RUN THEM OVER!
AND WHO CARES ABOUT THE TRAINING. THE TREES WILL STILL BE THERE. KIDS ARE HAPPY AS LONG AS YOU THROW THEM IN THE SANDBOX AND LET THEM PISS THEIR PANTS.
WOW, YOU'RE GONNA BE A GREAT MOM!!
HAVE ANY MORE PEARLS OF WISDOM I CAN WRITE DOWN?
YUP: KIDS NEED LOTS OF POCKET MONEY...
...TONS!
TOO LATE, WE'RE HERE!
SWEET...
LE CAMP DU LAC A
BAY 649
BAY 649

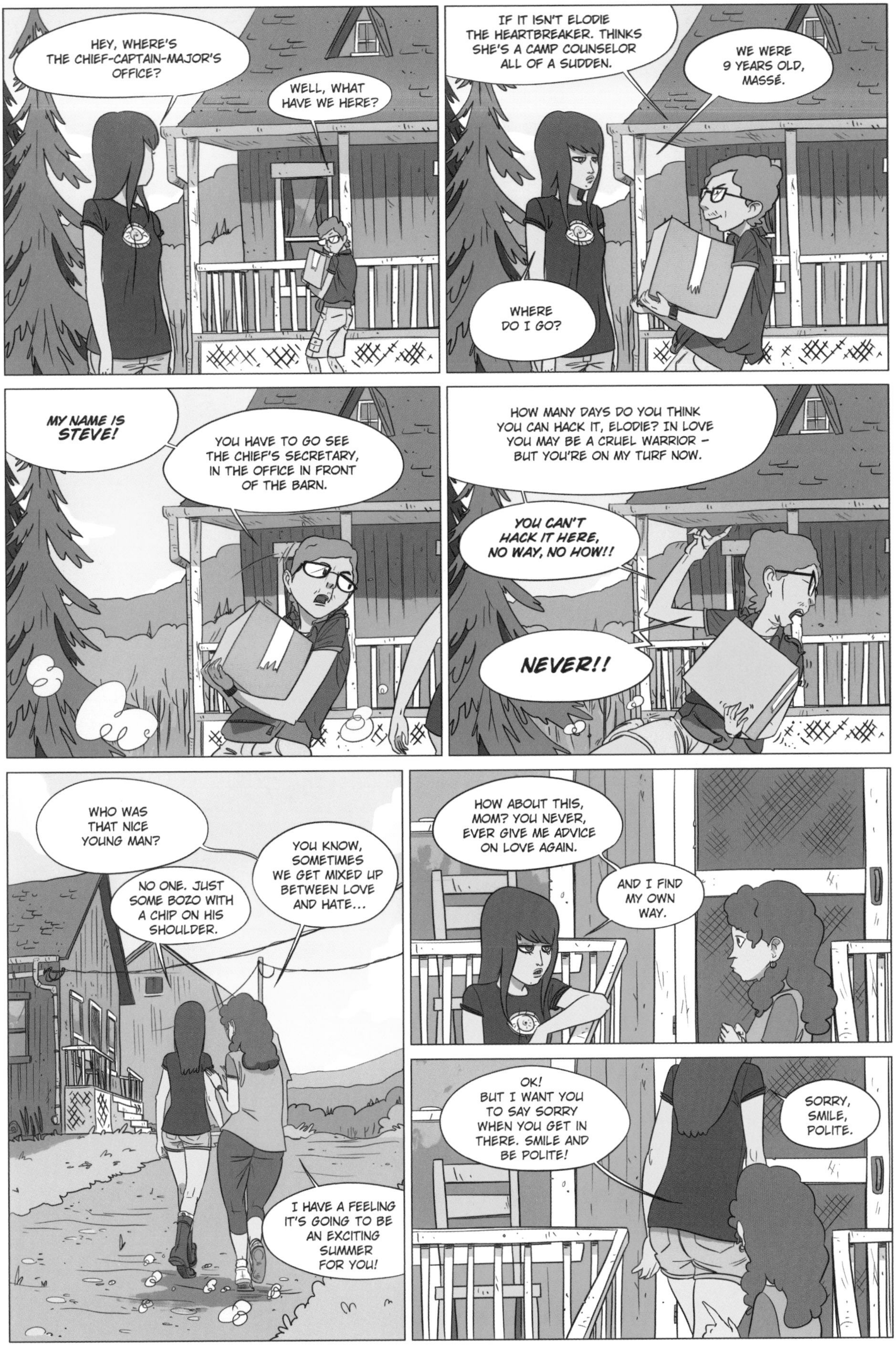
HEY, WHERE'S THE CHIEF-CAPTAIN-MAJOR'S OFFICE?
WELL, WHAT HAVE WE HERE?
IF IT ISN'T ELODIE THE HEARTBREAKER. THINKS SHE'S A CAMP COUNSELOR ALL OF A SUDDEN.
WE WERE 9 YEARS OLD, MASSÉ.
WHERE DO I GO?
MY NAME IS STEVE!
YOU HAVE TO GO SEE THE CHIEF'S SECRETARY, IN THE OFFICE IN FRONT OF THE BARN.
HOW MANY DAYS DO YOU THINK YOU CAN HACK IT, ELODIE? IN LOVE YOU MAY BE A CRUEL WARRIOR – BUT YOU'RE ON MY TURF NOW.
YOU CAN'T HACK IT HERE, NO WAY, NO HOW!!
NEVER!!
WHO WAS THAT NICE YOUNG MAN?
NO ONE. JUST SOME BOZO WITH A CHIP ON HIS SHOULDER.
YOU KNOW, SOMETIMES WE GET MIXED UP BETWEEN LOVE AND HATE...
I HAVE A FEELING IT'S GOING TO BE AN EXCITING SUMMER FOR YOU!
HOW ABOUT THIS, MOM? YOU NEVER, EVER GIVE ME ADVICE ON LOVE AGAIN.
AND I FIND MY OWN WAY.
OK! BUT I WANT YOU TO SAY SORRY WHEN YOU GET IN THERE. SMILE AND BE POLITE!
SORRY, SMILE, POLITE.

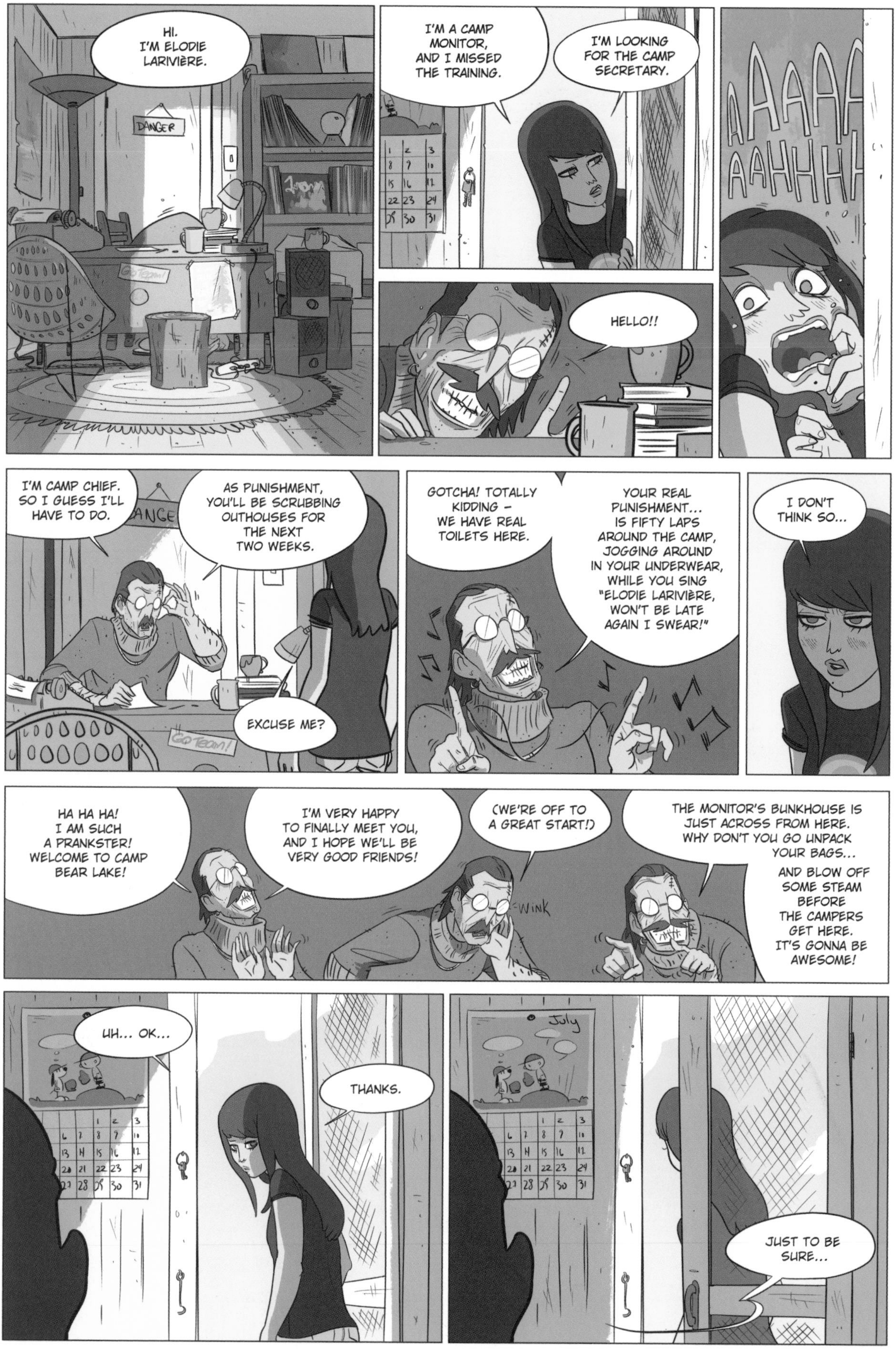
HI.
I'M ELODIE LARIVIÈRE.
DANGER
I'M A CAMP MONITOR, AND I MISSED THE TRAINING.
I'M LOOKING FOR THE CAMP SECRETARY.
AAAAAAHHHHH
HELLO!!
I'M CAMP CHIEF. SO I GUESS I'LL HAVE TO DO.
AS PUNISHMENT, YOU'LL BE SCRUBBING OUTHOUSES FOR THE NEXT TWO WEEKS.
EXCUSE ME?
GO TEAM!
GOTCHA! TOTALLY KIDDING – WE HAVE REAL TOILETS HERE.
YOUR REAL PUNISHMENT... IS FIFTY LAPS AROUND THE CAMP, JOGGING AROUND IN YOUR UNDERWEAR, WHILE YOU SING "ELODIE LARIVIÈRE, WON'T BE LATE AGAIN I SWEAR!"
I DON'T THINK SO...
HA HA HA! I AM SUCH A PRANKSTER! WELCOME TO CAMP BEAR LAKE!
I'M VERY HAPPY TO FINALLY MEET YOU, AND I HOPE WE'LL BE VERY GOOD FRIENDS!
(WE'RE OFF TO A GREAT START!)
WINK
THE MONITOR'S BUNKHOUSE IS JUST ACROSS FROM HERE. WHY DON'T YOU GO UNPACK YOUR BAGS...
AND BLOW OFF SOME STEAM BEFORE THE CAMPERS GET HERE. IT'S GONNA BE AWESOME!
UH... OK...
THANKS.
July
JUST TO BE SURE...

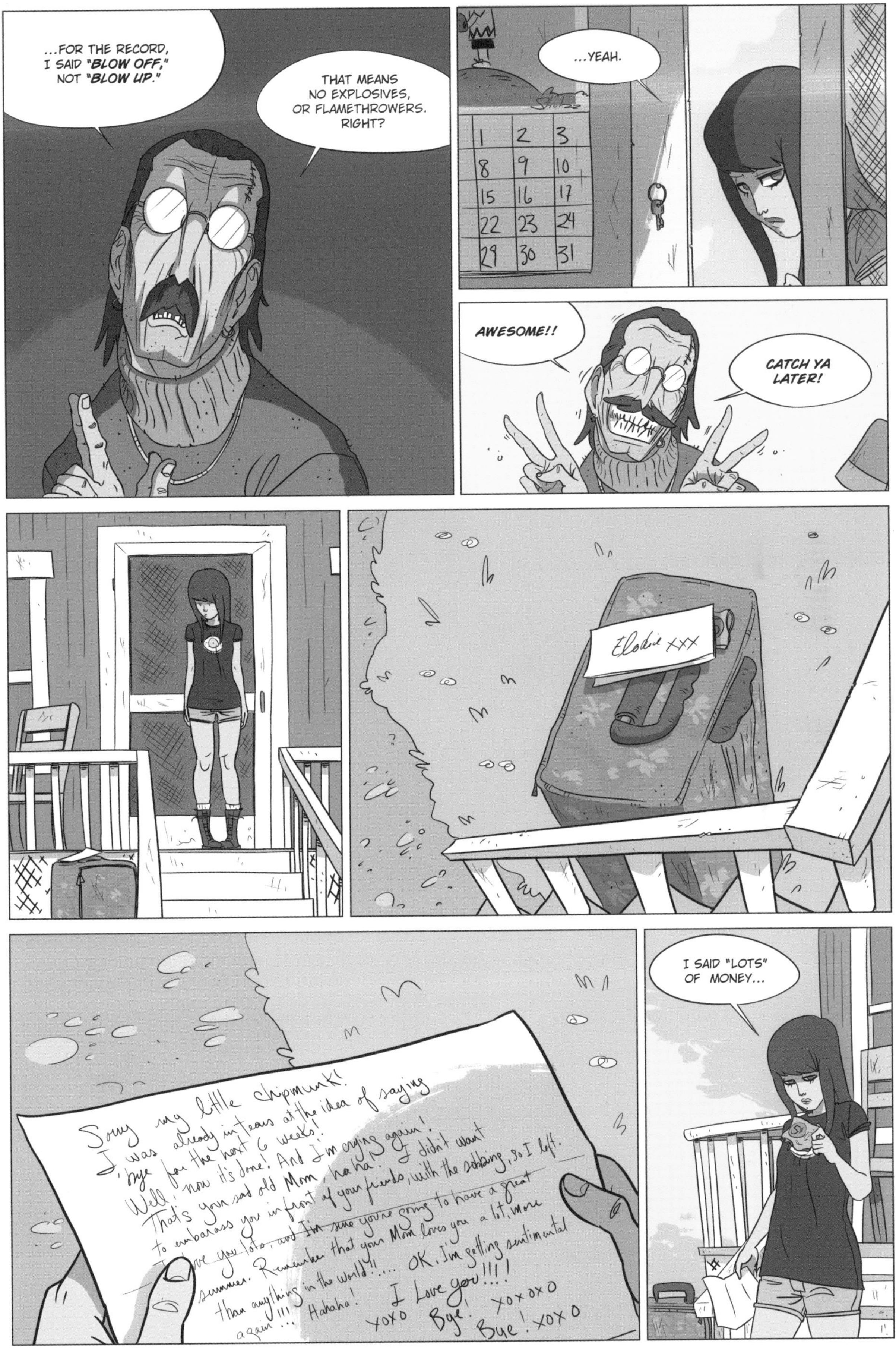

...FOR THE RECORD, I SAID "BLOW OFF," NOT "BLOW UP."
THAT MEANS NO EXPLOSIVES, OR FLAMETHROWERS. RIGHT?
...YEAH.
AWESOME!!
CATCH YA LATER!
Elodie xxx
Sorry my little chipmunk!
I was already in tears at the idea of saying
'bye for the next 6 weeks!
Well! now it's done! And I'm crying again!
That's your sad old Mom, haha! I didn't want
to embarass you in front of your friends, with the sobbing, so I left.
ve you lots, and I'm sure you're going to have a great
summer. Remember that your Mom loves you a lot, more
than anything in the world!!.... OK, I'm getting sentimental
again!!!... Hahaha! I Love you!!!!
xoxo Bye! xoxoxo
Bye! xoxo
I SAID "LOTS" OF MONEY...

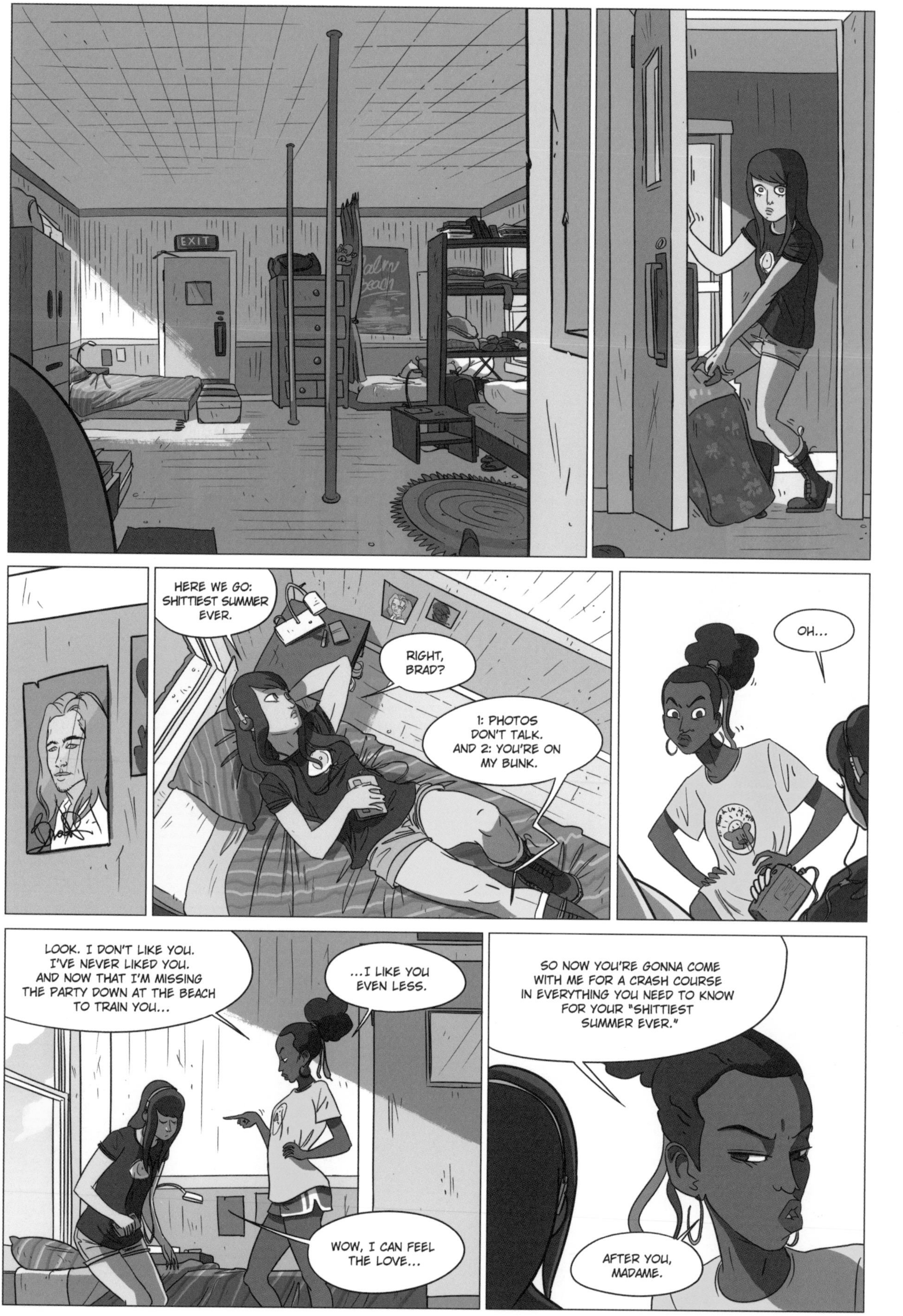
EXIT
HERE WE GO: SHITTIEST SUMMER EVER.
RIGHT, BRAD?
1: PHOTOS DON'T TALK. AND 2: YOU'RE ON MY BUNK.
OH...
LOOK. I DON'T LIKE YOU. I'VE NEVER LIKED YOU. AND NOW THAT I'M MISSING THE PARTY DOWN AT THE BEACH TO TRAIN YOU...
...I LIKE YOU EVEN LESS.
WOW, I CAN FEEL THE LOVE...
SO NOW YOU'RE GONNA COME WITH ME FOR A CRASH COURSE IN EVERYTHING YOU NEED TO KNOW FOR YOUR "SHITTIEST SUMMER EVER."
AFTER YOU, MADAME.

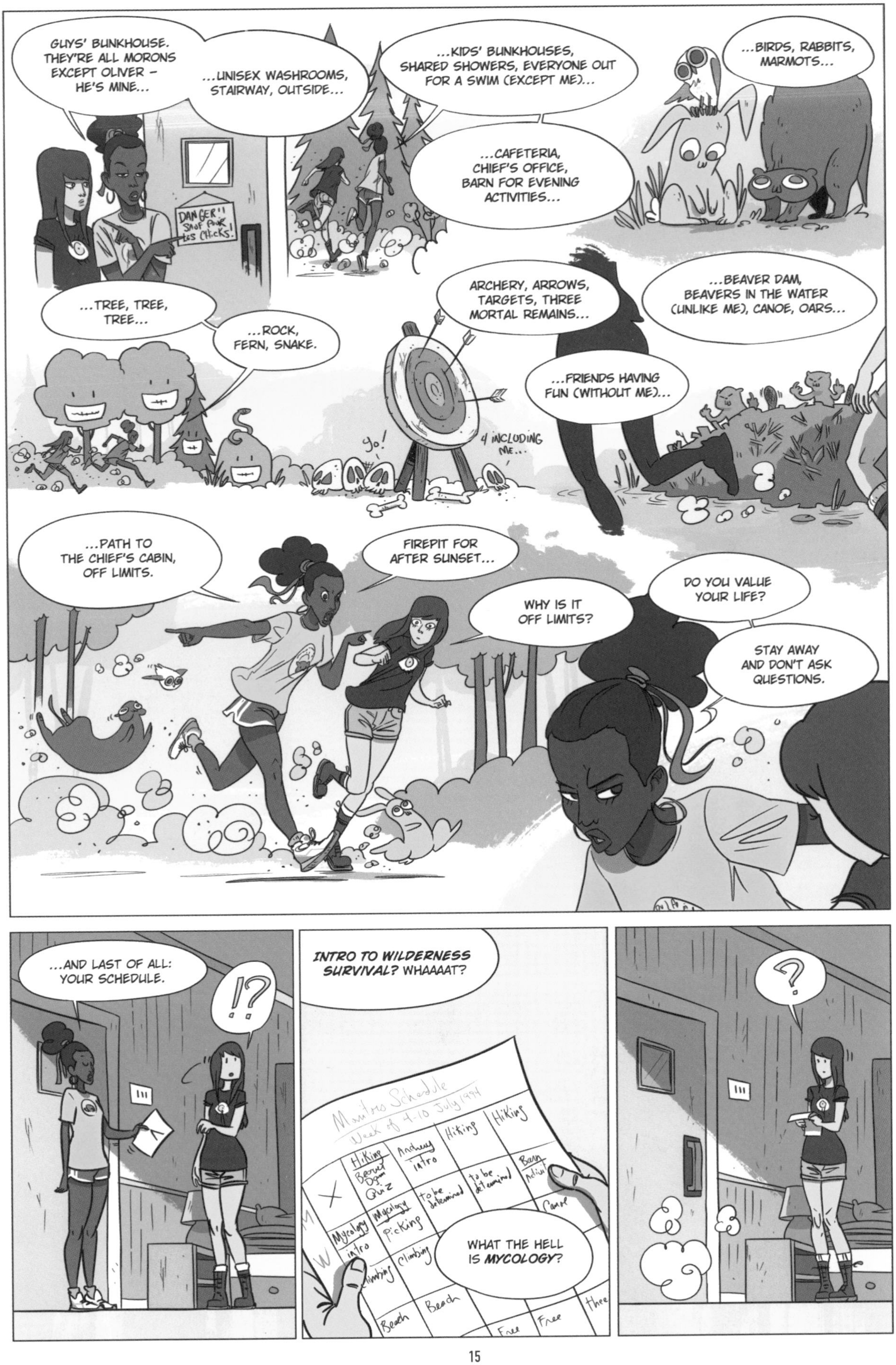
GUYS' BUNKHOUSE. THEY'RE ALL MORONS EXCEPT OLIVER – HE'S MINE...
...UNISEX WASHROOMS, STAIRWAY, OUTSIDE...
DANGER!! SAUF POUR LES CHICKS!
...KIDS' BUNKHOUSES, SHARED SHOWERS, EVERYONE OUT FOR A SWIM (EXCEPT ME)...
...CAFETERIA, CHIEF'S OFFICE, BARN FOR EVENING ACTIVITIES...
...BIRDS, RABBITS, MARMOTS...
...TREE, TREE, TREE...
...ROCK, FERN, SNAKE.
ARCHERY, ARROWS, TARGETS, THREE MORTAL REMAINS...
YO!
4 INCLUDING ME...
...FRIENDS HAVING FUN (WITHOUT ME)...
...BEAVER DAM, BEAVERS IN THE WATER (UNLIKE ME), CANOE, OARS...
...PATH TO THE CHIEF'S CABIN, OFF LIMITS.
FIREPIT FOR AFTER SUNSET...
WHY IS IT OFF LIMITS?
DO YOU VALUE YOUR LIFE?
STAY AWAY AND DON'T ASK QUESTIONS.
...AND LAST OF ALL: YOUR SCHEDULE.
!?
INTRO TO WILDERNESS SURVIVAL? WHAAAAT?
Monitors Schedule
Week of 4-10 July 1994
Hiking
Hiking
Archery intro
Hiking
Beaver Dam Quiz
to be determined
to be determined
Mycology picking
Mycology intro
Climbing
Climbing
Canoe
Beach
Beach
Free
Free
WHAT THE HELL IS MYCOLOGY?
?

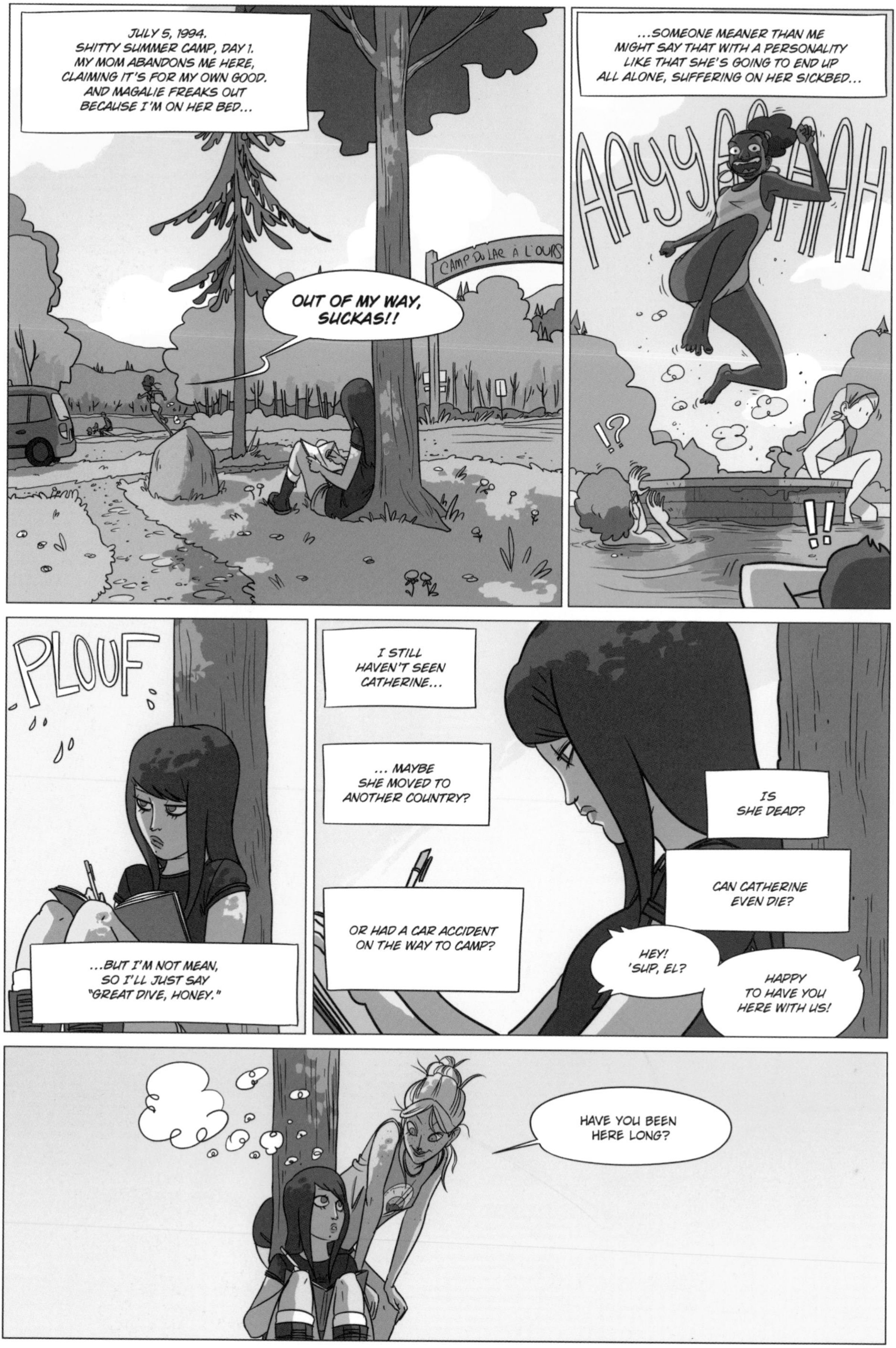
JULY 5, 1994.
SHITTY SUMMER CAMP, DAY 1.
MY MOM ABANDONS ME HERE, CLAIMING IT'S FOR MY OWN GOOD.
AND MAGALIE FREAKS OUT BECAUSE I'M ON HER BED...
CAMP DU LAC À L'OURS
OUT OF MY WAY, SUCKAS!!
...SOMEONE MEANER THAN ME MIGHT SAY THAT WITH A PERSONALITY LIKE THAT SHE'S GOING TO END UP ALL ALONE, SUFFERING ON HER SICKBED...
AAYYAAAAH
!?
!!
PLOUF
...BUT I'M NOT MEAN, SO I'LL JUST SAY "GREAT DIVE, HONEY."
I STILL HAVEN'T SEEN CATHERINE...
... MAYBE SHE MOVED TO ANOTHER COUNTRY?
OR HAD A CAR ACCIDENT ON THE WAY TO CAMP?
IS SHE DEAD?
CAN CATHERINE EVEN DIE?
HEY! 'SUP, EL?
HAPPY TO HAVE YOU HERE WITH US!
HAVE YOU BEEN HERE LONG?

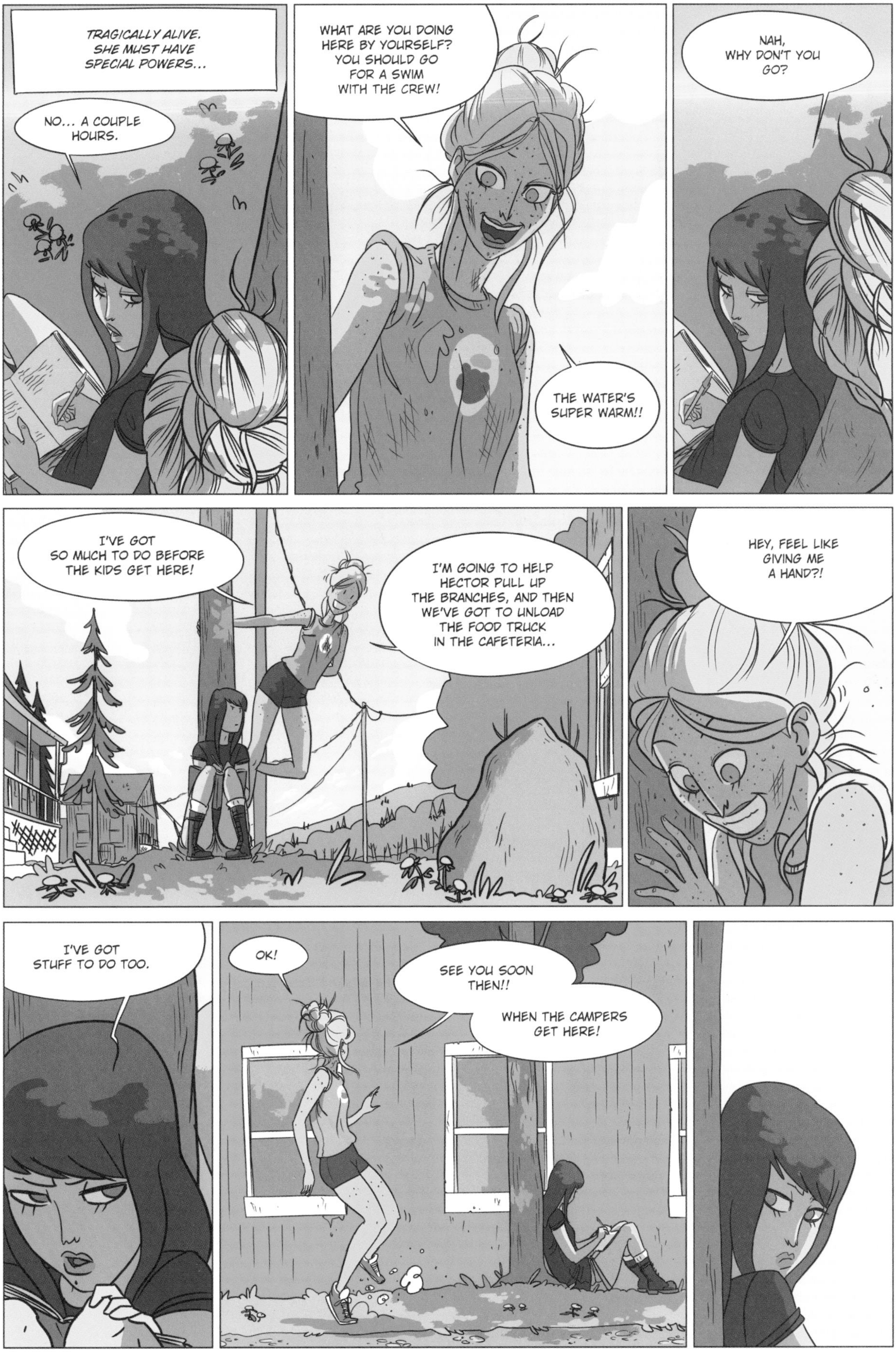
TRAGICALLY ALIVE. SHE MUST HAVE SPECIAL POWERS...
NO... A COUPLE HOURS.
WHAT ARE YOU DOING HERE BY YOURSELF? YOU SHOULD GO FOR A SWIM WITH THE CREW!
THE WATER'S SUPER WARM!!
NAH, WHY DON'T YOU GO?
I'VE GOT SO MUCH TO DO BEFORE THE KIDS GET HERE!
I'M GOING TO HELP HECTOR PULL UP THE BRANCHES, AND THEN WE'VE GOT TO UNLOAD THE FOOD TRUCK IN THE CAFETERIA...
HEY, FEEL LIKE GIVING ME A HAND?!
I'VE GOT STUFF TO DO TOO.
OK!
SEE YOU SOON THEN!!
WHEN THE CAMPERS GET HERE!

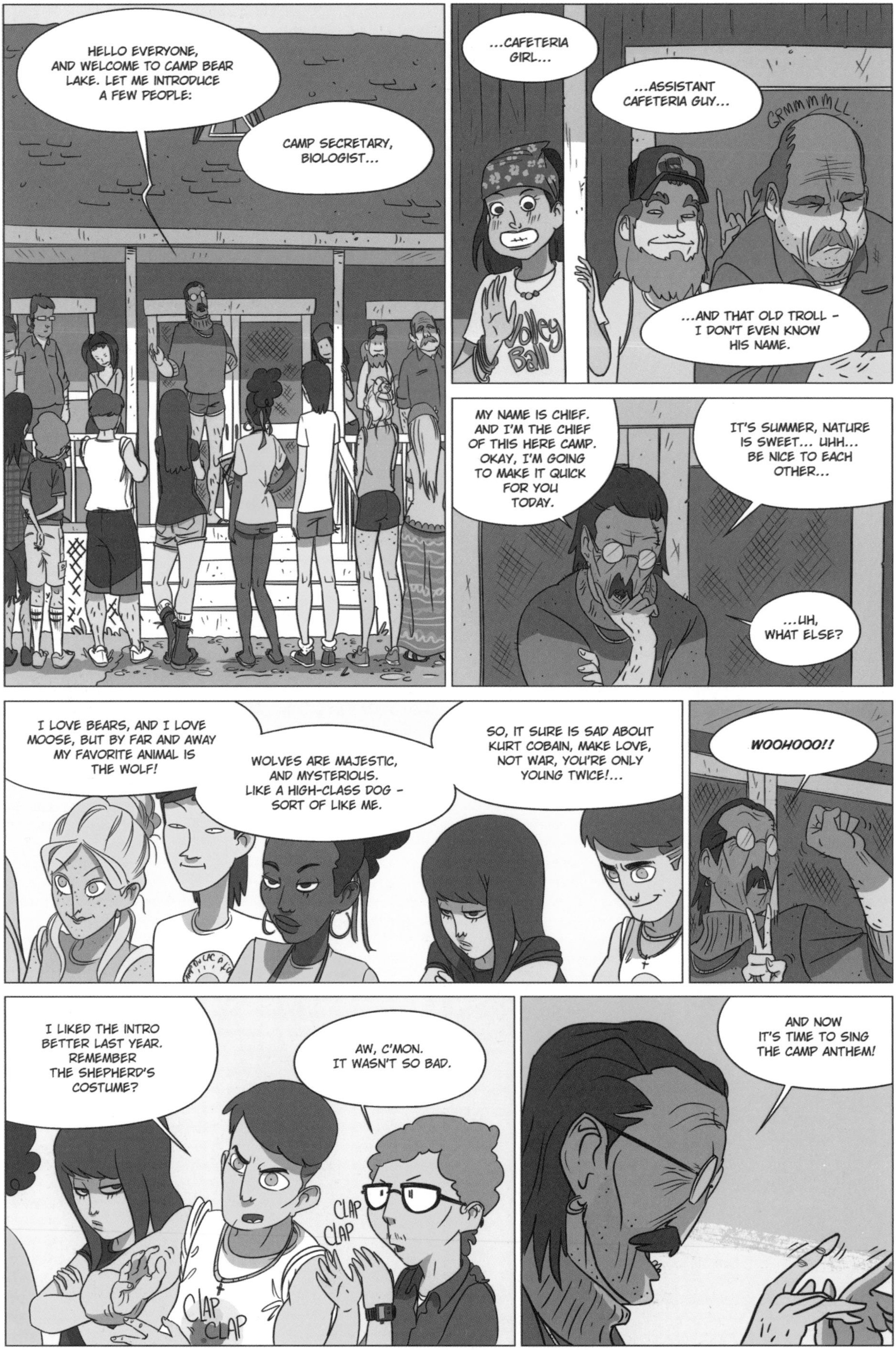
HELLO EVERYONE, AND WELCOME TO CAMP BEAR LAKE. LET ME INTRODUCE A FEW PEOPLE:
CAMP SECRETARY, BIOLOGIST...
...CAFETERIA GIRL...
...ASSISTANT CAFETERIA GUY...
GRMMMMLL...
...AND THAT OLD TROLL - I DON'T EVEN KNOW HIS NAME.
MY NAME IS CHIEF. AND I'M THE CHIEF OF THIS HERE CAMP. OKAY, I'M GOING TO MAKE IT QUICK FOR YOU TODAY.
IT'S SUMMER, NATURE IS SWEET... UHH... BE NICE TO EACH OTHER...
...UH, WHAT ELSE?
I LOVE BEARS, AND I LOVE MOOSE, BUT BY FAR AND AWAY MY FAVORITE ANIMAL IS THE WOLF!
WOLVES ARE MAJESTIC, AND MYSTERIOUS. LIKE A HIGH-CLASS DOG - SORT OF LIKE ME.
SO, IT SURE IS SAD ABOUT KURT COBAIN, MAKE LOVE, NOT WAR, YOU'RE ONLY YOUNG TWICE!...
WOOHOOO!!
I LIKED THE INTRO BETTER LAST YEAR. REMEMBER THE SHEPHERD'S COSTUME?
AW, C'MON. IT WASN'T SO BAD.
CLAP CLAP
CLAP CLAP
AND NOW IT'S TIME TO SING THE CAMP ANTHEM!

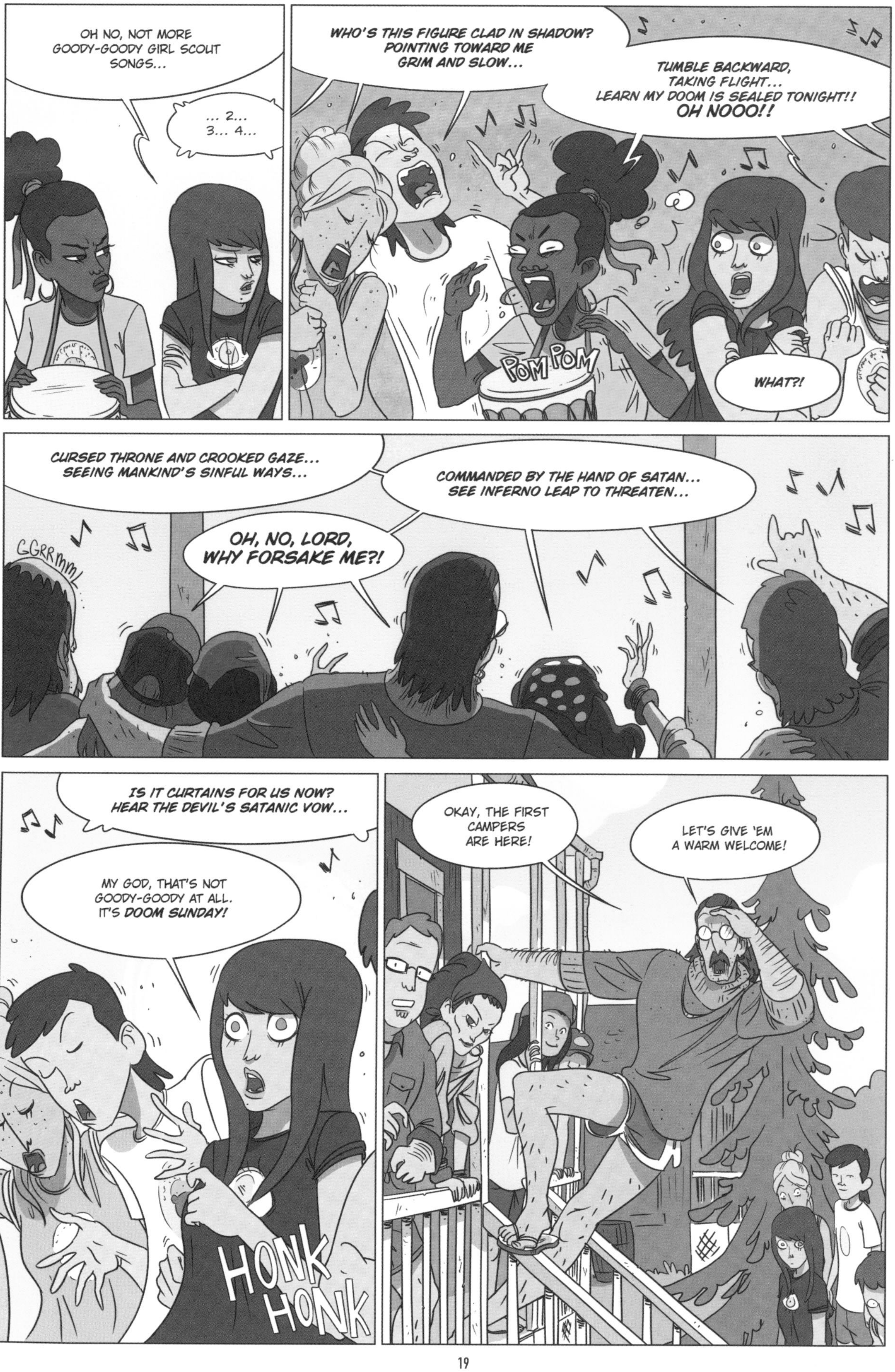

OH NO, NOT MORE GOODY-GOODY GIRL SCOUT SONGS...
... 2... 3... 4...
WHO'S THIS FIGURE CLAD IN SHADOW? POINTING TOWARD ME GRIM AND SLOW...
TUMBLE BACKWARD, TAKING FLIGHT... LEARN MY DOOM IS SEALED TONIGHT!! OH NOOO!!
POM POM
WHAT?!
CURSED THRONE AND CROOKED GAZE... SEEING MANKIND'S SINFUL WAYS...
COMMANDED BY THE HAND OF SATAN... SEE INFERNO LEAP TO THREATEN...
GGRRmm!
OH, NO, LORD, WHY FORSAKE ME?!
IS IT CURTAINS FOR US NOW? HEAR THE DEVIL'S SATANIC VOW...
MY GOD, THAT'S NOT GOODY-GOODY AT ALL. IT'S DOOM SUNDAY!
HONK HONK
OKAY, THE FIRST CAMPERS ARE HERE!
LET'S GIVE 'EM A WARM WELCOME!

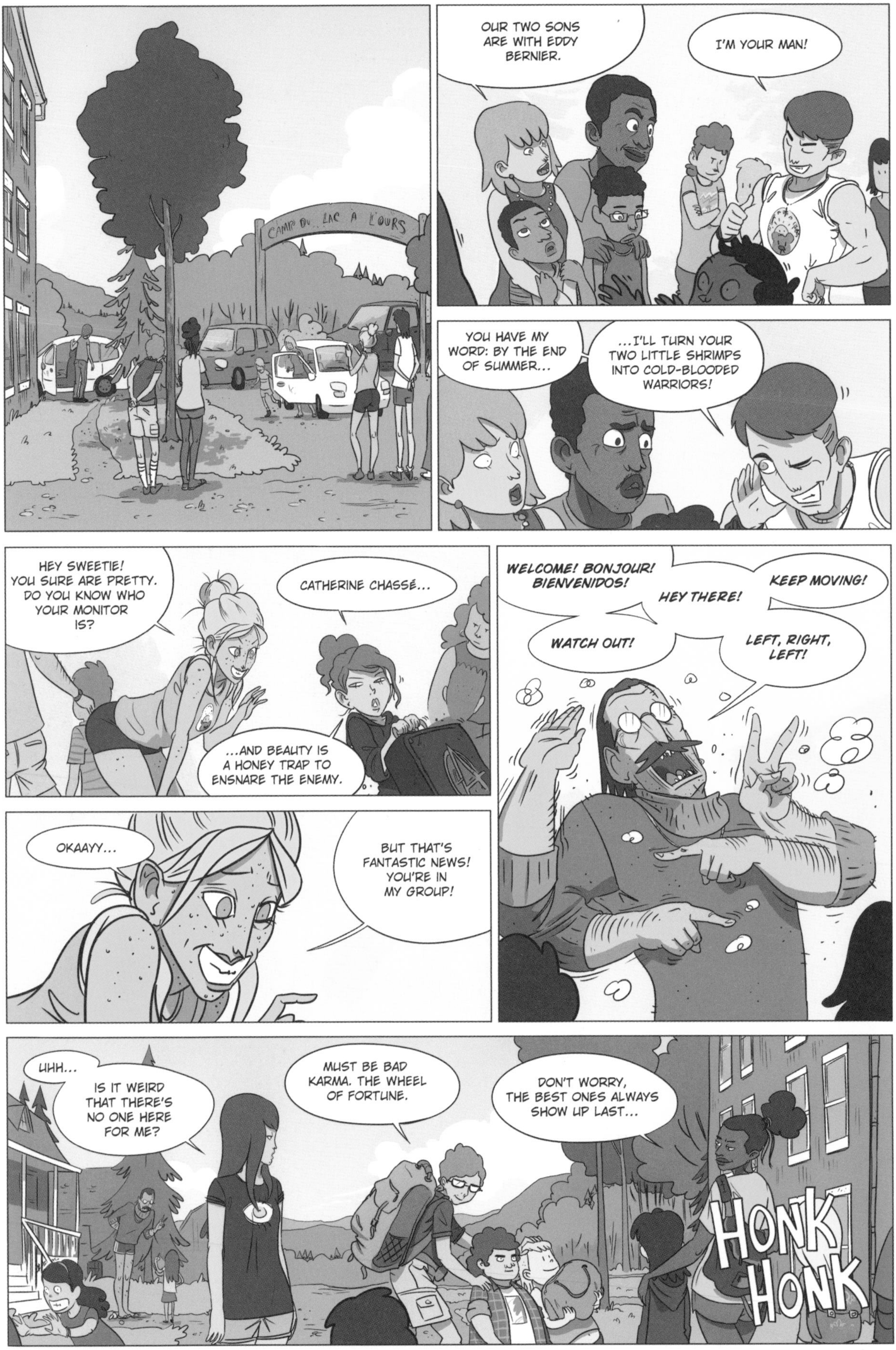
CAMP DU LAC À L'OURS
OUR TWO SONS ARE WITH EDDY BERNIER.
I'M YOUR MAN!
YOU HAVE MY WORD: BY THE END OF SUMMER...
...I'LL TURN YOUR TWO LITTLE SHRIMPS INTO COLD-BLOODED WARRIORS!
HEY SWEETIE! YOU SURE ARE PRETTY. DO YOU KNOW WHO YOUR MONITOR IS?
CATHERINE CHASSÉ...
...AND BEAUTY IS A HONEY TRAP TO ENSNARE THE ENEMY.
OKAAYY...
BUT THAT'S FANTASTIC NEWS! YOU'RE IN MY GROUP!
WELCOME! BONJOUR! BIENVENIDOS!
HEY THERE!
KEEP MOVING!
WATCH OUT!
LEFT, RIGHT, LEFT!
UHH...
IS IT WEIRD THAT THERE'S NO ONE HERE FOR ME?
MUST BE BAD KARMA. THE WHEEL OF FORTUNE.
DON'T WORRY, THE BEST ONES ALWAYS SHOW UP LAST...
HONK HONK

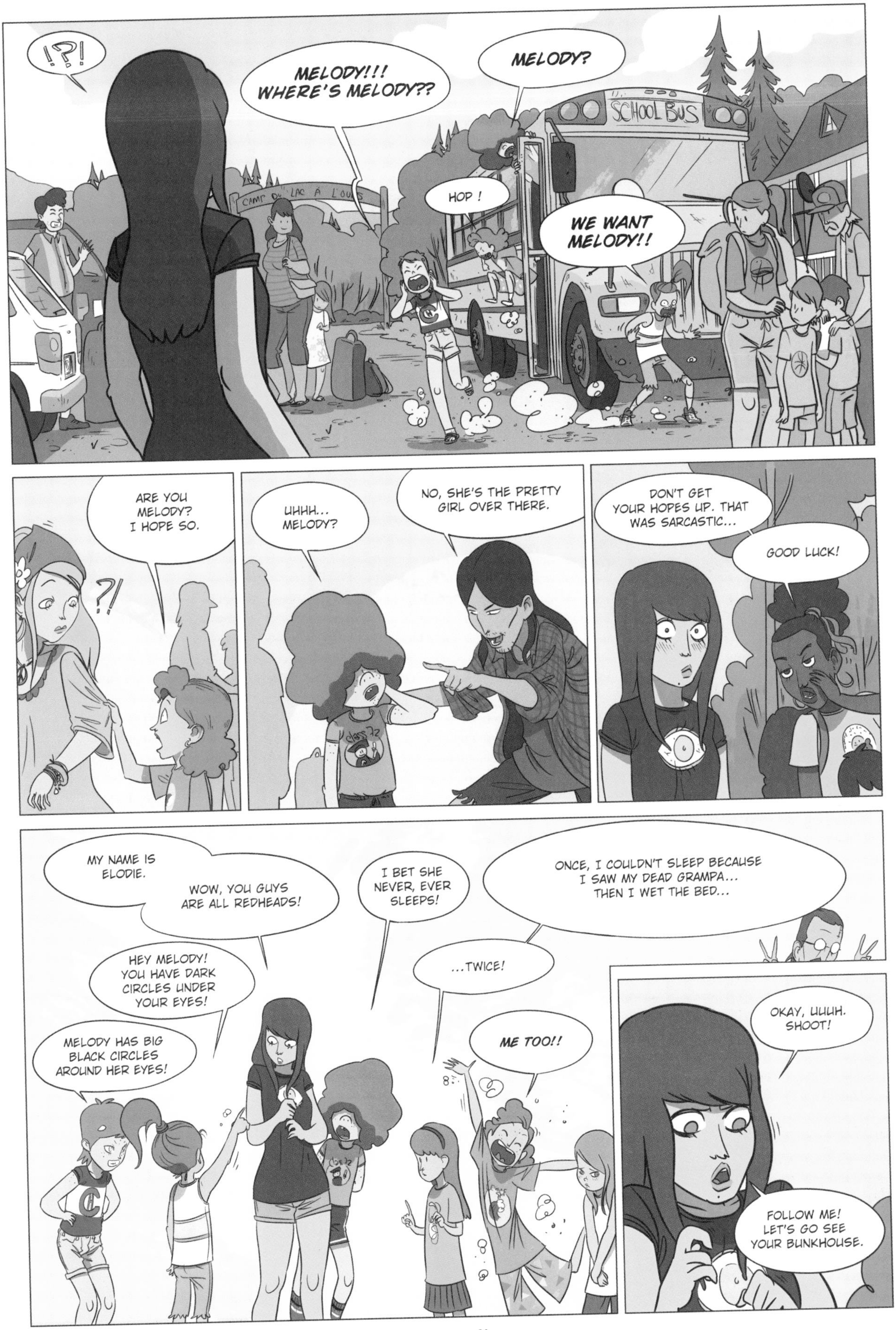
!?!
MELODY!!! WHERE'S MELODY??
MELODY?
SCHOOL BUS
CAMP DU LAC À L'OURS
HOP !
WE WANT MELODY!!
ARE YOU MELODY? I HOPE SO.
?!
UHHH... MELODY?
NO, SHE'S THE PRETTY GIRL OVER THERE.
DON'T GET YOUR HOPES UP. THAT WAS SARCASTIC...
GOOD LUCK!
MY NAME IS ELODIE.
WOW, YOU GUYS ARE ALL REDHEADS!
I BET SHE NEVER, EVER SLEEPS!
ONCE, I COULDN'T SLEEP BECAUSE I SAW MY DEAD GRAMPA... THEN I WET THE BED...
HEY MELODY! YOU HAVE DARK CIRCLES UNDER YOUR EYES!
...TWICE!
MELODY HAS BIG BLACK CIRCLES AROUND HER EYES!
ME TOO!!
OKAY, UUUH. SHOOT!
FOLLOW ME! LET'S GO SEE YOUR BUNKHOUSE.

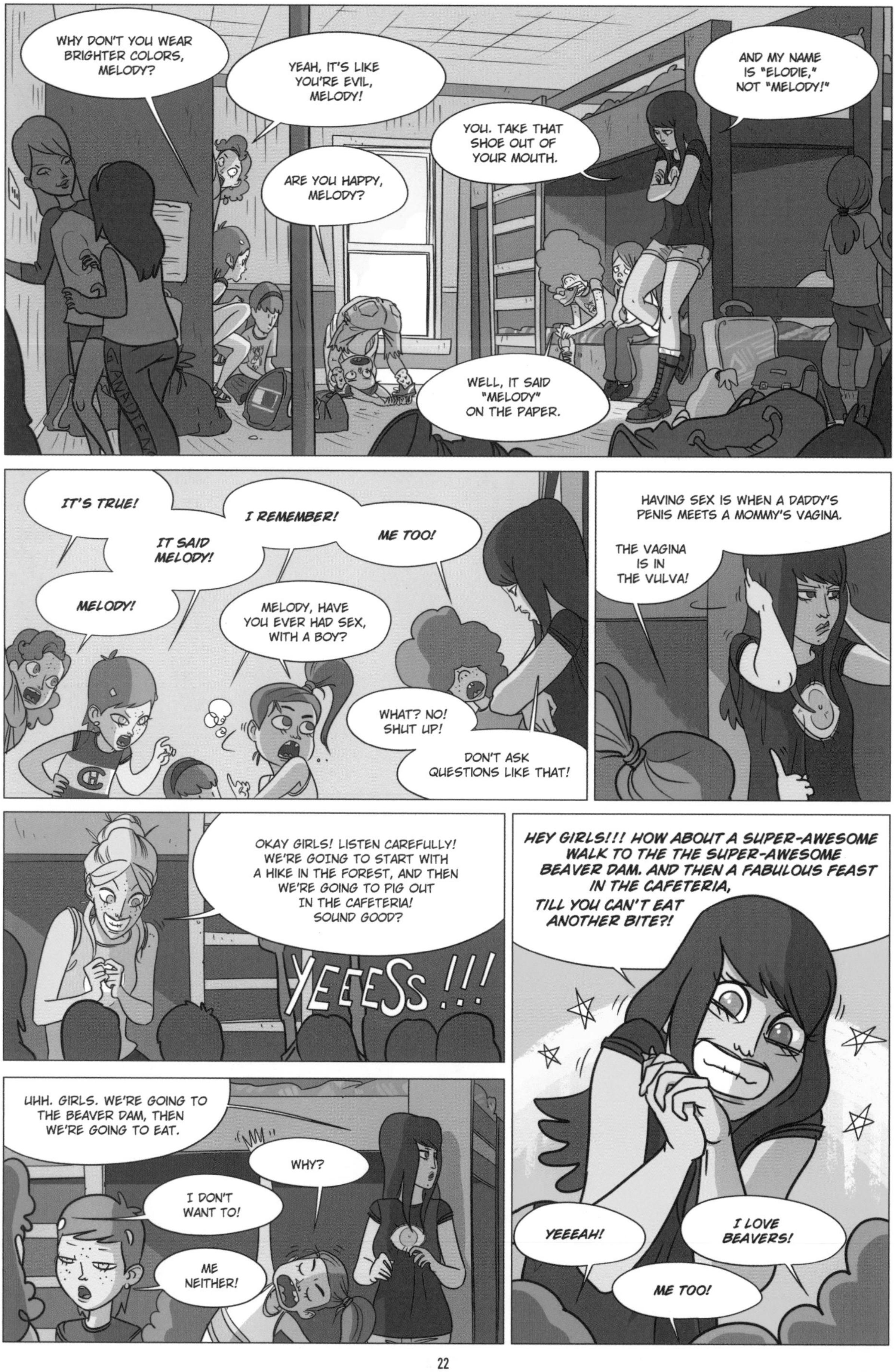
WHY DON'T YOU WEAR BRIGHTER COLORS, MELODY?
YEAH, IT'S LIKE YOU'RE EVIL, MELODY!
ARE YOU HAPPY, MELODY?
YOU. TAKE THAT SHOE OUT OF YOUR MOUTH.
AND MY NAME IS "ELODIE," NOT "MELODY!"
WELL, IT SAID "MELODY" ON THE PAPER.
IT'S TRUE!
I REMEMBER!
ME TOO!
IT SAID MELODY!
MELODY!
MELODY, HAVE YOU EVER HAD SEX, WITH A BOY?
WHAT? NO! SHUT UP!
DON'T ASK QUESTIONS LIKE THAT!
HAVING SEX IS WHEN A DADDY'S PENIS MEETS A MOMMY'S VAGINA.
THE VAGINA IS IN THE VULVA!
OKAY GIRLS! LISTEN CAREFULLY! WE'RE GOING TO START WITH A HIKE IN THE FOREST, AND THEN WE'RE GOING TO PIG OUT IN THE CAFETERIA! SOUND GOOD?
YEEESs!!!
HEY GIRLS!!! HOW ABOUT A SUPER-AWESOME WALK TO THE THE SUPER-AWESOME BEAVER DAM. AND THEN A FABULOUS FEAST IN THE CAFETERIA, TILL YOU CAN'T EAT ANOTHER BITE?!
YEEEAH!
I LOVE BEAVERS!
ME TOO!
UHH. GIRLS. WE'RE GOING TO THE BEAVER DAM, THEN WE'RE GOING TO EAT.
WHY?
I DON'T WANT TO!
ME NEITHER!

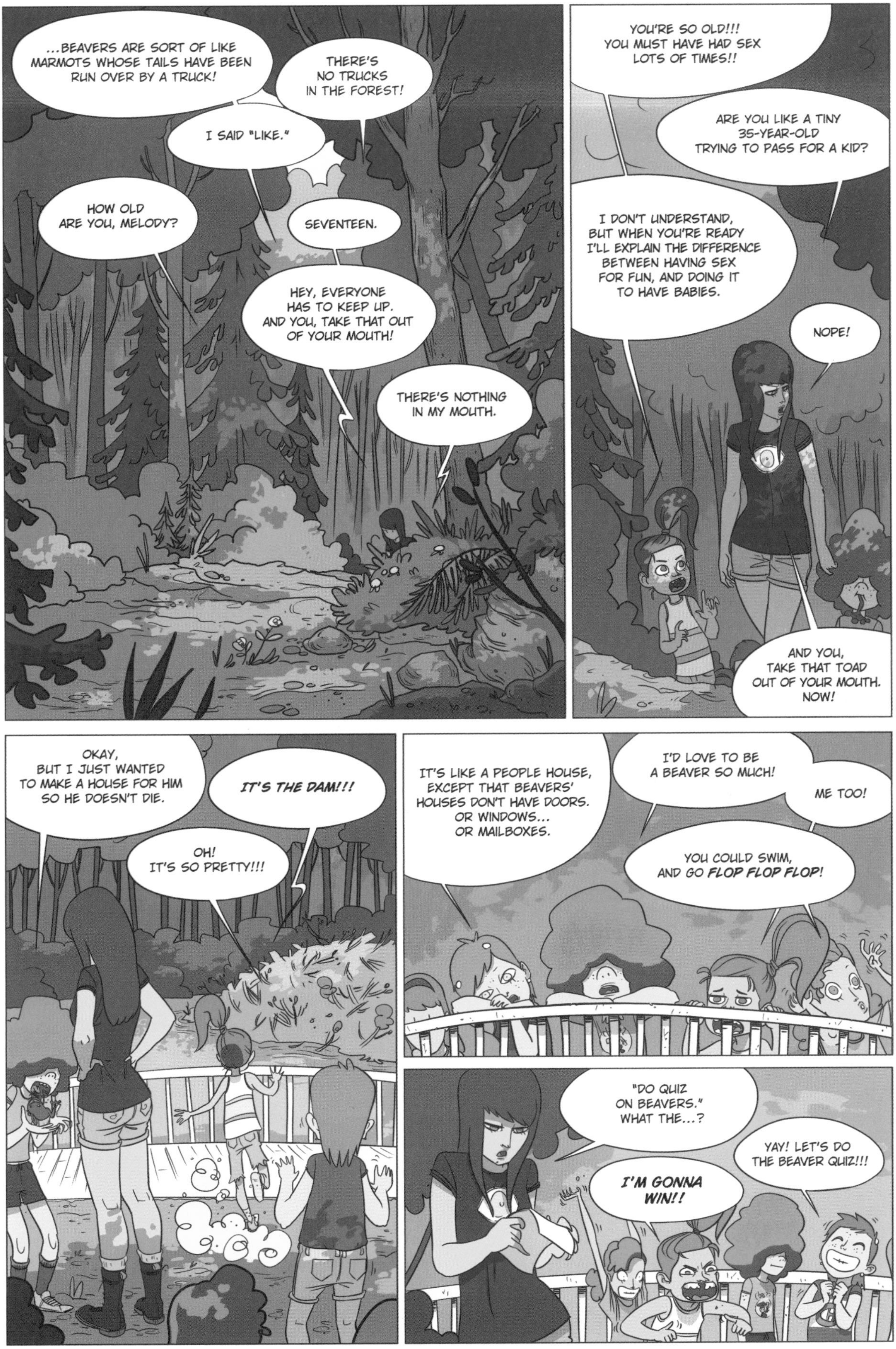
...BEAVERS ARE SORT OF LIKE MARMOTS WHOSE TAILS HAVE BEEN RUN OVER BY A TRUCK!
THERE'S NO TRUCKS IN THE FOREST!
I SAID "LIKE."
HOW OLD ARE YOU, MELODY?
SEVENTEEN.
HEY, EVERYONE HAS TO KEEP UP. AND YOU, TAKE THAT OUT OF YOUR MOUTH!
THERE'S NOTHING IN MY MOUTH.
YOU'RE SO OLD!!! YOU MUST HAVE HAD SEX LOTS OF TIMES!!
ARE YOU LIKE A TINY 35-YEAR-OLD TRYING TO PASS FOR A KID?
I DON'T UNDERSTAND, BUT WHEN YOU'RE READY I'LL EXPLAIN THE DIFFERENCE BETWEEN HAVING SEX FOR FUN, AND DOING IT TO HAVE BABIES.
NOPE!
AND YOU, TAKE THAT TOAD OUT OF YOUR MOUTH. NOW!
OKAY, BUT I JUST WANTED TO MAKE A HOUSE FOR HIM SO HE DOESN'T DIE.
IT'S THE DAM!!!
OH! IT'S SO PRETTY!!!
IT'S LIKE A PEOPLE HOUSE, EXCEPT THAT BEAVERS' HOUSES DON'T HAVE DOORS. OR WINDOWS... OR MAILBOXES.
I'D LOVE TO BE A BEAVER SO MUCH!
ME TOO!
YOU COULD SWIM, AND GO FLOP FLOP FLOP!
"DO QUIZ ON BEAVERS." WHAT THE...?
YAY! LET'S DO THE BEAVER QUIZ!!!
I'M GONNA WIN!!

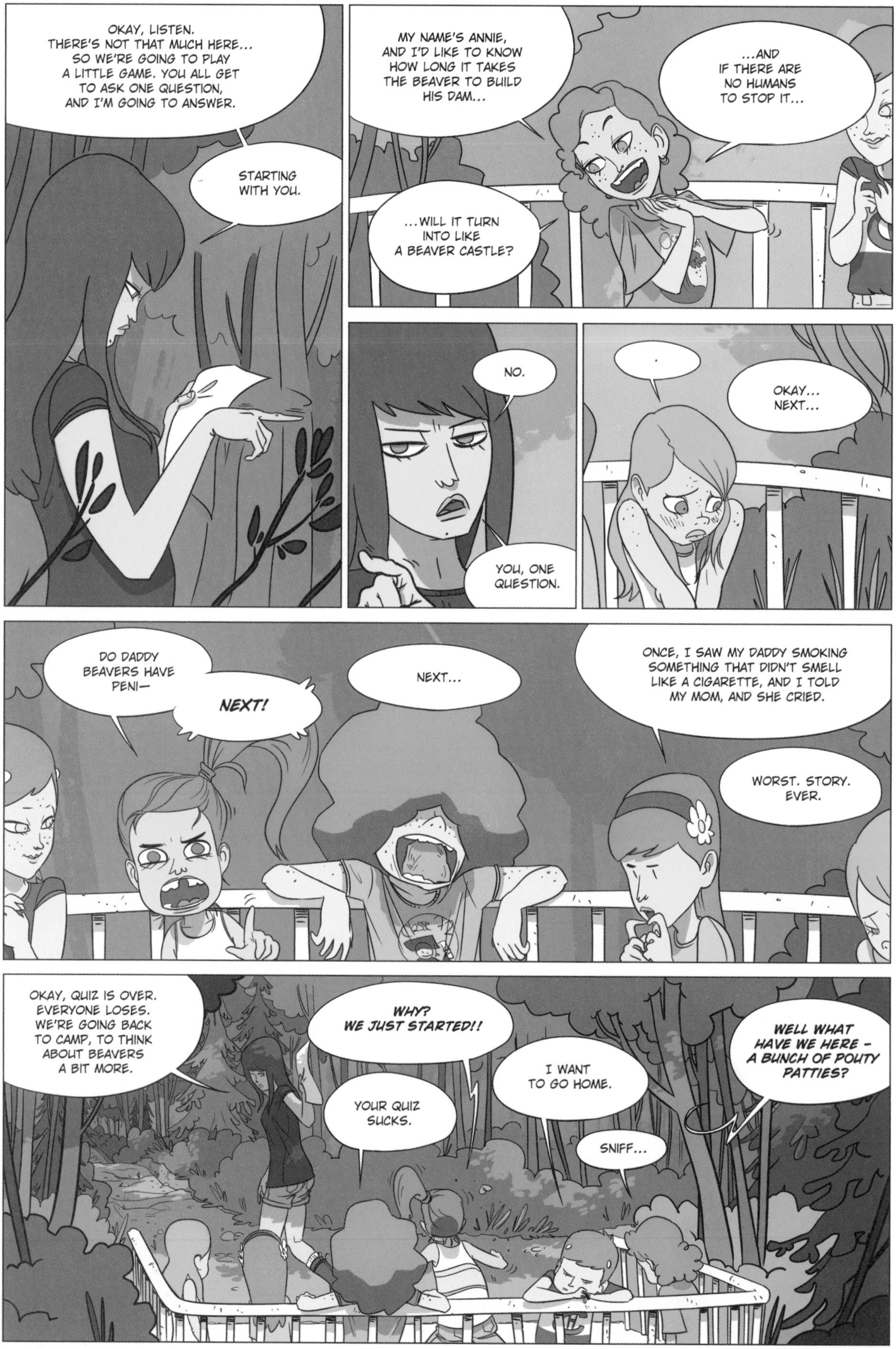
OKAY, LISTEN. THERE'S NOT THAT MUCH HERE... SO WE'RE GOING TO PLAY A LITTLE GAME. YOU ALL GET TO ASK ONE QUESTION, AND I'M GOING TO ANSWER.
STARTING WITH YOU.
MY NAME'S ANNIE, AND I'D LIKE TO KNOW HOW LONG IT TAKES THE BEAVER TO BUILD HIS DAM...
...AND IF THERE ARE NO HUMANS TO STOP IT...
...WILL IT TURN INTO LIKE A BEAVER CASTLE?
NO.
YOU, ONE QUESTION.
.
OKAY... NEXT...
DO DADDY BEAVERS HAVE PENI—
NEXT!
NEXT...
ONCE, I SAW MY DADDY SMOKING SOMETHING THAT DIDN'T SMELL LIKE A CIGARETTE, AND I TOLD MY MOM, AND SHE CRIED.
WORST. STORY. EVER.
OKAY, QUIZ IS OVER. EVERYONE LOSES. WE'RE GOING BACK TO CAMP, TO THINK ABOUT BEAVERS A BIT MORE.
WHY? WE JUST STARTED!!
YOUR QUIZ SUCKS.
I WANT TO GO HOME.
SNIFF...
WELL WHAT HAVE WE HERE - A BUNCH OF POUTY PATTIES?

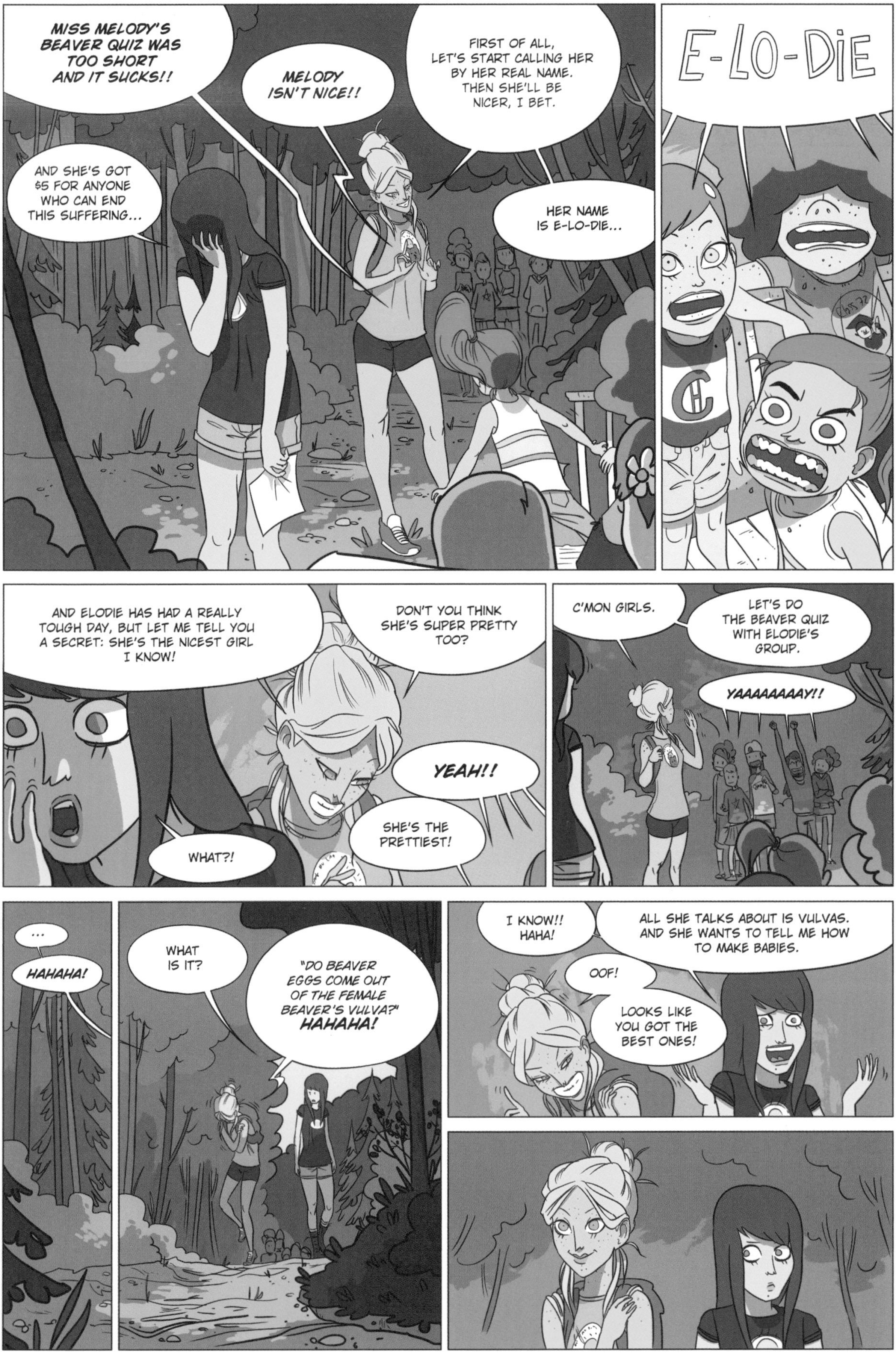
MISS MELODY'S BEAVER QUIZ WAS TOO SHORT AND IT SUCKS!!
MELODY ISN'T NICE!!
FIRST OF ALL, LET'S START CALLING HER BY HER REAL NAME. THEN SHE'LL BE NICER, I BET.
AND SHE'S GOT $5 FOR ANYONE WHO CAN END THIS SUFFERING...
HER NAME IS E-LO-DIE...
E-LO-DIE
AND ELODIE HAS HAD A REALLY TOUGH DAY, BUT LET ME TELL YOU A SECRET: SHE'S THE NICEST GIRL I KNOW!
DON'T YOU THINK SHE'S SUPER PRETTY TOO?
YEAH!!
SHE'S THE PRETTIEST!
WHAT?!
C'MON GIRLS.
LET'S DO THE BEAVER QUIZ WITH ELODIE'S GROUP.
YAAAAAAAAY!!
...
HAHAHA!
WHAT IS IT?
"DO BEAVER EGGS COME OUT OF THE FEMALE BEAVER'S VULVA?" HAHAHA!
I KNOW!! HAHA!
ALL SHE TALKS ABOUT IS VULVAS. AND SHE WANTS TO TELL ME HOW TO MAKE BABIES.
OOF!
LOOKS LIKE YOU GOT THE BEST ONES!

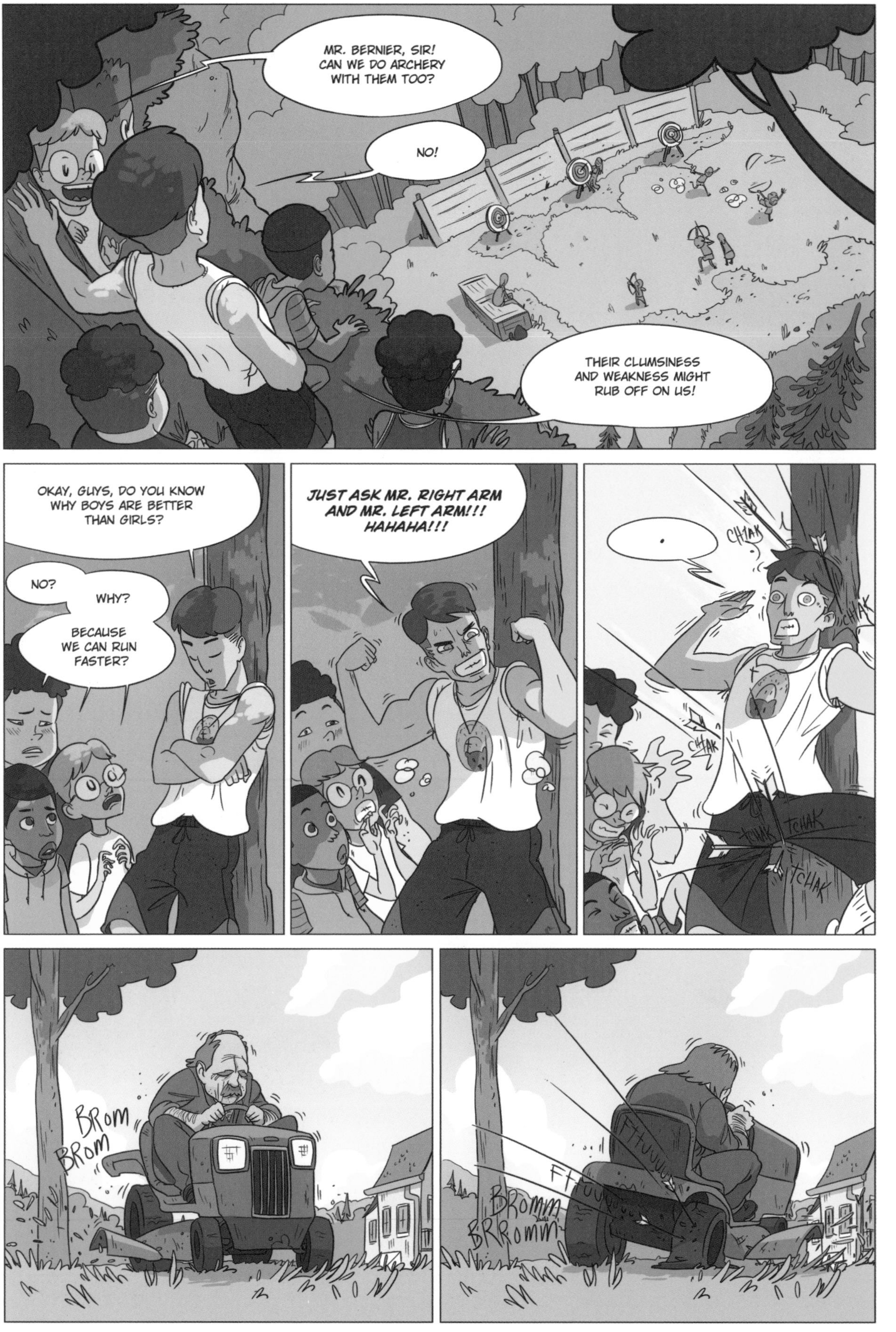
MR. BERNIER, SIR! CAN WE DO ARCHERY WITH THEM TOO?
NO!
THEIR CLUMSINESS AND WEAKNESS MIGHT RUB OFF ON US!
OKAY, GUYS, DO YOU KNOW WHY BOYS ARE BETTER THAN GIRLS?
NO?
WHY?
BECAUSE WE CAN RUN FASTER?
JUST ASK MR. RIGHT ARM AND MR. LEFT ARM!!! HAHAHA!!!
.
CHAK
CHAK
CHAK
TCHAK
TCHAK
TCHAK
BROM
BROM
FTUUUU
FT
BROMM
BRROMM

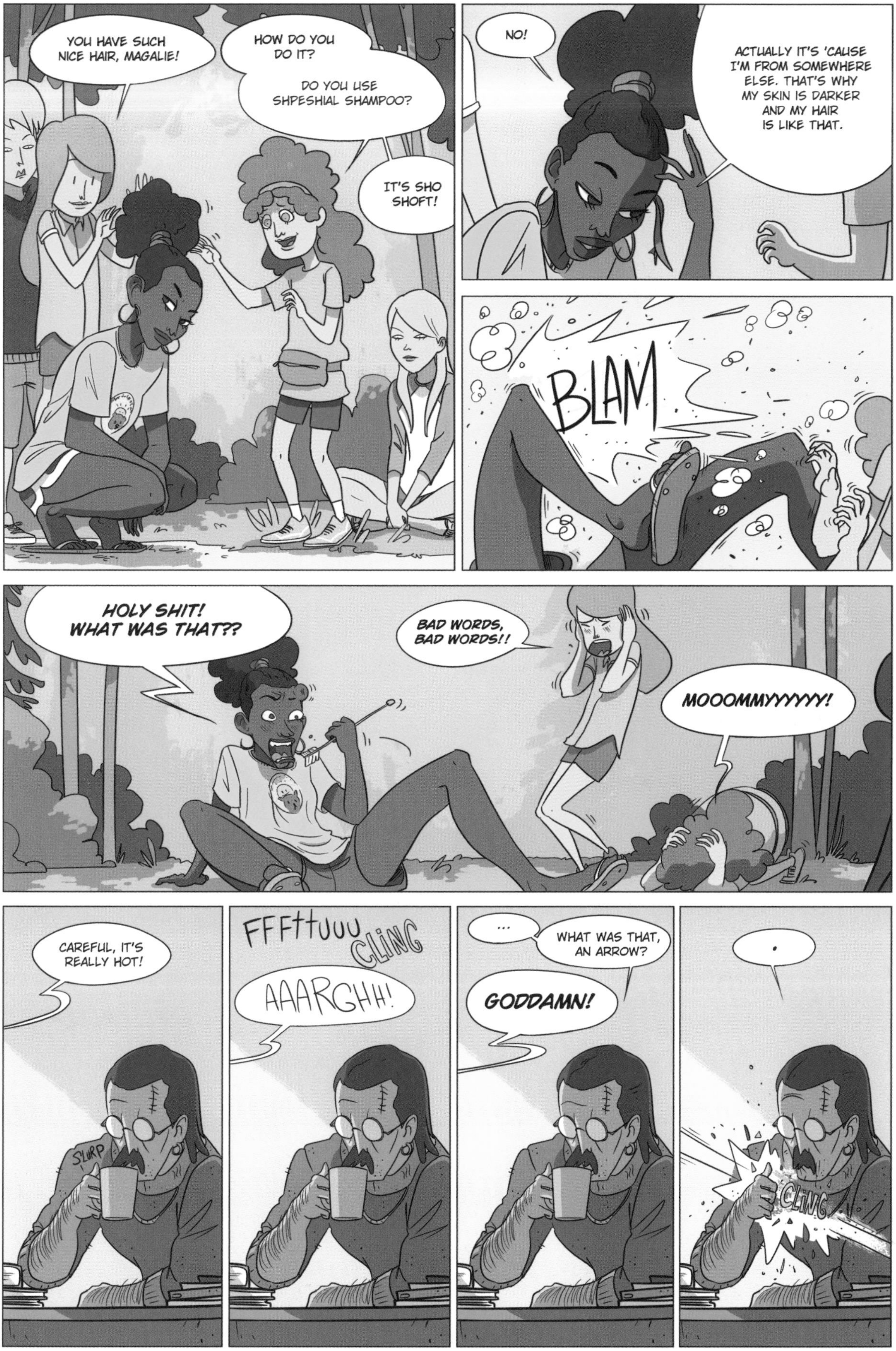

YOU HAVE SUCH NICE HAIR, MAGALIE!
HOW DO YOU DO IT?
DO YOU USE SHPESHIAL SHAMPOO?
IT'S SHO SHOFT!
NO!
ACTUALLY IT'S 'CAUSE I'M FROM SOMEWHERE ELSE. THAT'S WHY MY SKIN IS DARKER AND MY HAIR IS LIKE THAT.
BLAM
HOLY SHIT! WHAT WAS THAT??
BAD WORDS, BAD WORDS!!
MOOOMMYYYYYY!
CAREFUL, IT'S REALLY HOT!
SLURP
FFFttuuu
CLING
AAARGHH!
...
WHAT WAS THAT, AN ARROW?
GODDAMN!
.
CLING

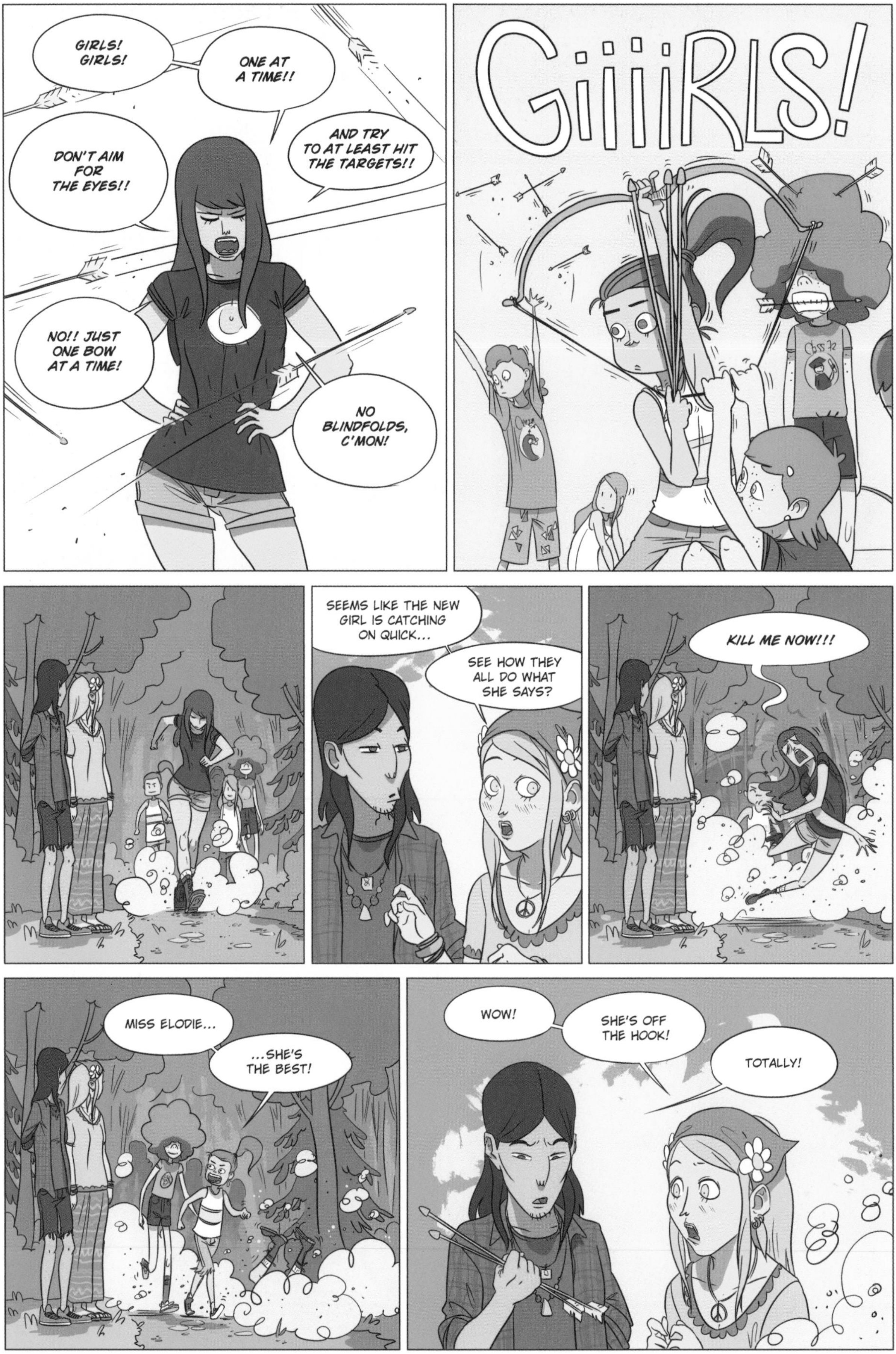
GIRLS! GIRLS!
ONE AT A TIME!!
DON'T AIM FOR THE EYES!!
AND TRY TO AT LEAST HIT THE TARGETS!!
NO!! JUST ONE BOW AT A TIME!
NO BLINDFOLDS, C'MON!
GiiiRLS!
SEEMS LIKE THE NEW GIRL IS CATCHING ON QUICK...
SEE HOW THEY ALL DO WHAT SHE SAYS?
KILL ME NOW!!!
MISS ELODIE...
...SHE'S THE BEST!
WOW!
SHE'S OFF THE HOOK!
TOTALLY!

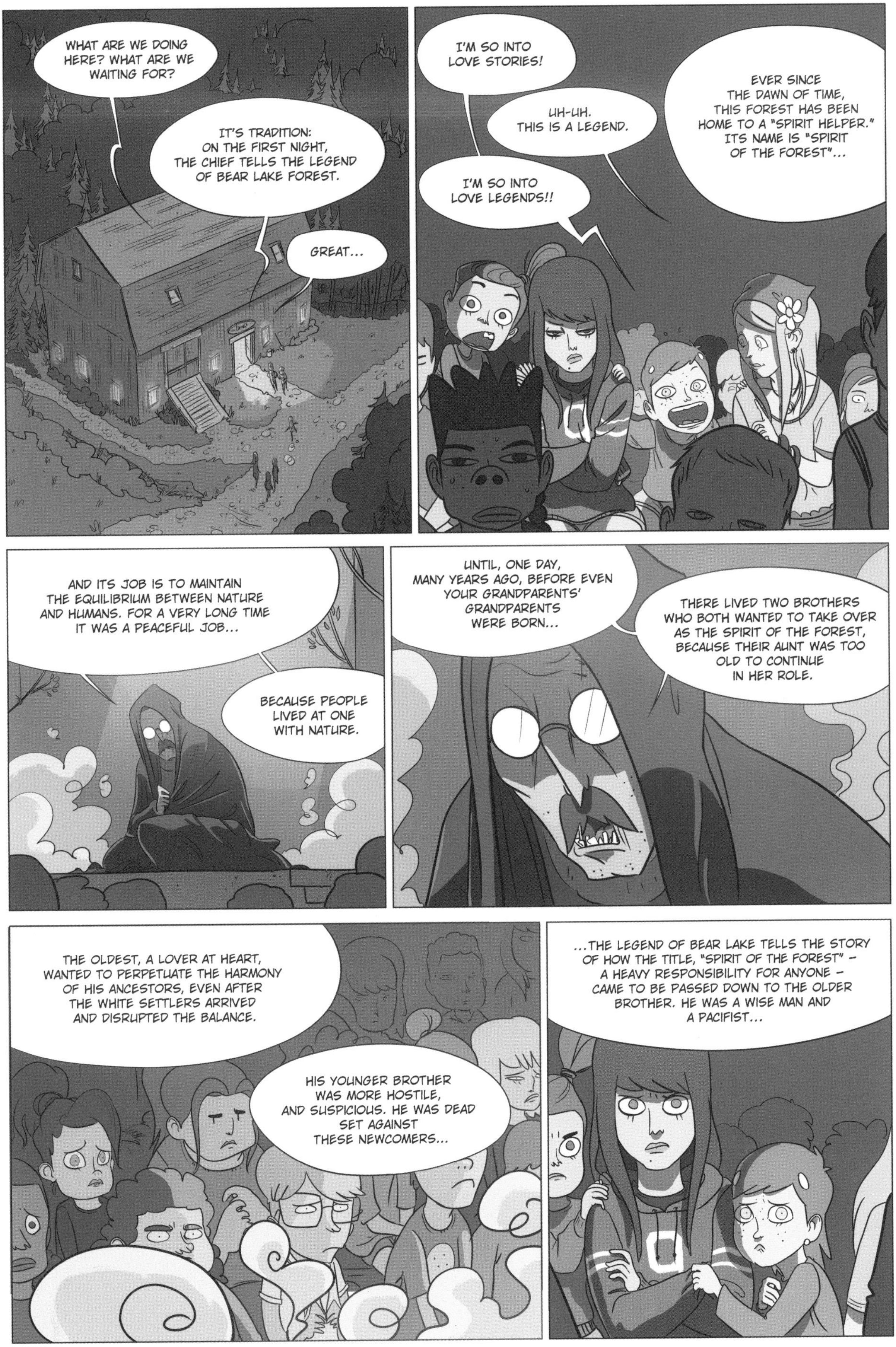
WHAT ARE WE DOING HERE? WHAT ARE WE WAITING FOR?
IT'S TRADITION: ON THE FIRST NIGHT, THE CHIEF TELLS THE LEGEND OF BEAR LAKE FOREST.
GREAT...
I'M SO INTO LOVE STORIES!
UH-UH. THIS IS A LEGEND.
I'M SO INTO LOVE LEGENDS!!
EVER SINCE THE DAWN OF TIME, THIS FOREST HAS BEEN HOME TO A "SPIRIT HELPER." ITS NAME IS "SPIRIT OF THE FOREST"...
AND ITS JOB IS TO MAINTAIN THE EQUILIBRIUM BETWEEN NATURE AND HUMANS. FOR A VERY LONG TIME IT WAS A PEACEFUL JOB...
BECAUSE PEOPLE LIVED AT ONE WITH NATURE.
UNTIL, ONE DAY, MANY YEARS AGO, BEFORE EVEN YOUR GRANDPARENTS' GRANDPARENTS WERE BORN...
THERE LIVED TWO BROTHERS WHO BOTH WANTED TO TAKE OVER AS THE SPIRIT OF THE FOREST, BECAUSE THEIR AUNT WAS TOO OLD TO CONTINUE IN HER ROLE.
THE OLDEST, A LOVER AT HEART, WANTED TO PERPETUATE THE HARMONY OF HIS ANCESTORS, EVEN AFTER THE WHITE SETTLERS ARRIVED AND DISRUPTED THE BALANCE.
HIS YOUNGER BROTHER WAS MORE HOSTILE, AND SUSPICIOUS. HE WAS DEAD SET AGAINST THESE NEWCOMERS...
...THE LEGEND OF BEAR LAKE TELLS THE STORY OF HOW THE TITLE, "SPIRIT OF THE FOREST" – A HEAVY RESPONSIBILITY FOR ANYONE – CAME TO BE PASSED DOWN TO THE OLDER BROTHER. HE WAS A WISE MAN AND A PACIFIST...

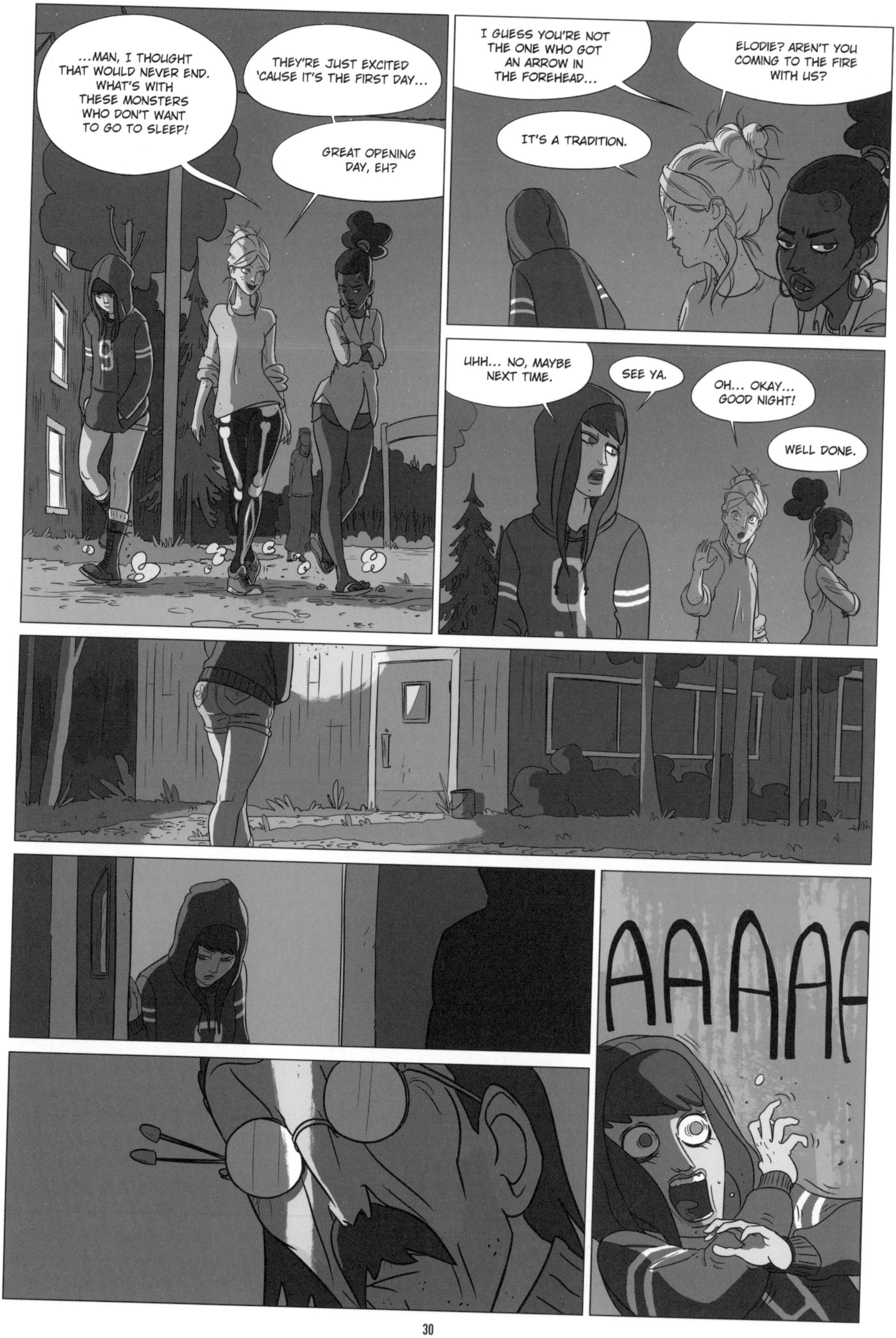

...MAN, I THOUGHT THAT WOULD NEVER END. WHAT'S WITH THESE MONSTERS WHO DON'T WANT TO GO TO SLEEP!
THEY'RE JUST EXCITED 'CAUSE IT'S THE FIRST DAY...
GREAT OPENING DAY, EH?
I GUESS YOU'RE NOT THE ONE WHO GOT AN ARROW IN THE FOREHEAD...
ELODIE? AREN'T YOU COMING TO THE FIRE WITH US?
IT'S A TRADITION.
UHH... NO, MAYBE NEXT TIME.
SEE YA.
OH... OKAY... GOOD NIGHT!
WELL DONE.
AAAAE

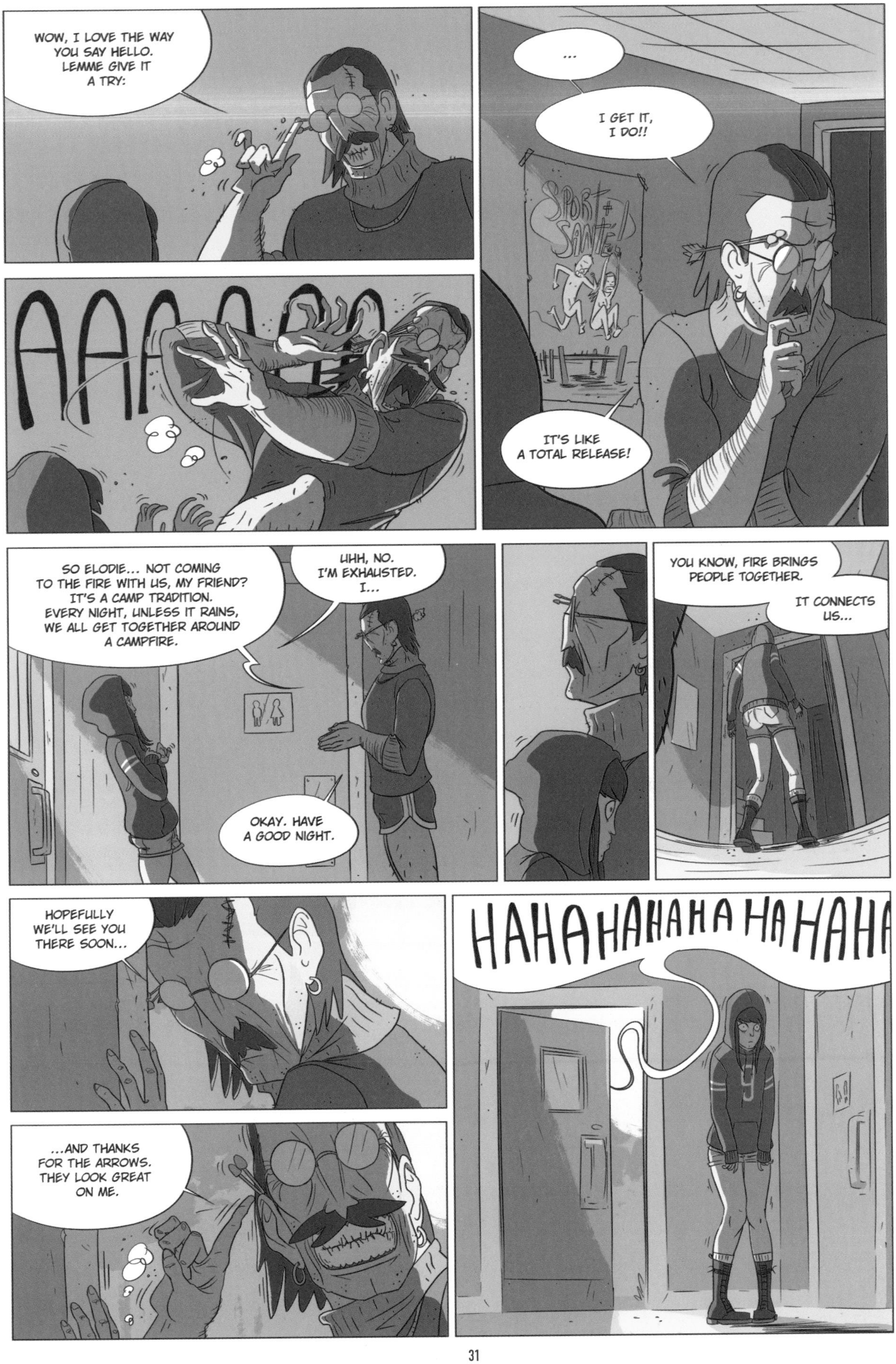
WOW, I LOVE THE WAY YOU SAY HELLO. LEMME GIVE IT A TRY:
AAAAAA
...
I GET IT, I DO!!
SPORT + SANTÉ!
IT'S LIKE A TOTAL RELEASE!
SO ELODIE... NOT COMING TO THE FIRE WITH US, MY FRIEND? IT'S A CAMP TRADITION. EVERY NIGHT, UNLESS IT RAINS, WE ALL GET TOGETHER AROUND A CAMPFIRE.
UHH, NO. I'M EXHAUSTED. I...
OKAY. HAVE A GOOD NIGHT.
YOU KNOW, FIRE BRINGS PEOPLE TOGETHER.
IT CONNECTS US...
HOPEFULLY WE'LL SEE YOU THERE SOON...
...AND THANKS FOR THE ARROWS. THEY LOOK GREAT ON ME.
HAHAHAHAHA HAHAHA

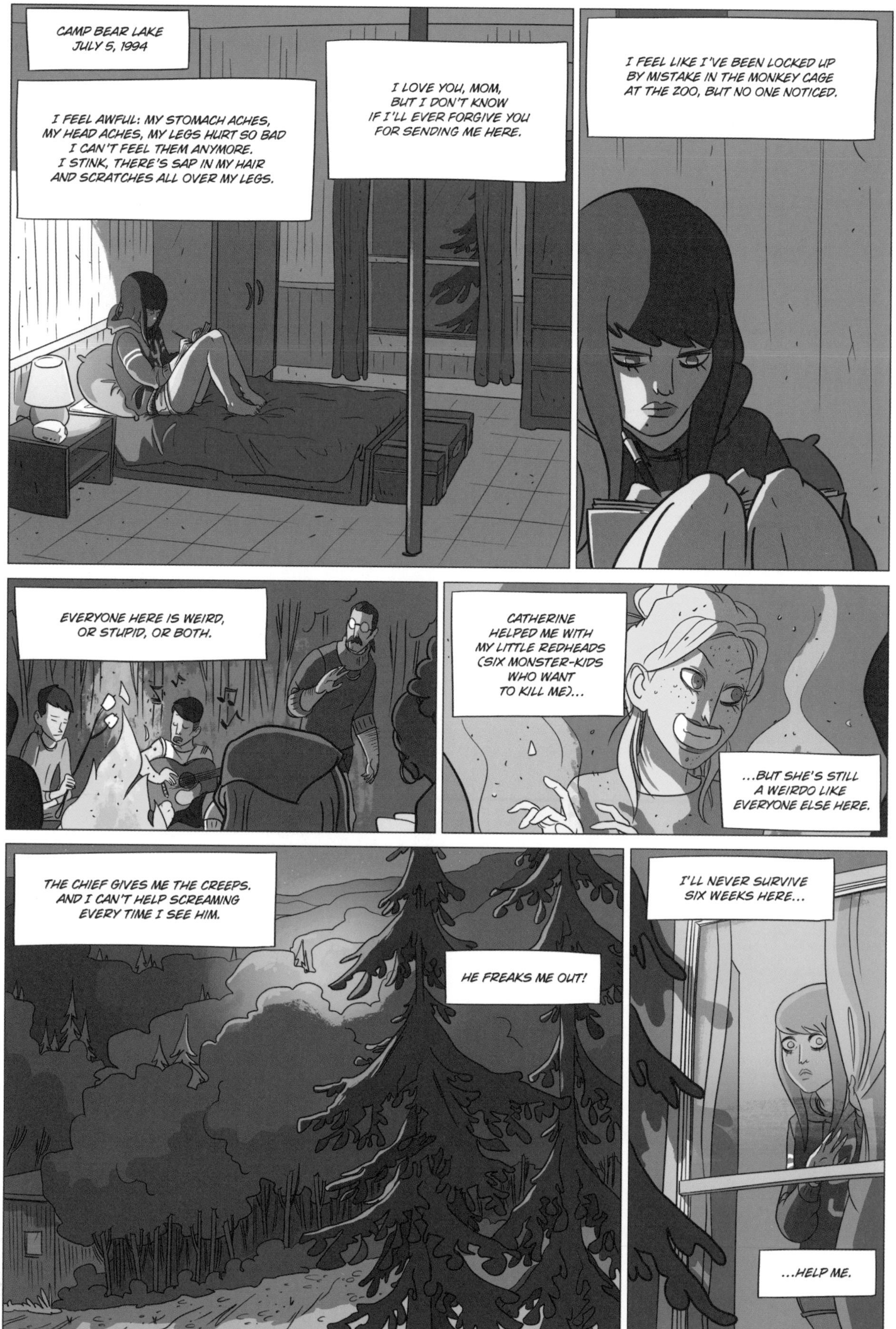
CAMP BEAR LAKE
JULY 5, 1994
I FEEL AWFUL: MY STOMACH ACHES, MY HEAD ACHES, MY LEGS HURT SO BAD I CAN'T FEEL THEM ANYMORE. I STINK, THERE'S SAP IN MY HAIR AND SCRATCHES ALL OVER MY LEGS.
I LOVE YOU, MOM, BUT I DON'T KNOW IF I'LL EVER FORGIVE YOU FOR SENDING ME HERE.
I FEEL LIKE I'VE BEEN LOCKED UP BY MISTAKE IN THE MONKEY CAGE AT THE ZOO, BUT NO ONE NOTICED.
EVERYONE HERE IS WEIRD, OR STUPID, OR BOTH.
CATHERINE HELPED ME WITH MY LITTLE REDHEADS (SIX MONSTER-KIDS WHO WANT TO KILL ME)...
...BUT SHE'S STILL A WEIRDO LIKE EVERYONE ELSE HERE.
THE CHIEF GIVES ME THE CREEPS. AND I CAN'T HELP SCREAMING EVERY TIME I SEE HIM.
HE FREAKS ME OUT!
I'LL NEVER SURVIVE SIX WEEKS HERE...
...HELP ME.

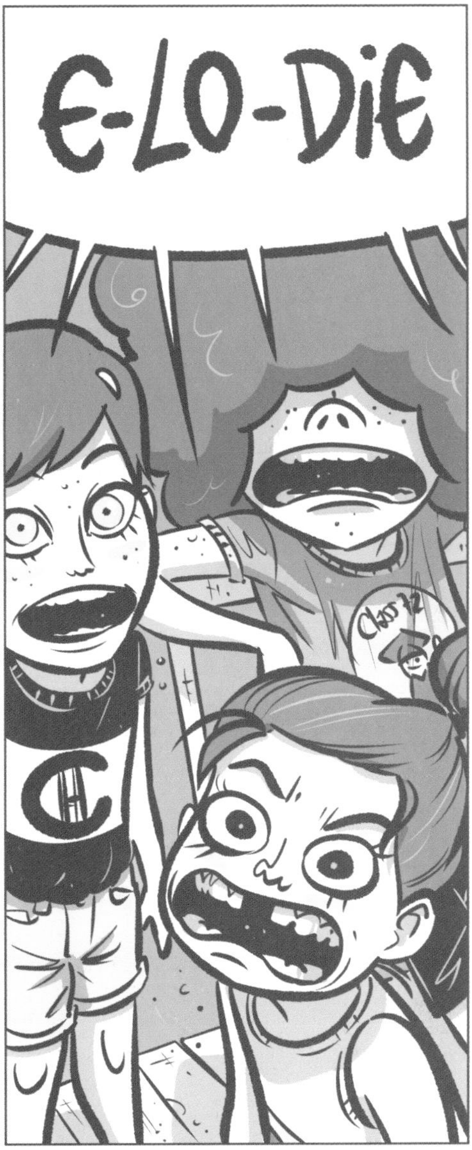
E-LO-DIE

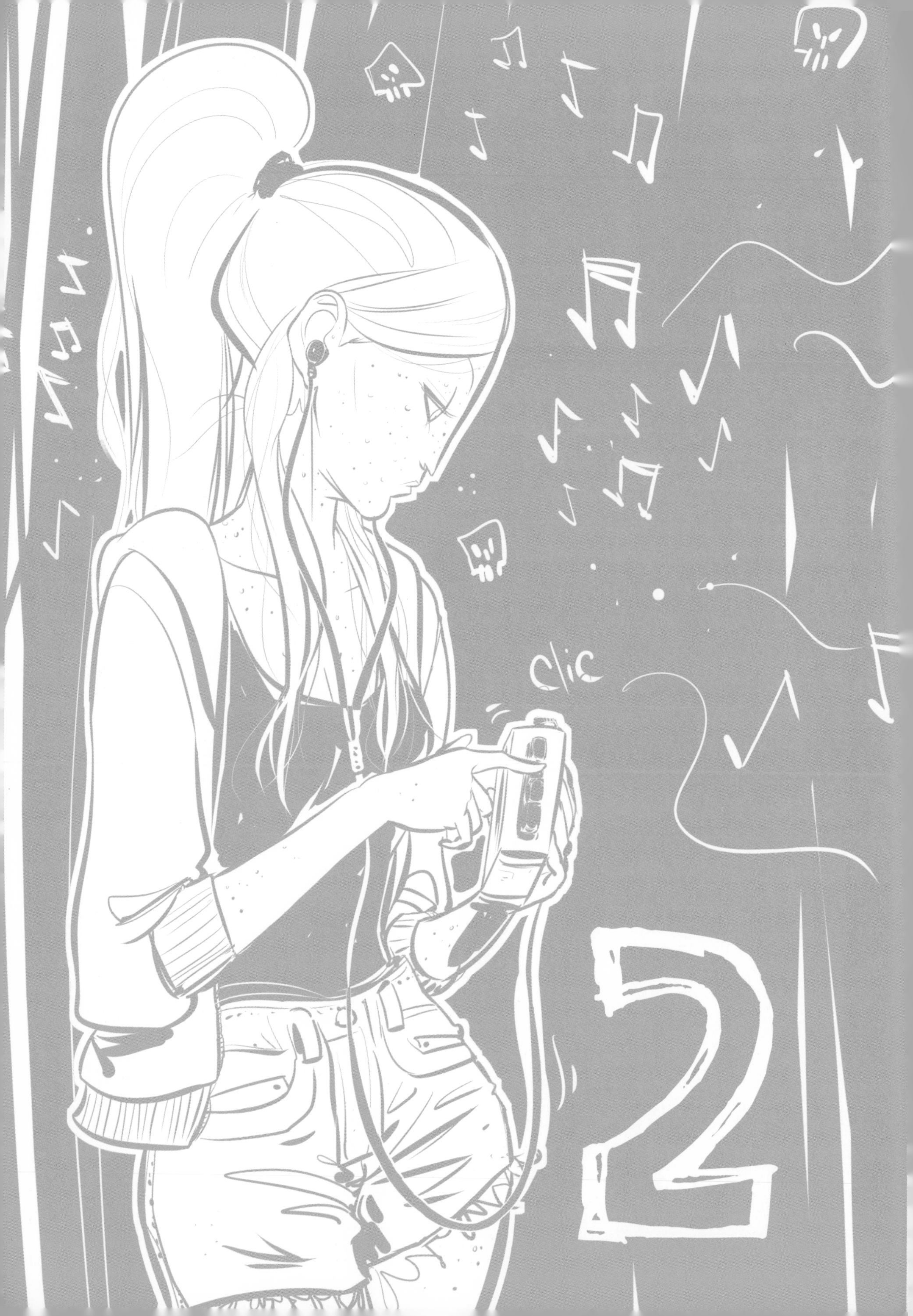
clic
2

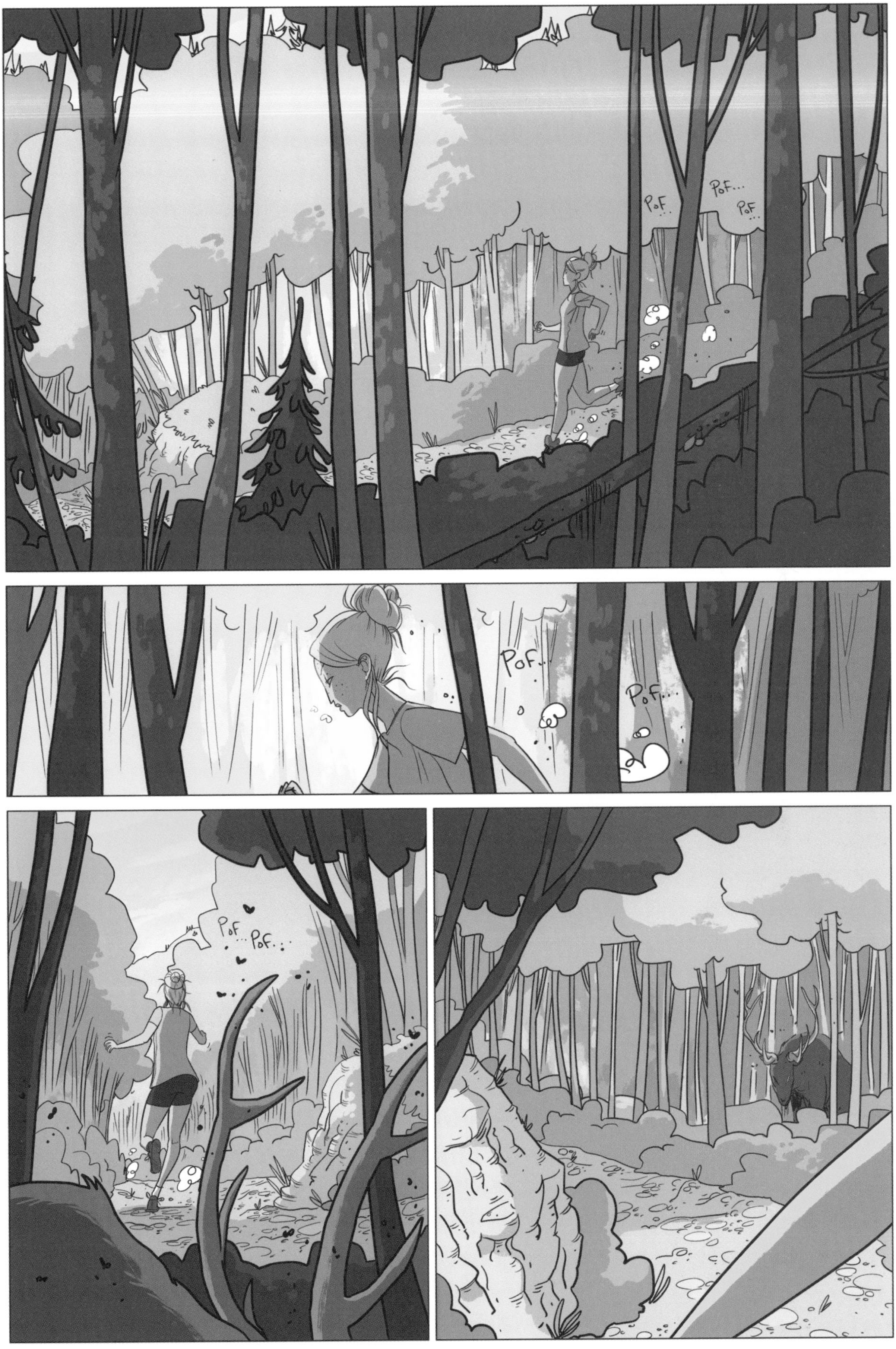
PoF...
PoF...
PoF...
PoF...
PoF...
PoF...
PoF...

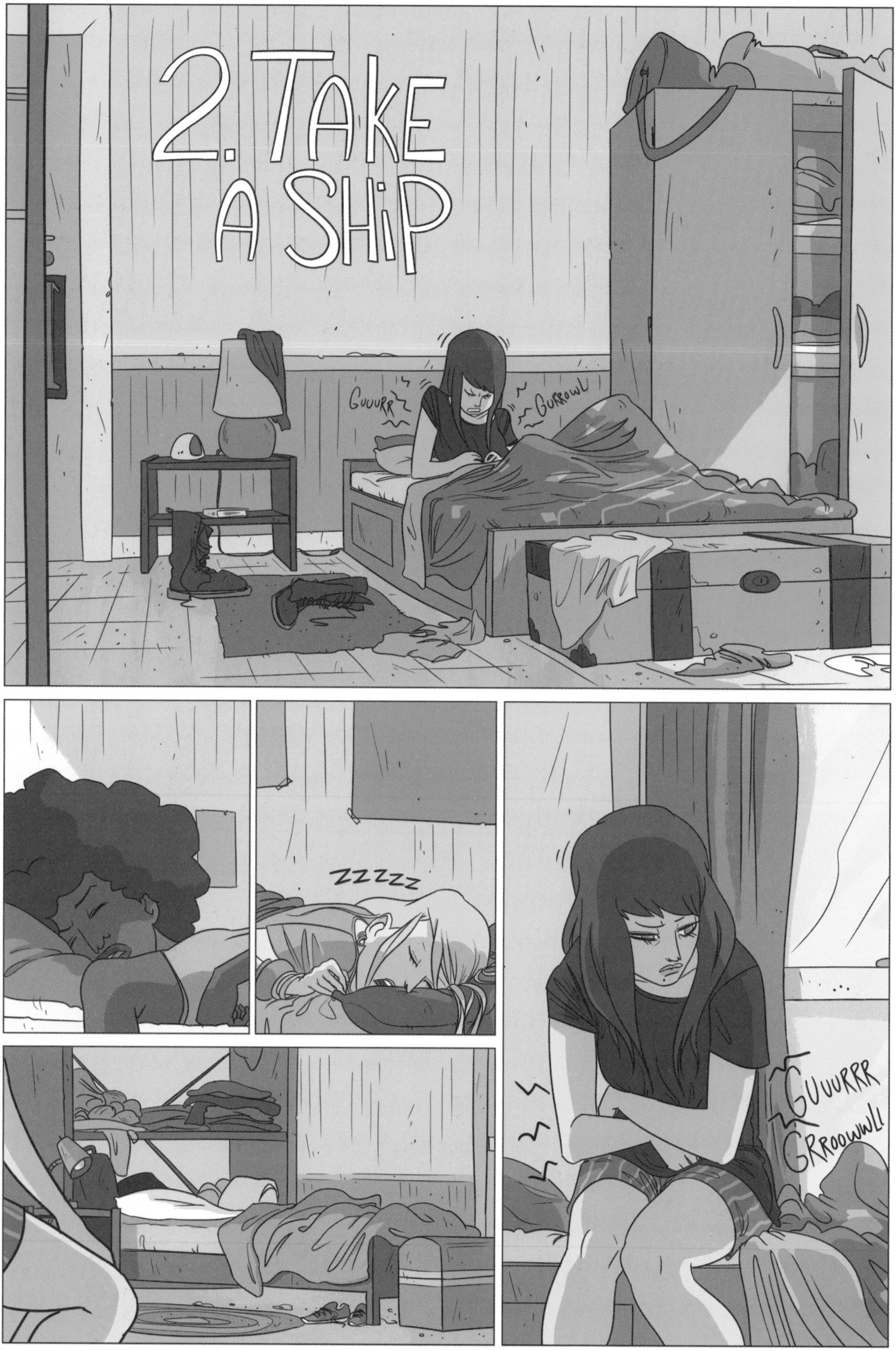
2. TAKE A SHIP
GUUURR
GURROWL
ZZZZZ
GUUURRR
GRROOWWL!

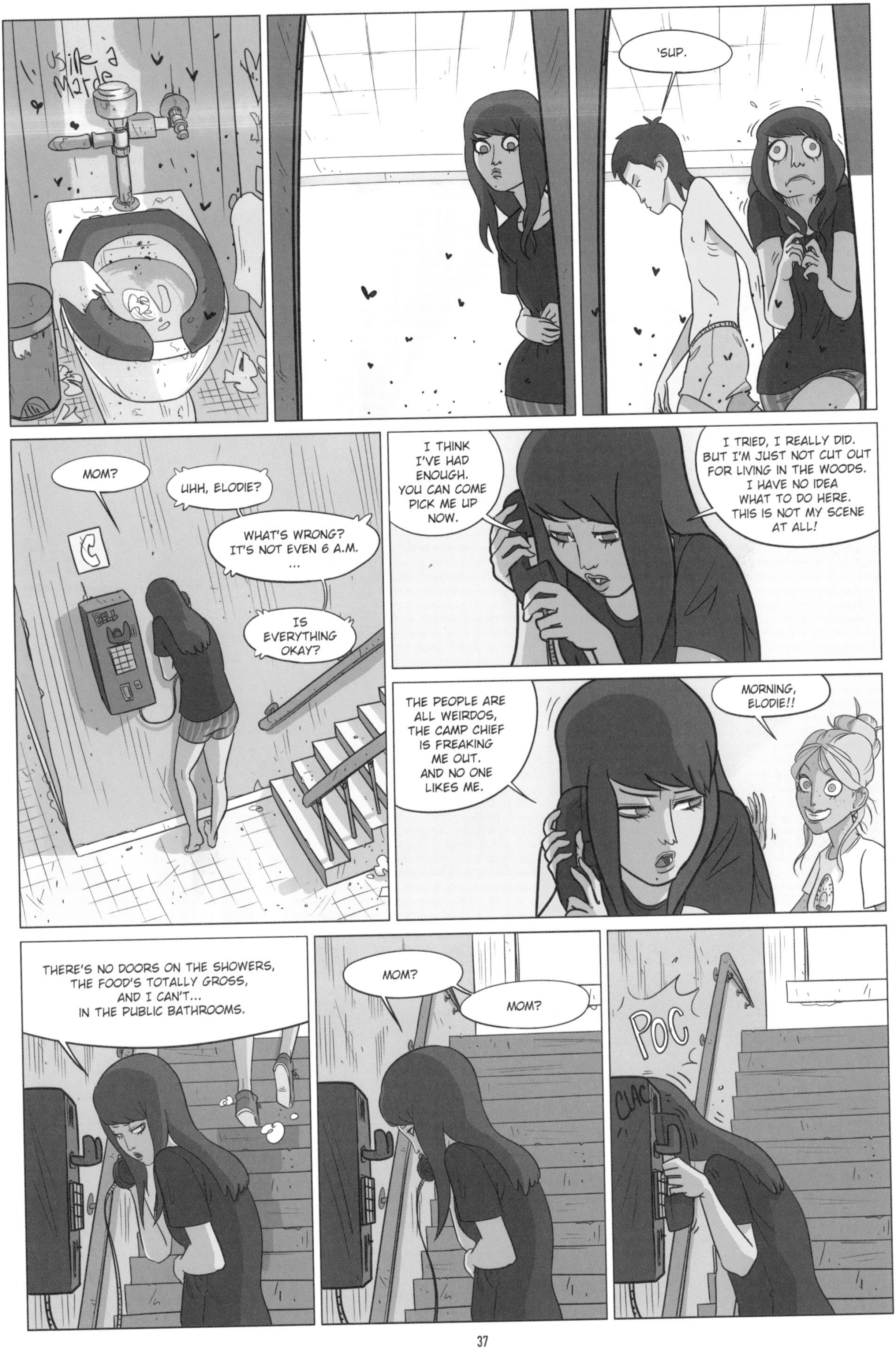
Usine à Marde
'SUP.
MOM?
UHH, ELODIE?
WHAT'S WRONG? IT'S NOT EVEN 6 A.M. ...
IS EVERYTHING OKAY?
BELL
I THINK I'VE HAD ENOUGH. YOU CAN COME PICK ME UP NOW.
I TRIED, I REALLY DID. BUT I'M JUST NOT CUT OUT FOR LIVING IN THE WOODS. I HAVE NO IDEA WHAT TO DO HERE. THIS IS NOT MY SCENE AT ALL!
THE PEOPLE ARE ALL WEIRDOS, THE CAMP CHIEF IS FREAKING ME OUT. AND NO ONE LIKES ME.
MORNING, ELODIE!!
THERE'S NO DOORS ON THE SHOWERS, THE FOOD'S TOTALLY GROSS, AND I CAN'T... IN THE PUBLIC BATHROOMS.
MOM?
MOM?
POC
CLAC

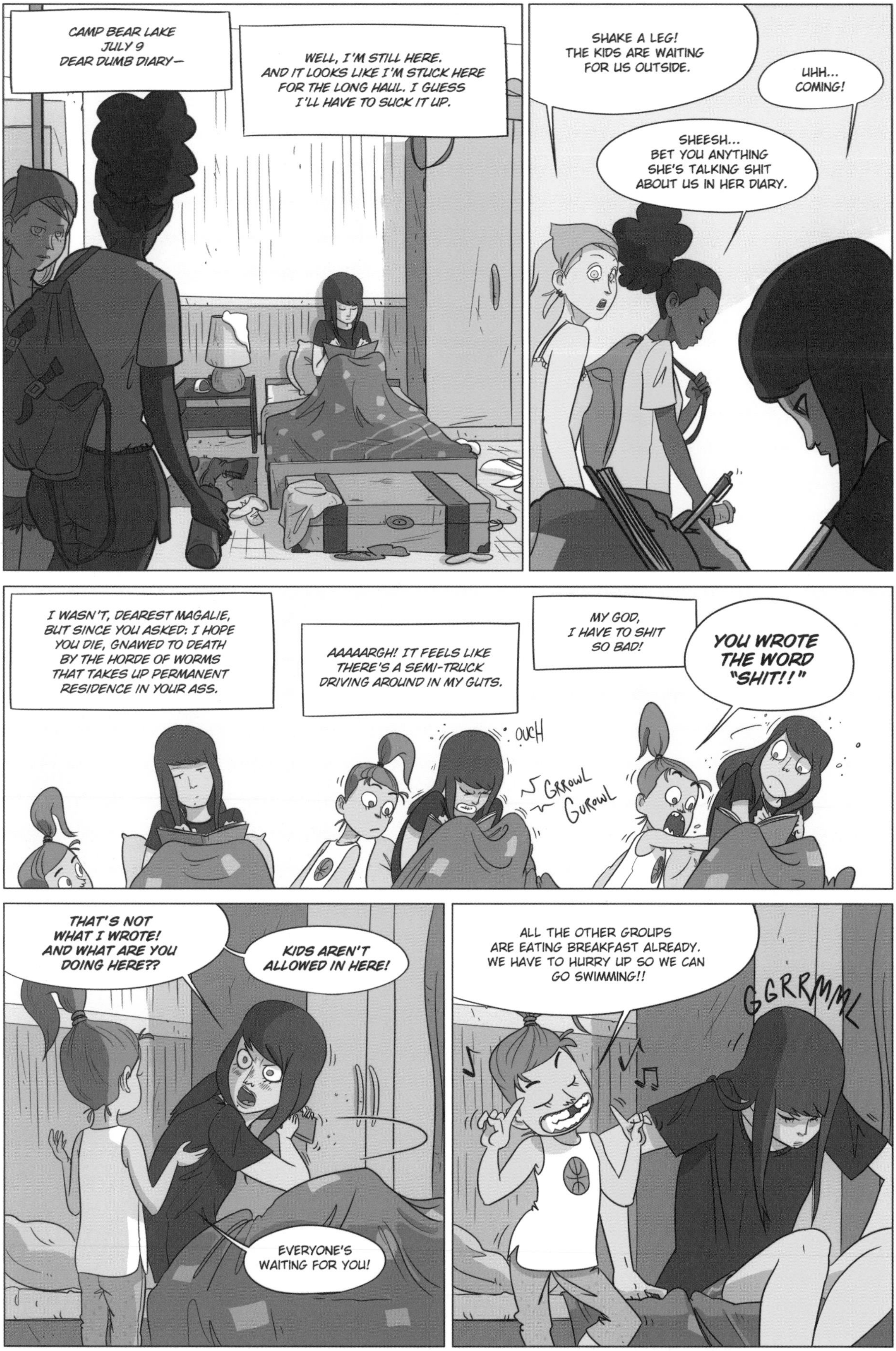
CAMP BEAR LAKE
JULY 9
DEAR DUMB DIARY—
WELL, I'M STILL HERE. AND IT LOOKS LIKE I'M STUCK HERE FOR THE LONG HAUL. I GUESS I'LL HAVE TO SUCK IT UP.
SHAKE A LEG! THE KIDS ARE WAITING FOR US OUTSIDE.
UHH... COMING!
SHEESH... BET YOU ANYTHING SHE'S TALKING SHIT ABOUT US IN HER DIARY.
I WASN'T, DEAREST MAGALIE, BUT SINCE YOU ASKED: I HOPE YOU DIE, GNAWED TO DEATH BY THE HORDE OF WORMS THAT TAKES UP PERMANENT RESIDENCE IN YOUR ASS.
AAAAARGH! IT FEELS LIKE THERE'S A SEMI-TRUCK DRIVING AROUND IN MY GUTS.
OUCH
GRROWL
GUROWL
MY GOD, I HAVE TO SHIT SO BAD!
YOU WROTE THE WORD "SHIT!!"
THAT'S NOT WHAT I WROTE! AND WHAT ARE YOU DOING HERE??
KIDS AREN'T ALLOWED IN HERE!
EVERYONE'S WAITING FOR YOU!
ALL THE OTHER GROUPS ARE EATING BREAKFAST ALREADY. WE HAVE TO HURRY UP SO WE CAN GO SWIMMING!!
GGRRMMML

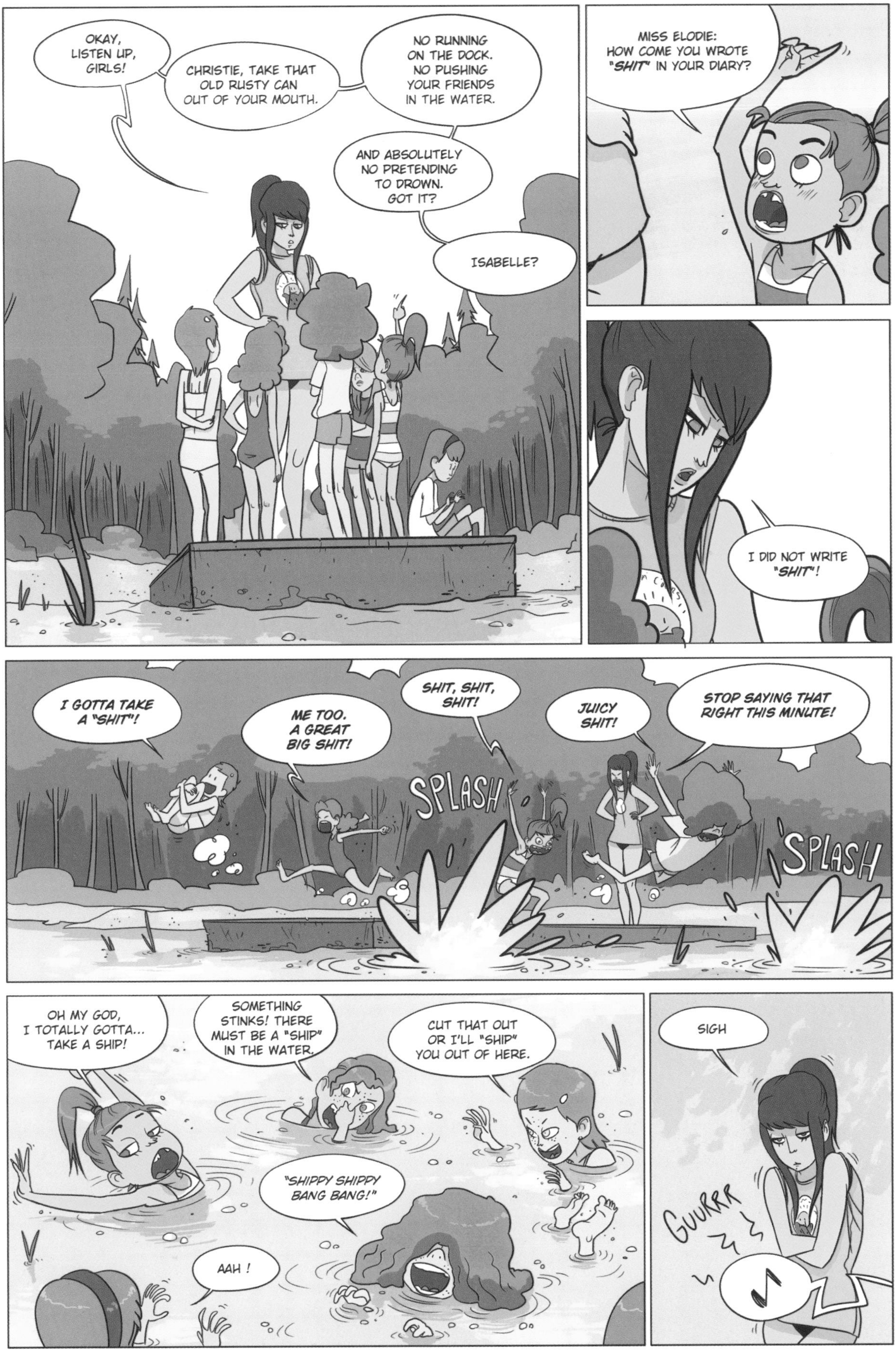
OKAY, LISTEN UP, GIRLS!
CHRISTIE, TAKE THAT OLD RUSTY CAN OUT OF YOUR MOUTH.
NO RUNNING ON THE DOCK. NO PUSHING YOUR FRIENDS IN THE WATER.
AND ABSOLUTELY NO PRETENDING TO DROWN. GOT IT?
ISABELLE?
MISS ELODIE: HOW COME YOU WROTE "SHIT" IN YOUR DIARY?
I DID NOT WRITE "SHIT"!
I GOTTA TAKE A "SHIT"!
ME TOO. A GREAT BIG SHIT!
SPLASH
SHIT, SHIT, SHIT!
JUICY SHIT!
STOP SAYING THAT RIGHT THIS MINUTE!
SPLASH
OH MY GOD, I TOTALLY GOTTA... TAKE A SHIP!
SOMETHING STINKS! THERE MUST BE A "SHIP" IN THE WATER.
CUT THAT OUT OR I'LL "SHIP" YOU OUT OF HERE.
"SHIPPY SHIPPY BANG BANG!"
AAH !
SIGH
GUURR

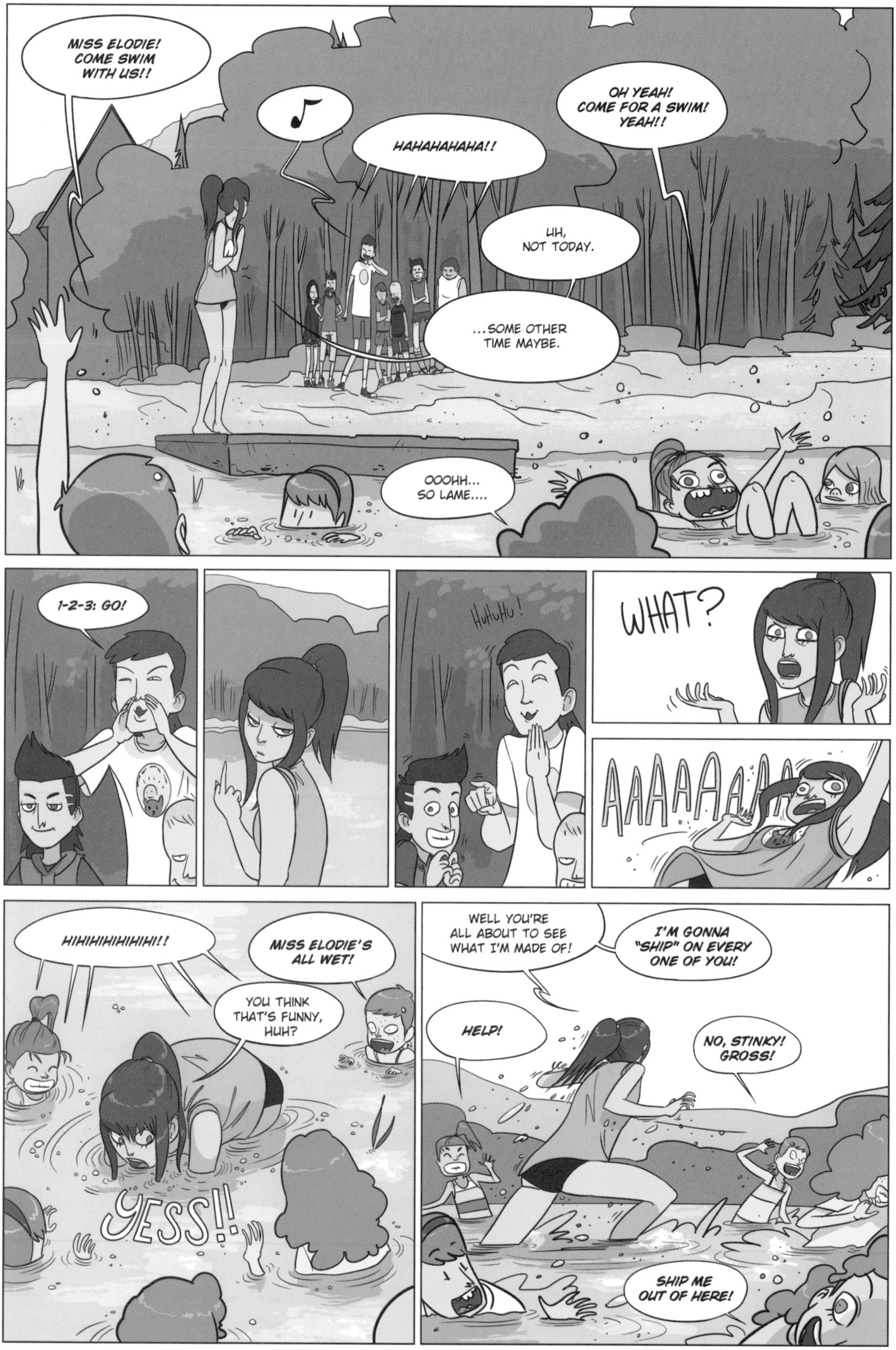
MISS ELODIE! COME SWIM WITH US!!
♪
HAHAHAHAHA!!
OH YEAH! COME FOR A SWIM! YEAH!!
UH, NOT TODAY.
...SOME OTHER TIME MAYBE.
OOOHH... SO LAME....
1-2-3: GO!
HUHUHU!
WHAT?
AAAAAAAA
HIHIHIHIHIHI!!
MISS ELODIE'S ALL WET!
YOU THINK THAT'S FUNNY, HUH?
YESS!!
WELL YOU'RE ALL ABOUT TO SEE WHAT I'M MADE OF!
I'M GONNA "SHIP" ON EVERY ONE OF YOU!
HELP!
NO, STINKY! GROSS!
SHIP ME OUT OF HERE!

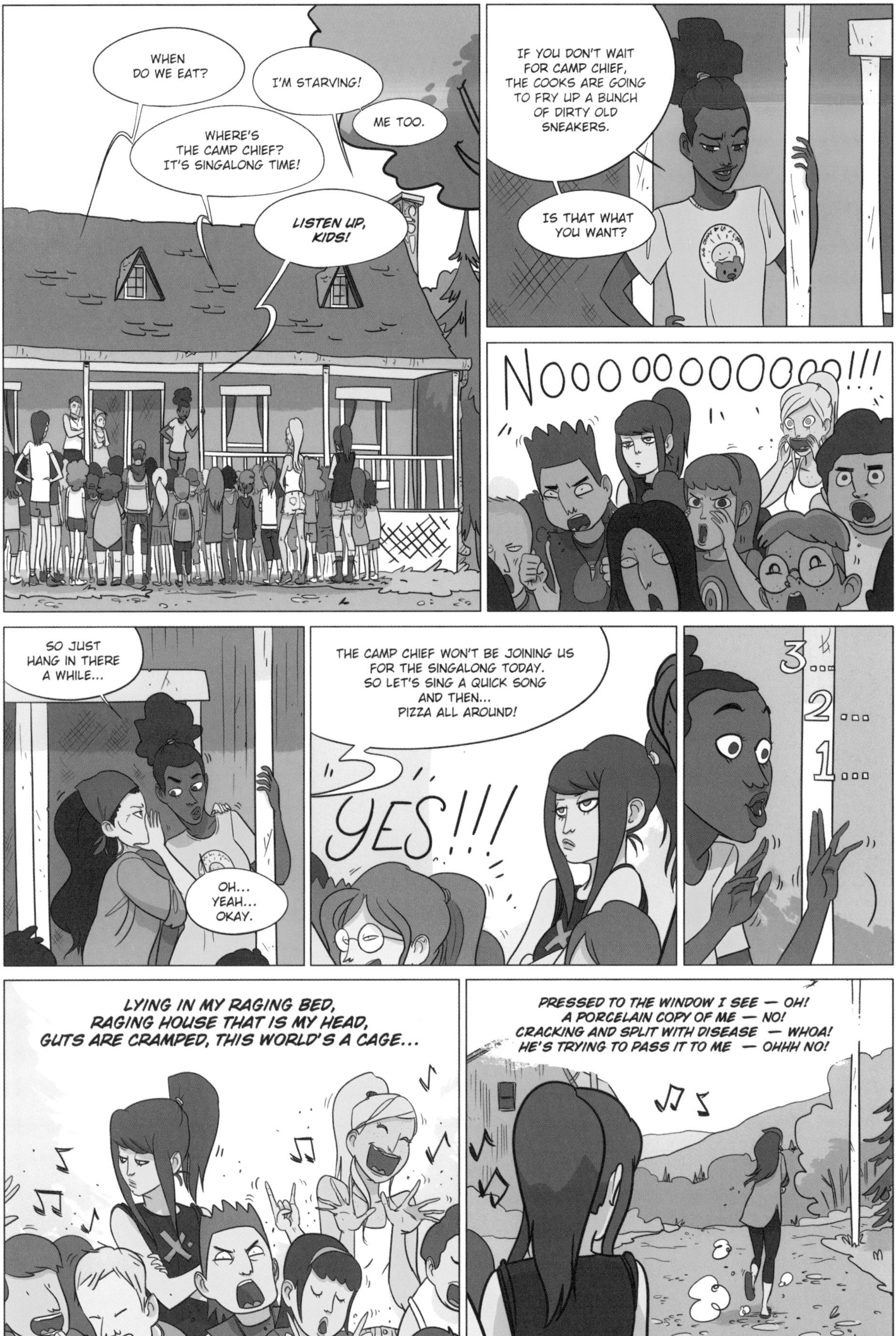
WHEN DO WE EAT?
I'M STARVING!
ME TOO.
WHERE'S THE CAMP CHIEF? IT'S SINGALONG TIME!
LISTEN UP, KIDS!
IF YOU DON'T WAIT FOR CAMP CHIEF, THE COOKS ARE GOING TO FRY UP A BUNCH OF DIRTY OLD SNEAKERS.
IS THAT WHAT YOU WANT?
NOOOOOOOOOOOO!!!
SO JUST HANG IN THERE A WHILE...
OH... YEAH... OKAY.
THE CAMP CHIEF WON'T BE JOINING US FOR THE SINGALONG TODAY. SO LET'S SING A QUICK SONG AND THEN... PIZZA ALL AROUND!
YES!!!
3...
2...
1...
LYING IN MY RAGING BED, RAGING HOUSE THAT IS MY HEAD, GUTS ARE CRAMPED, THIS WORLD'S A CAGE...
PRESSED TO THE WINDOW I SEE — OH! A PORCELAIN COPY OF ME — NO! CRACKING AND SPLIT WITH DISEASE — WHOA! HE'S TRYING TO PASS IT TO ME — OHHH NO!

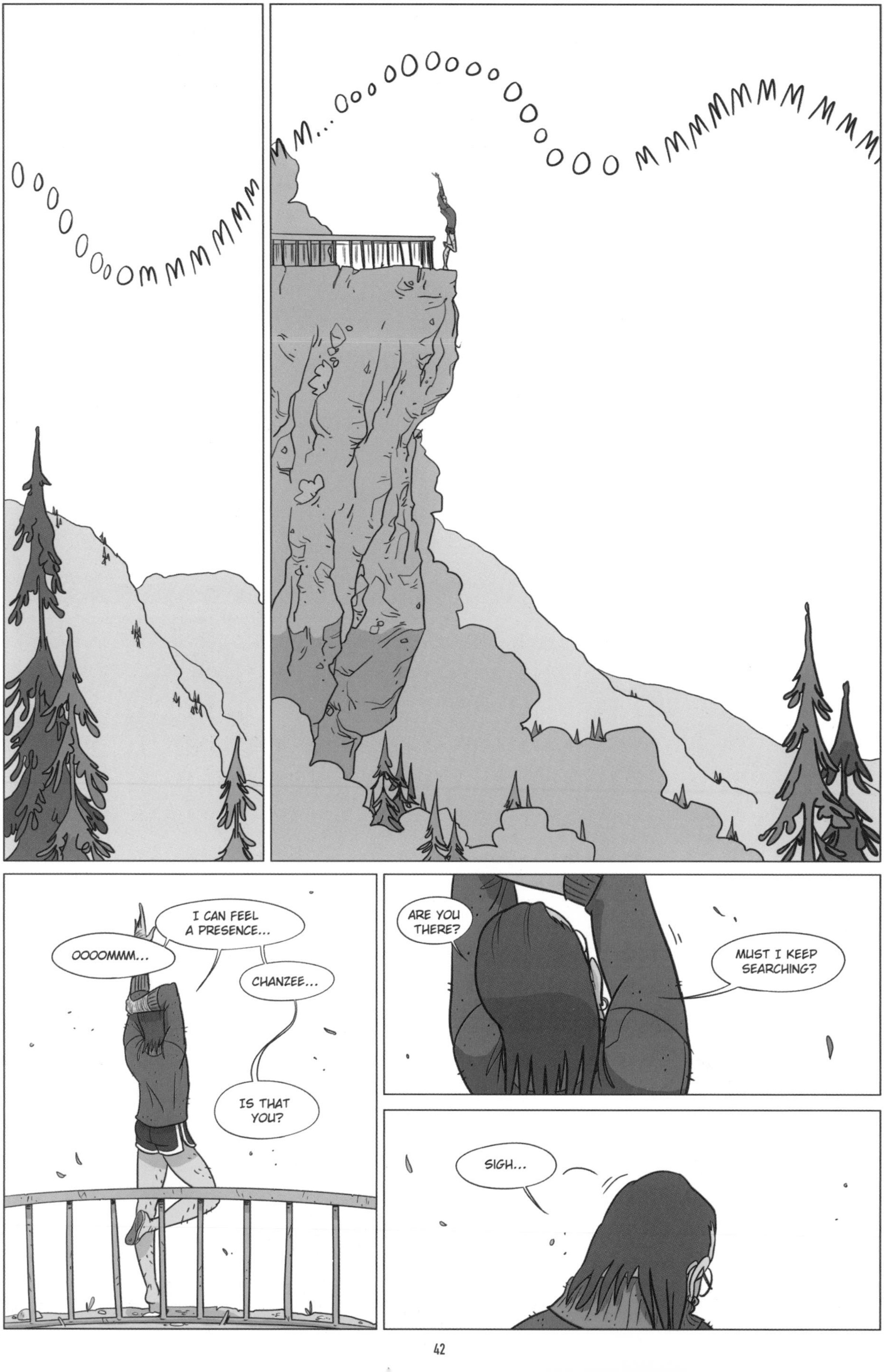

OOOOOOOOOMMMMMMMMMMM...OOOOOOOOOOOOOOOOOMMMMMMMMMMMM
OOOOMMM...
I CAN FEEL A PRESENCE...
CHANZEE...
IS THAT YOU?
ARE YOU THERE?
MUST I KEEP SEARCHING?
SIGH...

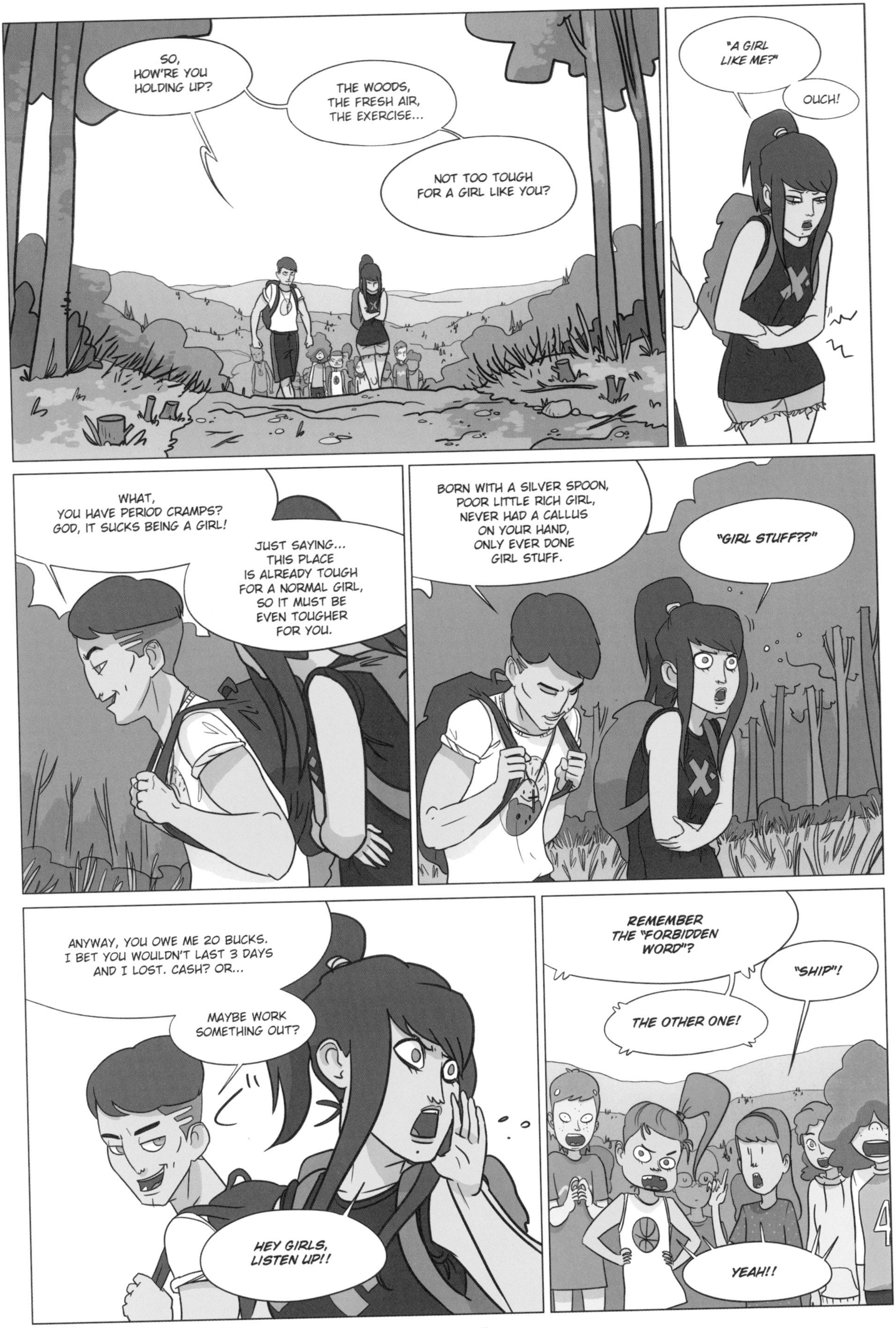

SO, HOW'RE YOU HOLDING UP?
THE WOODS, THE FRESH AIR, THE EXERCISE...
NOT TOO TOUGH FOR A GIRL LIKE YOU?
"A GIRL LIKE ME?"
OUCH!
WHAT, YOU HAVE PERIOD CRAMPS? GOD, IT SUCKS BEING A GIRL!
JUST SAYING... THIS PLACE IS ALREADY TOUGH FOR A NORMAL GIRL, SO IT MUST BE EVEN TOUGHER FOR YOU.
BORN WITH A SILVER SPOON, POOR LITTLE RICH GIRL, NEVER HAD A CALLUS ON YOUR HAND, ONLY EVER DONE GIRL STUFF.
"GIRL STUFF??"
ANYWAY, YOU OWE ME 20 BUCKS. I BET YOU WOULDN'T LAST 3 DAYS AND I LOST. CASH? OR...
MAYBE WORK SOMETHING OUT?
HEY GIRLS, LISTEN UP!!
REMEMBER THE "FORBIDDEN WORD"?
"SHIP"!
THE OTHER ONE!
YEAH!!

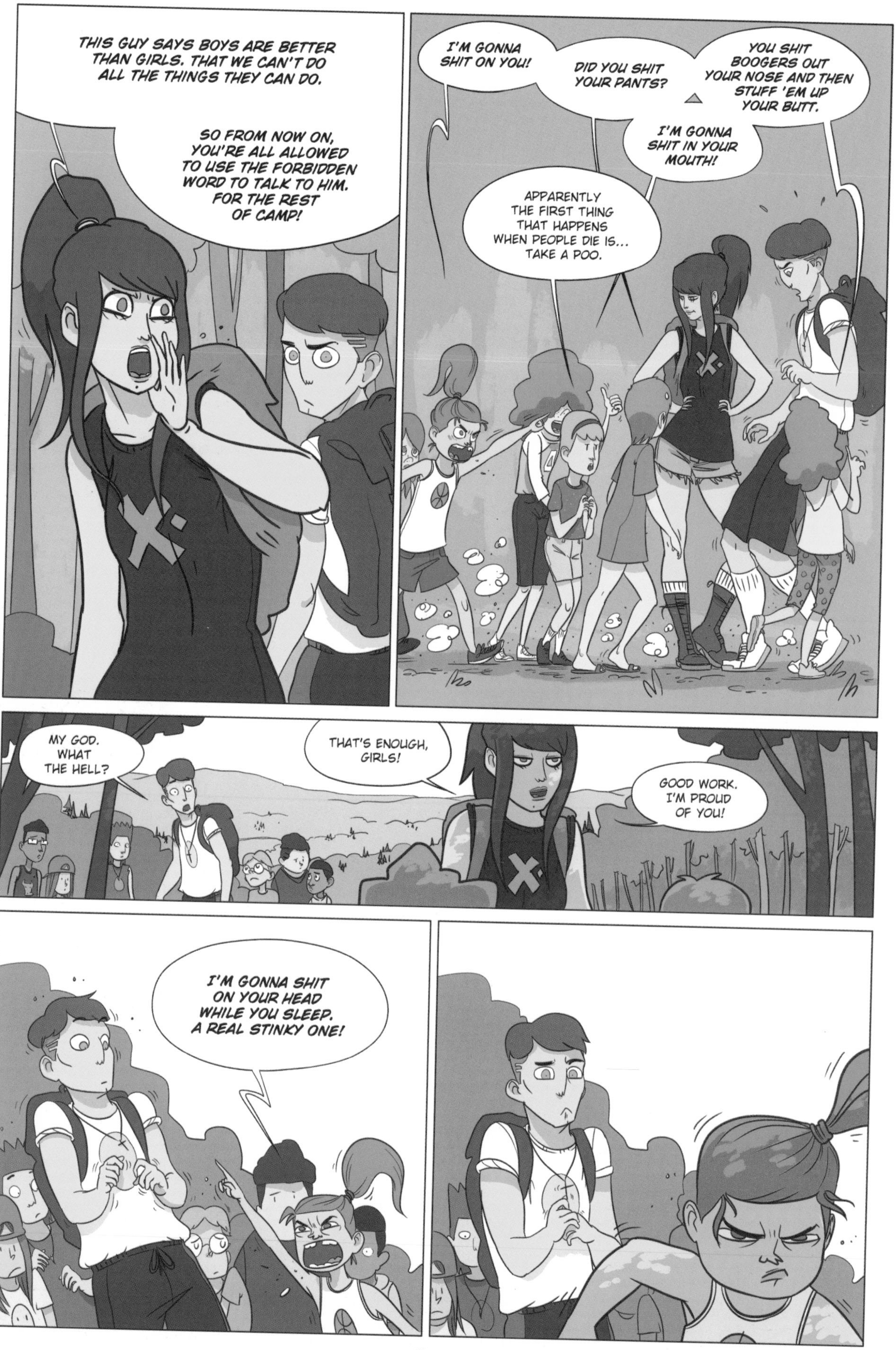
THIS GUY SAYS BOYS ARE BETTER THAN GIRLS. THAT WE CAN'T DO ALL THE THINGS THEY CAN DO.
SO FROM NOW ON, YOU'RE ALL ALLOWED TO USE THE FORBIDDEN WORD TO TALK TO HIM. FOR THE REST OF CAMP!
I'M GONNA SHIT ON YOU!
DID YOU SHIT YOUR PANTS?
YOU SHIT BOOGERS OUT YOUR NOSE AND THEN STUFF 'EM UP YOUR BUTT.
I'M GONNA SHIT IN YOUR MOUTH!
APPARENTLY THE FIRST THING THAT HAPPENS WHEN PEOPLE DIE IS... TAKE A POO.
MY GOD. WHAT THE HELL?
THAT'S ENOUGH, GIRLS!
GOOD WORK. I'M PROUD OF YOU!
I'M GONNA SHIT ON YOUR HEAD WHILE YOU SLEEP. A REAL STINKY ONE!

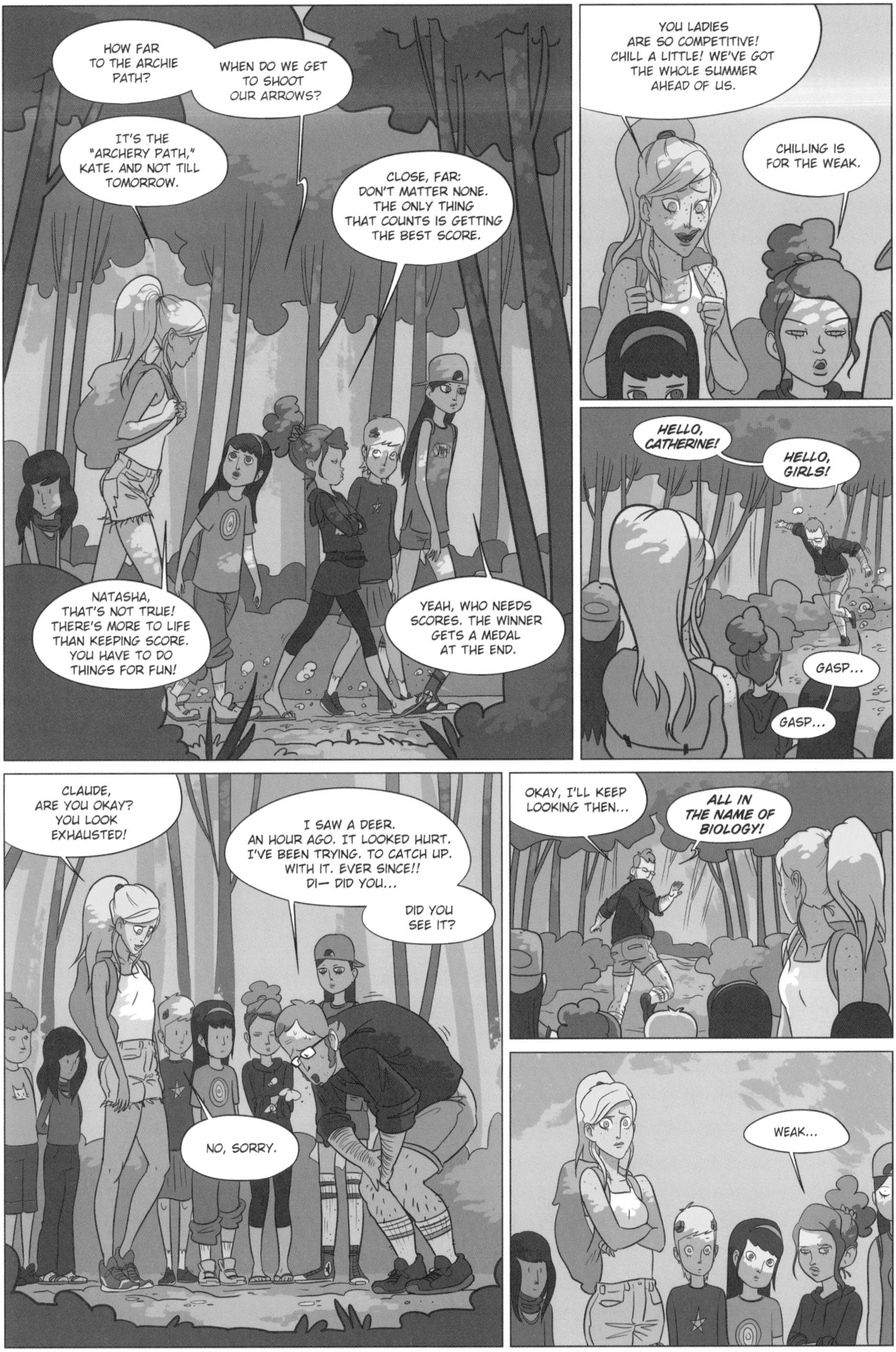
HOW FAR TO THE ARCHIE PATH?
WHEN DO WE GET TO SHOOT OUR ARROWS?
IT'S THE "ARCHERY PATH," KATE. AND NOT TILL TOMORROW.
CLOSE, FAR: DON'T MATTER NONE. THE ONLY THING THAT COUNTS IS GETTING THE BEST SCORE.
NATASHA, THAT'S NOT TRUE! THERE'S MORE TO LIFE THAN KEEPING SCORE. YOU HAVE TO DO THINGS FOR FUN!
YEAH, WHO NEEDS SCORES. THE WINNER GETS A MEDAL AT THE END.
YOU LADIES ARE SO COMPETITIVE! CHILL A LITTLE! WE'VE GOT THE WHOLE SUMMER AHEAD OF US.
CHILLING IS FOR THE WEAK.
HELLO, CATHERINE!
HELLO, GIRLS!
GASP...
GASP...
CLAUDE, ARE YOU OKAY? YOU LOOK EXHAUSTED!
I SAW A DEER. AN HOUR AGO. IT LOOKED HURT. I'VE BEEN TRYING. TO CATCH UP. WITH IT. EVER SINCE!! DI— DID YOU...
DID YOU SEE IT?
NO, SORRY.
OKAY, I'LL KEEP LOOKING THEN...
ALL IN THE NAME OF BIOLOGY!
WEAK...

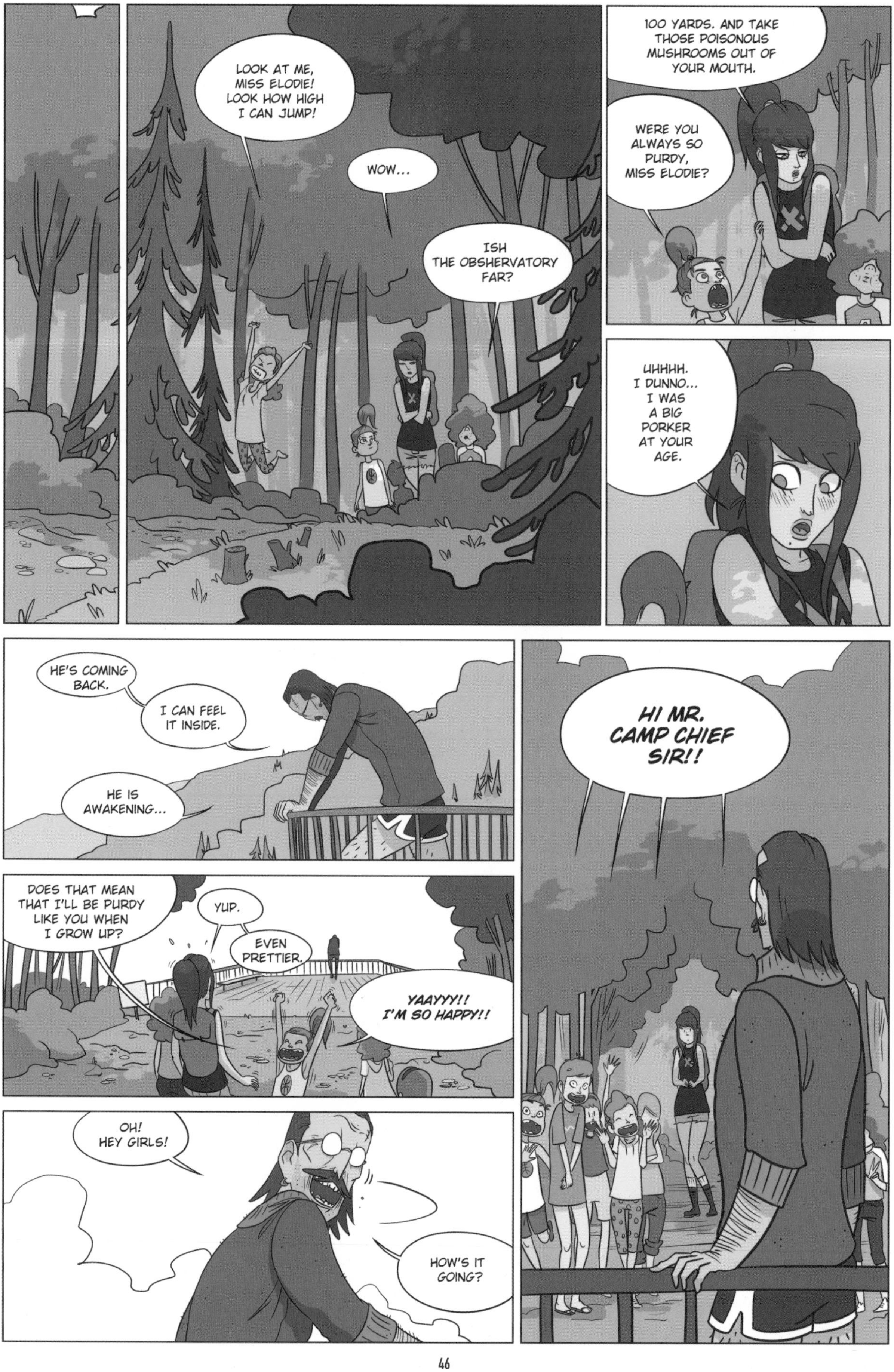
LOOK AT ME, MISS ELODIE! LOOK HOW HIGH I CAN JUMP!
WOW...
ISH THE OBSHERVATORY FAR?
100 YARDS. AND TAKE THOSE POISONOUS MUSHROOMS OUT OF YOUR MOUTH.
WERE YOU ALWAYS SO PURDY, MISS ELODIE?
UHHHH. I DUNNO... I WAS A BIG PORKER AT YOUR AGE.
HE'S COMING BACK.
I CAN FEEL IT INSIDE.
HE IS AWAKENING...
DOES THAT MEAN THAT I'LL BE PURDY LIKE YOU WHEN I GROW UP?
YUP.
EVEN PRETTIER.
YAAYYY!! I'M SO HAPPY!!
HI MR. CAMP CHIEF SIR!!
OH! HEY GIRLS!
HOW'S IT GOING?

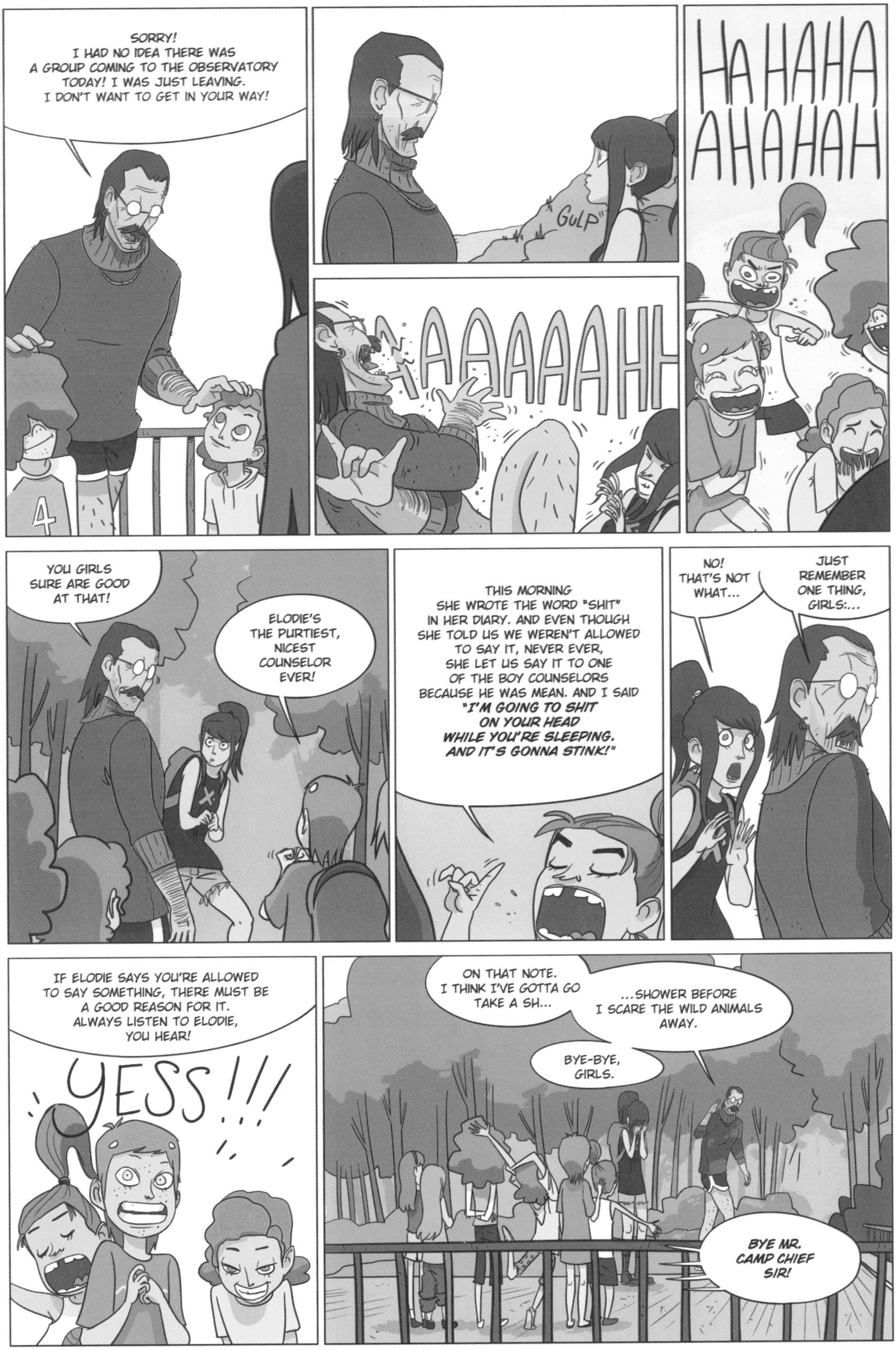
SORRY! I HAD NO IDEA THERE WAS A GROUP COMING TO THE OBSERVATORY TODAY! I WAS JUST LEAVING. I DON'T WANT TO GET IN YOUR WAY!
4
GULP
AAAAAAAHH
HA HAHA AHAHAH
YOU GIRLS SURE ARE GOOD AT THAT!
ELODIE'S THE PURTIEST, NICEST COUNSELOR EVER!
THIS MORNING SHE WROTE THE WORD "SHIT" IN HER DIARY. AND EVEN THOUGH SHE TOLD US WE WEREN'T ALLOWED TO SAY IT, NEVER EVER, SHE LET US SAY IT TO ONE OF THE BOY COUNSELORS BECAUSE HE WAS MEAN. AND I SAID "I'M GOING TO SHIT ON YOUR HEAD WHILE YOU'RE SLEEPING. AND IT'S GONNA STINK!"
NO! THAT'S NOT WHAT...
JUST REMEMBER ONE THING, GIRLS:...
IF ELODIE SAYS YOU'RE ALLOWED TO SAY SOMETHING, THERE MUST BE A GOOD REASON FOR IT. ALWAYS LISTEN TO ELODIE, YOU HEAR!
YESS!!!
ON THAT NOTE. I THINK I'VE GOTTA GO TAKE A SH...
...SHOWER BEFORE I SCARE THE WILD ANIMALS AWAY.
BYE-BYE, GIRLS.
BYE MR. CAMP CHIEF SIR!

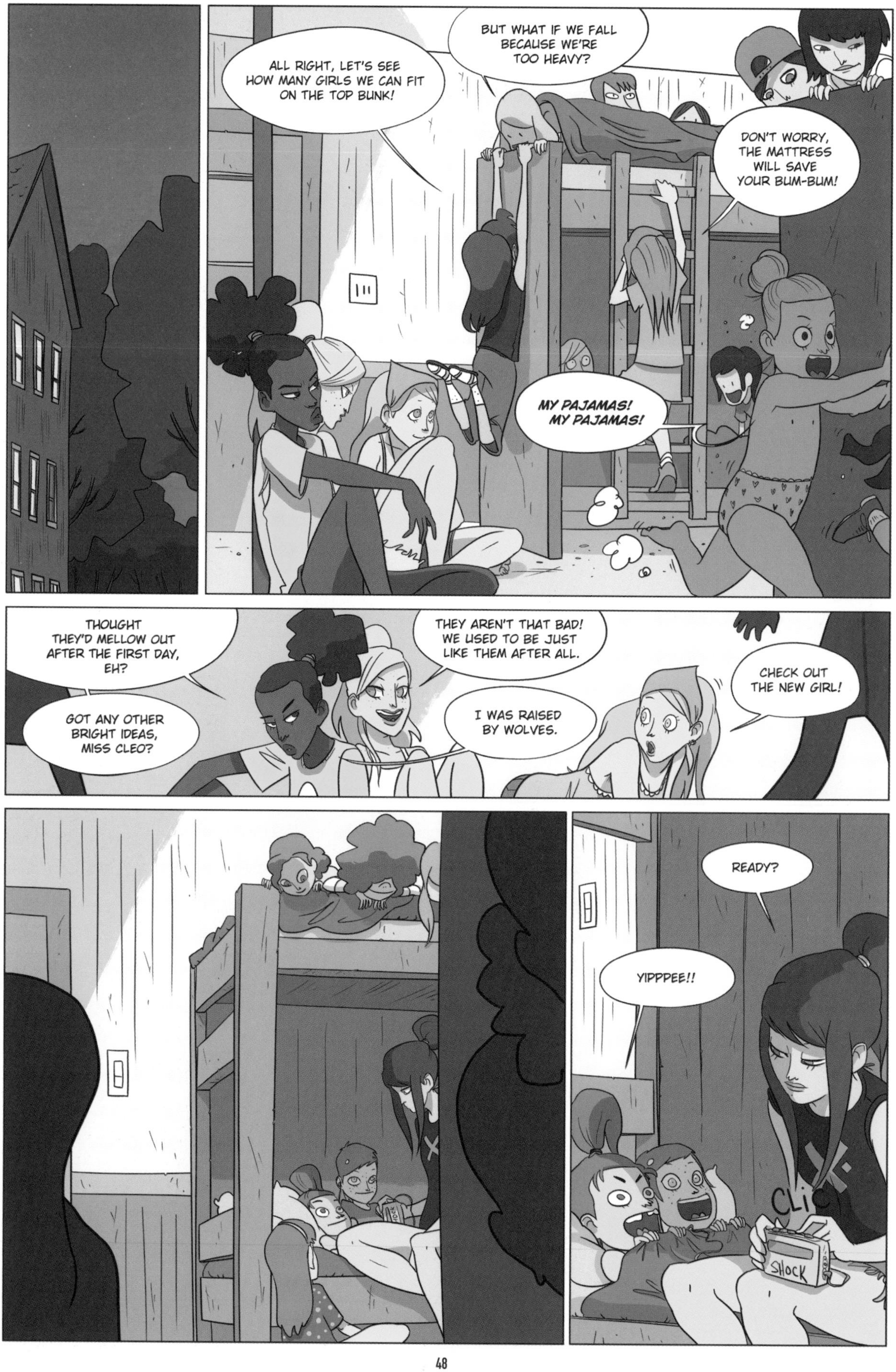
ALL RIGHT, LET'S SEE HOW MANY GIRLS WE CAN FIT ON THE TOP BUNK!
BUT WHAT IF WE FALL BECAUSE WE'RE TOO HEAVY?
DON'T WORRY, THE MATTRESS WILL SAVE YOUR BUM-BUM!
MY PAJAMAS! MY PAJAMAS!
THOUGHT THEY'D MELLOW OUT AFTER THE FIRST DAY, EH?
GOT ANY OTHER BRIGHT IDEAS, MISS CLEO?
THEY AREN'T THAT BAD! WE USED TO BE JUST LIKE THEM AFTER ALL.
I WAS RAISED BY WOLVES.
CHECK OUT THE NEW GIRL!
READY?
YIPPPEE!!
CLIC
SHOCK

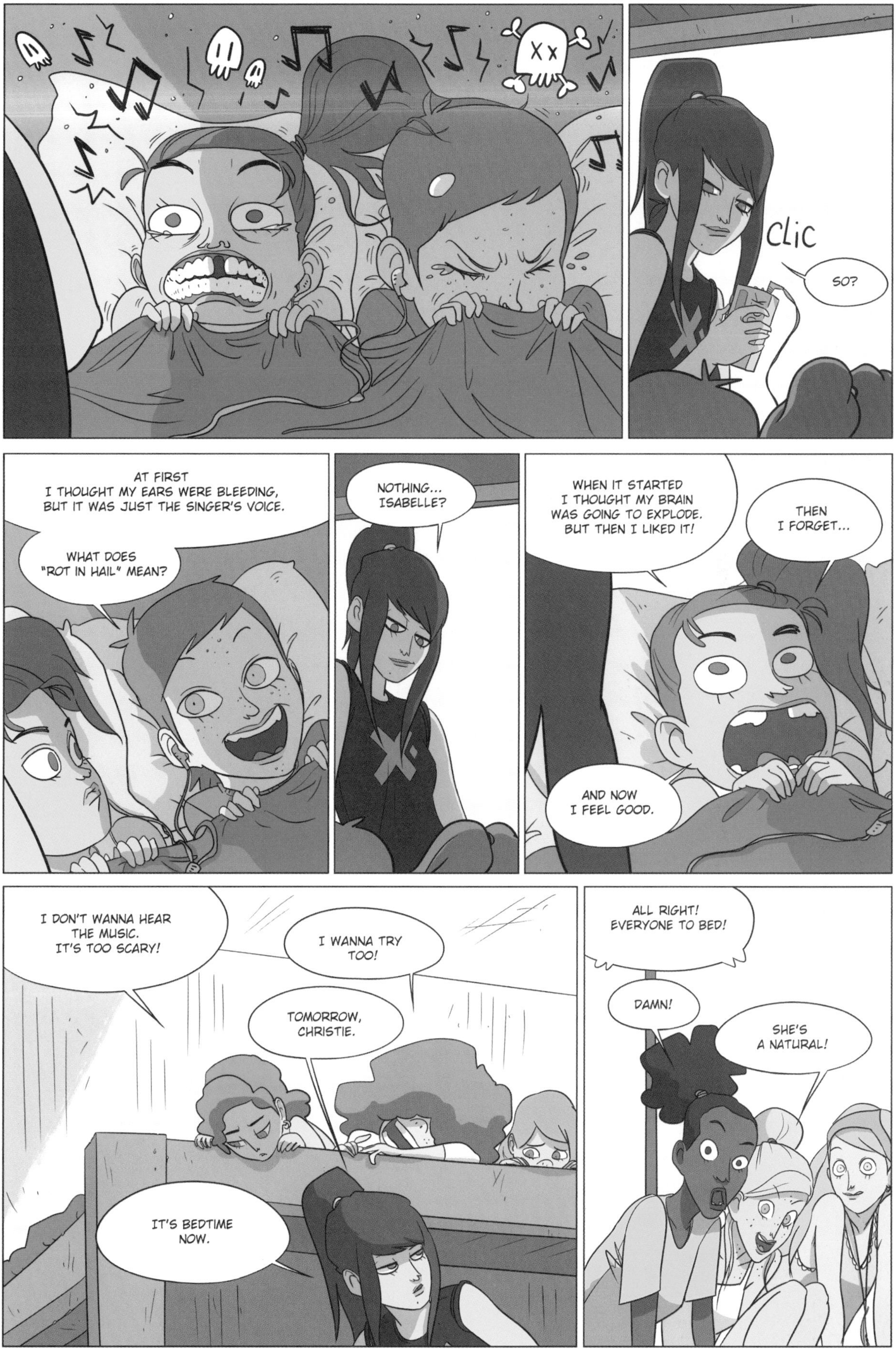
CLIC
SO?
AT FIRST I THOUGHT MY EARS WERE BLEEDING, BUT IT WAS JUST THE SINGER'S VOICE.
WHAT DOES "ROT IN HAIL" MEAN?
NOTHING... ISABELLE?
WHEN IT STARTED I THOUGHT MY BRAIN WAS GOING TO EXPLODE. BUT THEN I LIKED IT!
THEN I FORGET...
AND NOW I FEEL GOOD.
I DON'T WANNA HEAR THE MUSIC. IT'S TOO SCARY!
I WANNA TRY TOO!
TOMORROW, CHRISTIE.
IT'S BEDTIME NOW.
ALL RIGHT! EVERYONE TO BED!
DAMN!
SHE'S A NATURAL!

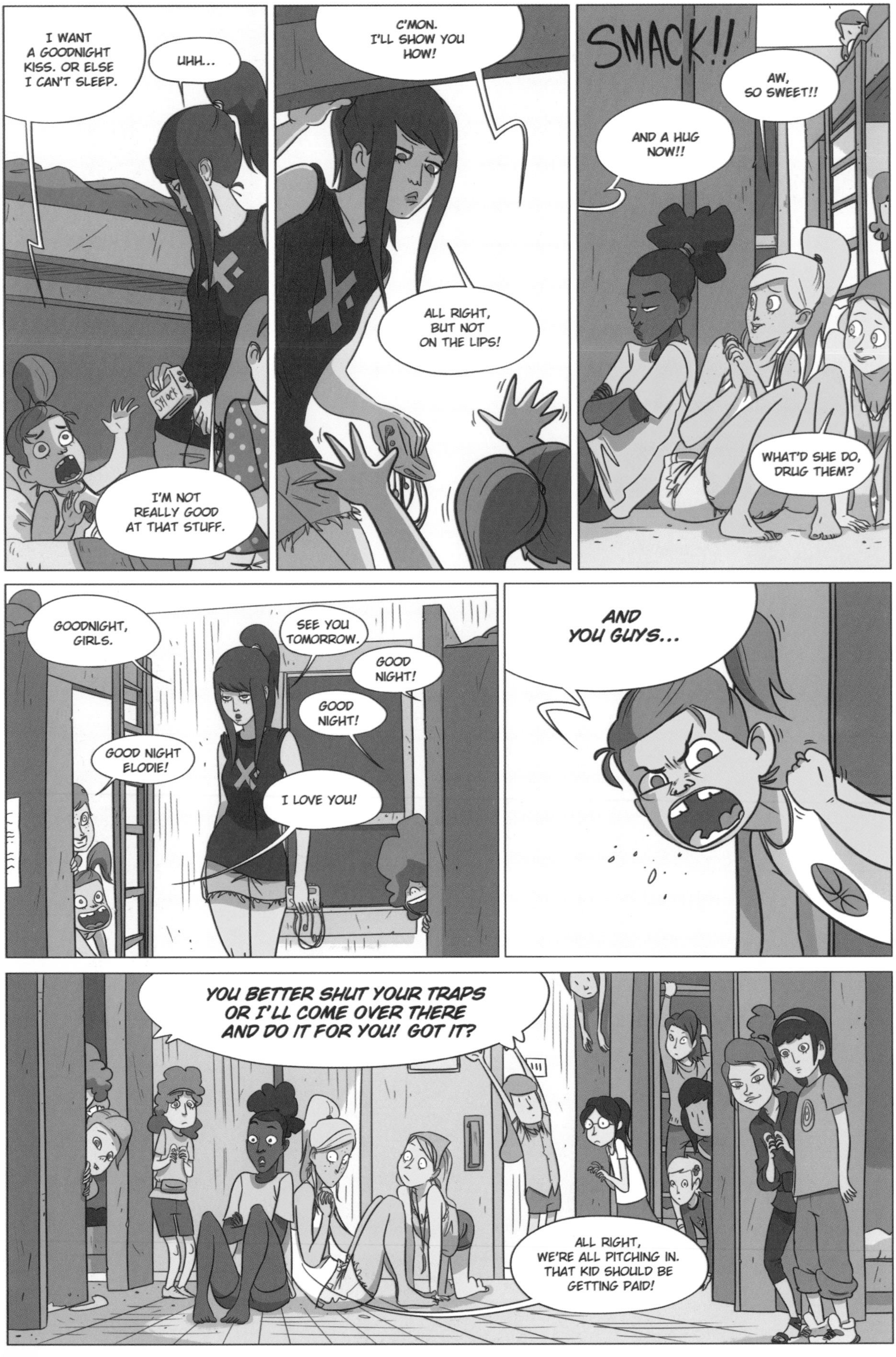
I WANT A GOODNIGHT KISS. OR ELSE I CAN'T SLEEP.
UHH...
I'M NOT REALLY GOOD AT THAT STUFF.
C'MON. I'LL SHOW YOU HOW!
ALL RIGHT, BUT NOT ON THE LIPS!
SMACK!!
AW, SO SWEET!!
AND A HUG NOW!!
WHAT'D SHE DO, DRUG THEM?
GOODNIGHT, GIRLS.
SEE YOU TOMORROW.
GOOD NIGHT!
GOOD NIGHT!
GOOD NIGHT ELODIE!
I LOVE YOU!
AND YOU GUYS...
YOU BETTER SHUT YOUR TRAPS OR I'LL COME OVER THERE AND DO IT FOR YOU! GOT IT?
ALL RIGHT, WE'RE ALL PITCHING IN. THAT KID SHOULD BE GETTING PAID!

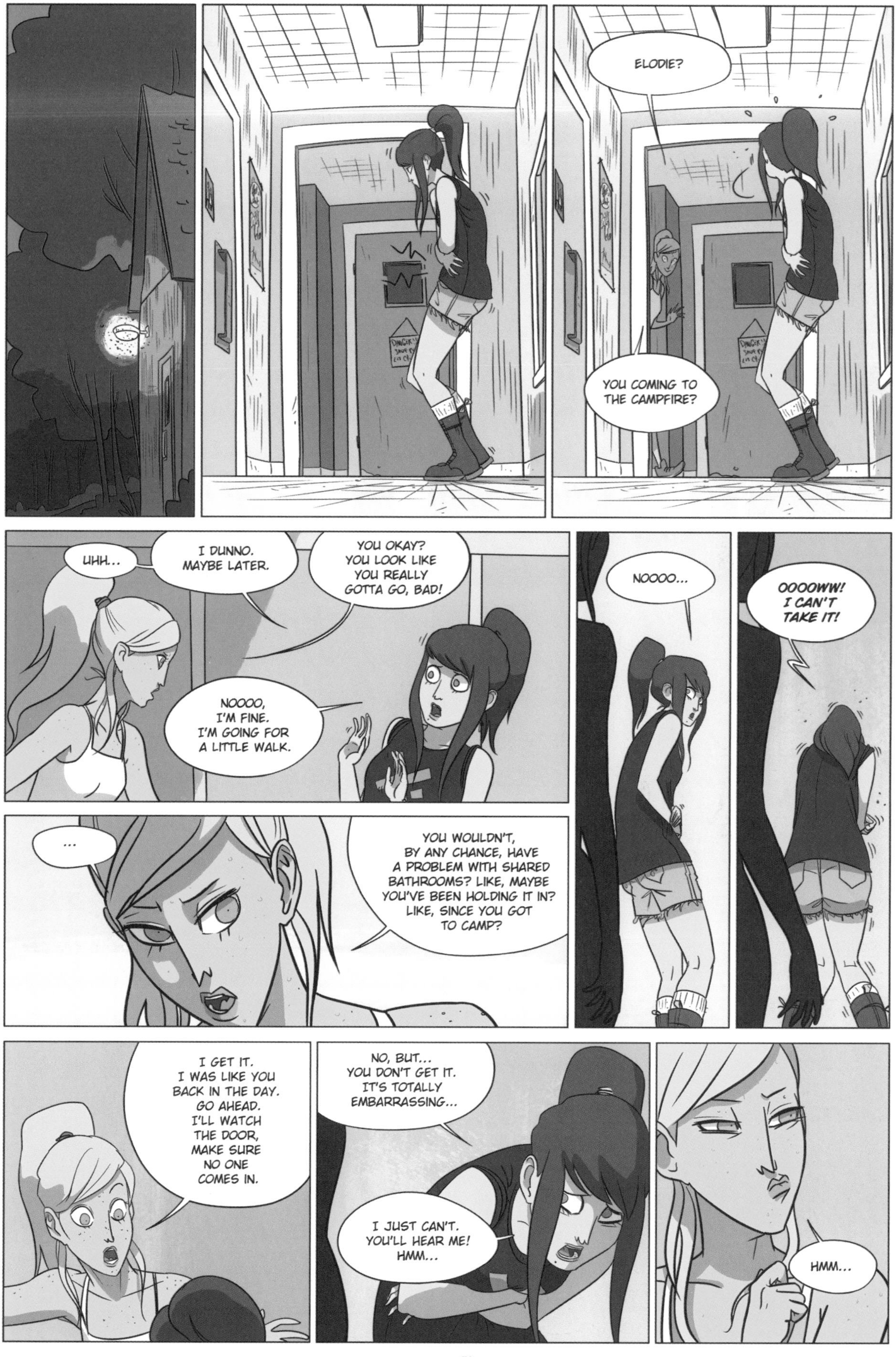
ELODIE?
YOU COMING TO THE CAMPFIRE?
UHH...
I DUNNO. MAYBE LATER.
YOU OKAY? YOU LOOK LIKE YOU REALLY GOTTA GO, BAD!
NOOOO, I'M FINE. I'M GOING FOR A LITTLE WALK.
NOOOO...
OOOOWW! I CAN'T TAKE IT!
...
YOU WOULDN'T, BY ANY CHANCE, HAVE A PROBLEM WITH SHARED BATHROOMS? LIKE, MAYBE YOU'VE BEEN HOLDING IT IN? LIKE, SINCE YOU GOT TO CAMP?
I GET IT. I WAS LIKE YOU BACK IN THE DAY. GO AHEAD. I'LL WATCH THE DOOR, MAKE SURE NO ONE COMES IN.
NO, BUT... YOU DON'T GET IT. IT'S TOTALLY EMBARRASSING...
I JUST CAN'T. YOU'LL HEAR ME! HMM...
HMM...

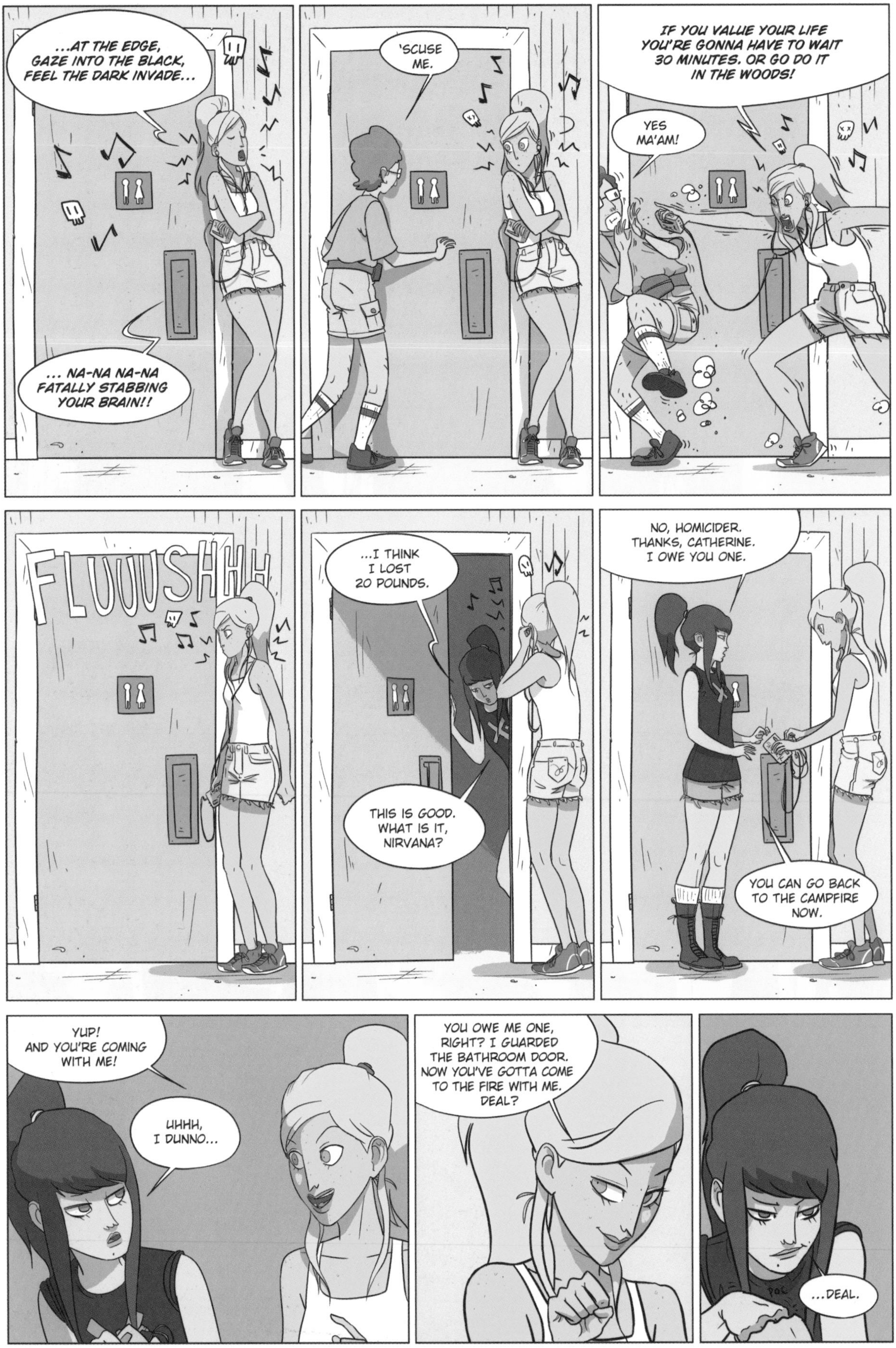
...AT THE EDGE, GAZE INTO THE BLACK, FEEL THE DARK INVADE...
... NA-NA NA-NA FATALLY STABBING YOUR BRAIN!!
'SCUSE ME.
IF YOU VALUE YOUR LIFE YOU'RE GONNA HAVE TO WAIT 30 MINUTES. OR GO DO IT IN THE WOODS!
YES MA'AM!
FLUUUSHHH
...I THINK I LOST 20 POUNDS.
THIS IS GOOD. WHAT IS IT, NIRVANA?
NO, HOMICIDER. THANKS, CATHERINE. I OWE YOU ONE.
YOU CAN GO BACK TO THE CAMPFIRE NOW.
YUP! AND YOU'RE COMING WITH ME!
UHHH, I DUNNO...
YOU OWE ME ONE, RIGHT? I GUARDED THE BATHROOM DOOR. NOW YOU'VE GOTTA COME TO THE FIRE WITH ME. DEAL?
...DEAL.

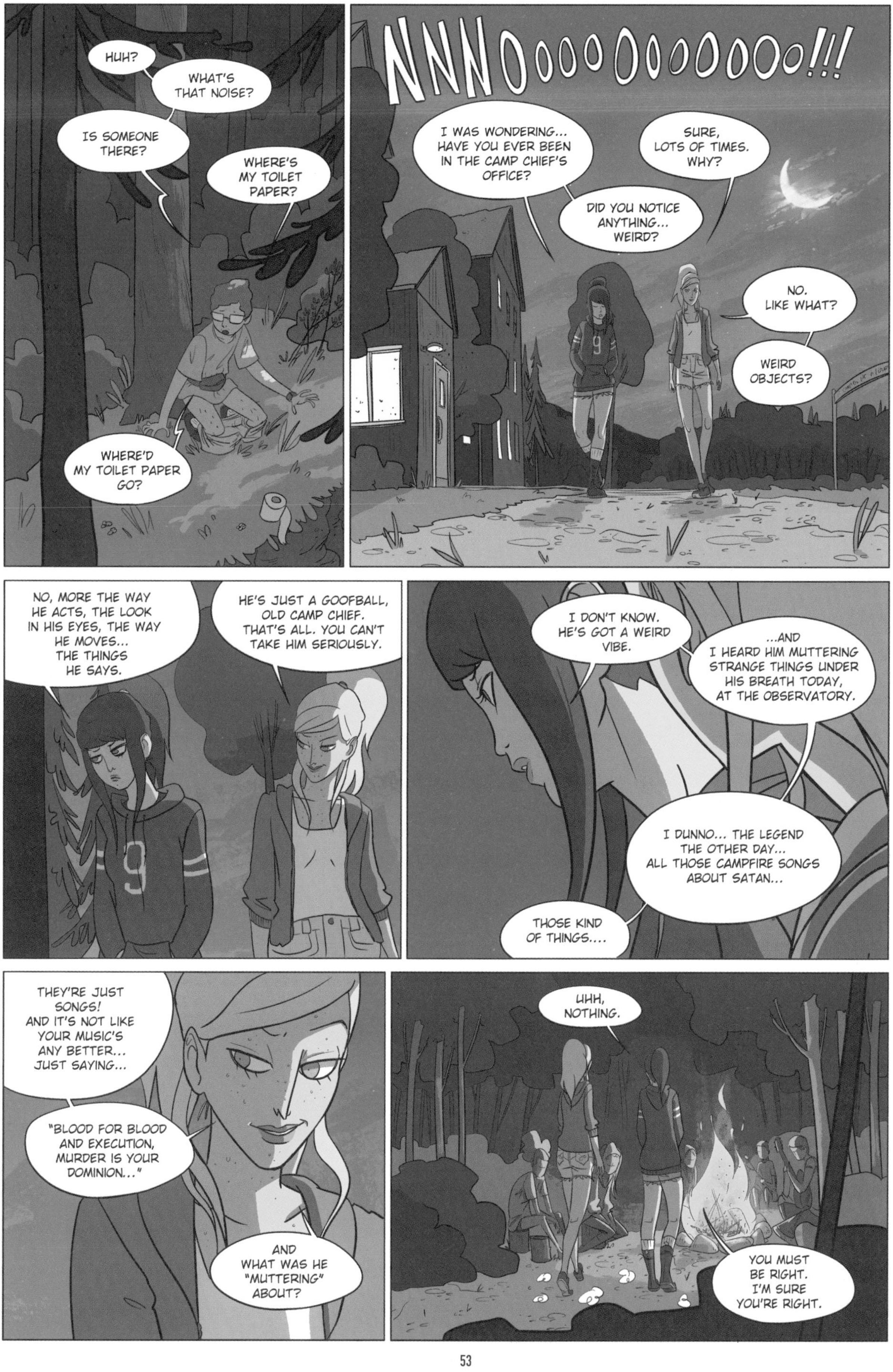

HUH?
WHAT'S THAT NOISE?
IS SOMEONE THERE?
WHERE'S MY TOILET PAPER?
WHERE'D MY TOILET PAPER GO?
NNNOooooOOOOOOOo!!!
I WAS WONDERING... HAVE YOU EVER BEEN IN THE CAMP CHIEF'S OFFICE?
SURE, LOTS OF TIMES. WHY?
DID YOU NOTICE ANYTHING... WEIRD?
NO. LIKE WHAT?
WEIRD OBJECTS?
NO, MORE THE WAY HE ACTS, THE LOOK IN HIS EYES, THE WAY HE MOVES... THE THINGS HE SAYS.
HE'S JUST A GOOFBALL, OLD CAMP CHIEF. THAT'S ALL. YOU CAN'T TAKE HIM SERIOUSLY.
I DON'T KNOW. HE'S GOT A WEIRD VIBE.
...AND I HEARD HIM MUTTERING STRANGE THINGS UNDER HIS BREATH TODAY, AT THE OBSERVATORY.
I DUNNO... THE LEGEND THE OTHER DAY... ALL THOSE CAMPFIRE SONGS ABOUT SATAN...
THOSE KIND OF THINGS....
THEY'RE JUST SONGS! AND IT'S NOT LIKE YOUR MUSIC'S ANY BETTER... JUST SAYING...
"BLOOD FOR BLOOD AND EXECUTION, MURDER IS YOUR DOMINION..."
AND WHAT WAS HE "MUTTERING" ABOUT?
UHH, NOTHING.
YOU MUST BE RIGHT. I'M SURE YOU'RE RIGHT.

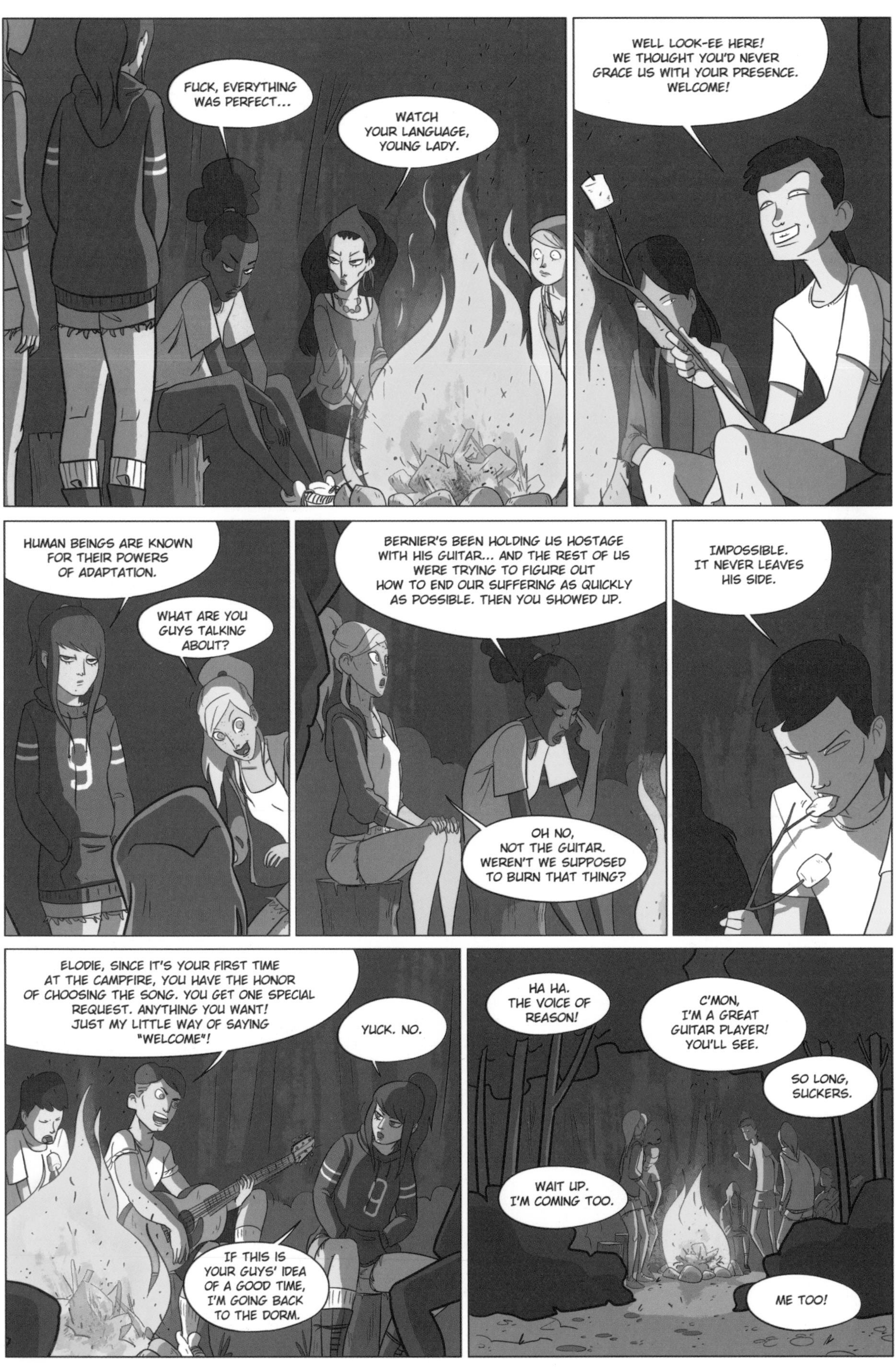
FUCK, EVERYTHING WAS PERFECT...
WATCH YOUR LANGUAGE, YOUNG LADY.
WELL LOOK-EE HERE! WE THOUGHT YOU'D NEVER GRACE US WITH YOUR PRESENCE. WELCOME!
HUMAN BEINGS ARE KNOWN FOR THEIR POWERS OF ADAPTATION.
WHAT ARE YOU GUYS TALKING ABOUT?
BERNIER'S BEEN HOLDING US HOSTAGE WITH HIS GUITAR... AND THE REST OF US WERE TRYING TO FIGURE OUT HOW TO END OUR SUFFERING AS QUICKLY AS POSSIBLE. THEN YOU SHOWED UP.
OH NO, NOT THE GUITAR. WEREN'T WE SUPPOSED TO BURN THAT THING?
IMPOSSIBLE. IT NEVER LEAVES HIS SIDE.
ELODIE, SINCE IT'S YOUR FIRST TIME AT THE CAMPFIRE, YOU HAVE THE HONOR OF CHOOSING THE SONG. YOU GET ONE SPECIAL REQUEST. ANYTHING YOU WANT! JUST MY LITTLE WAY OF SAYING "WELCOME"!
YUCK. NO.
IF THIS IS YOUR GUYS' IDEA OF A GOOD TIME, I'M GOING BACK TO THE DORM.
HA HA. THE VOICE OF REASON!
C'MON, I'M A GREAT GUITAR PLAYER! YOU'LL SEE.
SO LONG, SUCKERS.
WAIT UP. I'M COMING TOO.
ME TOO!

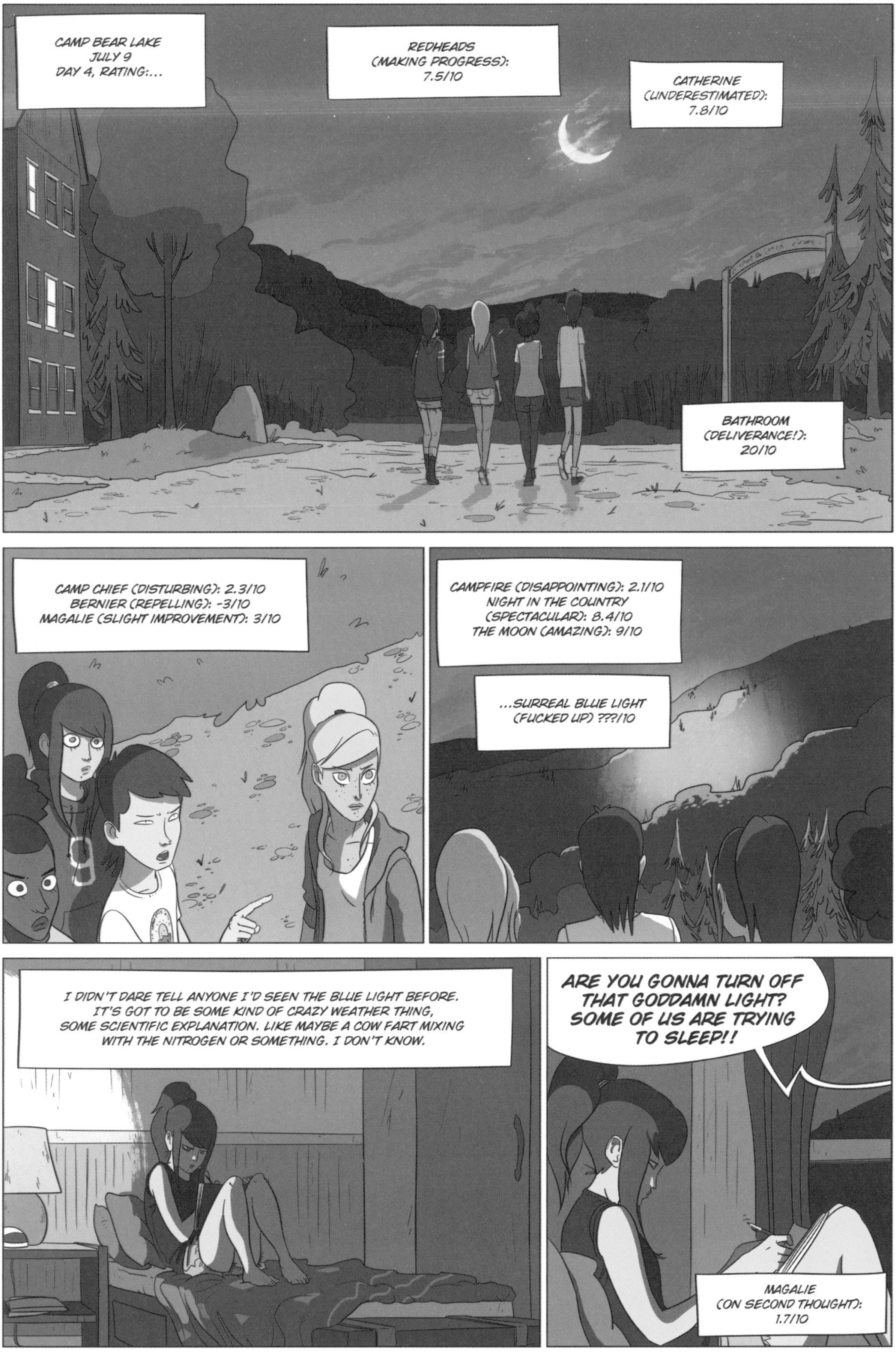
CAMP BEAR LAKE
JULY 9
DAY 4, RATING:...
REDHEADS
(MAKING PROGRESS):
7.5/10
CATHERINE
(UNDERESTIMATED):
7.8/10
BATHROOM
(DELIVERANCE!):
20/10
CAMP CHIEF (DISTURBING): 2.3/10
BERNIER (REPELLING): -3/10
MAGALIE (SLIGHT IMPROVEMENT): 3/10
CAMPFIRE (DISAPPOINTING): 2.1/10
NIGHT IN THE COUNTRY
(SPECTACULAR): 8.4/10
THE MOON (AMAZING): 9/10
...SURREAL BLUE LIGHT
(FUCKED UP) ???/10
I DIDN'T DARE TELL ANYONE I'D SEEN THE BLUE LIGHT BEFORE. IT'S GOT TO BE SOME KIND OF CRAZY WEATHER THING, SOME SCIENTIFIC EXPLANATION. LIKE MAYBE A COW FART MIXING WITH THE NITROGEN OR SOMETHING. I DON'T KNOW.
ARE YOU GONNA TURN OFF THAT GODDAMN LIGHT? SOME OF US ARE TRYING TO SLEEP!!
MAGALIE
(ON SECOND THOUGHT):
1.7/10

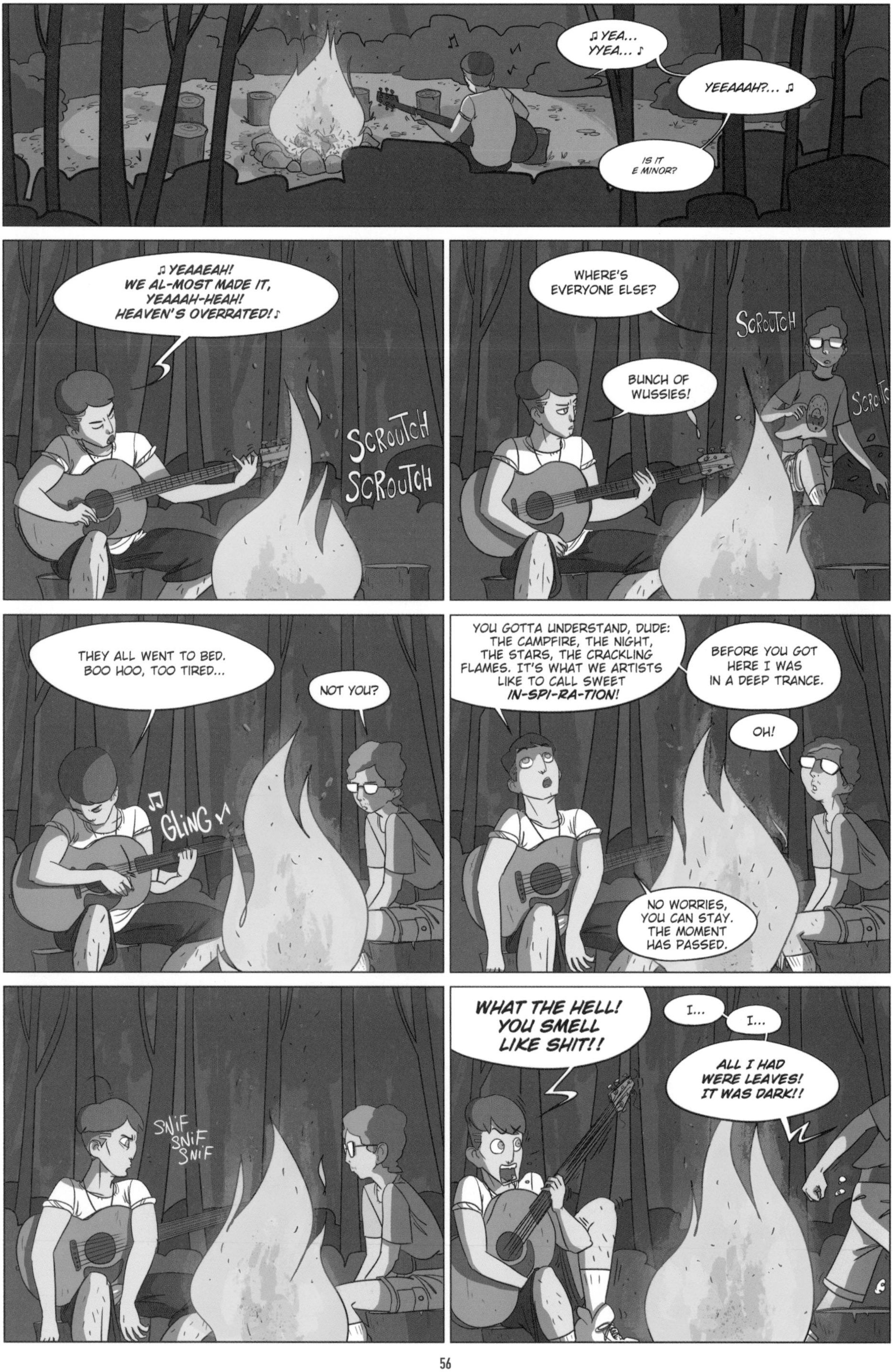
♫ YEA... YYEA... ♪
YEEAAAH?... ♫
IS IT E MINOR?
♫ YEAAAEAH! WE AL-MOST MADE IT, YEAAAH-HEAH! HEAVEN'S OVERRATED! ♪
SCROUTCH
SCROUTCH
WHERE'S EVERYONE ELSE?
SCROUTCH
SCROUTCH
BUNCH OF WUSSIES!
THEY ALL WENT TO BED. BOO HOO, TOO TIRED...
GLING
NOT YOU?
YOU GOTTA UNDERSTAND, DUDE: THE CAMPFIRE, THE NIGHT, THE STARS, THE CRACKLING FLAMES. IT'S WHAT WE ARTISTS LIKE TO CALL SWEET IN-SPI-RA-TION!
BEFORE YOU GOT HERE I WAS IN A DEEP TRANCE.
OH!
NO WORRIES, YOU CAN STAY. THE MOMENT HAS PASSED.
SNIF SNIF SNIF
WHAT THE HELL! YOU SMELL LIKE SHIT!!
I...
I...
ALL I HAD WERE LEAVES! IT WAS DARK!!

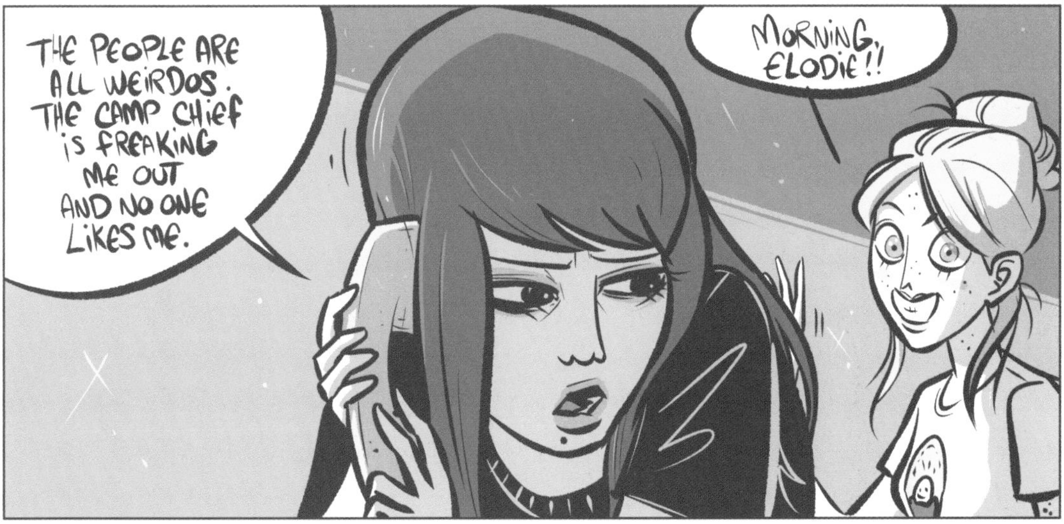
THE PEOPLE ARE ALL WEIRDOS. THE CAMP CHIEF IS FREAKING ME OUT AND NO ONE LIKES ME.
MORNING, ELODIE!!

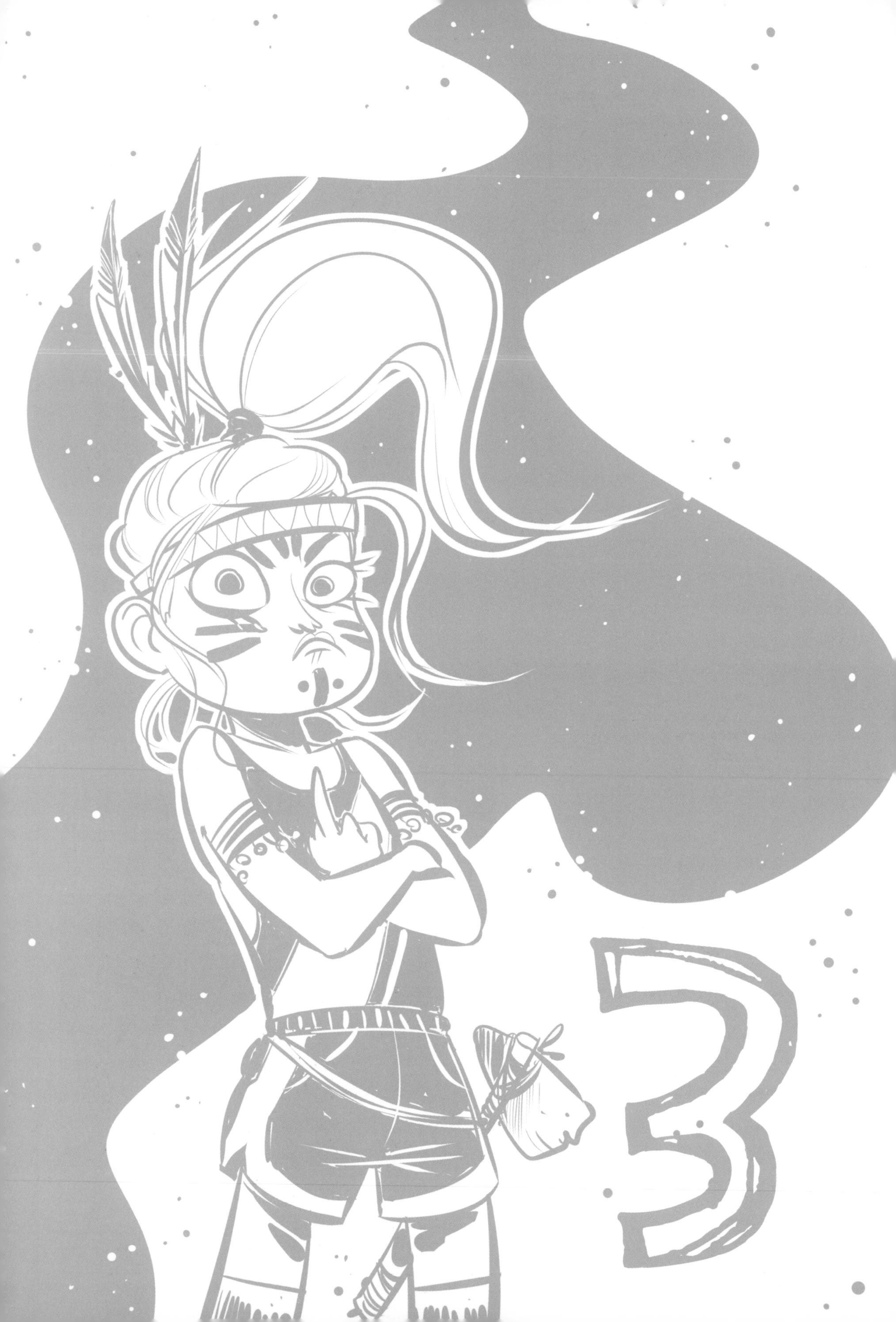
3

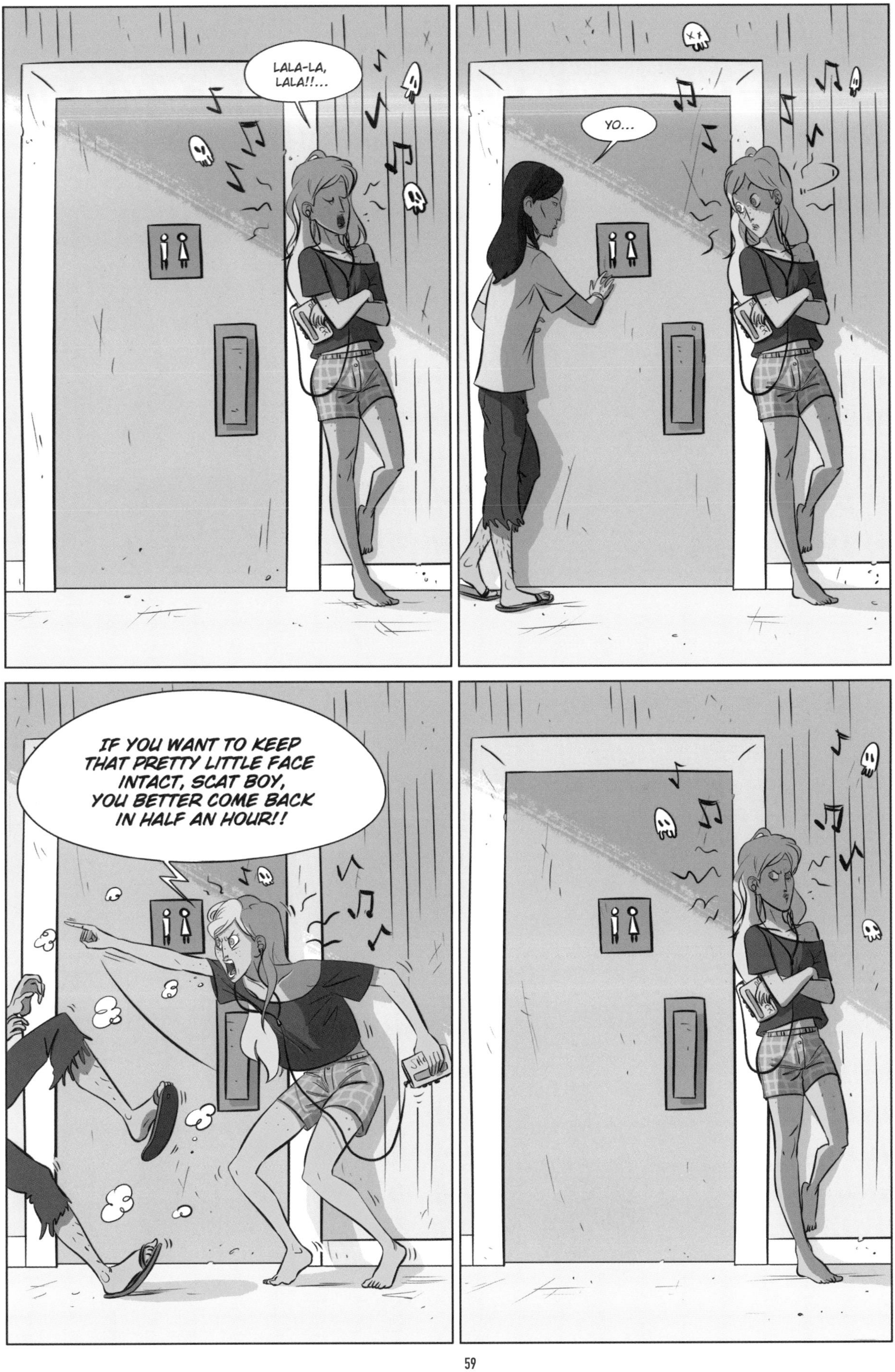
LALA-LA, LALA!!...
YO...
IF YOU WANT TO KEEP THAT PRETTY LITTLE FACE INTACT, SCAT BOY, YOU BETTER COME BACK IN HALF AN HOUR!!

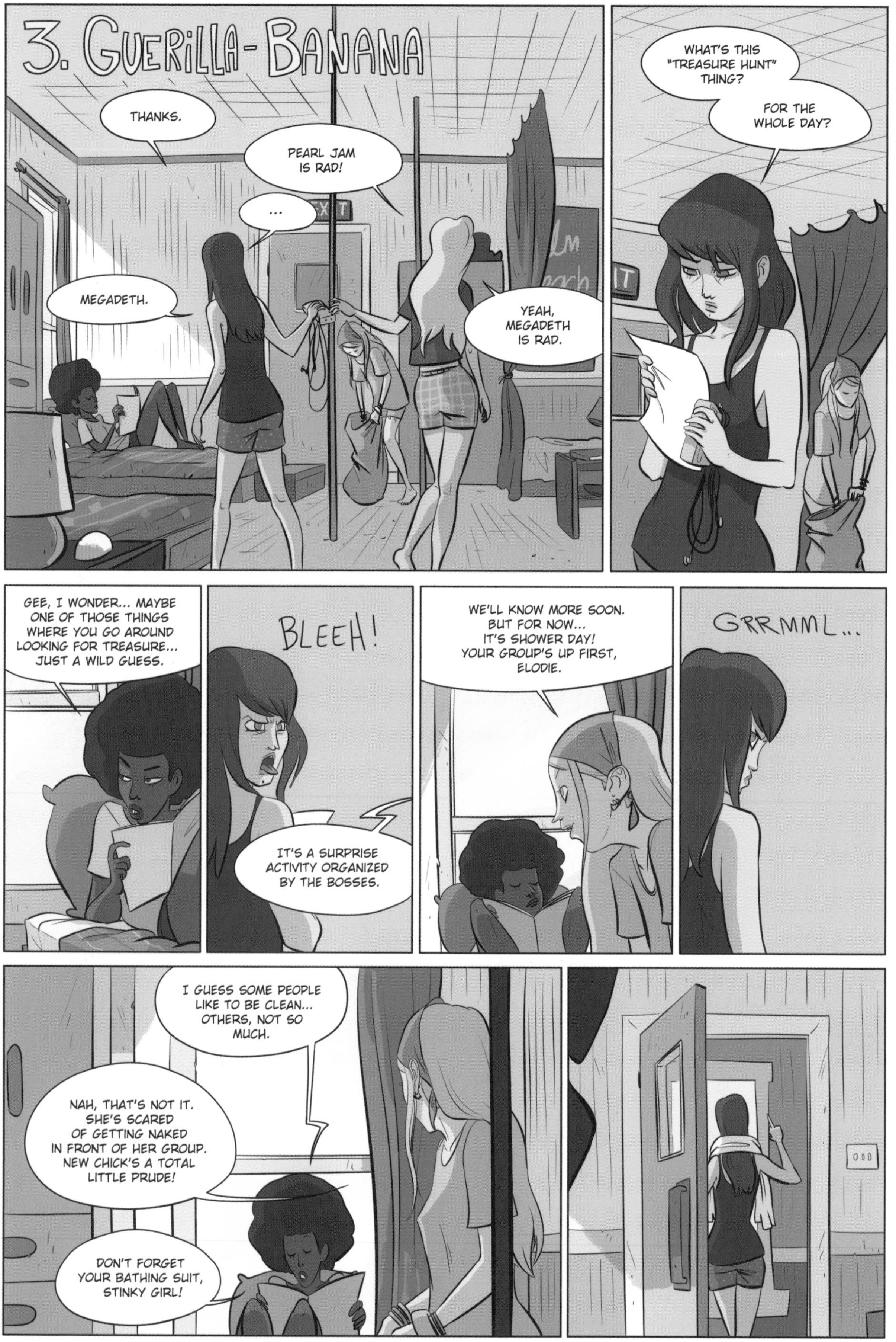
3. GUERILLA-BANANA
THANKS.
PEARL JAM IS RAD!
...
MEGADETH.
YEAH, MEGADETH IS RAD.
WHAT'S THIS "TREASURE HUNT" THING?
FOR THE WHOLE DAY?
GEE, I WONDER... MAYBE ONE OF THOSE THINGS WHERE YOU GO AROUND LOOKING FOR TREASURE... JUST A WILD GUESS.
BLEEH!
IT'S A SURPRISE ACTIVITY ORGANIZED BY THE BOSSES.
WE'LL KNOW MORE SOON. BUT FOR NOW... IT'S SHOWER DAY! YOUR GROUP'S UP FIRST, ELODIE.
GRRMML...
I GUESS SOME PEOPLE LIKE TO BE CLEAN... OTHERS, NOT SO MUCH.
NAH, THAT'S NOT IT. SHE'S SCARED OF GETTING NAKED IN FRONT OF HER GROUP. NEW CHICK'S A TOTAL LITTLE PRUDE!
DON'T FORGET YOUR BATHING SUIT, STINKY GIRL!

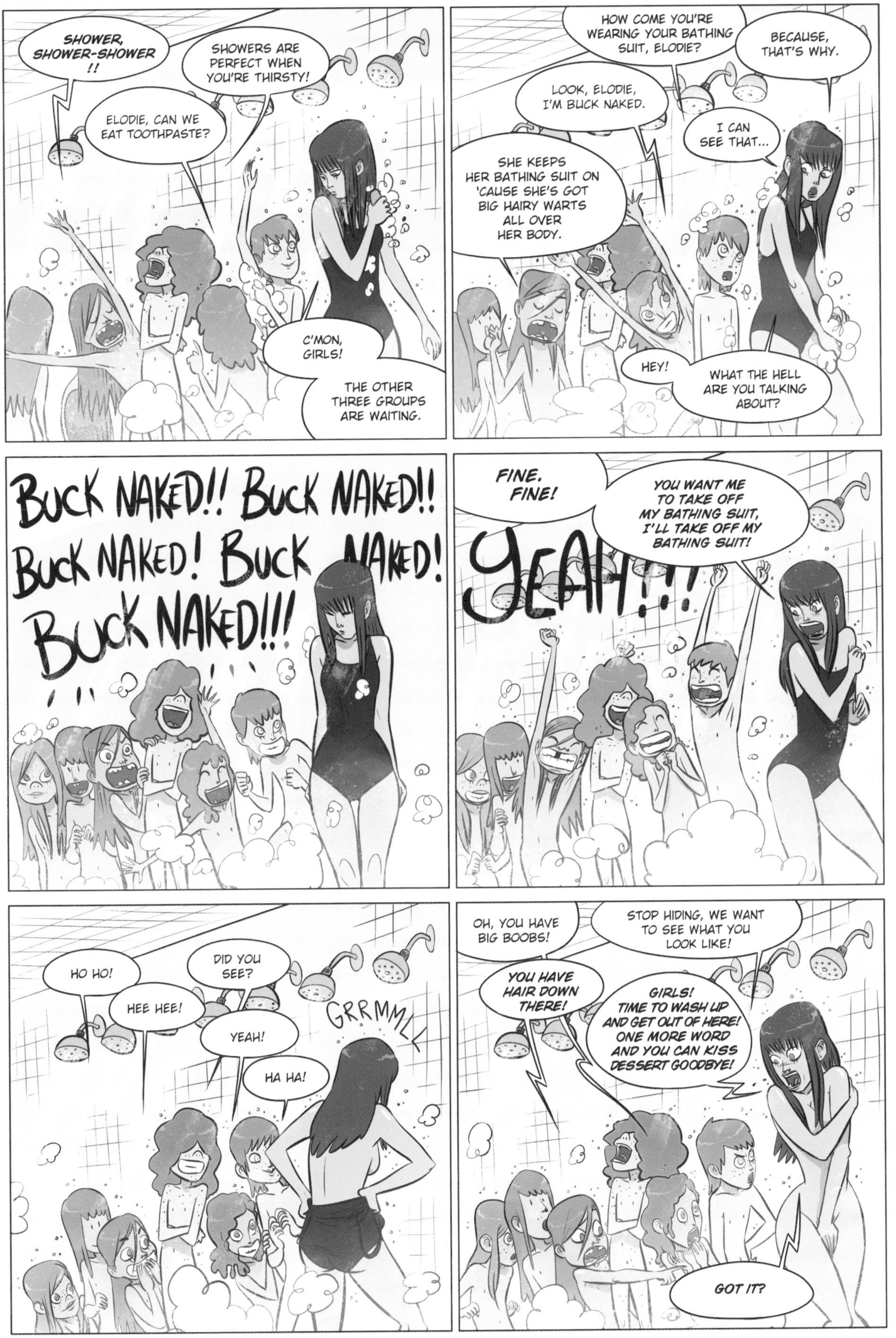
SHOWER, SHOWER-SHOWER !!
SHOWERS ARE PERFECT WHEN YOU'RE THIRSTY!
ELODIE, CAN WE EAT TOOTHPASTE?
C'MON, GIRLS!
THE OTHER THREE GROUPS ARE WAITING.
HOW COME YOU'RE WEARING YOUR BATHING SUIT, ELODIE?
BECAUSE, THAT'S WHY.
LOOK, ELODIE, I'M BUCK NAKED.
I CAN SEE THAT...
SHE KEEPS HER BATHING SUIT ON 'CAUSE SHE'S GOT BIG HAIRY WARTS ALL OVER HER BODY.
HEY!
WHAT THE HELL ARE YOU TALKING ABOUT?
BUCK NAKED!! BUCK NAKED!!
BUCK NAKED! BUCK NAKED!
BUCK NAKED!!!
FINE. FINE!
YOU WANT ME TO TAKE OFF MY BATHING SUIT, I'LL TAKE OFF MY BATHING SUIT!
YEAH!!!
HO HO!
DID YOU SEE?
HEE HEE!
YEAH!
HA HA!
GRRMMLL
OH, YOU HAVE BIG BOOBS!
STOP HIDING, WE WANT TO SEE WHAT YOU LOOK LIKE!
YOU HAVE HAIR DOWN THERE!
GIRLS! TIME TO WASH UP AND GET OUT OF HERE! ONE MORE WORD AND YOU CAN KISS DESSERT GOODBYE!
GOT IT?

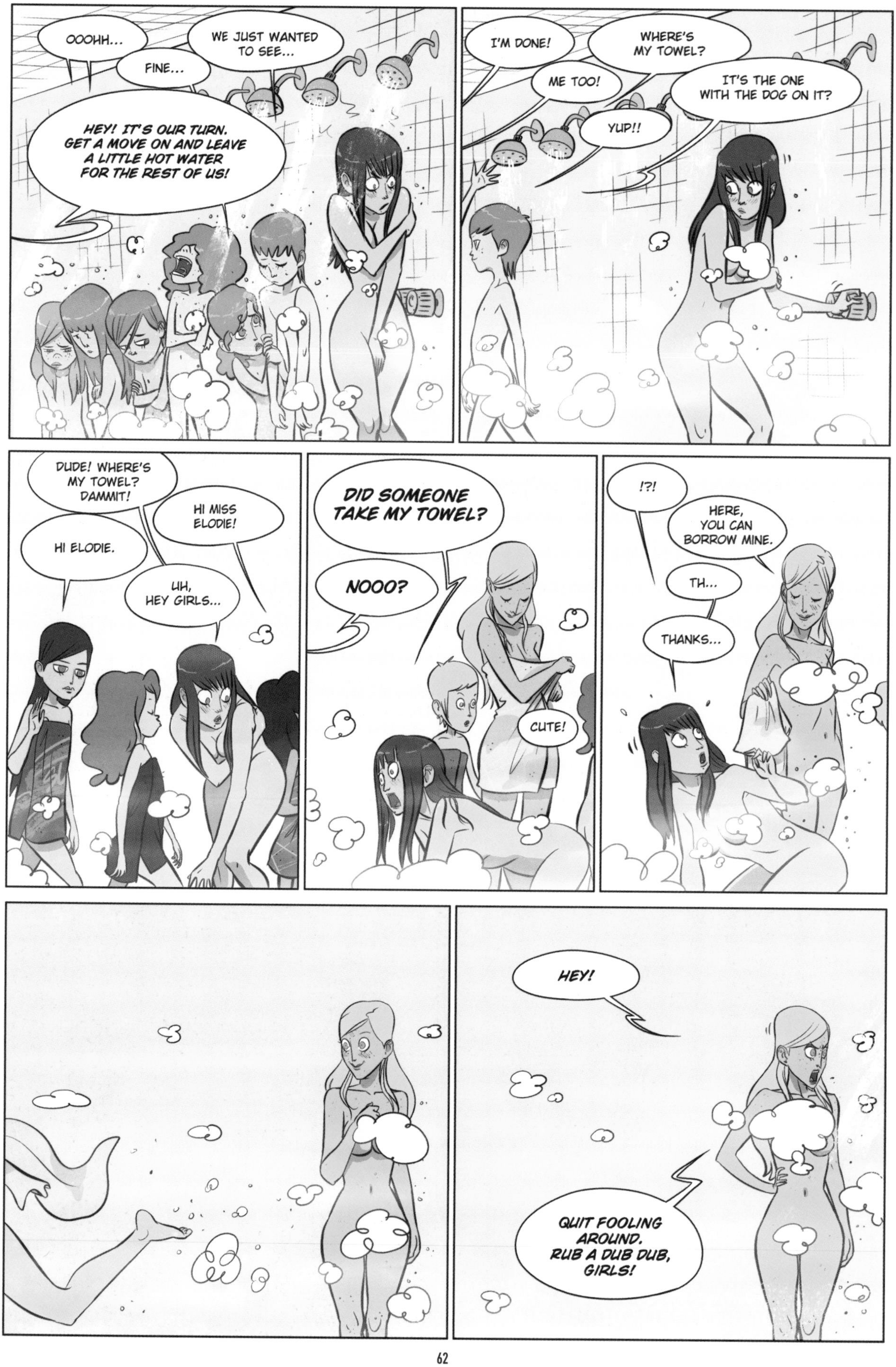
OOOHH...
FINE...
WE JUST WANTED TO SEE...
HEY! IT'S OUR TURN. GET A MOVE ON AND LEAVE A LITTLE HOT WATER FOR THE REST OF US!
I'M DONE!
WHERE'S MY TOWEL?
ME TOO!
IT'S THE ONE WITH THE DOG ON IT?
YUP!!
DUDE! WHERE'S MY TOWEL? DAMMIT!
HI MISS ELODIE!
HI ELODIE.
UH, HEY GIRLS...
DID SOMEONE TAKE MY TOWEL?
NOOO?
CUTE!
!?!
HERE, YOU CAN BORROW MINE.
TH...
THANKS...
HEY!
QUIT FOOLING AROUND. RUB A DUB DUB, GIRLS!

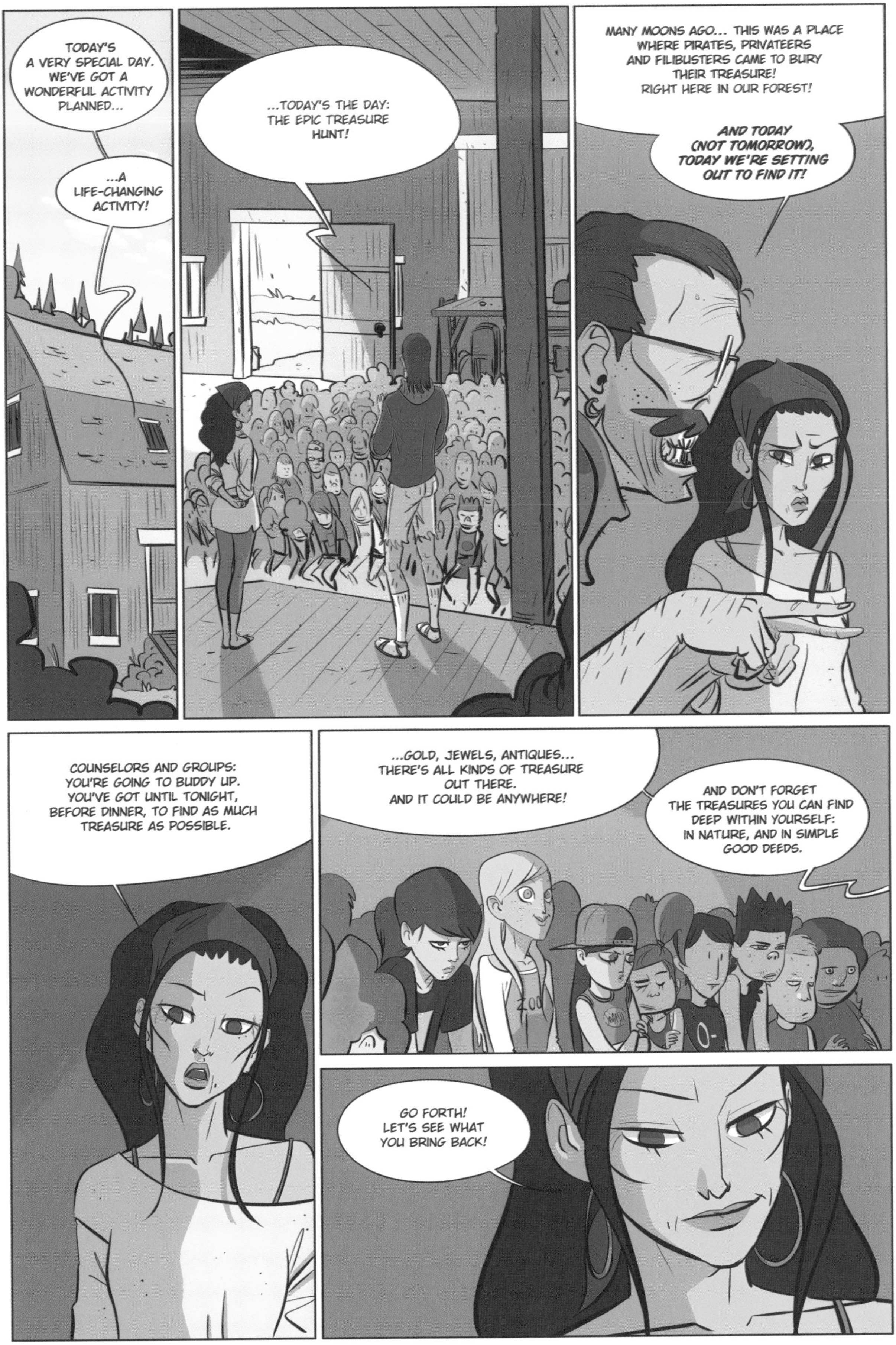
TODAY'S A VERY SPECIAL DAY. WE'VE GOT A WONDERFUL ACTIVITY PLANNED...
...A LIFE-CHANGING ACTIVITY!
...TODAY'S THE DAY: THE EPIC TREASURE HUNT!
MANY MOONS AGO... THIS WAS A PLACE WHERE PIRATES, PRIVATEERS AND FILIBUSTERS CAME TO BURY THEIR TREASURE! RIGHT HERE IN OUR FOREST!
AND TODAY (NOT TOMORROW), TODAY WE'RE SETTING OUT TO FIND IT!
COUNSELORS AND GROUPS: YOU'RE GOING TO BUDDY UP. YOU'VE GOT UNTIL TONIGHT, BEFORE DINNER, TO FIND AS MUCH TREASURE AS POSSIBLE.
...GOLD, JEWELS, ANTIQUES... THERE'S ALL KINDS OF TREASURE OUT THERE. AND IT COULD BE ANYWHERE!
AND DON'T FORGET THE TREASURES YOU CAN FIND DEEP WITHIN YOURSELF: IN NATURE, AND IN SIMPLE GOOD DEEDS.
GO FORTH! LET'S SEE WHAT YOU BRING BACK!

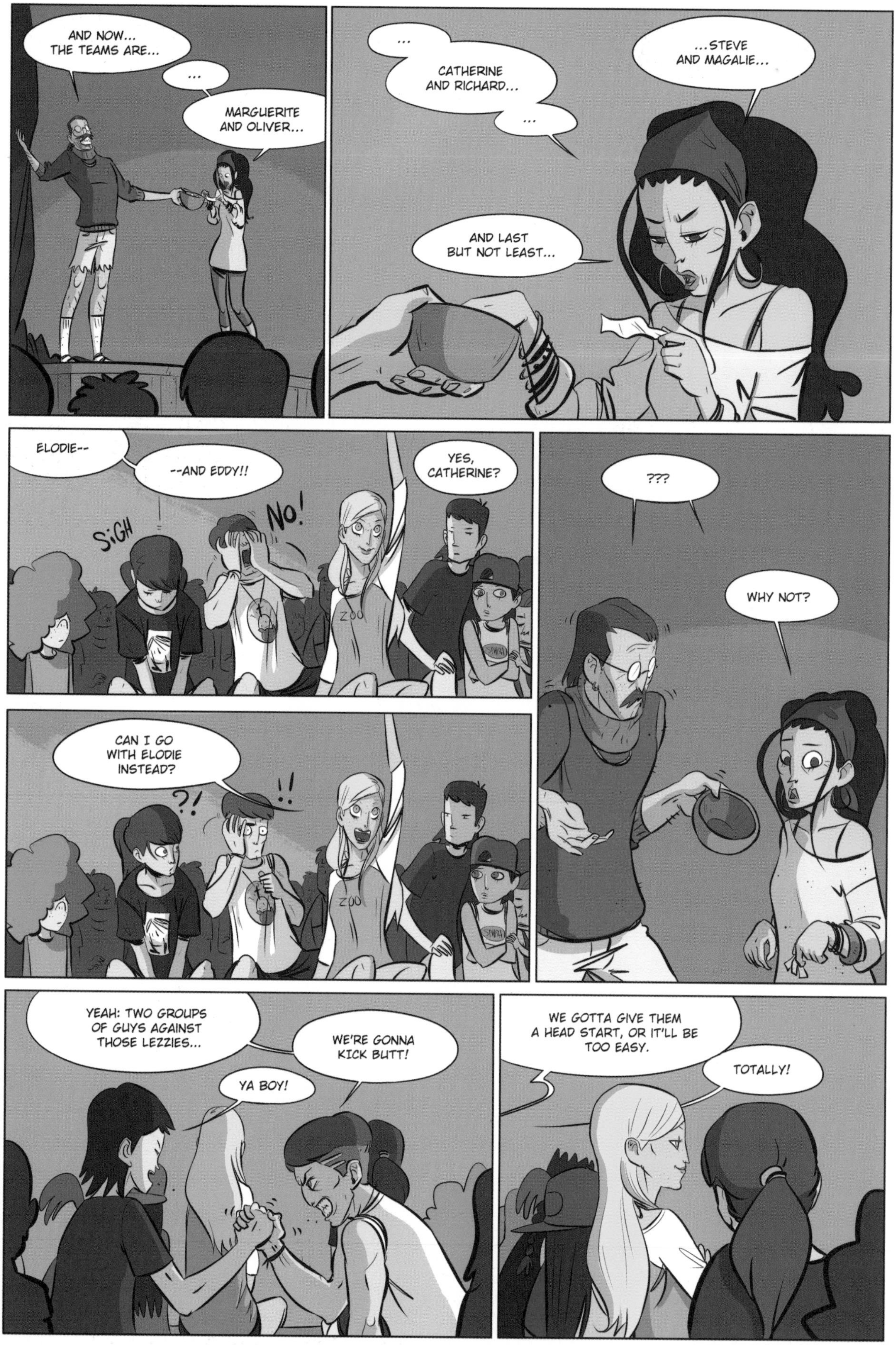
AND NOW... THE TEAMS ARE...
...
MARGUERITE AND OLIVER...
...
CATHERINE AND RICHARD...
...
...STEVE AND MAGALIE...
AND LAST BUT NOT LEAST...
ELODIE--
--AND EDDY!!
SIGH
NO!
YES, CATHERINE?
???
WHY NOT?
CAN I GO WITH ELODIE INSTEAD?
?!
!!
YEAH: TWO GROUPS OF GUYS AGAINST THOSE LEZZIES...
WE'RE GONNA KICK BUTT!
YA BOY!
WE GOTTA GIVE THEM A HEAD START, OR IT'LL BE TOO EASY.
TOTALLY!

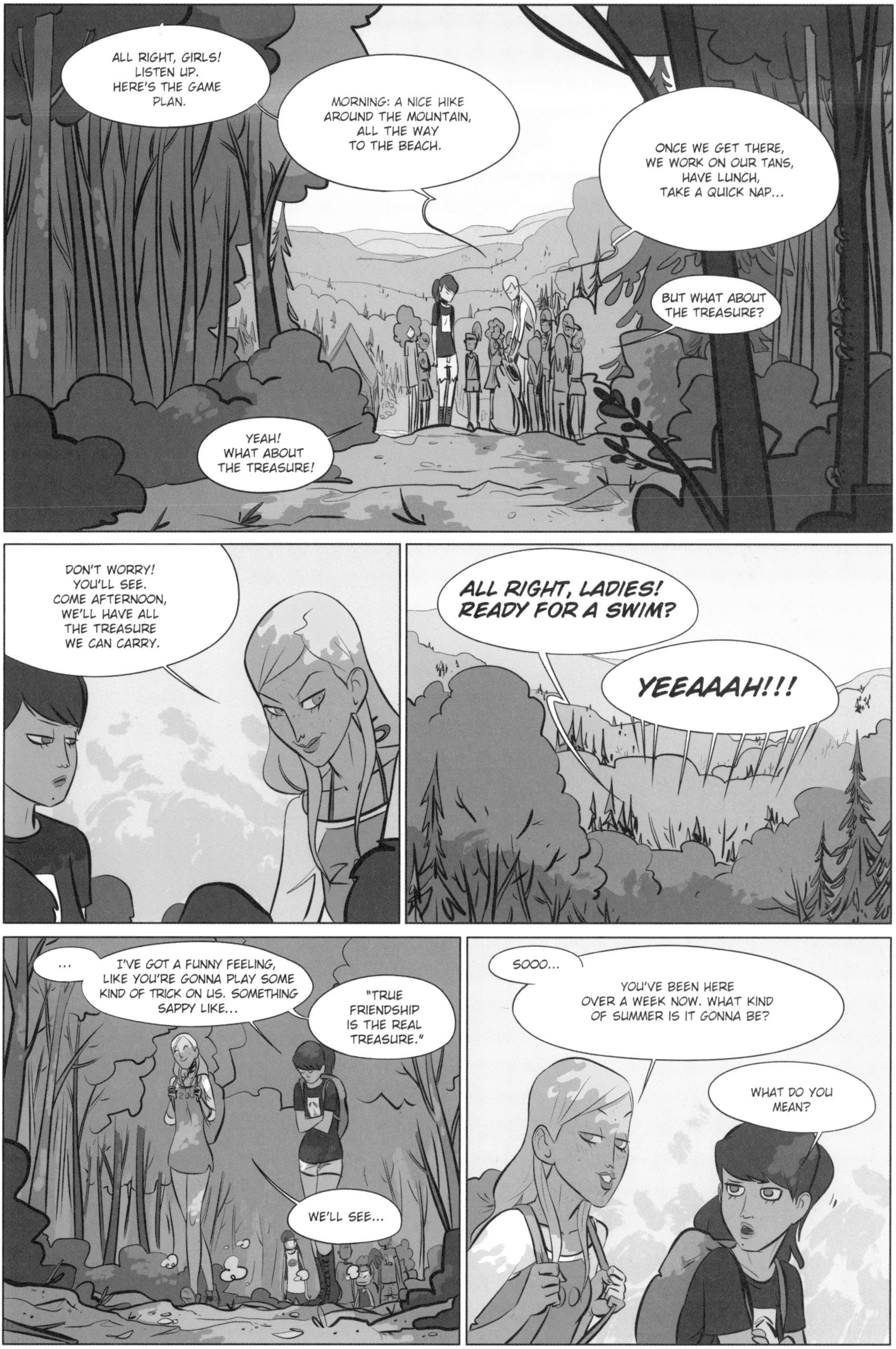
ALL RIGHT, GIRLS! LISTEN UP. HERE'S THE GAME PLAN.
MORNING: A NICE HIKE AROUND THE MOUNTAIN, ALL THE WAY TO THE BEACH.
ONCE WE GET THERE, WE WORK ON OUR TANS, HAVE LUNCH, TAKE A QUICK NAP...
BUT WHAT ABOUT THE TREASURE?
YEAH! WHAT ABOUT THE TREASURE!
DON'T WORRY! YOU'LL SEE. COME AFTERNOON, WE'LL HAVE ALL THE TREASURE WE CAN CARRY.
ALL RIGHT, LADIES! READY FOR A SWIM?
YEEAAAH!!!
...
I'VE GOT A FUNNY FEELING, LIKE YOU'RE GONNA PLAY SOME KIND OF TRICK ON US. SOMETHING SAPPY LIKE...
"TRUE FRIENDSHIP IS THE REAL TREASURE."
WE'LL SEE...
SOOO...
YOU'VE BEEN HERE OVER A WEEK NOW. WHAT KIND OF SUMMER IS IT GONNA BE?
WHAT DO YOU MEAN?

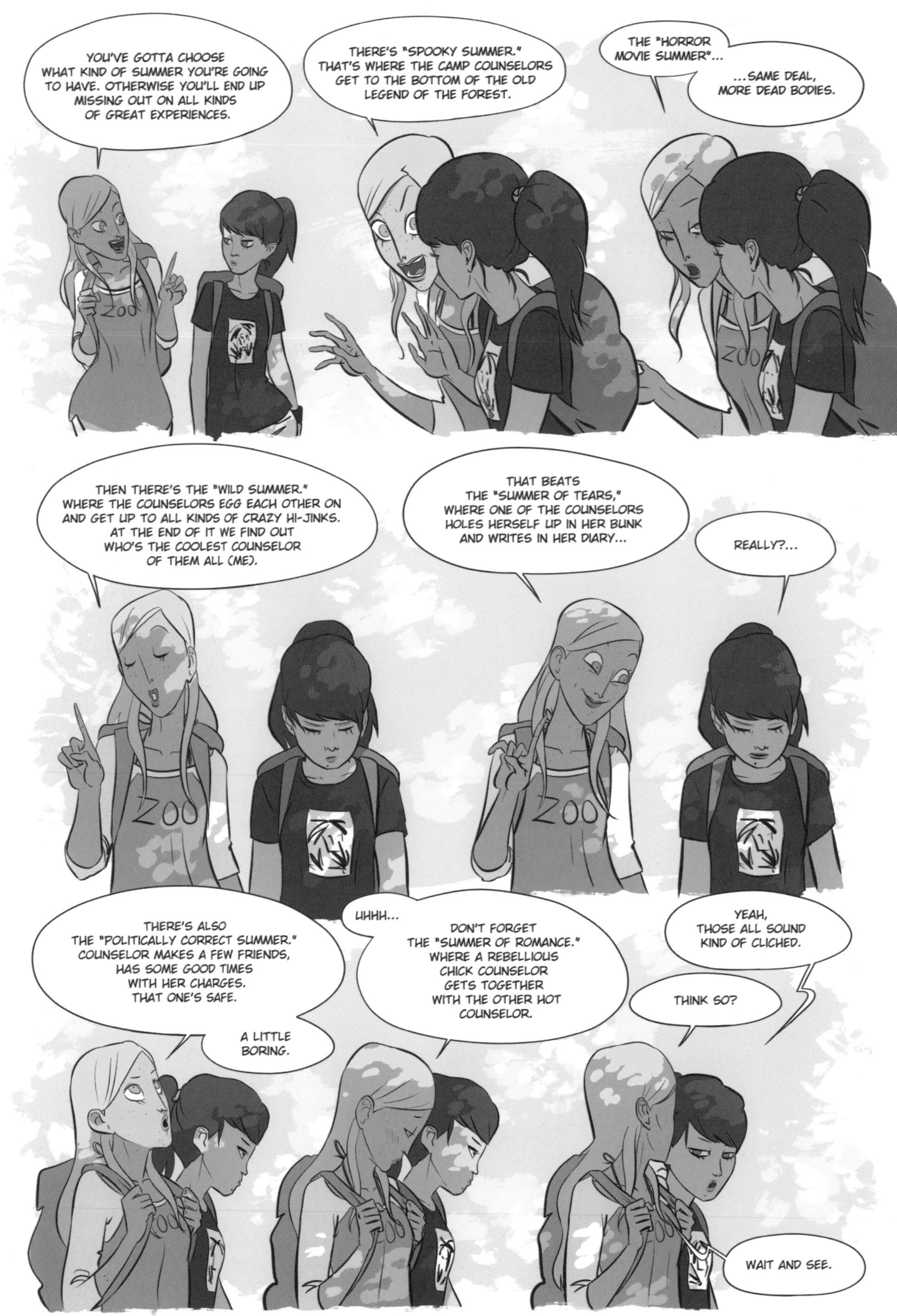
YOU'VE GOTTA CHOOSE WHAT KIND OF SUMMER YOU'RE GOING TO HAVE. OTHERWISE YOU'LL END UP MISSING OUT ON ALL KINDS OF GREAT EXPERIENCES.
THERE'S "SPOOKY SUMMER." THAT'S WHERE THE CAMP COUNSELORS GET TO THE BOTTOM OF THE OLD LEGEND OF THE FOREST.
THE "HORROR MOVIE SUMMER"...
...SAME DEAL, MORE DEAD BODIES.
THEN THERE'S THE "WILD SUMMER." WHERE THE COUNSELORS EGG EACH OTHER ON AND GET UP TO ALL KINDS OF CRAZY HI-JINKS. AT THE END OF IT WE FIND OUT WHO'S THE COOLEST COUNSELOR OF THEM ALL (ME).
THAT BEATS THE "SUMMER OF TEARS," WHERE ONE OF THE COUNSELORS HOLES HERSELF UP IN HER BUNK AND WRITES IN HER DIARY...
REALLY?...
ZOO
ZOO
THERE'S ALSO THE "POLITICALLY CORRECT SUMMER." COUNSELOR MAKES A FEW FRIENDS, HAS SOME GOOD TIMES WITH HER CHARGES. THAT ONE'S SAFE.
A LITTLE BORING.
UHHH...
DON'T FORGET THE "SUMMER OF ROMANCE." WHERE A REBELLIOUS CHICK COUNSELOR GETS TOGETHER WITH THE OTHER HOT COUNSELOR.
YEAH, THOSE ALL SOUND KIND OF CLICHED.
THINK SO?
WAIT AND SEE.

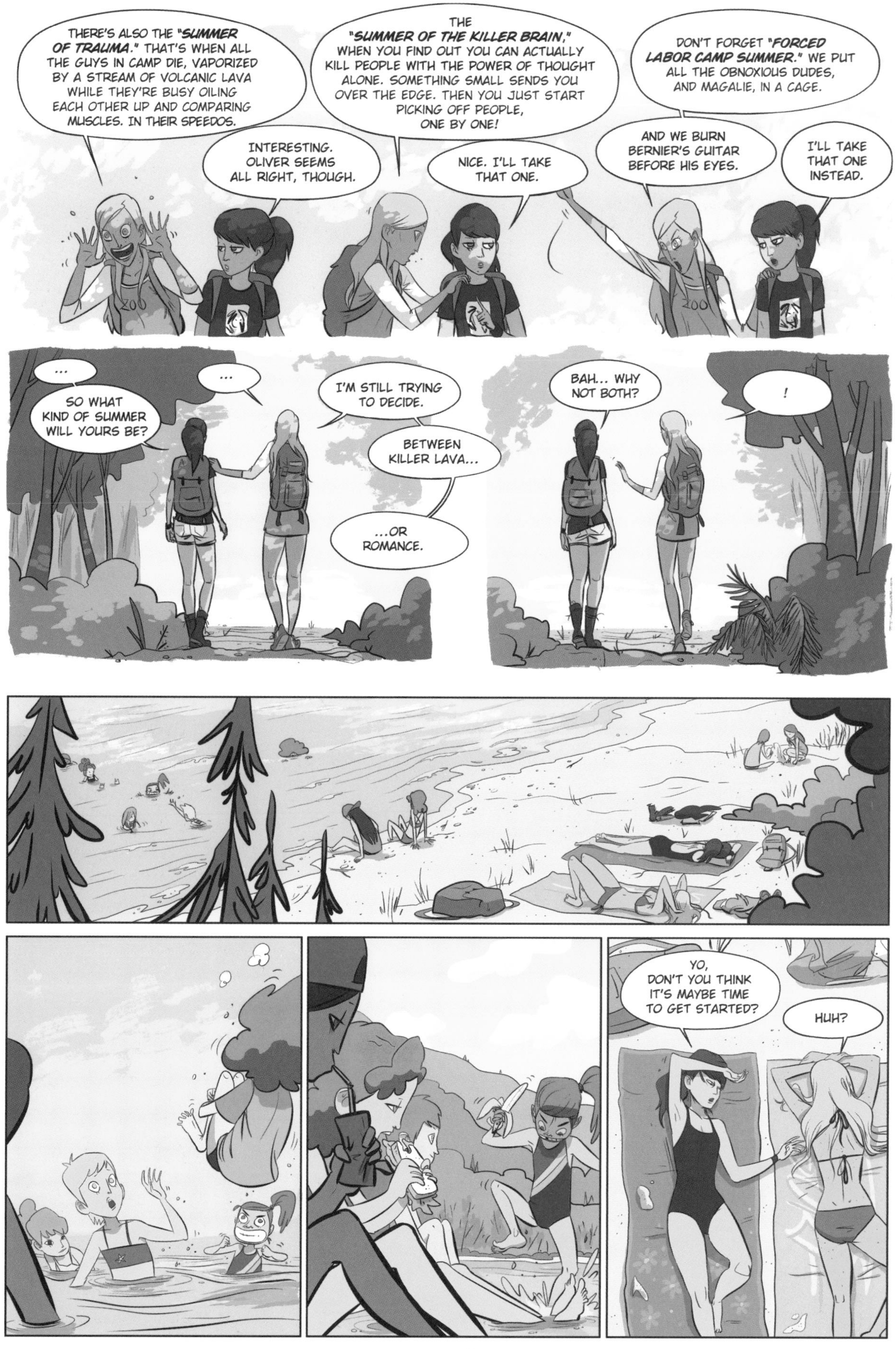
THERE'S ALSO THE "SUMMER OF TRAUMA." THAT'S WHEN ALL THE GUYS IN CAMP DIE, VAPORIZED BY A STREAM OF VOLCANIC LAVA WHILE THEY'RE BUSY OILING EACH OTHER UP AND COMPARING MUSCLES. IN THEIR SPEEDOS.
INTERESTING. OLIVER SEEMS ALL RIGHT, THOUGH.
THE "SUMMER OF THE KILLER BRAIN," WHEN YOU FIND OUT YOU CAN ACTUALLY KILL PEOPLE WITH THE POWER OF THOUGHT ALONE. SOMETHING SMALL SENDS YOU OVER THE EDGE. THEN YOU JUST START PICKING OFF PEOPLE, ONE BY ONE!
NICE. I'LL TAKE THAT ONE.
DON'T FORGET "FORCED LABOR CAMP SUMMER." WE PUT ALL THE OBNOXIOUS DUDES, AND MAGALIE, IN A CAGE.
AND WE BURN BERNIER'S GUITAR BEFORE HIS EYES.
I'LL TAKE THAT ONE INSTEAD.
...
SO WHAT KIND OF SUMMER WILL YOURS BE?
...
I'M STILL TRYING TO DECIDE.
BETWEEN KILLER LAVA...
...OR ROMANCE.
BAH... WHY NOT BOTH?
!
YO, DON'T YOU THINK IT'S MAYBE TIME TO GET STARTED?
HUH?

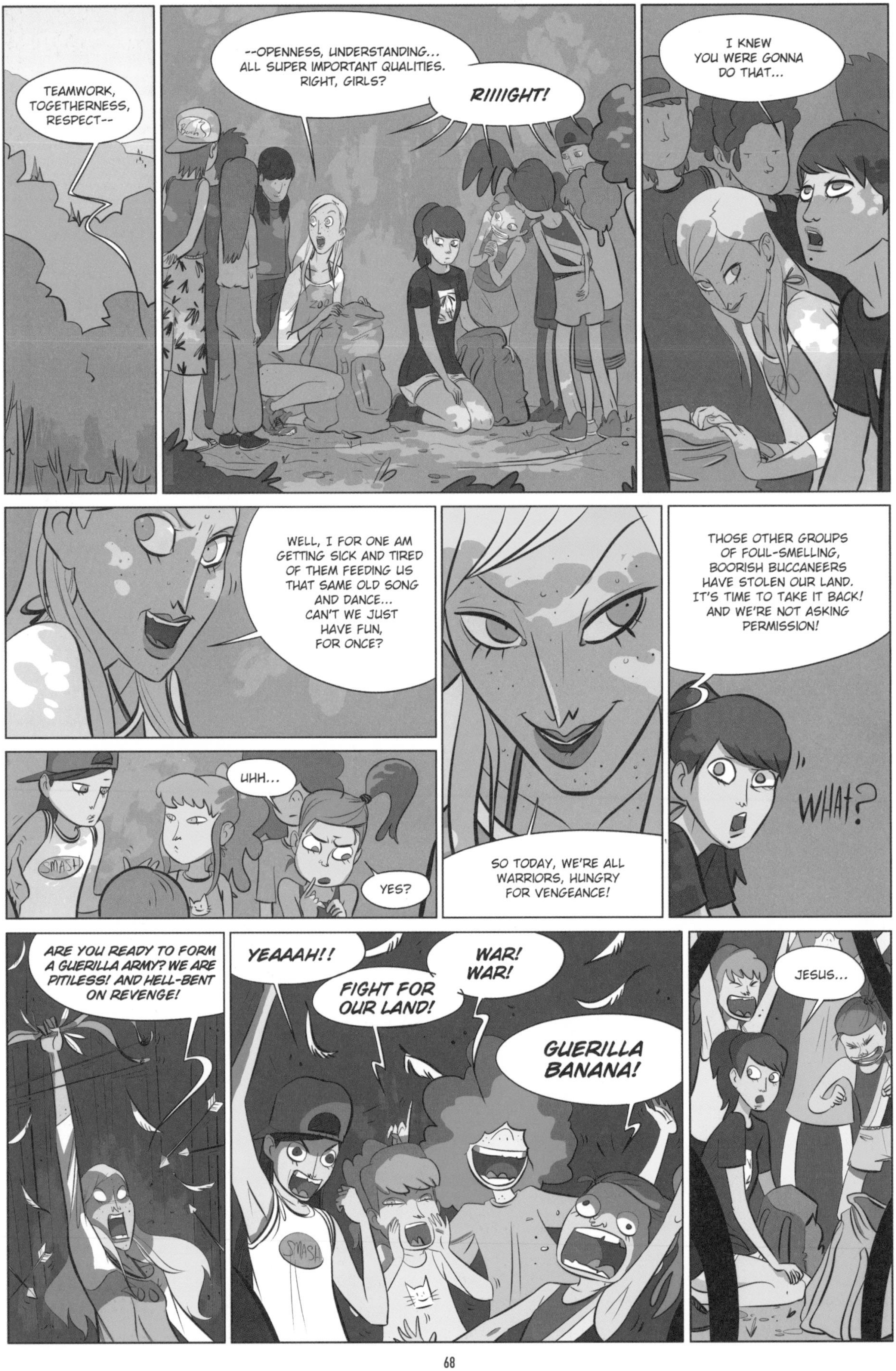
TEAMWORK, TOGETHERNESS, RESPECT--
--OPENNESS, UNDERSTANDING... ALL SUPER IMPORTANT QUALITIES. RIGHT, GIRLS?
RIIIGHT!
I KNEW YOU WERE GONNA DO THAT...
WELL, I FOR ONE AM GETTING SICK AND TIRED OF THEM FEEDING US THAT SAME OLD SONG AND DANCE... CAN'T WE JUST HAVE FUN, FOR ONCE?
THOSE OTHER GROUPS OF FOUL-SMELLING, BOORISH BUCCANEERS HAVE STOLEN OUR LAND. IT'S TIME TO TAKE IT BACK! AND WE'RE NOT ASKING PERMISSION!
UHH...
YES?
SO TODAY, WE'RE ALL WARRIORS, HUNGRY FOR VENGEANCE!
WHAT?
ARE YOU READY TO FORM A GUERILLA ARMY? WE ARE PITILESS! AND HELL-BENT ON REVENGE!
YEAAAH!!
FIGHT FOR OUR LAND!
WAR! WAR!
GUERILLA BANANA!
JESUS...

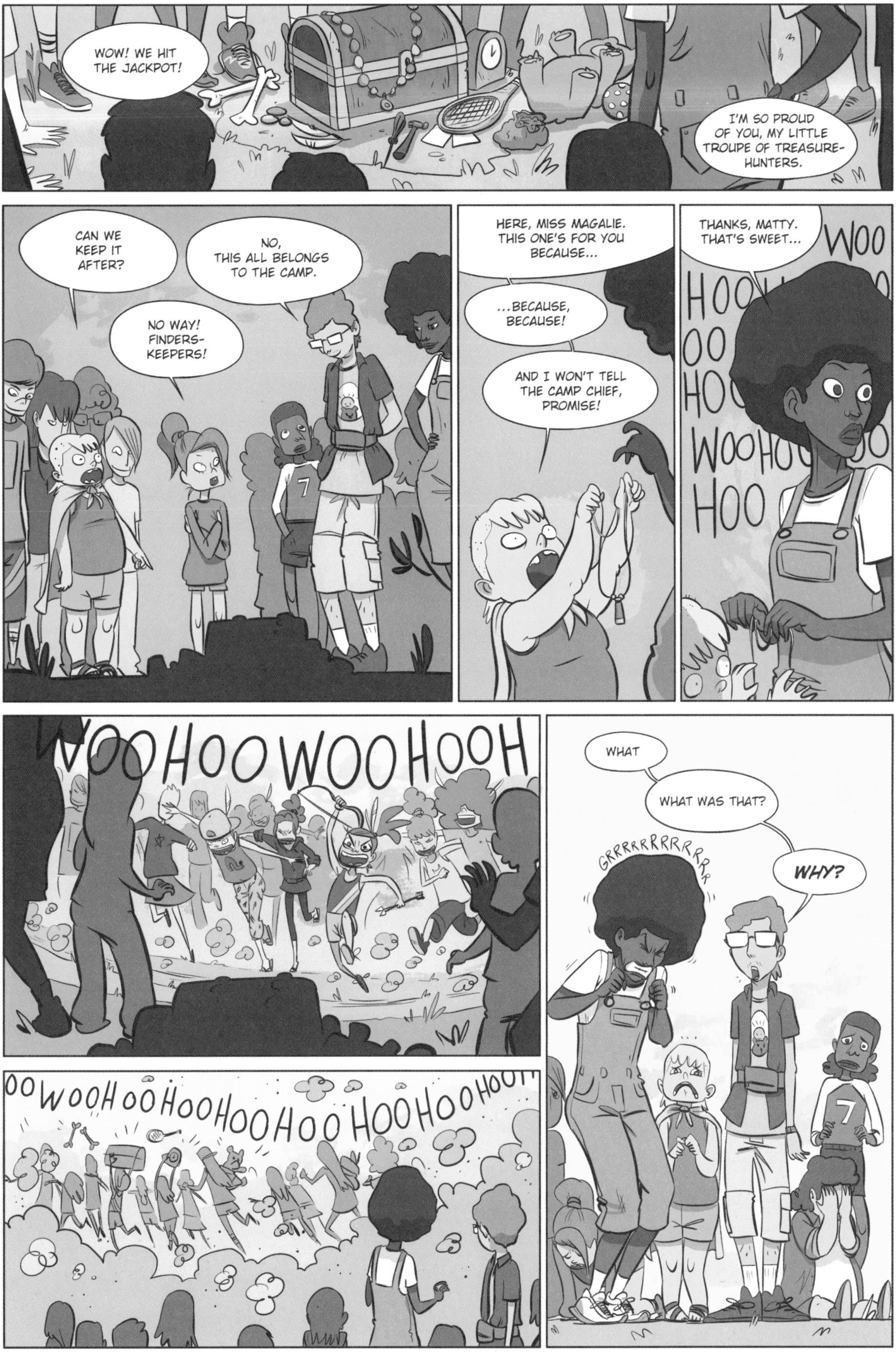
WOW! WE HIT THE JACKPOT!
I'M SO PROUD OF YOU, MY LITTLE TROUPE OF TREASURE-HUNTERS.
CAN WE KEEP IT AFTER?
NO, THIS ALL BELONGS TO THE CAMP.
NO WAY! FINDERS-KEEPERS!
HERE, MISS MAGALIE. THIS ONE'S FOR YOU BECAUSE...
...BECAUSE, BECAUSE!
AND I WON'T TELL THE CAMP CHIEF, PROMISE!
THANKS, MATTY. THAT'S SWEET...
WOOHOOOOHOOWOOHOOHOO
WOOHOOWOOHOOH
OOWOOHOOHOOHOOHOOHOOHOOHOO
WHAT
WHAT WAS THAT?
GRRRRRRRRRRRR
WHY?

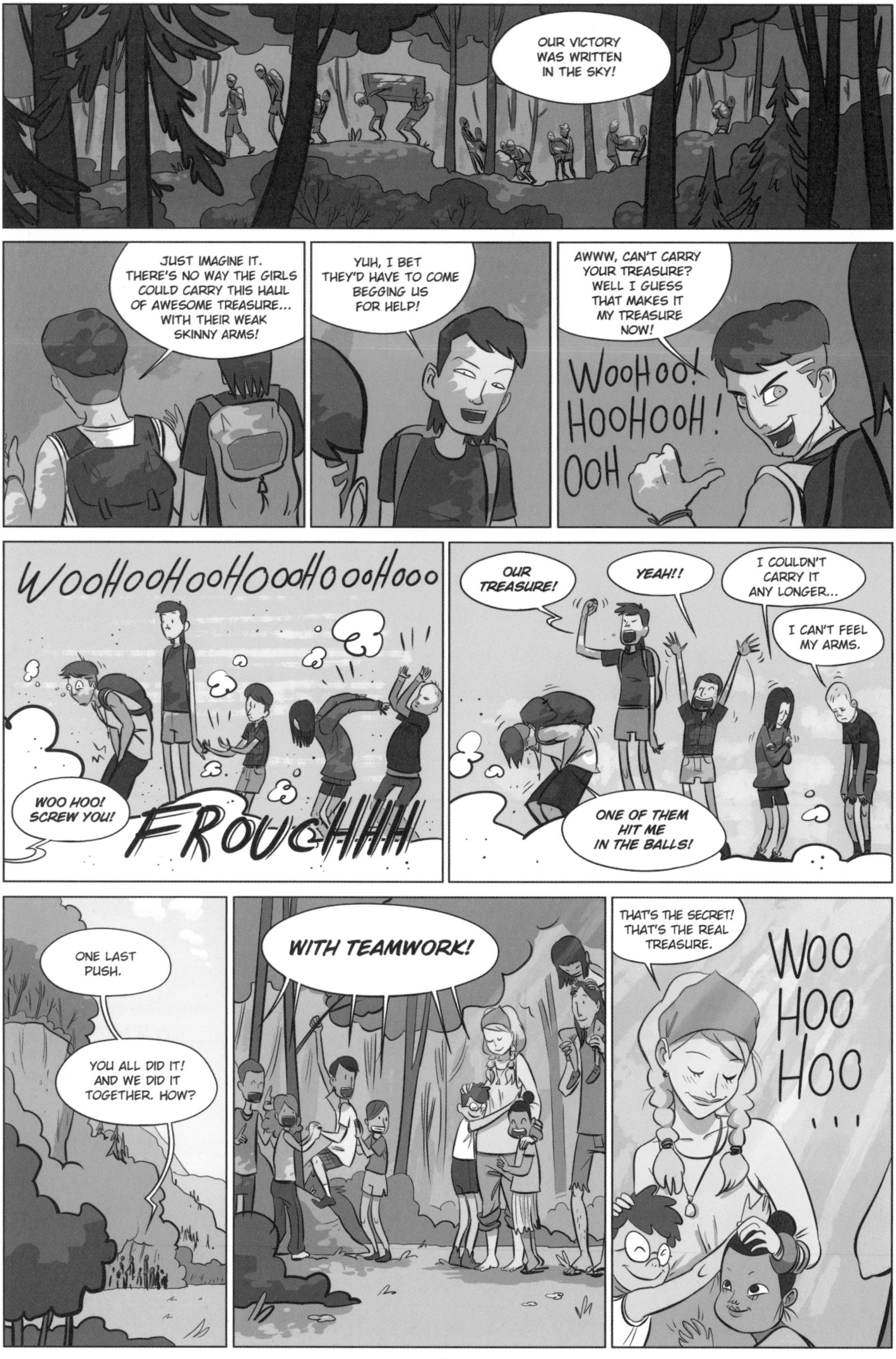

OUR VICTORY WAS WRITTEN IN THE SKY!
JUST IMAGINE IT. THERE'S NO WAY THE GIRLS COULD CARRY THIS HAUL OF AWESOME TREASURE... WITH THEIR WEAK SKINNY ARMS!
YUH, I BET THEY'D HAVE TO COME BEGGING US FOR HELP!
AWWW, CAN'T CARRY YOUR TREASURE? WELL I GUESS THAT MAKES IT MY TREASURE NOW!
WooHoo! HOOHOOH! OOH
WooHooHooHoooHoooHooo
WOO HOO! SCREW YOU!
FROUCHHH
OUR TREASURE!
YEAH!!
I COULDN'T CARRY IT ANY LONGER...
I CAN'T FEEL MY ARMS.
ONE OF THEM HIT ME IN THE BALLS!
ONE LAST PUSH.
YOU ALL DID IT! AND WE DID IT TOGETHER. HOW?
WITH TEAMWORK!
THAT'S THE SECRET! THAT'S THE REAL TREASURE.
WOO HOO HOO HOO ...

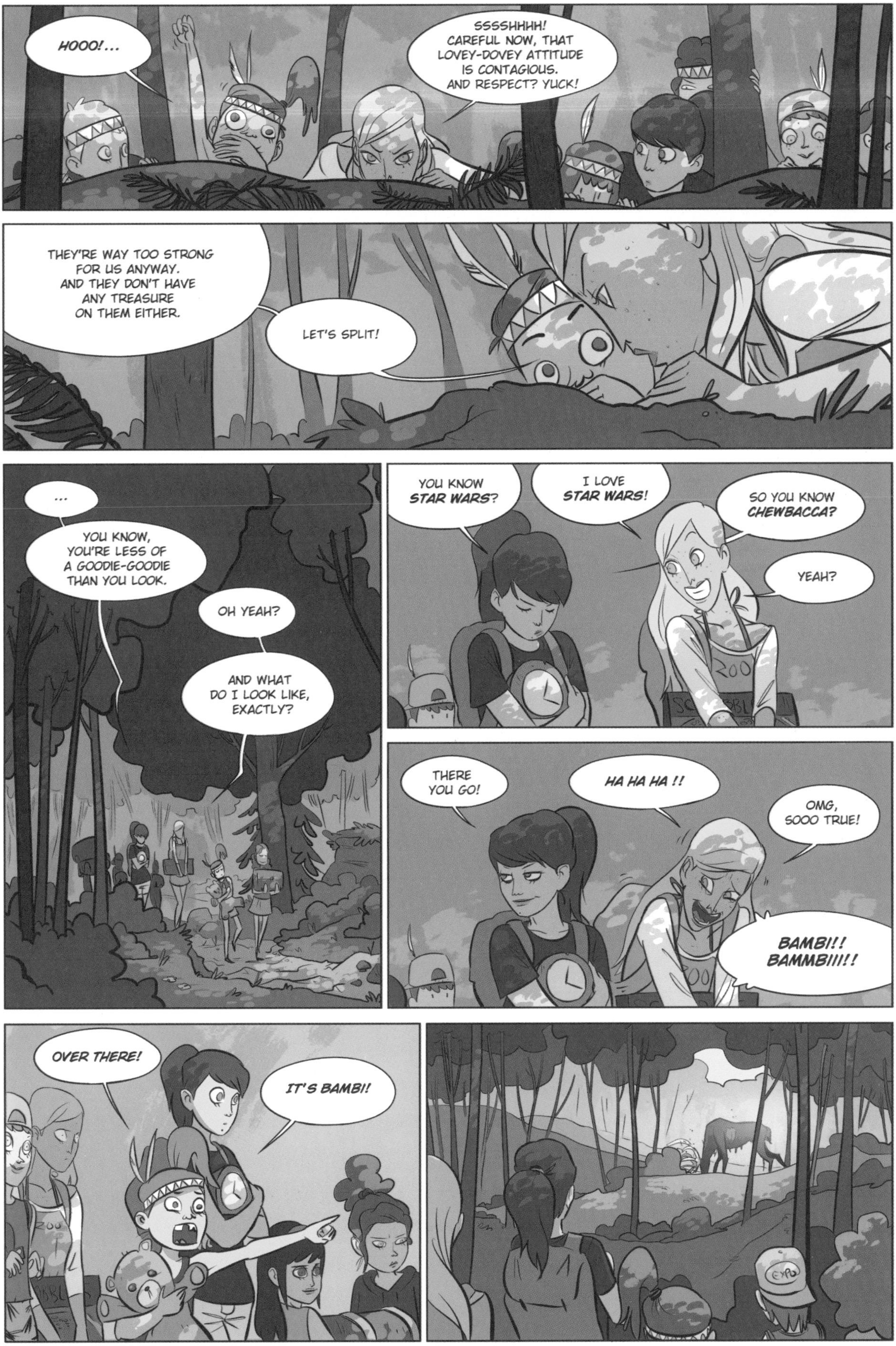
HOOO!...
SSSSHHHH! CAREFUL NOW, THAT LOVEY-DOVEY ATTITUDE IS CONTAGIOUS. AND RESPECT? YUCK!
THEY'RE WAY TOO STRONG FOR US ANYWAY. AND THEY DON'T HAVE ANY TREASURE ON THEM EITHER.
LET'S SPLIT!
...
YOU KNOW, YOU'RE LESS OF A GOODIE-GOODIE THAN YOU LOOK.
OH YEAH?
AND WHAT DO I LOOK LIKE, EXACTLY?
YOU KNOW STAR WARS?
I LOVE STAR WARS!
SO YOU KNOW CHEWBACCA?
YEAH?
THERE YOU GO!
HA HA HA !!
OMG, SOOO TRUE!
BAMBI!! BAMMBI!!!!
OVER THERE!
IT'S BAMBI!

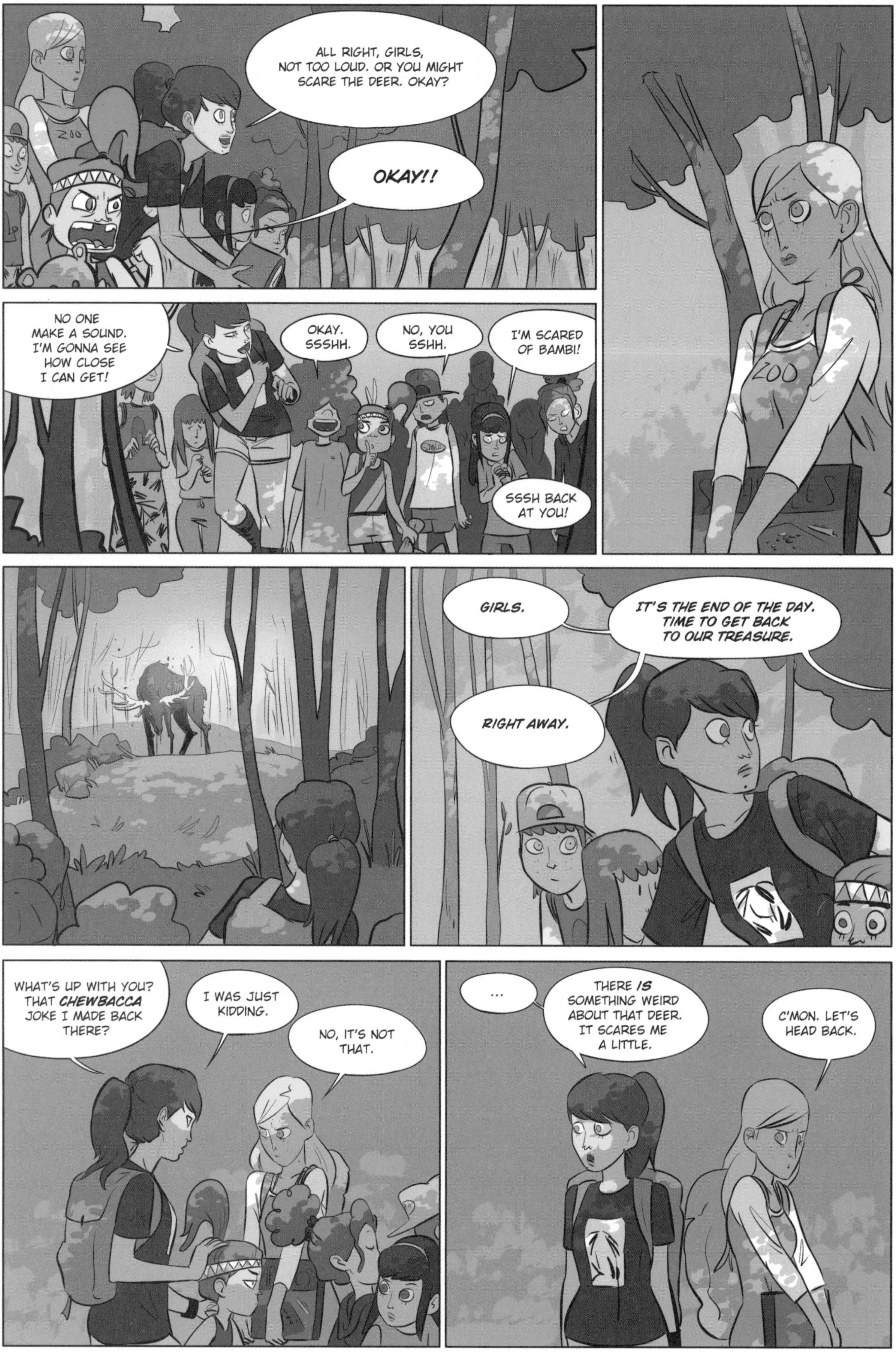
ALL RIGHT, GIRLS, NOT TOO LOUD. OR YOU MIGHT SCARE THE DEER. OKAY?
OKAY!!
NO ONE MAKE A SOUND. I'M GONNA SEE HOW CLOSE I CAN GET!
OKAY. SSSHH.
NO, YOU SSHH.
I'M SCARED OF BAMBI!
SSSH BACK AT YOU!
GIRLS.
IT'S THE END OF THE DAY. TIME TO GET BACK TO OUR TREASURE.
RIGHT AWAY.
WHAT'S UP WITH YOU? THAT CHEWBACCA JOKE I MADE BACK THERE?
I WAS JUST KIDDING.
NO, IT'S NOT THAT.
...
THERE IS SOMETHING WEIRD ABOUT THAT DEER. IT SCARES ME A LITTLE.
C'MON. LET'S HEAD BACK.

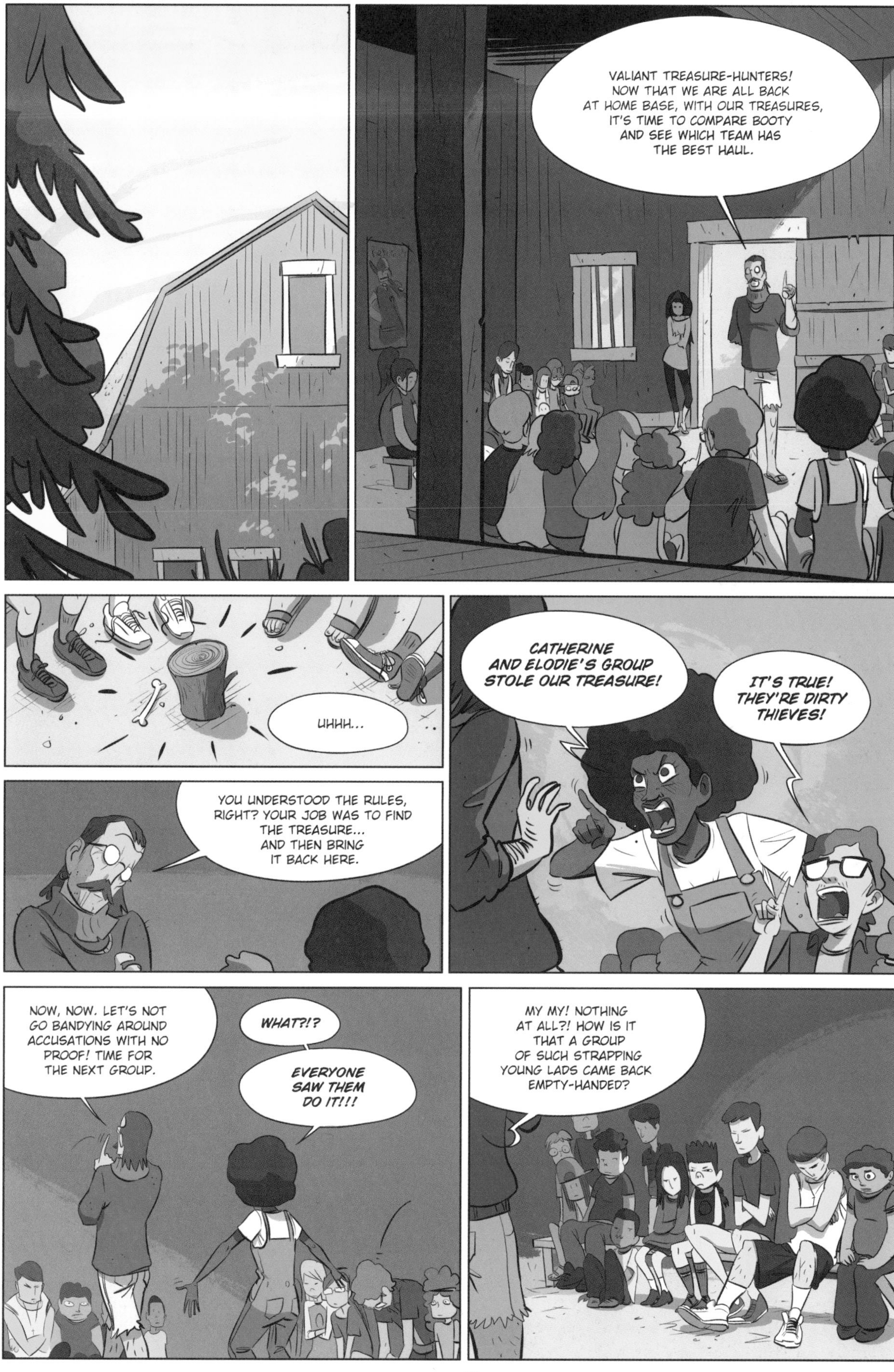
VALIANT TREASURE-HUNTERS! NOW THAT WE ARE ALL BACK AT HOME BASE, WITH OUR TREASURES, IT'S TIME TO COMPARE BOOTY AND SEE WHICH TEAM HAS THE BEST HAUL.
UHHH...
YOU UNDERSTOOD THE RULES, RIGHT? YOUR JOB WAS TO FIND THE TREASURE... AND THEN BRING IT BACK HERE.
CATHERINE AND ELODIE'S GROUP STOLE OUR TREASURE!
IT'S TRUE! THEY'RE DIRTY THIEVES!
NOW, NOW. LET'S NOT GO BANDYING AROUND ACCUSATIONS WITH NO PROOF! TIME FOR THE NEXT GROUP.
WHAT?!?
EVERYONE SAW THEM DO IT!!!
MY MY! NOTHING AT ALL?! HOW IS IT THAT A GROUP OF SUCH STRAPPING YOUNG LADS CAME BACK EMPTY-HANDED?

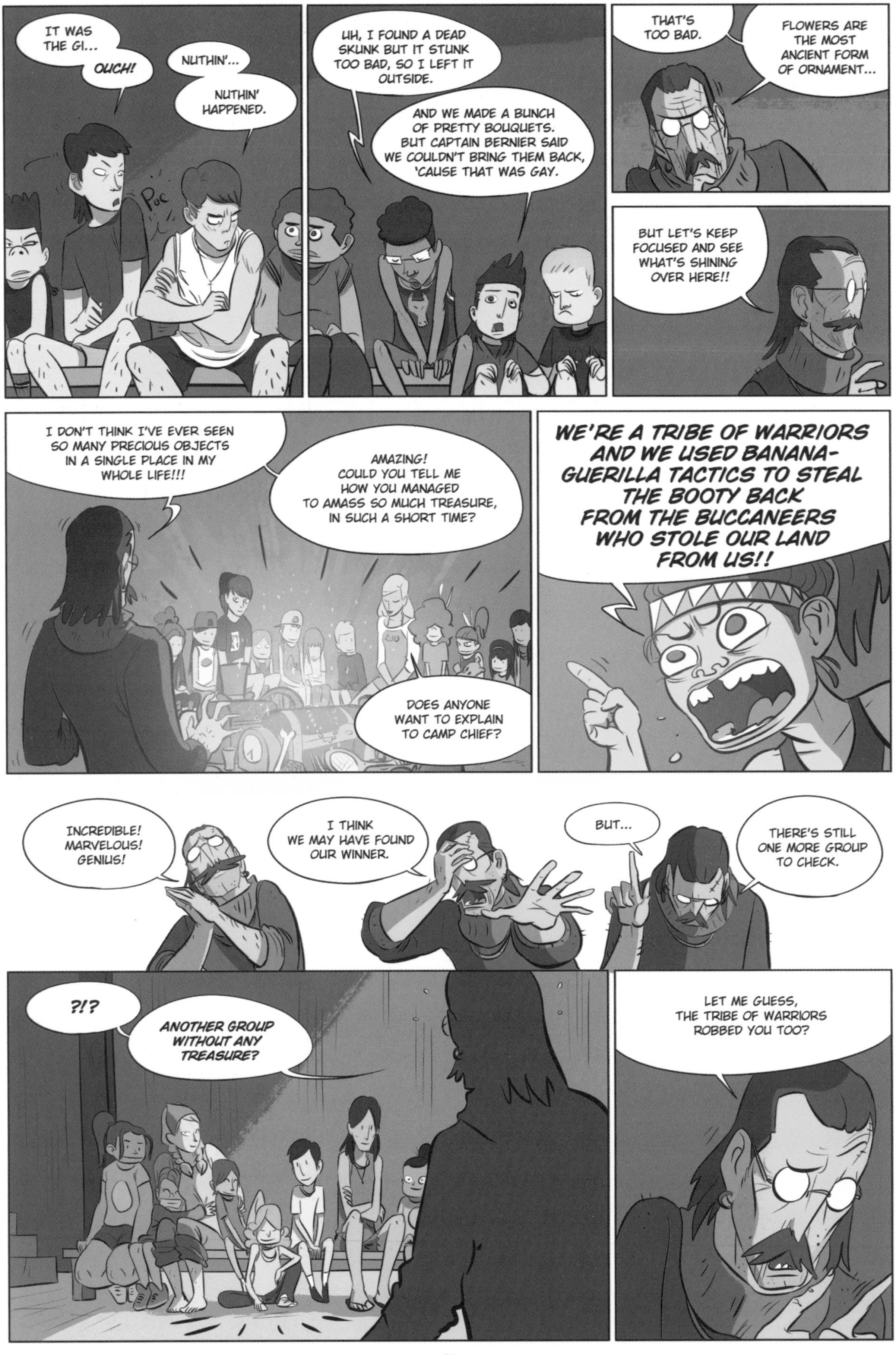

IT WAS THE GI... OUCH!
NUTHIN'...
NUTHIN' HAPPENED.
PAC
UH, I FOUND A DEAD SKUNK BUT IT STUNK TOO BAD, SO I LEFT IT OUTSIDE.
AND WE MADE A BUNCH OF PRETTY BOUQUETS. BUT CAPTAIN BERNIER SAID WE COULDN'T BRING THEM BACK, 'CAUSE THAT WAS GAY.
THAT'S TOO BAD.
FLOWERS ARE THE MOST ANCIENT FORM OF ORNAMENT...
BUT LET'S KEEP FOCUSED AND SEE WHAT'S SHINING OVER HERE!!
I DON'T THINK I'VE EVER SEEN SO MANY PRECIOUS OBJECTS IN A SINGLE PLACE IN MY WHOLE LIFE!!!
AMAZING! COULD YOU TELL ME HOW YOU MANAGED TO AMASS SO MUCH TREASURE, IN SUCH A SHORT TIME?
DOES ANYONE WANT TO EXPLAIN TO CAMP CHIEF?
WE'RE A TRIBE OF WARRIORS AND WE USED BANANA-GUERILLA TACTICS TO STEAL THE BOOTY BACK FROM THE BUCCANEERS WHO STOLE OUR LAND FROM US!!
INCREDIBLE! MARVELOUS! GENIUS!
I THINK WE MAY HAVE FOUND OUR WINNER.
BUT...
THERE'S STILL ONE MORE GROUP TO CHECK.
?!?
ANOTHER GROUP WITHOUT ANY TREASURE?
LET ME GUESS, THE TRIBE OF WARRIORS ROBBED YOU TOO?

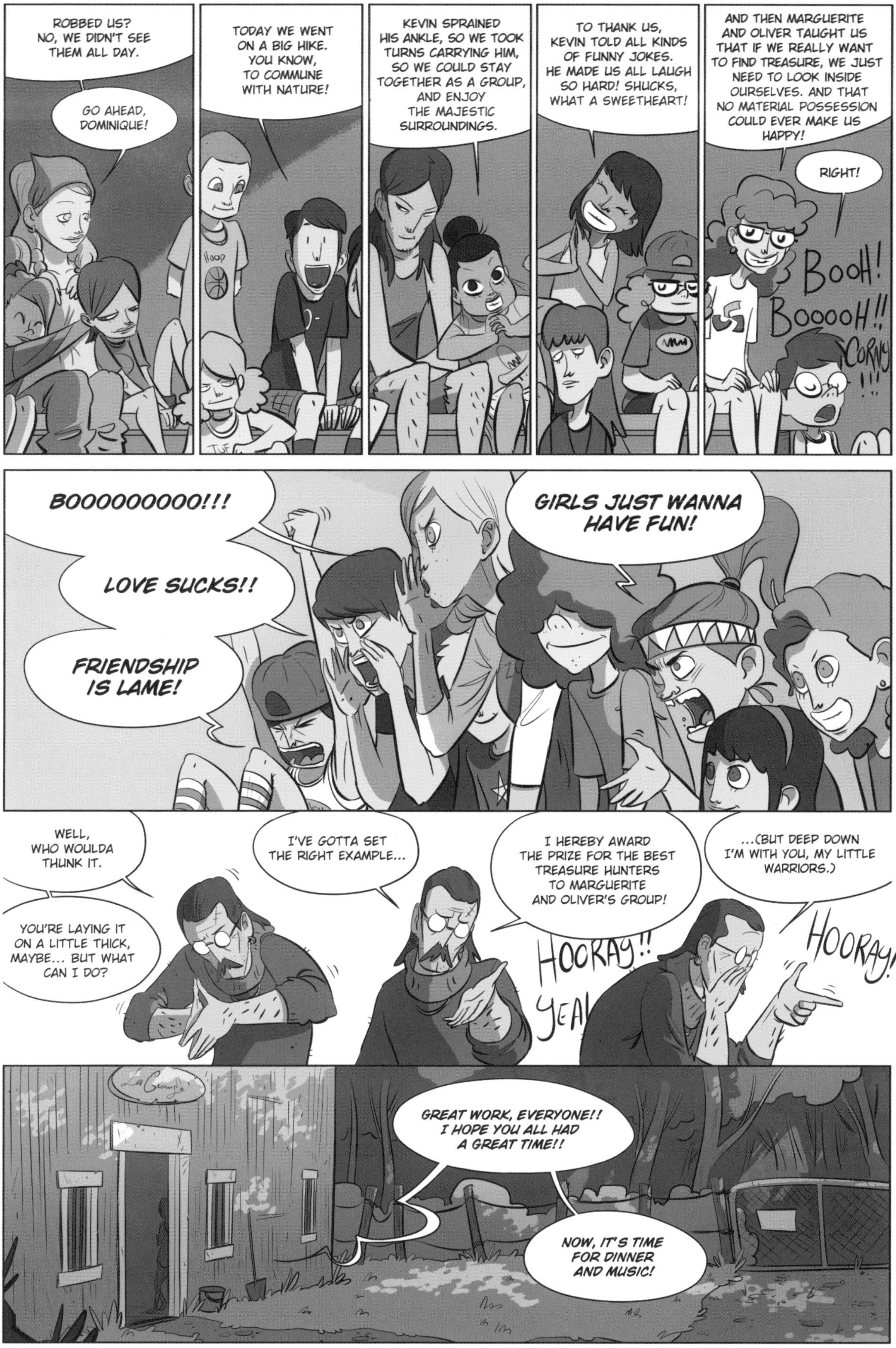

ROBBED US? NO, WE DIDN'T SEE THEM ALL DAY.
GO AHEAD, DOMINIQUE!
TODAY WE WENT ON A BIG HIKE. YOU KNOW, TO COMMUNE WITH NATURE!
KEVIN SPRAINED HIS ANKLE, SO WE TOOK TURNS CARRYING HIM, SO WE COULD STAY TOGETHER AS A GROUP, AND ENJOY THE MAJESTIC SURROUNDINGS.
TO THANK US, KEVIN TOLD ALL KINDS OF FUNNY JOKES. HE MADE US ALL LAUGH SO HARD! SHUCKS, WHAT A SWEETHEART!
AND THEN MARGUERITE AND OLIVER TAUGHT US THAT IF WE REALLY WANT TO FIND TREASURE, WE JUST NEED TO LOOK INSIDE OURSELVES. AND THAT NO MATERIAL POSSESSION COULD EVER MAKE US HAPPY!
RIGHT!
BOOH!
BOOOOH!!
CORNY!!!
BOOOOOOOOO!!!
LOVE SUCKS!!
FRIENDSHIP IS LAME!
GIRLS JUST WANNA HAVE FUN!
WELL, WHO WOULDA THUNK IT.
YOU'RE LAYING IT ON A LITTLE THICK, MAYBE... BUT WHAT CAN I DO?
I'VE GOTTA SET THE RIGHT EXAMPLE...
I HEREBY AWARD THE PRIZE FOR THE BEST TREASURE HUNTERS TO MARGUERITE AND OLIVER'S GROUP!
HOORAY!!
YEA!
...(BUT DEEP DOWN I'M WITH YOU, MY LITTLE WARRIORS.)
HOORAY!
GREAT WORK, EVERYONE!! I HOPE YOU ALL HAD A GREAT TIME!!
NOW, IT'S TIME FOR DINNER AND MUSIC!

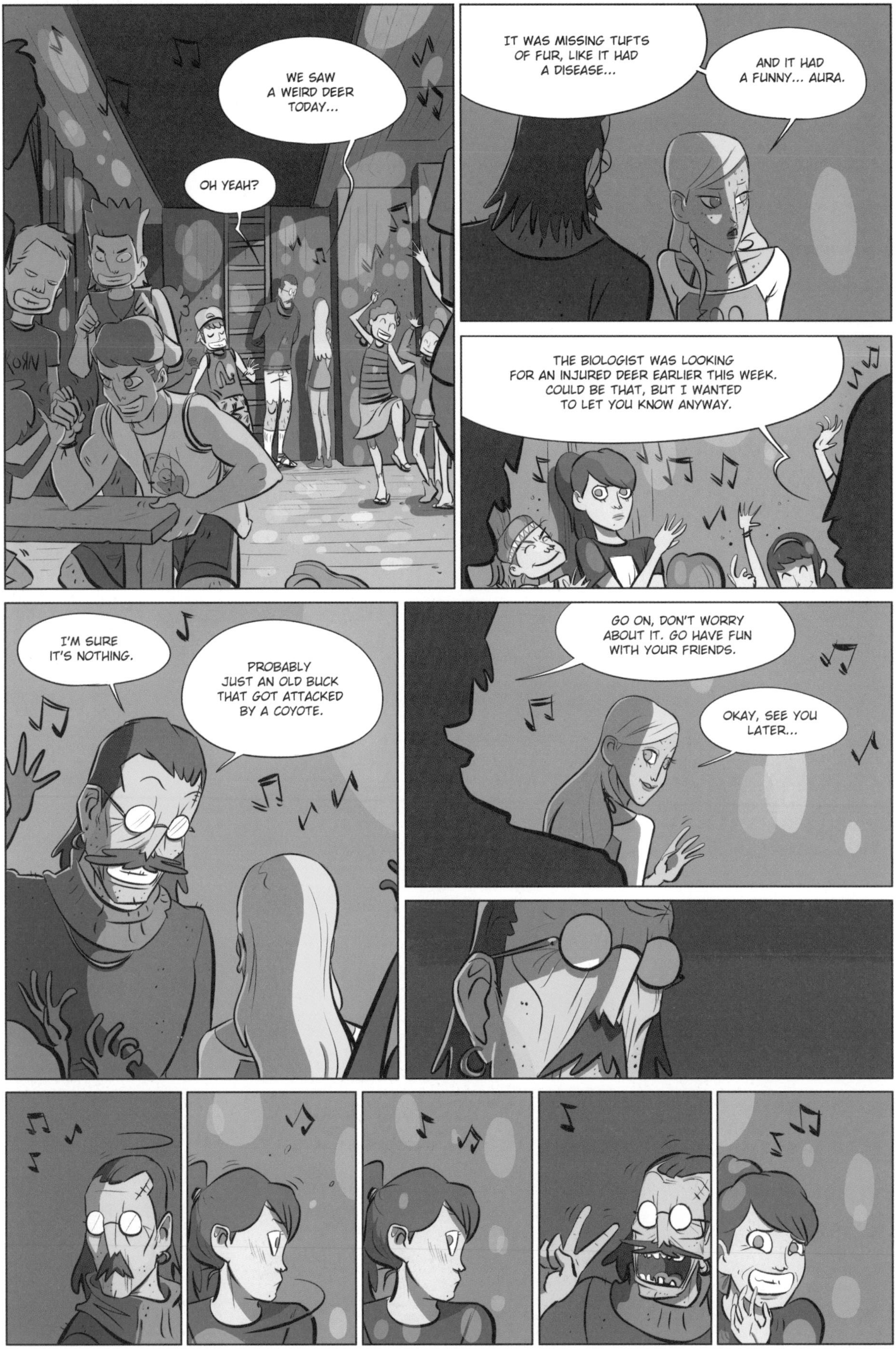

WE SAW A WEIRD DEER TODAY...
OH YEAH?
IT WAS MISSING TUFTS OF FUR, LIKE IT HAD A DISEASE...
AND IT HAD A FUNNY... AURA.
THE BIOLOGIST WAS LOOKING FOR AN INJURED DEER EARLIER THIS WEEK. COULD BE THAT, BUT I WANTED TO LET YOU KNOW ANYWAY.
I'M SURE IT'S NOTHING.
PROBABLY JUST AN OLD BUCK THAT GOT ATTACKED BY A COYOTE.
GO ON, DON'T WORRY ABOUT IT. GO HAVE FUN WITH YOUR FRIENDS.
OKAY, SEE YOU LATER...

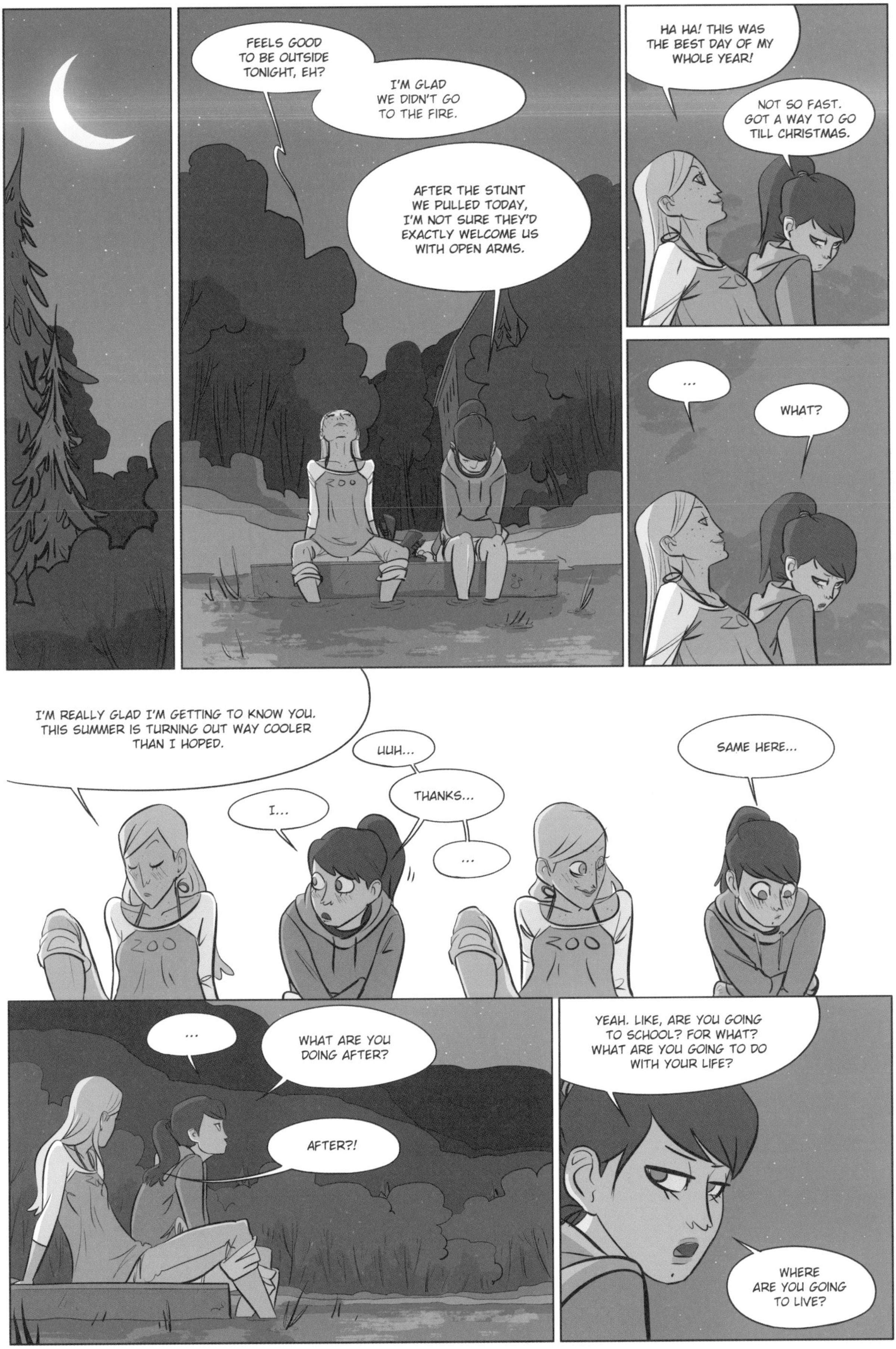
FEELS GOOD TO BE OUTSIDE TONIGHT, EH?
I'M GLAD WE DIDN'T GO TO THE FIRE.
AFTER THE STUNT WE PULLED TODAY, I'M NOT SURE THEY'D EXACTLY WELCOME US WITH OPEN ARMS.
HA HA! THIS WAS THE BEST DAY OF MY WHOLE YEAR!
NOT SO FAST. GOT A WAY TO GO TILL CHRISTMAS.
...
WHAT?
I'M REALLY GLAD I'M GETTING TO KNOW YOU. THIS SUMMER IS TURNING OUT WAY COOLER THAN I HOPED.
UUH...
I...
THANKS...
...
SAME HERE...
...
WHAT ARE YOU DOING AFTER?
AFTER?!
YEAH. LIKE, ARE YOU GOING TO SCHOOL? FOR WHAT? WHAT ARE YOU GOING TO DO WITH YOUR LIFE?
WHERE ARE YOU GOING TO LIVE?

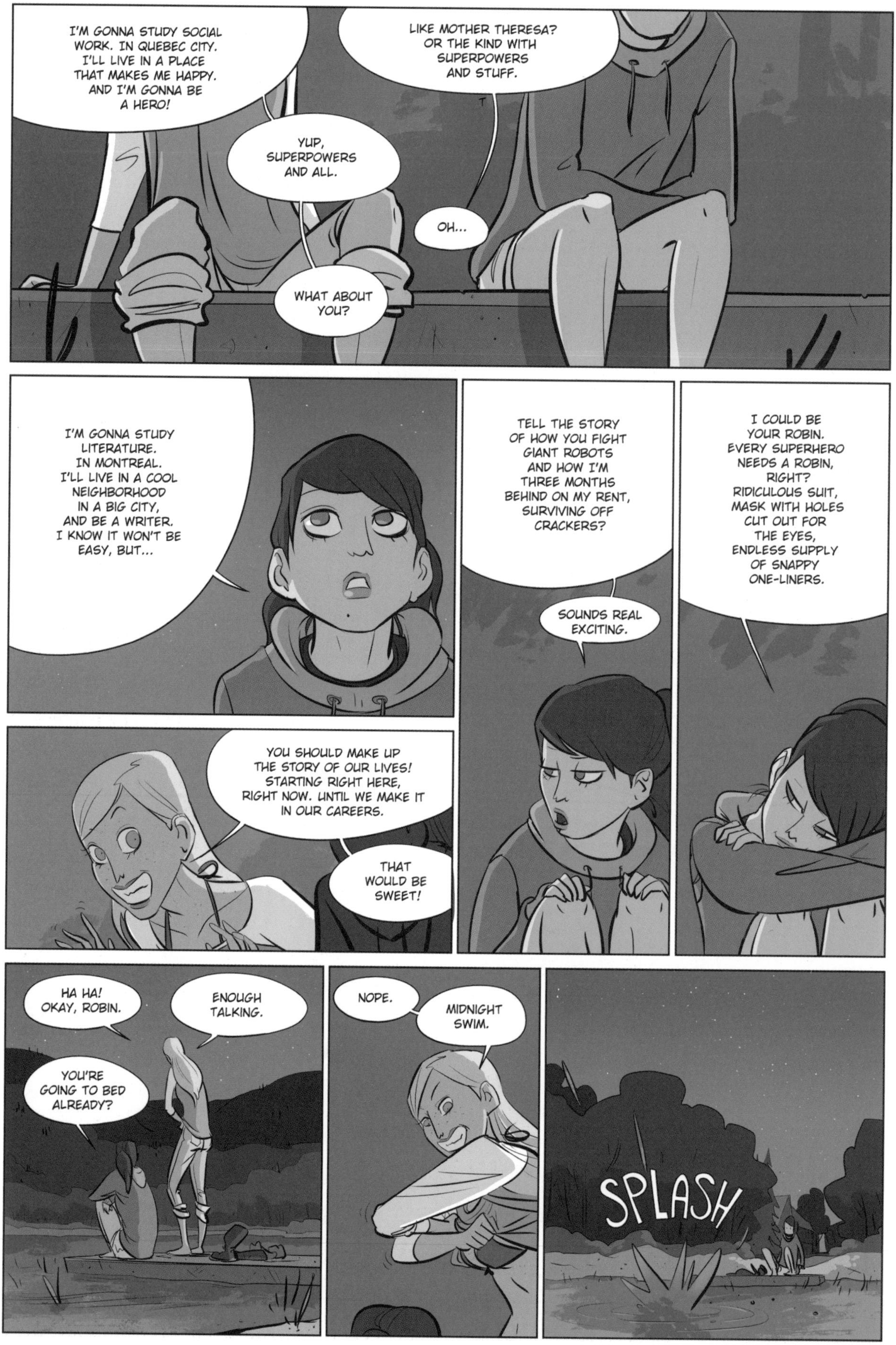
I'M GONNA STUDY SOCIAL WORK. IN QUEBEC CITY. I'LL LIVE IN A PLACE THAT MAKES ME HAPPY. AND I'M GONNA BE A HERO!
LIKE MOTHER THERESA? OR THE KIND WITH SUPERPOWERS AND STUFF.
YUP, SUPERPOWERS AND ALL.
OH...
WHAT ABOUT YOU?
I'M GONNA STUDY LITERATURE. IN MONTREAL. I'LL LIVE IN A COOL NEIGHBORHOOD IN A BIG CITY, AND BE A WRITER. I KNOW IT WON'T BE EASY, BUT...
YOU SHOULD MAKE UP THE STORY OF OUR LIVES! STARTING RIGHT HERE, RIGHT NOW. UNTIL WE MAKE IT IN OUR CAREERS.
THAT WOULD BE SWEET!
TELL THE STORY OF HOW YOU FIGHT GIANT ROBOTS AND HOW I'M THREE MONTHS BEHIND ON MY RENT, SURVIVING OFF CRACKERS?
SOUNDS REAL EXCITING.
I COULD BE YOUR ROBIN. EVERY SUPERHERO NEEDS A ROBIN, RIGHT? RIDICULOUS SUIT, MASK WITH HOLES CUT OUT FOR THE EYES, ENDLESS SUPPLY OF SNAPPY ONE-LINERS.
HA HA! OKAY, ROBIN.
ENOUGH TALKING.
YOU'RE GOING TO BED ALREADY?
NOPE.
MIDNIGHT SWIM.
SPLASH

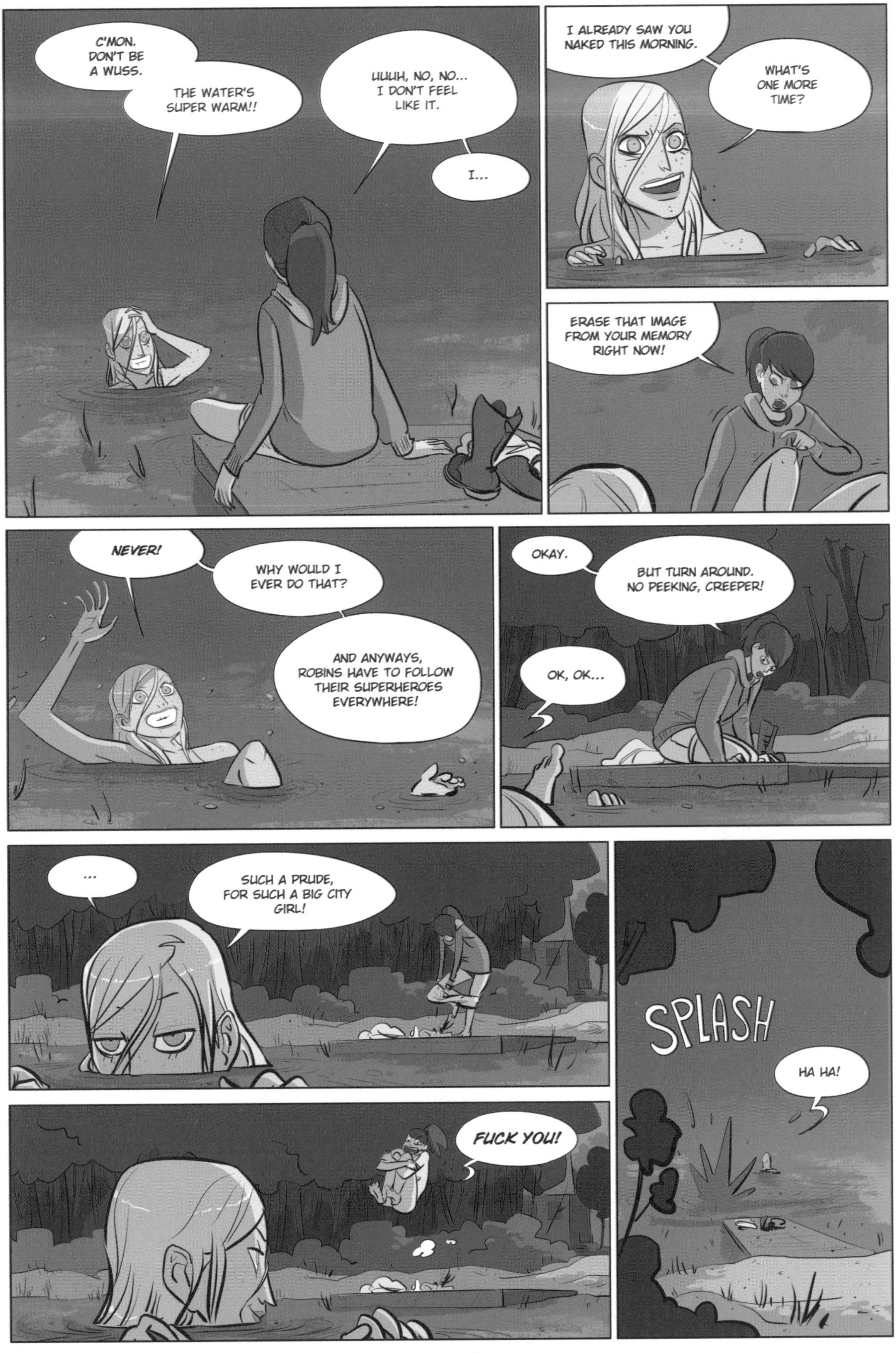
C'MON. DON'T BE A WUSS.
THE WATER'S SUPER WARM!!
UUUH, NO, NO... I DON'T FEEL LIKE IT.
I...
I ALREADY SAW YOU NAKED THIS MORNING.
WHAT'S ONE MORE TIME?
ERASE THAT IMAGE FROM YOUR MEMORY RIGHT NOW!
NEVER!
WHY WOULD I EVER DO THAT?
AND ANYWAYS, ROBINS HAVE TO FOLLOW THEIR SUPERHEROES EVERYWHERE!
OKAY.
BUT TURN AROUND. NO PEEKING, CREEPER!
OK, OK...
...
SUCH A PRUDE, FOR SUCH A BIG CITY GIRL!
FUCK YOU!
SPLASH
HA HA!

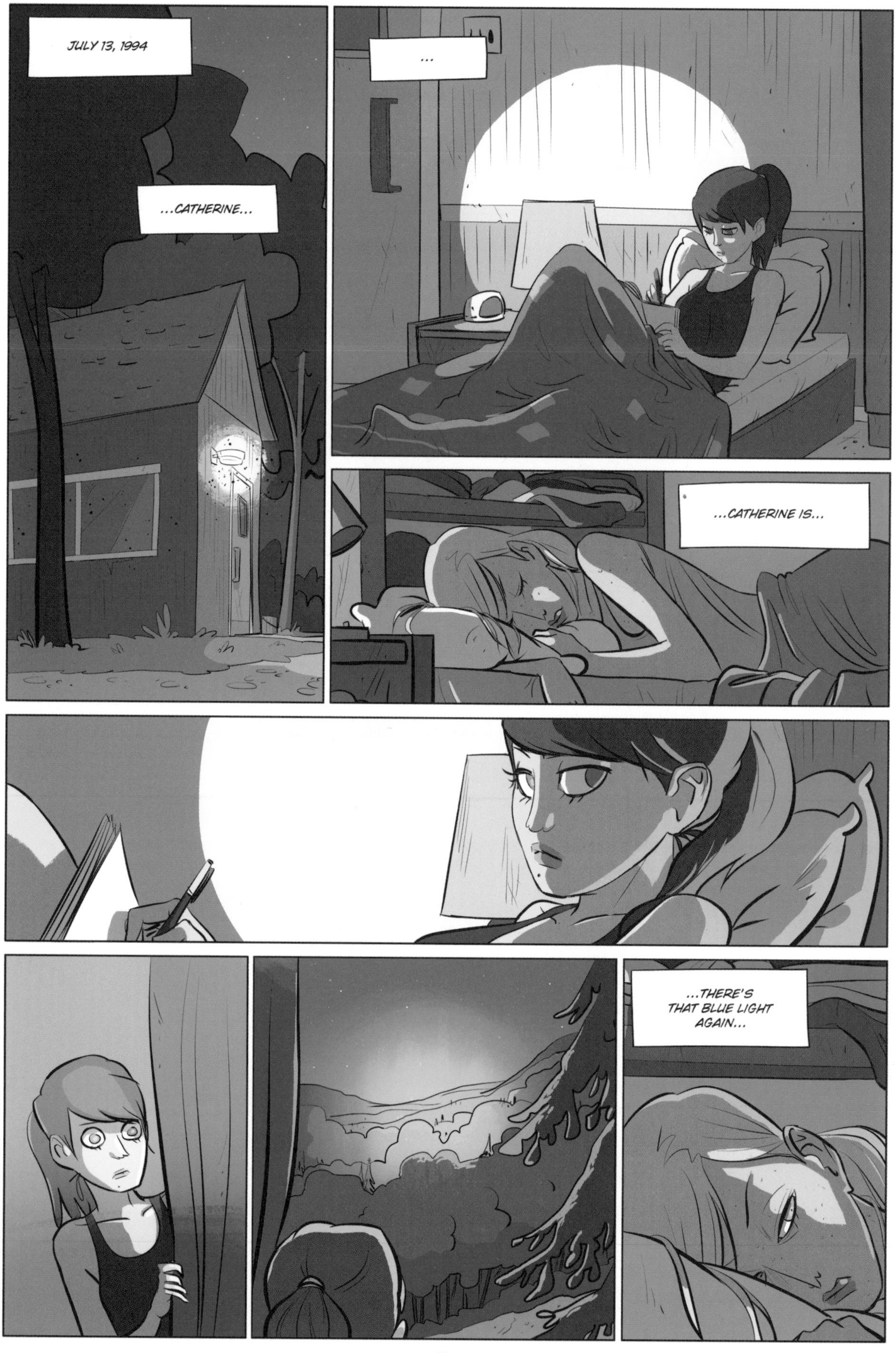
JULY 13, 1994
...CATHERINE...
...
...CATHERINE IS...
...THERE'S THAT BLUE LIGHT AGAIN...

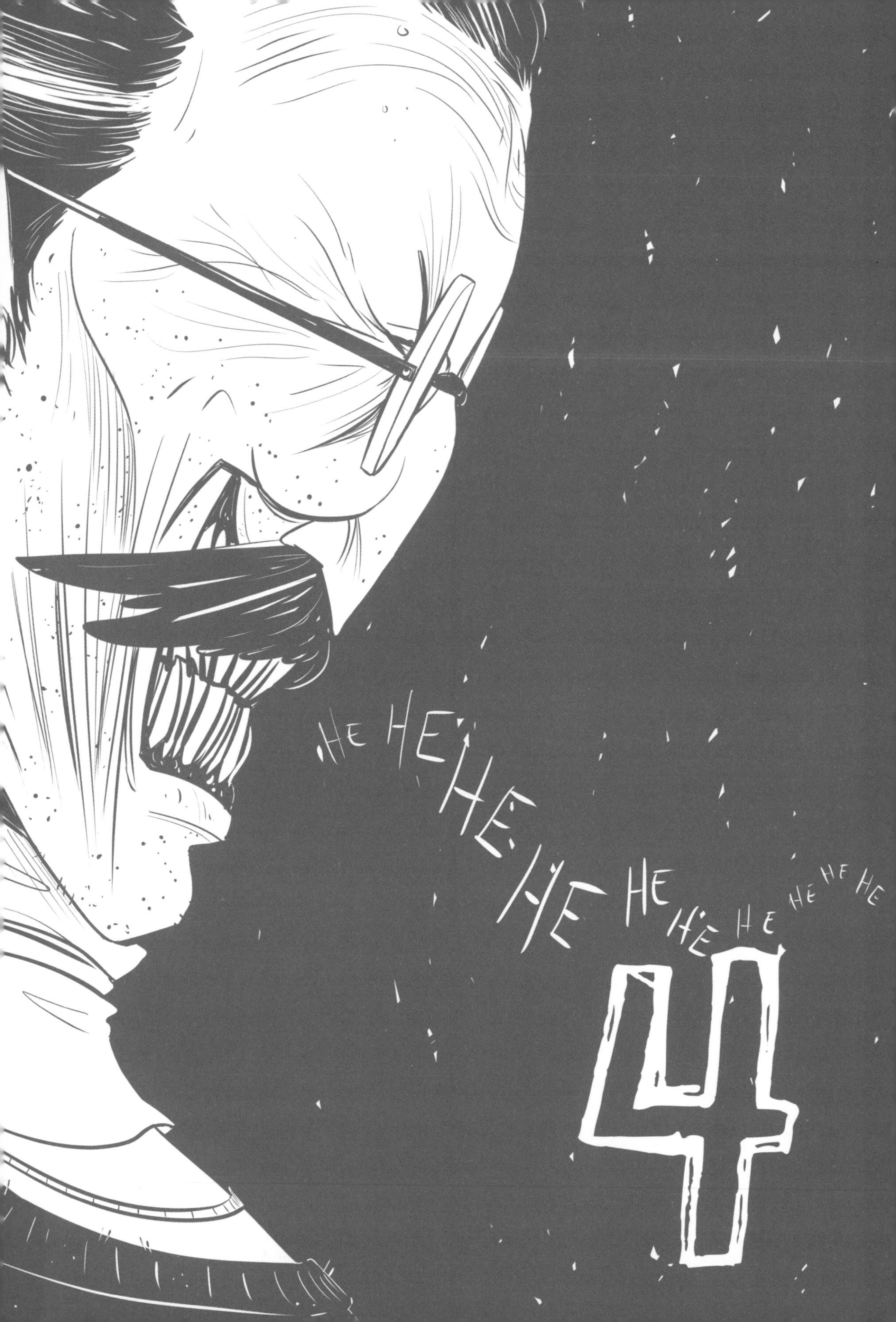
HE HE HE HE HE HE HE HE HE HE HE HE
4

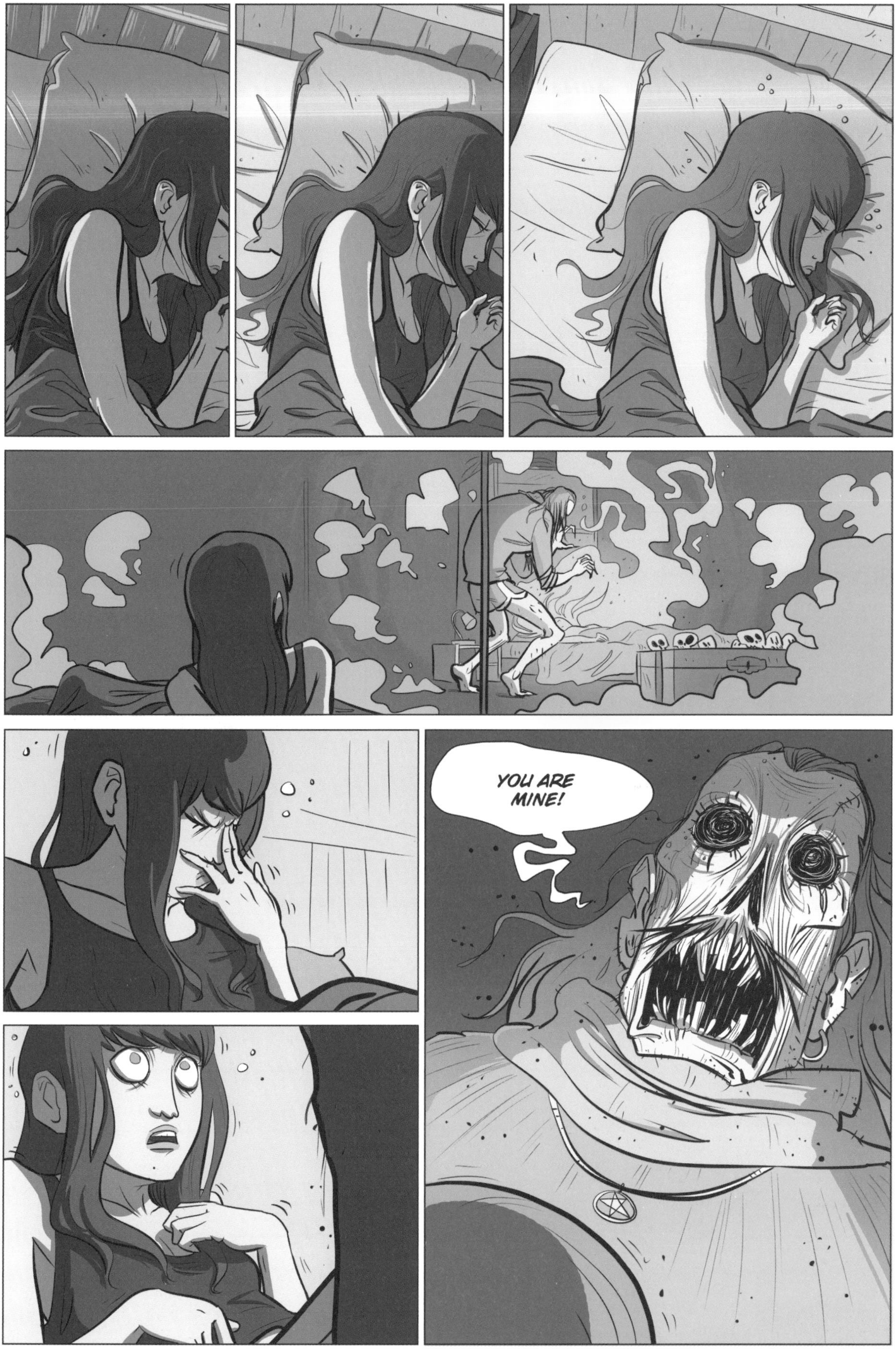
YOU ARE MINE!

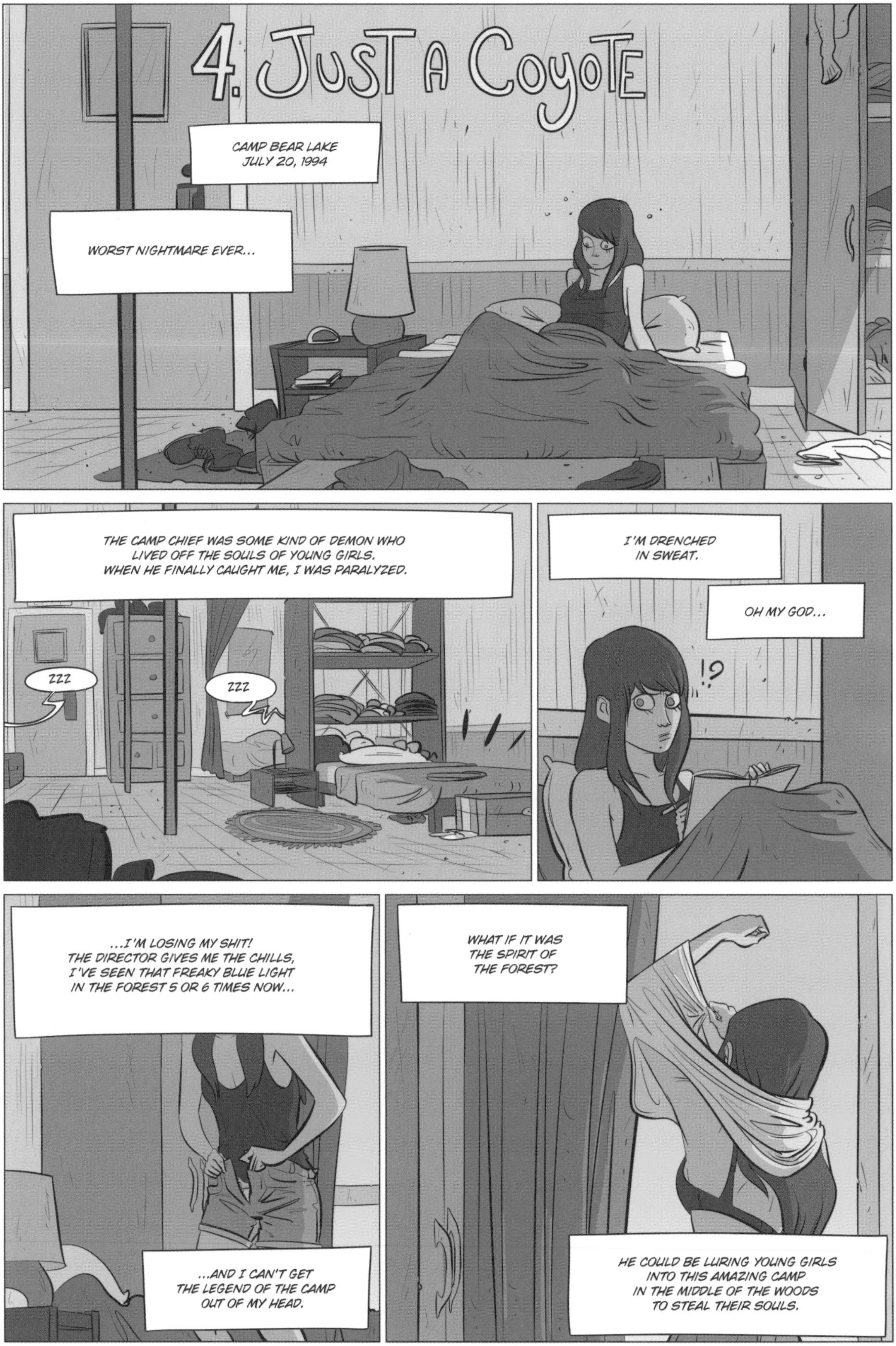
4. JUST A COYOTE
CAMP BEAR LAKE
JULY 20, 1994
WORST NIGHTMARE EVER...
THE CAMP CHIEF WAS SOME KIND OF DEMON WHO LIVED OFF THE SOULS OF YOUNG GIRLS. WHEN HE FINALLY CAUGHT ME, I WAS PARALYZED.
ZZZ
ZZZ
I'M DRENCHED IN SWEAT.
OH MY GOD...
!?
...I'M LOSING MY SHIT! THE DIRECTOR GIVES ME THE CHILLS, I'VE SEEN THAT FREAKY BLUE LIGHT IN THE FOREST 5 OR 6 TIMES NOW...
...AND I CAN'T GET THE LEGEND OF THE CAMP OUT OF MY HEAD.
WHAT IF IT WAS THE SPIRIT OF THE FOREST?
HE COULD BE LURING YOUNG GIRLS INTO THIS AMAZING CAMP IN THE MIDDLE OF THE WOODS TO STEAL THEIR SOULS.

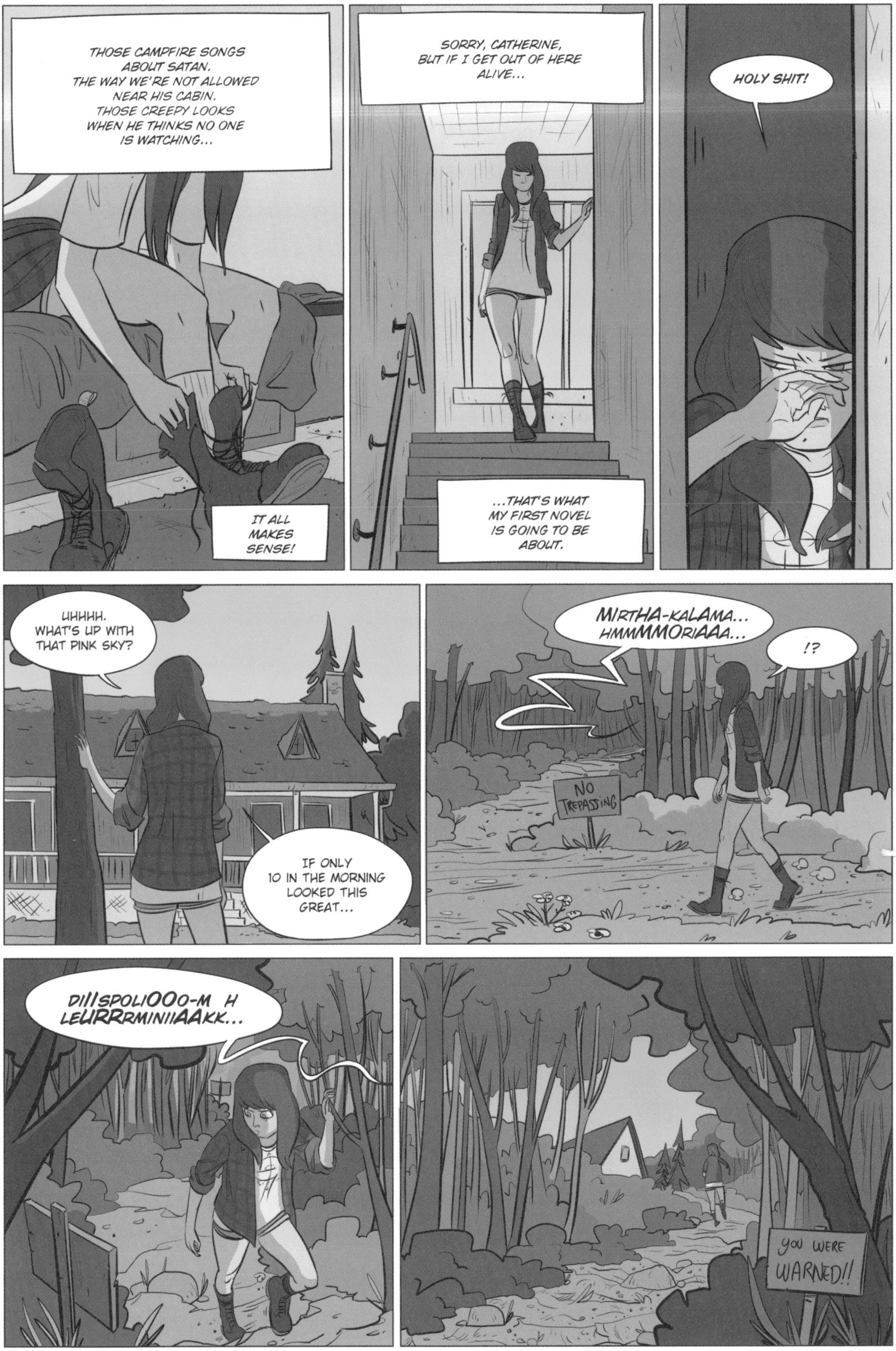

THOSE CAMPFIRE SONGS ABOUT SATAN. THE WAY WE'RE NOT ALLOWED NEAR HIS CABIN. THOSE CREEPY LOOKS WHEN HE THINKS NO ONE IS WATCHING...
IT ALL MAKES SENSE!
SORRY, CATHERINE, BUT IF I GET OUT OF HERE ALIVE...
...THAT'S WHAT MY FIRST NOVEL IS GOING TO BE ABOUT.
HOLY SHIT!
UHHHH. WHAT'S UP WITH THAT PINK SKY?
IF ONLY 10 IN THE MORNING LOOKED THIS GREAT...
MIRTHA-KALAMA... HMMMMORIAAA...
!?
NO TRESPASSING
DIIISPOLIOOO-M H LEURRRMINIIAAKK...
YOU WERE WARNED!!

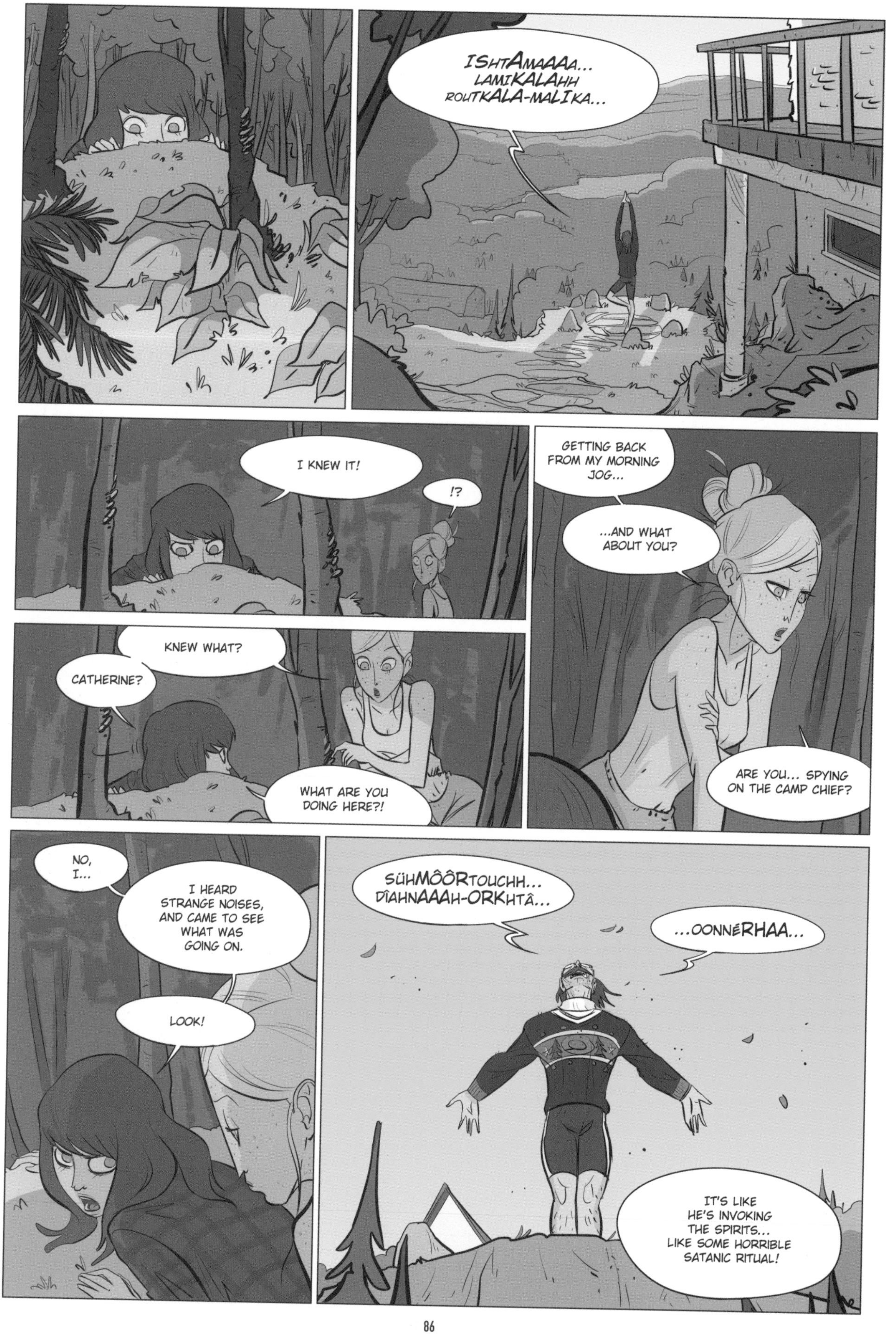
ISHTAMAAAA...
LAMIKALAHH
ROUTKALA-MALIKA...
I KNEW IT!
!?
KNEW WHAT?
CATHERINE?
WHAT ARE YOU DOING HERE?!
GETTING BACK FROM MY MORNING JOG...
...AND WHAT ABOUT YOU?
ARE YOU... SPYING ON THE CAMP CHIEF?
NO, I...
I HEARD STRANGE NOISES, AND CAME TO SEE WHAT WAS GOING ON.
LOOK!
SÜHMÔÔRTOUCHH... DÎAHNAAAH-ORKHTÂ...
...OONNÉRHAA...
IT'S LIKE HE'S INVOKING THE SPIRITS... LIKE SOME HORRIBLE SATANIC RITUAL!

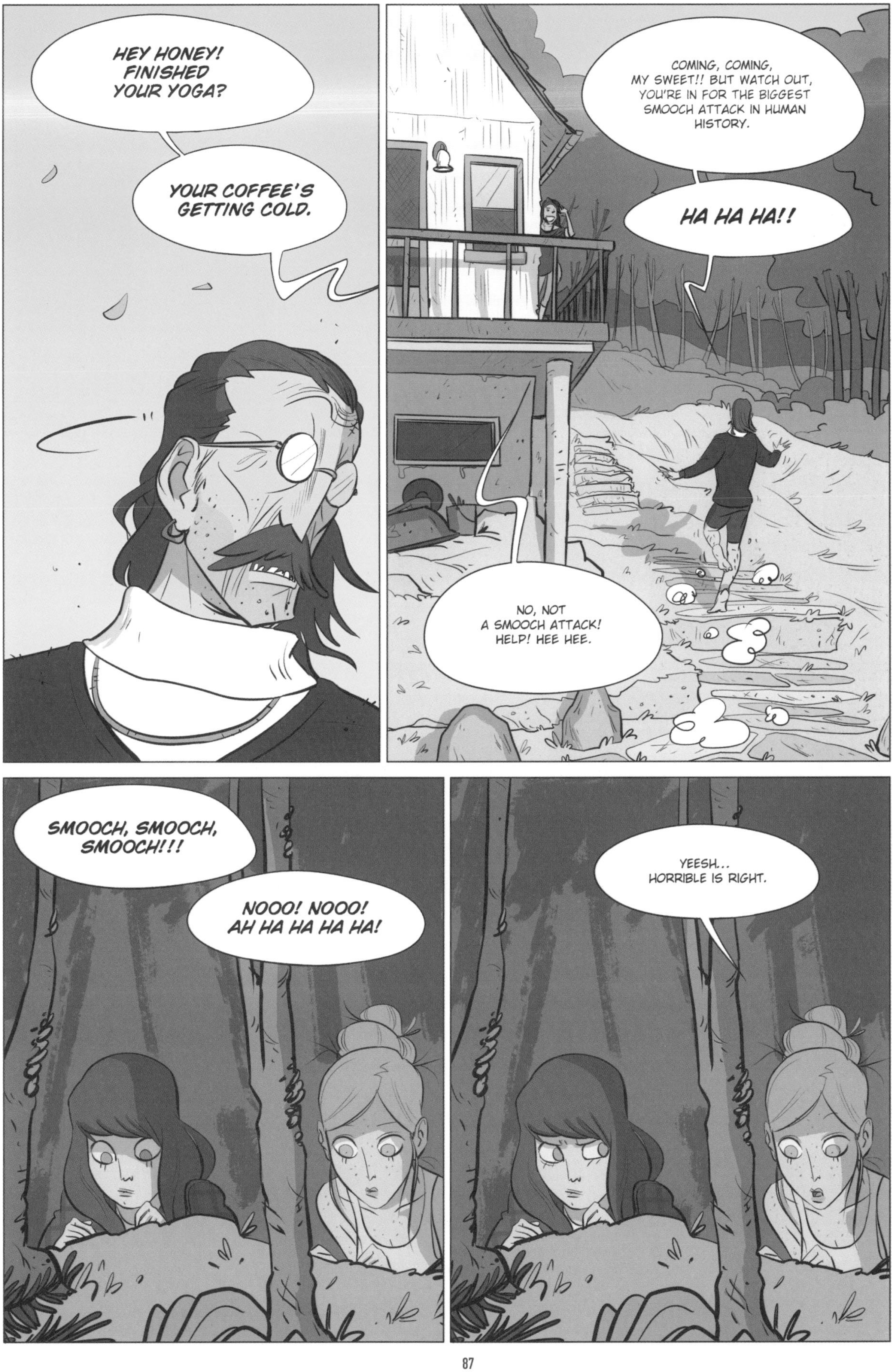
HEY HONEY! FINISHED YOUR YOGA?
YOUR COFFEE'S GETTING COLD.
COMING, COMING, MY SWEET!! BUT WATCH OUT, YOU'RE IN FOR THE BIGGEST SMOOCH ATTACK IN HUMAN HISTORY.
HA HA HA!!
NO, NOT A SMOOCH ATTACK! HELP! HEE HEE.
SMOOCH, SMOOCH, SMOOCH!!!
NOOO! NOOO! AH HA HA HA HA!
YEESH... HORRIBLE IS RIGHT.

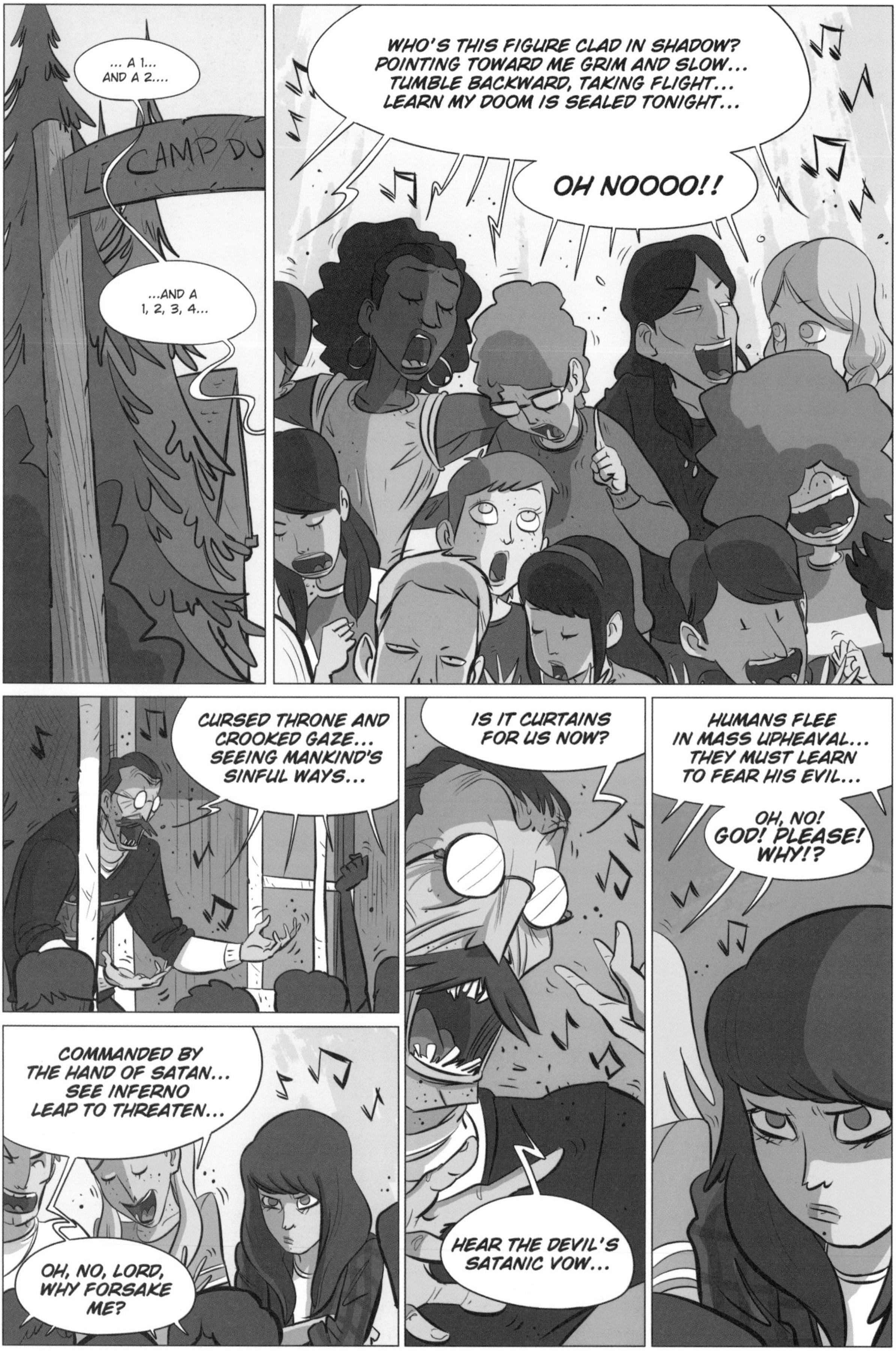

... A 1...
AND A 2....
...AND A 1, 2, 3, 4...
LE CAMP DU
WHO'S THIS FIGURE CLAD IN SHADOW? POINTING TOWARD ME GRIM AND SLOW... TUMBLE BACKWARD, TAKING FLIGHT... LEARN MY DOOM IS SEALED TONIGHT...
OH NOOOO!!
CURSED THRONE AND CROOKED GAZE... SEEING MANKIND'S SINFUL WAYS...
IS IT CURTAINS FOR US NOW?
HUMANS FLEE IN MASS UPHEAVAL... THEY MUST LEARN TO FEAR HIS EVIL...
OH, NO! GOD! PLEASE! WHY!?
COMMANDED BY THE HAND OF SATAN... SEE INFERNO LEAP TO THREATEN...
OH, NO, LORD, WHY FORSAKE ME?
HEAR THE DEVIL'S SATANIC VOW...

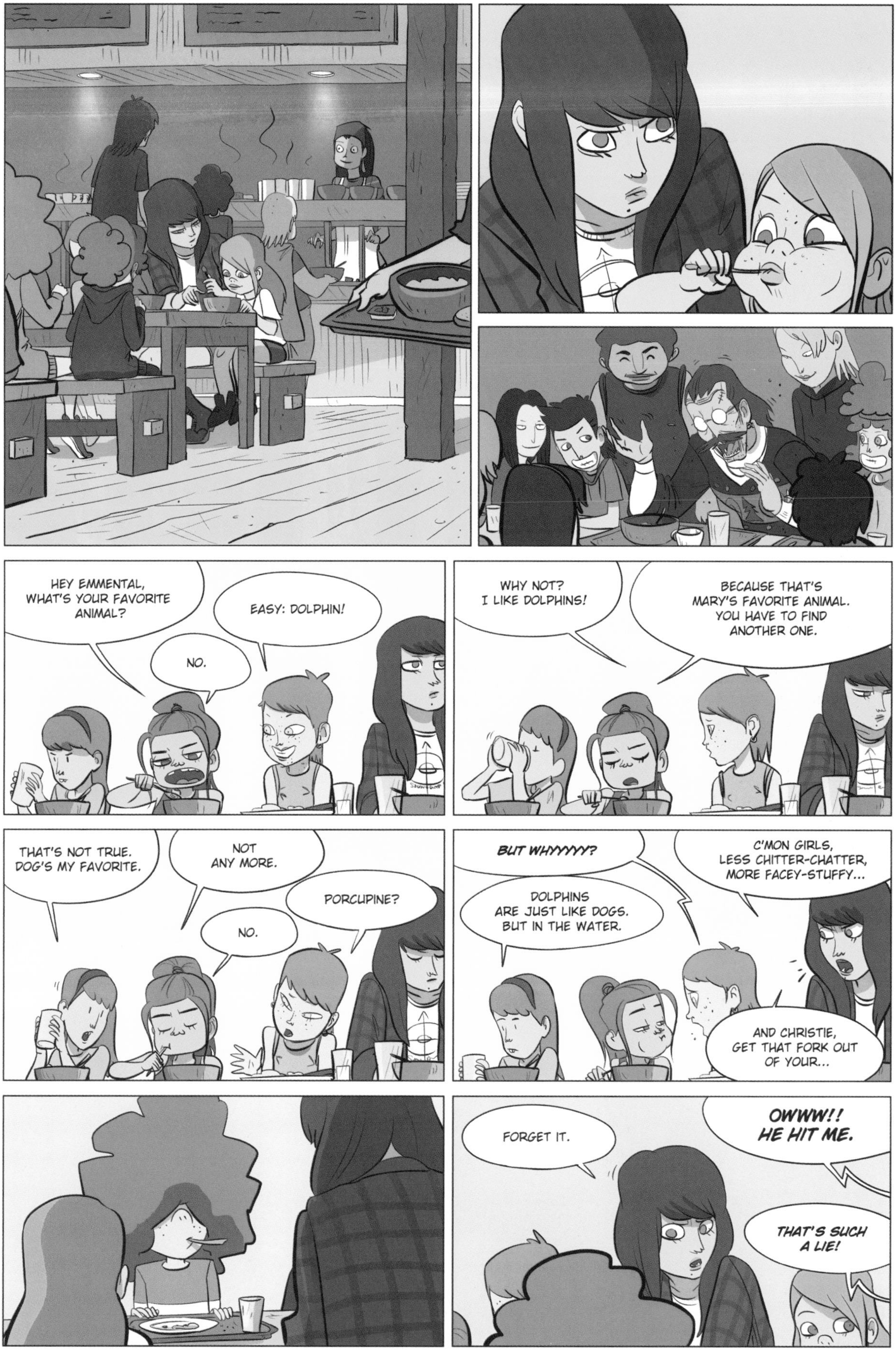
HEY EMMENTAL, WHAT'S YOUR FAVORITE ANIMAL?
NO.
EASY: DOLPHIN!
WHY NOT? I LIKE DOLPHINS!
BECAUSE THAT'S MARY'S FAVORITE ANIMAL. YOU HAVE TO FIND ANOTHER ONE.
THAT'S NOT TRUE. DOG'S MY FAVORITE.
NOT ANY MORE.
PORCUPINE?
NO.
BUT WHYYYYY?
DOLPHINS ARE JUST LIKE DOGS. BUT IN THE WATER.
C'MON GIRLS, LESS CHITTER-CHATTER, MORE FACEY-STUFFY...
AND CHRISTIE, GET THAT FORK OUT OF YOUR...
FORGET IT.
OWWW!! HE HIT ME.
THAT'S SUCH A LIE!

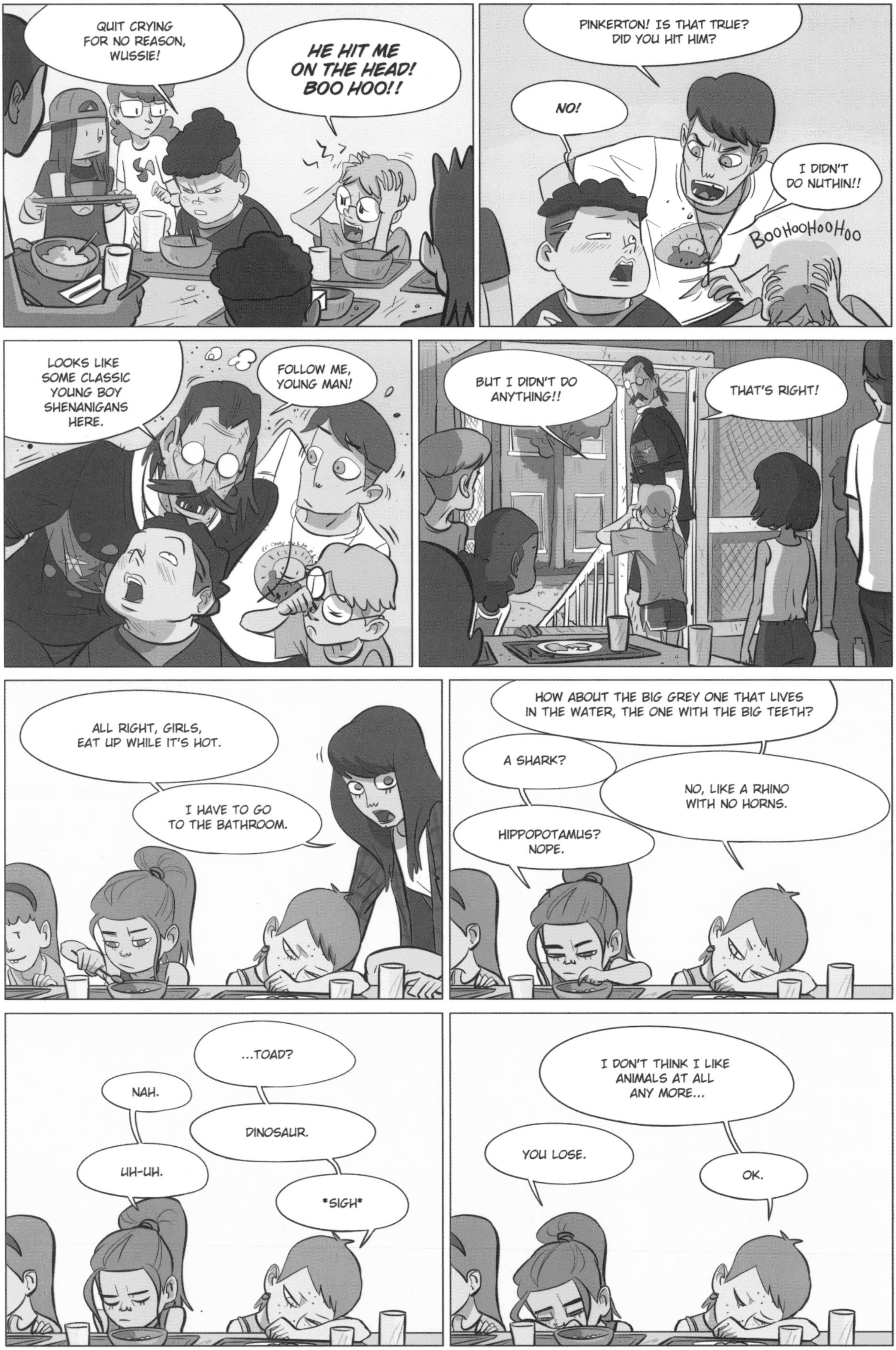
QUIT CRYING FOR NO REASON, WUSSIE!
HE HIT ME ON THE HEAD! BOO HOO!!
PINKERTON! IS THAT TRUE? DID YOU HIT HIM?
NO!
I DIDN'T DO NUTHIN!!
BooHooHooHoo
LOOKS LIKE SOME CLASSIC YOUNG BOY SHENANIGANS HERE.
FOLLOW ME, YOUNG MAN!
BUT I DIDN'T DO ANYTHING!!
THAT'S RIGHT!
ALL RIGHT, GIRLS, EAT UP WHILE IT'S HOT.
I HAVE TO GO TO THE BATHROOM.
HOW ABOUT THE BIG GREY ONE THAT LIVES IN THE WATER, THE ONE WITH THE BIG TEETH?
A SHARK?
NO, LIKE A RHINO WITH NO HORNS.
HIPPOPOTAMUS? NOPE.
...TOAD?
NAH.
DINOSAUR.
UH-UH.
SIGH
I DON'T THINK I LIKE ANIMALS AT ALL ANY MORE...
YOU LOSE.
OK.

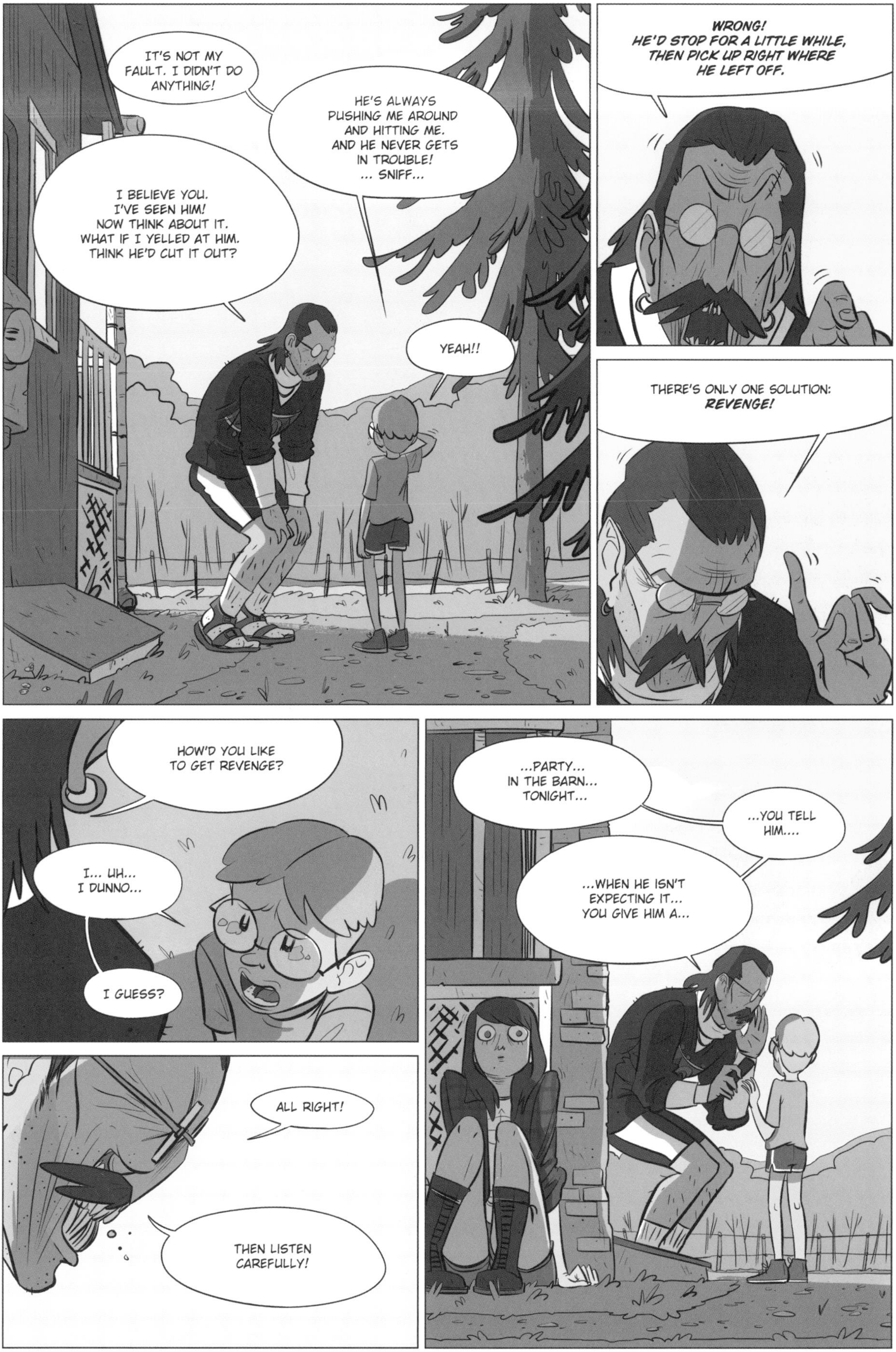
IT'S NOT MY FAULT. I DIDN'T DO ANYTHING!
HE'S ALWAYS PUSHING ME AROUND AND HITTING ME. AND HE NEVER GETS IN TROUBLE! ... SNIFF...
I BELIEVE YOU. I'VE SEEN HIM! NOW THINK ABOUT IT. WHAT IF I YELLED AT HIM. THINK HE'D CUT IT OUT?
YEAH!!
WRONG! HE'D STOP FOR A LITTLE WHILE, THEN PICK UP RIGHT WHERE HE LEFT OFF.
THERE'S ONLY ONE SOLUTION: REVENGE!
HOW'D YOU LIKE TO GET REVENGE?
I... UH... I DUNNO...
I GUESS?
ALL RIGHT!
THEN LISTEN CAREFULLY!
...PARTY... IN THE BARN... TONIGHT...
...YOU TELL HIM....
...WHEN HE ISN'T EXPECTING IT... YOU GIVE HIM A...

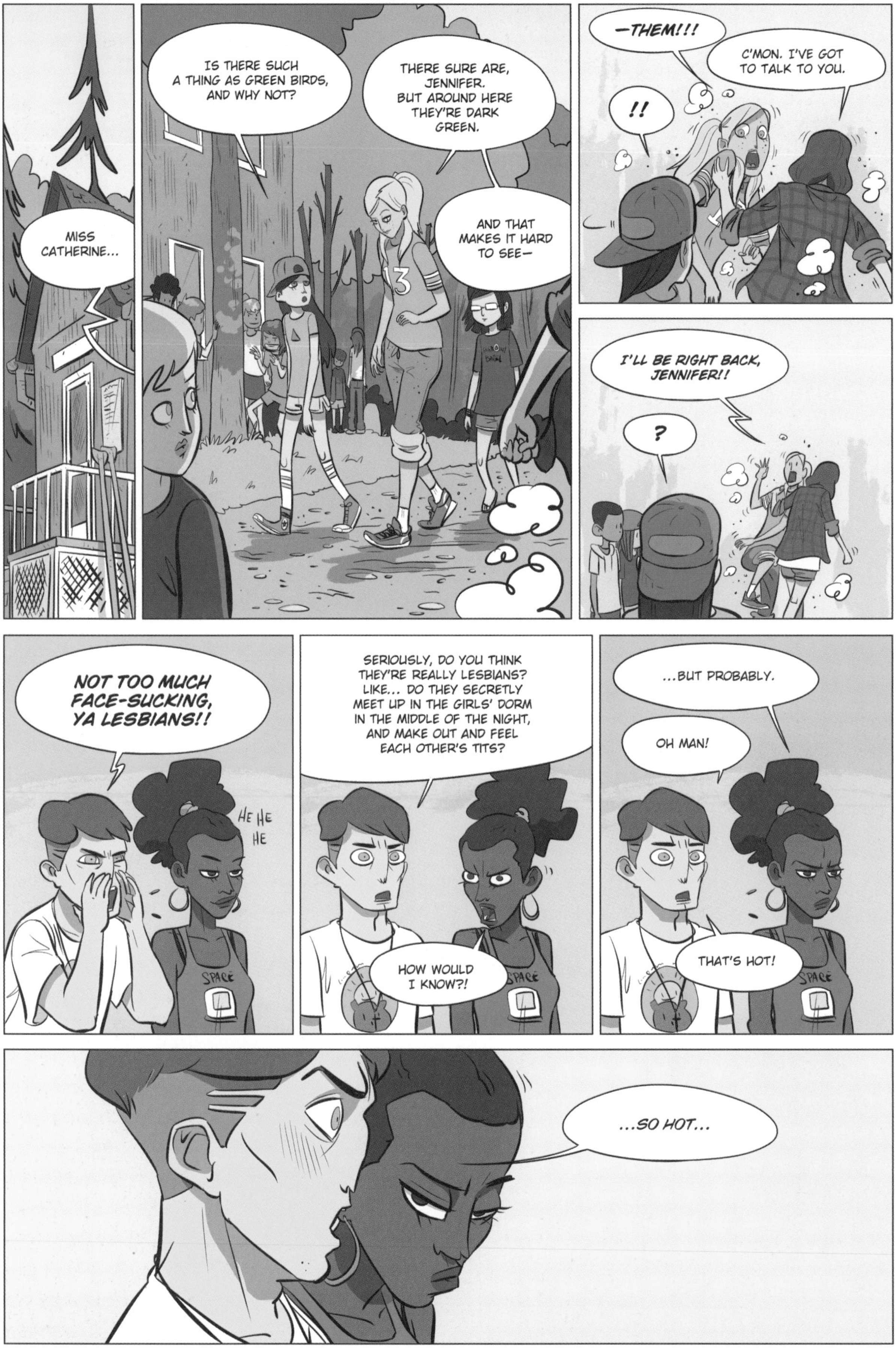

MISS CATHERINE...
IS THERE SUCH A THING AS GREEN BIRDS, AND WHY NOT?
THERE SURE ARE, JENNIFER. BUT AROUND HERE THEY'RE DARK GREEN.
AND THAT MAKES IT HARD TO SEE—
—THEM!!!
C'MON. I'VE GOT TO TALK TO YOU.
!!
I'LL BE RIGHT BACK, JENNIFER!!
?
NOT TOO MUCH FACE-SUCKING, YA LESBIANS!!
HE HE HE
SERIOUSLY, DO YOU THINK THEY'RE REALLY LESBIANS? LIKE... DO THEY SECRETLY MEET UP IN THE GIRLS' DORM IN THE MIDDLE OF THE NIGHT, AND MAKE OUT AND FEEL EACH OTHER'S TITS?
HOW WOULD I KNOW?!
...BUT PROBABLY.
OH MAN!
THAT'S HOT!
...SO HOT...

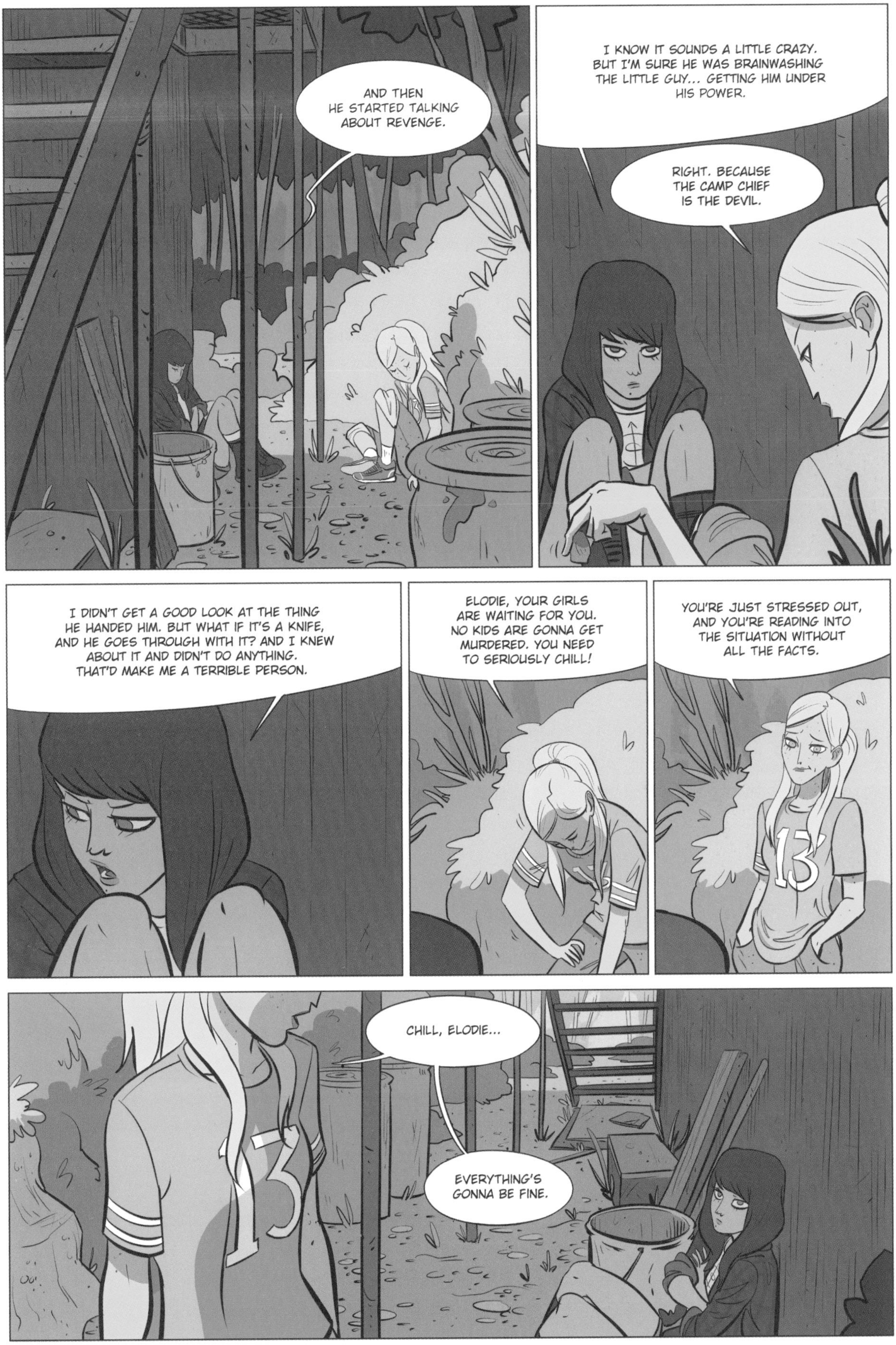
AND THEN HE STARTED TALKING ABOUT REVENGE.
I KNOW IT SOUNDS A LITTLE CRAZY. BUT I'M SURE HE WAS BRAINWASHING THE LITTLE GUY... GETTING HIM UNDER HIS POWER.
RIGHT. BECAUSE THE CAMP CHIEF IS THE DEVIL.
I DIDN'T GET A GOOD LOOK AT THE THING HE HANDED HIM. BUT WHAT IF IT'S A KNIFE, AND HE GOES THROUGH WITH IT? AND I KNEW ABOUT IT AND DIDN'T DO ANYTHING. THAT'D MAKE ME A TERRIBLE PERSON.
ELODIE, YOUR GIRLS ARE WAITING FOR YOU. NO KIDS ARE GONNA GET MURDERED. YOU NEED TO SERIOUSLY CHILL!
YOU'RE JUST STRESSED OUT, AND YOU'RE READING INTO THE SITUATION WITHOUT ALL THE FACTS.
CHILL, ELODIE...
EVERYTHING'S GONNA BE FINE.

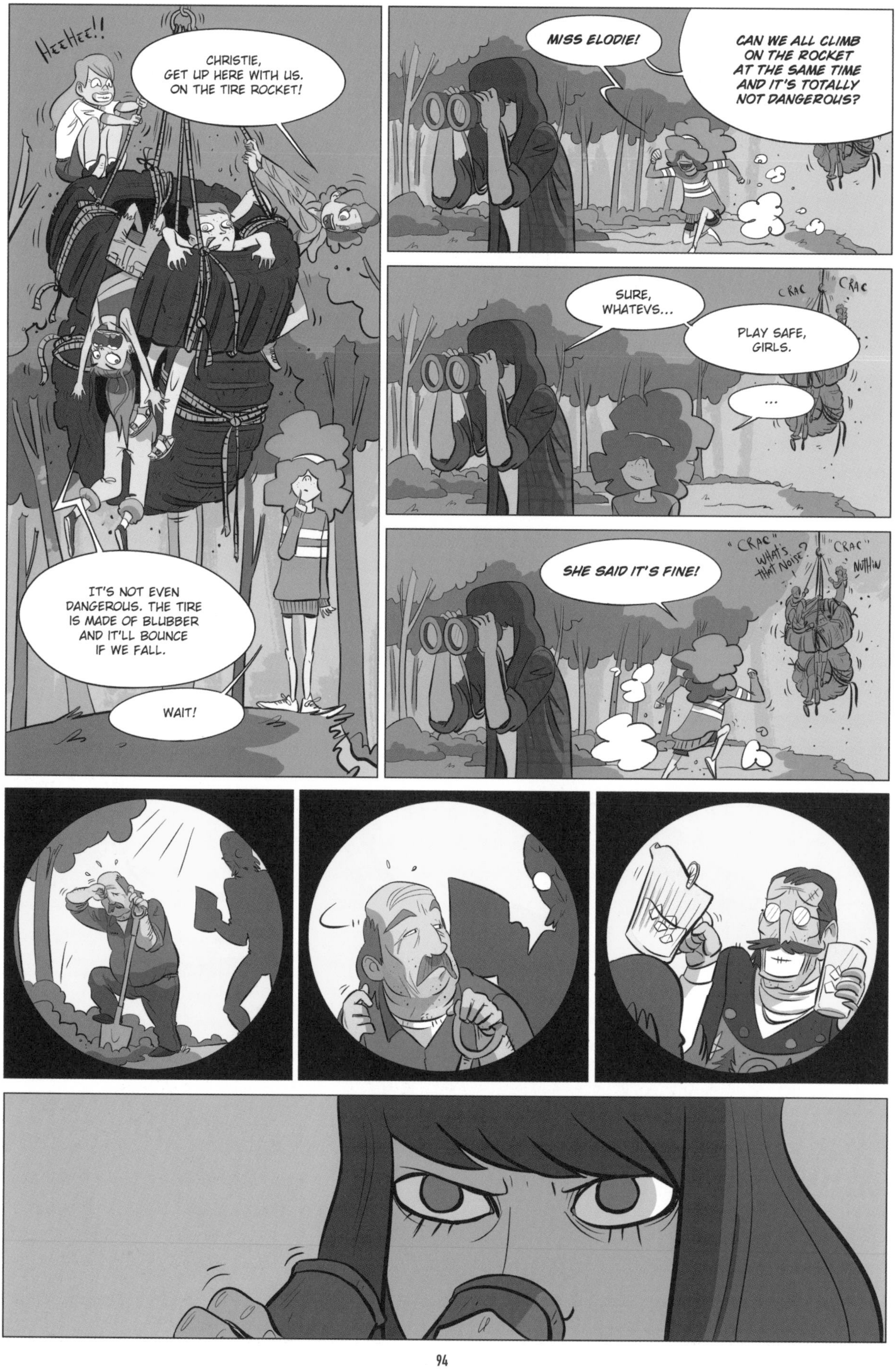
HEEHEE!!
CHRISTIE, GET UP HERE WITH US. ON THE TIRE ROCKET!
IT'S NOT EVEN DANGEROUS. THE TIRE IS MADE OF BLUBBER AND IT'LL BOUNCE IF WE FALL.
WAIT!
MISS ELODIE!
CAN WE ALL CLIMB ON THE ROCKET AT THE SAME TIME AND IT'S TOTALLY NOT DANGEROUS?
SURE, WHATEVS...
PLAY SAFE, GIRLS.
...
CRAC
CRAC
SHE SAID IT'S FINE!
"CRAC"
WHAT'S THAT NOISE?
"CRAC"
NUTHIN

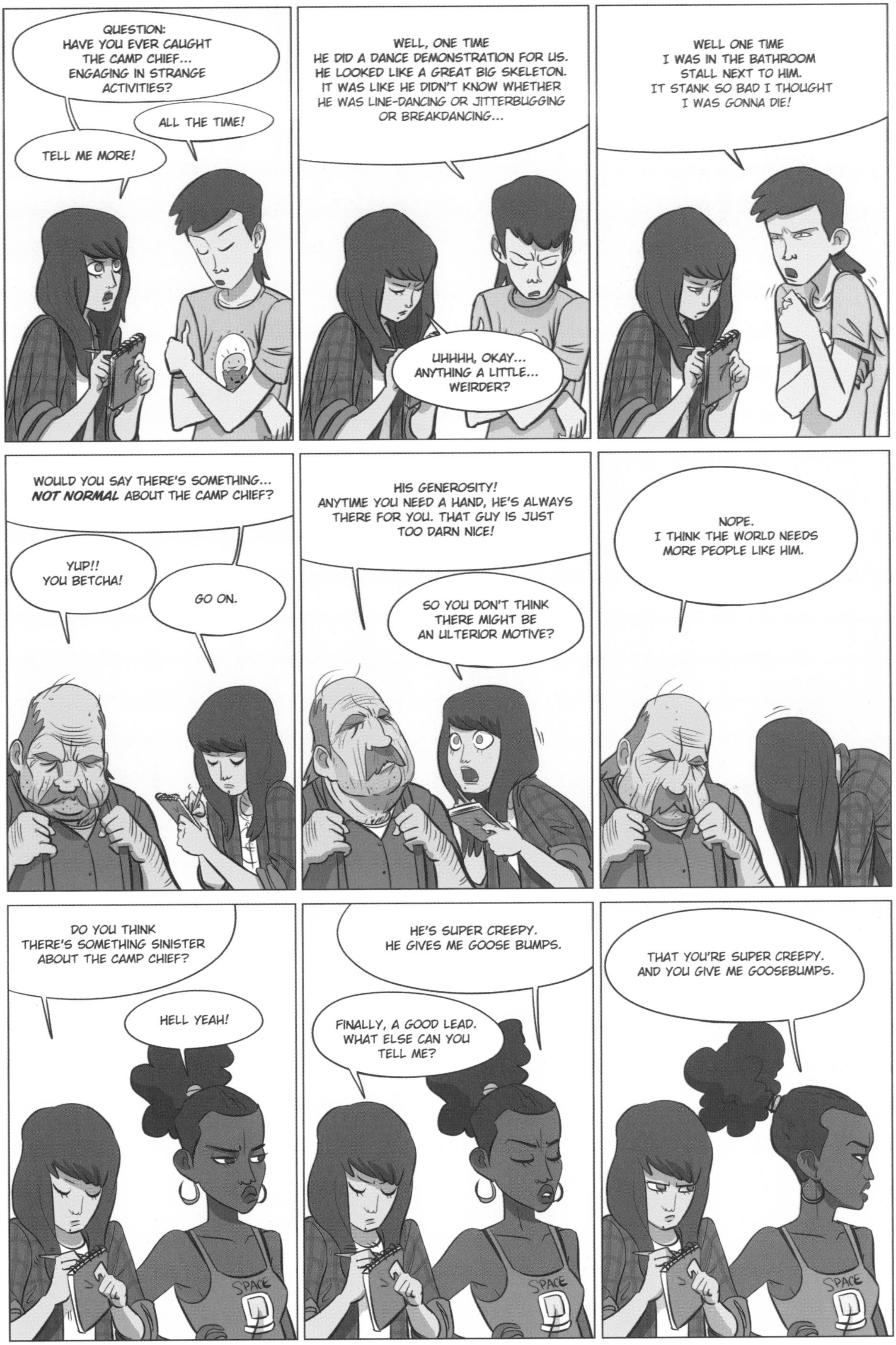
QUESTION: HAVE YOU EVER CAUGHT THE CAMP CHIEF... ENGAGING IN STRANGE ACTIVITIES?
ALL THE TIME!
TELL ME MORE!
WELL, ONE TIME HE DID A DANCE DEMONSTRATION FOR US. HE LOOKED LIKE A GREAT BIG SKELETON. IT WAS LIKE HE DIDN'T KNOW WHETHER HE WAS LINE-DANCING OR JITTERBUGGING OR BREAKDANCING...
UHHHH, OKAY... ANYTHING A LITTLE... WEIRDER?
WELL ONE TIME I WAS IN THE BATHROOM STALL NEXT TO HIM. IT STANK SO BAD I THOUGHT I WAS GONNA DIE!
WOULD YOU SAY THERE'S SOMETHING... ***NOT NORMAL*** ABOUT THE CAMP CHIEF?
YUP!! YOU BETCHA!
GO ON.
HIS GENEROSITY! ANYTIME YOU NEED A HAND, HE'S ALWAYS THERE FOR YOU. THAT GUY IS JUST TOO DARN NICE!
SO YOU DON'T THINK THERE MIGHT BE AN ULTERIOR MOTIVE?
NOPE. I THINK THE WORLD NEEDS MORE PEOPLE LIKE HIM.
DO YOU THINK THERE'S SOMETHING SINISTER ABOUT THE CAMP CHIEF?
HELL YEAH!
HE'S SUPER CREEPY. HE GIVES ME GOOSE BUMPS.
FINALLY, A GOOD LEAD. WHAT ELSE CAN YOU TELL ME?
THAT YOU'RE SUPER CREEPY. AND YOU GIVE ME GOOSEBUMPS.
SPACE
SPACE
SPACE

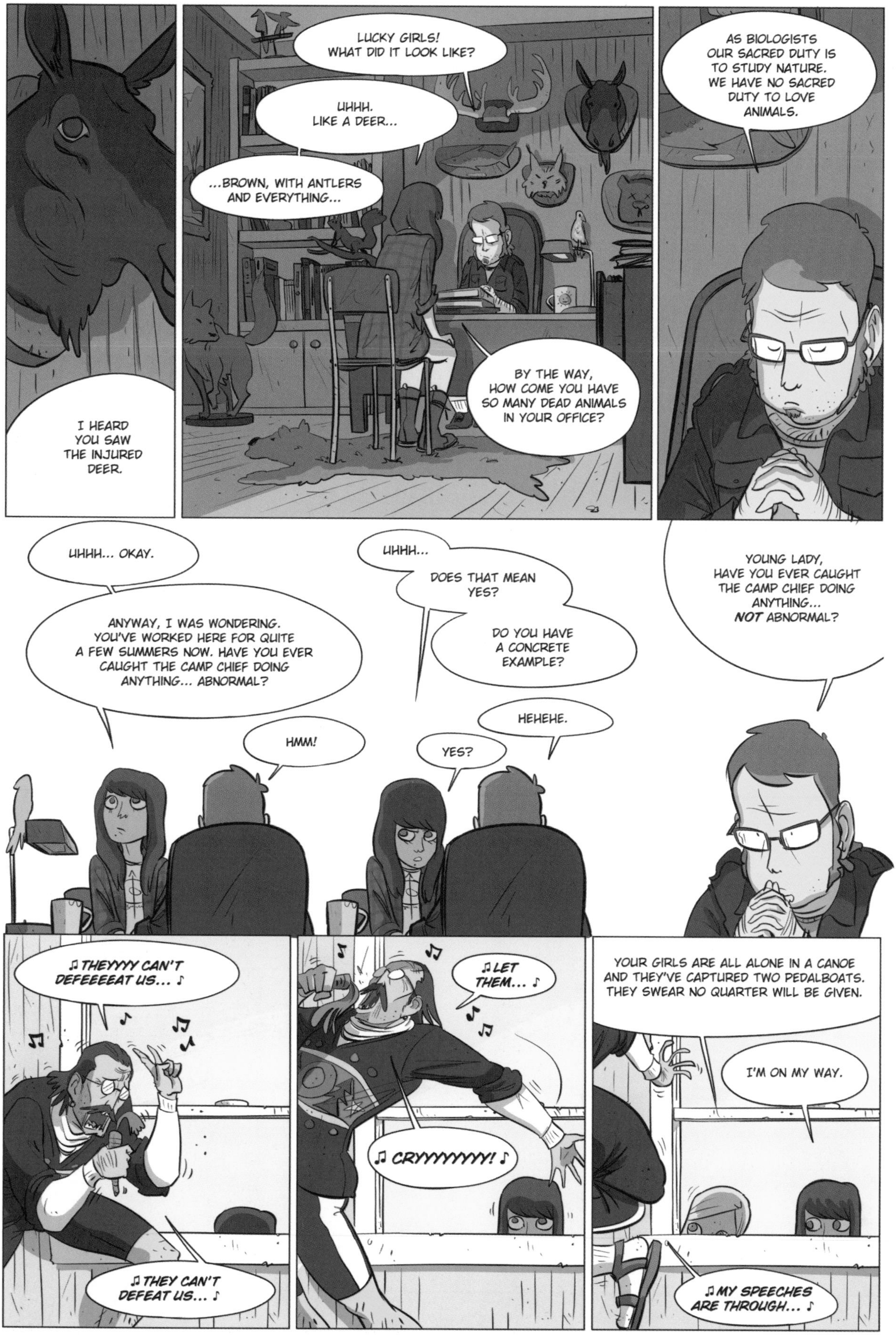
I HEARD YOU SAW THE INJURED DEER.
LUCKY GIRLS! WHAT DID IT LOOK LIKE?
UHHH. LIKE A DEER...
...BROWN, WITH ANTLERS AND EVERYTHING...
BY THE WAY, HOW COME YOU HAVE SO MANY DEAD ANIMALS IN YOUR OFFICE?
AS BIOLOGISTS OUR SACRED DUTY IS TO STUDY NATURE. WE HAVE NO SACRED DUTY TO LOVE ANIMALS.
UHHH... OKAY.
ANYWAY, I WAS WONDERING. YOU'VE WORKED HERE FOR QUITE A FEW SUMMERS NOW. HAVE YOU EVER CAUGHT THE CAMP CHIEF DOING ANYTHING... ABNORMAL?
HMM!
UHHH...
DOES THAT MEAN YES?
DO YOU HAVE A CONCRETE EXAMPLE?
YES?
HEHEHE.
YOUNG LADY, HAVE YOU EVER CAUGHT THE CAMP CHIEF DOING ANYTHING... *NOT* ABNORMAL?
♫ THEYYYY CAN'T DEFEEEEAT US... ♪
♫ THEY CAN'T DEFEAT US... ♪
♫ LET THEM... ♪
♫ CRYYYYYYYY! ♪
YOUR GIRLS ARE ALL ALONE IN A CANOE AND THEY'VE CAPTURED TWO PEDALBOATS. THEY SWEAR NO QUARTER WILL BE GIVEN.
I'M ON MY WAY.
♫ MY SPEECHES ARE THROUGH... ♪

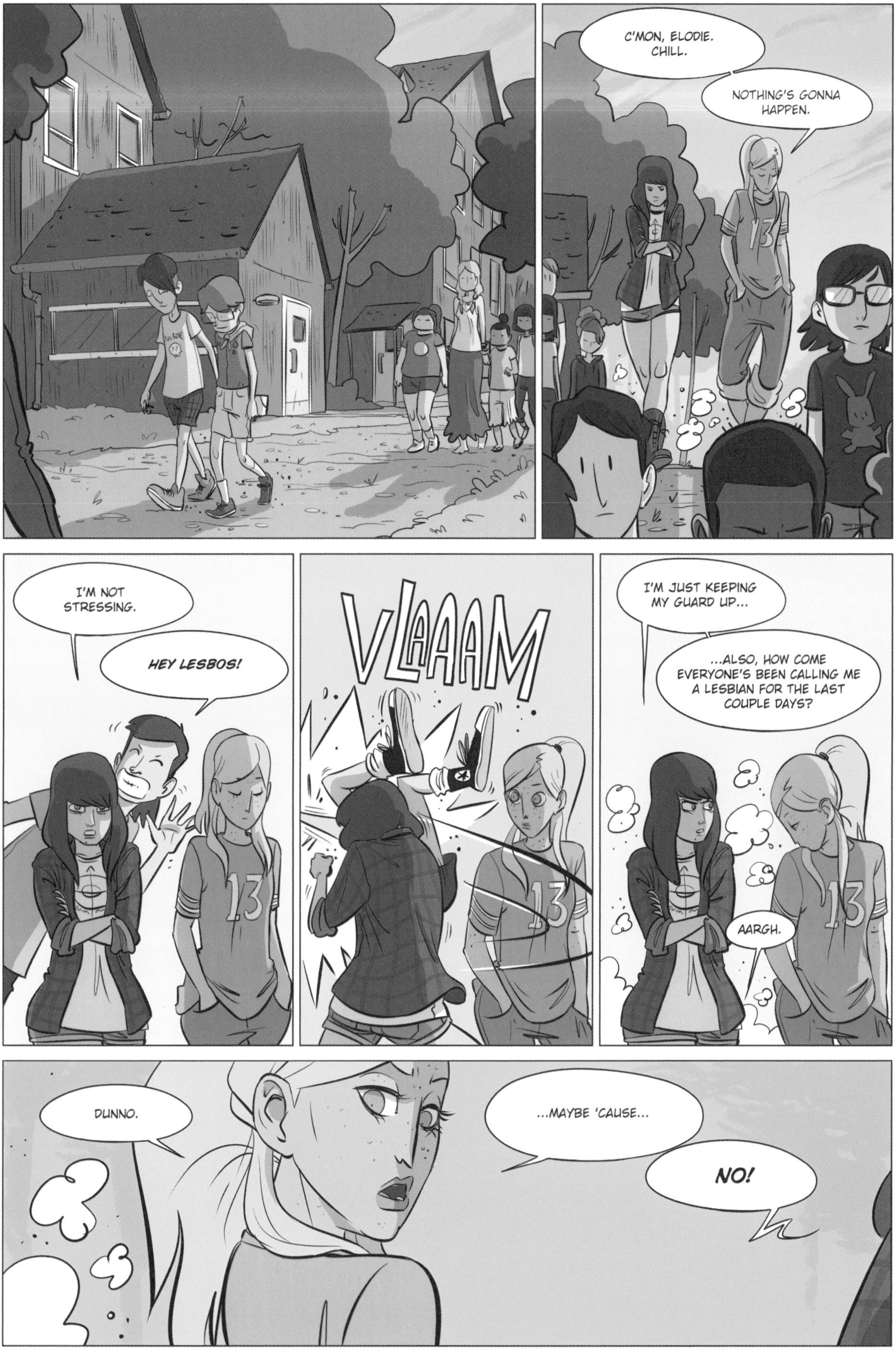
C'MON, ELODIE. CHILL.
NOTHING'S GONNA HAPPEN.
I'M NOT STRESSING.
HEY LESBOS!
VLAAAM
I'M JUST KEEPING MY GUARD UP...
...ALSO, HOW COME EVERYONE'S BEEN CALLING ME A LESBIAN FOR THE LAST COUPLE DAYS?
AARGH.
DUNNO.
...MAYBE 'CAUSE...
NO!

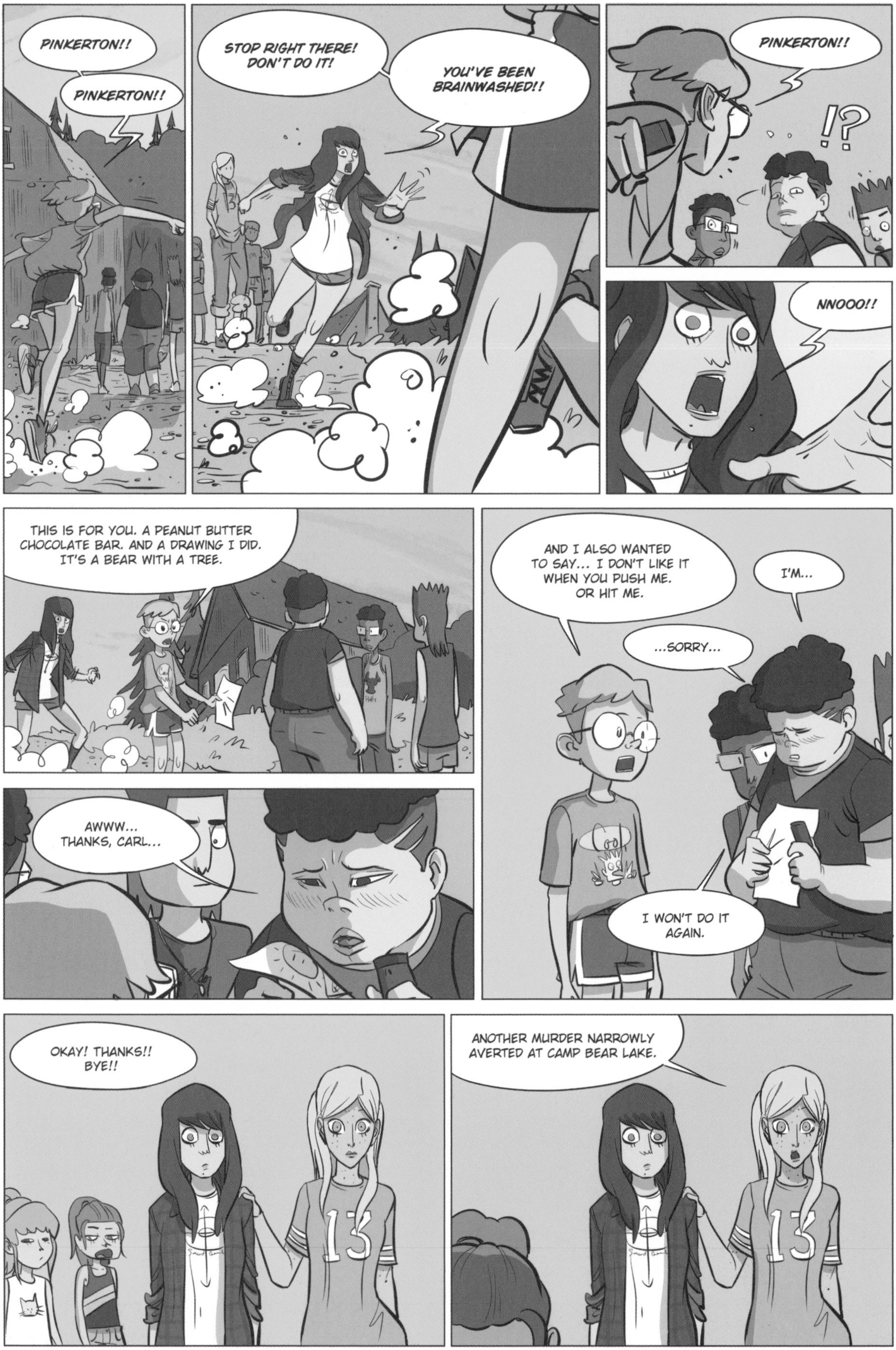
PINKERTON!!
PINKERTON!!
STOP RIGHT THERE! DON'T DO IT!
YOU'VE BEEN BRAINWASHED!!
PINKERTON!!
!?
NNOOO!!
THIS IS FOR YOU. A PEANUT BUTTER CHOCOLATE BAR. AND A DRAWING I DID. IT'S A BEAR WITH A TREE.
AWWW... THANKS, CARL...
AND I ALSO WANTED TO SAY... I DON'T LIKE IT WHEN YOU PUSH ME. OR HIT ME.
I'M...
...SORRY...
I WON'T DO IT AGAIN.
OKAY! THANKS!! BYE!!
ANOTHER MURDER NARROWLY AVERTED AT CAMP BEAR LAKE.

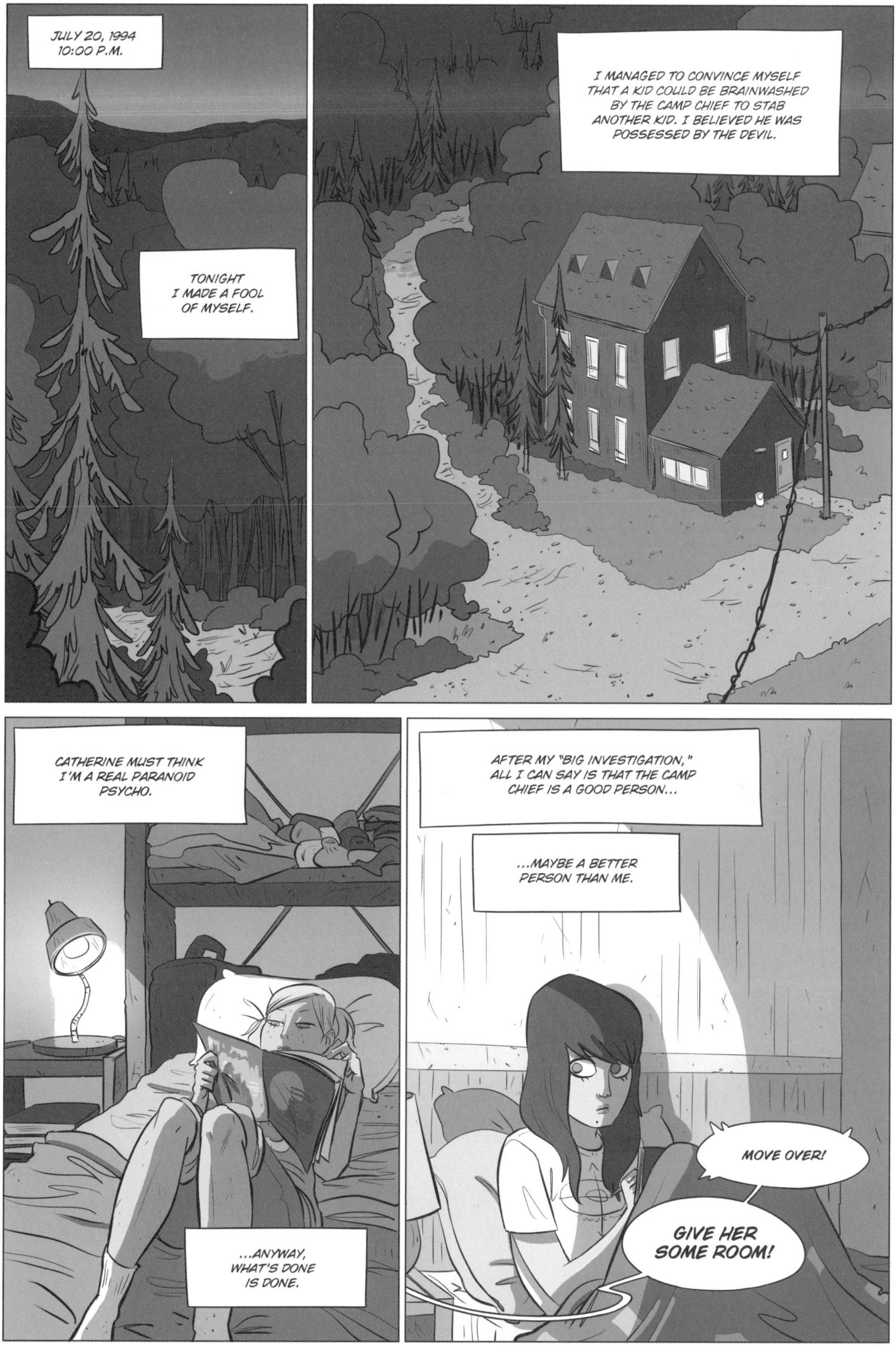
JULY 20, 1994
10:00 P.M.
TONIGHT I MADE A FOOL OF MYSELF.
I MANAGED TO CONVINCE MYSELF THAT A KID COULD BE BRAINWASHED BY THE CAMP CHIEF TO STAB ANOTHER KID. I BELIEVED HE WAS POSSESSED BY THE DEVIL.
CATHERINE MUST THINK I'M A REAL PARANOID PSYCHO.
...ANYWAY, WHAT'S DONE IS DONE.
AFTER MY "BIG INVESTIGATION," ALL I CAN SAY IS THAT THE CAMP CHIEF IS A GOOD PERSON...
...MAYBE A BETTER PERSON THAN ME.
MOVE OVER!
GIVE HER SOME ROOM!

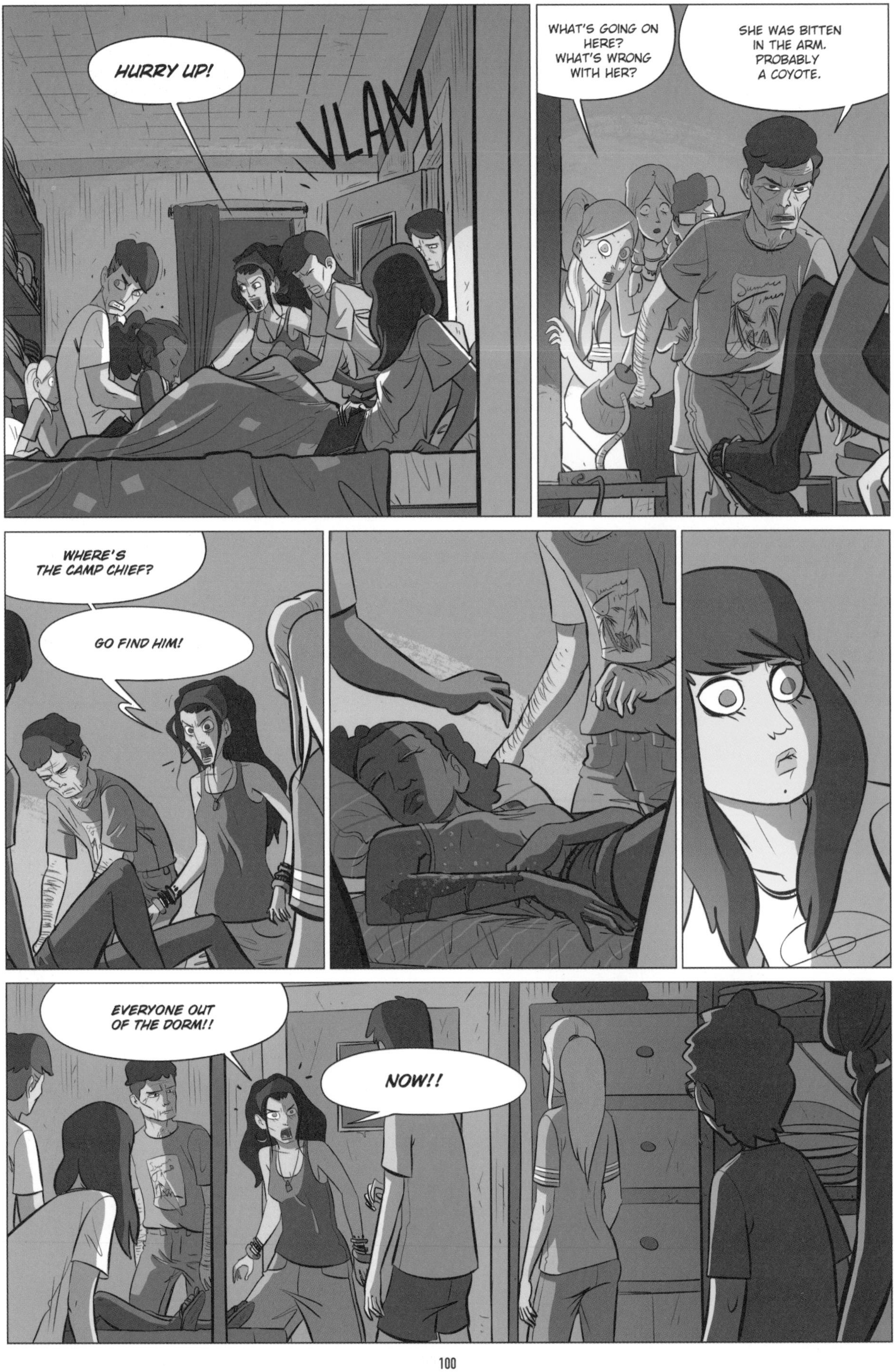
HURRY UP!
VLAM
WHAT'S GOING ON HERE? WHAT'S WRONG WITH HER?
SHE WAS BITTEN IN THE ARM. PROBABLY A COYOTE.
WHERE'S THE CAMP CHIEF?
GO FIND HIM!
EVERYONE OUT OF THE DORM!!
NOW!!

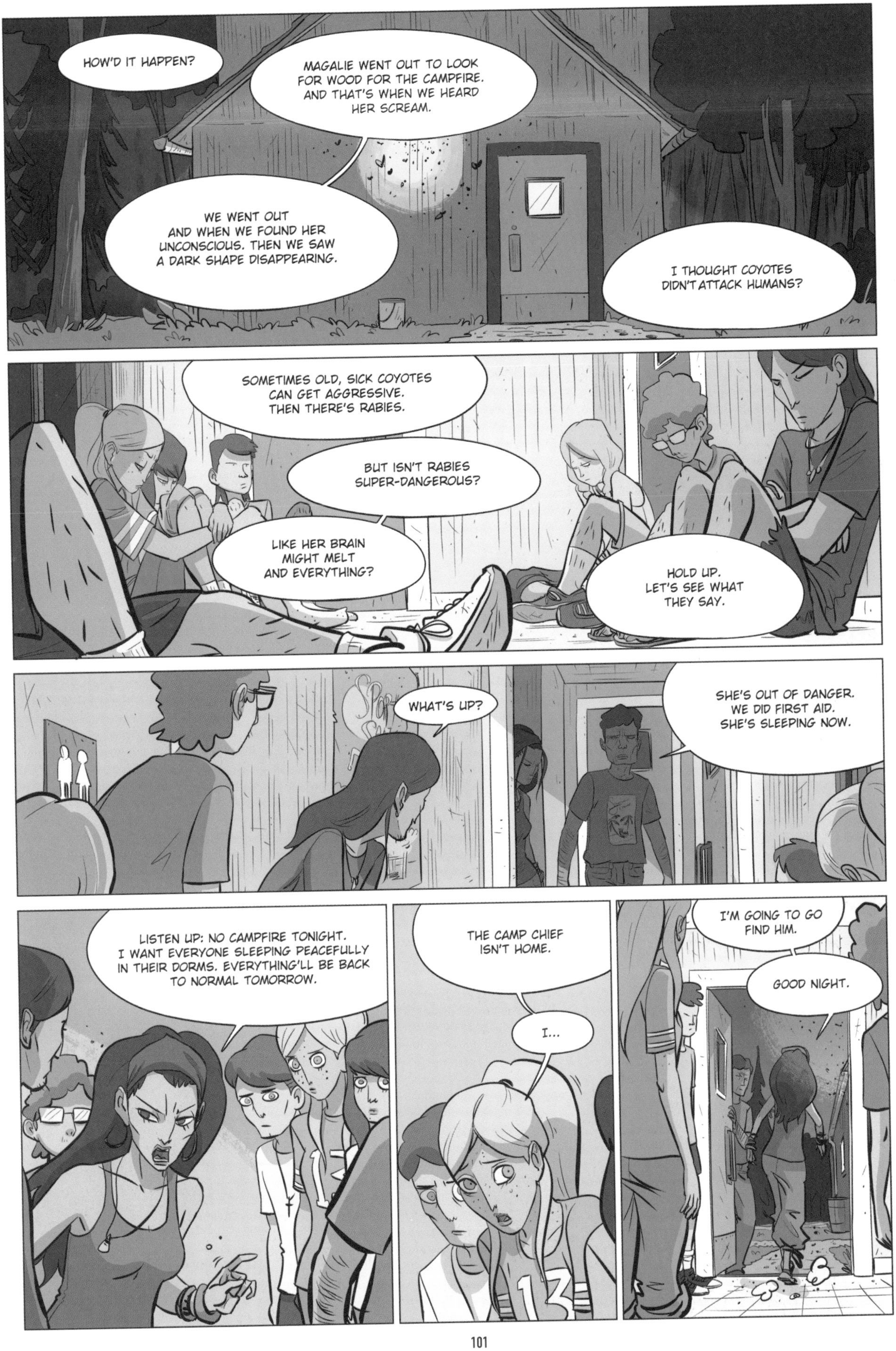
HOW'D IT HAPPEN?
MAGALIE WENT OUT TO LOOK FOR WOOD FOR THE CAMPFIRE. AND THAT'S WHEN WE HEARD HER SCREAM.
WE WENT OUT AND WHEN WE FOUND HER UNCONSCIOUS. THEN WE SAW A DARK SHAPE DISAPPEARING.
I THOUGHT COYOTES DIDN'T ATTACK HUMANS?
SOMETIMES OLD, SICK COYOTES CAN GET AGGRESSIVE. THEN THERE'S RABIES.
BUT ISN'T RABIES SUPER-DANGEROUS?
LIKE HER BRAIN MIGHT MELT AND EVERYTHING?
HOLD UP. LET'S SEE WHAT THEY SAY.
WHAT'S UP?
SHE'S OUT OF DANGER. WE DID FIRST AID. SHE'S SLEEPING NOW.
LISTEN UP: NO CAMPFIRE TONIGHT. I WANT EVERYONE SLEEPING PEACEFULLY IN THEIR DORMS. EVERYTHING'LL BE BACK TO NORMAL TOMORROW.
THE CAMP CHIEF ISN'T HOME.
I...
I'M GOING TO GO FIND HIM.
GOOD NIGHT.

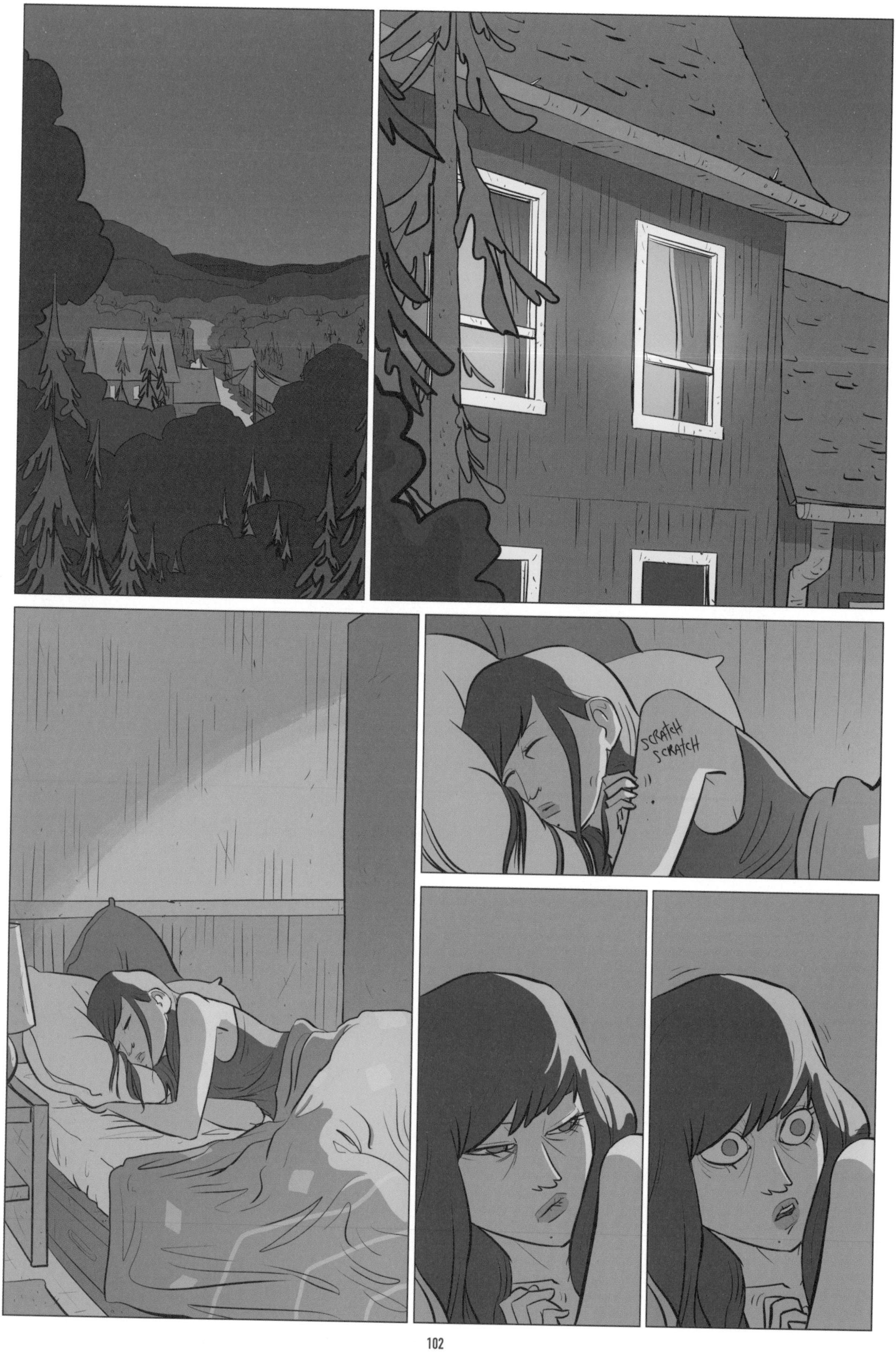
SCRATCH
SCRATCH

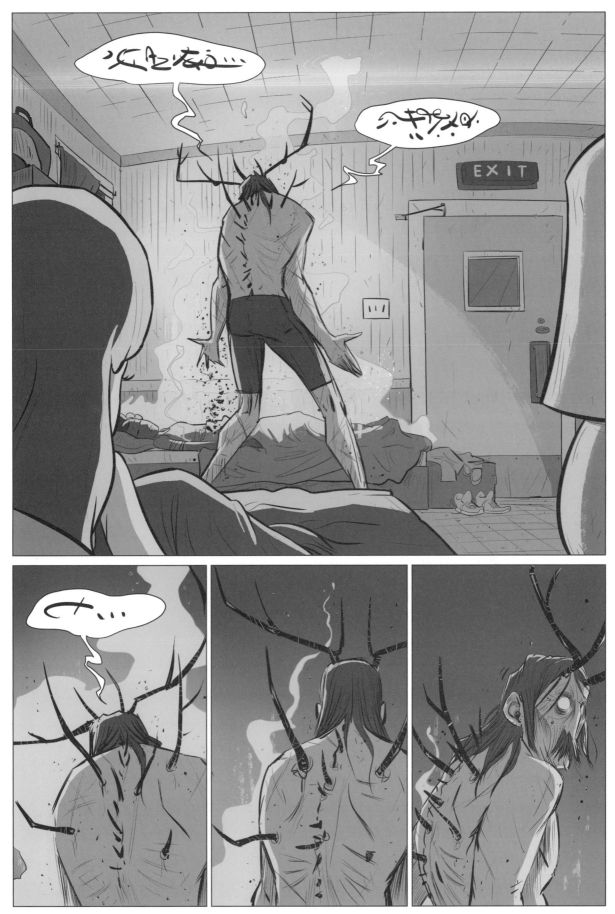

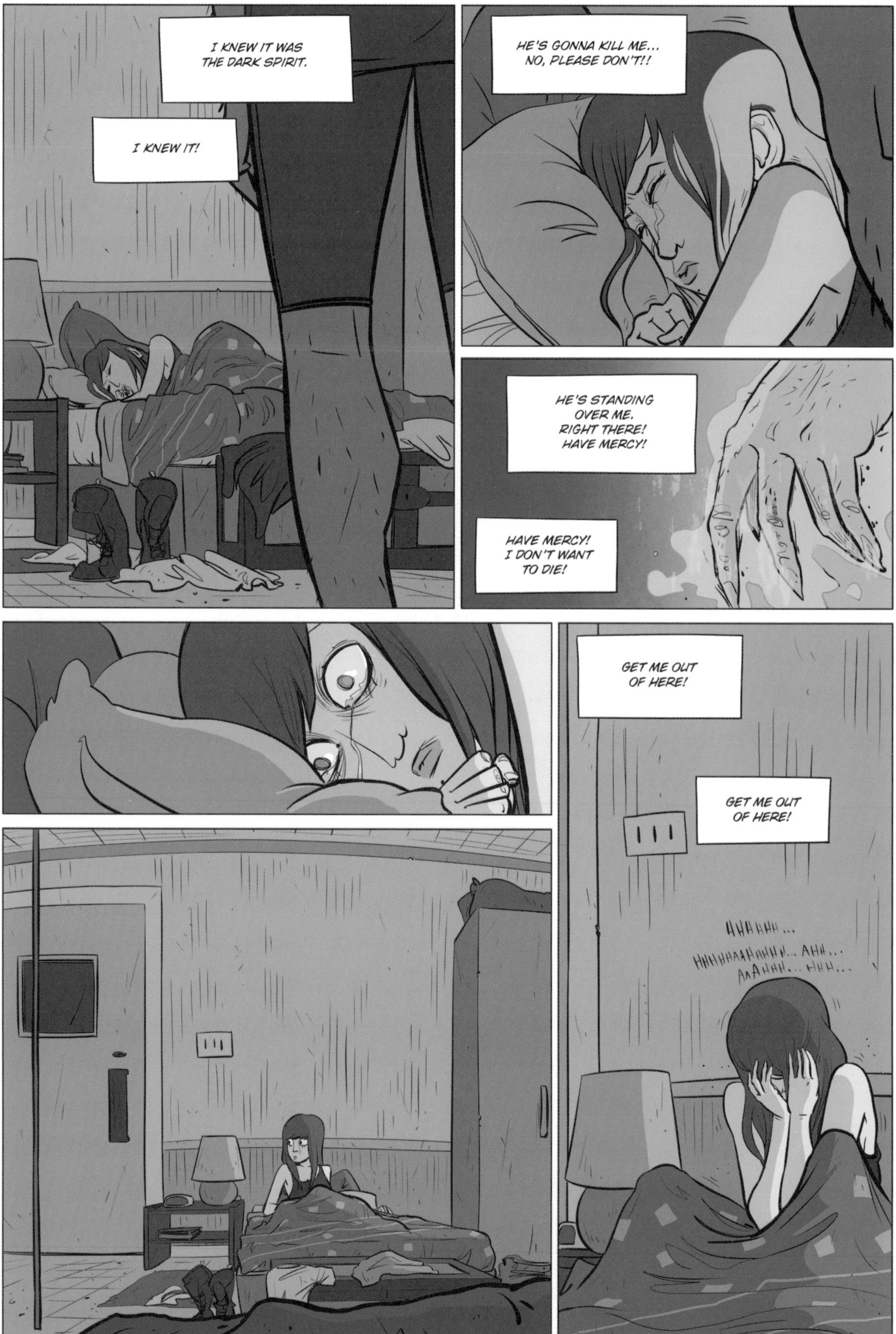
I KNEW IT WAS THE DARK SPIRIT.
I KNEW IT!
HE'S GONNA KILL ME... NO, PLEASE DON'T!!
HE'S STANDING OVER ME. RIGHT THERE! HAVE MERCY!
HAVE MERCY! I DON'T WANT TO DIE!
GET ME OUT OF HERE!
GET ME OUT OF HERE!
HHHHHH...
HHHHHAAHHHH... AHH...
AAAHHH... HHH...

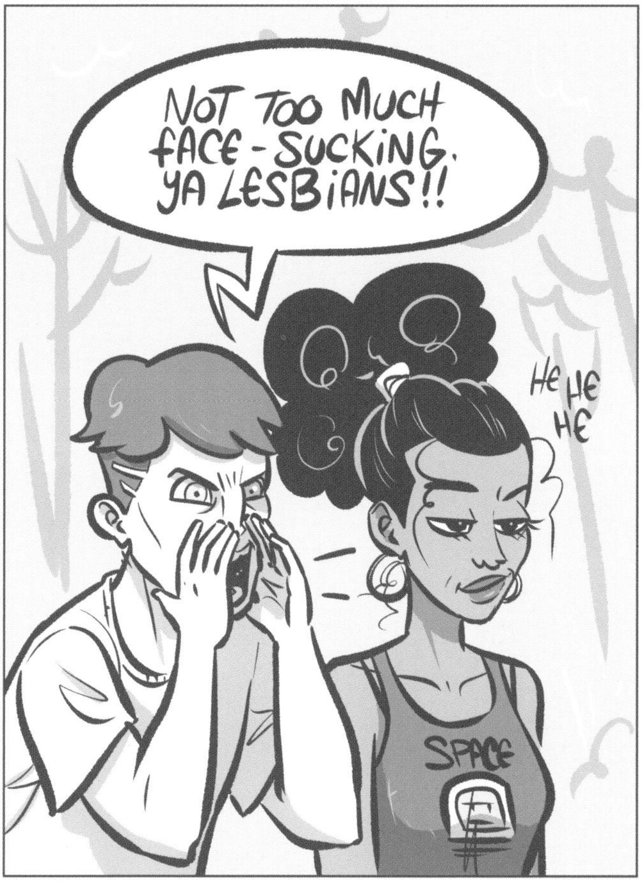
NOT TOO MUCH FACE-SUCKING, YA LESBIANS!!
HE HE HE
SPACE

5

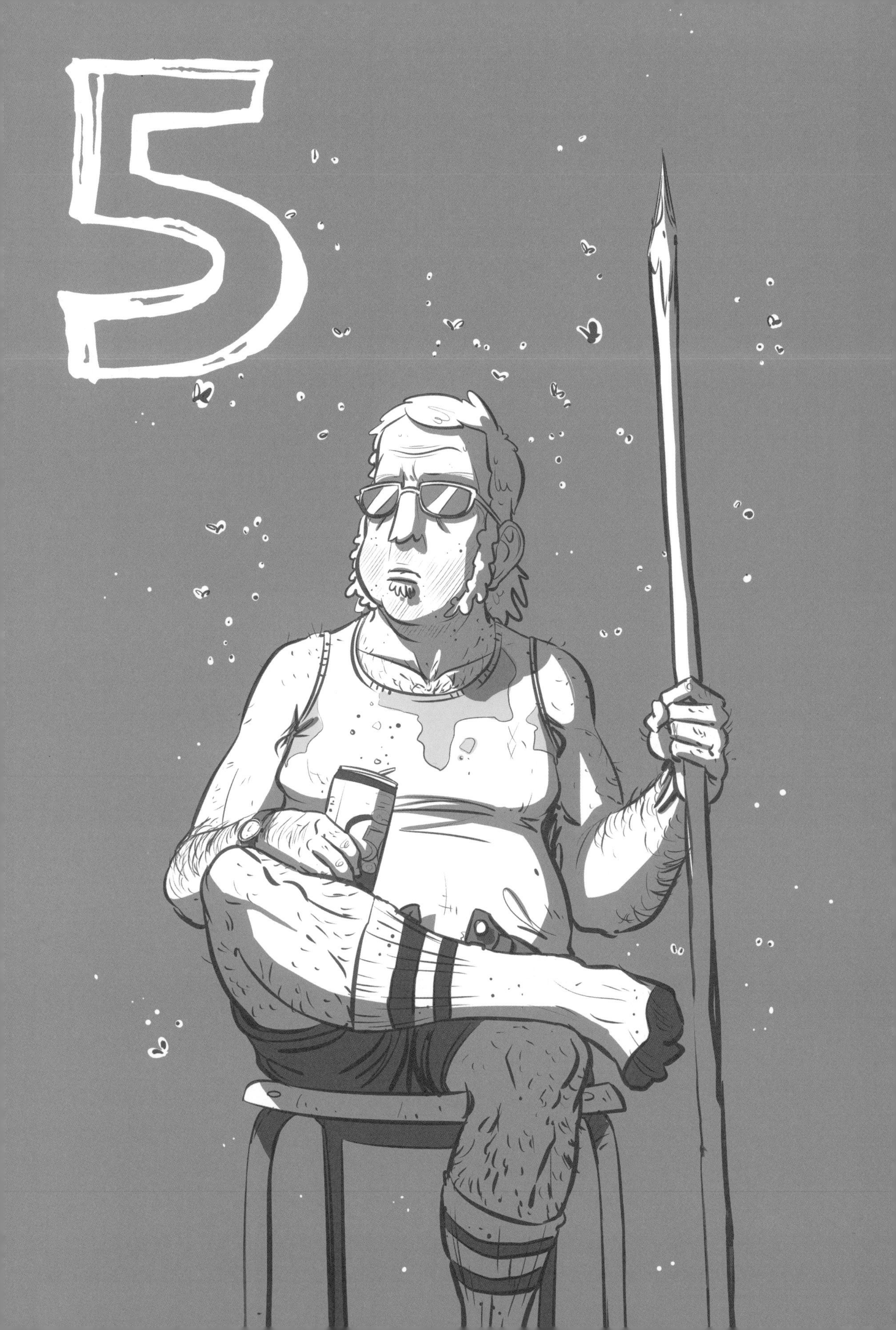

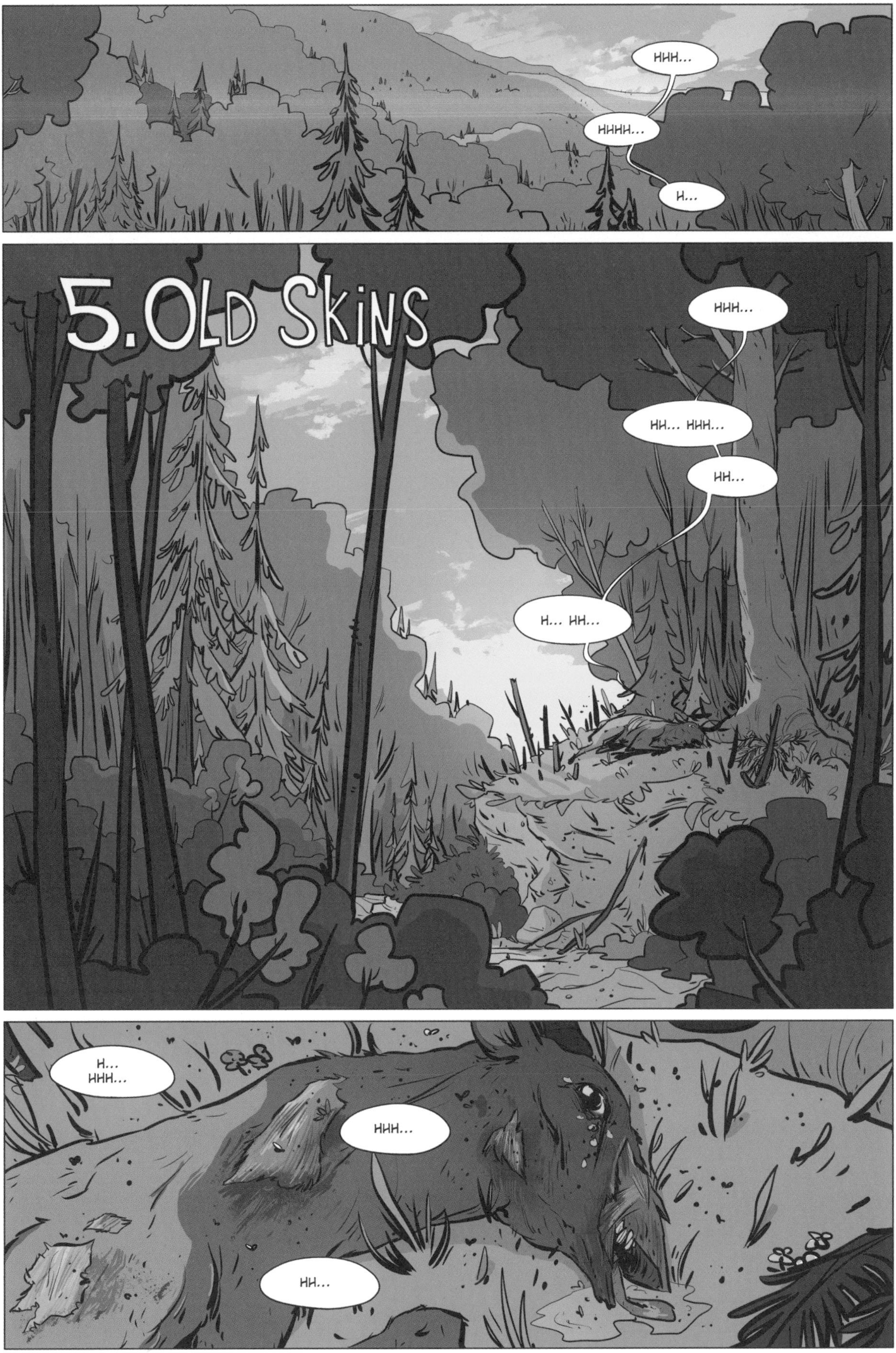
HHH...
HHHH...
H...
5. OLD SKINS
HHH...
HH... HHH...
HH...
H... HH...
H...
HHH...
HHH...
HH...

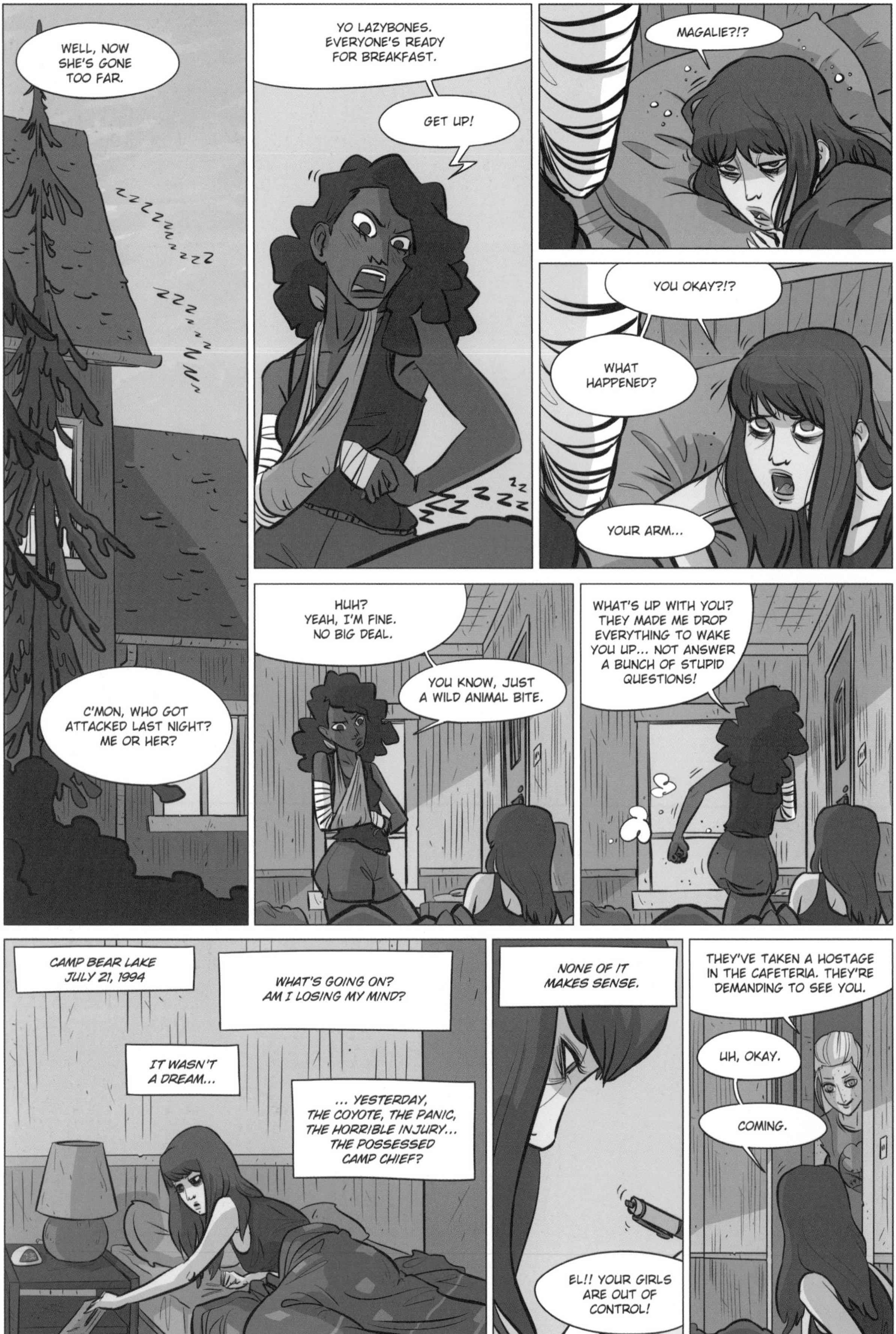
WELL, NOW SHE'S GONE TOO FAR.
YO LAZYBONES. EVERYONE'S READY FOR BREAKFAST.
GET UP!
MAGALIE?!?
YOU OKAY?!?
WHAT HAPPENED?
YOUR ARM...
C'MON, WHO GOT ATTACKED LAST NIGHT? ME OR HER?
HUH? YEAH, I'M FINE. NO BIG DEAL.
YOU KNOW, JUST A WILD ANIMAL BITE.
WHAT'S UP WITH YOU? THEY MADE ME DROP EVERYTHING TO WAKE YOU UP... NOT ANSWER A BUNCH OF STUPID QUESTIONS!
CAMP BEAR LAKE JULY 21, 1994
WHAT'S GOING ON? AM I LOSING MY MIND?
IT WASN'T A DREAM...
... YESTERDAY, THE COYOTE, THE PANIC, THE HORRIBLE INJURY... THE POSSESSED CAMP CHIEF?
NONE OF IT MAKES SENSE.
EL!! YOUR GIRLS ARE OUT OF CONTROL!
THEY'VE TAKEN A HOSTAGE IN THE CAFETERIA. THEY'RE DEMANDING TO SEE YOU.
UH, OKAY.
COMING.

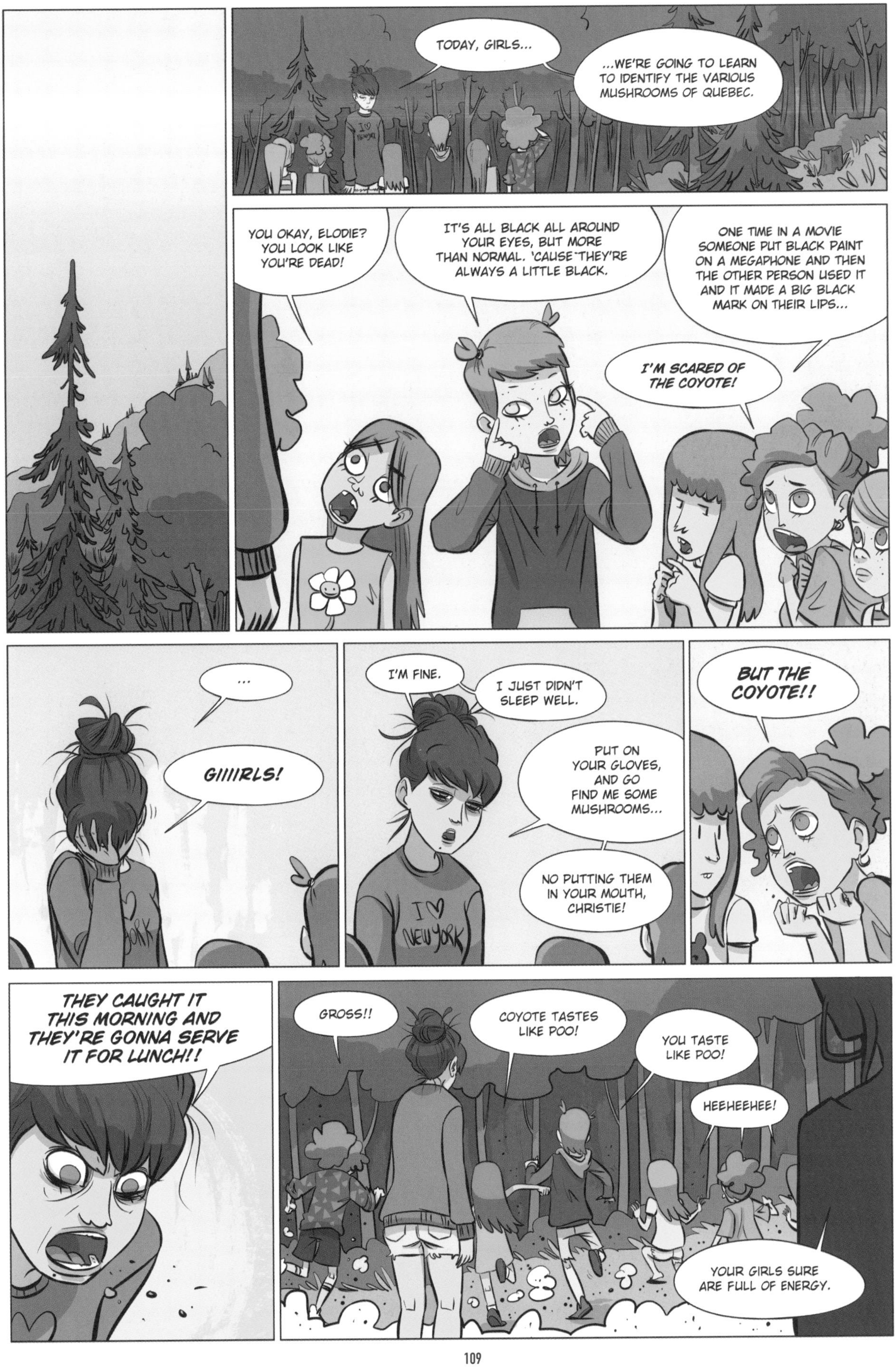
TODAY, GIRLS...
...WE'RE GOING TO LEARN TO IDENTIFY THE VARIOUS MUSHROOMS OF QUEBEC.
YOU OKAY, ELODIE? YOU LOOK LIKE YOU'RE DEAD!
IT'S ALL BLACK ALL AROUND YOUR EYES, BUT MORE THAN NORMAL. 'CAUSE THEY'RE ALWAYS A LITTLE BLACK.
ONE TIME IN A MOVIE SOMEONE PUT BLACK PAINT ON A MEGAPHONE AND THEN THE OTHER PERSON USED IT AND IT MADE A BIG BLACK MARK ON THEIR LIPS...
I'M SCARED OF THE COYOTE!
...
GIIIRLS!
I'M FINE.
I JUST DIDN'T SLEEP WELL.
PUT ON YOUR GLOVES, AND GO FIND ME SOME MUSHROOMS...
NO PUTTING THEM IN YOUR MOUTH, CHRISTIE!
BUT THE COYOTE!!
THEY CAUGHT IT THIS MORNING AND THEY'RE GONNA SERVE IT FOR LUNCH!!
GROSS!!
COYOTE TASTES LIKE POO!
YOU TASTE LIKE POO!
HEEHEEHEE!
YOUR GIRLS SURE ARE FULL OF ENERGY.

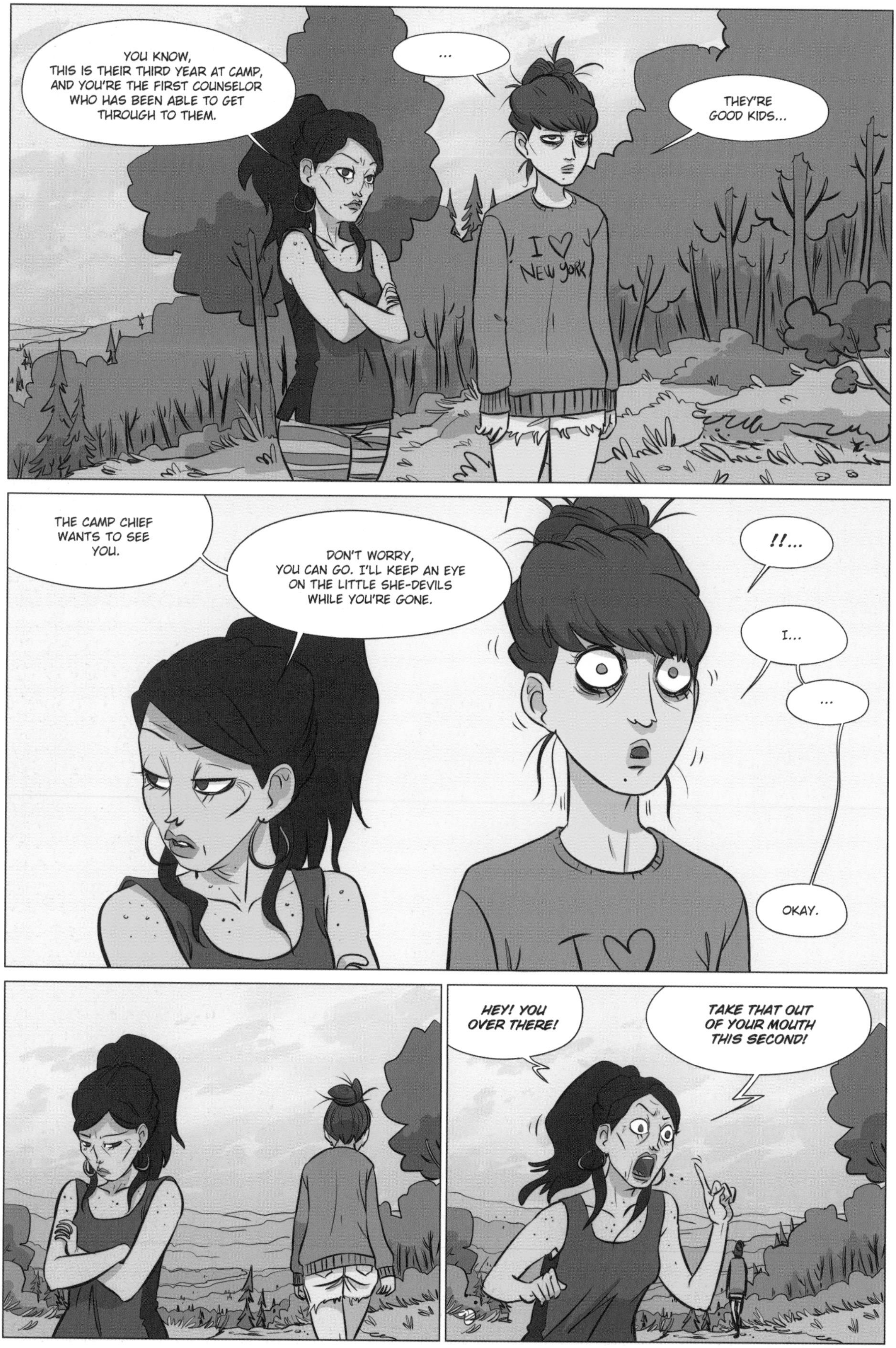
YOU KNOW,
THIS IS THEIR THIRD YEAR AT CAMP,
AND YOU'RE THE FIRST COUNSELOR
WHO HAS BEEN ABLE TO GET
THROUGH TO THEM.
...
THEY'RE
GOOD KIDS...
I ♥
NEW YORK
THE CAMP CHIEF
WANTS TO SEE
YOU.
DON'T WORRY,
YOU CAN GO. I'LL KEEP AN EYE
ON THE LITTLE SHE-DEVILS
WHILE YOU'RE GONE.
!!...
I...
...
OKAY.
I ♥
HEY! YOU
OVER THERE!
TAKE THAT OUT
OF YOUR MOUTH
THIS SECOND!

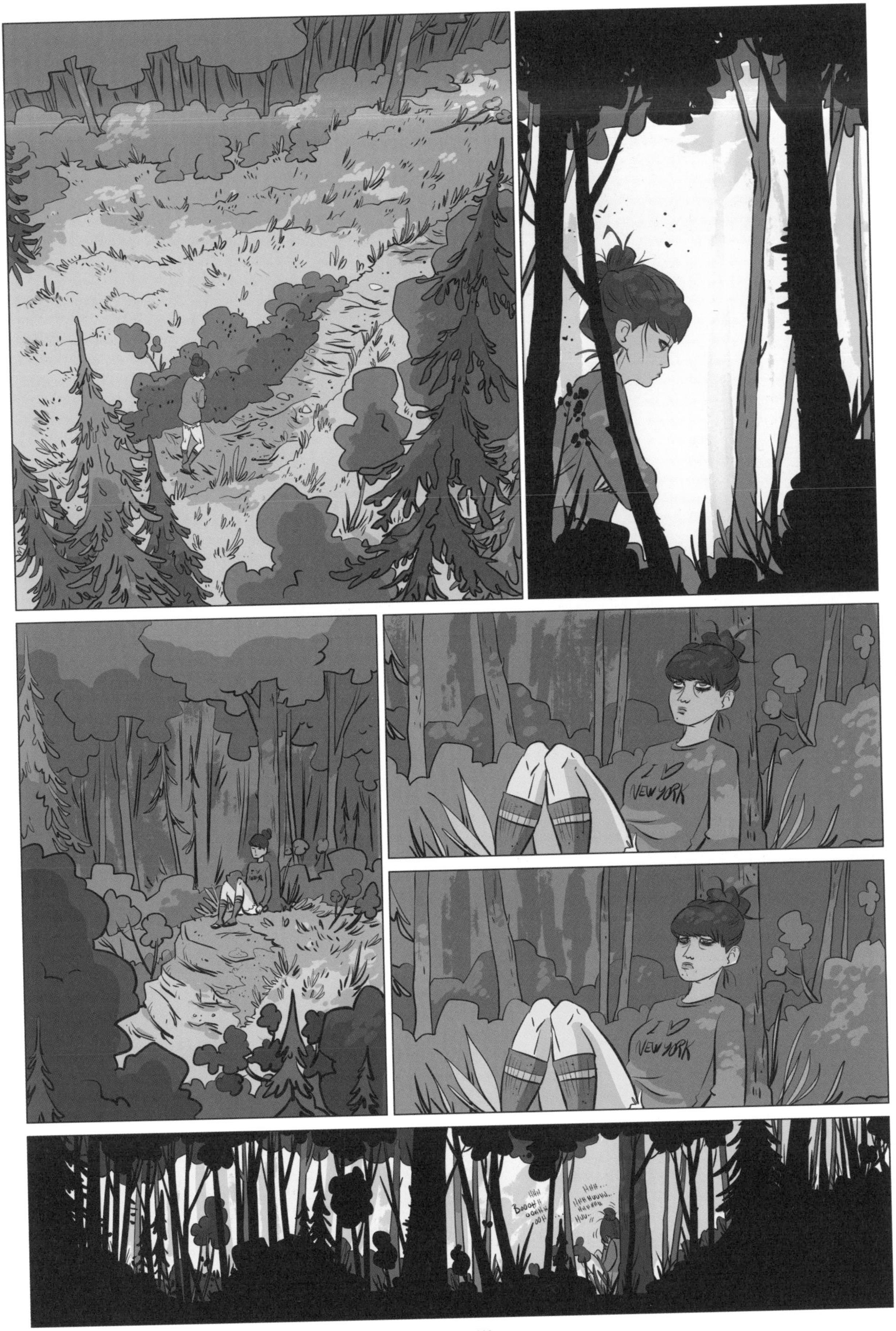
I ♥ NEW YORK
I ♥ NEW YORK
HHH
BOOOHHH
OOHHH
OOH...
HHH...
HHHHUUUH...
HHHHHH
HUU..

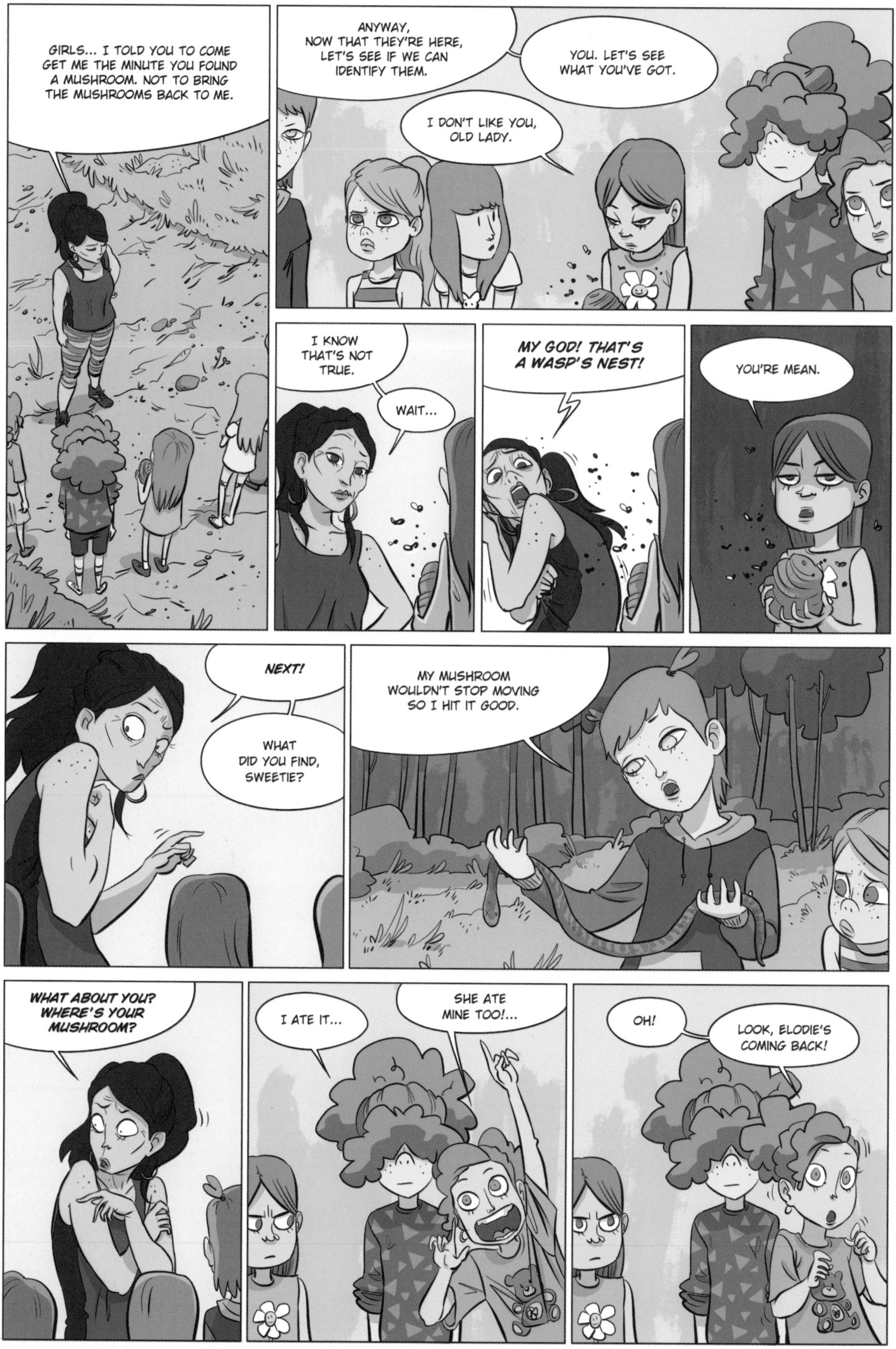
GIRLS... I TOLD YOU TO COME GET ME THE MINUTE YOU FOUND A MUSHROOM. NOT TO BRING THE MUSHROOMS BACK TO ME.
ANYWAY, NOW THAT THEY'RE HERE, LET'S SEE IF WE CAN IDENTIFY THEM.
YOU. LET'S SEE WHAT YOU'VE GOT.
I DON'T LIKE YOU, OLD LADY.
I KNOW THAT'S NOT TRUE.
WAIT...
MY GOD! THAT'S A WASP'S NEST!
YOU'RE MEAN.
NEXT!
WHAT DID YOU FIND, SWEETIE?
MY MUSHROOM WOULDN'T STOP MOVING SO I HIT IT GOOD.
WHAT ABOUT YOU? WHERE'S YOUR MUSHROOM?
I ATE IT...
SHE ATE MINE TOO!...
OH!
LOOK, ELODIE'S COMING BACK!

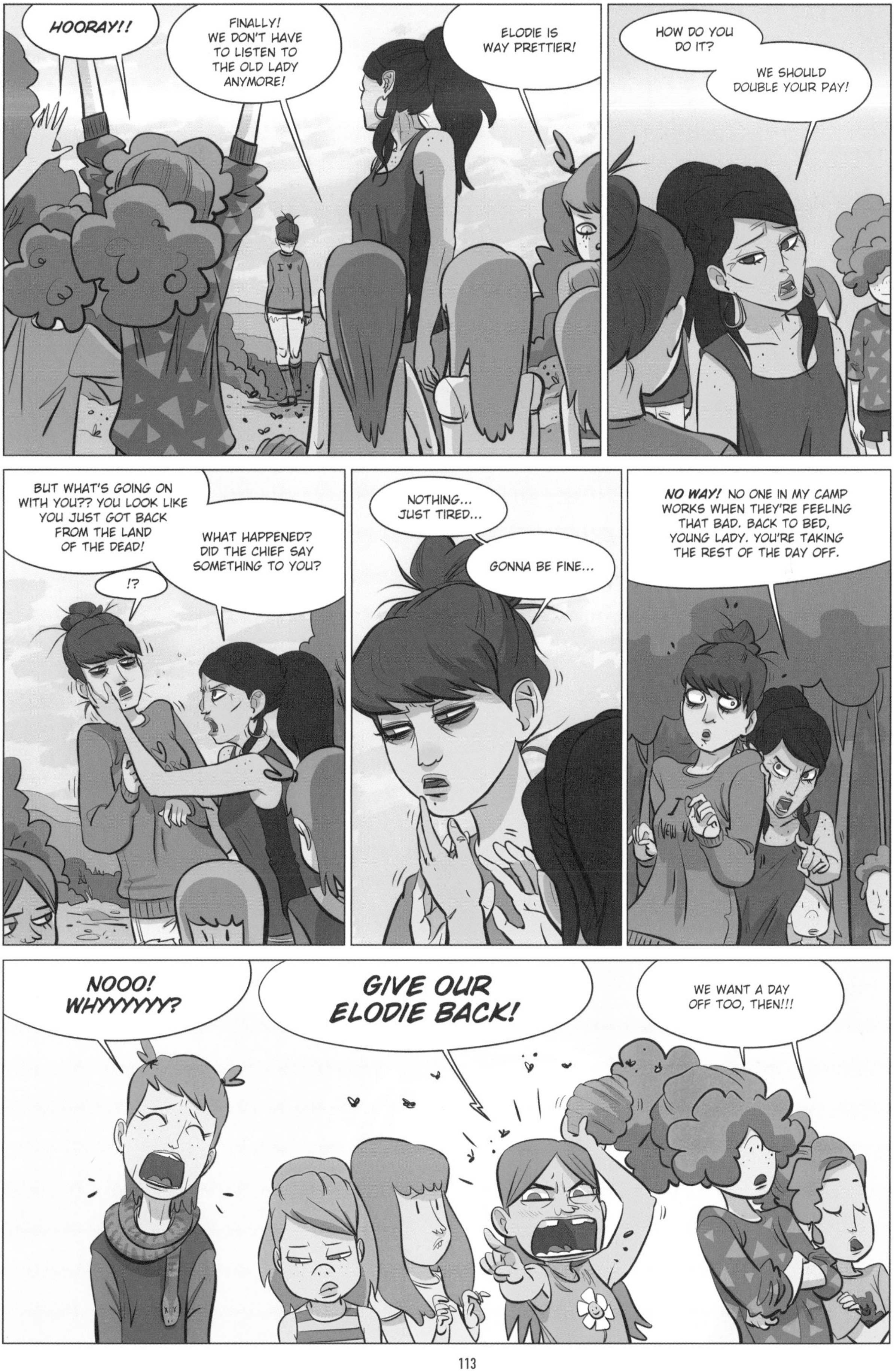
HOORAY!!
FINALLY! WE DON'T HAVE TO LISTEN TO THE OLD LADY ANYMORE!
ELODIE IS WAY PRETTIER!
HOW DO YOU DO IT?
WE SHOULD DOUBLE YOUR PAY!
BUT WHAT'S GOING ON WITH YOU?? YOU LOOK LIKE YOU JUST GOT BACK FROM THE LAND OF THE DEAD!
WHAT HAPPENED? DID THE CHIEF SAY SOMETHING TO YOU?
!?
NOTHING... JUST TIRED...
GONNA BE FINE...
NO WAY! NO ONE IN MY CAMP WORKS WHEN THEY'RE FEELING THAT BAD. BACK TO BED, YOUNG LADY. YOU'RE TAKING THE REST OF THE DAY OFF.
NOOO! WHYYYYYY?
GIVE OUR ELODIE BACK!
WE WANT A DAY OFF TOO, THEN!!!

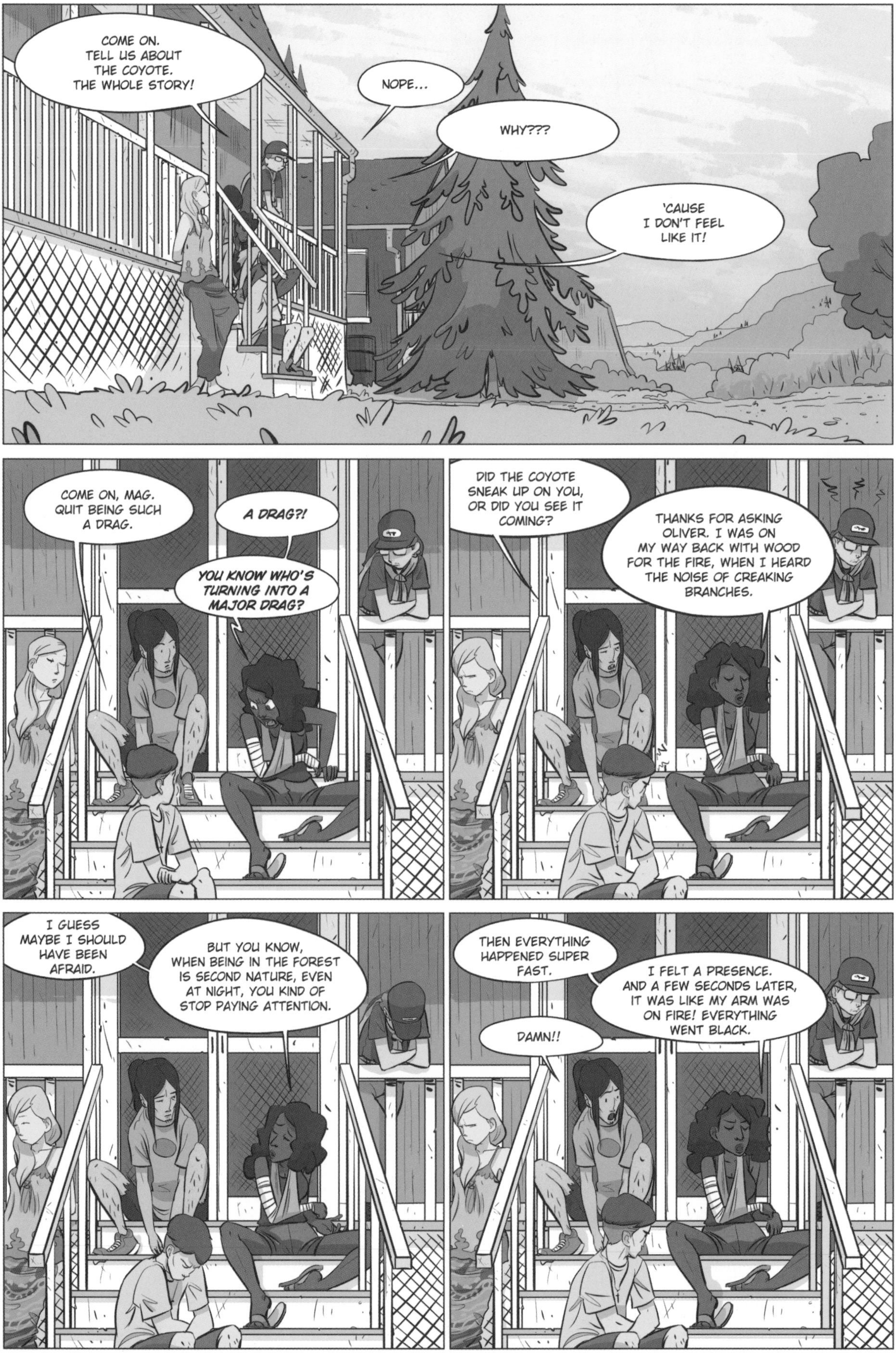
COME ON. TELL US ABOUT THE COYOTE. THE WHOLE STORY!
NOPE...
WHY???
'CAUSE I DON'T FEEL LIKE IT!
COME ON, MAG. QUIT BEING SUCH A DRAG.
A DRAG?!
YOU KNOW WHO'S TURNING INTO A MAJOR DRAG?
DID THE COYOTE SNEAK UP ON YOU, OR DID YOU SEE IT COMING?
THANKS FOR ASKING OLIVER. I WAS ON MY WAY BACK WITH WOOD FOR THE FIRE, WHEN I HEARD THE NOISE OF CREAKING BRANCHES.
I GUESS MAYBE I SHOULD HAVE BEEN AFRAID.
BUT YOU KNOW, WHEN BEING IN THE FOREST IS SECOND NATURE, EVEN AT NIGHT, YOU KIND OF STOP PAYING ATTENTION.
THEN EVERYTHING HAPPENED SUPER FAST.
I FELT A PRESENCE. AND A FEW SECONDS LATER, IT WAS LIKE MY ARM WAS ON FIRE! EVERYTHING WENT BLACK.
DAMN!!

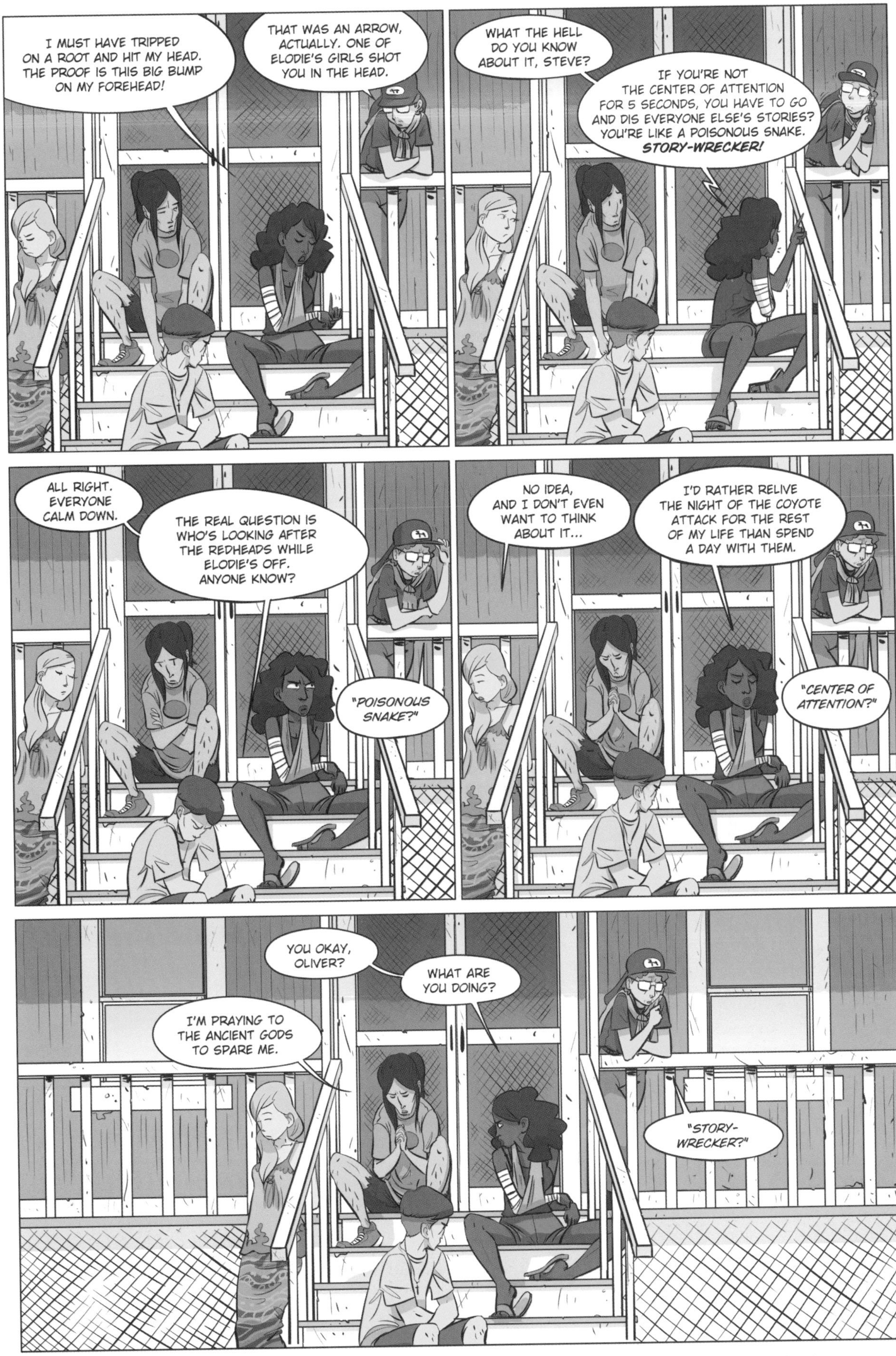
I MUST HAVE TRIPPED ON A ROOT AND HIT MY HEAD. THE PROOF IS THIS BIG BUMP ON MY FOREHEAD!
THAT WAS AN ARROW, ACTUALLY. ONE OF ELODIE'S GIRLS SHOT YOU IN THE HEAD.
WHAT THE HELL DO YOU KNOW ABOUT IT, STEVE?
IF YOU'RE NOT THE CENTER OF ATTENTION FOR 5 SECONDS, YOU HAVE TO GO AND DIS EVERYONE ELSE'S STORIES? YOU'RE LIKE A POISONOUS SNAKE. STORY-WRECKER!
ALL RIGHT. EVERYONE CALM DOWN.
THE REAL QUESTION IS WHO'S LOOKING AFTER THE REDHEADS WHILE ELODIE'S OFF. ANYONE KNOW?
"POISONOUS SNAKE?"
NO IDEA, AND I DON'T EVEN WANT TO THINK ABOUT IT...
I'D RATHER RELIVE THE NIGHT OF THE COYOTE ATTACK FOR THE REST OF MY LIFE THAN SPEND A DAY WITH THEM.
"CENTER OF ATTENTION?"
YOU OKAY, OLIVER?
WHAT ARE YOU DOING?
I'M PRAYING TO THE ANCIENT GODS TO SPARE ME.
"STORY-WRECKER?"

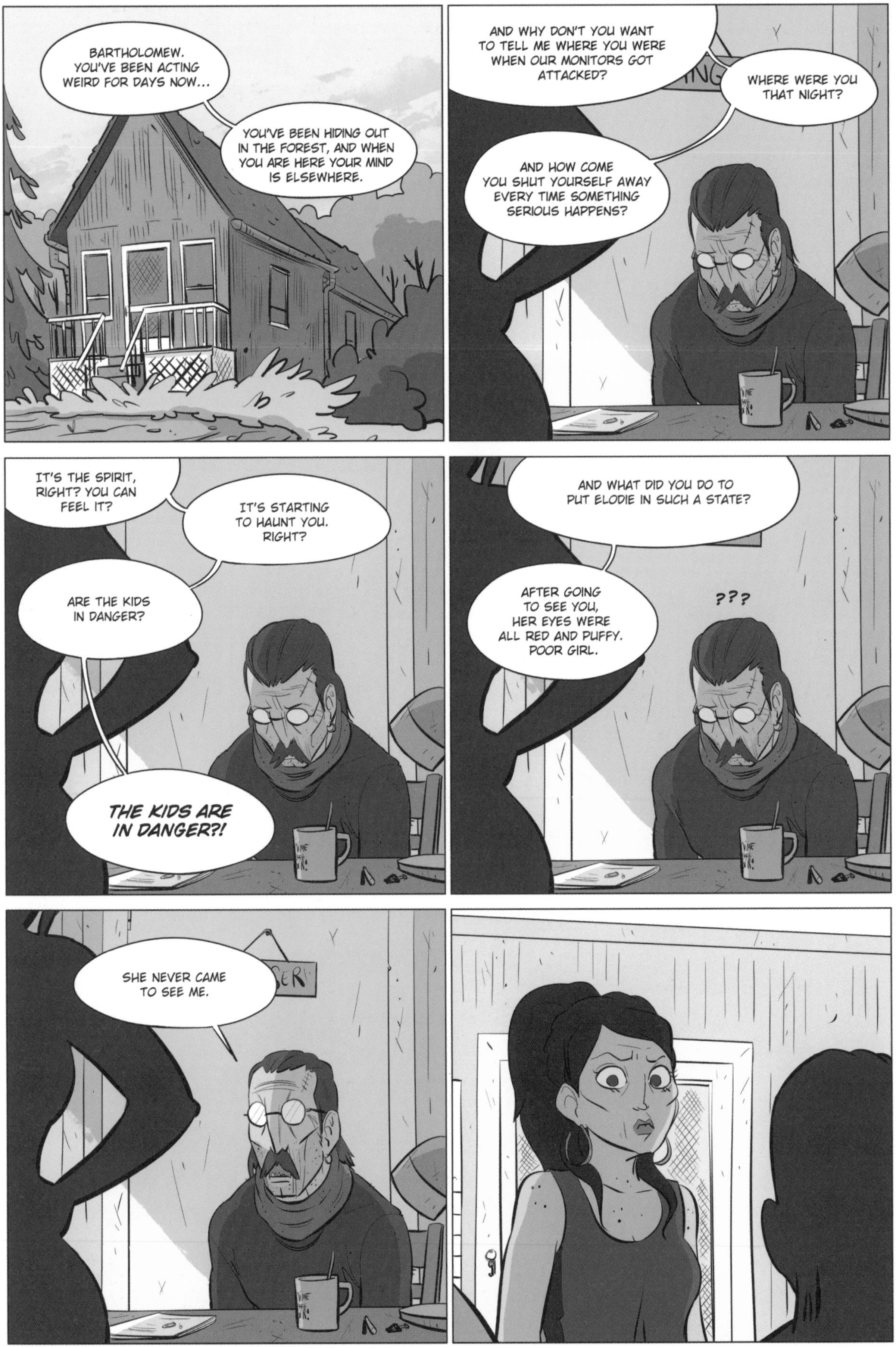
BARTHOLOMEW. YOU'VE BEEN ACTING WEIRD FOR DAYS NOW...
YOU'VE BEEN HIDING OUT IN THE FOREST, AND WHEN YOU ARE HERE YOUR MIND IS ELSEWHERE.
AND WHY DON'T YOU WANT TO TELL ME WHERE YOU WERE WHEN OUR MONITORS GOT ATTACKED?
WHERE WERE YOU THAT NIGHT?
AND HOW COME YOU SHUT YOURSELF AWAY EVERY TIME SOMETHING SERIOUS HAPPENS?
IT'S THE SPIRIT, RIGHT? YOU CAN FEEL IT?
IT'S STARTING TO HAUNT YOU. RIGHT?
ARE THE KIDS IN DANGER?
THE KIDS ARE IN DANGER?!
AND WHAT DID YOU DO TO PUT ELODIE IN SUCH A STATE?
AFTER GOING TO SEE YOU, HER EYES WERE ALL RED AND PUFFY. POOR GIRL.
???
SHE NEVER CAME TO SEE ME.

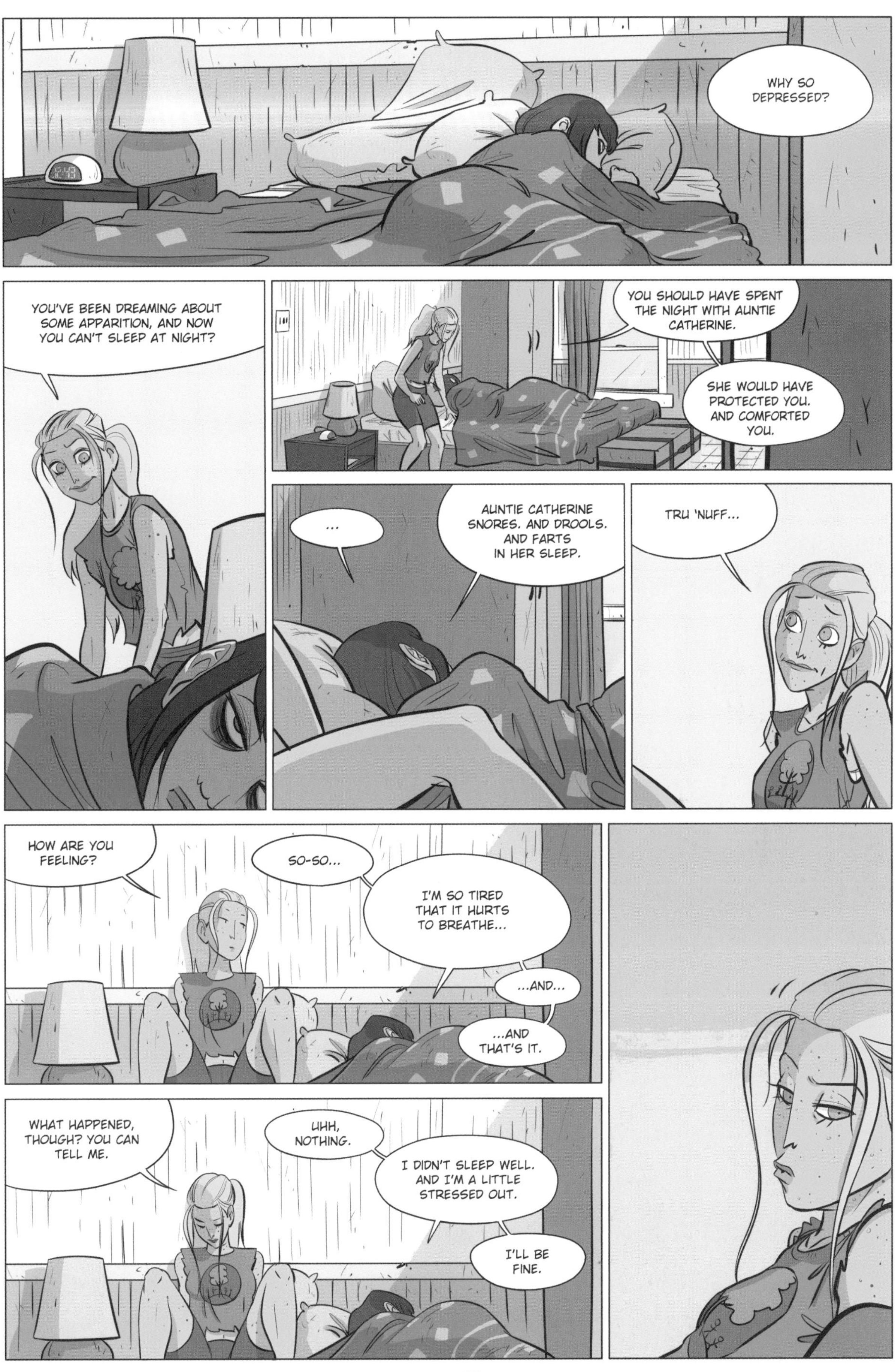
WHY SO DEPRESSED?
YOU'VE BEEN DREAMING ABOUT SOME APPARITION, AND NOW YOU CAN'T SLEEP AT NIGHT?
YOU SHOULD HAVE SPENT THE NIGHT WITH AUNTIE CATHERINE.
SHE WOULD HAVE PROTECTED YOU. AND COMFORTED YOU.
...
AUNTIE CATHERINE SNORES. AND DROOLS. AND FARTS IN HER SLEEP.
TRU 'NUFF...
HOW ARE YOU FEELING?
SO-SO...
I'M SO TIRED THAT IT HURTS TO BREATHE...
...AND...
...AND THAT'S IT.
WHAT HAPPENED, THOUGH? YOU CAN TELL ME.
UHH, NOTHING.
I DIDN'T SLEEP WELL. AND I'M A LITTLE STRESSED OUT.
I'LL BE FINE.

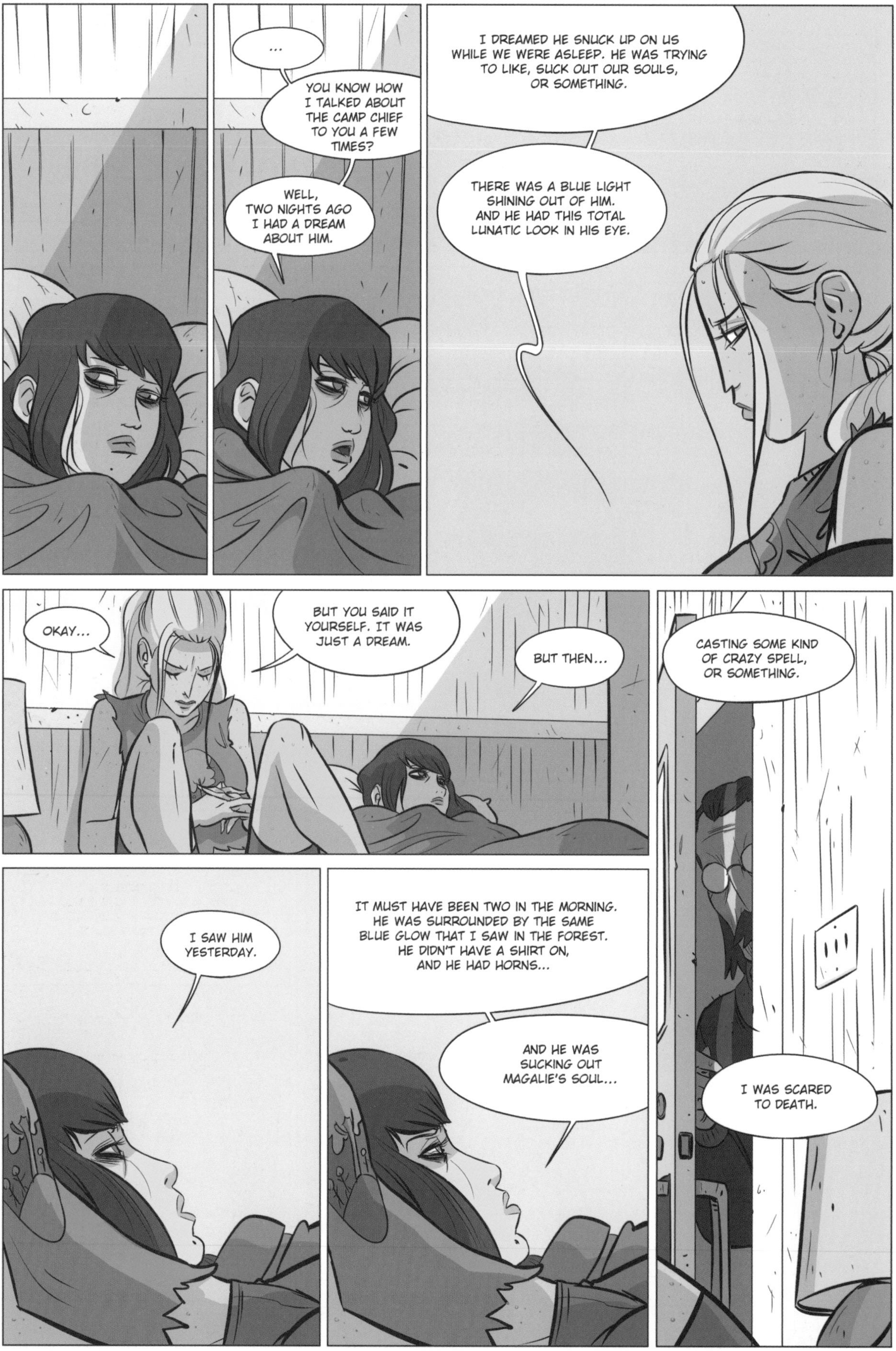
...
YOU KNOW HOW I TALKED ABOUT THE CAMP CHIEF TO YOU A FEW TIMES?
WELL, TWO NIGHTS AGO I HAD A DREAM ABOUT HIM.
I DREAMED HE SNUCK UP ON US WHILE WE WERE ASLEEP. HE WAS TRYING TO LIKE, SUCK OUT OUR SOULS, OR SOMETHING.
THERE WAS A BLUE LIGHT SHINING OUT OF HIM. AND HE HAD THIS TOTAL LUNATIC LOOK IN HIS EYE.
OKAY...
BUT YOU SAID IT YOURSELF. IT WAS JUST A DREAM.
BUT THEN...
I SAW HIM YESTERDAY.
IT MUST HAVE BEEN TWO IN THE MORNING. HE WAS SURROUNDED BY THE SAME BLUE GLOW THAT I SAW IN THE FOREST. HE DIDN'T HAVE A SHIRT ON, AND HE HAD HORNS...
AND HE WAS SUCKING OUT MAGALIE'S SOUL...
CASTING SOME KIND OF CRAZY SPELL, OR SOMETHING.
I WAS SCARED TO DEATH.

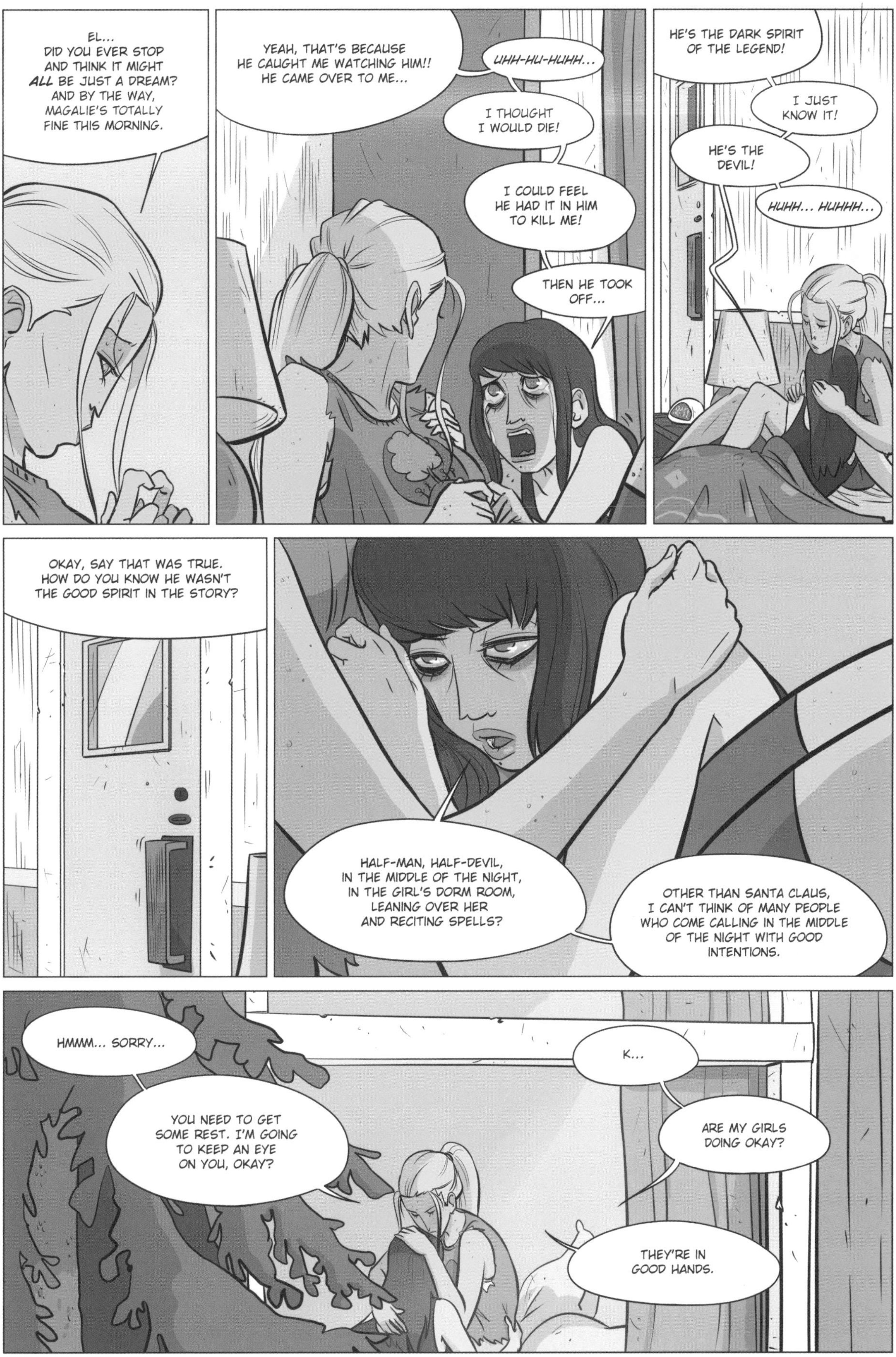
EL... DID YOU EVER STOP AND THINK IT MIGHT ALL BE JUST A DREAM? AND BY THE WAY, MAGALIE'S TOTALLY FINE THIS MORNING.
YEAH, THAT'S BECAUSE HE CAUGHT ME WATCHING HIM!! HE CAME OVER TO ME...
UHH-HU-HUHH...
I THOUGHT I WOULD DIE!
I COULD FEEL HE HAD IT IN HIM TO KILL ME!
THEN HE TOOK OFF...
HE'S THE DARK SPIRIT OF THE LEGEND!
I JUST KNOW IT!
HE'S THE DEVIL!
HUHH... HUHHH...
OKAY, SAY THAT WAS TRUE. HOW DO YOU KNOW HE WASN'T THE GOOD SPIRIT IN THE STORY?
HALF-MAN, HALF-DEVIL, IN THE MIDDLE OF THE NIGHT, IN THE GIRL'S DORM ROOM, LEANING OVER HER AND RECITING SPELLS?
OTHER THAN SANTA CLAUS, I CAN'T THINK OF MANY PEOPLE WHO COME CALLING IN THE MIDDLE OF THE NIGHT WITH GOOD INTENTIONS.
HMMM... SORRY...
YOU NEED TO GET SOME REST. I'M GOING TO KEEP AN EYE ON YOU, OKAY?
K...
ARE MY GIRLS DOING OKAY?
THEY'RE IN GOOD HANDS.

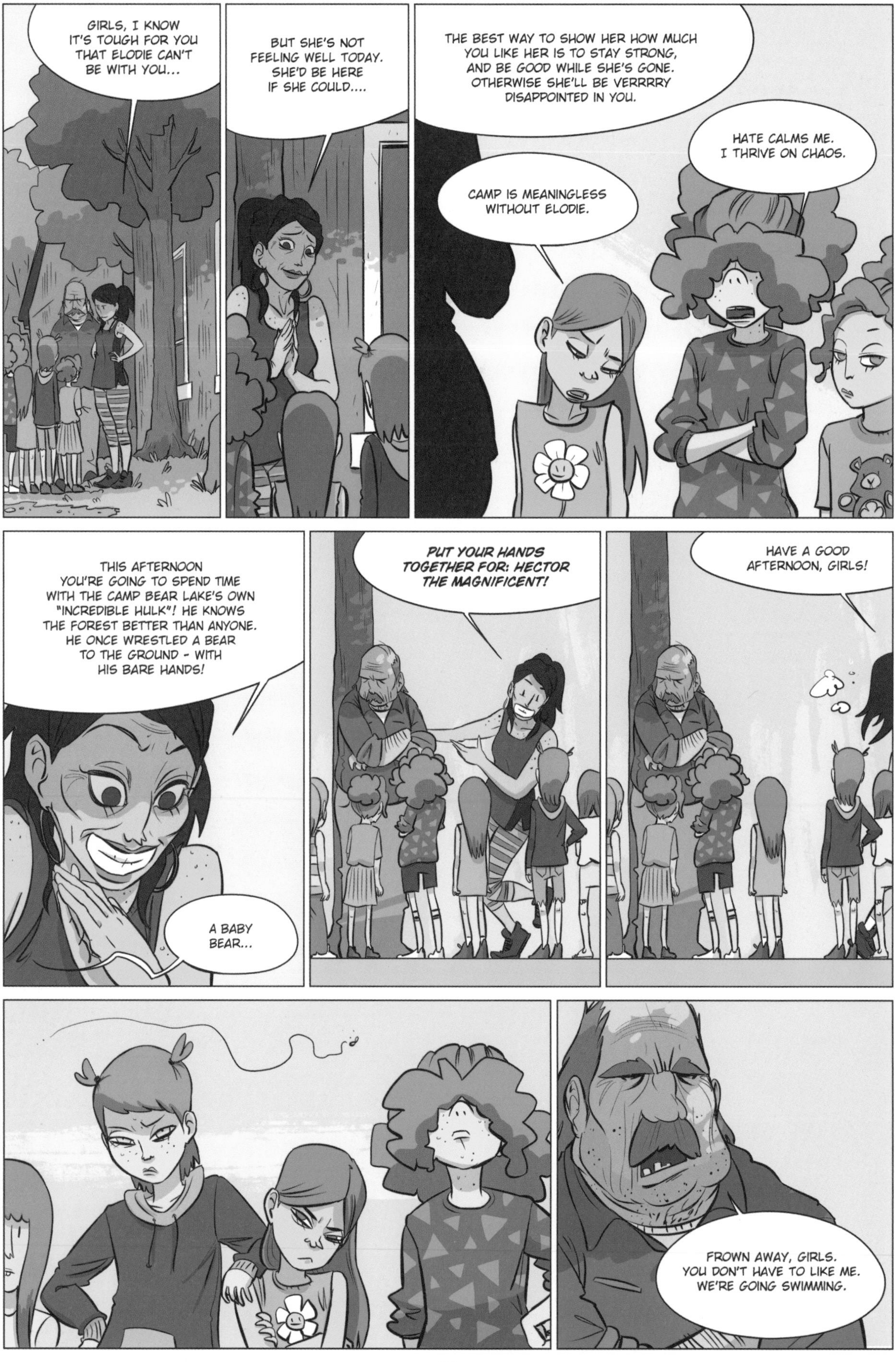
GIRLS, I KNOW IT'S TOUGH FOR YOU THAT ELODIE CAN'T BE WITH YOU...
BUT SHE'S NOT FEELING WELL TODAY. SHE'D BE HERE IF SHE COULD....
THE BEST WAY TO SHOW HER HOW MUCH YOU LIKE HER IS TO STAY STRONG, AND BE GOOD WHILE SHE'S GONE. OTHERWISE SHE'LL BE VERRRRY DISAPPOINTED IN YOU.
CAMP IS MEANINGLESS WITHOUT ELODIE.
HATE CALMS ME. I THRIVE ON CHAOS.
THIS AFTERNOON YOU'RE GOING TO SPEND TIME WITH THE CAMP BEAR LAKE'S OWN "INCREDIBLE HULK"! HE KNOWS THE FOREST BETTER THAN ANYONE. HE ONCE WRESTLED A BEAR TO THE GROUND - WITH HIS BARE HANDS!
A BABY BEAR...
PUT YOUR HANDS TOGETHER FOR: HECTOR THE MAGNIFICENT!
HAVE A GOOD AFTERNOON, GIRLS!
FROWN AWAY, GIRLS. YOU DON'T HAVE TO LIKE ME. WE'RE GOING SWIMMING.

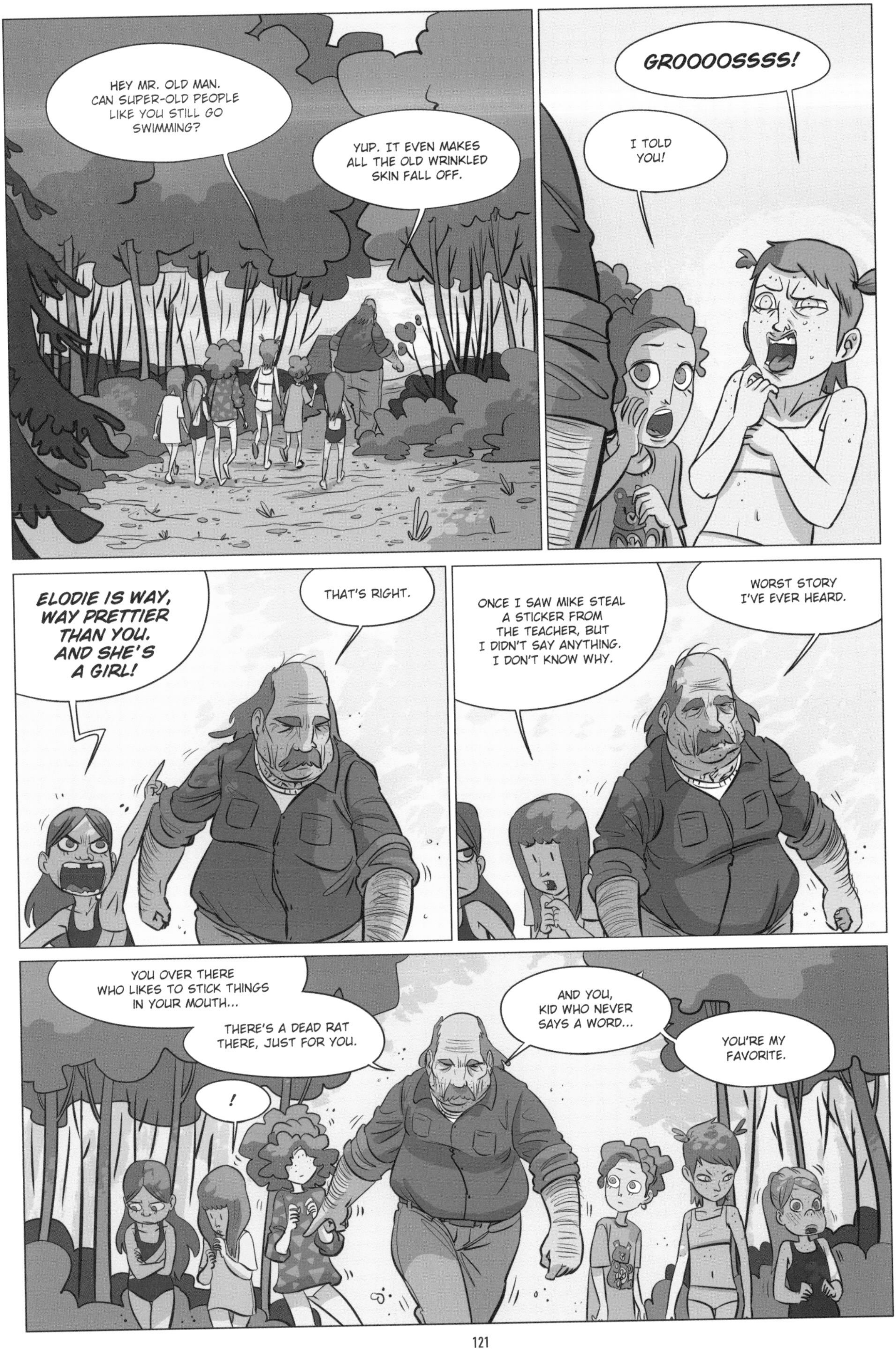
HEY MR. OLD MAN. CAN SUPER-OLD PEOPLE LIKE YOU STILL GO SWIMMING?
YUP. IT EVEN MAKES ALL THE OLD WRINKLED SKIN FALL OFF.
GROOOOSSSS!
I TOLD YOU!
ELODIE IS WAY, WAY PRETTIER THAN YOU. AND SHE'S A GIRL!
THAT'S RIGHT.
ONCE I SAW MIKE STEAL A STICKER FROM THE TEACHER, BUT I DIDN'T SAY ANYTHING. I DON'T KNOW WHY.
WORST STORY I'VE EVER HEARD.
YOU OVER THERE WHO LIKES TO STICK THINGS IN YOUR MOUTH...
THERE'S A DEAD RAT THERE, JUST FOR YOU.
!
AND YOU, KID WHO NEVER SAYS A WORD...
YOU'RE MY FAVORITE.

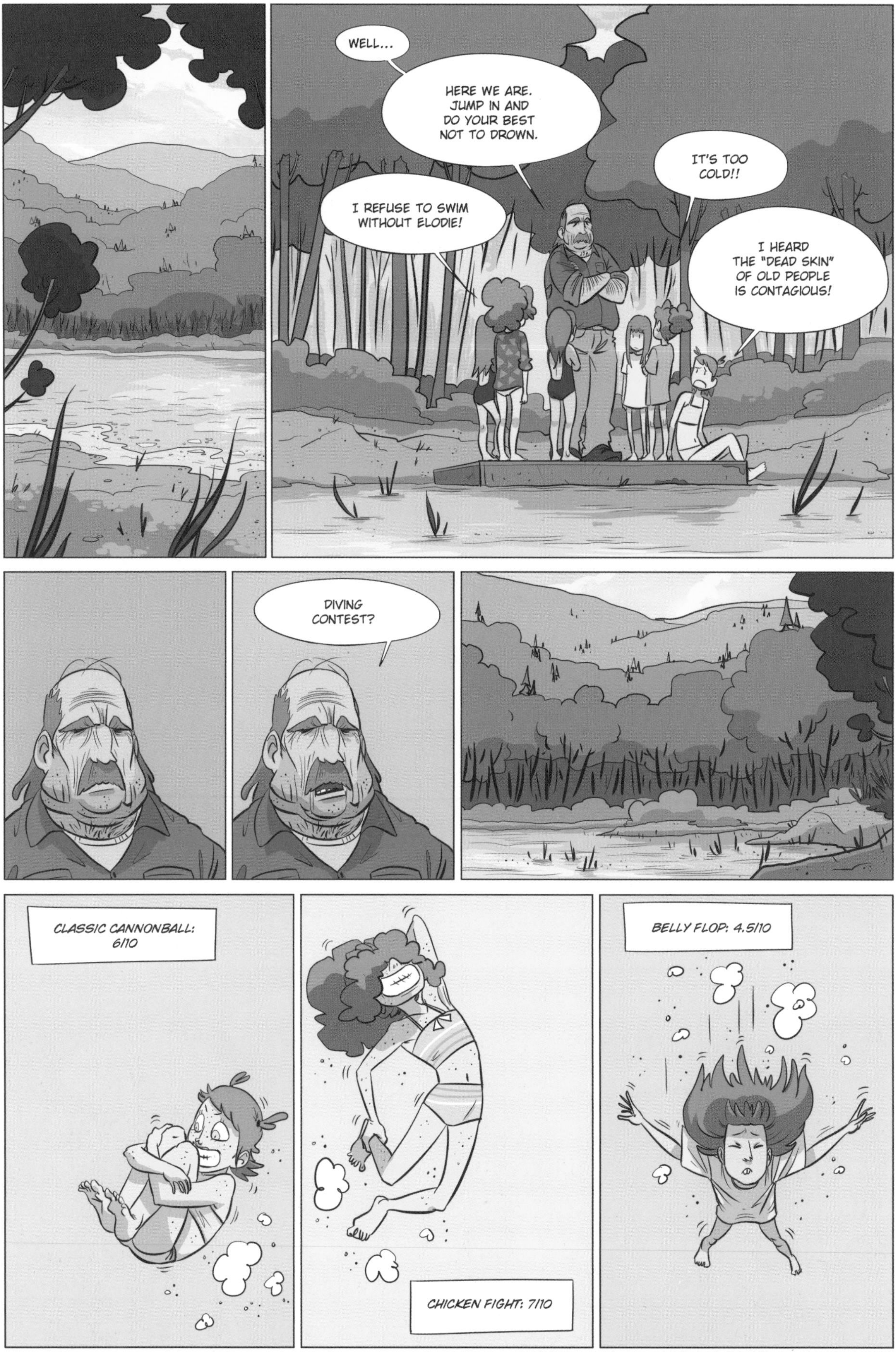
WELL...
HERE WE ARE. JUMP IN AND DO YOUR BEST NOT TO DROWN.
I REFUSE TO SWIM WITHOUT ELODIE!
IT'S TOO COLD!!
I HEARD THE "DEAD SKIN" OF OLD PEOPLE IS CONTAGIOUS!
DIVING CONTEST?
CLASSIC CANNONBALL: 6/10
CHICKEN FIGHT: 7/10
BELLY FLOP: 4.5/10

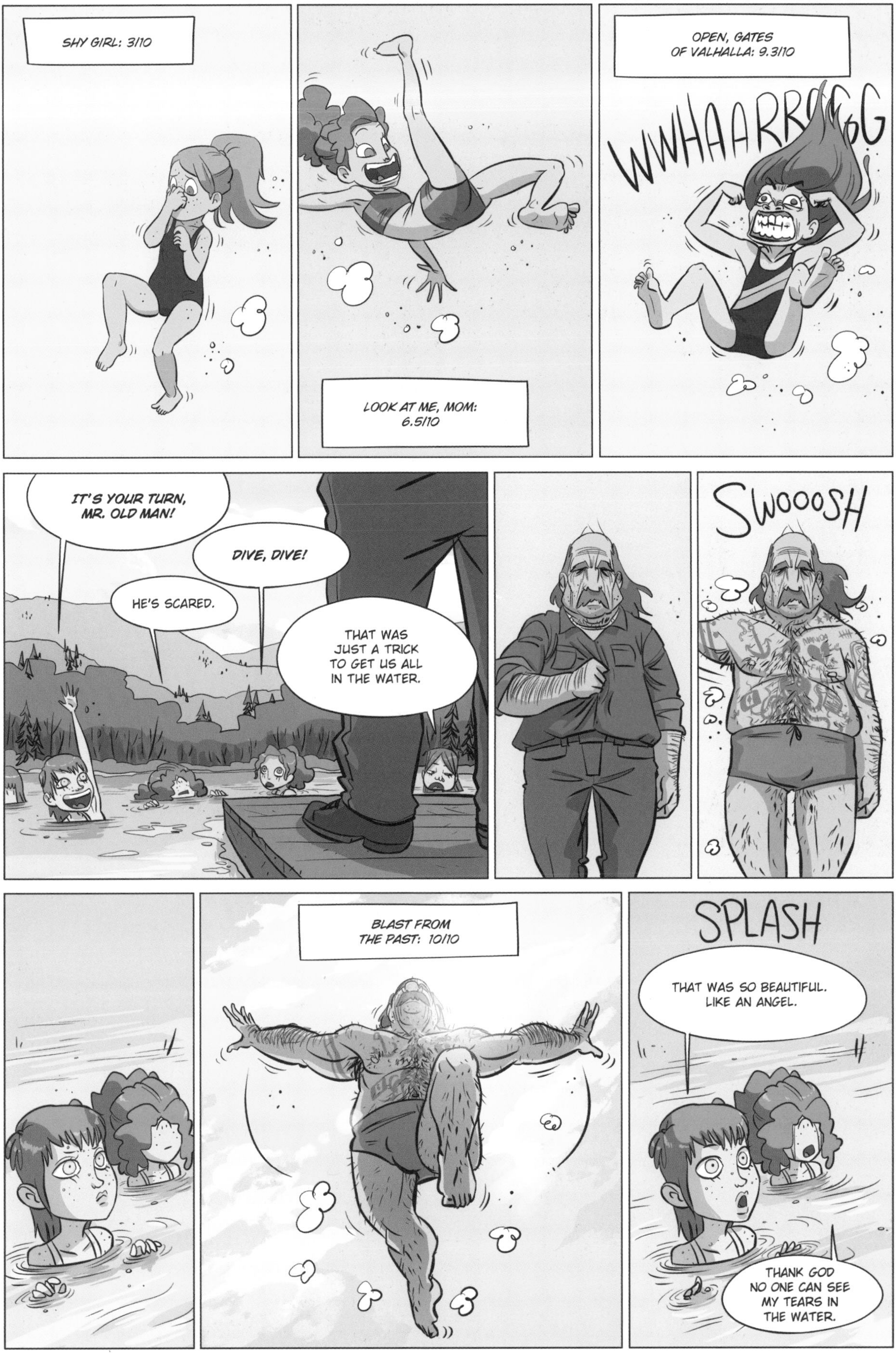
SHY GIRL: 3/10
LOOK AT ME, MOM: 6.5/10
OPEN, GATES OF VALHALLA: 9.3/10
WWHAARRGG
IT'S YOUR TURN, MR. OLD MAN!
HE'S SCARED.
DIVE, DIVE!
THAT WAS JUST A TRICK TO GET US ALL IN THE WATER.
SWOOOSH
BLAST FROM THE PAST: 10/10
SPLASH
THAT WAS SO BEAUTIFUL. LIKE AN ANGEL.
THANK GOD NO ONE CAN SEE MY TEARS IN THE WATER.

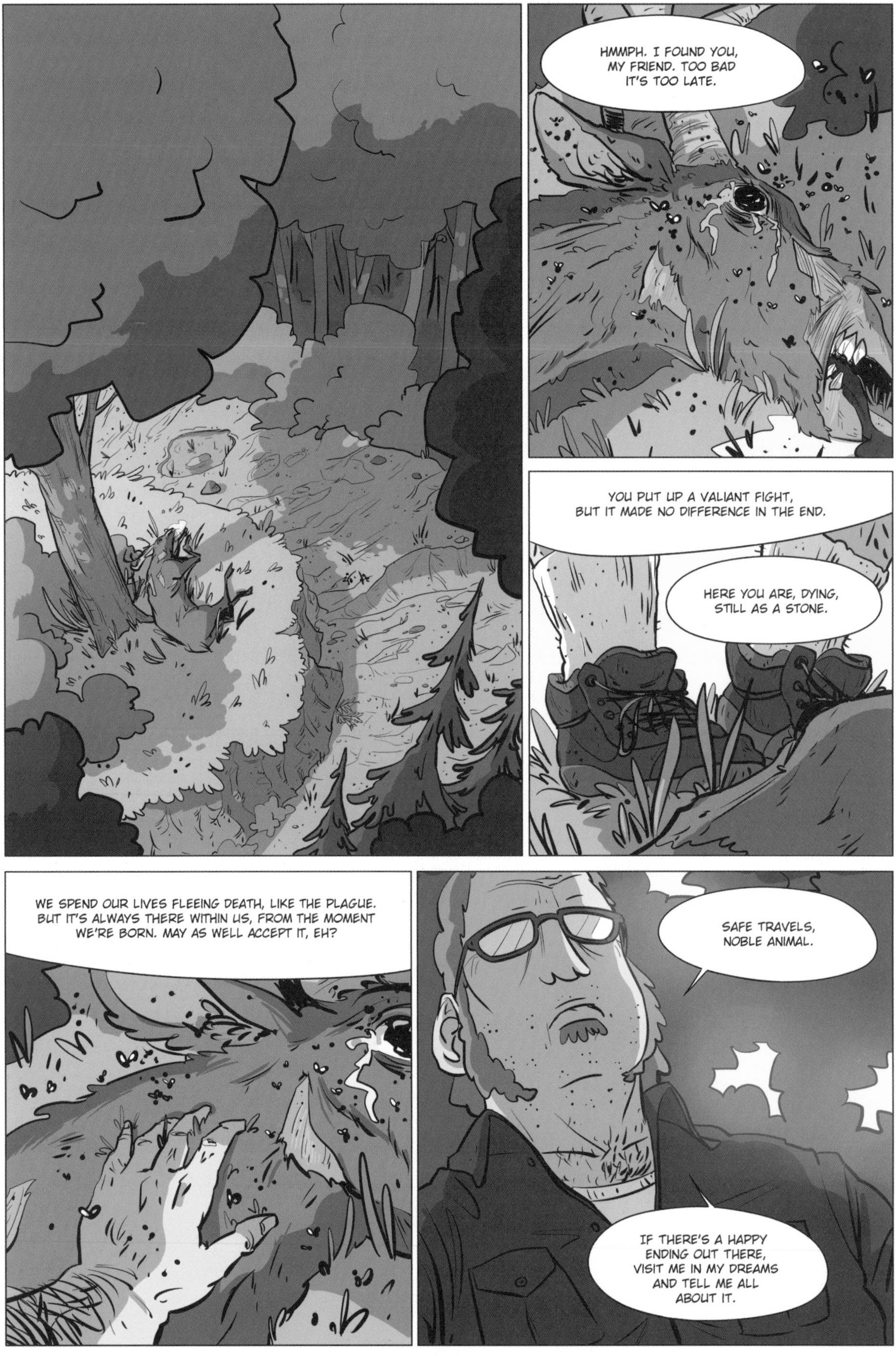
HMMPH. I FOUND YOU, MY FRIEND. TOO BAD IT'S TOO LATE.
YOU PUT UP A VALIANT FIGHT, BUT IT MADE NO DIFFERENCE IN THE END.
HERE YOU ARE, DYING, STILL AS A STONE.
WE SPEND OUR LIVES FLEEING DEATH, LIKE THE PLAGUE. BUT IT'S ALWAYS THERE WITHIN US, FROM THE MOMENT WE'RE BORN. MAY AS WELL ACCEPT IT, EH?
SAFE TRAVELS, NOBLE ANIMAL.
IF THERE'S A HAPPY ENDING OUT THERE, VISIT ME IN MY DREAMS AND TELL ME ALL ABOUT IT.

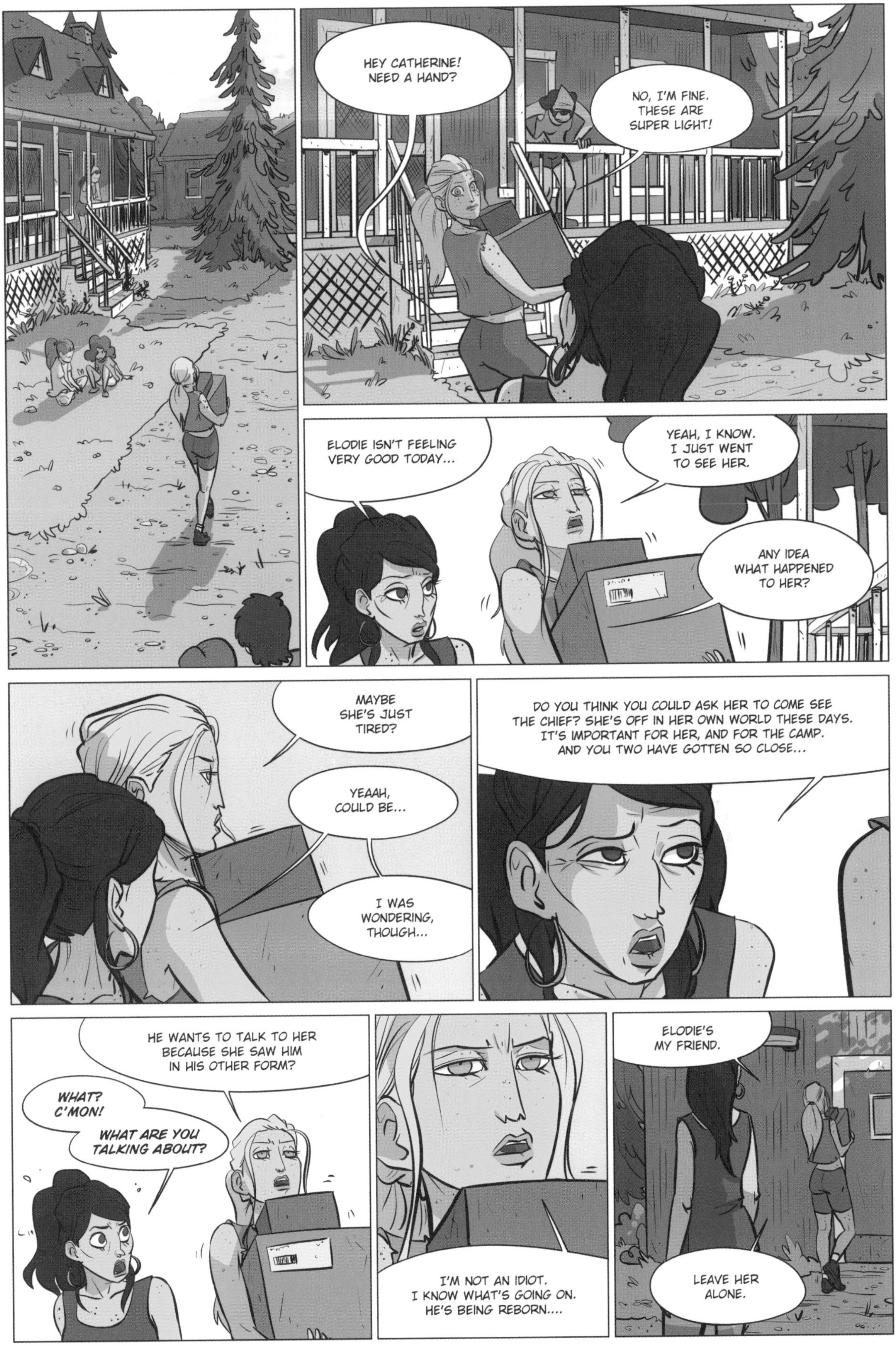
HEY CATHERINE! NEED A HAND?
NO, I'M FINE. THESE ARE SUPER LIGHT!
ELODIE ISN'T FEELING VERY GOOD TODAY...
YEAH, I KNOW. I JUST WENT TO SEE HER.
ANY IDEA WHAT HAPPENED TO HER?
MAYBE SHE'S JUST TIRED?
YEAAH, COULD BE...
I WAS WONDERING, THOUGH...
DO YOU THINK YOU COULD ASK HER TO COME SEE THE CHIEF? SHE'S OFF IN HER OWN WORLD THESE DAYS. IT'S IMPORTANT FOR HER, AND FOR THE CAMP. AND YOU TWO HAVE GOTTEN SO CLOSE...
HE WANTS TO TALK TO HER BECAUSE SHE SAW HIM IN HIS OTHER FORM?
WHAT? C'MON!
WHAT ARE YOU TALKING ABOUT?
I'M NOT AN IDIOT. I KNOW WHAT'S GOING ON. HE'S BEING REBORN....
ELODIE'S MY FRIEND.
LEAVE HER ALONE.

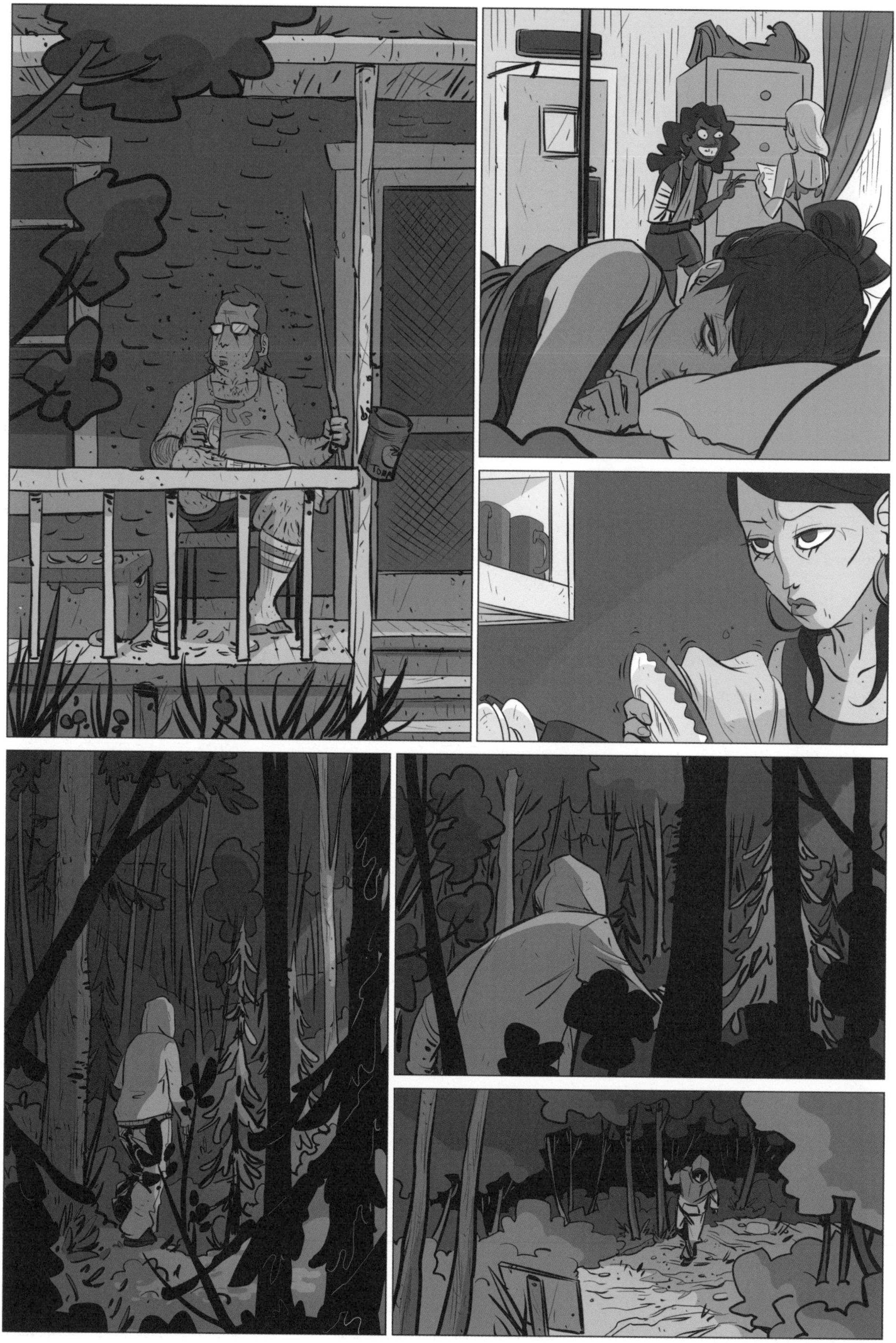

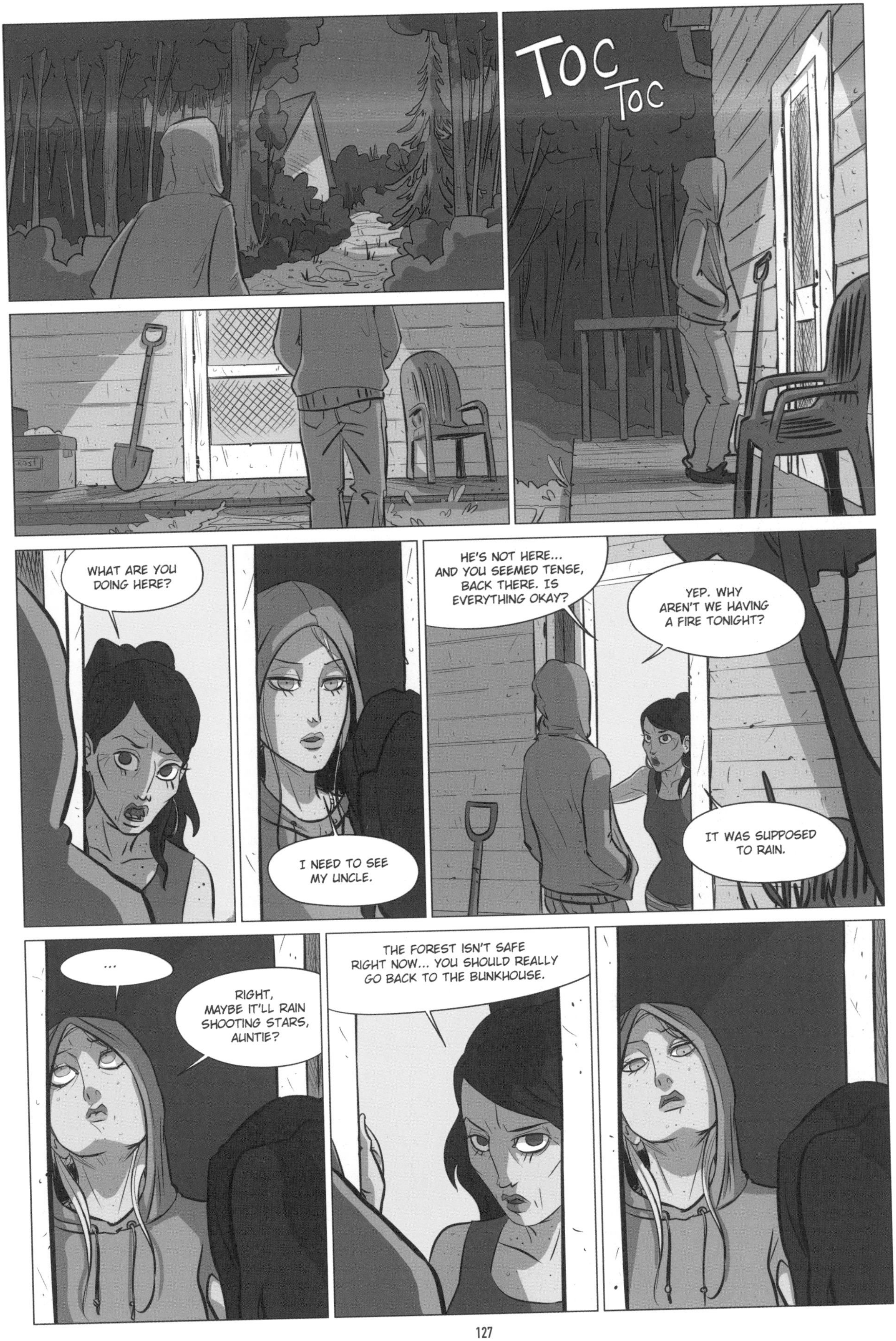
TOC TOC
WHAT ARE YOU DOING HERE?
I NEED TO SEE MY UNCLE.
HE'S NOT HERE... AND YOU SEEMED TENSE, BACK THERE. IS EVERYTHING OKAY?
YEP. WHY AREN'T WE HAVING A FIRE TONIGHT?
IT WAS SUPPOSED TO RAIN.
...
RIGHT, MAYBE IT'LL RAIN SHOOTING STARS, AUNTIE?
THE FOREST ISN'T SAFE RIGHT NOW... YOU SHOULD REALLY GO BACK TO THE BUNKHOUSE.

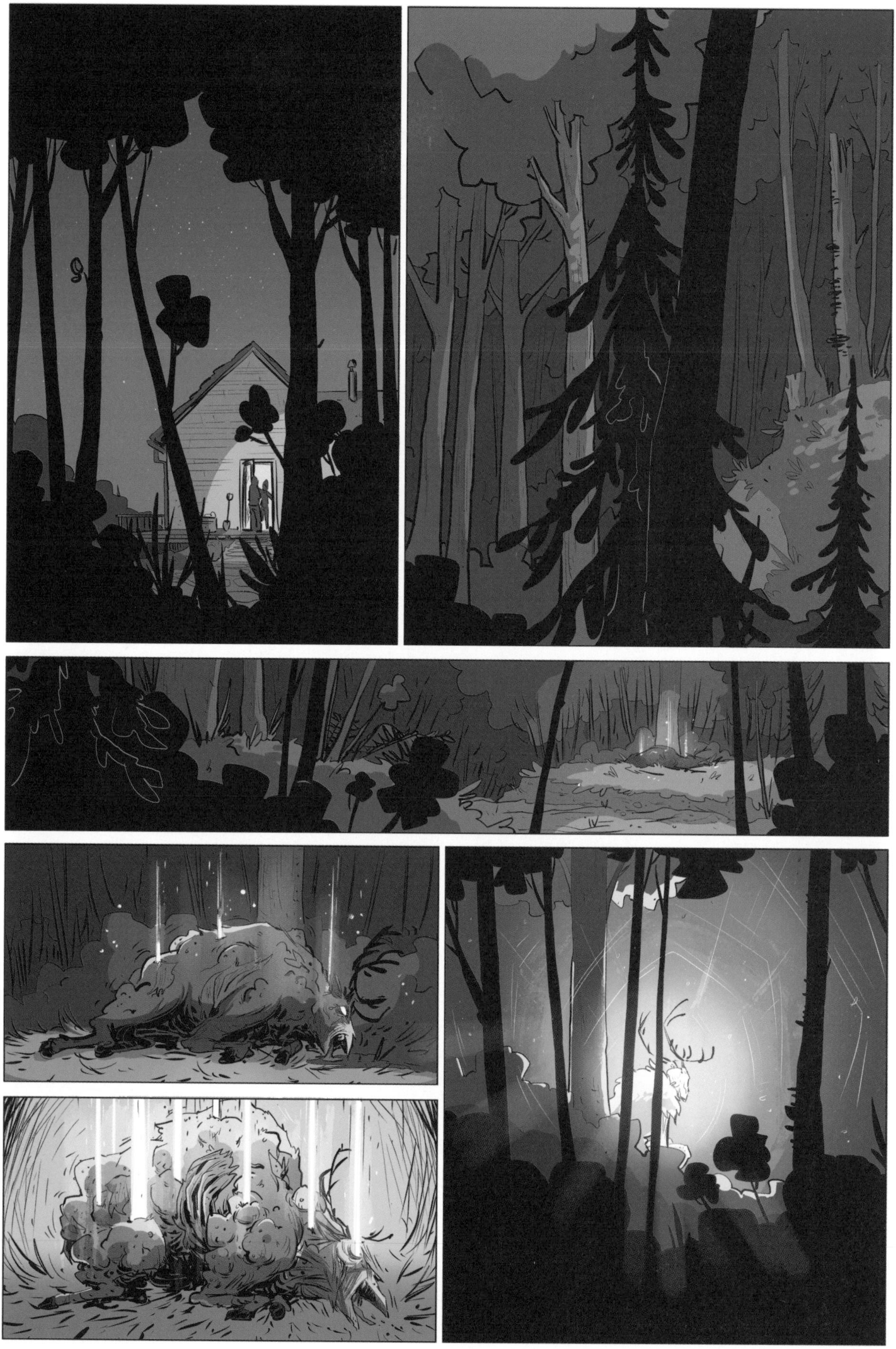

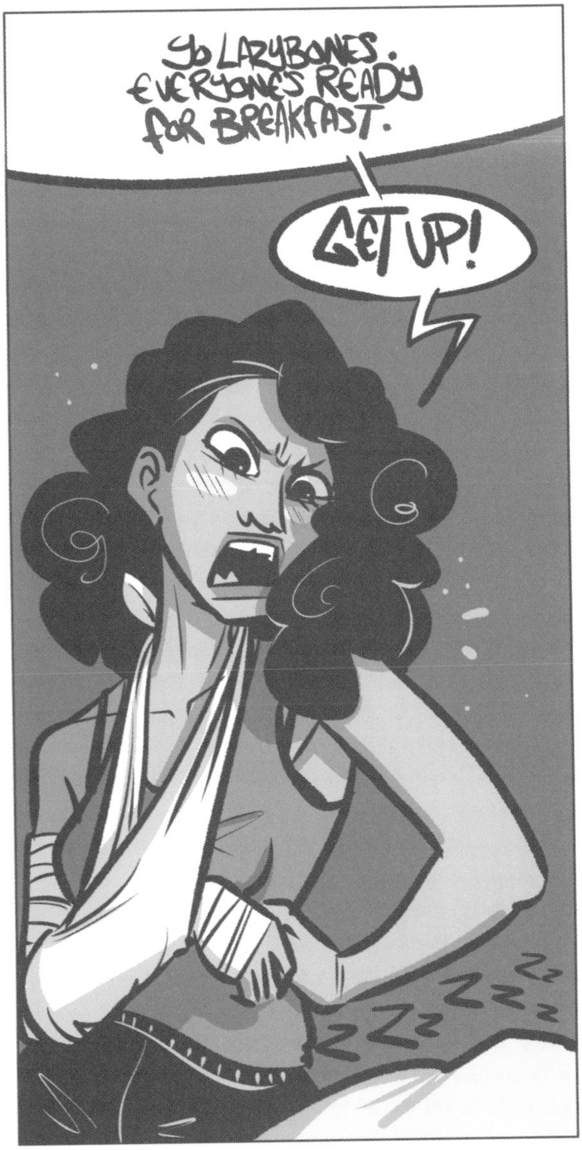
YO LAZYBONES. EVERYONE'S READY FOR BREAKFAST.
GET UP!
ZZZ
ZZZ

6

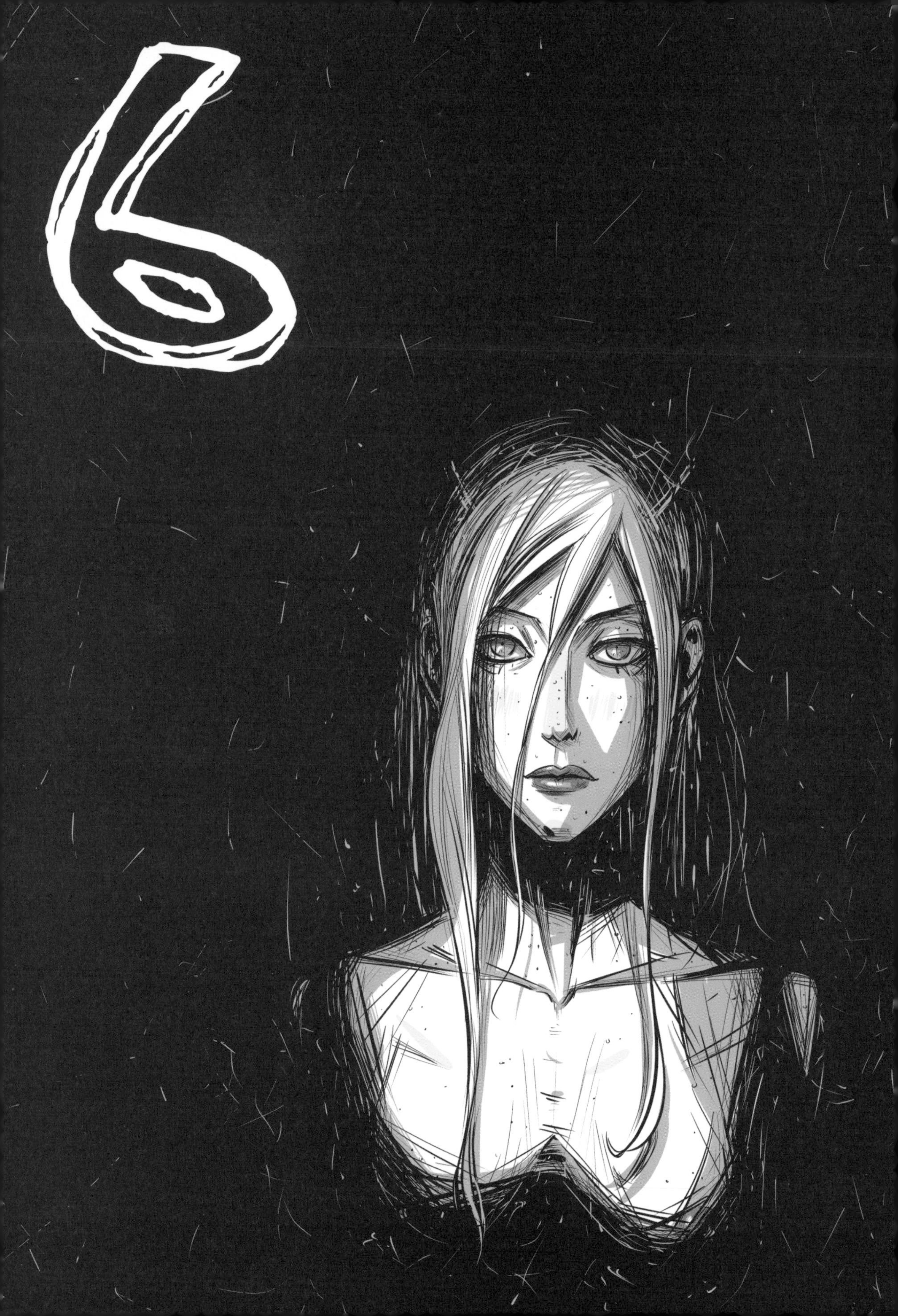

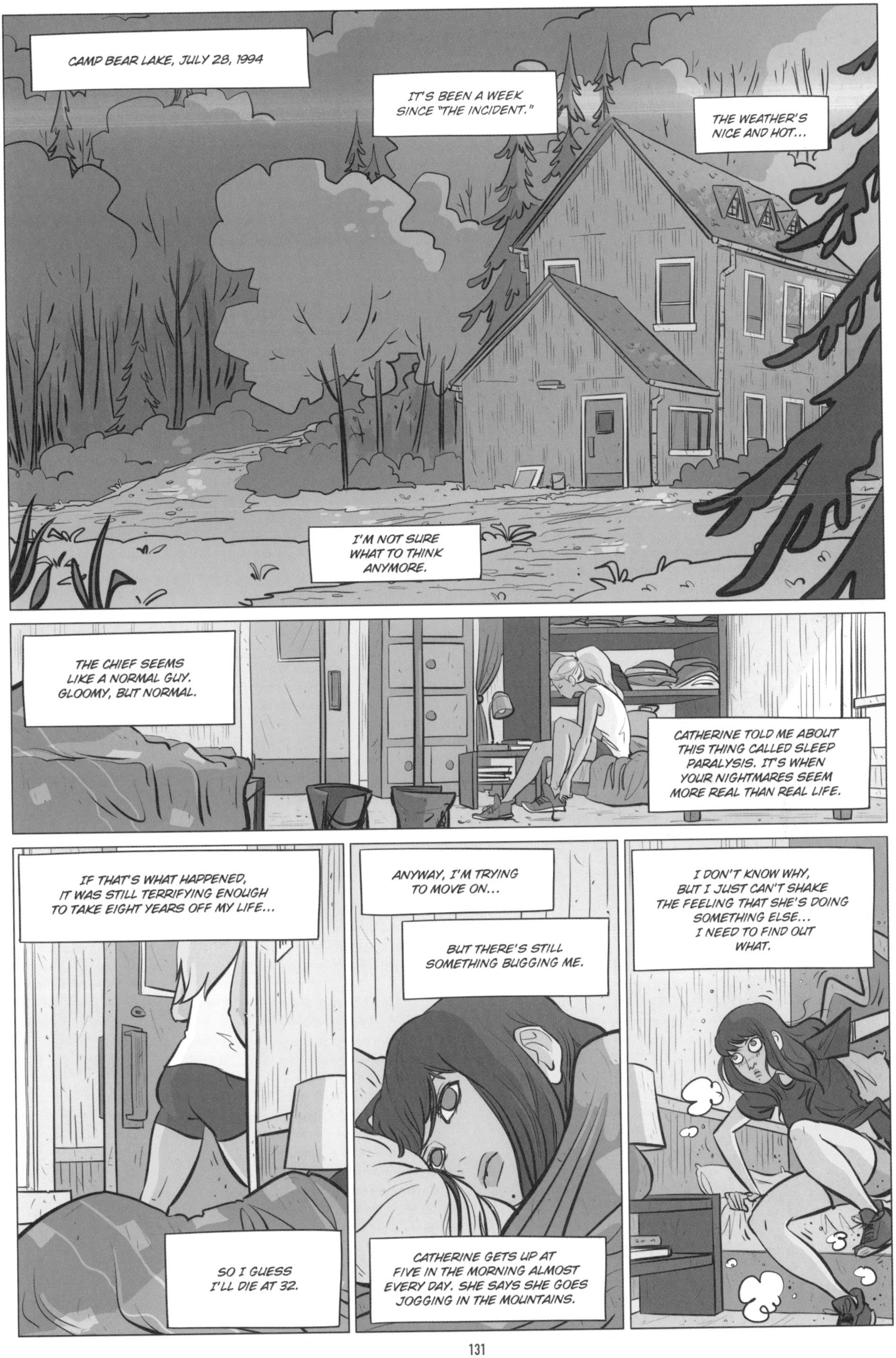
CAMP BEAR LAKE, JULY 28, 1994
IT'S BEEN A WEEK SINCE "THE INCIDENT."
THE WEATHER'S NICE AND HOT...
I'M NOT SURE WHAT TO THINK ANYMORE.
THE CHIEF SEEMS LIKE A NORMAL GUY. GLOOMY, BUT NORMAL.
CATHERINE TOLD ME ABOUT THIS THING CALLED SLEEP PARALYSIS. IT'S WHEN YOUR NIGHTMARES SEEM MORE REAL THAN REAL LIFE.
IF THAT'S WHAT HAPPENED, IT WAS STILL TERRIFYING ENOUGH TO TAKE EIGHT YEARS OFF MY LIFE...
SO I GUESS I'LL DIE AT 32.
ANYWAY, I'M TRYING TO MOVE ON...
BUT THERE'S STILL SOMETHING BUGGING ME.
CATHERINE GETS UP AT FIVE IN THE MORNING ALMOST EVERY DAY. SHE SAYS SHE GOES JOGGING IN THE MOUNTAINS.
I DON'T KNOW WHY, BUT I JUST CAN'T SHAKE THE FEELING THAT SHE'S DOING SOMETHING ELSE... I NEED TO FIND OUT WHAT.

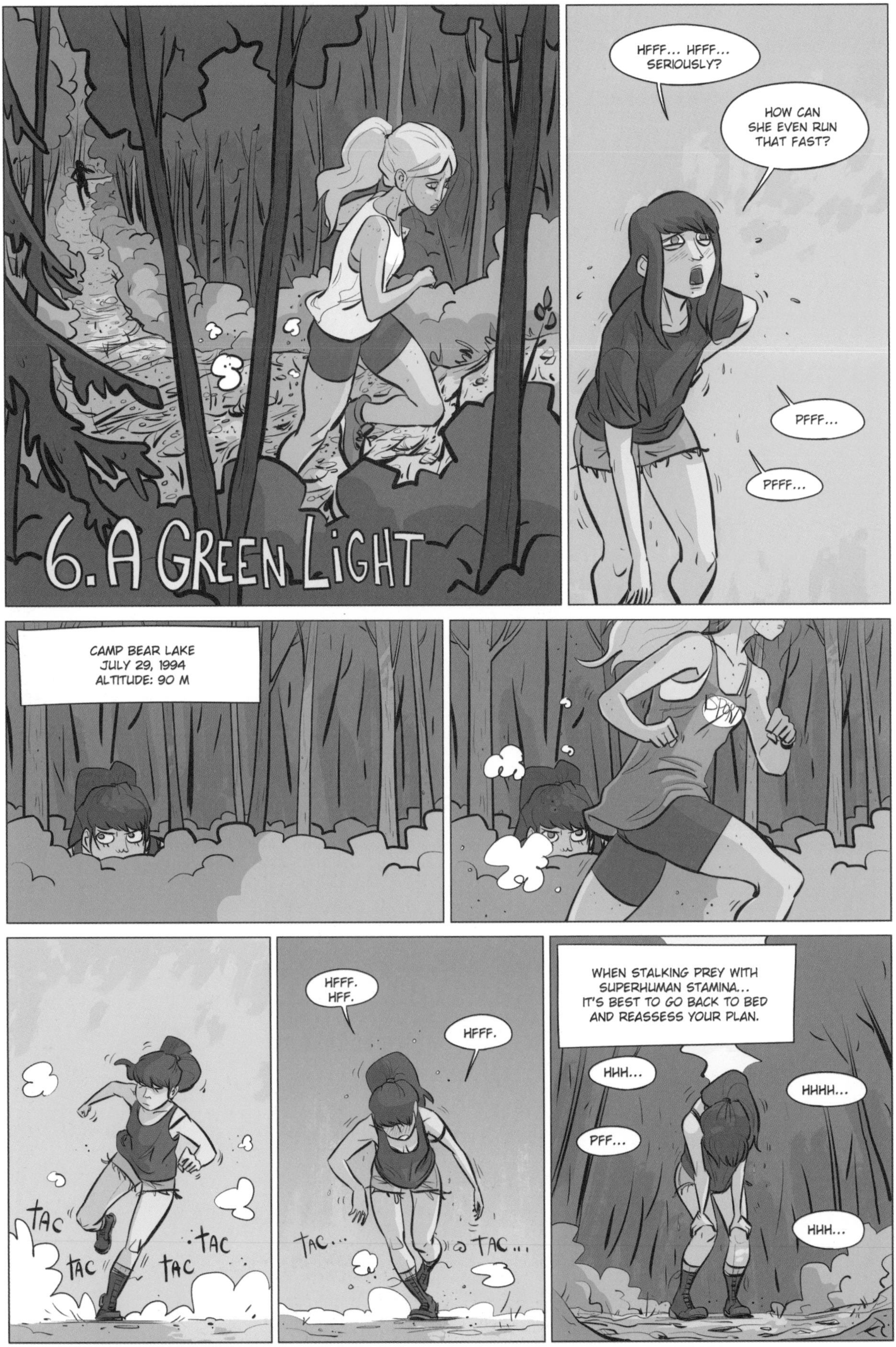
6. A GREEN LIGHT
HFFF... HFFF... SERIOUSLY?
HOW CAN SHE EVEN RUN THAT FAST?
PFFF...
PFFF...
CAMP BEAR LAKE
JULY 29, 1994
ALTITUDE: 90 M
TAC
TAC
TAC
TAC
HFFF. HFF.
HFFF.
TAC...
TAC...
WHEN STALKING PREY WITH SUPERHUMAN STAMINA... IT'S BEST TO GO BACK TO BED AND REASSESS YOUR PLAN.
HHH...
HHHH...
PFF...
HHH...

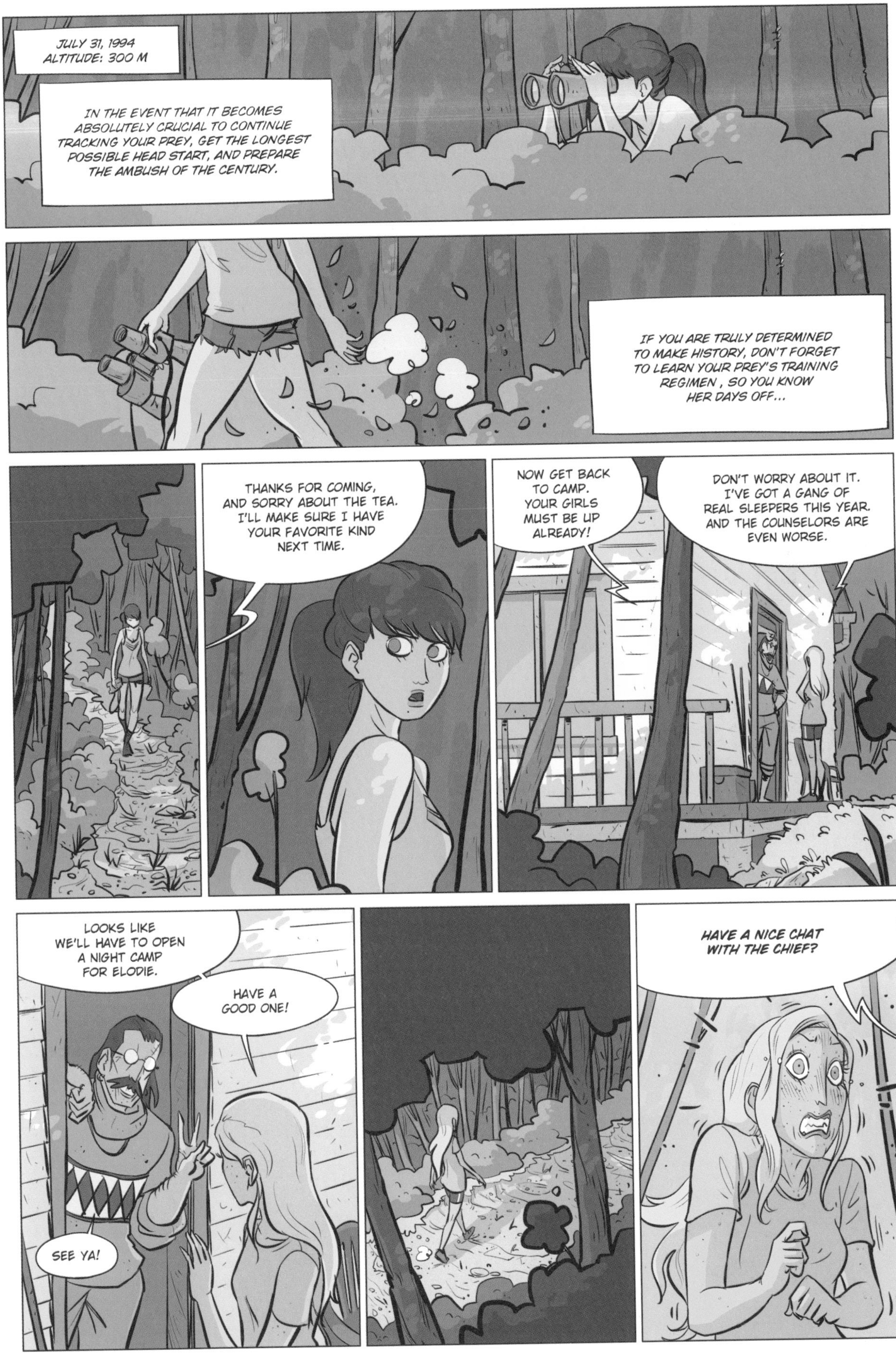
JULY 31, 1994
ALTITUDE: 300 M
IN THE EVENT THAT IT BECOMES ABSOLUTELY CRUCIAL TO CONTINUE TRACKING YOUR PREY, GET THE LONGEST POSSIBLE HEAD START, AND PREPARE THE AMBUSH OF THE CENTURY.
IF YOU ARE TRULY DETERMINED TO MAKE HISTORY, DON'T FORGET TO LEARN YOUR PREY'S TRAINING REGIMEN , SO YOU KNOW HER DAYS OFF...
THANKS FOR COMING, AND SORRY ABOUT THE TEA. I'LL MAKE SURE I HAVE YOUR FAVORITE KIND NEXT TIME.
NOW GET BACK TO CAMP. YOUR GIRLS MUST BE UP ALREADY!
DON'T WORRY ABOUT IT. I'VE GOT A GANG OF REAL SLEEPERS THIS YEAR. AND THE COUNSELORS ARE EVEN WORSE.
LOOKS LIKE WE'LL HAVE TO OPEN A NIGHT CAMP FOR ELODIE.
HAVE A GOOD ONE!
SEE YA!
HAVE A NICE CHAT WITH THE CHIEF?

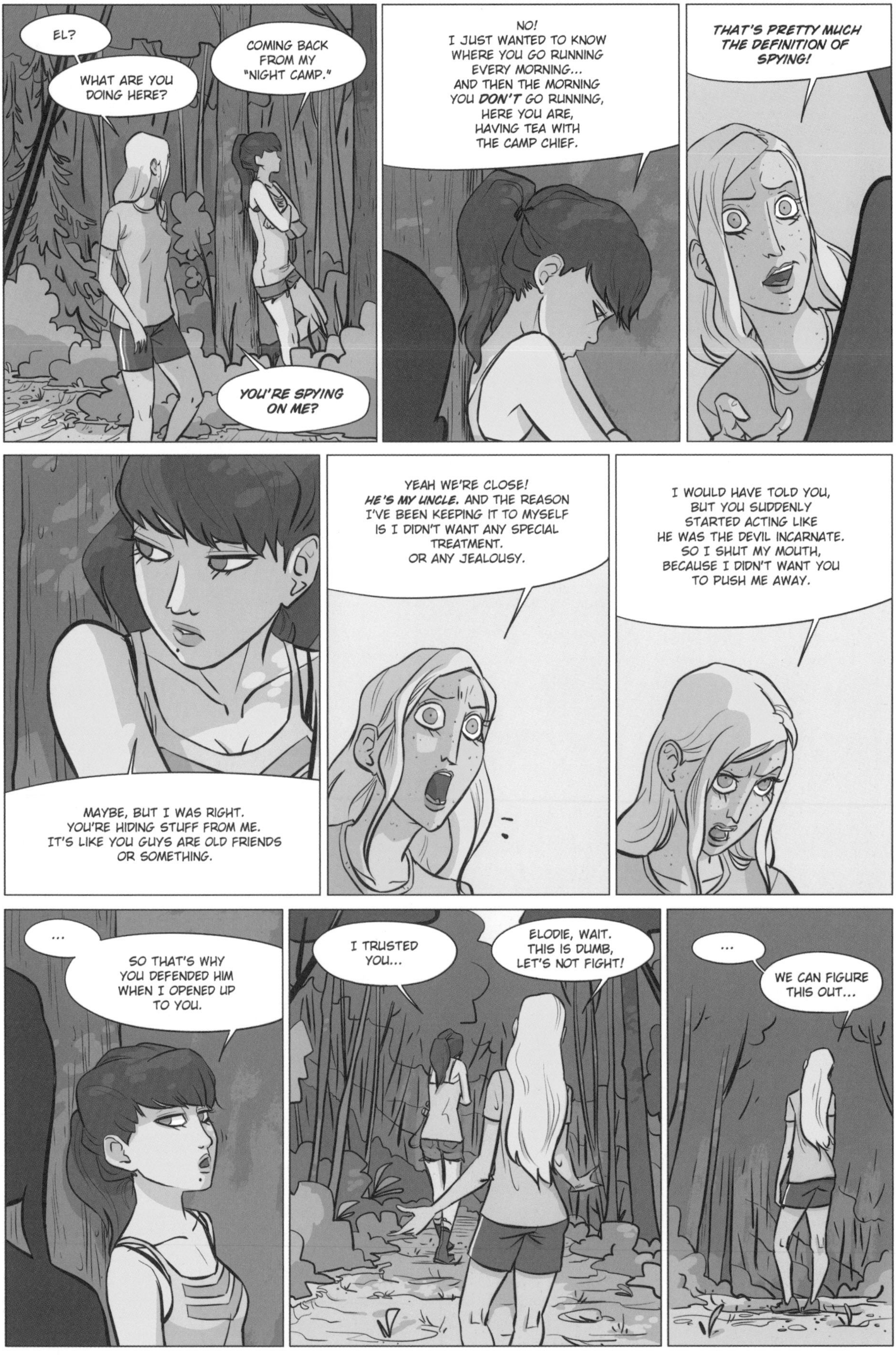
EL?
WHAT ARE YOU DOING HERE?
COMING BACK FROM MY "NIGHT CAMP."
YOU'RE SPYING ON ME?
NO! I JUST WANTED TO KNOW WHERE YOU GO RUNNING EVERY MORNING... AND THEN THE MORNING YOU DON'T GO RUNNING, HERE YOU ARE, HAVING TEA WITH THE CAMP CHIEF.
THAT'S PRETTY MUCH THE DEFINITION OF SPYING!
MAYBE, BUT I WAS RIGHT. YOU'RE HIDING STUFF FROM ME. IT'S LIKE YOU GUYS ARE OLD FRIENDS OR SOMETHING.
YEAH WE'RE CLOSE! HE'S MY UNCLE. AND THE REASON I'VE BEEN KEEPING IT TO MYSELF IS I DIDN'T WANT ANY SPECIAL TREATMENT. OR ANY JEALOUSY.
I WOULD HAVE TOLD YOU, BUT YOU SUDDENLY STARTED ACTING LIKE HE WAS THE DEVIL INCARNATE. SO I SHUT MY MOUTH, BECAUSE I DIDN'T WANT YOU TO PUSH ME AWAY.
...
SO THAT'S WHY YOU DEFENDED HIM WHEN I OPENED UP TO YOU.
I TRUSTED YOU...
ELODIE, WAIT. THIS IS DUMB, LET'S NOT FIGHT!
...
WE CAN FIGURE THIS OUT...

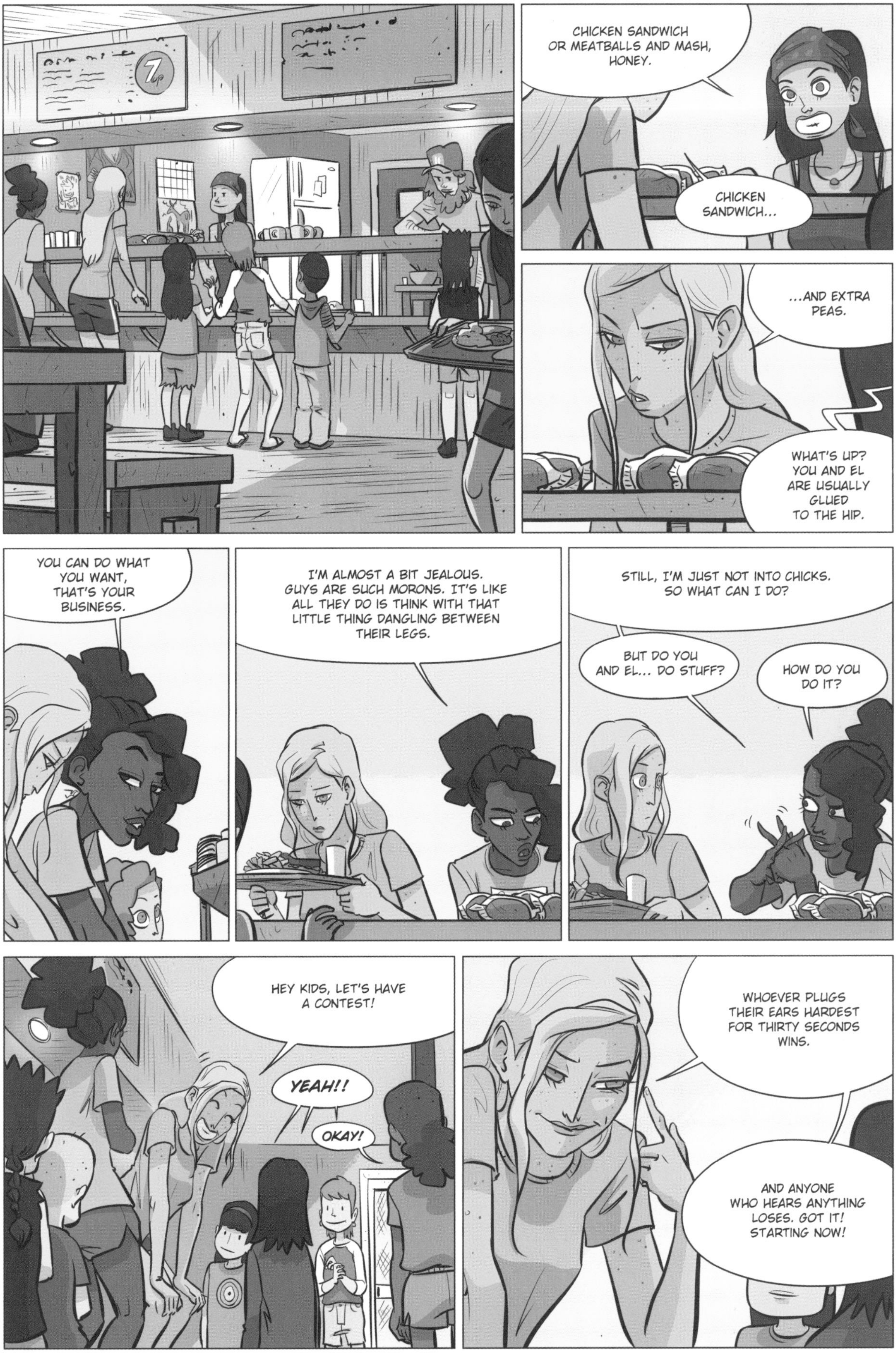
CHICKEN SANDWICH OR MEATBALLS AND MASH, HONEY.
CHICKEN SANDWICH...
...AND EXTRA PEAS.
WHAT'S UP? YOU AND EL ARE USUALLY GLUED TO THE HIP.
YOU CAN DO WHAT YOU WANT, THAT'S YOUR BUSINESS.
I'M ALMOST A BIT JEALOUS. GUYS ARE SUCH MORONS. IT'S LIKE ALL THEY DO IS THINK WITH THAT LITTLE THING DANGLING BETWEEN THEIR LEGS.
STILL, I'M JUST NOT INTO CHICKS. SO WHAT CAN I DO?
BUT DO YOU AND EL... DO STUFF?
HOW DO YOU DO IT?
HEY KIDS, LET'S HAVE A CONTEST!
YEAH!!
OKAY!
WHOEVER PLUGS THEIR EARS HARDEST FOR THIRTY SECONDS WINS.
AND ANYONE WHO HEARS ANYTHING LOSES. GOT IT! STARTING NOW!

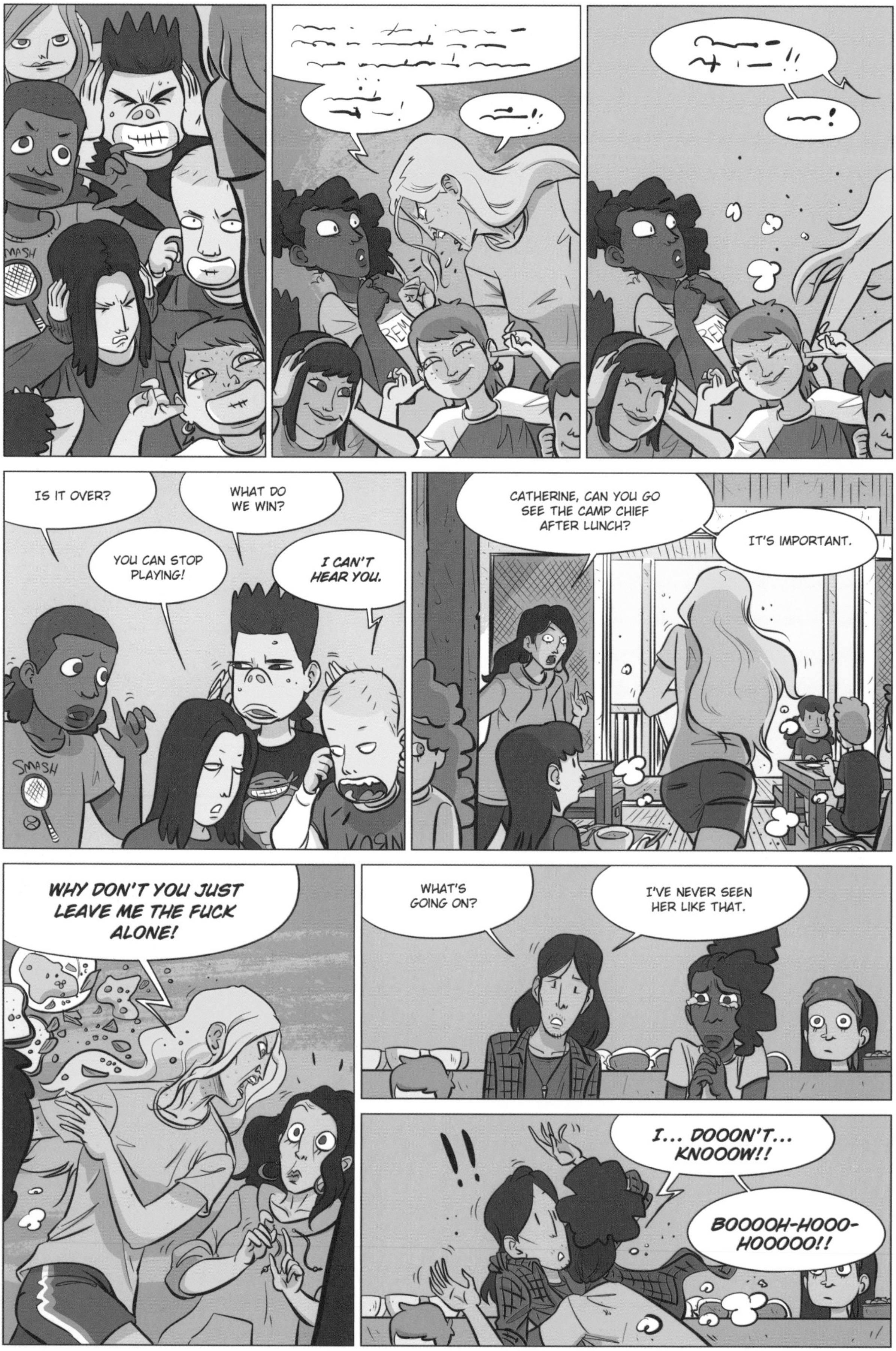
IS IT OVER?
WHAT DO WE WIN?
YOU CAN STOP PLAYING!
I CAN'T HEAR YOU.
CATHERINE, CAN YOU GO SEE THE CAMP CHIEF AFTER LUNCH?
IT'S IMPORTANT.
WHY DON'T YOU JUST LEAVE ME THE FUCK ALONE!
WHAT'S GOING ON?
I'VE NEVER SEEN HER LIKE THAT.
I... DOOON'T... KNOOOW!!
BOOOOH-HOOO-HOOOOO!!

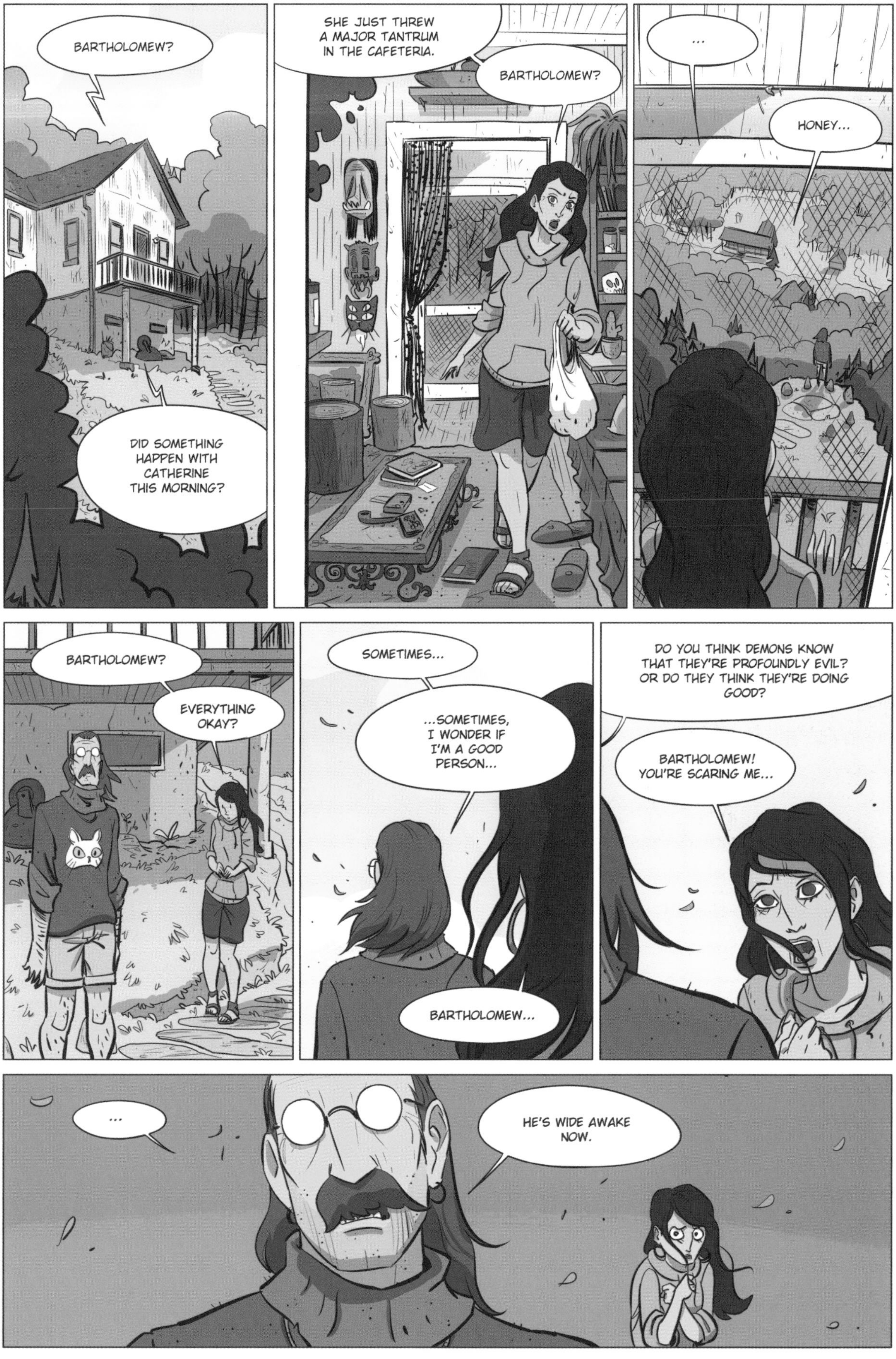
BARTHOLOMEW?
DID SOMETHING HAPPEN WITH CATHERINE THIS MORNING?
SHE JUST THREW A MAJOR TANTRUM IN THE CAFETERIA.
BARTHOLOMEW?
...
HONEY...
BARTHOLOMEW?
EVERYTHING OKAY?
SOMETIMES...
...SOMETIMES, I WONDER IF I'M A GOOD PERSON...
BARTHOLOMEW...
DO YOU THINK DEMONS KNOW THAT THEY'RE PROFOUNDLY EVIL? OR DO THEY THINK THEY'RE DOING GOOD?
BARTHOLOMEW! YOU'RE SCARING ME...
...
HE'S WIDE AWAKE NOW.

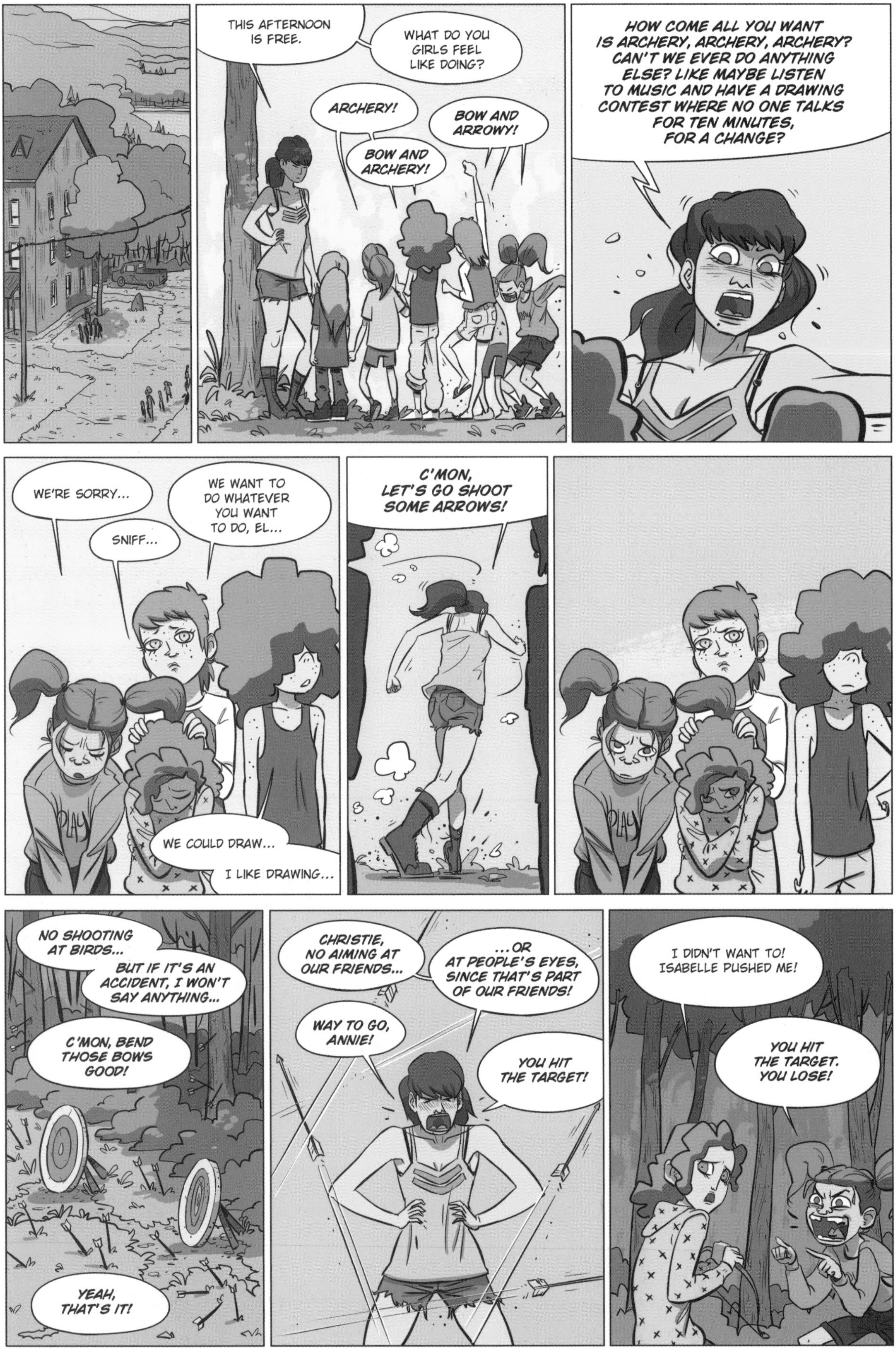
THIS AFTERNOON IS FREE.
WHAT DO YOU GIRLS FEEL LIKE DOING?
ARCHERY!
BOW AND ARCHERY!
BOW AND ARROWY!
HOW COME ALL YOU WANT IS ARCHERY, ARCHERY, ARCHERY? CAN'T WE EVER DO ANYTHING ELSE? LIKE MAYBE LISTEN TO MUSIC AND HAVE A DRAWING CONTEST WHERE NO ONE TALKS FOR TEN MINUTES, FOR A CHANGE?
WE'RE SORRY...
SNIFF...
WE WANT TO DO WHATEVER YOU WANT TO DO, EL...
WE COULD DRAW...
I LIKE DRAWING...
C'MON, LET'S GO SHOOT SOME ARROWS!
NO SHOOTING AT BIRDS...
BUT IF IT'S AN ACCIDENT, I WON'T SAY ANYTHING...
C'MON, BEND THOSE BOWS GOOD!
YEAH, THAT'S IT!
CHRISTIE, NO AIMING AT OUR FRIENDS...
...OR AT PEOPLE'S EYES, SINCE THAT'S PART OF OUR FRIENDS!
WAY TO GO, ANNIE!
YOU HIT THE TARGET!
I DIDN'T WANT TO! ISABELLE PUSHED ME!
YOU HIT THE TARGET. YOU LOSE!

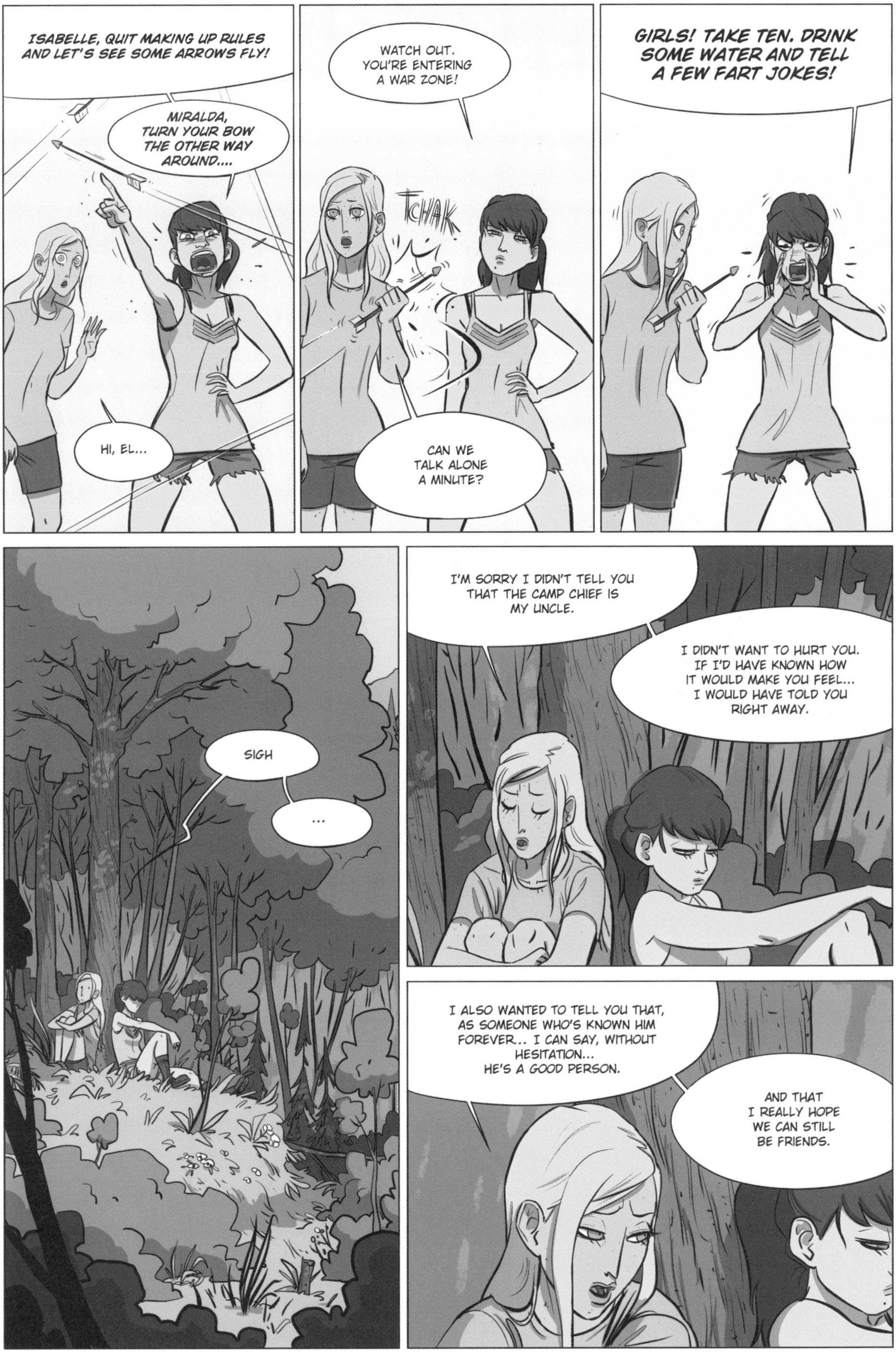
ISABELLE, QUIT MAKING UP RULES AND LET'S SEE SOME ARROWS FLY!
MIRALDA, TURN YOUR BOW THE OTHER WAY AROUND....
HI, EL...
WATCH OUT. YOU'RE ENTERING A WAR ZONE!
TCHAK
CAN WE TALK ALONE A MINUTE?
GIRLS! TAKE TEN. DRINK SOME WATER AND TELL A FEW FART JOKES!
SIGH
...
I'M SORRY I DIDN'T TELL YOU THAT THE CAMP CHIEF IS MY UNCLE.
I DIDN'T WANT TO HURT YOU. IF I'D HAVE KNOWN HOW IT WOULD MAKE YOU FEEL... I WOULD HAVE TOLD YOU RIGHT AWAY.
I ALSO WANTED TO TELL YOU THAT, AS SOMEONE WHO'S KNOWN HIM FOREVER... I CAN SAY, WITHOUT HESITATION... HE'S A GOOD PERSON.
AND THAT I REALLY HOPE WE CAN STILL BE FRIENDS.

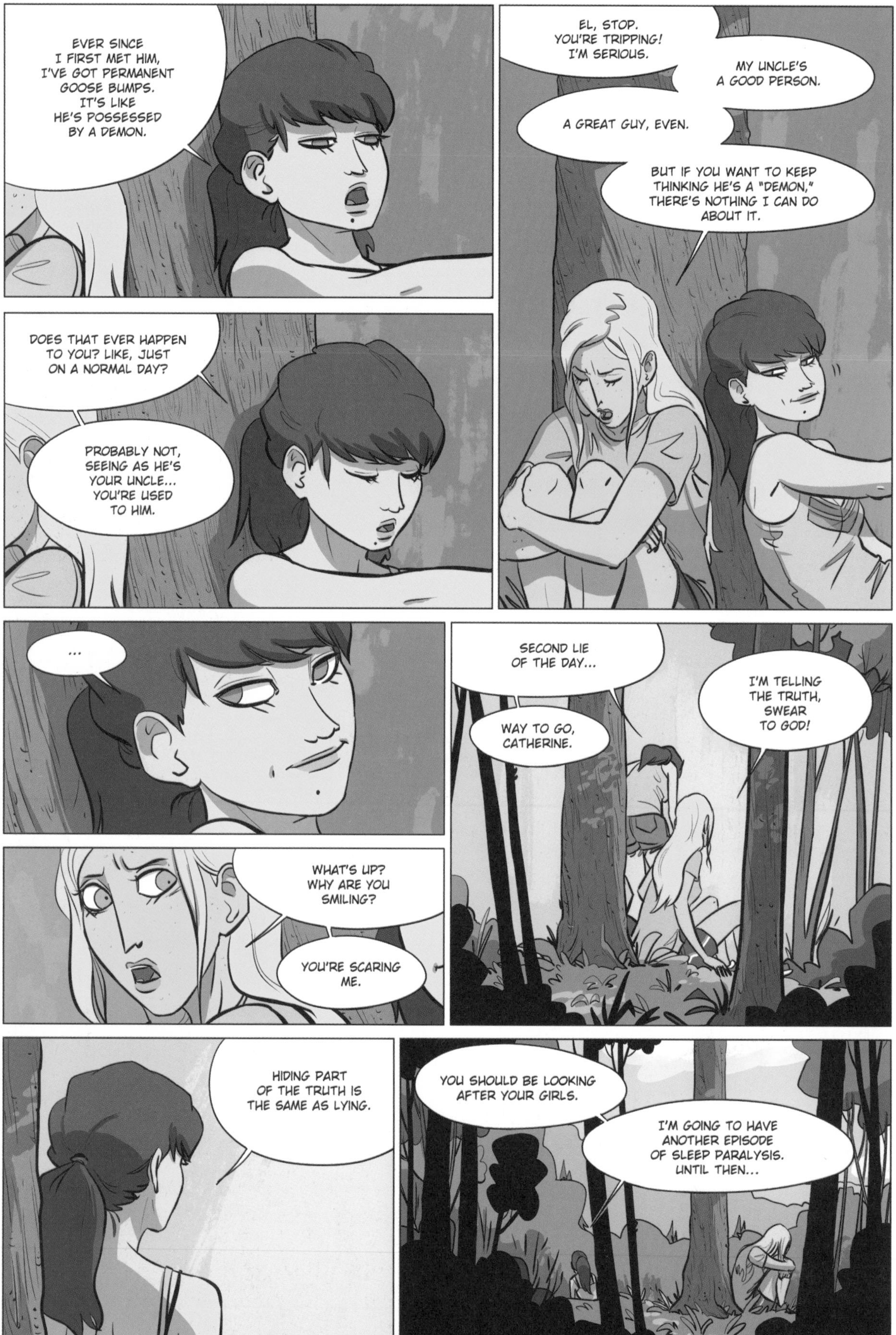
EVER SINCE I FIRST MET HIM, I'VE GOT PERMANENT GOOSE BUMPS. IT'S LIKE HE'S POSSESSED BY A DEMON.
EL, STOP. YOU'RE TRIPPING! I'M SERIOUS.
MY UNCLE'S A GOOD PERSON.
A GREAT GUY, EVEN.
BUT IF YOU WANT TO KEEP THINKING HE'S A "DEMON," THERE'S NOTHING I CAN DO ABOUT IT.
DOES THAT EVER HAPPEN TO YOU? LIKE, JUST ON A NORMAL DAY?
PROBABLY NOT, SEEING AS HE'S YOUR UNCLE... YOU'RE USED TO HIM.
...
WHAT'S UP? WHY ARE YOU SMILING?
YOU'RE SCARING ME.
SECOND LIE OF THE DAY...
WAY TO GO, CATHERINE.
I'M TELLING THE TRUTH, SWEAR TO GOD!
HIDING PART OF THE TRUTH IS THE SAME AS LYING.
YOU SHOULD BE LOOKING AFTER YOUR GIRLS.
I'M GOING TO HAVE ANOTHER EPISODE OF SLEEP PARALYSIS. UNTIL THEN...

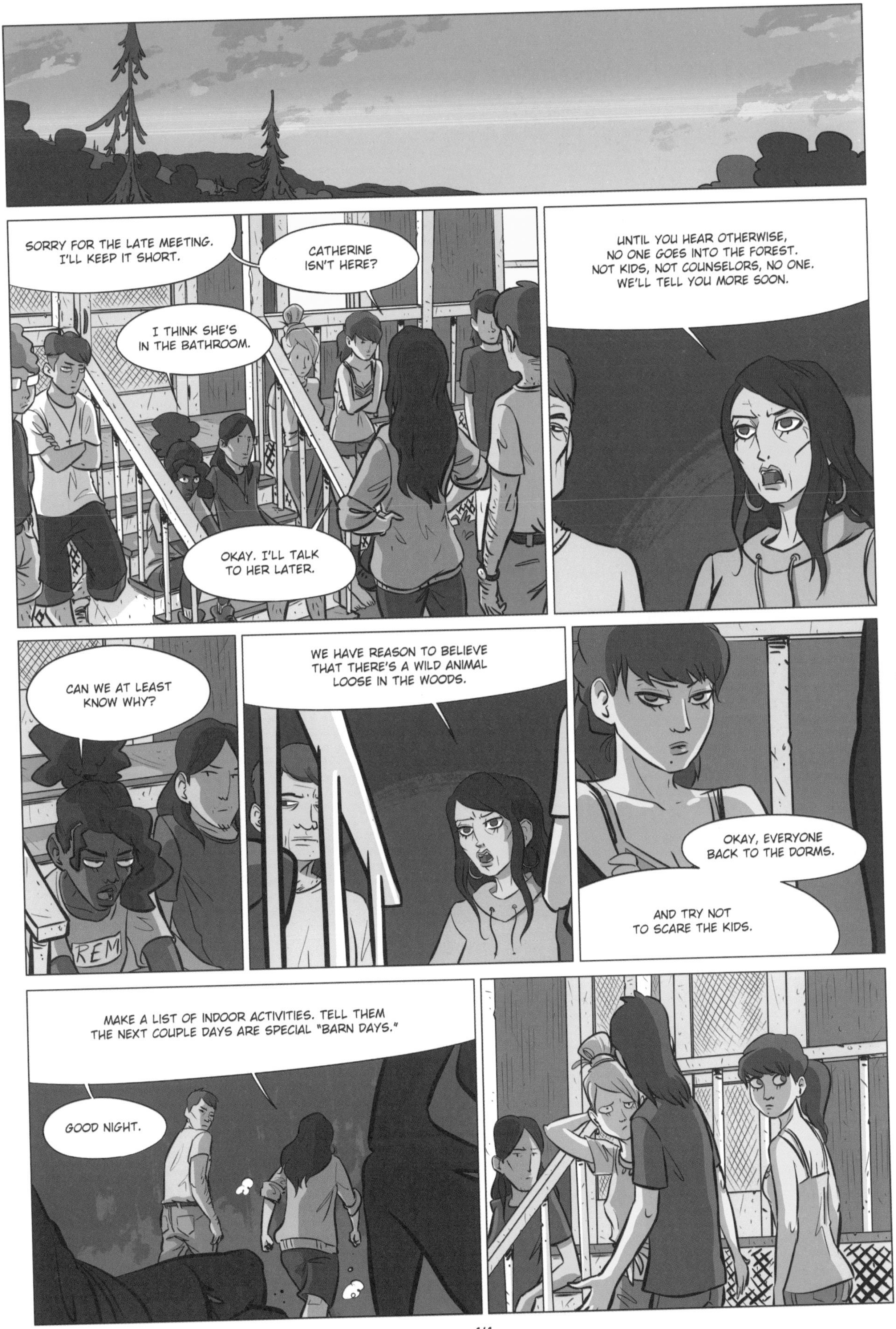
SORRY FOR THE LATE MEETING. I'LL KEEP IT SHORT.
CATHERINE ISN'T HERE?
I THINK SHE'S IN THE BATHROOM.
OKAY. I'LL TALK TO HER LATER.
UNTIL YOU HEAR OTHERWISE, NO ONE GOES INTO THE FOREST. NOT KIDS, NOT COUNSELORS, NO ONE. WE'LL TELL YOU MORE SOON.
CAN WE AT LEAST KNOW WHY?
REM
WE HAVE REASON TO BELIEVE THAT THERE'S A WILD ANIMAL LOOSE IN THE WOODS.
OKAY, EVERYONE BACK TO THE DORMS.
AND TRY NOT TO SCARE THE KIDS.
MAKE A LIST OF INDOOR ACTIVITIES. TELL THEM THE NEXT COUPLE DAYS ARE SPECIAL "BARN DAYS."
GOOD NIGHT.

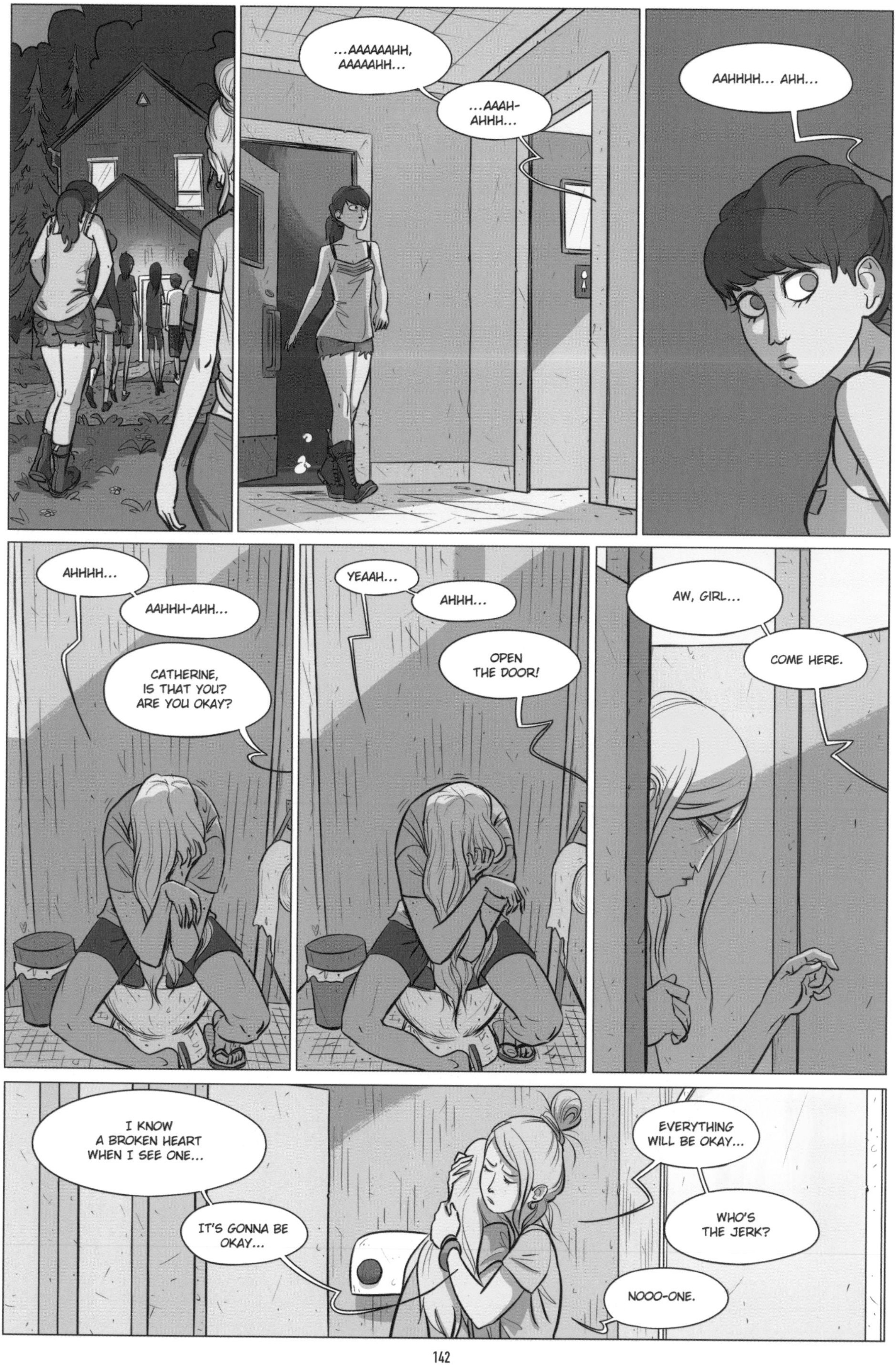
...AAAAAAHH,
AAAAAHH...
...AAAH-
AHHH...
AAHHHH... AHH...
AHHHH...
AAHHH-AHH...
CATHERINE,
IS THAT YOU?
ARE YOU OKAY?
YEAAH...
AHHH...
OPEN
THE DOOR!
AW, GIRL...
COME HERE.
I KNOW
A BROKEN HEART
WHEN I SEE ONE...
IT'S GONNA BE
OKAY...
EVERYTHING
WILL BE OKAY...
WHO'S
THE JERK?
NOOO-ONE.

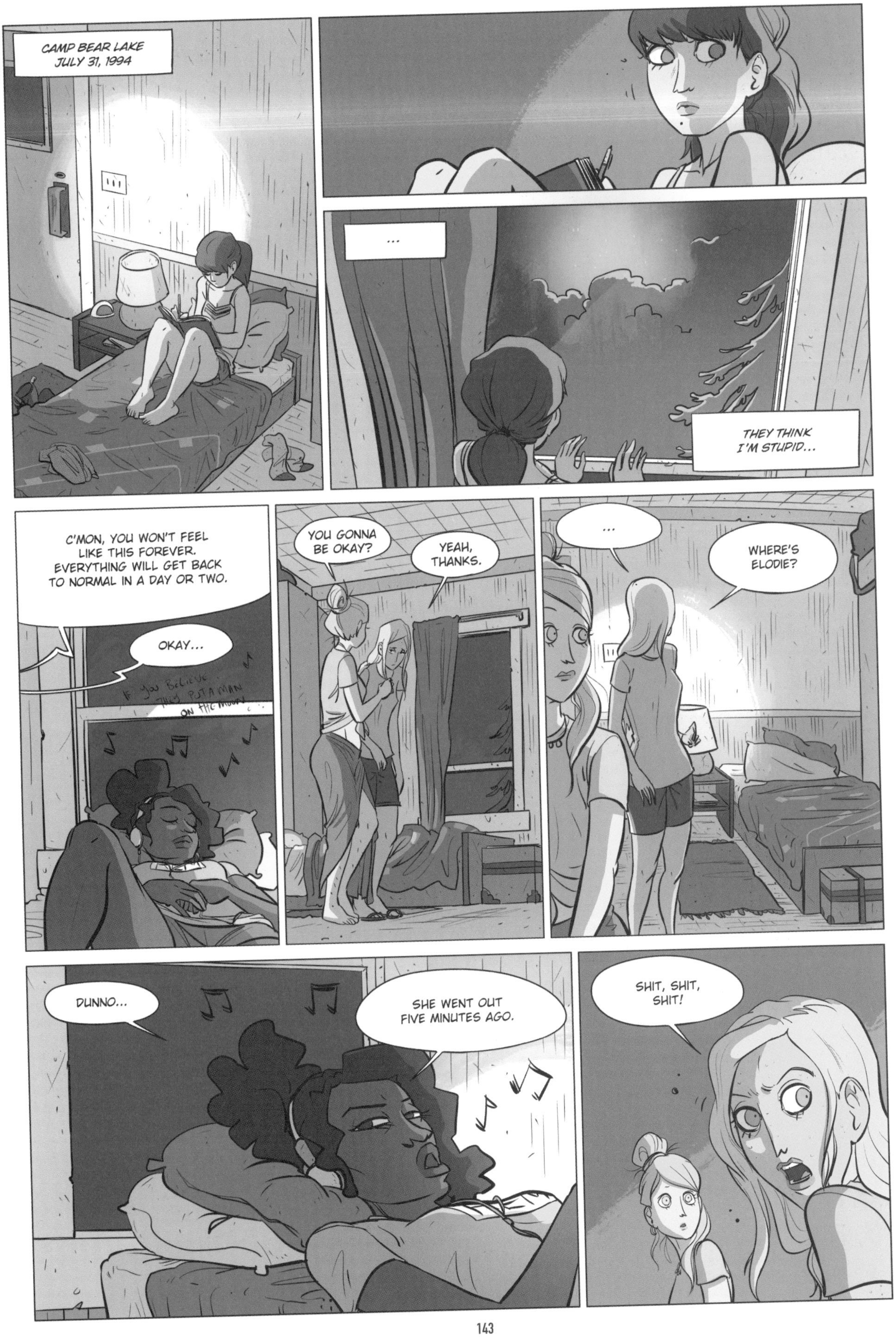
CAMP BEAR LAKE
JULY 31, 1994
...
THEY THINK I'M STUPID...
C'MON, YOU WON'T FEEL LIKE THIS FOREVER. EVERYTHING WILL GET BACK TO NORMAL IN A DAY OR TWO.
OKAY...
IF YOU BELIEVE THEY PUT A MAN ON THE MOON
YOU GONNA BE OKAY?
YEAH, THANKS.
...
WHERE'S ELODIE?
DUNNO...
SHE WENT OUT FIVE MINUTES AGO.
SHIT, SHIT, SHIT!

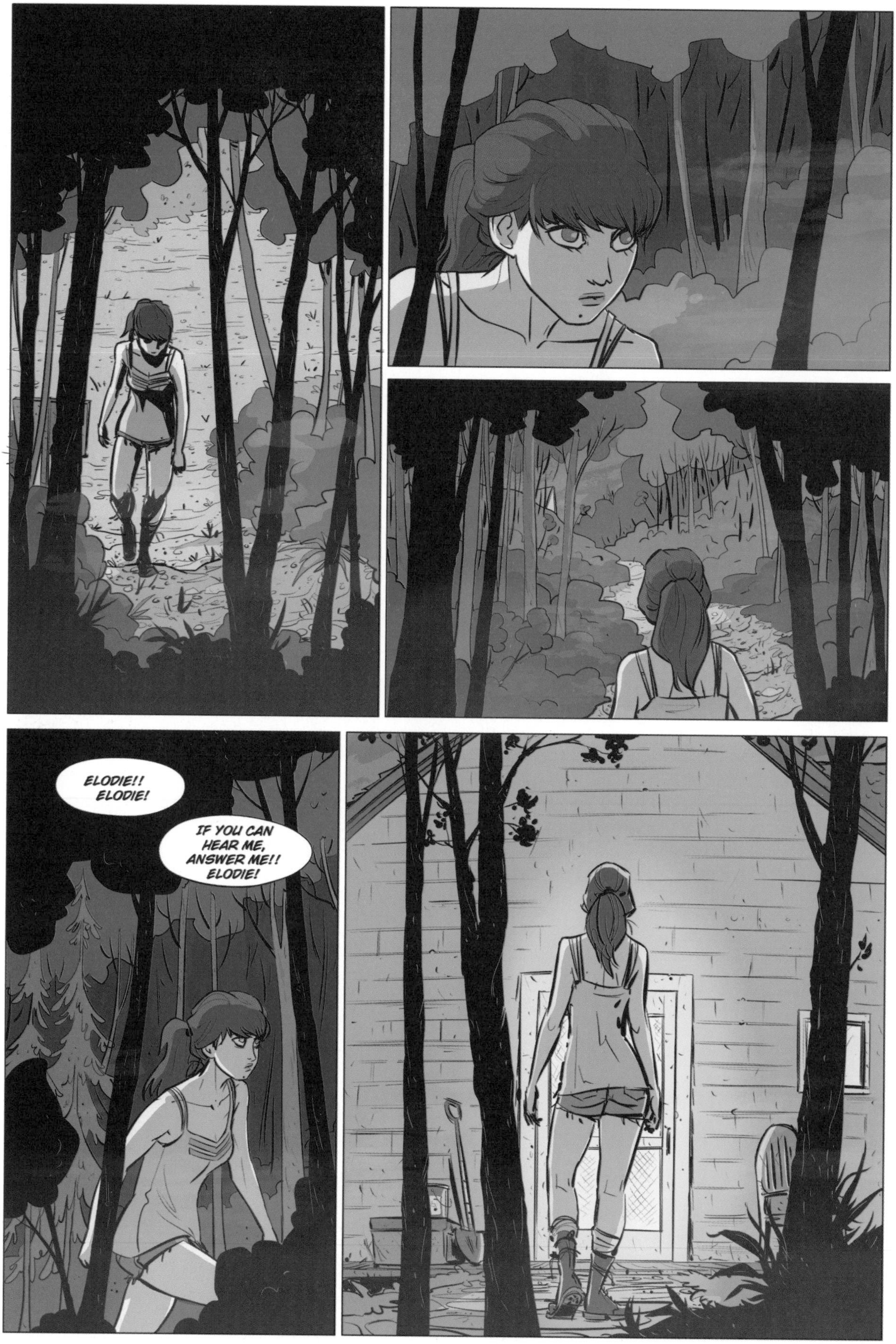
ELODIE!! ELODIE!
IF YOU CAN HEAR ME, ANSWER ME!! ELODIE!

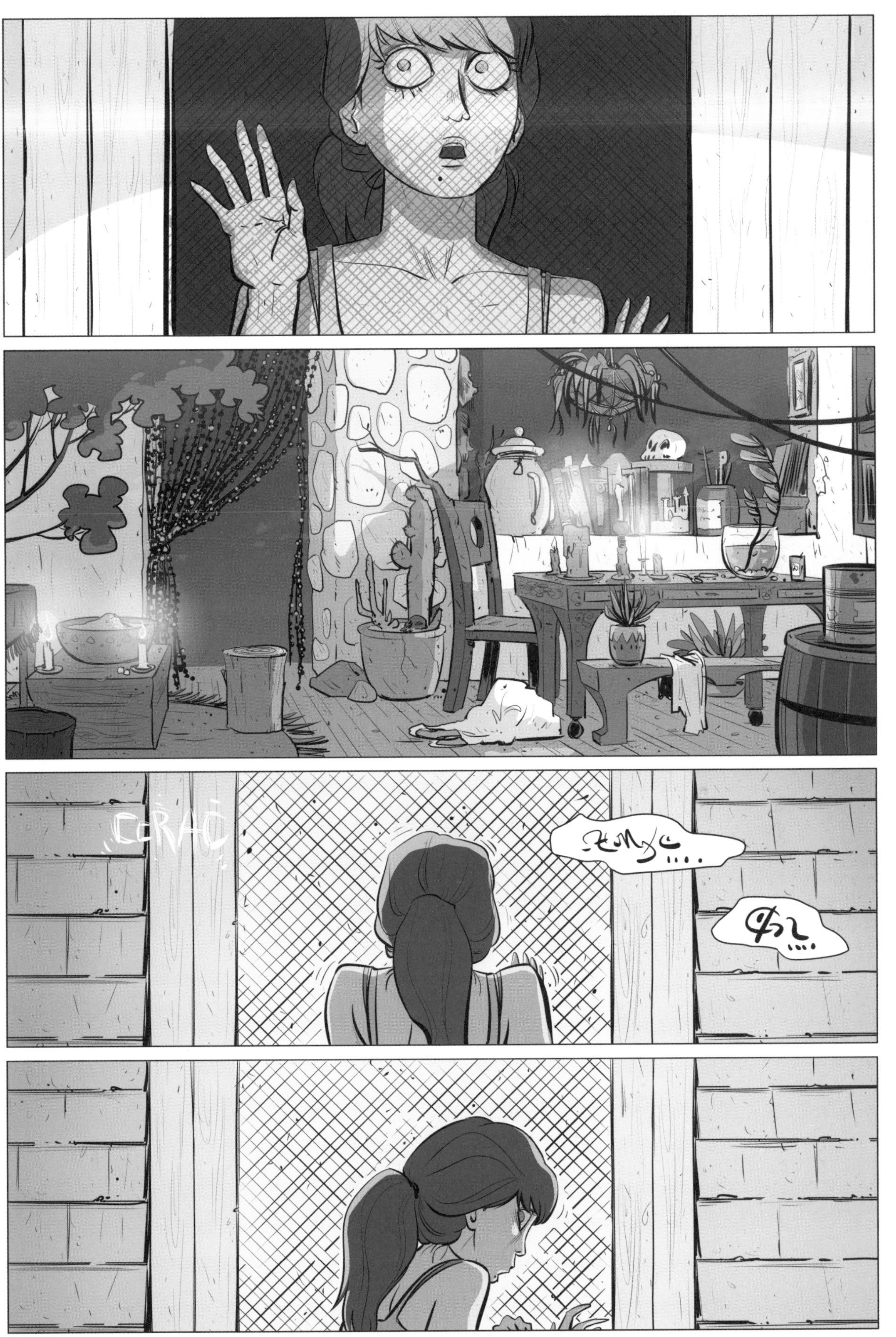
CRAC

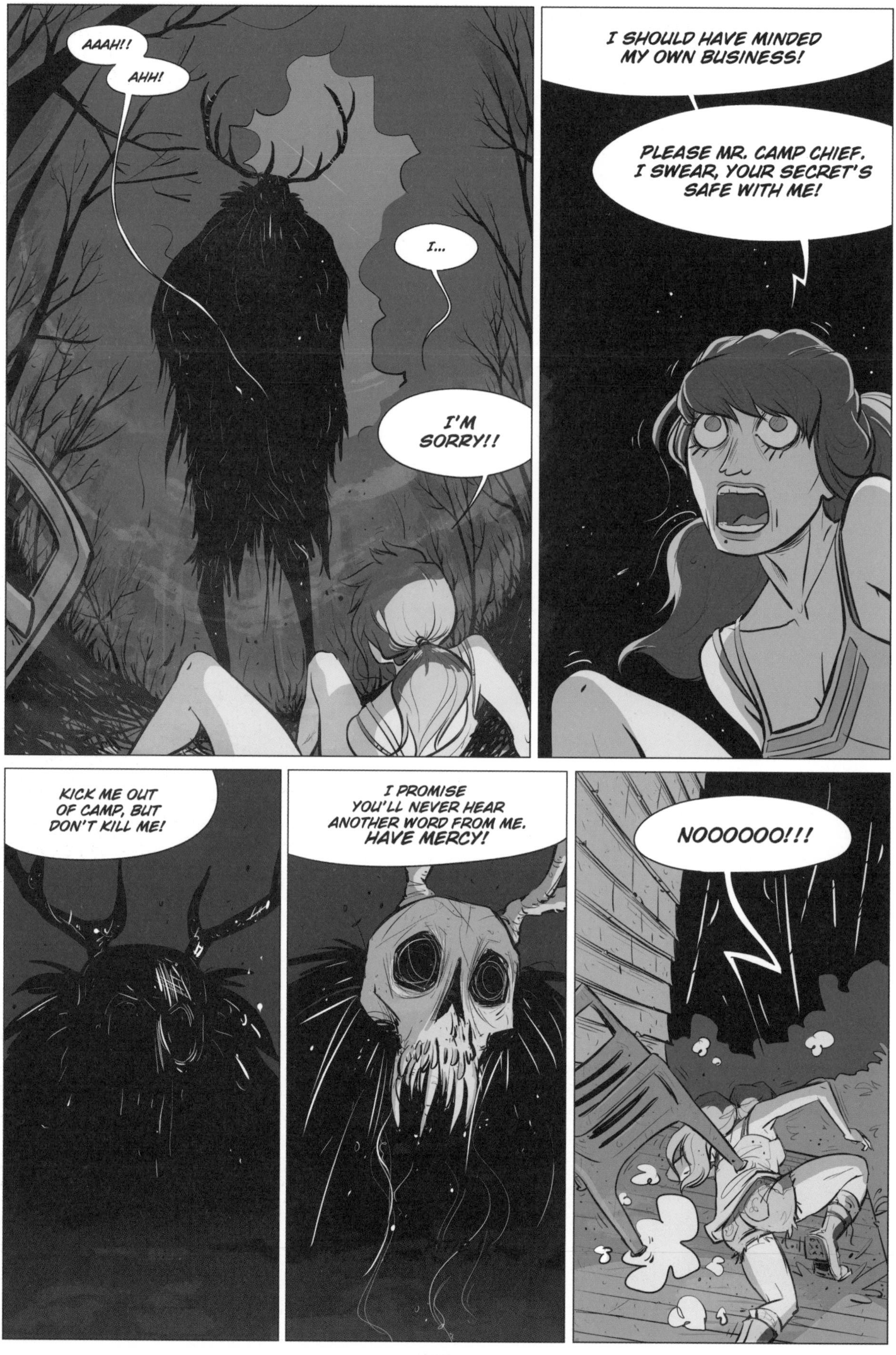
AAAH!!
AHH!
I...
I'M SORRY!!
I SHOULD HAVE MINDED MY OWN BUSINESS!
PLEASE MR. CAMP CHIEF. I SWEAR, YOUR SECRET'S SAFE WITH ME!
KICK ME OUT OF CAMP, BUT DON'T KILL ME!
I PROMISE YOU'LL NEVER HEAR ANOTHER WORD FROM ME. HAVE MERCY!
NOOOOOO!!!

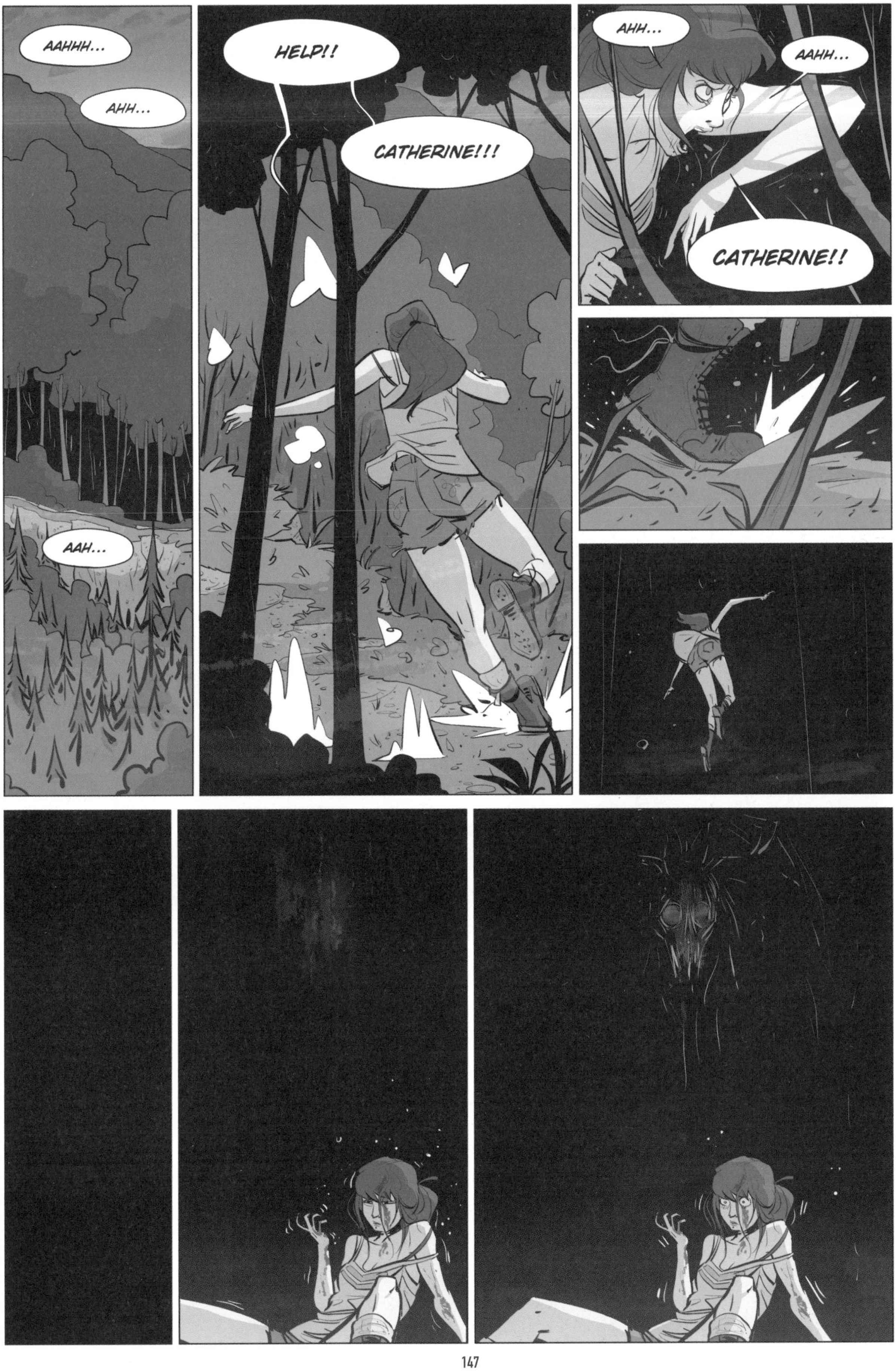
AAHHH...
AHH...
AAH...
HELP!!
CATHERINE!!!
AHH...
AAHH...
CATHERINE!!

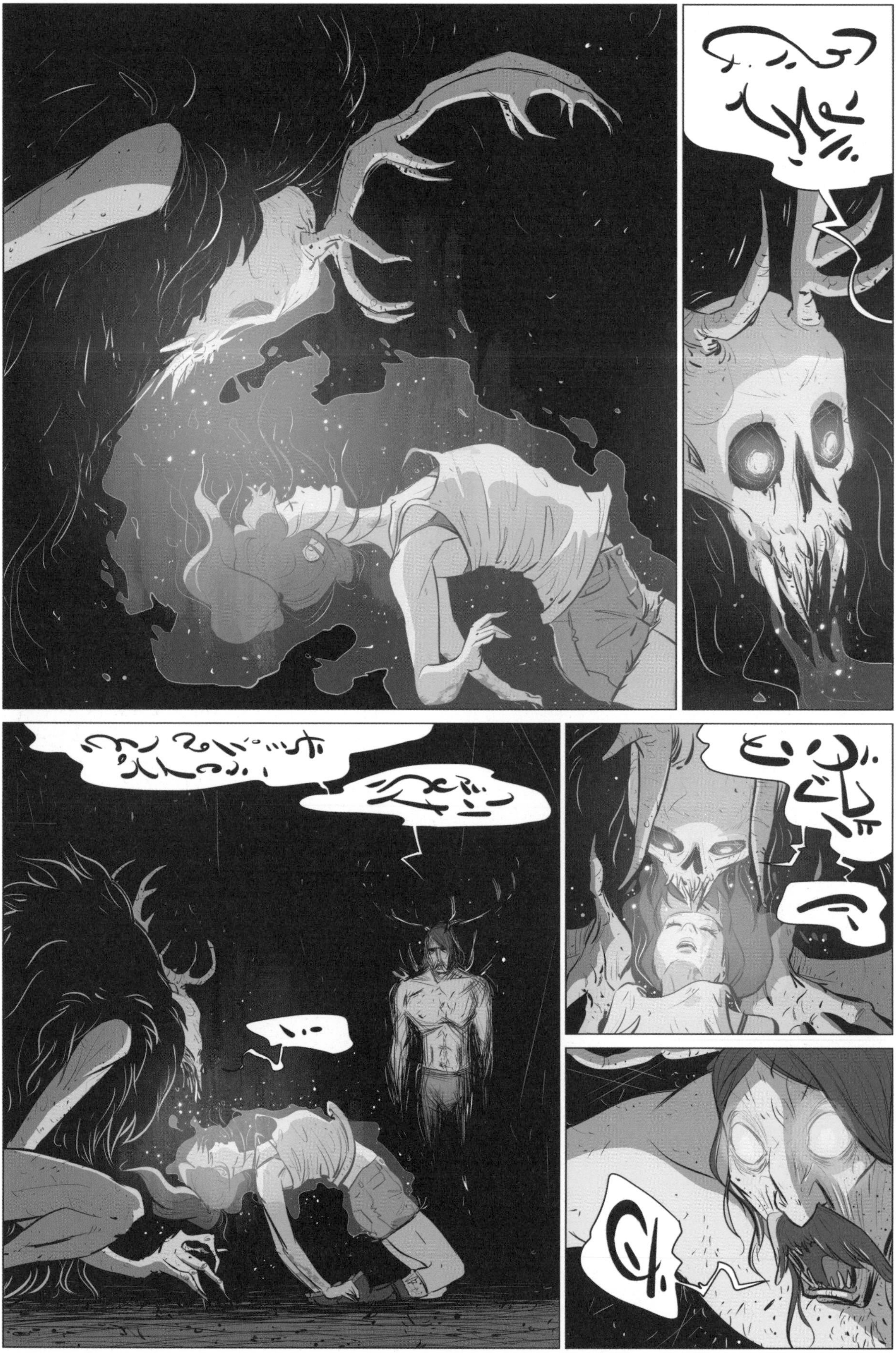

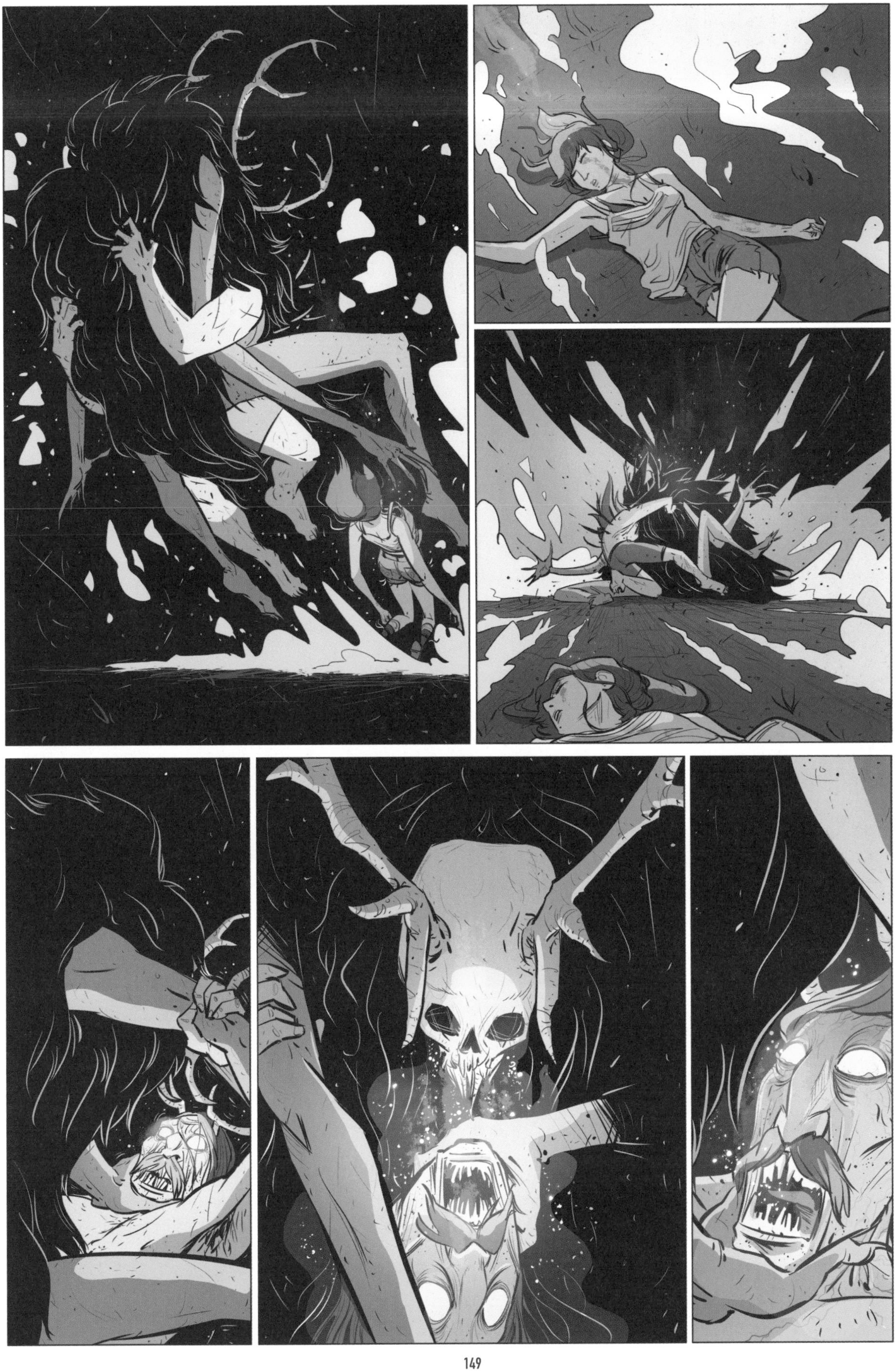

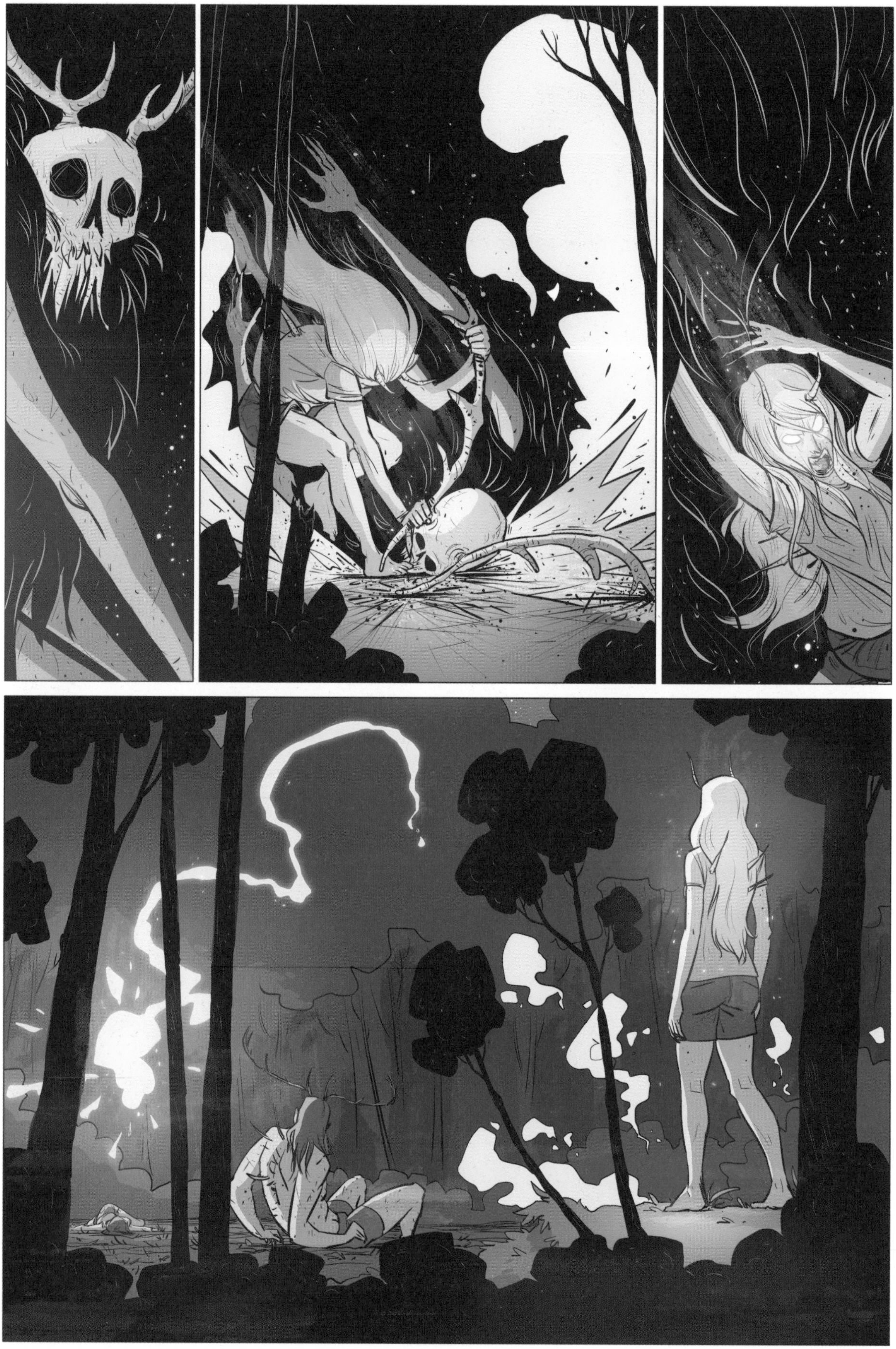

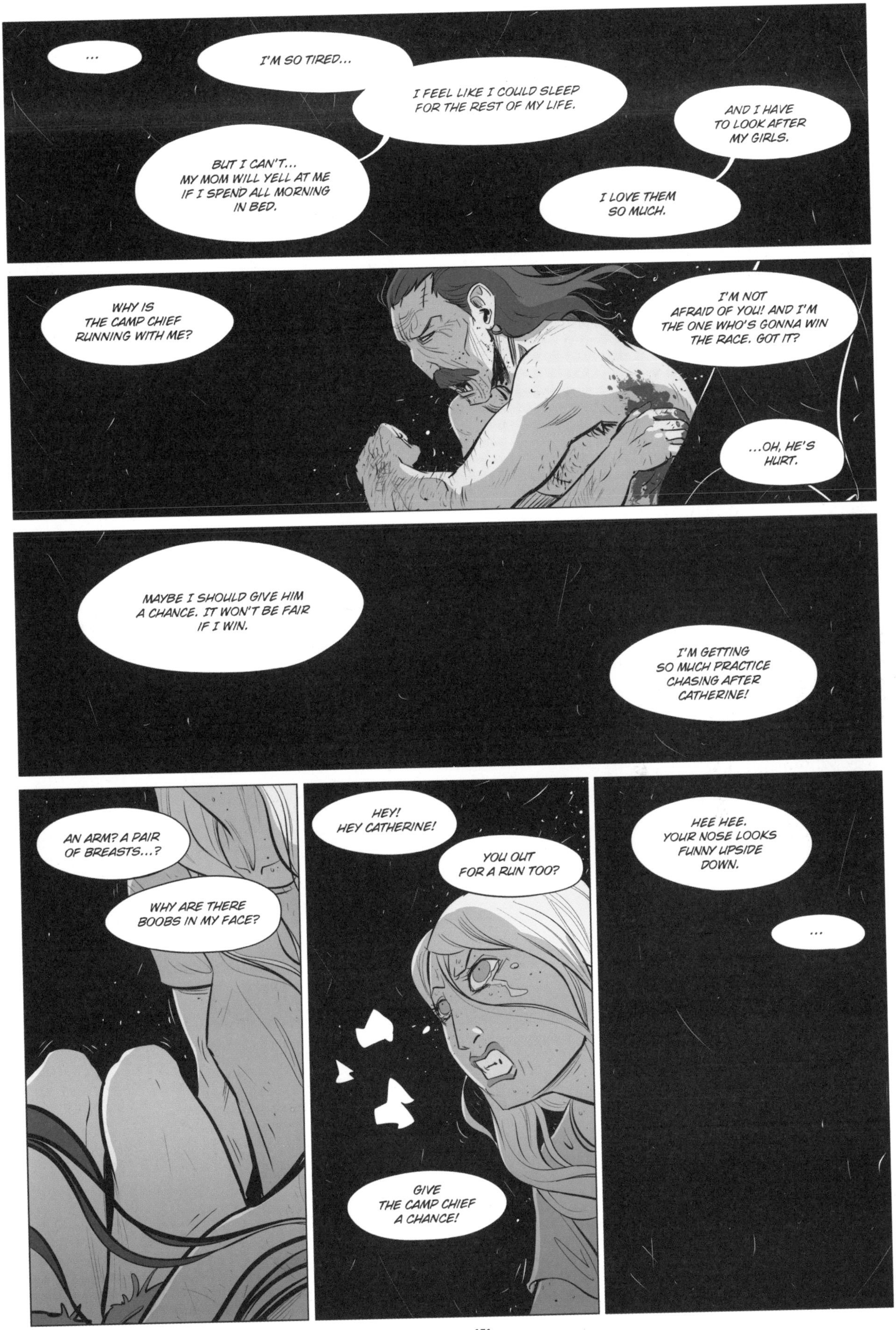
...
I'M SO TIRED...
I FEEL LIKE I COULD SLEEP FOR THE REST OF MY LIFE.
BUT I CAN'T... MY MOM WILL YELL AT ME IF I SPEND ALL MORNING IN BED.
AND I HAVE TO LOOK AFTER MY GIRLS.
I LOVE THEM SO MUCH.
WHY IS THE CAMP CHIEF RUNNING WITH ME?
I'M NOT AFRAID OF YOU! AND I'M THE ONE WHO'S GONNA WIN THE RACE. GOT IT?
...OH, HE'S HURT.
MAYBE I SHOULD GIVE HIM A CHANCE. IT WON'T BE FAIR IF I WIN.
I'M GETTING SO MUCH PRACTICE CHASING AFTER CATHERINE!
AN ARM? A PAIR OF BREASTS...?
WHY ARE THERE BOOBS IN MY FACE?
HEY! HEY CATHERINE!
YOU OUT FOR A RUN TOO?
GIVE THE CAMP CHIEF A CHANCE!
HEE HEE. YOUR NOSE LOOKS FUNNY UPSIDE DOWN.
...

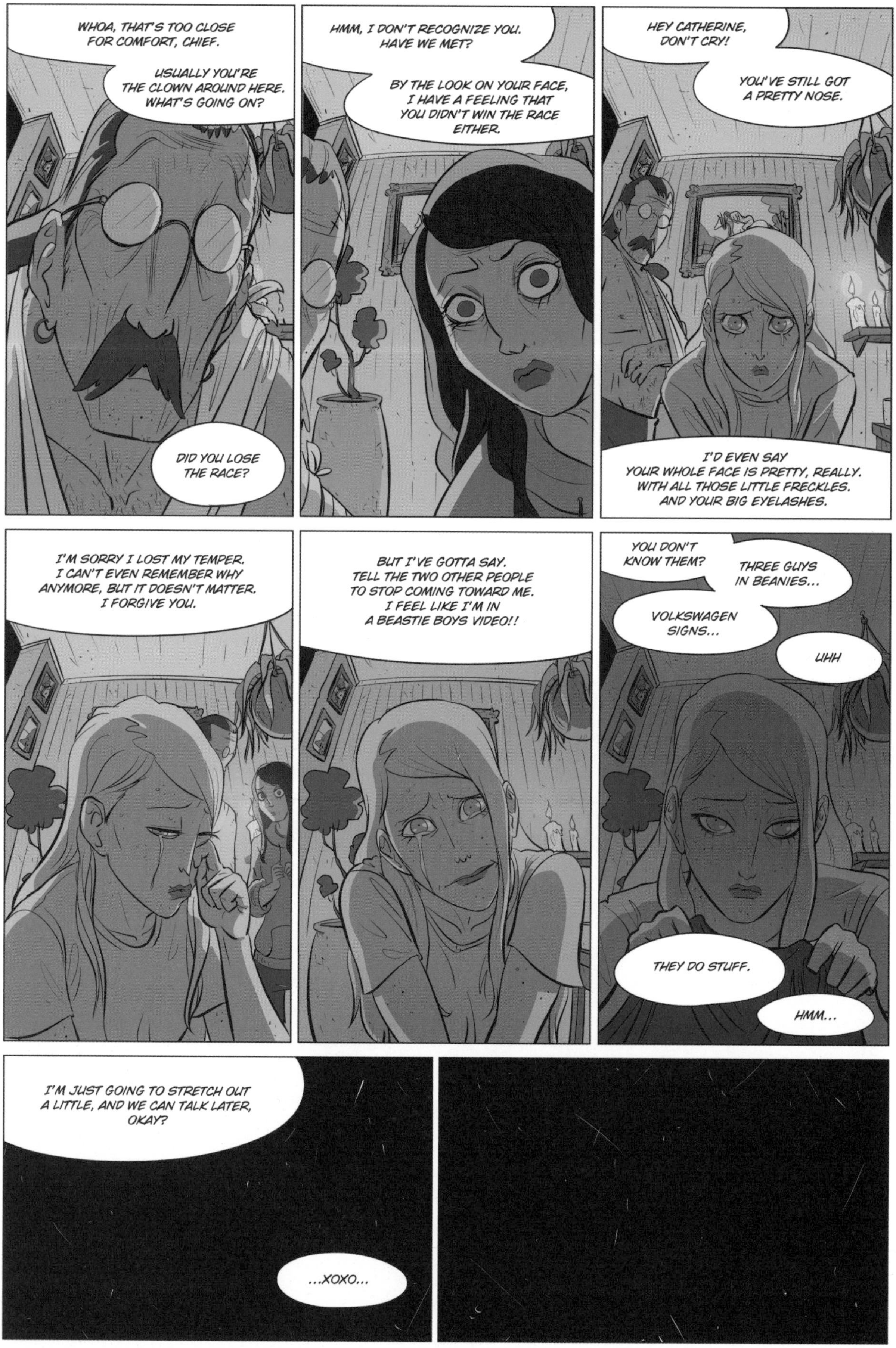
WHOA, THAT'S TOO CLOSE FOR COMFORT, CHIEF.
USUALLY YOU'RE THE CLOWN AROUND HERE. WHAT'S GOING ON?
DID YOU LOSE THE RACE?
HMM, I DON'T RECOGNIZE YOU. HAVE WE MET?
BY THE LOOK ON YOUR FACE, I HAVE A FEELING THAT YOU DIDN'T WIN THE RACE EITHER.
HEY CATHERINE, DON'T CRY!
YOU'VE STILL GOT A PRETTY NOSE.
I'D EVEN SAY YOUR WHOLE FACE IS PRETTY, REALLY. WITH ALL THOSE LITTLE FRECKLES. AND YOUR BIG EYELASHES.
I'M SORRY I LOST MY TEMPER. I CAN'T EVEN REMEMBER WHY ANYMORE, BUT IT DOESN'T MATTER. I FORGIVE YOU.
BUT I'VE GOTTA SAY. TELL THE TWO OTHER PEOPLE TO STOP COMING TOWARD ME. I FEEL LIKE I'M IN A BEASTIE BOYS VIDEO!!
YOU DON'T KNOW THEM?
THREE GUYS IN BEANIES...
VOLKSWAGEN SIGNS...
UHH
THEY DO STUFF.
HMM...
I'M JUST GOING TO STRETCH OUT A LITTLE, AND WE CAN TALK LATER, OKAY?
...XOXO...

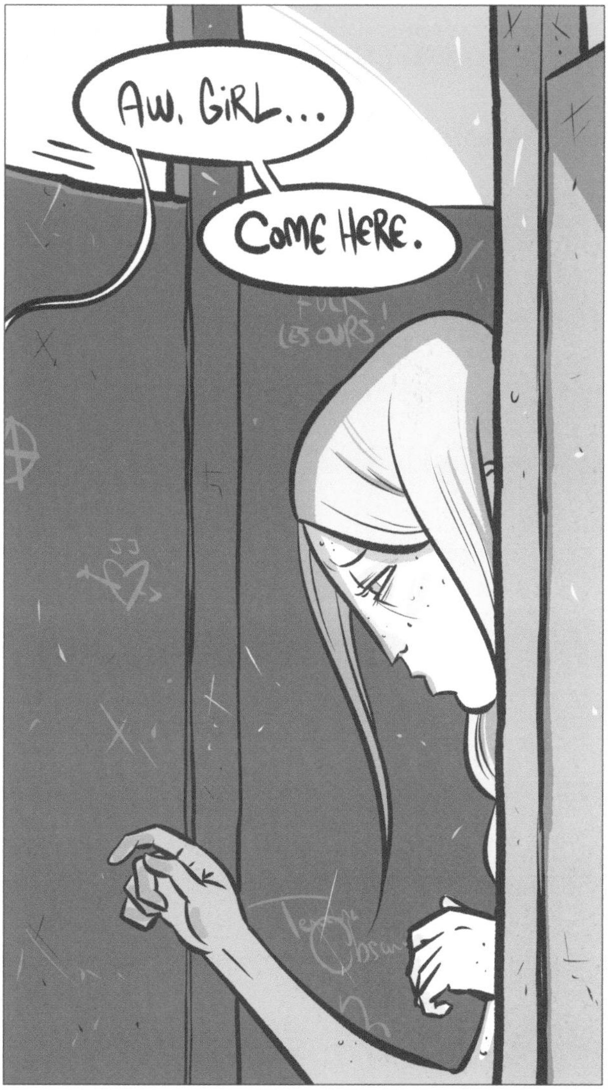
AW, GIRL...
COME HERE.

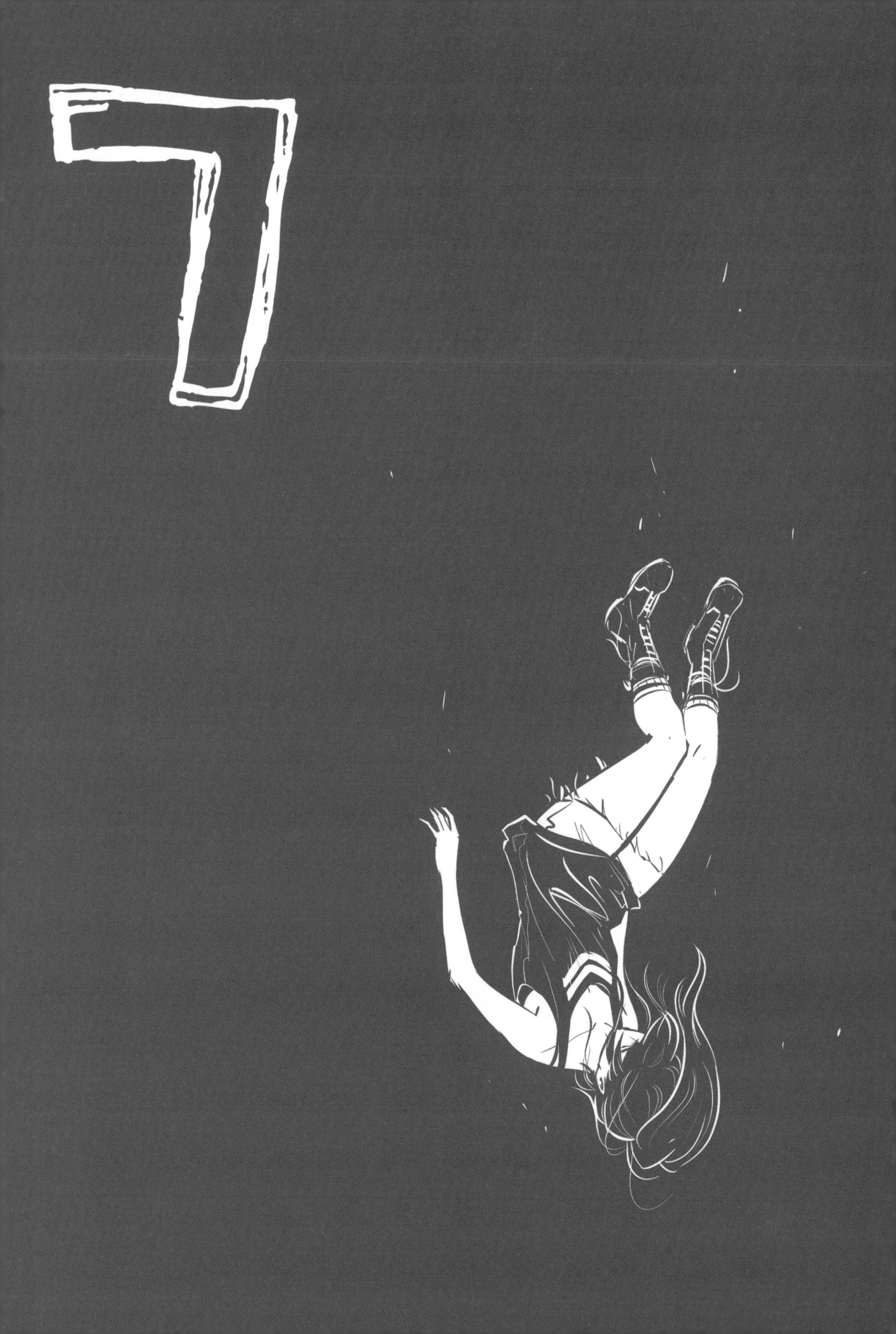
7

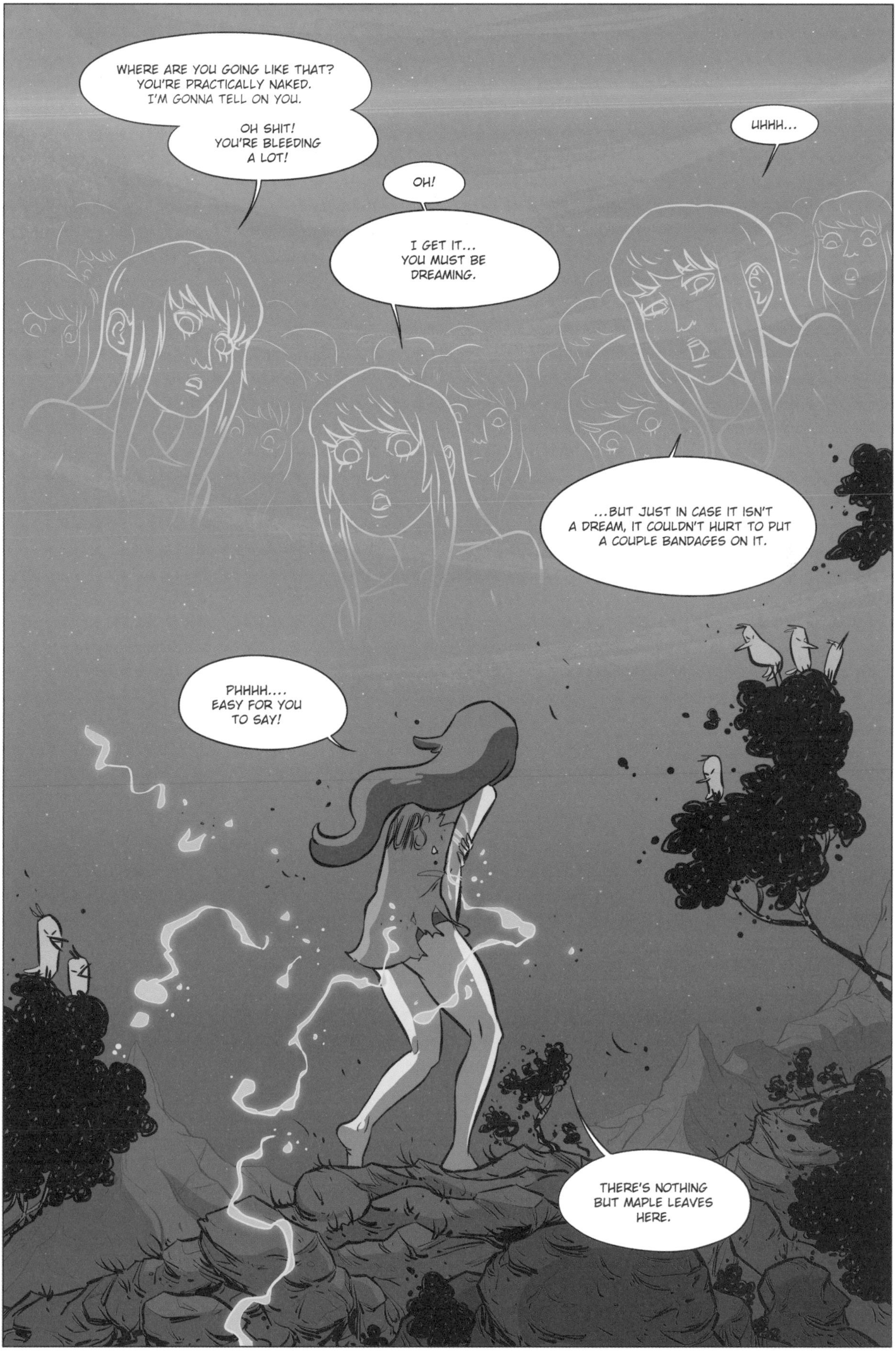

WHERE ARE YOU GOING LIKE THAT? YOU'RE PRACTICALLY NAKED. I'M GONNA TELL ON YOU.
OH SHIT! YOU'RE BLEEDING A LOT!
OH!
I GET IT... YOU MUST BE DREAMING.
UHHH...
...BUT JUST IN CASE IT ISN'T A DREAM, IT COULDN'T HURT TO PUT A COUPLE BANDAGES ON IT.
PHHHH.... EASY FOR YOU TO SAY!
OURS
THERE'S NOTHING BUT MAPLE LEAVES HERE.

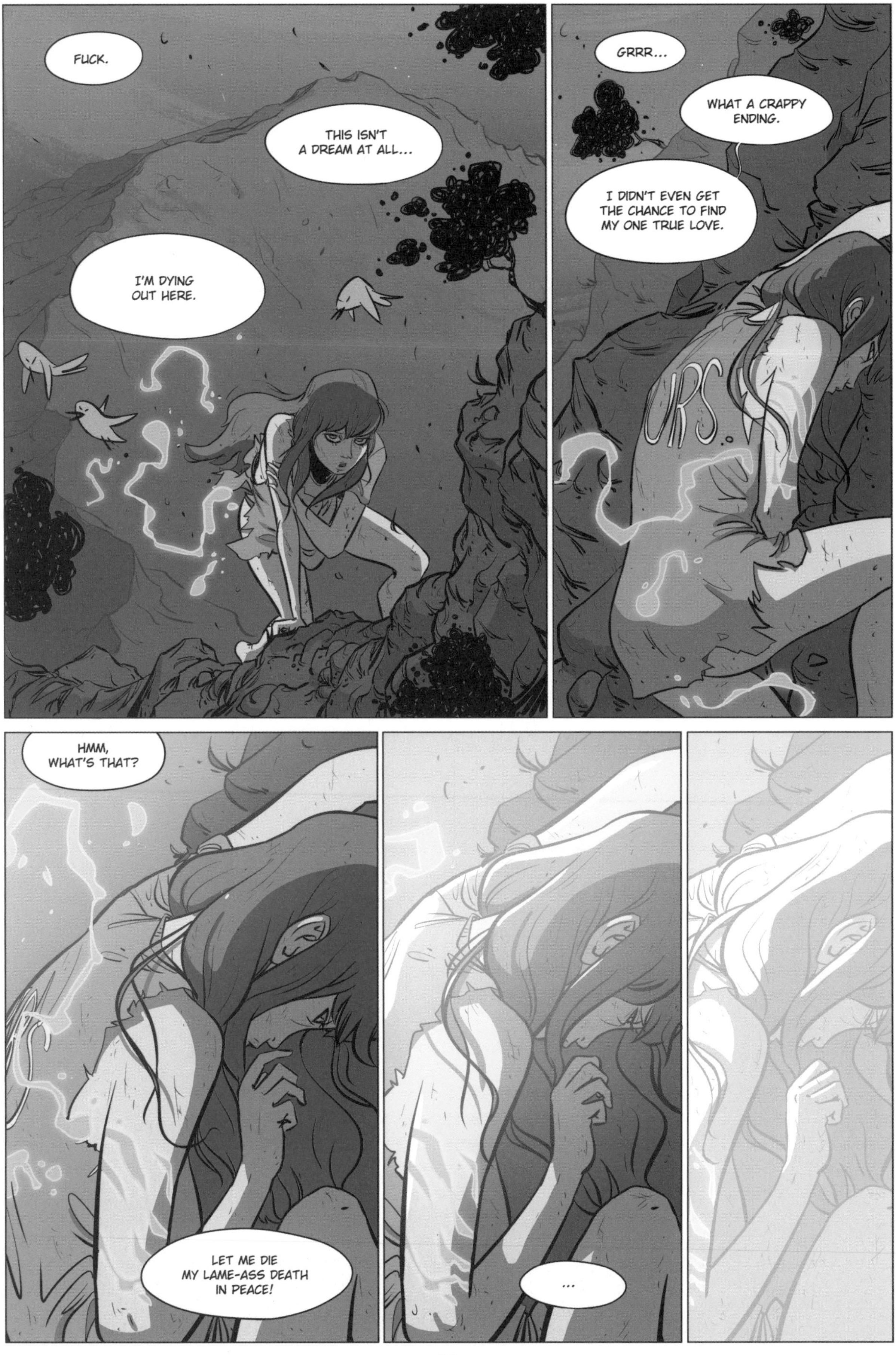
FUCK.
THIS ISN'T A DREAM AT ALL...
I'M DYING OUT HERE.
GRRR...
WHAT A CRAPPY ENDING.
I DIDN'T EVEN GET THE CHANCE TO FIND MY ONE TRUE LOVE.
HMM, WHAT'S THAT?
LET ME DIE MY LAME-ASS DEATH IN PEACE!
...

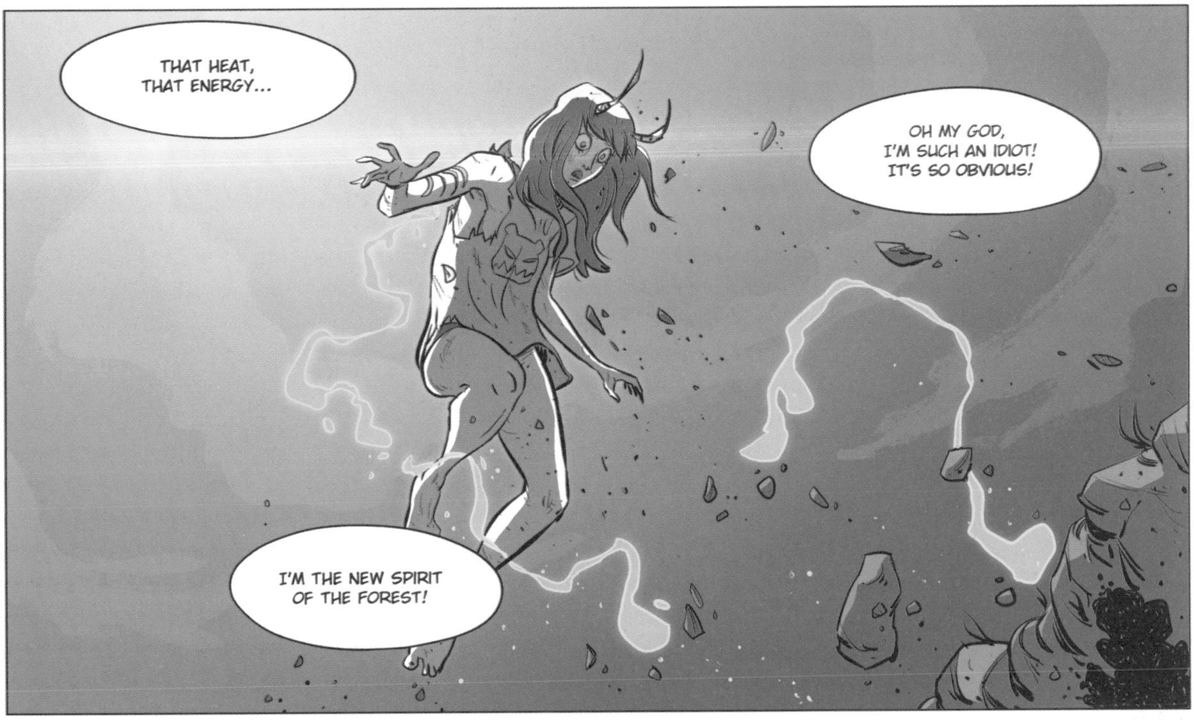
THAT HEAT, THAT ENERGY...
OH MY GOD, I'M SUCH AN IDIOT! IT'S SO OBVIOUS!
I'M THE NEW SPIRIT OF THE FOREST!

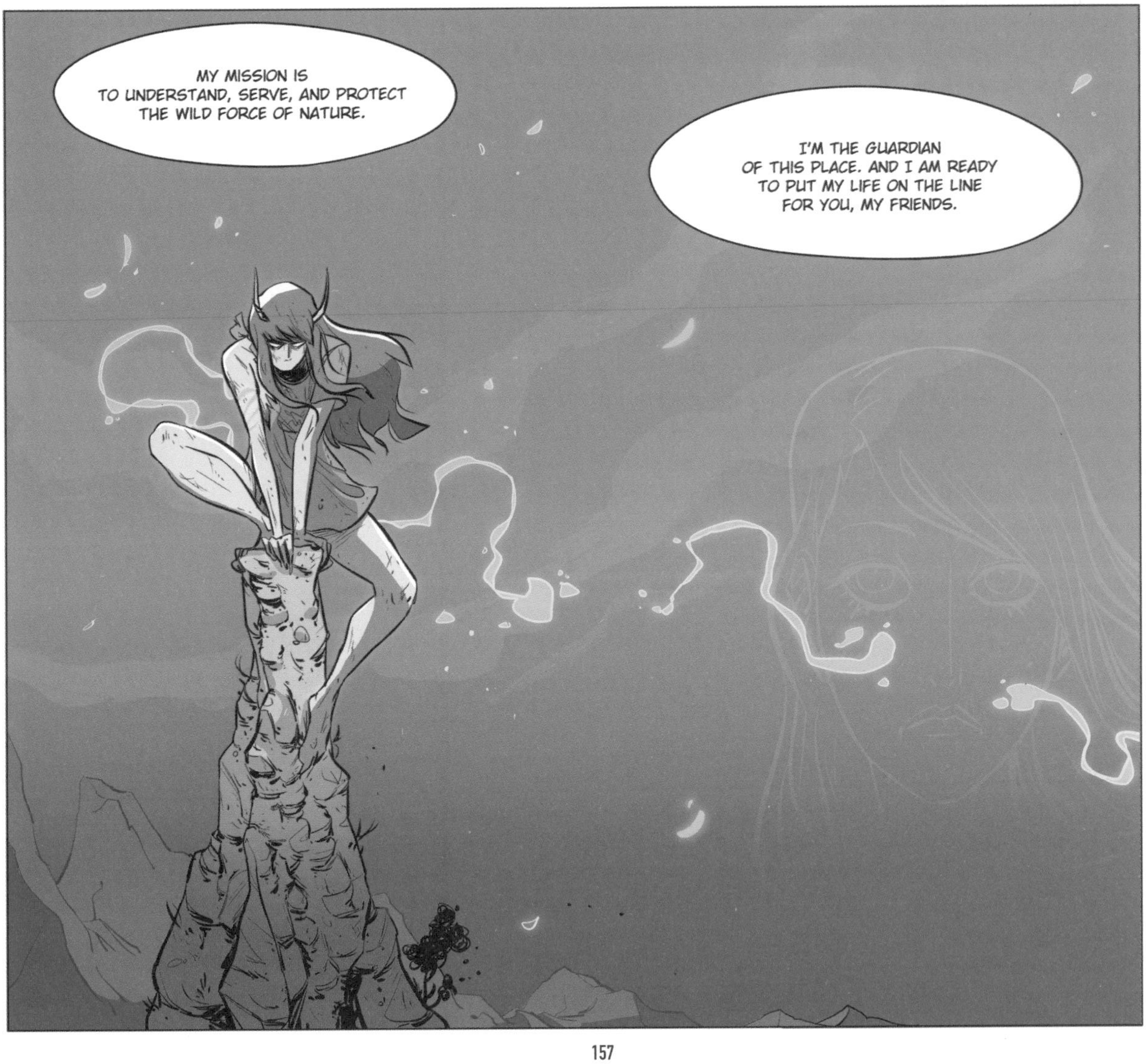
MY MISSION IS TO UNDERSTAND, SERVE, AND PROTECT THE WILD FORCE OF NATURE.
I'M THE GUARDIAN OF THIS PLACE. AND I AM READY TO PUT MY LIFE ON THE LINE FOR YOU, MY FRIENDS.

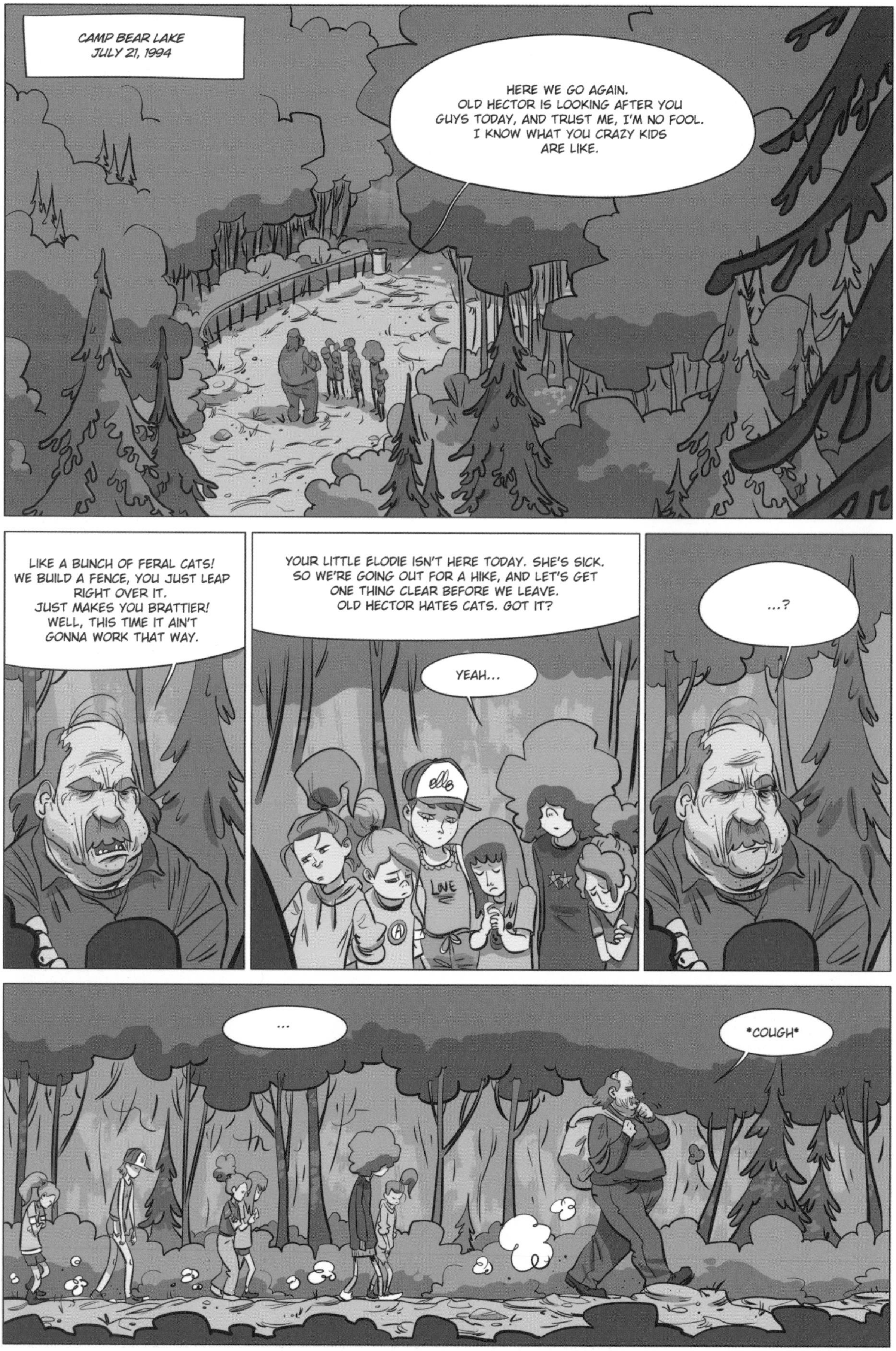
CAMP BEAR LAKE
JULY 21, 1994
HERE WE GO AGAIN. OLD HECTOR IS LOOKING AFTER YOU GUYS TODAY, AND TRUST ME, I'M NO FOOL. I KNOW WHAT YOU CRAZY KIDS ARE LIKE.
LIKE A BUNCH OF FERAL CATS! WE BUILD A FENCE, YOU JUST LEAP RIGHT OVER IT. JUST MAKES YOU BRATTIER! WELL, THIS TIME IT AIN'T GONNA WORK THAT WAY.
YOUR LITTLE ELODIE ISN'T HERE TODAY. SHE'S SICK. SO WE'RE GOING OUT FOR A HIKE, AND LET'S GET ONE THING CLEAR BEFORE WE LEAVE. OLD HECTOR HATES CATS. GOT IT?
YEAH...
...?
...
COUGH

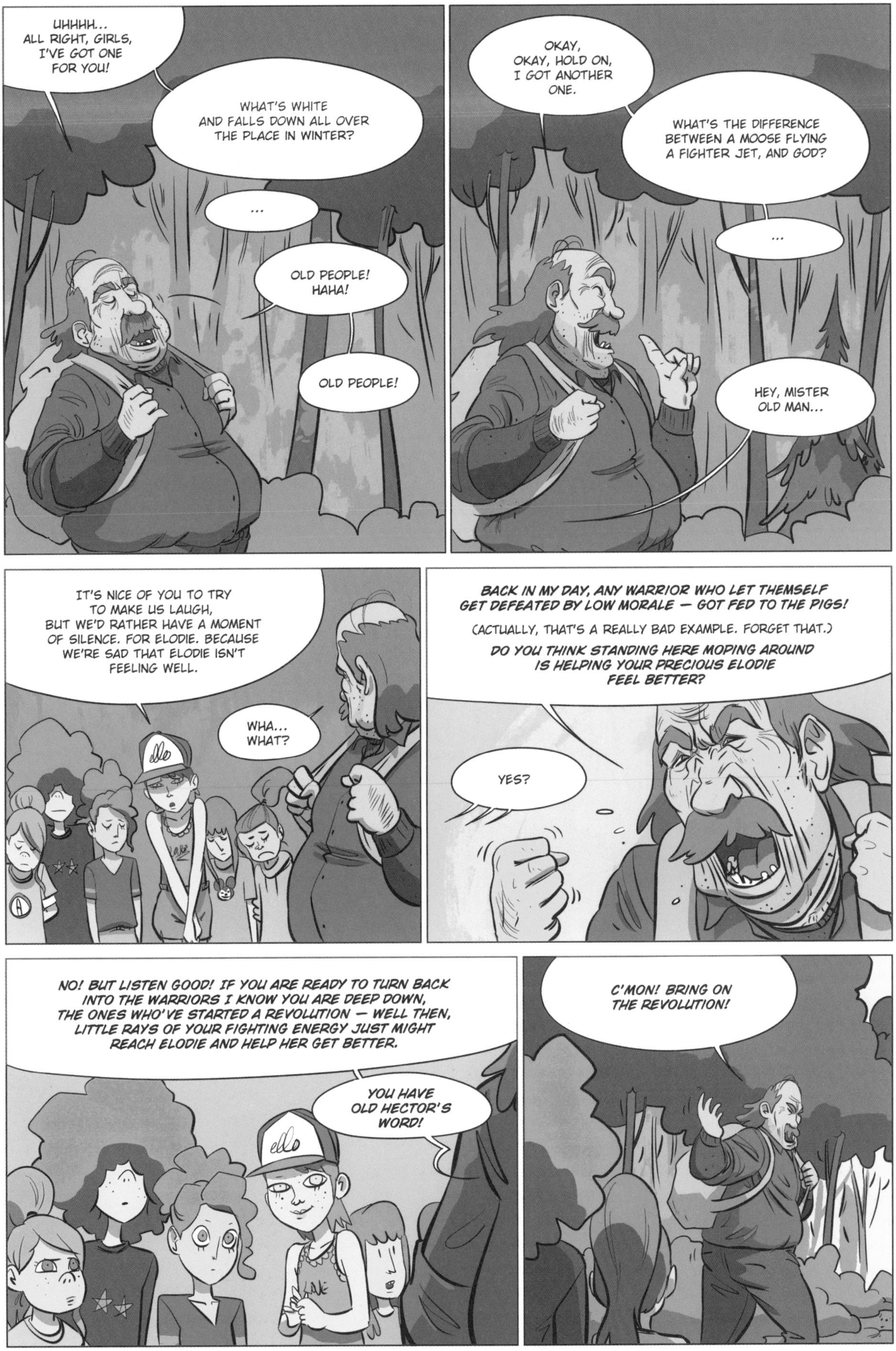
UHHHH... ALL RIGHT, GIRLS, I'VE GOT ONE FOR YOU!
WHAT'S WHITE AND FALLS DOWN ALL OVER THE PLACE IN WINTER?
...
OLD PEOPLE! HAHA!
OLD PEOPLE!
OKAY, OKAY, HOLD ON, I GOT ANOTHER ONE.
WHAT'S THE DIFFERENCE BETWEEN A MOOSE FLYING A FIGHTER JET, AND GOD?
...
HEY, MISTER OLD MAN...
IT'S NICE OF YOU TO TRY TO MAKE US LAUGH, BUT WE'D RATHER HAVE A MOMENT OF SILENCE. FOR ELODIE. BECAUSE WE'RE SAD THAT ELODIE ISN'T FEELING WELL.
WHA... WHAT?
BACK IN MY DAY, ANY WARRIOR WHO LET THEMSELF GET DEFEATED BY LOW MORALE — GOT FED TO THE PIGS!
(ACTUALLY, THAT'S A REALLY BAD EXAMPLE. FORGET THAT.)
DO YOU THINK STANDING HERE MOPING AROUND IS HELPING YOUR PRECIOUS ELODIE FEEL BETTER?
YES?
NO! BUT LISTEN GOOD! IF YOU ARE READY TO TURN BACK INTO THE WARRIORS I KNOW YOU ARE DEEP DOWN, THE ONES WHO'VE STARTED A REVOLUTION — WELL THEN, LITTLE RAYS OF YOUR FIGHTING ENERGY JUST MIGHT REACH ELODIE AND HELP HER GET BETTER.
YOU HAVE OLD HECTOR'S WORD!
C'MON! BRING ON THE REVOLUTION!

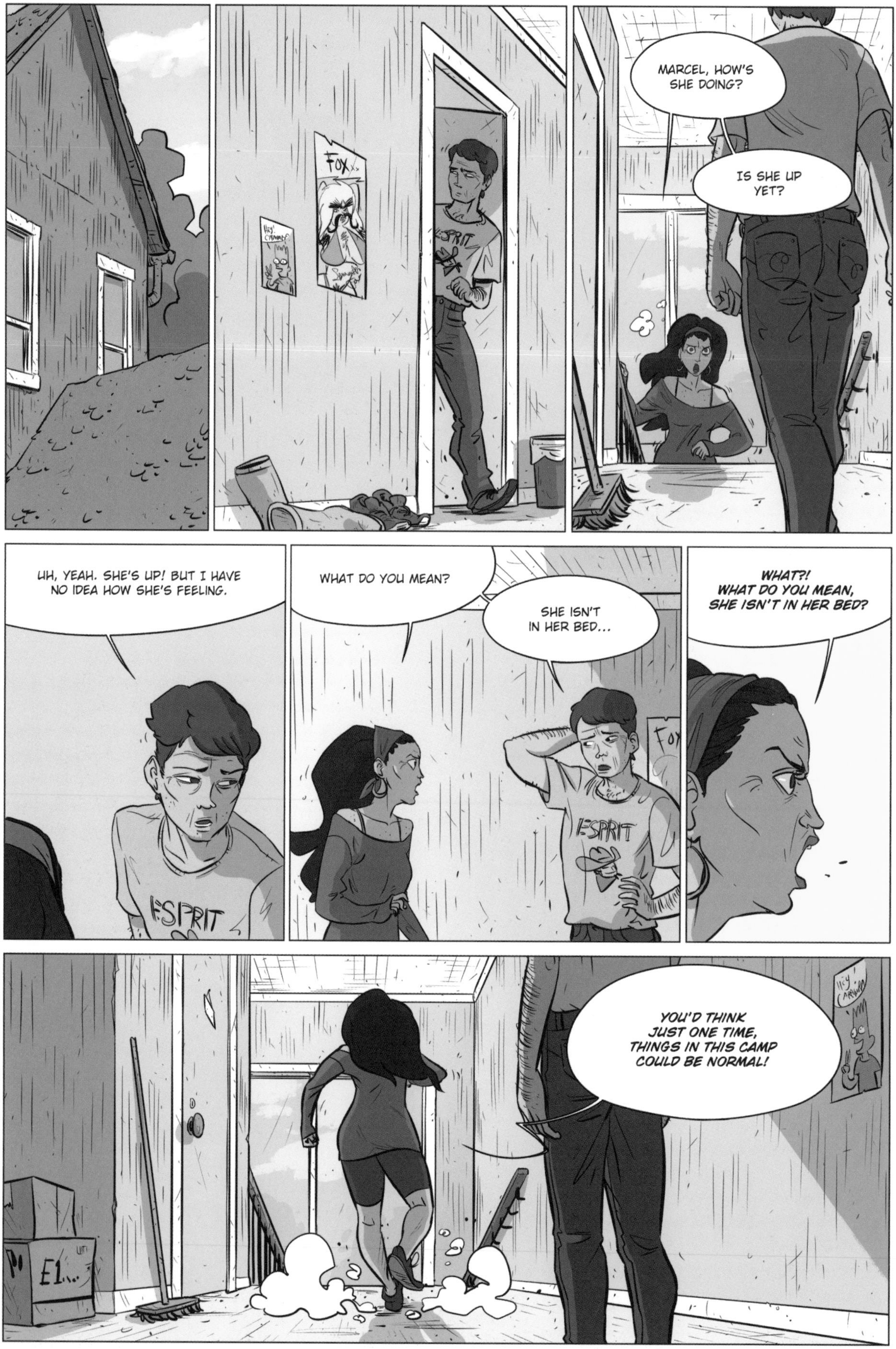

FOX
MARCEL, HOW'S SHE DOING?
IS SHE UP YET?
UH, YEAH. SHE'S UP! BUT I HAVE NO IDEA HOW SHE'S FEELING.
ESPRIT
WHAT DO YOU MEAN?
SHE ISN'T IN HER BED...
ESPRIT
FOX
WHAT?! WHAT DO YOU MEAN, SHE ISN'T IN HER BED?
YOU'D THINK JUST ONE TIME, THINGS IN THIS CAMP COULD BE NORMAL!

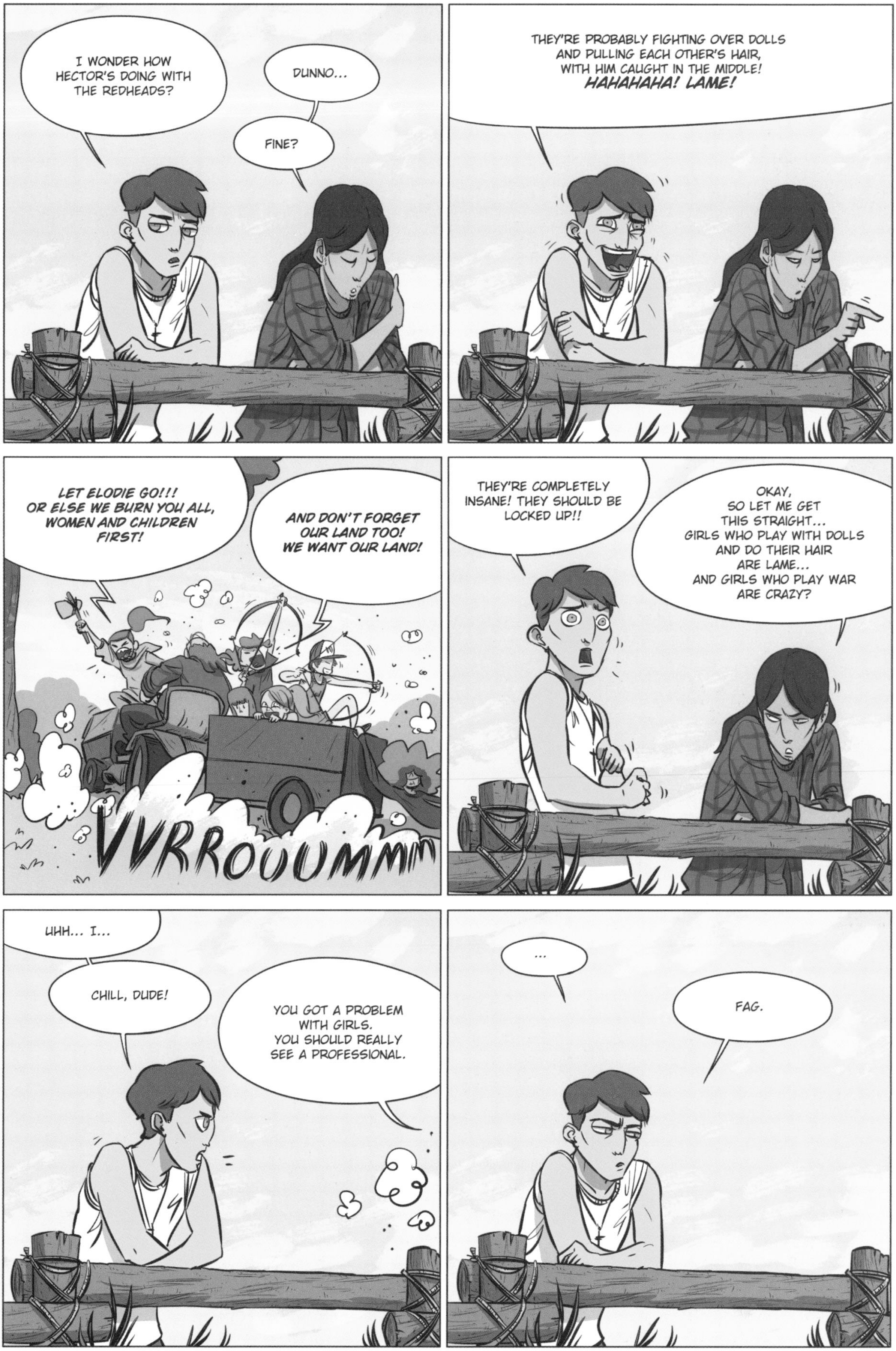
I WONDER HOW HECTOR'S DOING WITH THE REDHEADS?
DUNNO...
FINE?
THEY'RE PROBABLY FIGHTING OVER DOLLS AND PULLING EACH OTHER'S HAIR, WITH HIM CAUGHT IN THE MIDDLE! HAHAHAHA! LAME!
LET ELODIE GO!!! OR ELSE WE BURN YOU ALL, WOMEN AND CHILDREN FIRST!
AND DON'T FORGET OUR LAND TOO! WE WANT OUR LAND!
VVRROOUMMM
THEY'RE COMPLETELY INSANE! THEY SHOULD BE LOCKED UP!!
OKAY, SO LET ME GET THIS STRAIGHT... GIRLS WHO PLAY WITH DOLLS AND DO THEIR HAIR ARE LAME... AND GIRLS WHO PLAY WAR ARE CRAZY?
UHH... I...
CHILL, DUDE!
YOU GOT A PROBLEM WITH GIRLS. YOU SHOULD REALLY SEE A PROFESSIONAL.
...
FAG.

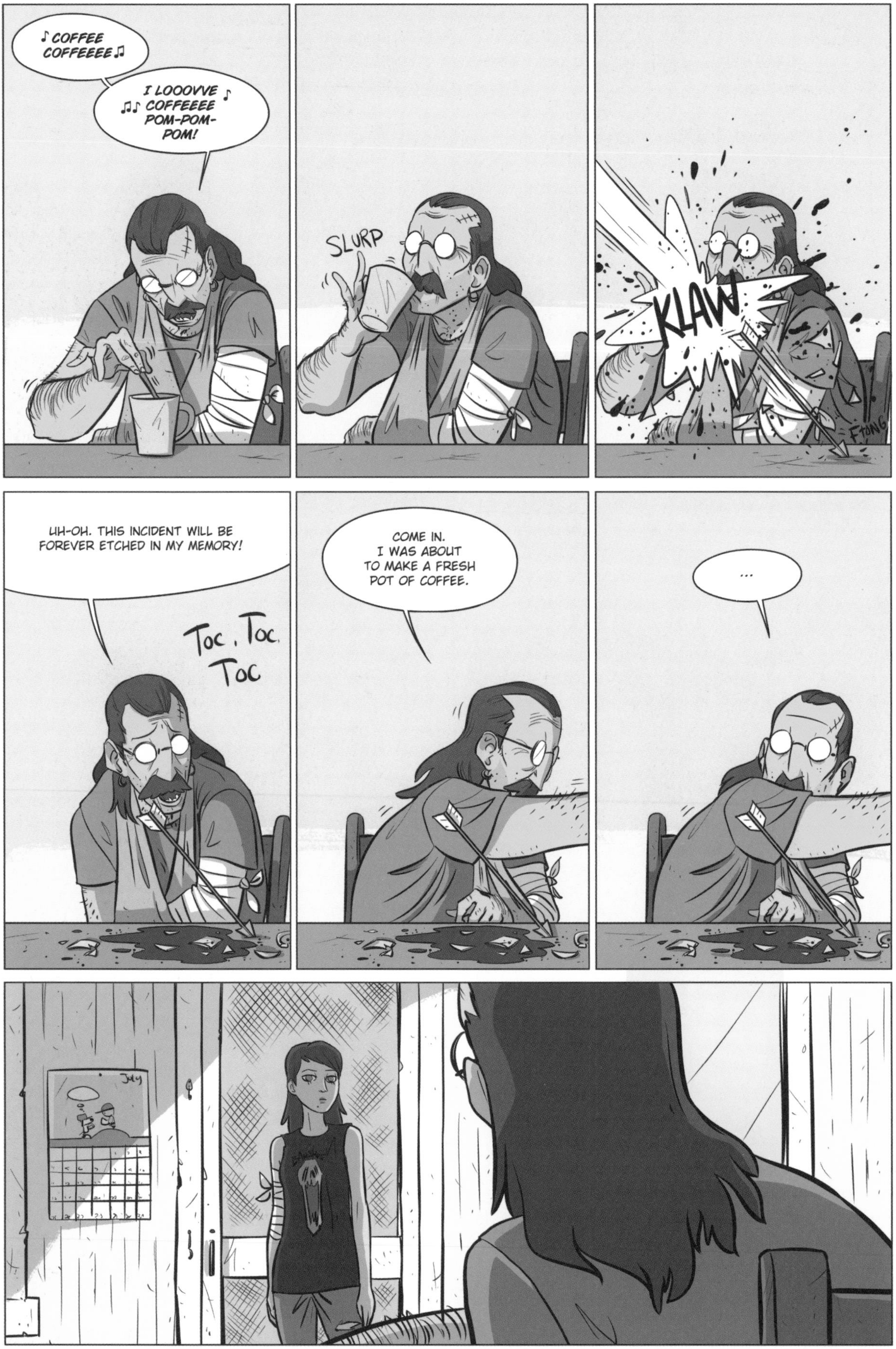
♪ COFFEE COFFEEEE ♫
I LOOOVVE ♪ ♫♪ COFFEEEE POM-POM-POM!
SLURP
KLAW
FTONG
UH-OH. THIS INCIDENT WILL BE FOREVER ETCHED IN MY MEMORY!
Toc. Toc. Toc
COME IN. I WAS ABOUT TO MAKE A FRESH POT OF COFFEE.
...

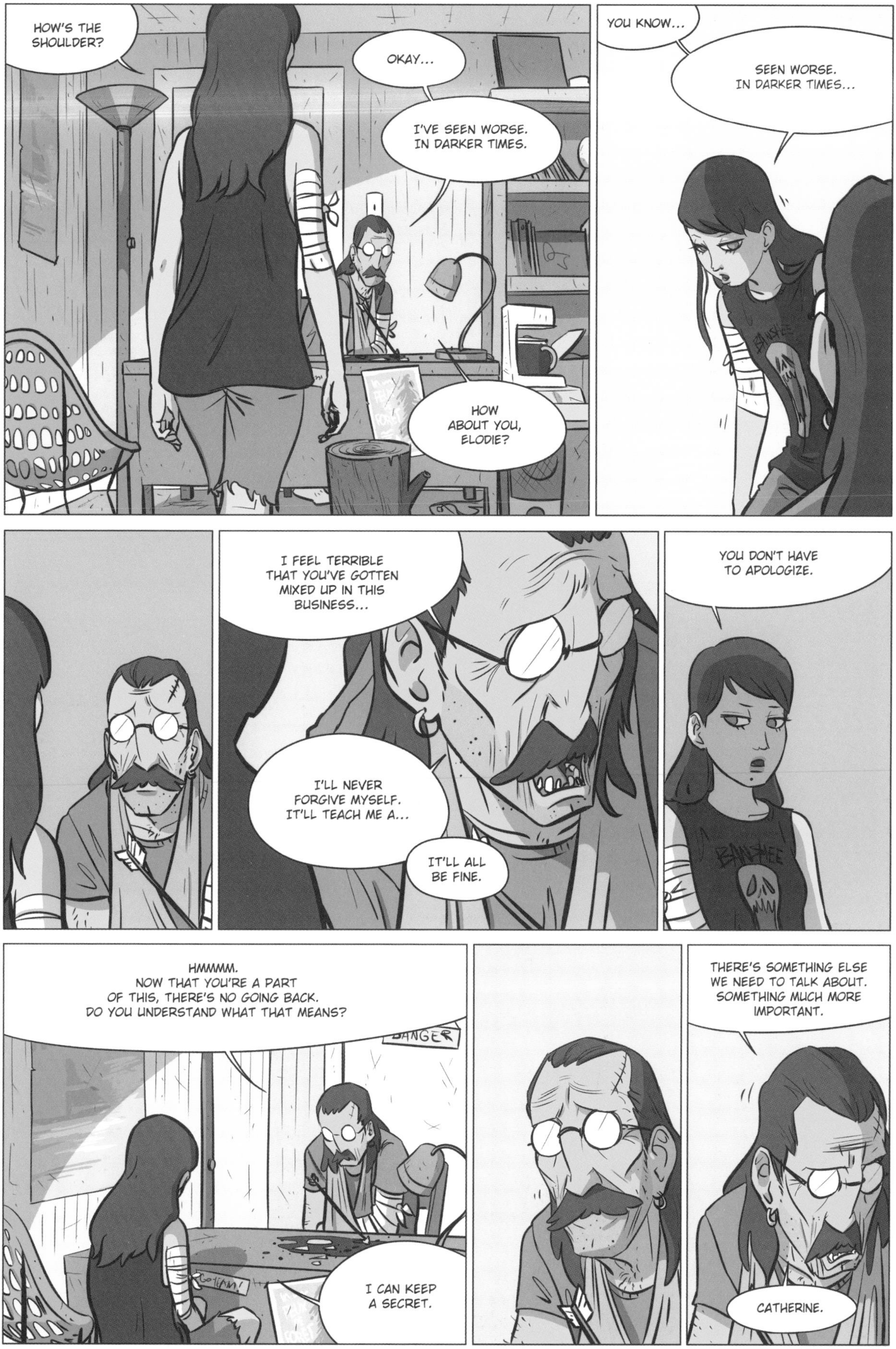
HOW'S THE SHOULDER?
OKAY...
I'VE SEEN WORSE. IN DARKER TIMES.
HOW ABOUT YOU, ELODIE?
YOU KNOW...
SEEN WORSE. IN DARKER TIMES...
I FEEL TERRIBLE THAT YOU'VE GOTTEN MIXED UP IN THIS BUSINESS...
I'LL NEVER FORGIVE MYSELF. IT'LL TEACH ME A...
IT'LL ALL BE FINE.
YOU DON'T HAVE TO APOLOGIZE.
HMMMM. NOW THAT YOU'RE A PART OF THIS, THERE'S NO GOING BACK. DO YOU UNDERSTAND WHAT THAT MEANS?
DANGER
I CAN KEEP A SECRET.
THERE'S SOMETHING ELSE WE NEED TO TALK ABOUT. SOMETHING MUCH MORE IMPORTANT.
CATHERINE.

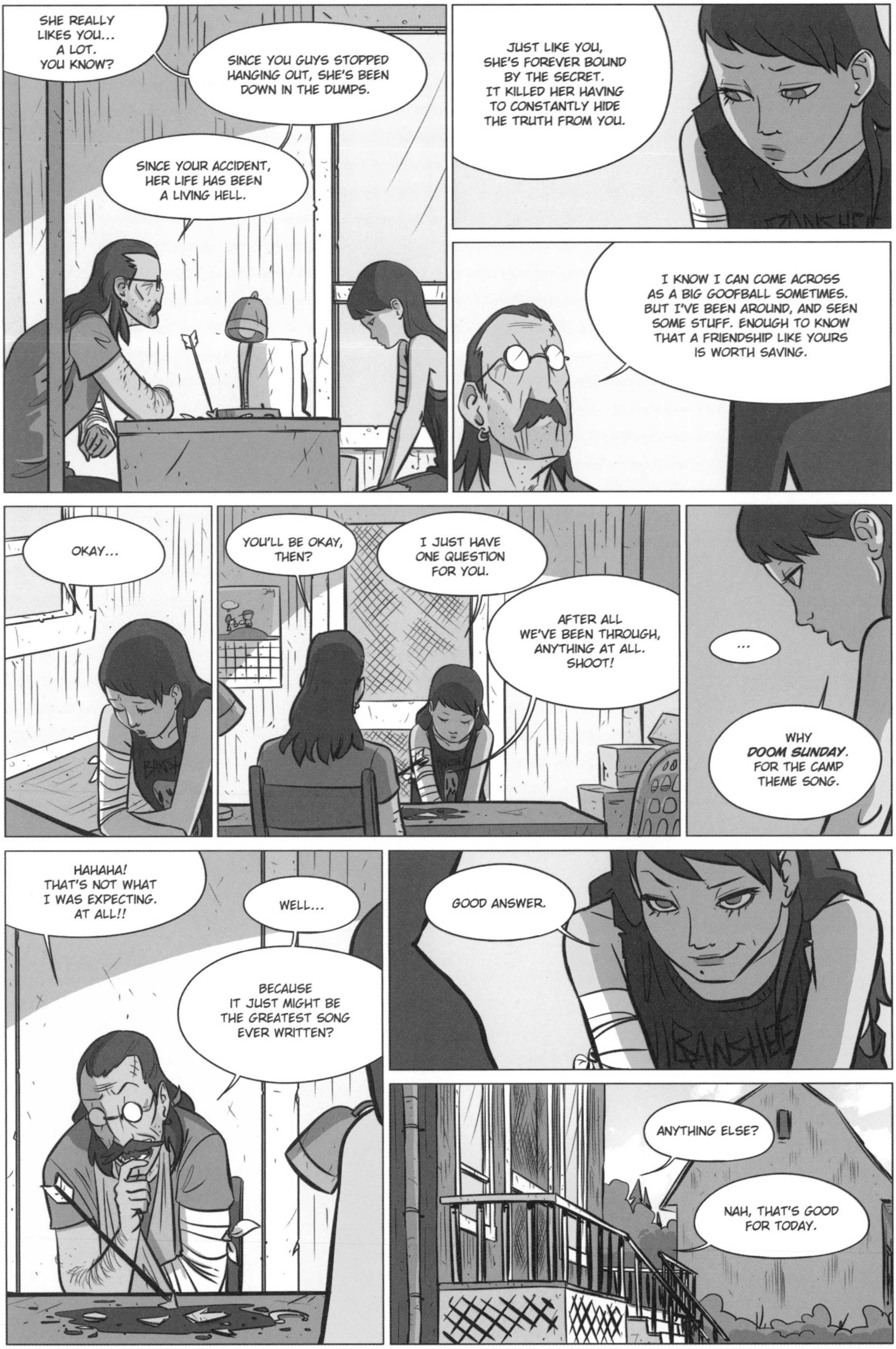
SHE REALLY LIKES YOU... A LOT. YOU KNOW?
SINCE YOU GUYS STOPPED HANGING OUT, SHE'S BEEN DOWN IN THE DUMPS.
SINCE YOUR ACCIDENT, HER LIFE HAS BEEN A LIVING HELL.
JUST LIKE YOU, SHE'S FOREVER BOUND BY THE SECRET. IT KILLED HER HAVING TO CONSTANTLY HIDE THE TRUTH FROM YOU.
I KNOW I CAN COME ACROSS AS A BIG GOOFBALL SOMETIMES. BUT I'VE BEEN AROUND, AND SEEN SOME STUFF. ENOUGH TO KNOW THAT A FRIENDSHIP LIKE YOURS IS WORTH SAVING.
OKAY...
YOU'LL BE OKAY, THEN?
I JUST HAVE ONE QUESTION FOR YOU.
AFTER ALL WE'VE BEEN THROUGH, ANYTHING AT ALL. SHOOT!
...
WHY ***DOOM SUNDAY***. FOR THE CAMP THEME SONG.
HAHAHA! THAT'S NOT WHAT I WAS EXPECTING. AT ALL!!
WELL...
BECAUSE IT JUST MIGHT BE THE GREATEST SONG EVER WRITTEN?
GOOD ANSWER.
ANYTHING ELSE?
NAH, THAT'S GOOD FOR TODAY.

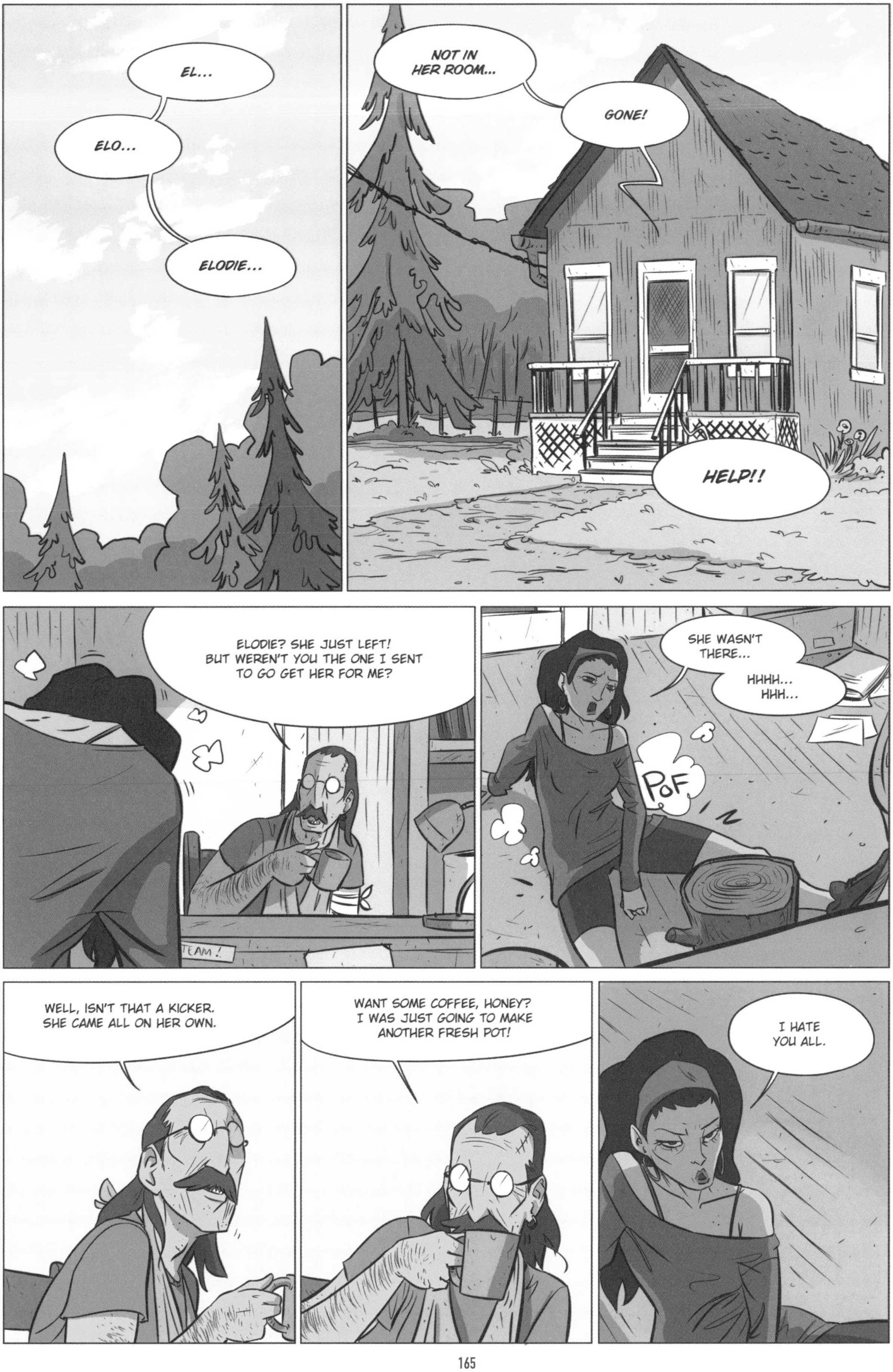
EL...
ELO...
ELODIE...
NOT IN HER ROOM...
GONE!
HELP!!
ELODIE? SHE JUST LEFT! BUT WEREN'T YOU THE ONE I SENT TO GO GET HER FOR ME?
TEAM!
SHE WASN'T THERE...
HHHH... HHH...
POF
WELL, ISN'T THAT A KICKER. SHE CAME ALL ON HER OWN.
WANT SOME COFFEE, HONEY? I WAS JUST GOING TO MAKE ANOTHER FRESH POT!
I HATE YOU ALL.

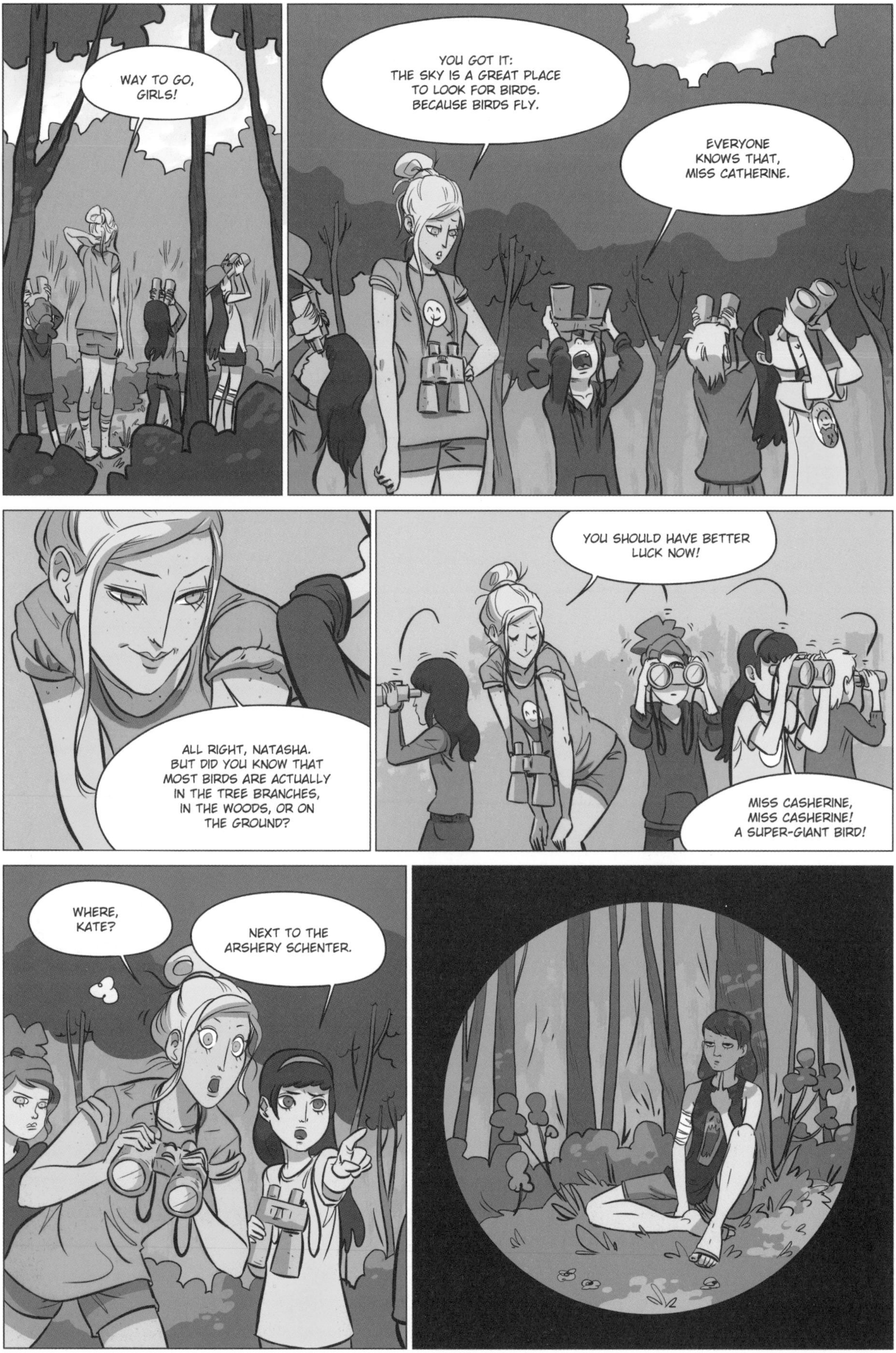
WAY TO GO, GIRLS!
YOU GOT IT: THE SKY IS A GREAT PLACE TO LOOK FOR BIRDS. BECAUSE BIRDS FLY.
EVERYONE KNOWS THAT, MISS CATHERINE.
ALL RIGHT, NATASHA. BUT DID YOU KNOW THAT MOST BIRDS ARE ACTUALLY IN THE TREE BRANCHES, IN THE WOODS, OR ON THE GROUND?
YOU SHOULD HAVE BETTER LUCK NOW!
MISS CASHERINE, MISS CASHERINE! A SUPER-GIANT BIRD!
WHERE, KATE?
NEXT TO THE ARSHERY SCHENTER.

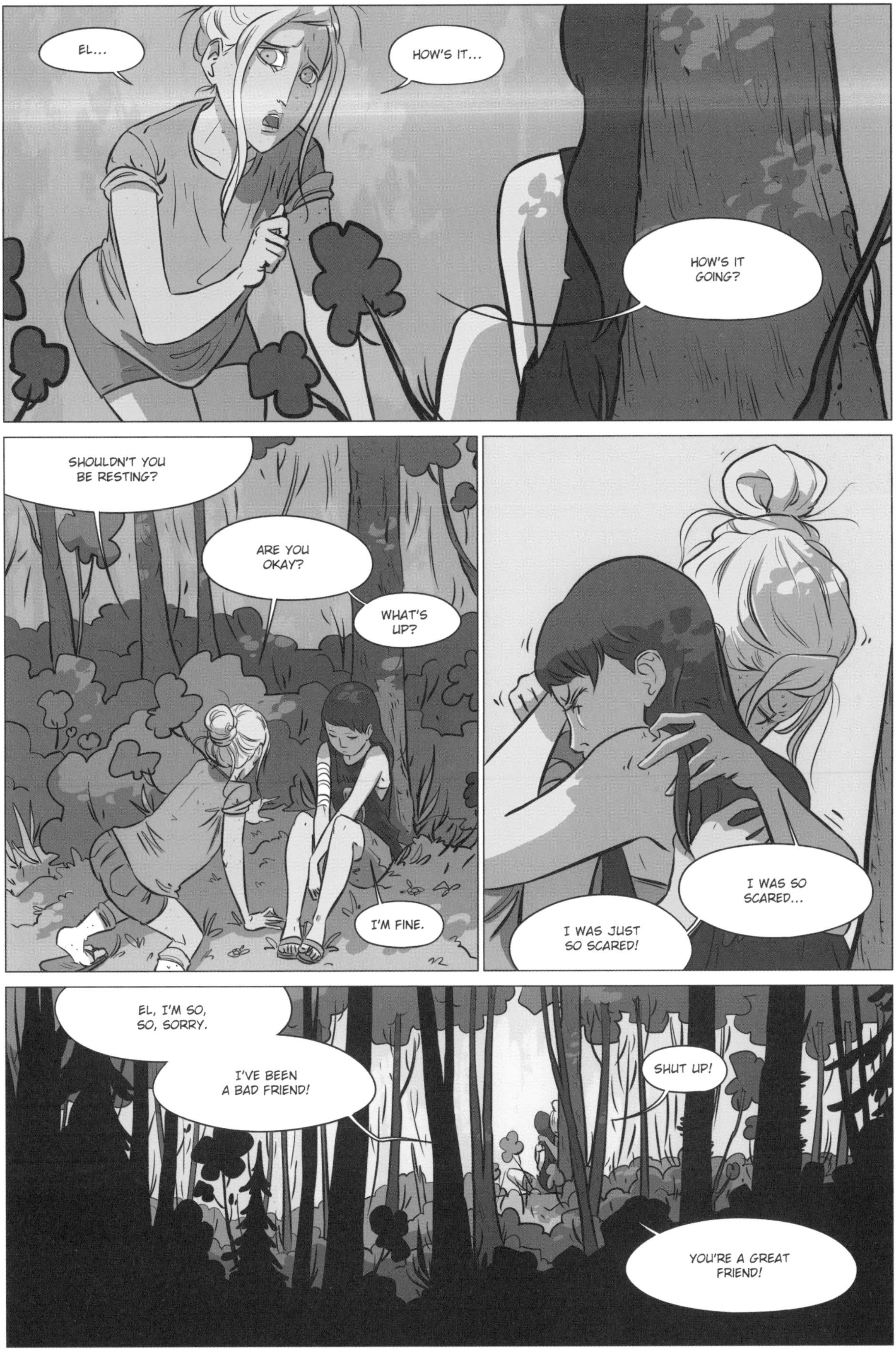
EL...
HOW'S IT...
HOW'S IT GOING?
SHOULDN'T YOU BE RESTING?
ARE YOU OKAY?
WHAT'S UP?
I'M FINE.
I WAS SO SCARED...
I WAS JUST SO SCARED!
EL, I'M SO, SO, SORRY.
I'VE BEEN A BAD FRIEND!
SHUT UP!
YOU'RE A GREAT FRIEND!

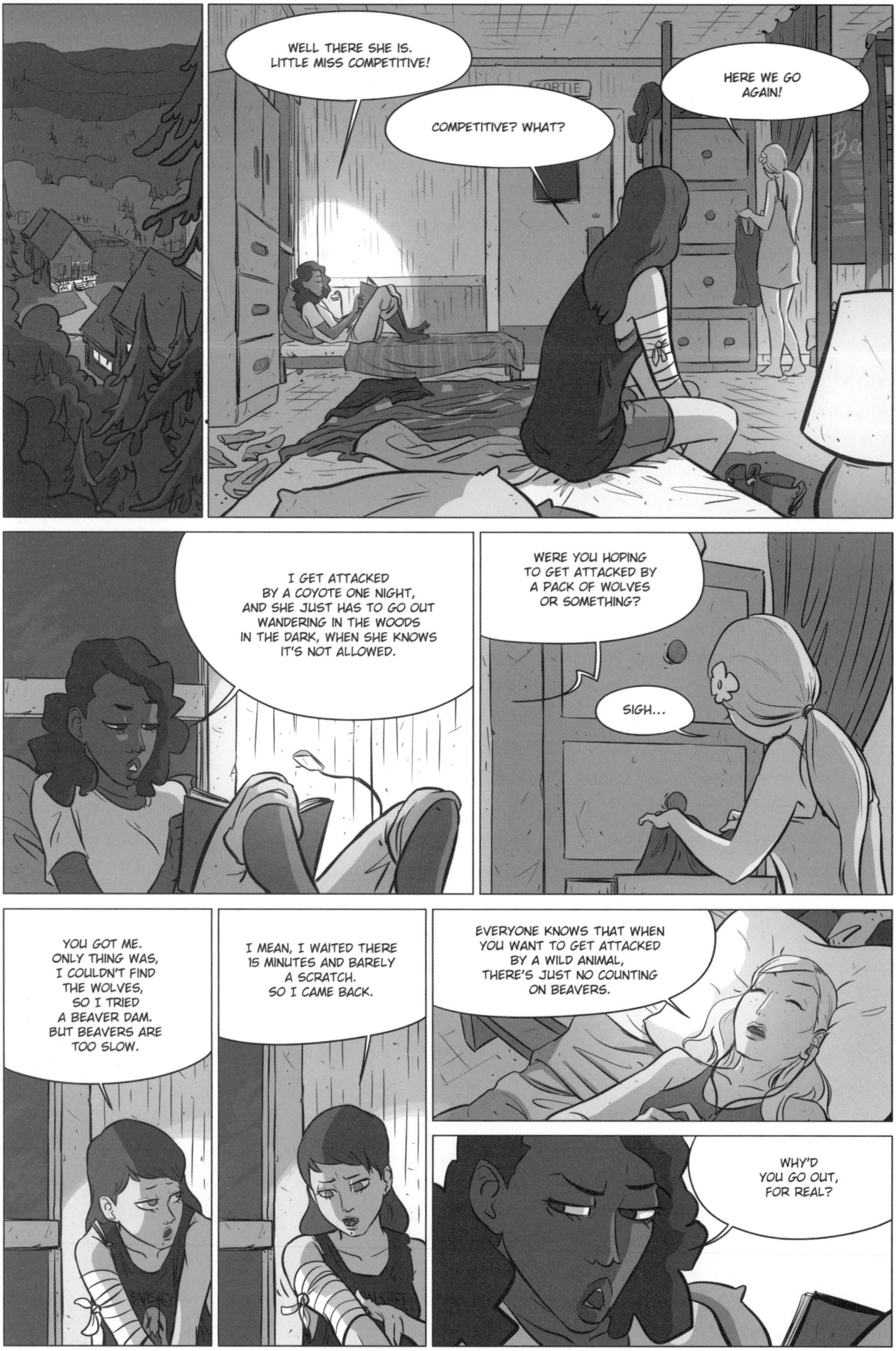
WELL THERE SHE IS. LITTLE MISS COMPETITIVE!
COMPETITIVE? WHAT?
HERE WE GO AGAIN!
I GET ATTACKED BY A COYOTE ONE NIGHT, AND SHE JUST HAS TO GO OUT WANDERING IN THE WOODS IN THE DARK, WHEN SHE KNOWS IT'S NOT ALLOWED.
WERE YOU HOPING TO GET ATTACKED BY A PACK OF WOLVES OR SOMETHING?
SIGH...
YOU GOT ME. ONLY THING WAS, I COULDN'T FIND THE WOLVES, SO I TRIED A BEAVER DAM. BUT BEAVERS ARE TOO SLOW.
I MEAN, I WAITED THERE 15 MINUTES AND BARELY A SCRATCH. SO I CAME BACK.
EVERYONE KNOWS THAT WHEN YOU WANT TO GET ATTACKED BY A WILD ANIMAL, THERE'S JUST NO COUNTING ON BEAVERS.
WHY'D YOU GO OUT, FOR REAL?

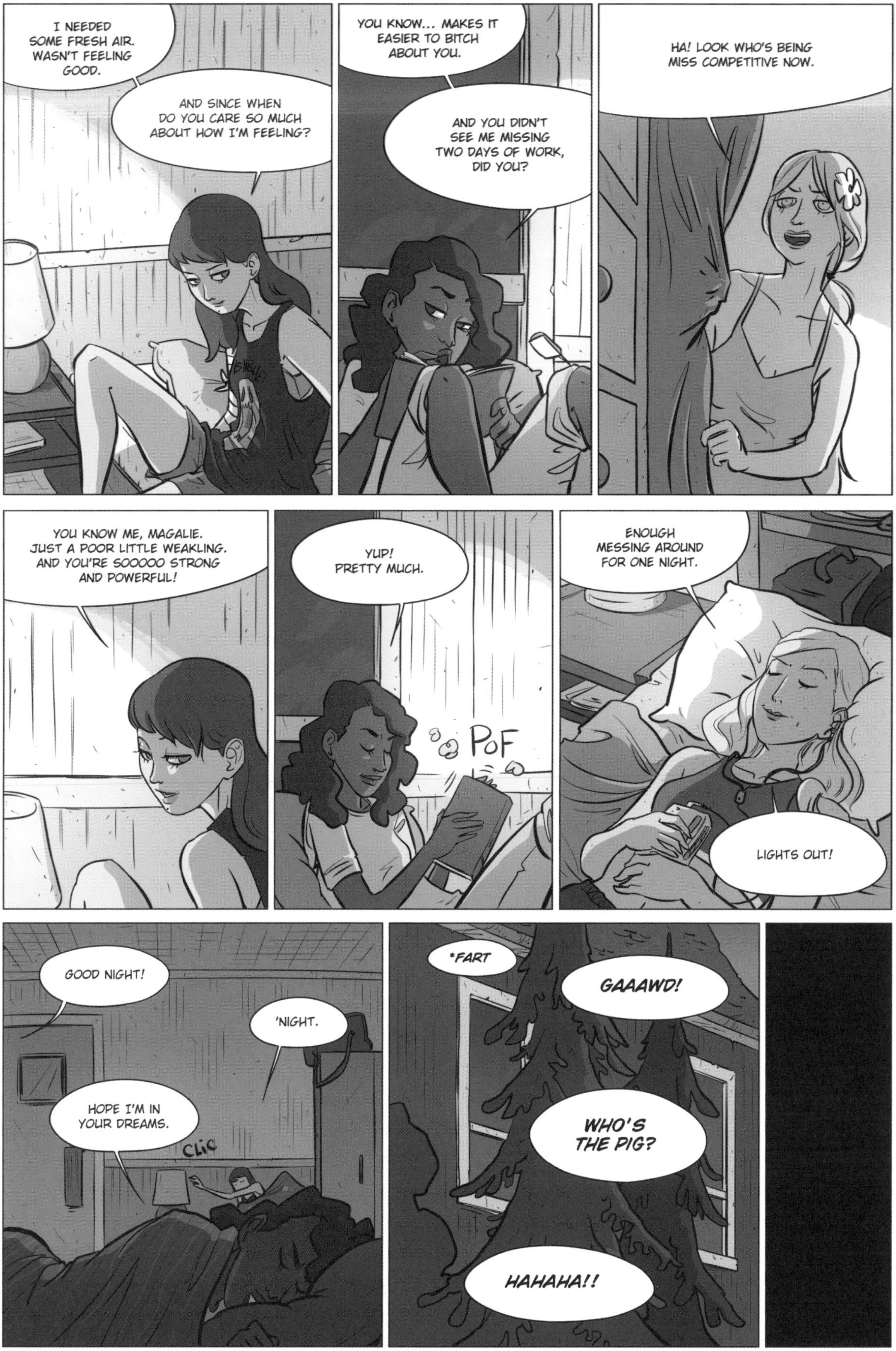
I NEEDED SOME FRESH AIR. WASN'T FEELING GOOD.
AND SINCE WHEN DO YOU CARE SO MUCH ABOUT HOW I'M FEELING?
YOU KNOW... MAKES IT EASIER TO BITCH ABOUT YOU.
AND YOU DIDN'T SEE ME MISSING TWO DAYS OF WORK, DID YOU?
HA! LOOK WHO'S BEING MISS COMPETITIVE NOW.
YOU KNOW ME, MAGALIE. JUST A POOR LITTLE WEAKLING. AND YOU'RE SOOOOO STRONG AND POWERFUL!
YUP! PRETTY MUCH.
POF
ENOUGH MESSING AROUND FOR ONE NIGHT.
LIGHTS OUT!
GOOD NIGHT!
'NIGHT.
HOPE I'M IN YOUR DREAMS.
CLIC
*FART
GAAAWD!
WHO'S THE PIG?
HAHAHA!!

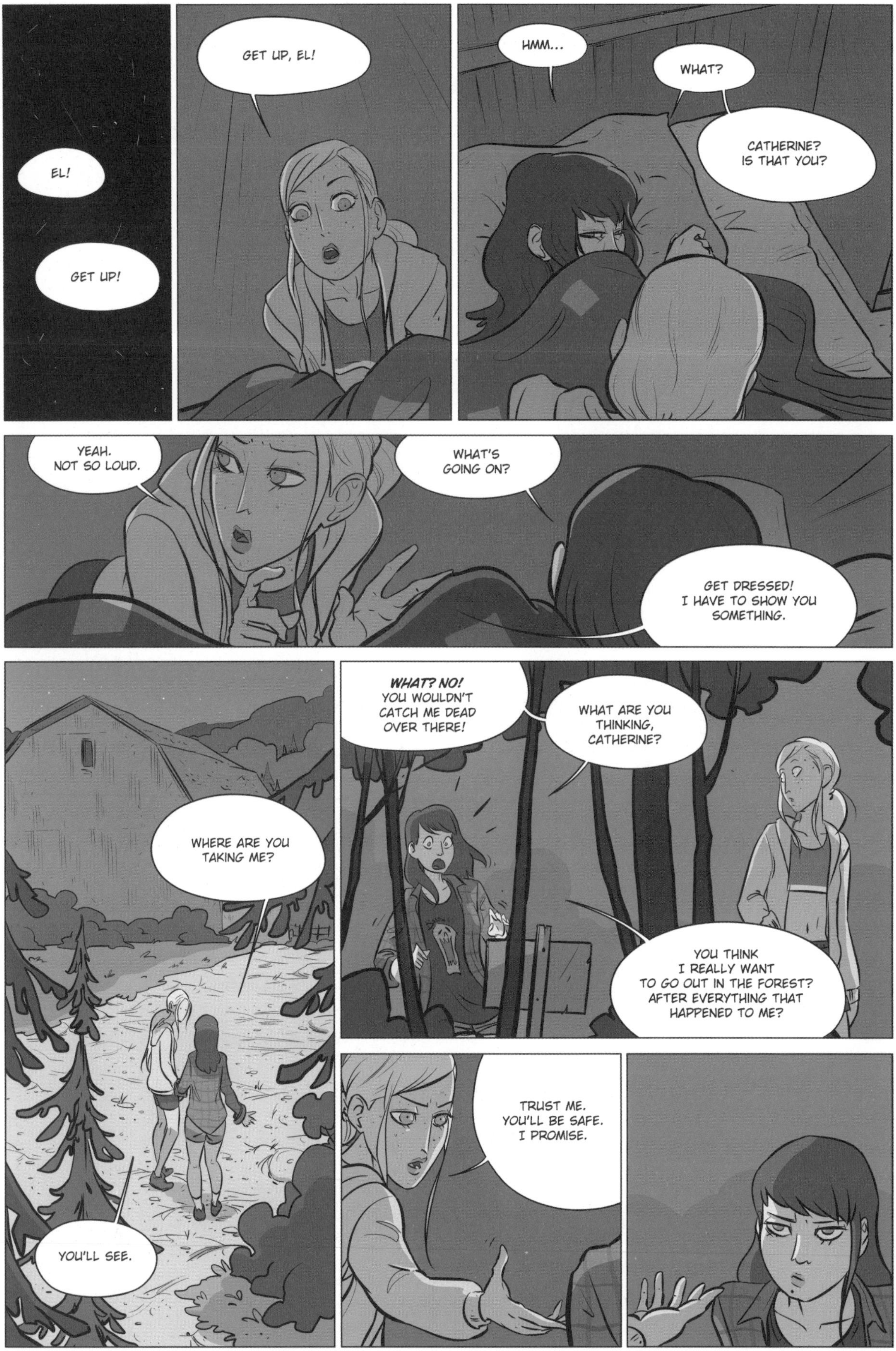
EL!
GET UP!
GET UP, EL!
HMM...
WHAT?
CATHERINE? IS THAT YOU?
YEAH. NOT SO LOUD.
WHAT'S GOING ON?
GET DRESSED! I HAVE TO SHOW YOU SOMETHING.
WHERE ARE YOU TAKING ME?
YOU'LL SEE.
WHAT? NO! YOU WOULDN'T CATCH ME DEAD OVER THERE!
WHAT ARE YOU THINKING, CATHERINE?
YOU THINK I REALLY WANT TO GO OUT IN THE FOREST? AFTER EVERYTHING THAT HAPPENED TO ME?
TRUST ME. YOU'LL BE SAFE. I PROMISE.

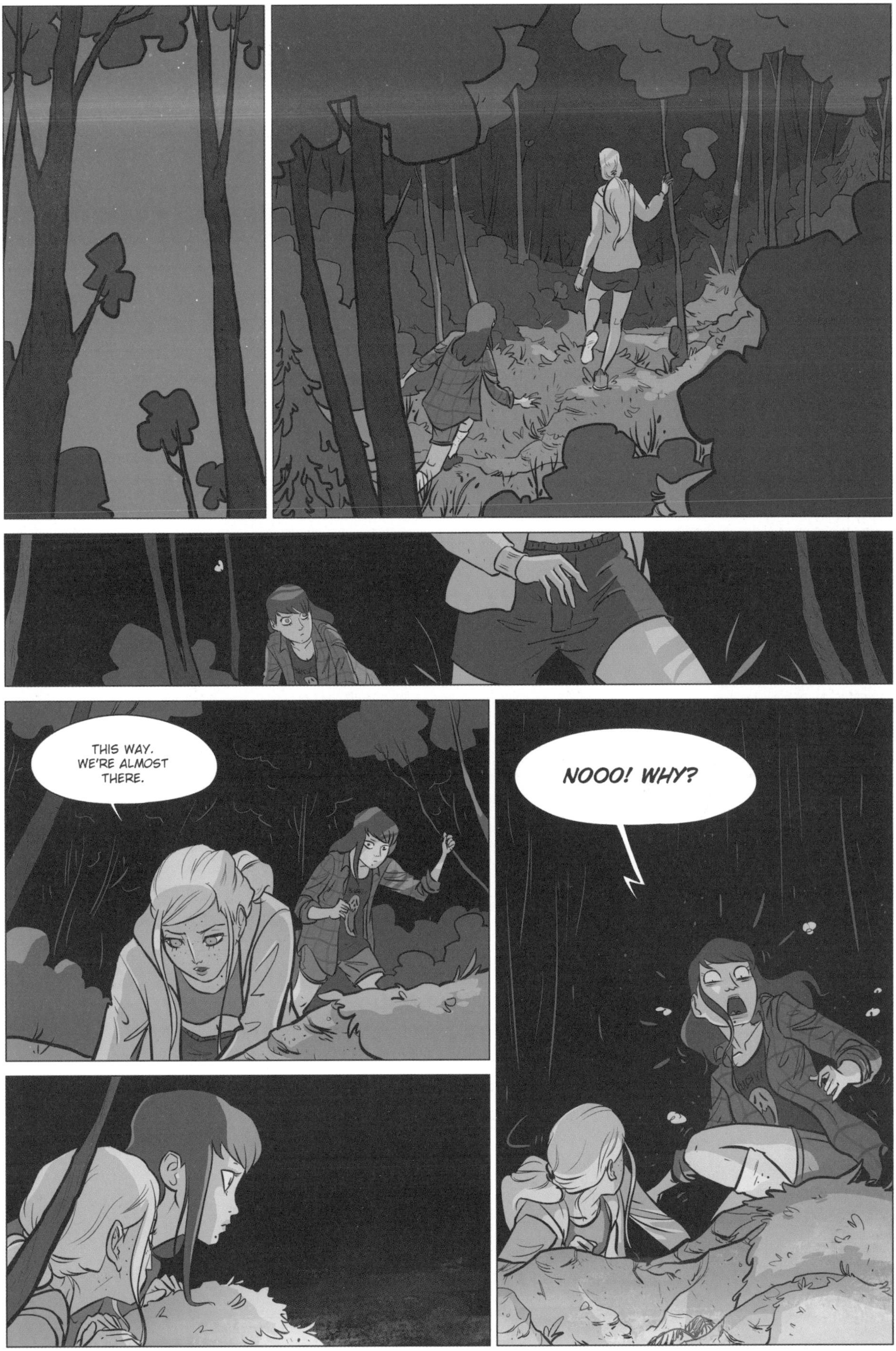
THIS WAY. WE'RE ALMOST THERE.
NOOO! WHY?

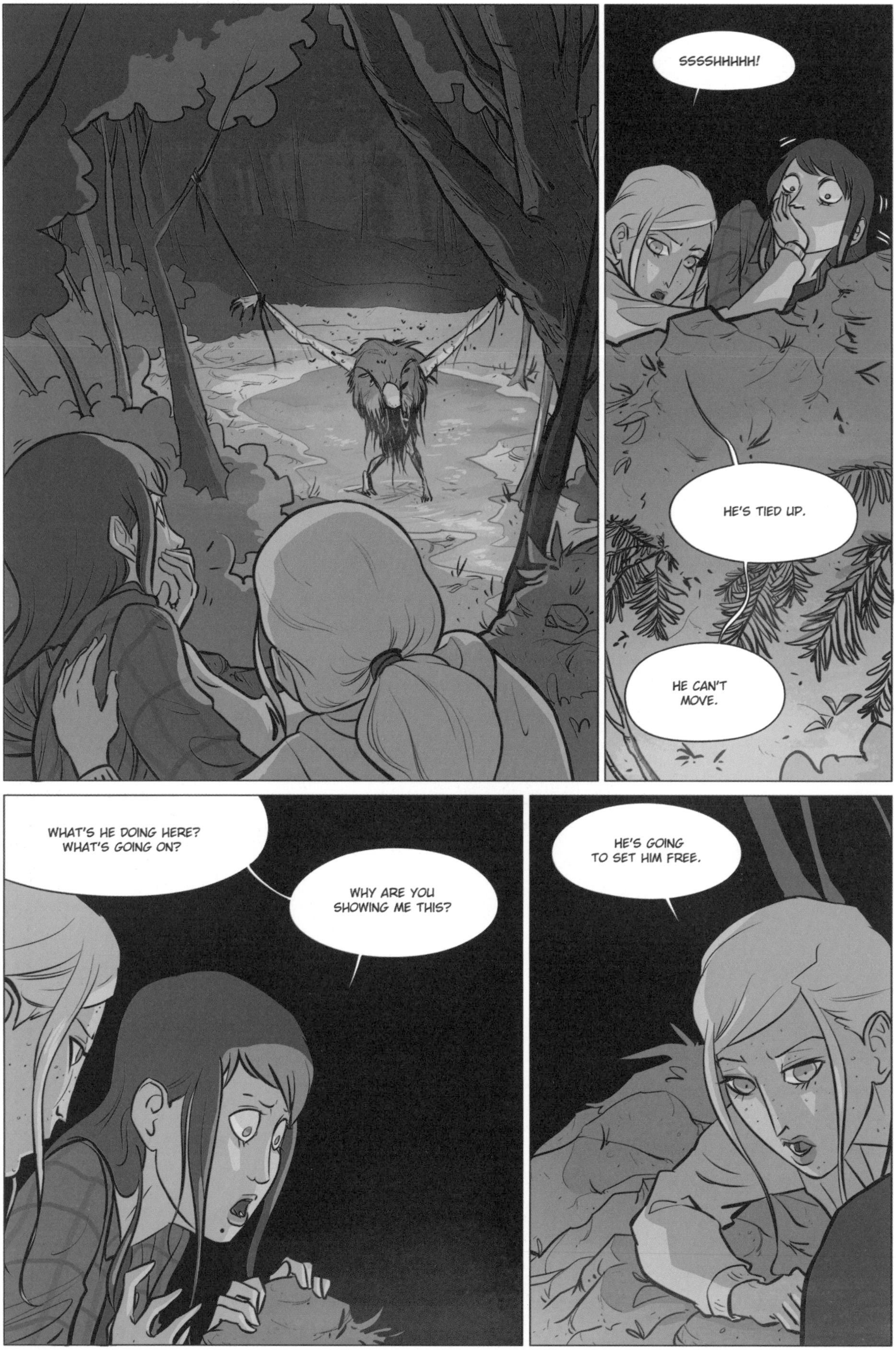
SSSSHHHHH!
HE'S TIED UP.
HE CAN'T MOVE.
WHAT'S HE DOING HERE? WHAT'S GOING ON?
WHY ARE YOU SHOWING ME THIS?
HE'S GOING TO SET HIM FREE.

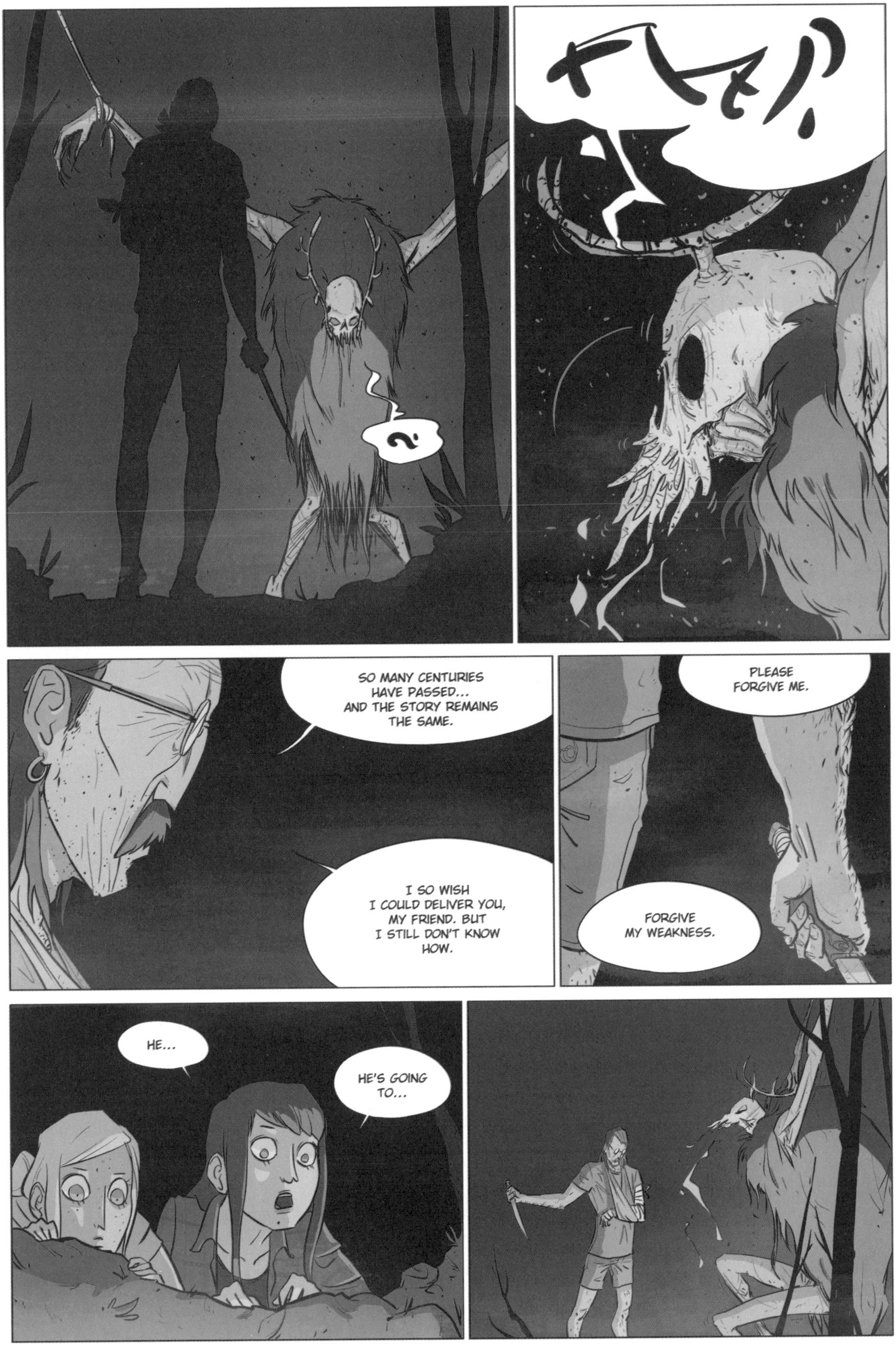

?
SO MANY CENTURIES HAVE PASSED... AND THE STORY REMAINS THE SAME.
I SO WISH I COULD DELIVER YOU, MY FRIEND. BUT I STILL DON'T KNOW HOW.
PLEASE FORGIVE ME.
FORGIVE MY WEAKNESS.
HE...
HE'S GOING TO...

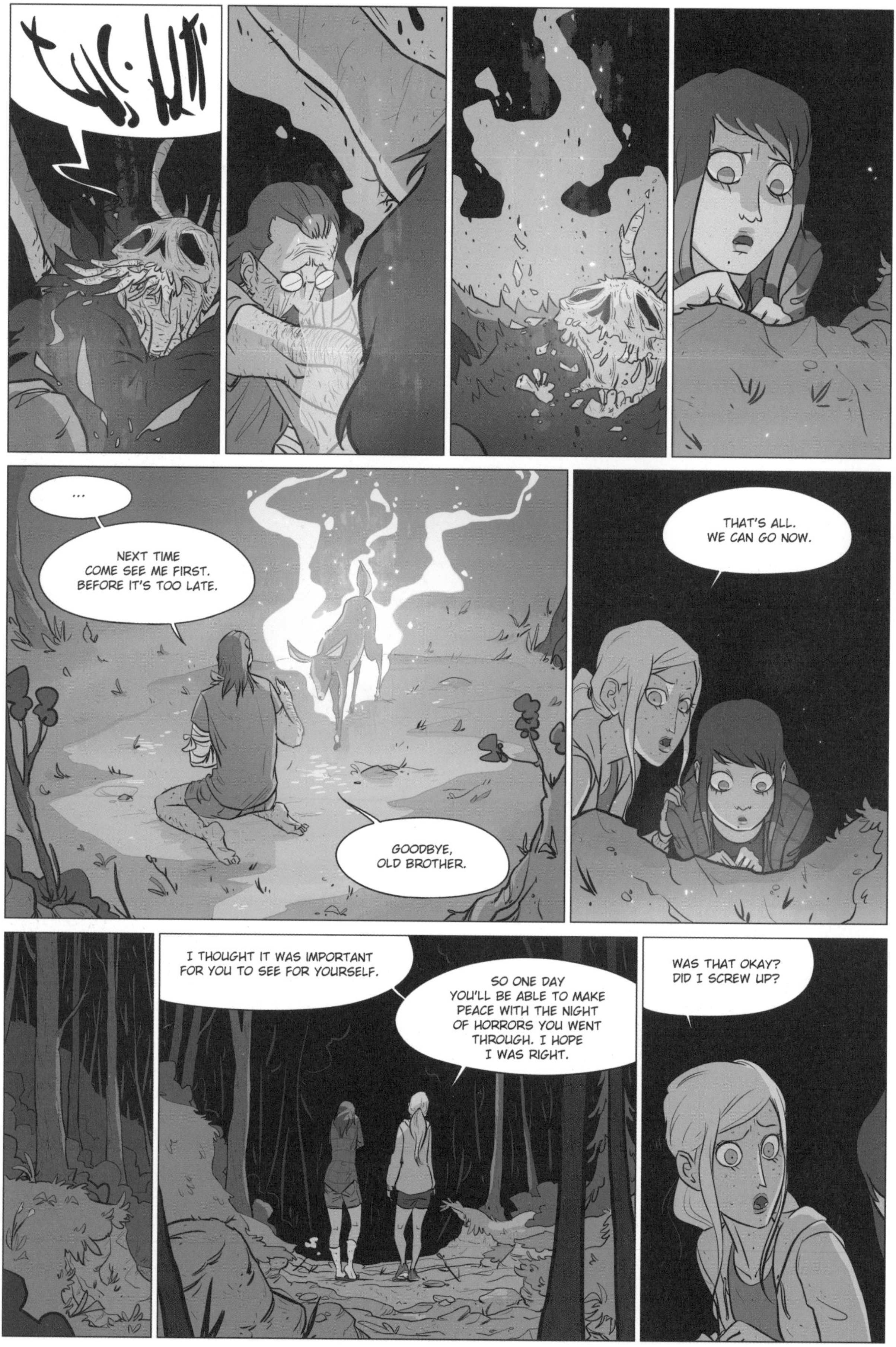
...
NEXT TIME COME SEE ME FIRST. BEFORE IT'S TOO LATE.
GOODBYE, OLD BROTHER.
THAT'S ALL. WE CAN GO NOW.
I THOUGHT IT WAS IMPORTANT FOR YOU TO SEE FOR YOURSELF.
SO ONE DAY YOU'LL BE ABLE TO MAKE PEACE WITH THE NIGHT OF HORRORS YOU WENT THROUGH. I HOPE I WAS RIGHT.
WAS THAT OKAY? DID I SCREW UP?

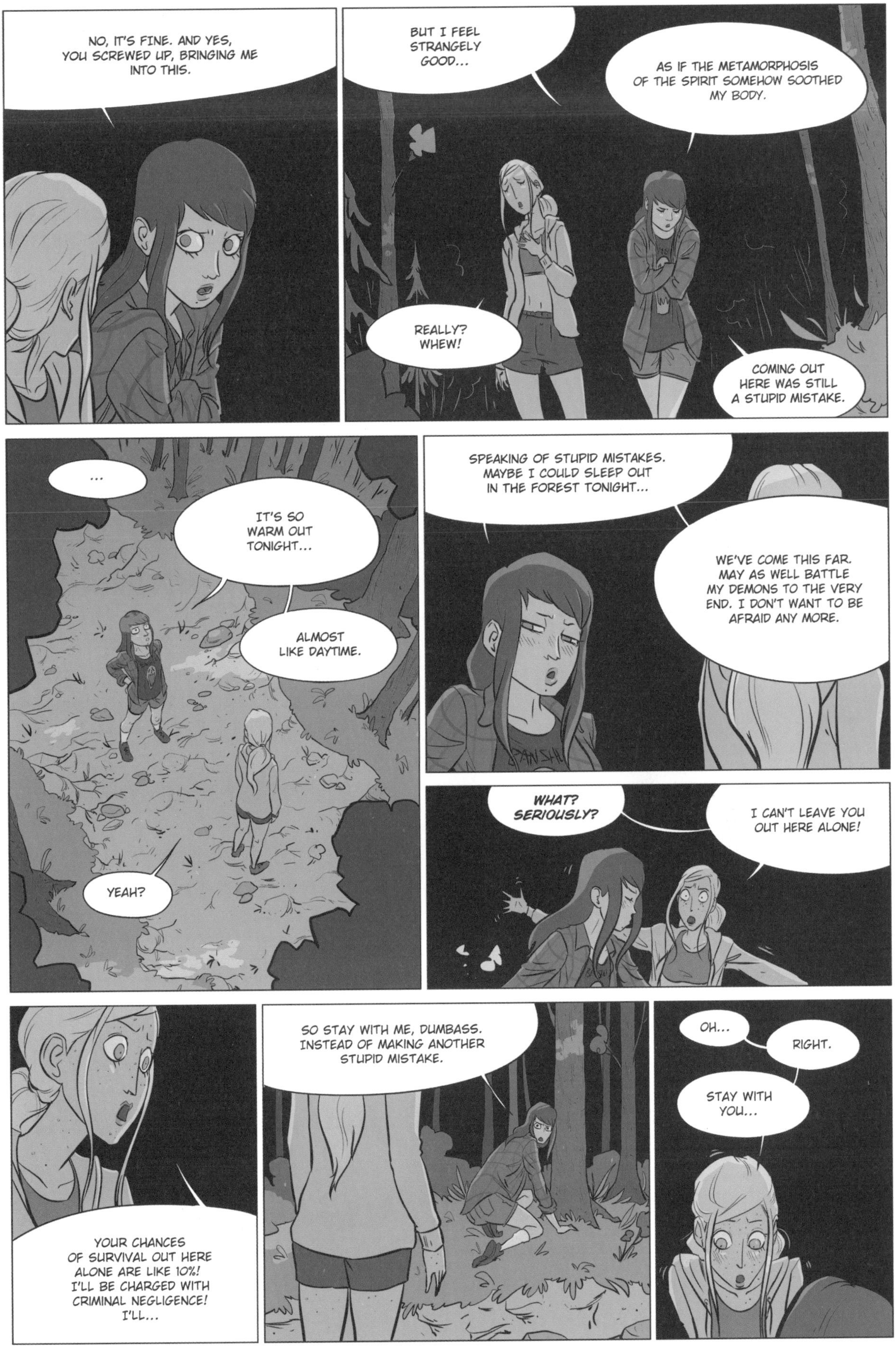
NO, IT'S FINE. AND YES, YOU SCREWED UP, BRINGING ME INTO THIS.
BUT I FEEL STRANGELY GOOD...
AS IF THE METAMORPHOSIS OF THE SPIRIT SOMEHOW SOOTHED MY BODY.
REALLY? WHEW!
COMING OUT HERE WAS STILL A STUPID MISTAKE.
...
IT'S SO WARM OUT TONIGHT...
ALMOST LIKE DAYTIME.
YEAH?
SPEAKING OF STUPID MISTAKES. MAYBE I COULD SLEEP OUT IN THE FOREST TONIGHT...
WE'VE COME THIS FAR. MAY AS WELL BATTLE MY DEMONS TO THE VERY END. I DON'T WANT TO BE AFRAID ANY MORE.
WHAT? SERIOUSLY?
I CAN'T LEAVE YOU OUT HERE ALONE!
YOUR CHANCES OF SURVIVAL OUT HERE ALONE ARE LIKE 10%! I'LL BE CHARGED WITH CRIMINAL NEGLIGENCE! I'LL...
SO STAY WITH ME, DUMBASS. INSTEAD OF MAKING ANOTHER STUPID MISTAKE.
OH...
RIGHT.
STAY WITH YOU...

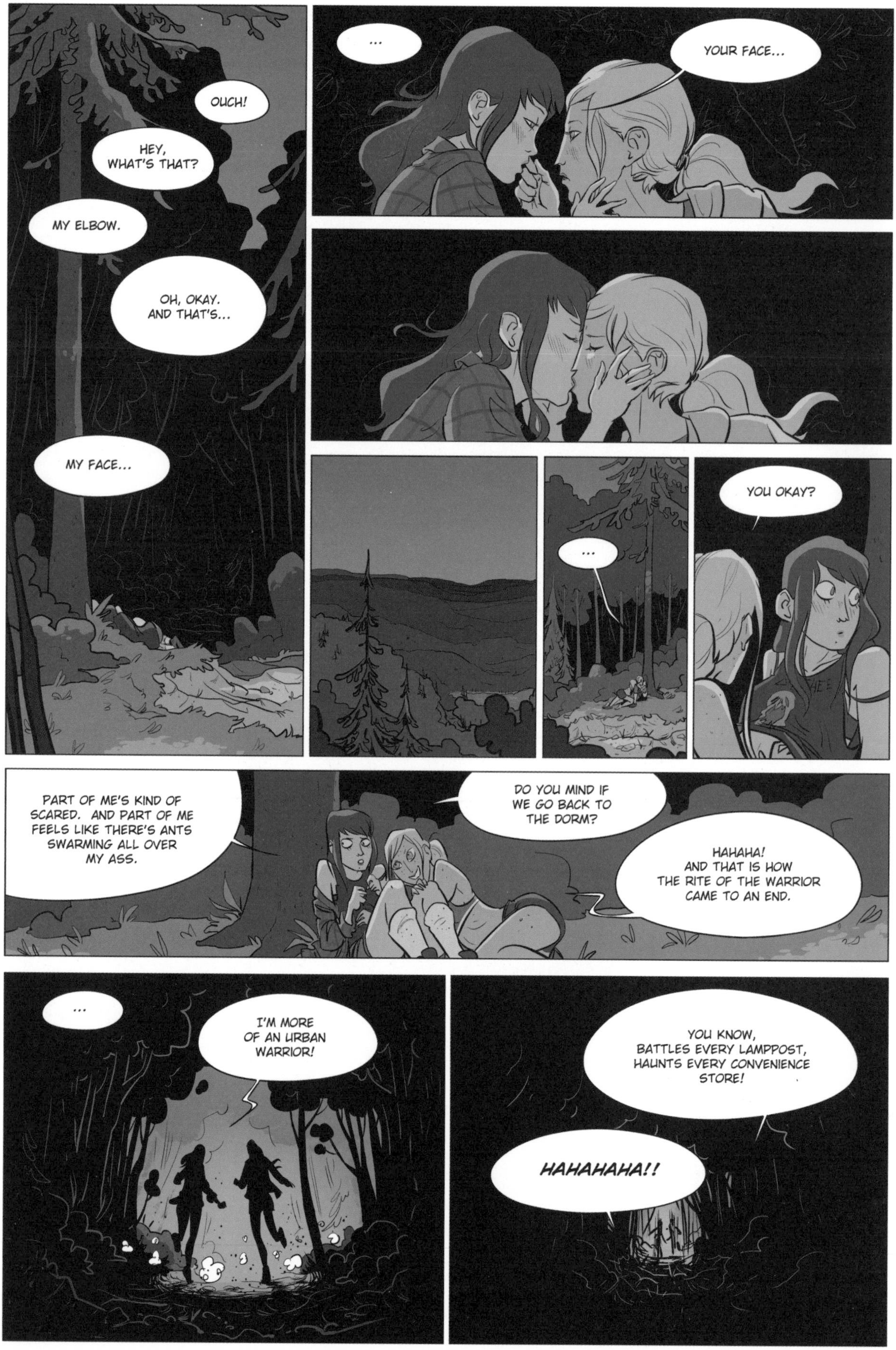
OUCH!
HEY, WHAT'S THAT?
MY ELBOW.
OH, OKAY. AND THAT'S...
MY FACE...
...
YOUR FACE...
...
YOU OKAY?
PART OF ME'S KIND OF SCARED. AND PART OF ME FEELS LIKE THERE'S ANTS SWARMING ALL OVER MY ASS.
DO YOU MIND IF WE GO BACK TO THE DORM?
HAHAHA! AND THAT IS HOW THE RITE OF THE WARRIOR CAME TO AN END.
...
I'M MORE OF AN URBAN WARRIOR!
YOU KNOW, BATTLES EVERY LAMPPOST, HAUNTS EVERY CONVENIENCE STORE!
HAHAHAHA!!

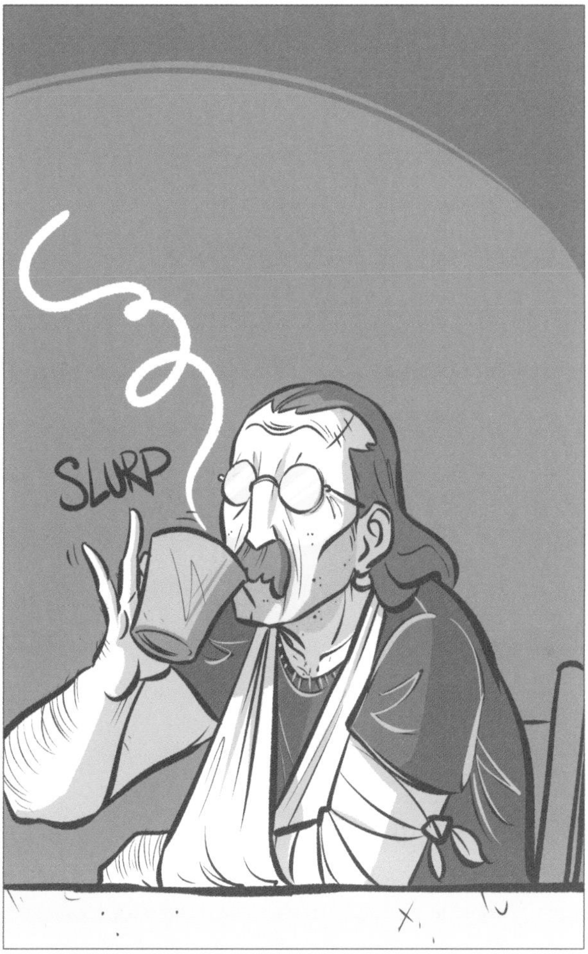
SLURP

8

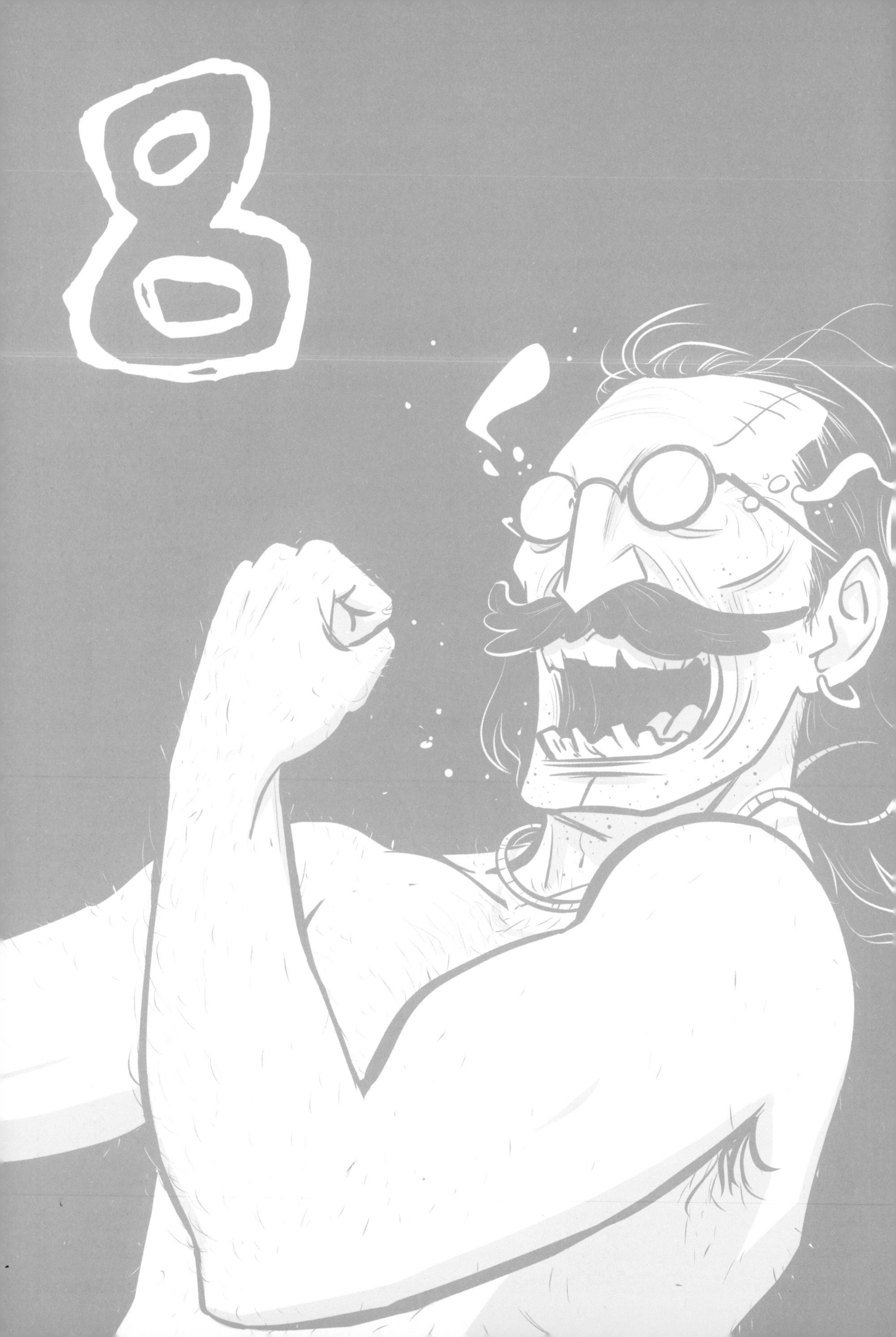

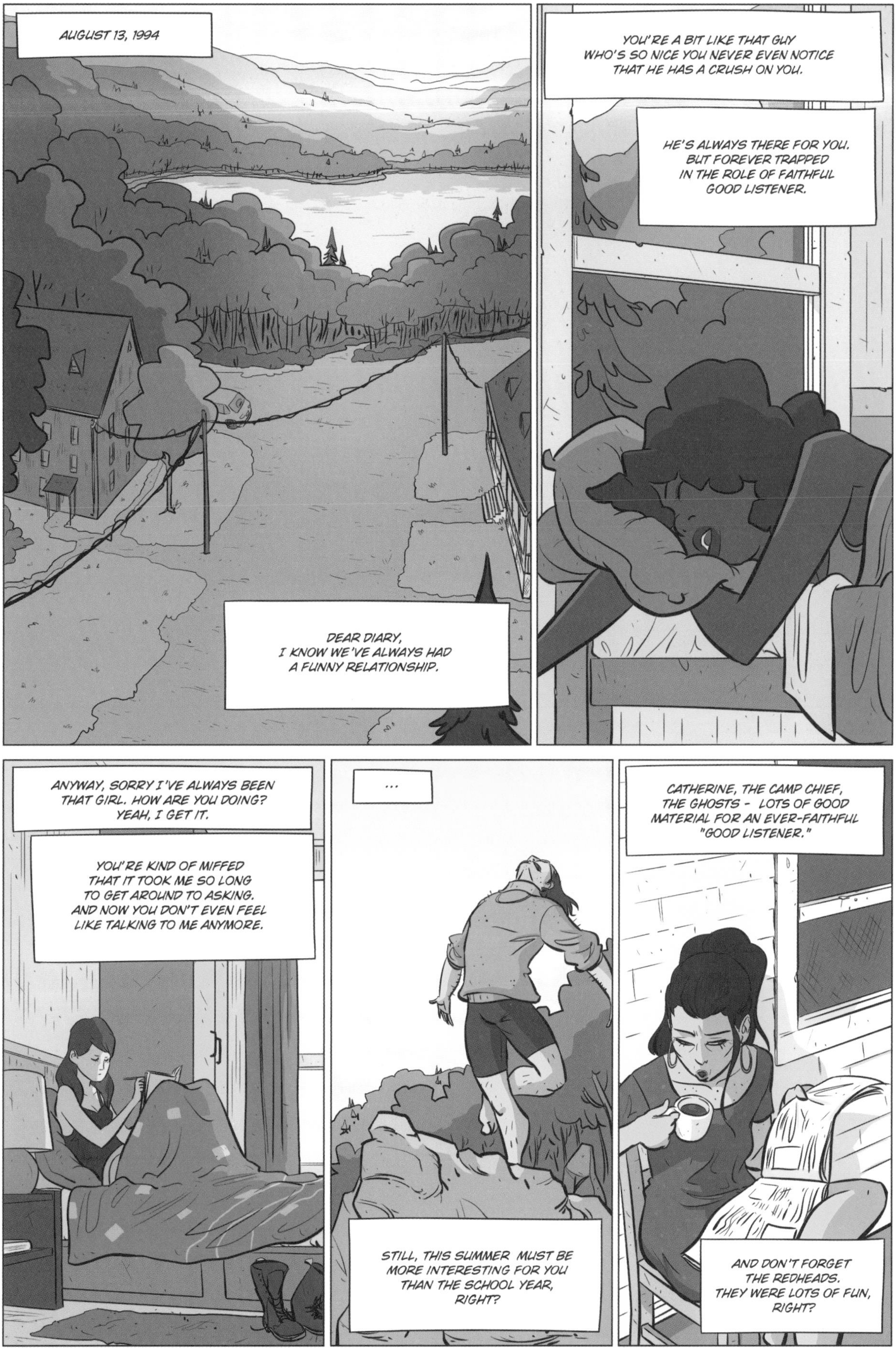
AUGUST 13, 1994
DEAR DIARY, I KNOW WE'VE ALWAYS HAD A FUNNY RELATIONSHIP.
YOU'RE A BIT LIKE THAT GUY WHO'S SO NICE YOU NEVER EVEN NOTICE THAT HE HAS A CRUSH ON YOU.
HE'S ALWAYS THERE FOR YOU. BUT FOREVER TRAPPED IN THE ROLE OF FAITHFUL GOOD LISTENER.
ANYWAY, SORRY I'VE ALWAYS BEEN THAT GIRL. HOW ARE YOU DOING? YEAH, I GET IT.
YOU'RE KIND OF MIFFED THAT IT TOOK ME SO LONG TO GET AROUND TO ASKING. AND NOW YOU DON'T EVEN FEEL LIKE TALKING TO ME ANYMORE.
...
STILL, THIS SUMMER MUST BE MORE INTERESTING FOR YOU THAN THE SCHOOL YEAR, RIGHT?
CATHERINE, THE CAMP CHIEF, THE GHOSTS - LOTS OF GOOD MATERIAL FOR AN EVER-FAITHFUL "GOOD LISTENER."
AND DON'T FORGET THE REDHEADS. THEY WERE LOTS OF FUN, RIGHT?

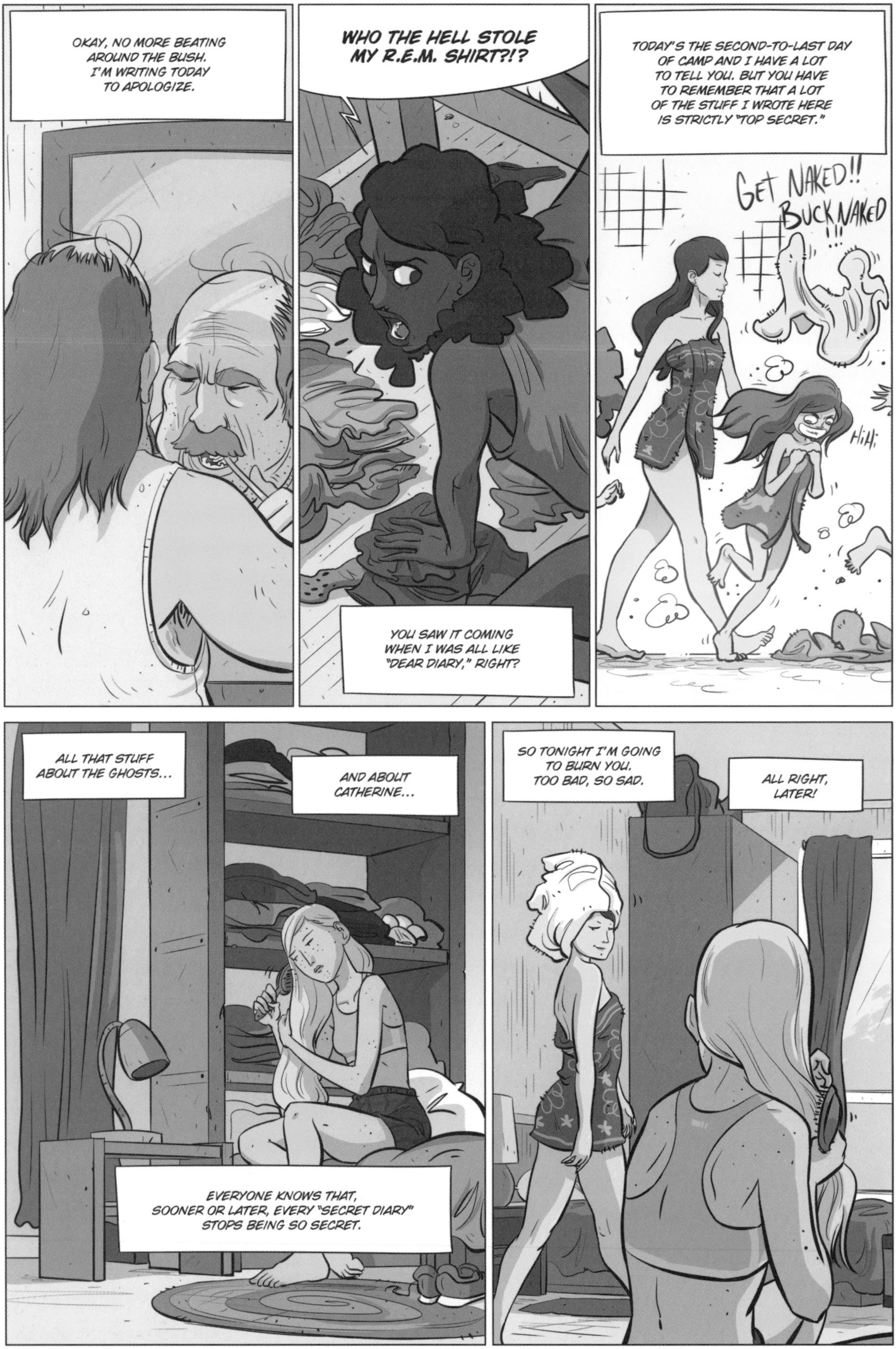
OKAY, NO MORE BEATING AROUND THE BUSH. I'M WRITING TODAY TO APOLOGIZE.
WHO THE HELL STOLE MY R.E.M. SHIRT?!?
YOU SAW IT COMING WHEN I WAS ALL LIKE "DEAR DIARY," RIGHT?
TODAY'S THE SECOND-TO-LAST DAY OF CAMP AND I HAVE A LOT TO TELL YOU. BUT YOU HAVE TO REMEMBER THAT A LOT OF THE STUFF I WROTE HERE IS STRICTLY "TOP SECRET."
GET NAKED!! BUCK NAKED!!!
HIHI
ALL THAT STUFF ABOUT THE GHOSTS...
AND ABOUT CATHERINE...
EVERYONE KNOWS THAT, SOONER OR LATER, EVERY "SECRET DIARY" STOPS BEING SO SECRET.
SO TONIGHT I'M GOING TO BURN YOU. TOO BAD, SO SAD.
ALL RIGHT, LATER!

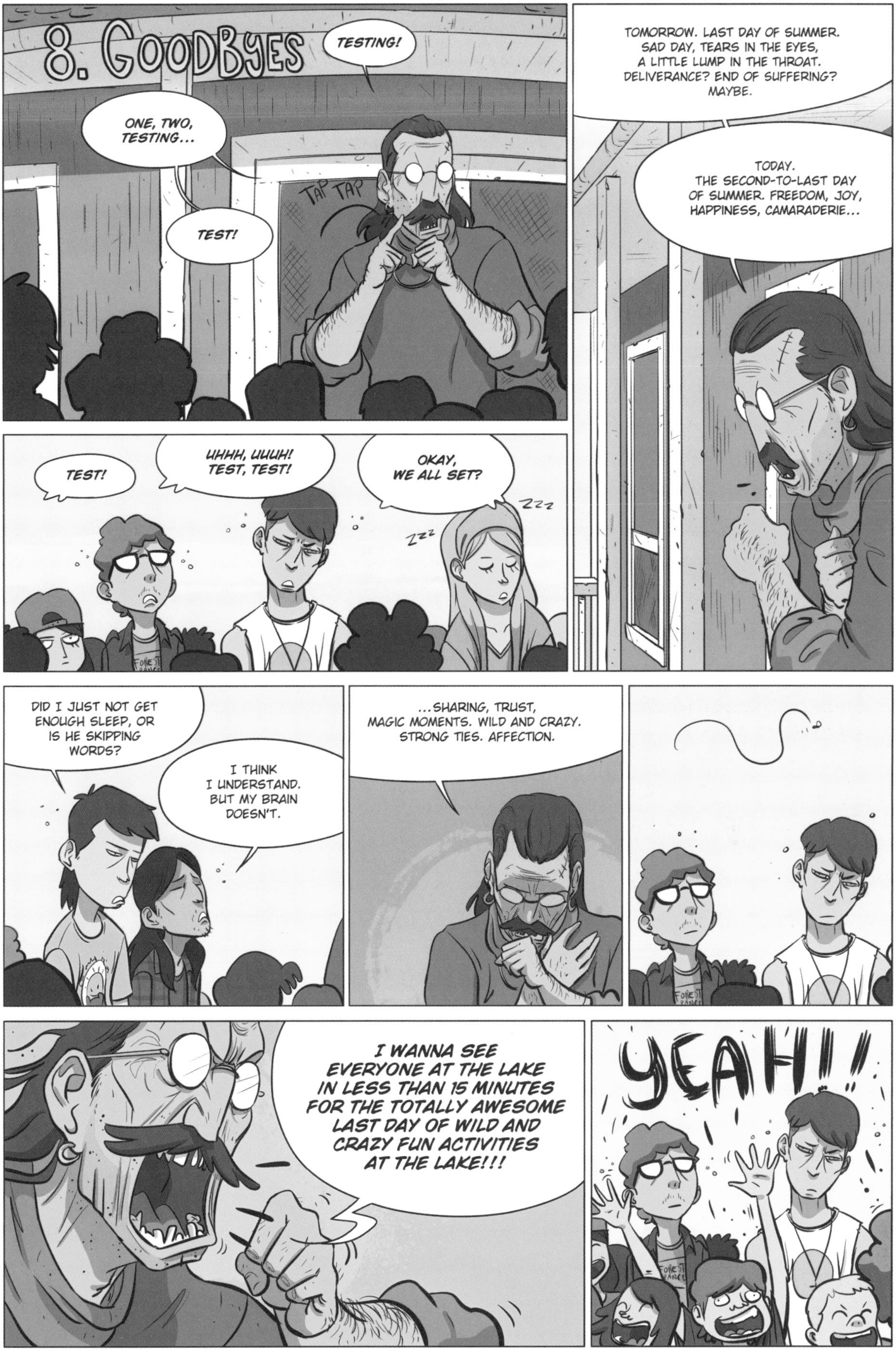
8. GOODBYES
TESTING!
ONE, TWO, TESTING...
TEST!
TAP TAP
TOMORROW. LAST DAY OF SUMMER. SAD DAY, TEARS IN THE EYES, A LITTLE LUMP IN THE THROAT. DELIVERANCE? END OF SUFFERING? MAYBE.
TODAY. THE SECOND-TO-LAST DAY OF SUMMER. FREEDOM, JOY, HAPPINESS, CAMARADERIE...
TEST!
UHHH, UUUH! TEST, TEST!
OKAY, WE ALL SET?
ZZZ
ZZZ
DID I JUST NOT GET ENOUGH SLEEP, OR IS HE SKIPPING WORDS?
I THINK I UNDERSTAND. BUT MY BRAIN DOESN'T.
...SHARING, TRUST, MAGIC MOMENTS. WILD AND CRAZY. STRONG TIES. AFFECTION.
I WANNA SEE EVERYONE AT THE LAKE IN LESS THAN 15 MINUTES FOR THE TOTALLY AWESOME LAST DAY OF WILD AND CRAZY FUN ACTIVITIES AT THE LAKE!!!
YEAH!!

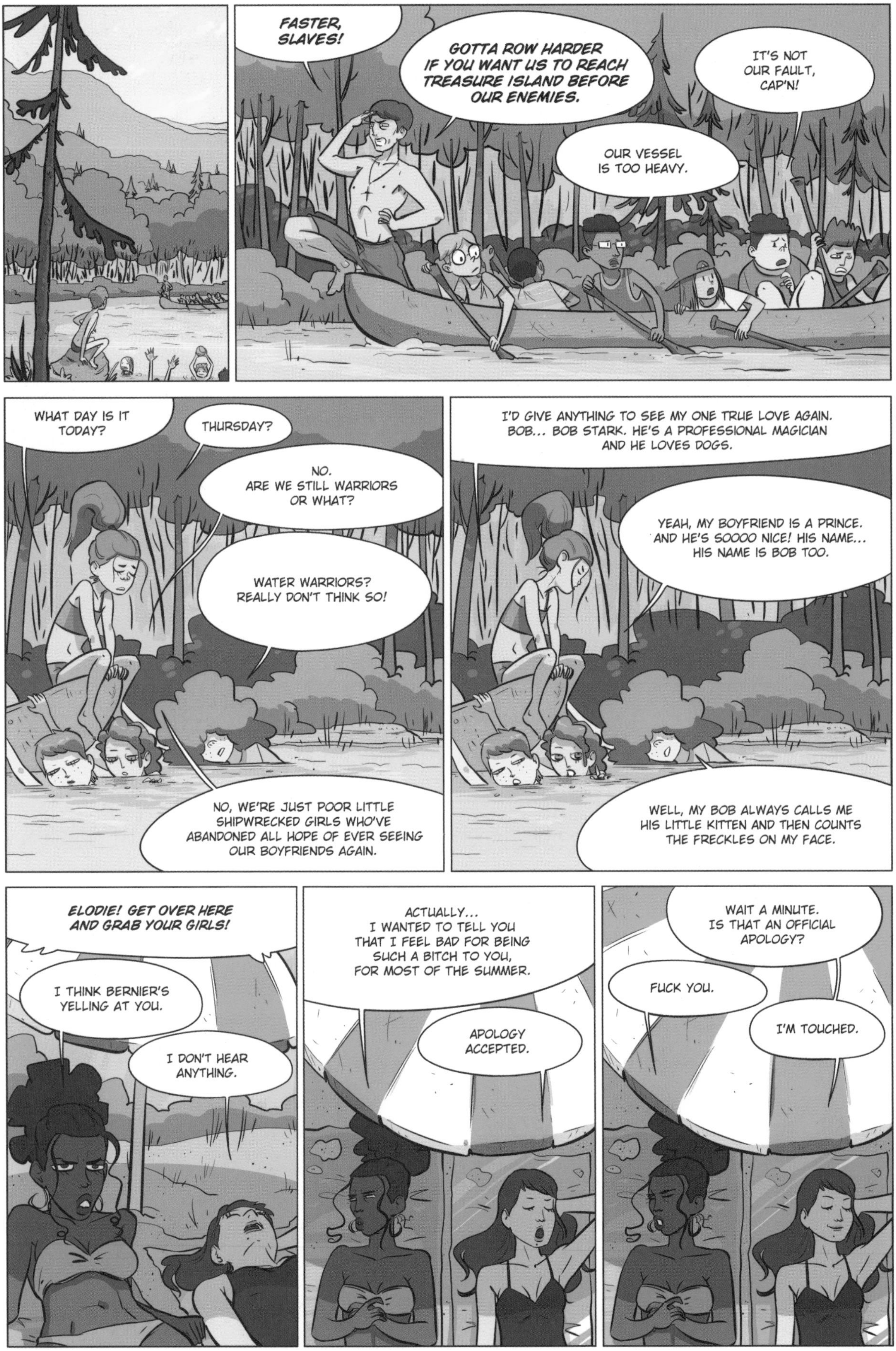
FASTER, SLAVES!
GOTTA ROW HARDER IF YOU WANT US TO REACH TREASURE ISLAND BEFORE OUR ENEMIES.
IT'S NOT OUR FAULT, CAP'N!
OUR VESSEL IS TOO HEAVY.
WHAT DAY IS IT TODAY?
THURSDAY?
NO. ARE WE STILL WARRIORS OR WHAT?
WATER WARRIORS? REALLY DON'T THINK SO!
NO, WE'RE JUST POOR LITTLE SHIPWRECKED GIRLS WHO'VE ABANDONED ALL HOPE OF EVER SEEING OUR BOYFRIENDS AGAIN.
I'D GIVE ANYTHING TO SEE MY ONE TRUE LOVE AGAIN. BOB... BOB STARK. HE'S A PROFESSIONAL MAGICIAN AND HE LOVES DOGS.
YEAH, MY BOYFRIEND IS A PRINCE. AND HE'S SOOOO NICE! HIS NAME... HIS NAME IS BOB TOO.
WELL, MY BOB ALWAYS CALLS ME HIS LITTLE KITTEN AND THEN COUNTS THE FRECKLES ON MY FACE.
ELODIE! GET OVER HERE AND GRAB YOUR GIRLS!
I THINK BERNIER'S YELLING AT YOU.
I DON'T HEAR ANYTHING.
ACTUALLY... I WANTED TO TELL YOU THAT I FEEL BAD FOR BEING SUCH A BITCH TO YOU, FOR MOST OF THE SUMMER.
APOLOGY ACCEPTED.
WAIT A MINUTE. IS THAT AN OFFICIAL APOLOGY?
FUCK YOU.
I'M TOUCHED.

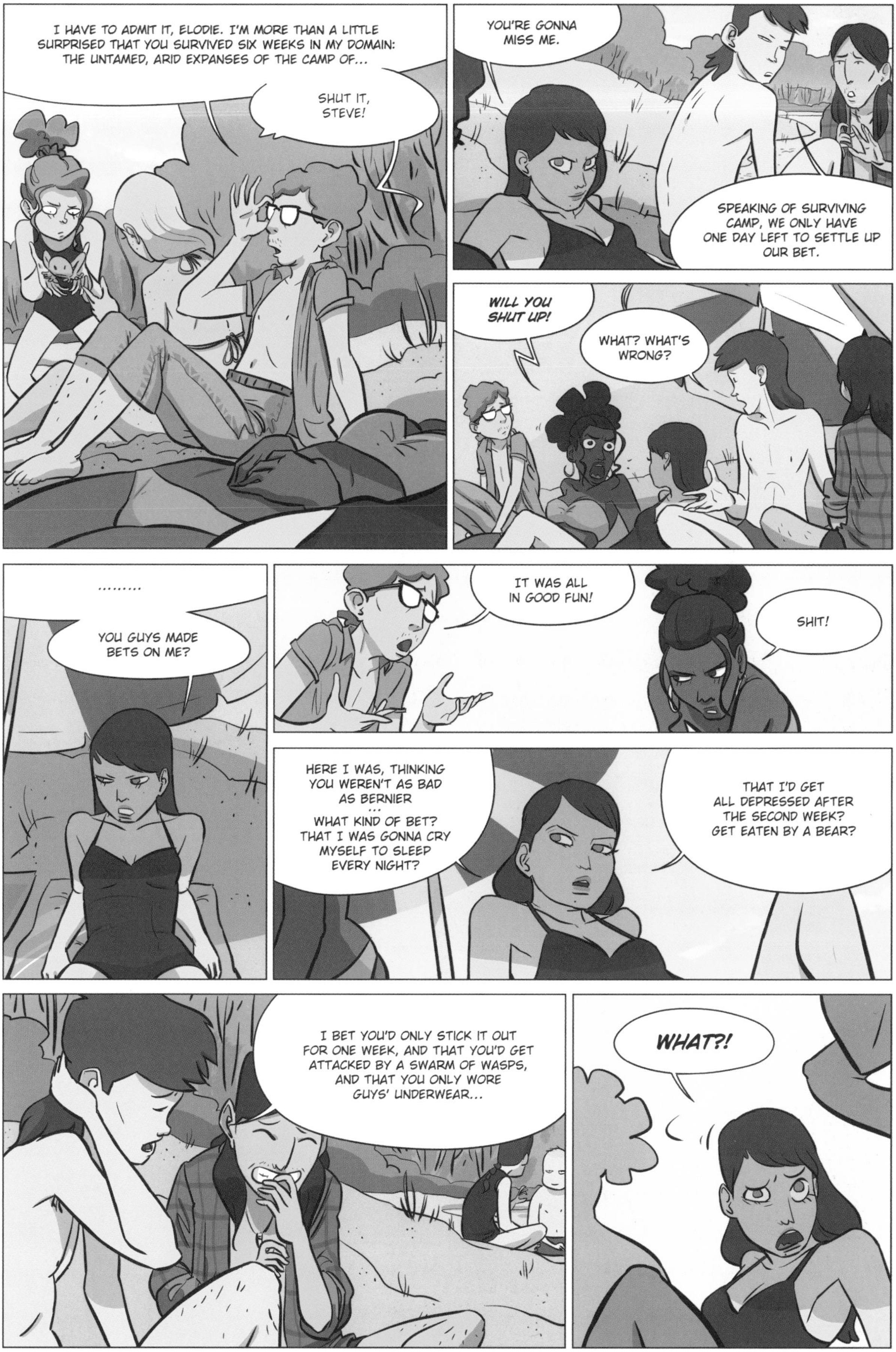
I HAVE TO ADMIT IT, ELODIE. I'M MORE THAN A LITTLE SURPRISED THAT YOU SURVIVED SIX WEEKS IN MY DOMAIN: THE UNTAMED, ARID EXPANSES OF THE CAMP OF...
SHUT IT, STEVE!
YOU'RE GONNA MISS ME.
SPEAKING OF SURVIVING CAMP, WE ONLY HAVE ONE DAY LEFT TO SETTLE UP OUR BET.
WILL YOU SHUT UP!
WHAT? WHAT'S WRONG?
....
YOU GUYS MADE BETS ON ME?
IT WAS ALL IN GOOD FUN!
SHIT!
HERE I WAS, THINKING YOU WEREN'T AS BAD AS BERNIER ... WHAT KIND OF BET? THAT I WAS GONNA CRY MYSELF TO SLEEP EVERY NIGHT?
THAT I'D GET ALL DEPRESSED AFTER THE SECOND WEEK? GET EATEN BY A BEAR?
I BET YOU'D ONLY STICK IT OUT FOR ONE WEEK, AND THAT YOU'D GET ATTACKED BY A SWARM OF WASPS, AND THAT YOU ONLY WORE GUYS' UNDERWEAR...
WHAT?!

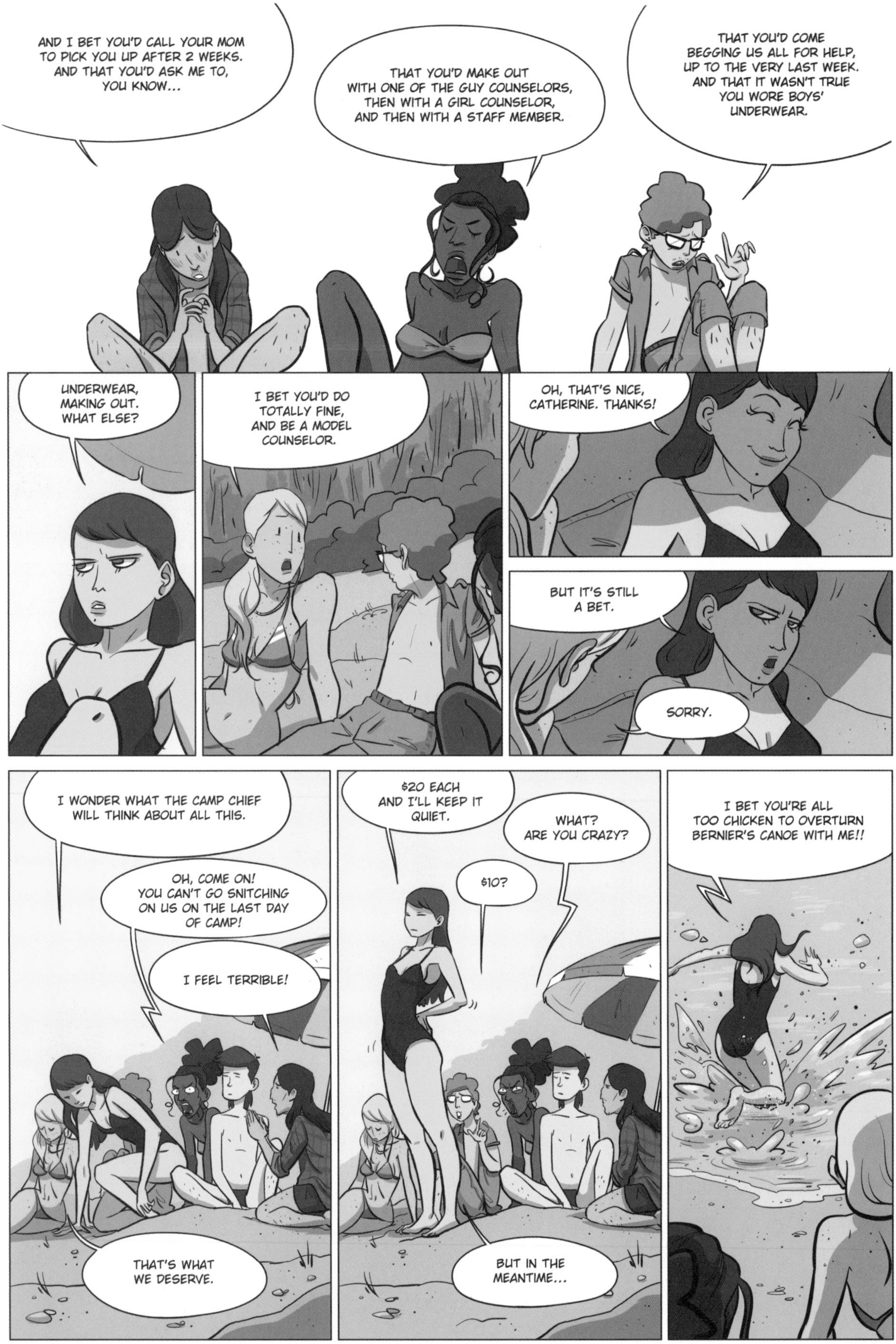
AND I BET YOU'D CALL YOUR MOM TO PICK YOU UP AFTER 2 WEEKS. AND THAT YOU'D ASK ME TO, YOU KNOW...
THAT YOU'D MAKE OUT WITH ONE OF THE GUY COUNSELORS, THEN WITH A GIRL COUNSELOR, AND THEN WITH A STAFF MEMBER.
THAT YOU'D COME BEGGING US ALL FOR HELP, UP TO THE VERY LAST WEEK. AND THAT IT WASN'T TRUE YOU WORE BOYS' UNDERWEAR.
UNDERWEAR, MAKING OUT. WHAT ELSE?
I BET YOU'D DO TOTALLY FINE, AND BE A MODEL COUNSELOR.
OH, THAT'S NICE, CATHERINE. THANKS!
BUT IT'S STILL A BET.
SORRY.
I WONDER WHAT THE CAMP CHIEF WILL THINK ABOUT ALL THIS.
OH, COME ON! YOU CAN'T GO SNITCHING ON US ON THE LAST DAY OF CAMP!
I FEEL TERRIBLE!
THAT'S WHAT WE DESERVE.
$20 EACH AND I'LL KEEP IT QUIET.
WHAT? ARE YOU CRAZY?
$10?
BUT IN THE MEANTIME...
I BET YOU'RE ALL TOO CHICKEN TO OVERTURN BERNIER'S CANOE WITH ME!!

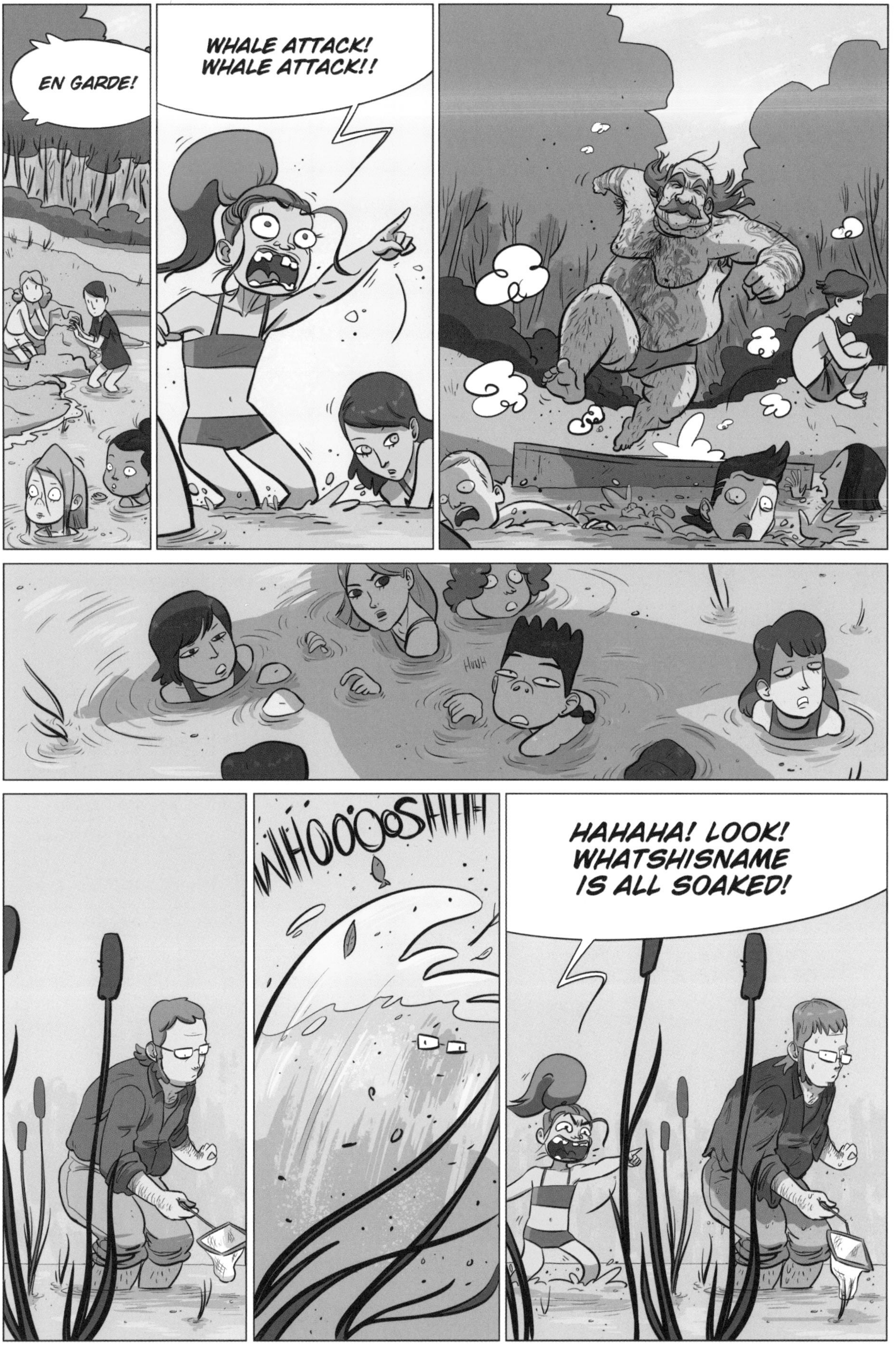
EN GARDE!
WHALE ATTACK! WHALE ATTACK!!
HUNH
WHOOOOOSHHHH
HAHAHA! LOOK! WHATSHISNAME IS ALL SOAKED!

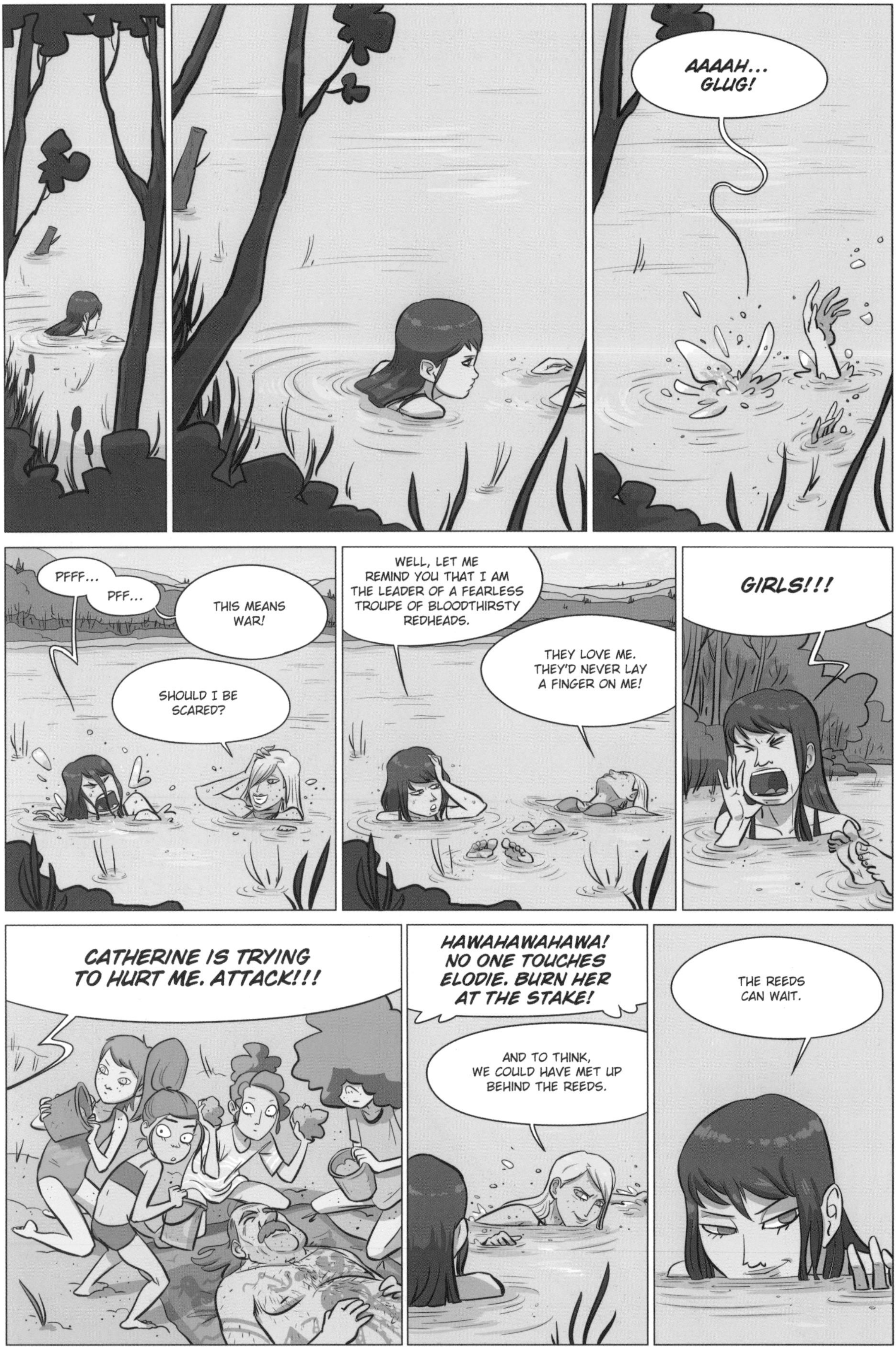
AAAAH... GLUG!
PFFF...
PFF...
THIS MEANS WAR!
SHOULD I BE SCARED?
WELL, LET ME REMIND YOU THAT I AM THE LEADER OF A FEARLESS TROUPE OF BLOODTHIRSTY REDHEADS.
THEY LOVE ME. THEY'D NEVER LAY A FINGER ON ME!
GIRLS!!!
CATHERINE IS TRYING TO HURT ME. ATTACK!!!
HAWAHAHAWAHAWA! NO ONE TOUCHES ELODIE. BURN HER AT THE STAKE!
AND TO THINK, WE COULD HAVE MET UP BEHIND THE REEDS.
THE REEDS CAN WAIT.

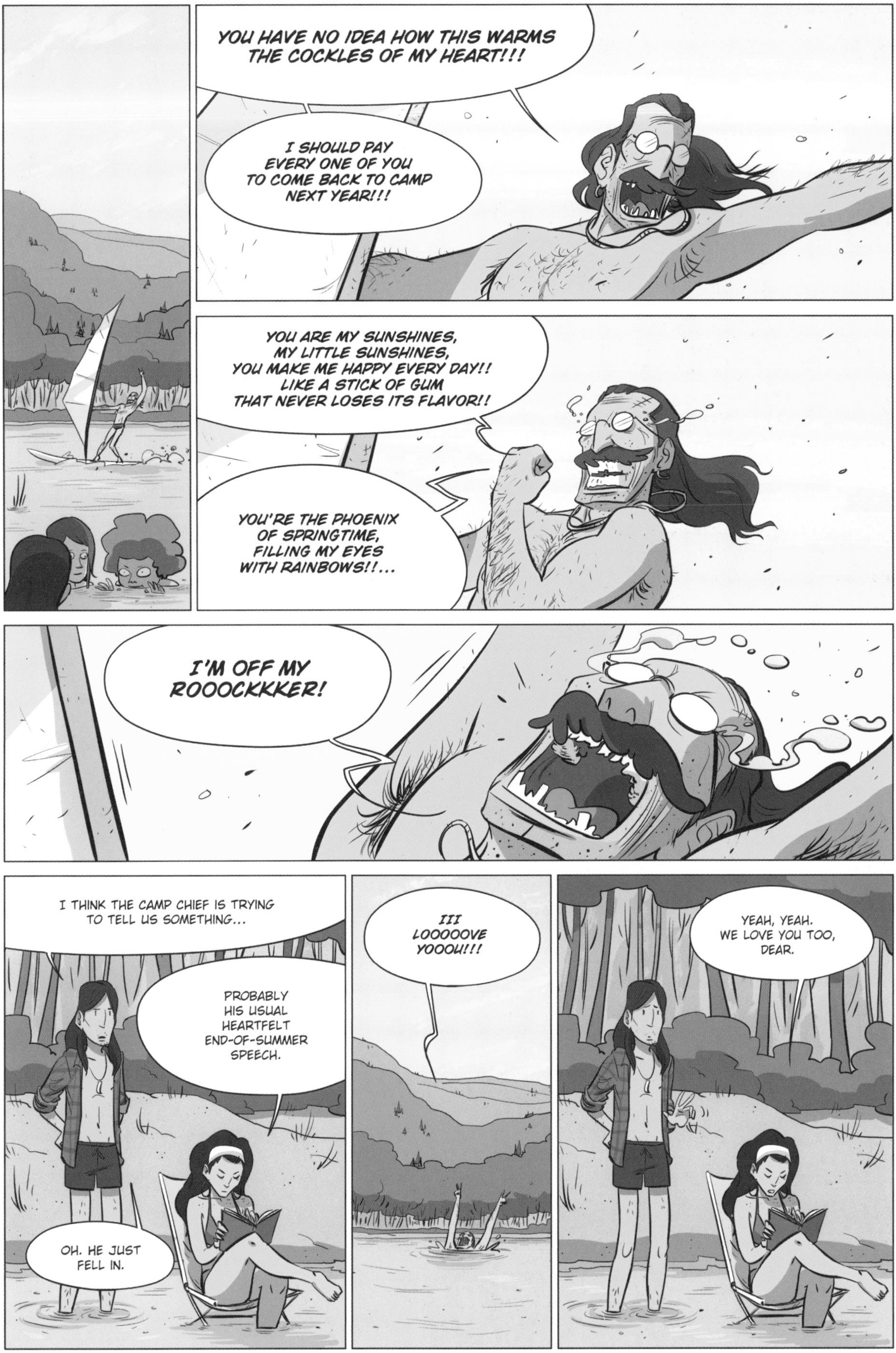
YOU HAVE NO IDEA HOW THIS WARMS THE COCKLES OF MY HEART!!!
I SHOULD PAY EVERY ONE OF YOU TO COME BACK TO CAMP NEXT YEAR!!!
YOU ARE MY SUNSHINES, MY LITTLE SUNSHINES, YOU MAKE ME HAPPY EVERY DAY!! LIKE A STICK OF GUM THAT NEVER LOSES ITS FLAVOR!!
YOU'RE THE PHOENIX OF SPRINGTIME, FILLING MY EYES WITH RAINBOWS!!...
I'M OFF MY ROOOCKKKER!
I THINK THE CAMP CHIEF IS TRYING TO TELL US SOMETHING...
PROBABLY HIS USUAL HEARTFELT END-OF-SUMMER SPEECH.
OH. HE JUST FELL IN.
III LOOOOOVE YOOOU!!!
YEAH, YEAH. WE LOVE YOU TOO, DEAR.

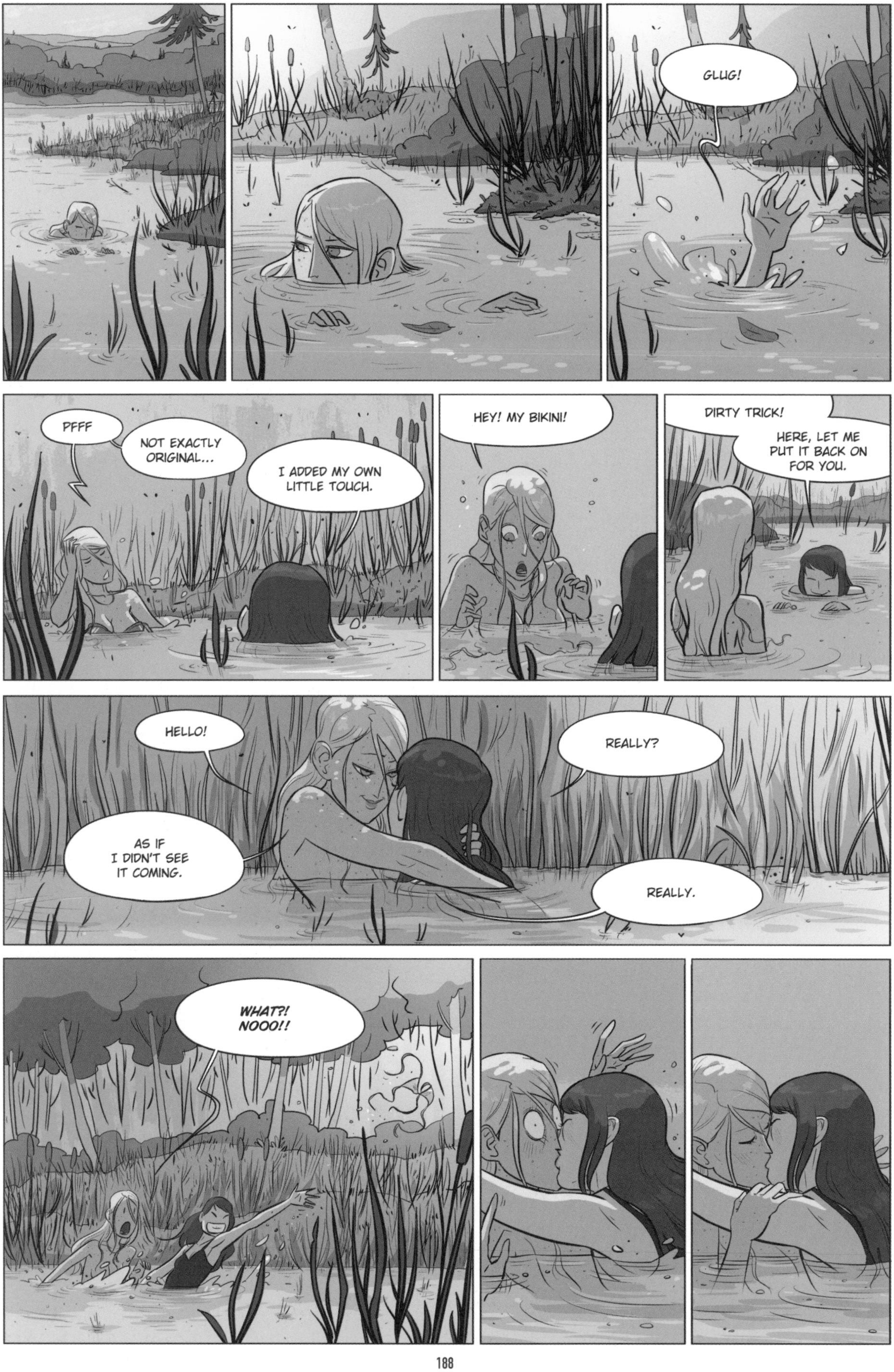

GLUG!
PFFF
NOT EXACTLY ORIGINAL...
I ADDED MY OWN LITTLE TOUCH.
HEY! MY BIKINI!
DIRTY TRICK!
HERE, LET ME PUT IT BACK ON FOR YOU.
HELLO!
AS IF I DIDN'T SEE IT COMING.
REALLY?
REALLY.
WHAT?! NOOO!!

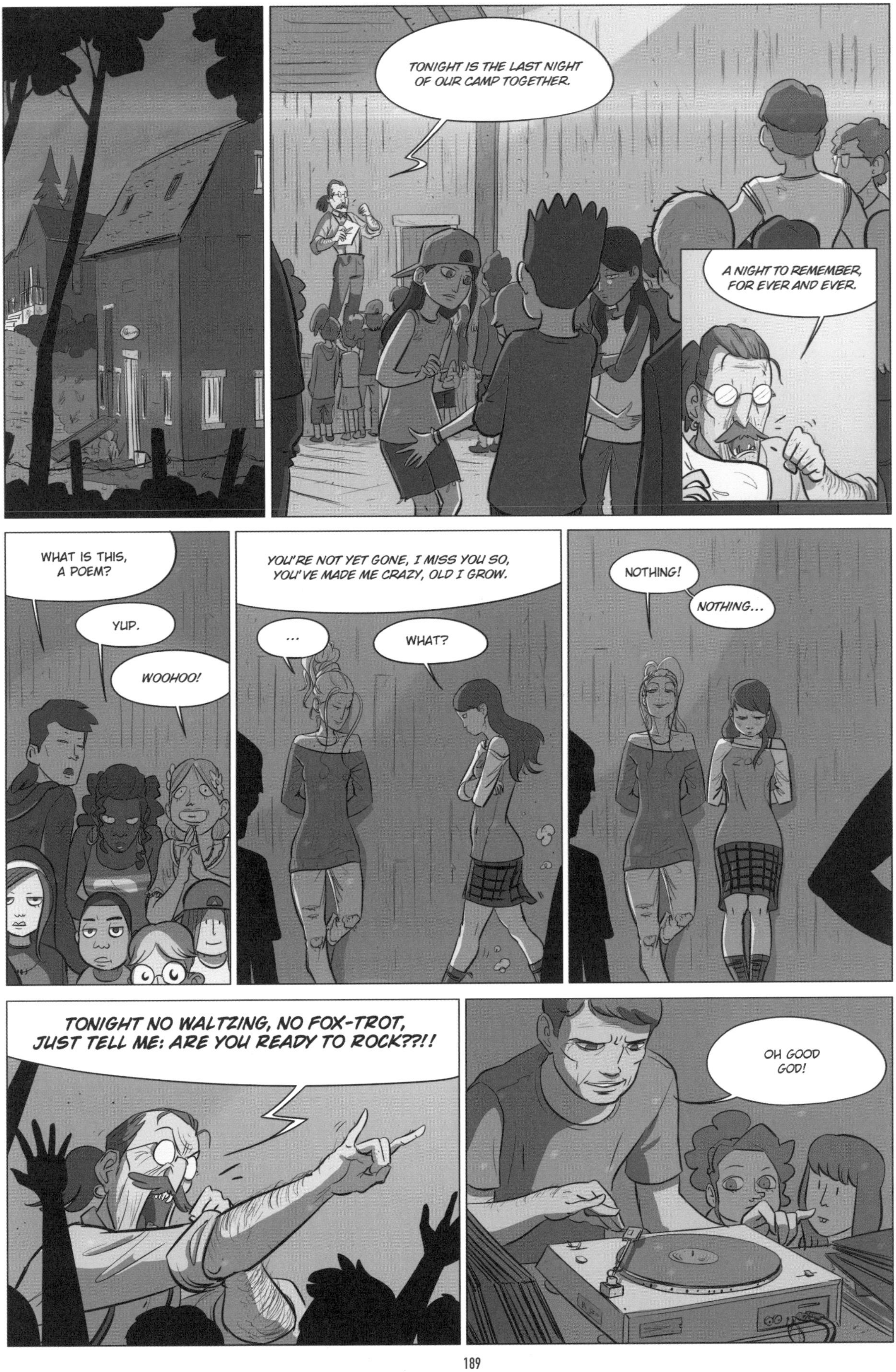
TONIGHT IS THE LAST NIGHT OF OUR CAMP TOGETHER.
A NIGHT TO REMEMBER, FOR EVER AND EVER.
WHAT IS THIS, A POEM?
YUP.
WOOHOO!
YOU'RE NOT YET GONE, I MISS YOU SO, YOU'VE MADE ME CRAZY, OLD I GROW.
...
WHAT?
NOTHING!
NOTHING...
TONIGHT NO WALTZING, NO FOX-TROT, JUST TELL ME: ARE YOU READY TO ROCK??!!
OH GOOD GOD!

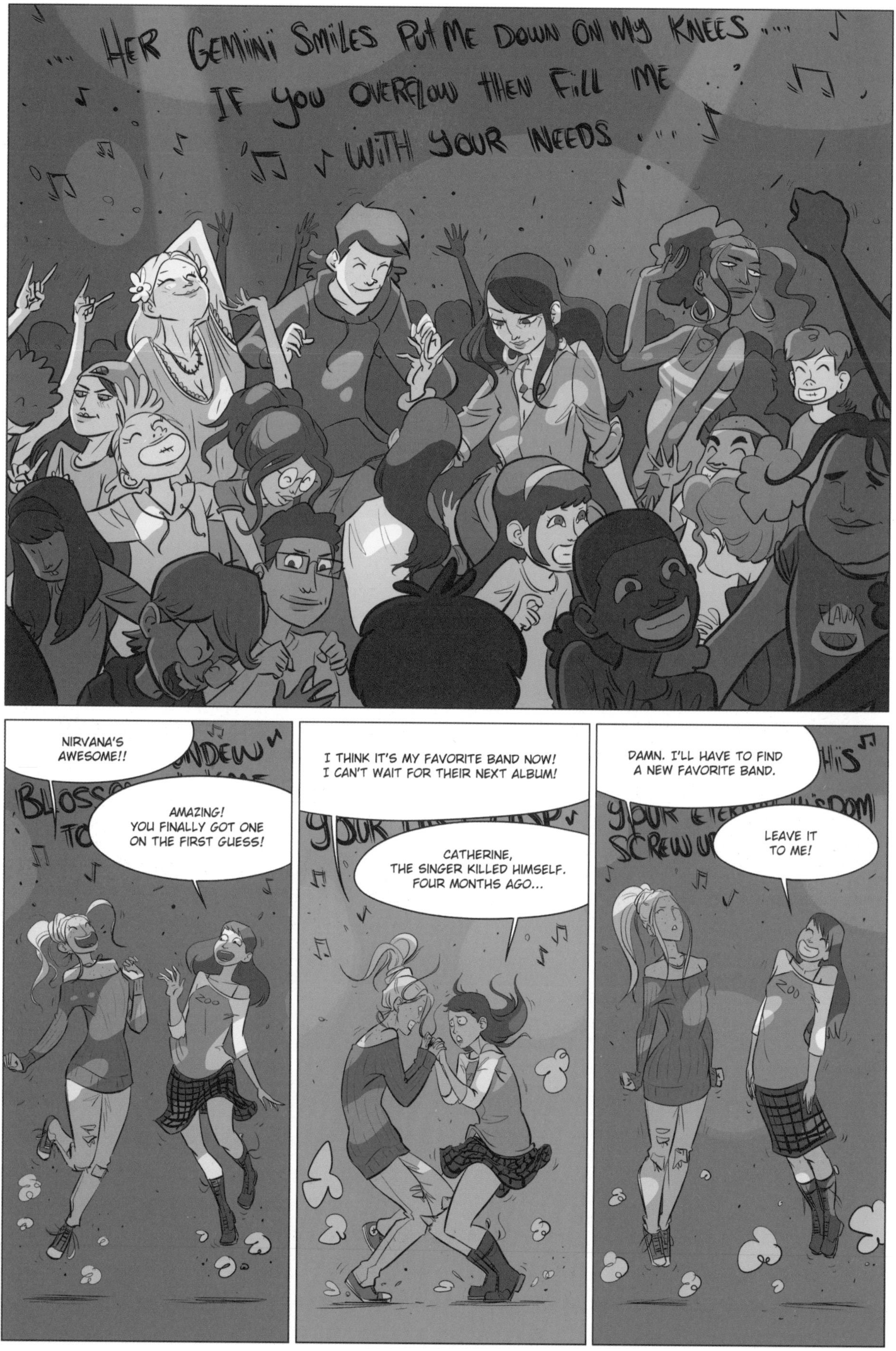
HER GEMINI SMILES PUT ME DOWN ON MY KNEES ...
IF YOU OVERFLOW THEN FILL ME
WITH YOUR NEEDS
NIRVANA'S AWESOME!!
AMAZING! YOU FINALLY GOT ONE ON THE FIRST GUESS!
I THINK IT'S MY FAVORITE BAND NOW! I CAN'T WAIT FOR THEIR NEXT ALBUM!
CATHERINE, THE SINGER KILLED HIMSELF. FOUR MONTHS AGO...
DAMN. I'LL HAVE TO FIND A NEW FAVORITE BAND.
LEAVE IT TO ME!

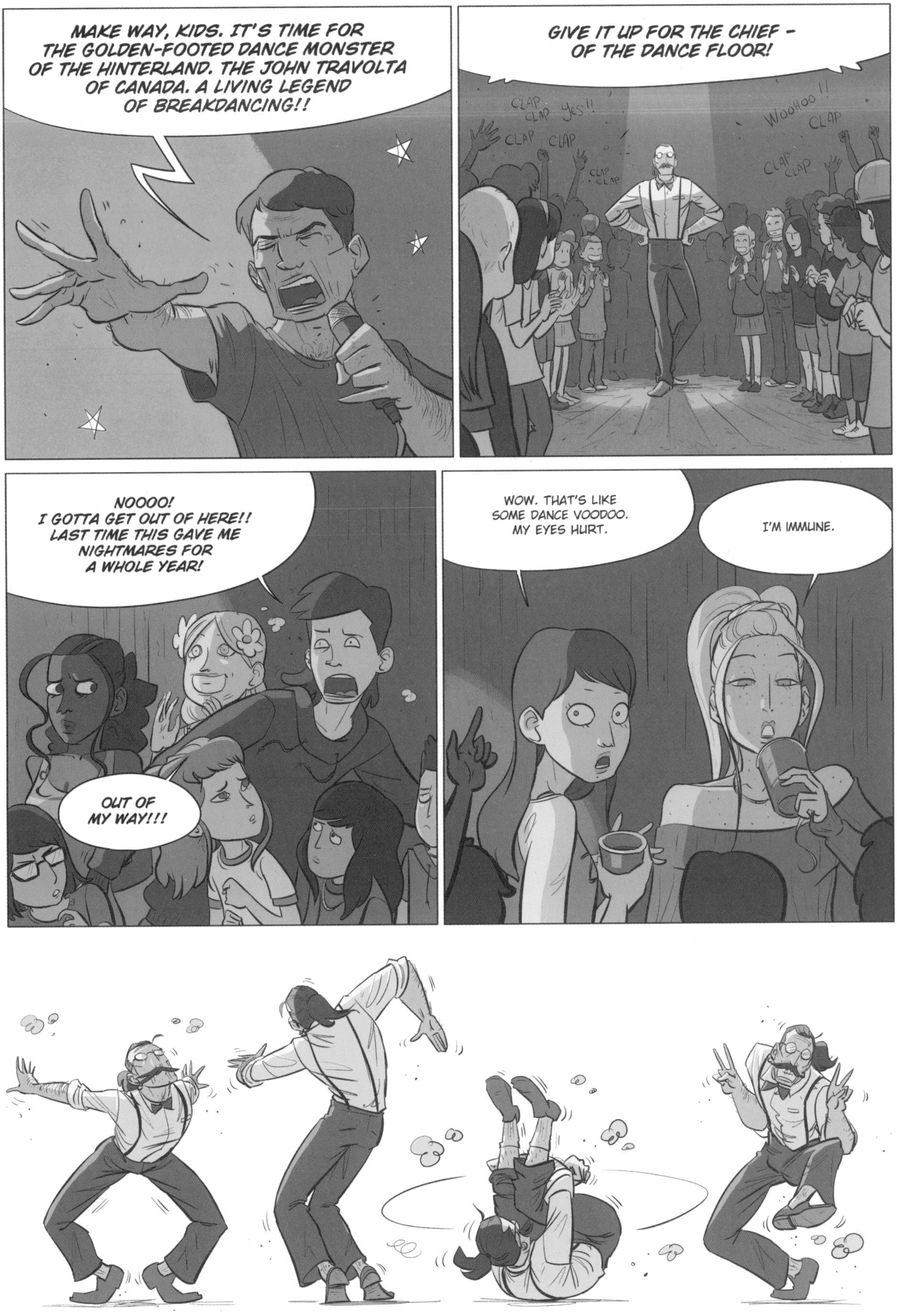
MAKE WAY, KIDS. IT'S TIME FOR THE GOLDEN-FOOTED DANCE MONSTER OF THE HINTERLAND. THE JOHN TRAVOLTA OF CANADA. A LIVING LEGEND OF BREAKDANCING!!
GIVE IT UP FOR THE CHIEF - OF THE DANCE FLOOR!
CLAP CLAP
YES!!
CLAP
CLAP
CLAP CLAP
WOOHOO!!
CLAP
CLAP CLAP
NOOOO! I GOTTA GET OUT OF HERE!! LAST TIME THIS GAVE ME NIGHTMARES FOR A WHOLE YEAR!
OUT OF MY WAY!!!
WOW. THAT'S LIKE SOME DANCE VOODOO. MY EYES HURT.
I'M IMMUNE.

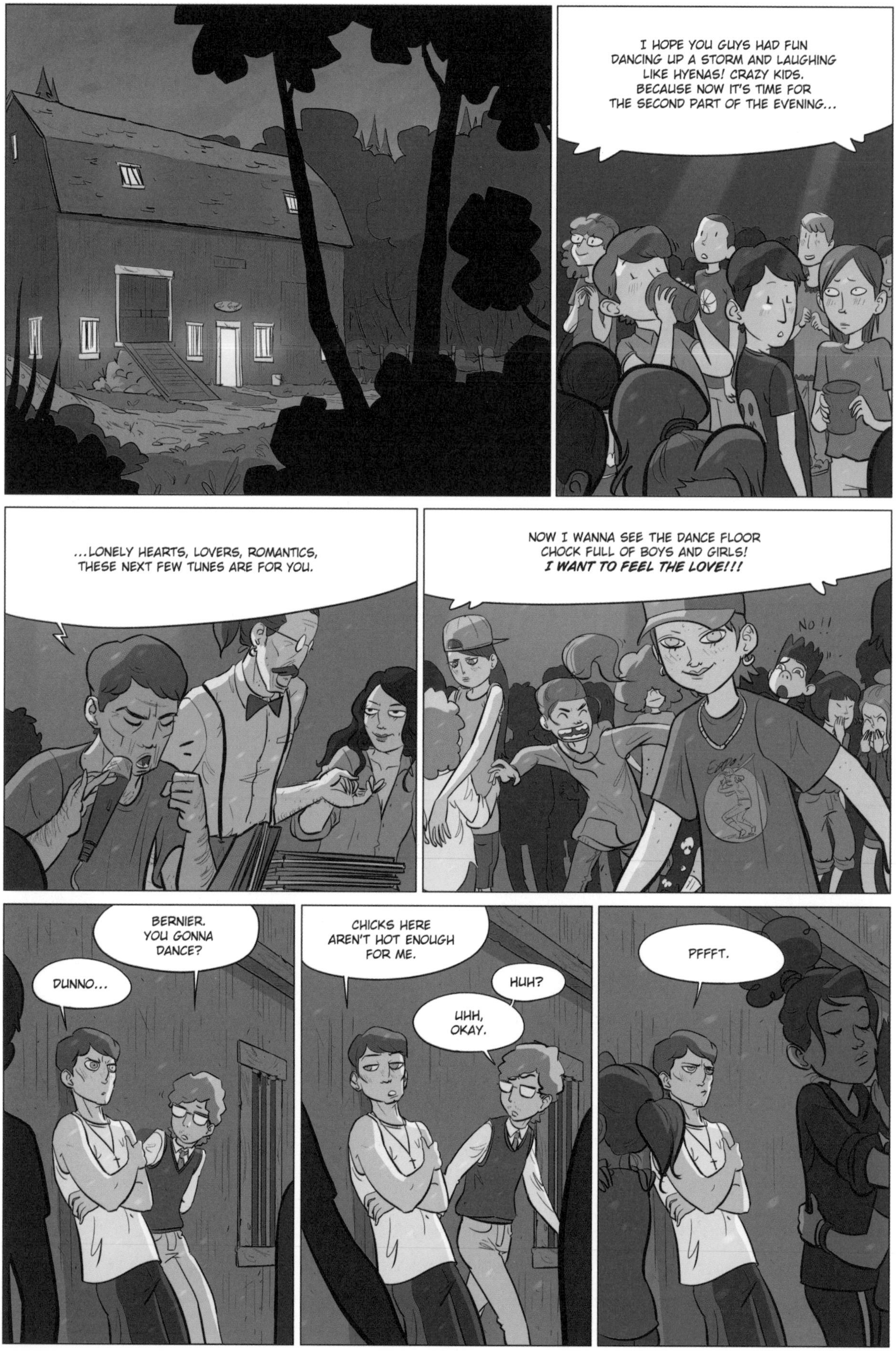
I HOPE YOU GUYS HAD FUN DANCING UP A STORM AND LAUGHING LIKE HYENAS! CRAZY KIDS. BECAUSE NOW IT'S TIME FOR THE SECOND PART OF THE EVENING...
...LONELY HEARTS, LOVERS, ROMANTICS, THESE NEXT FEW TUNES ARE FOR YOU.
NOW I WANNA SEE THE DANCE FLOOR CHOCK FULL OF BOYS AND GIRLS! I WANT TO FEEL THE LOVE!!!
NO!!
BERNIER. YOU GONNA DANCE?
DUNNO...
CHICKS HERE AREN'T HOT ENOUGH FOR ME.
HUH?
UHH, OKAY.
PFFFT.

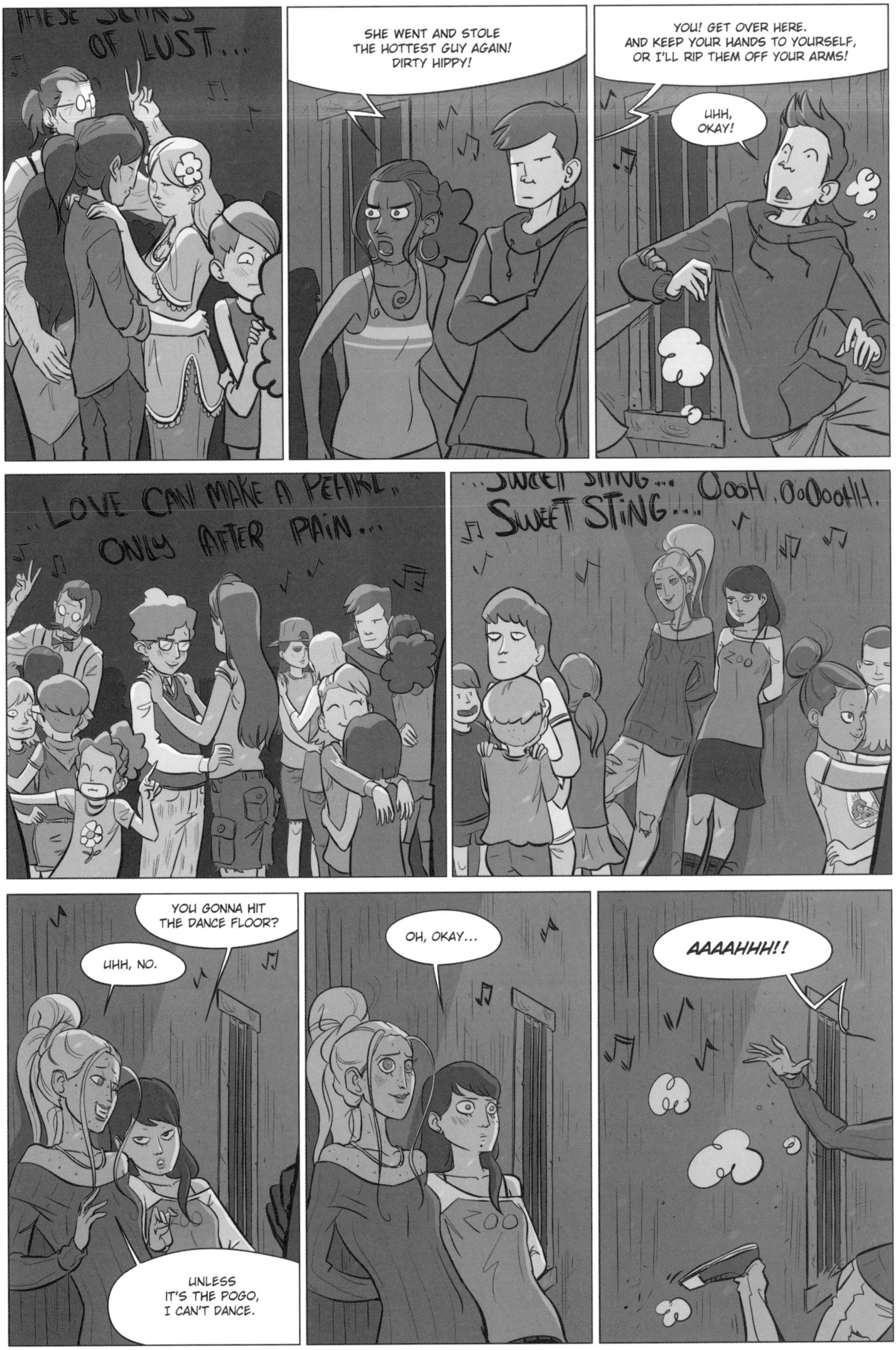
THESE SCARS OF LUST...
SHE WENT AND STOLE THE HOTTEST GUY AGAIN! DIRTY HIPPY!
YOU! GET OVER HERE. AND KEEP YOUR HANDS TO YOURSELF, OR I'LL RIP THEM OFF YOUR ARMS!
UHH, OKAY!
...LOVE CAN MAKE A PEARL, ONLY AFTER PAIN...
...SWEET STING... SWEET STING... OOOH, OOOOOHH.
ZOO
YOU GONNA HIT THE DANCE FLOOR?
UHH, NO.
UNLESS IT'S THE POGO, I CAN'T DANCE.
OH, OKAY...
AAAAHHH!!

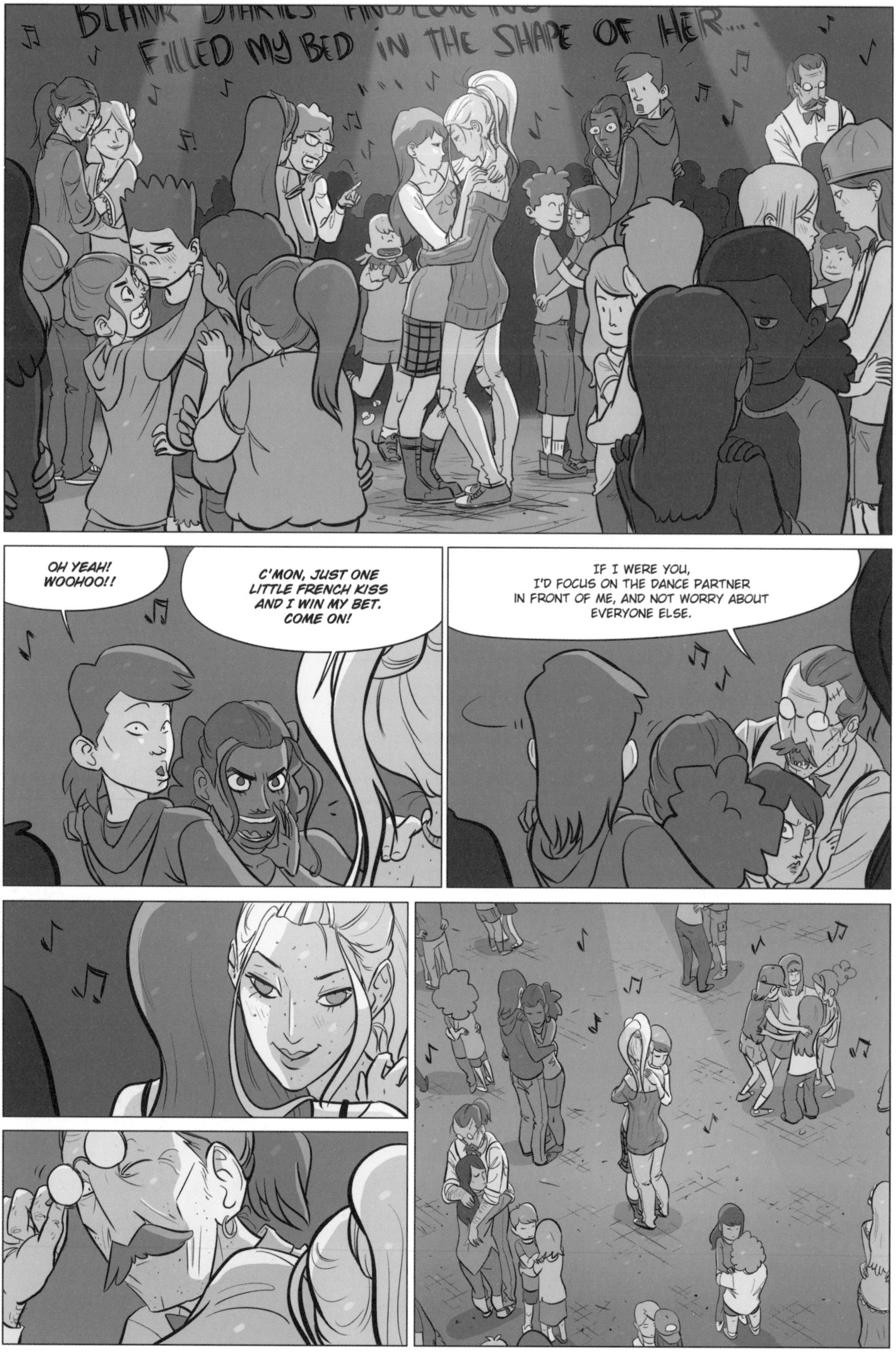
FILLED MY BED IN THE SHAPE OF HER....
OH YEAH! WOOHOO!!
C'MON, JUST ONE LITTLE FRENCH KISS AND I WIN MY BET. COME ON!
IF I WERE YOU, I'D FOCUS ON THE DANCE PARTNER IN FRONT OF ME, AND NOT WORRY ABOUT EVERYONE ELSE.

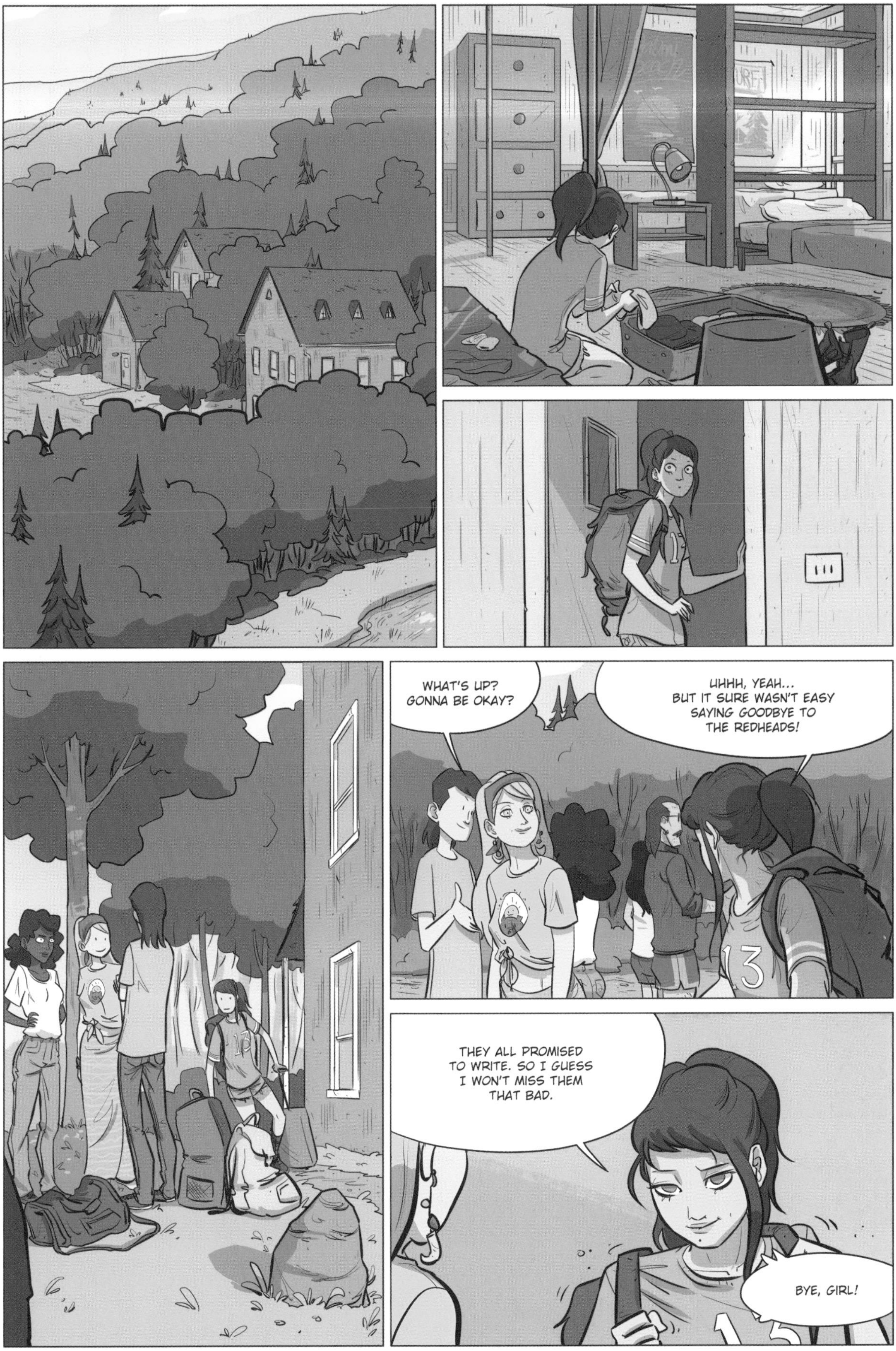
WHAT'S UP? GONNA BE OKAY?
UHHH, YEAH... BUT IT SURE WASN'T EASY SAYING GOODBYE TO THE REDHEADS!
THEY ALL PROMISED TO WRITE. SO I GUESS I WON'T MISS THEM THAT BAD.
BYE, GIRL!

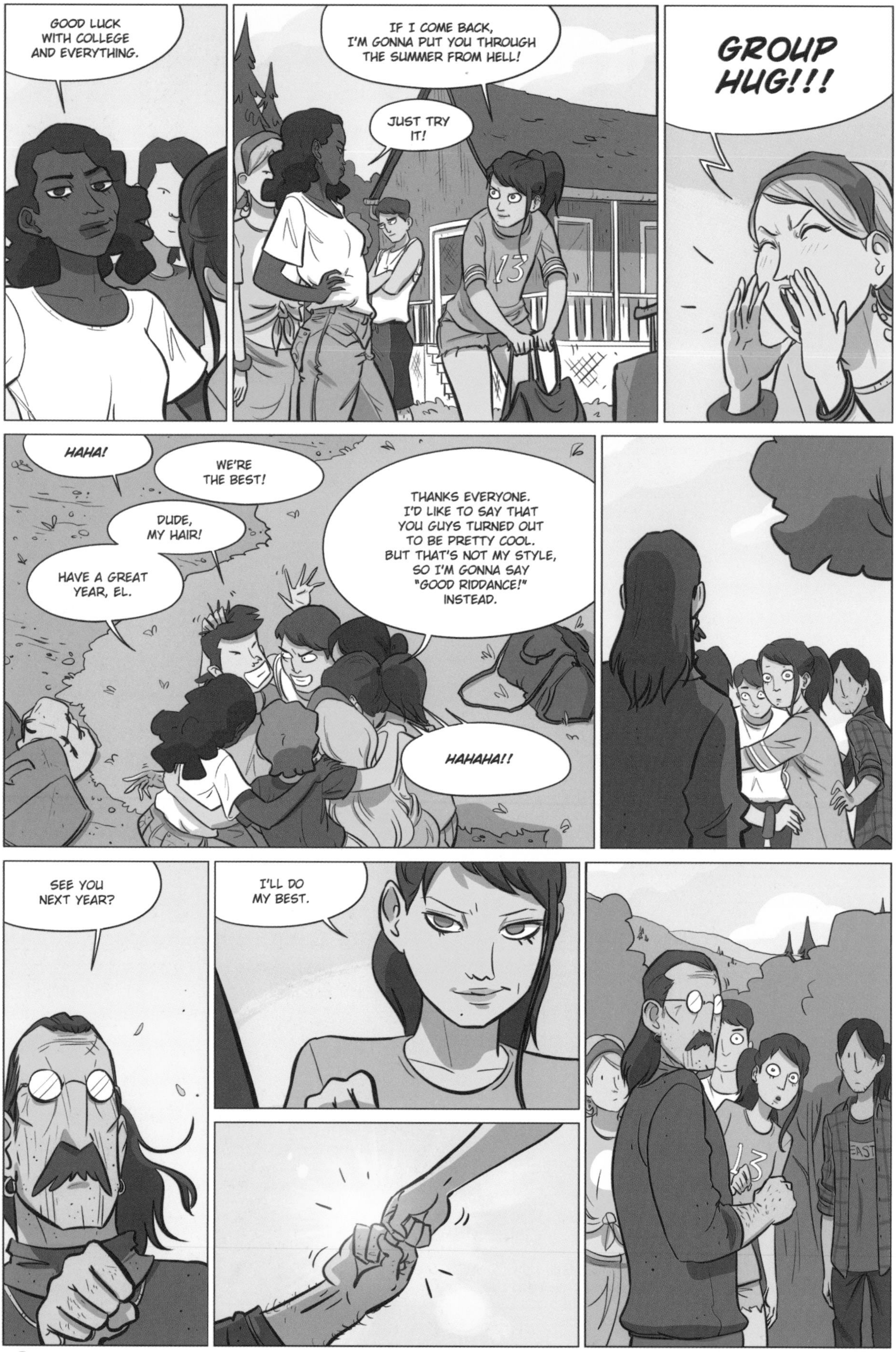
GOOD LUCK WITH COLLEGE AND EVERYTHING.
IF I COME BACK, I'M GONNA PUT YOU THROUGH THE SUMMER FROM HELL!
JUST TRY IT!
GROUP HUG!!!
HAHA!
WE'RE THE BEST!
DUDE, MY HAIR!
HAVE A GREAT YEAR, EL.
THANKS EVERYONE. I'D LIKE TO SAY THAT YOU GUYS TURNED OUT TO BE PRETTY COOL. BUT THAT'S NOT MY STYLE, SO I'M GONNA SAY "GOOD RIDDANCE!" INSTEAD.
HAHAHA!!
SEE YOU NEXT YEAR?
I'LL DO MY BEST.

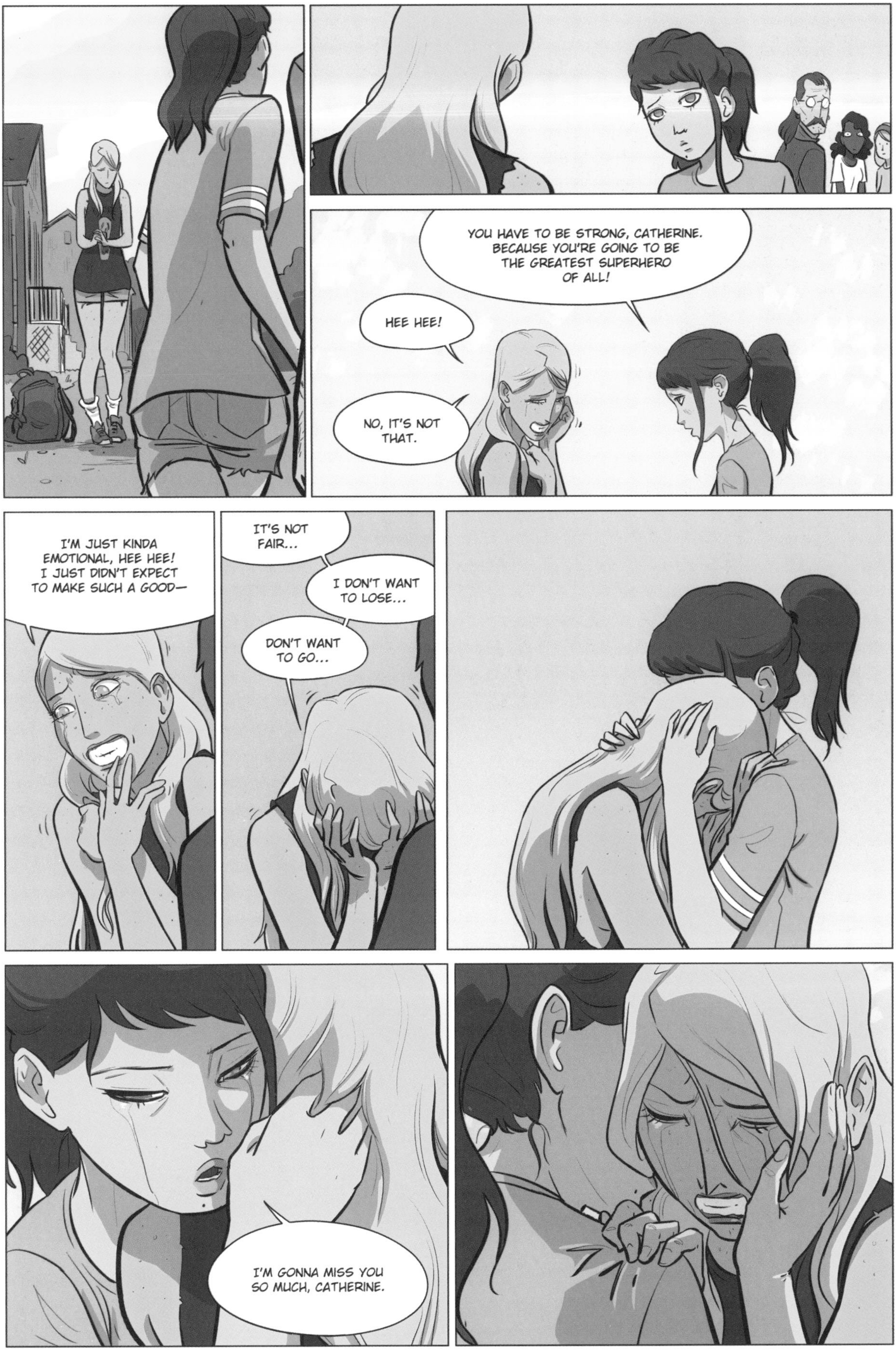
YOU HAVE TO BE STRONG, CATHERINE. BECAUSE YOU'RE GOING TO BE THE GREATEST SUPERHERO OF ALL!
HEE HEE!
NO, IT'S NOT THAT.
I'M JUST KINDA EMOTIONAL, HEE HEE! I JUST DIDN'T EXPECT TO MAKE SUCH A GOOD—
IT'S NOT FAIR...
I DON'T WANT TO LOSE...
DON'T WANT TO GO...
I'M GONNA MISS YOU SO MUCH, CATHERINE.

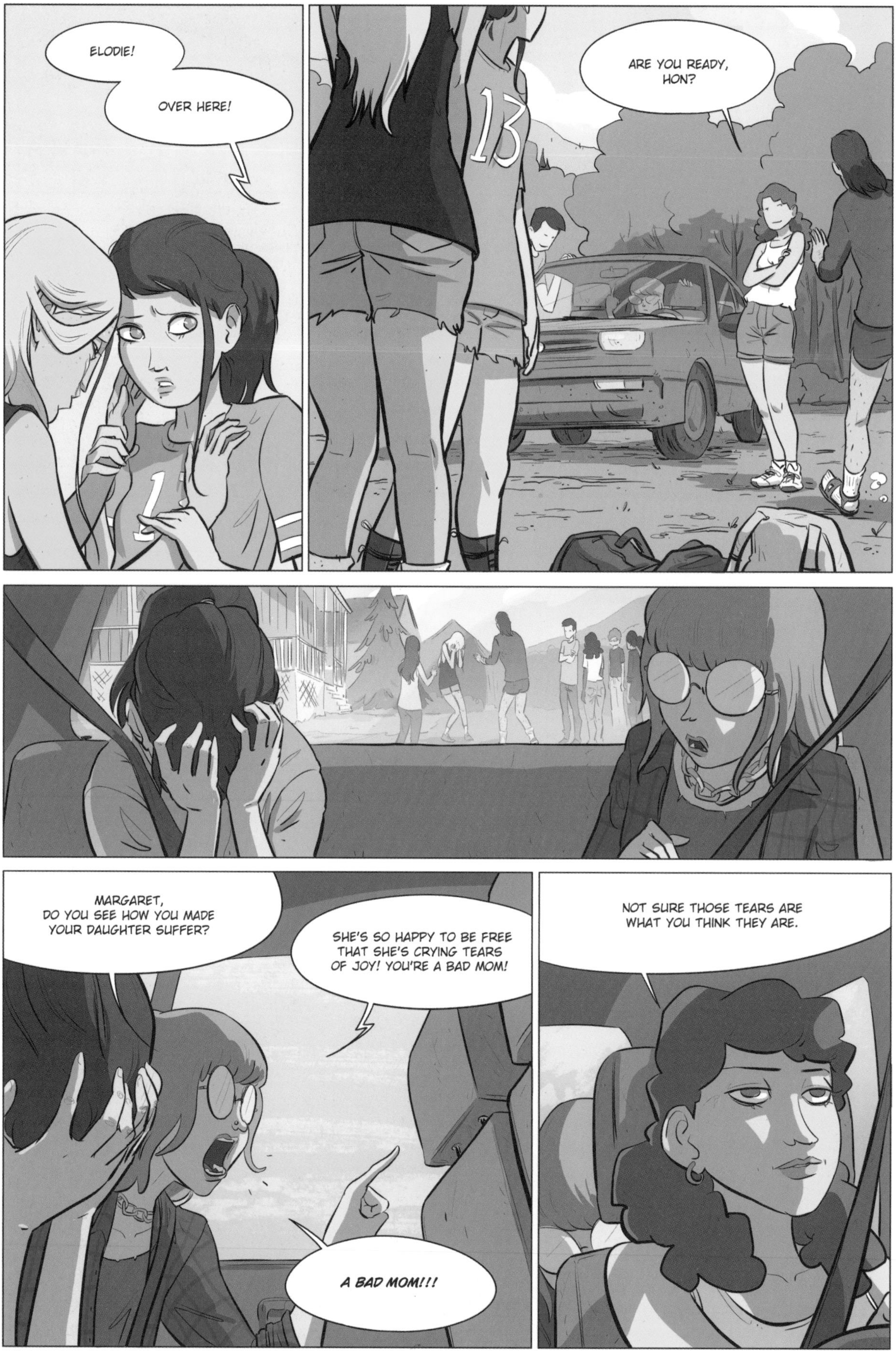
ELODIE!
OVER HERE!
ARE YOU READY, HON?
MARGARET, DO YOU SEE HOW YOU MADE YOUR DAUGHTER SUFFER?
SHE'S SO HAPPY TO BE FREE THAT SHE'S CRYING TEARS OF JOY! YOU'RE A BAD MOM!
A BAD MOM!!!
NOT SURE THOSE TEARS ARE WHAT YOU THINK THEY ARE.

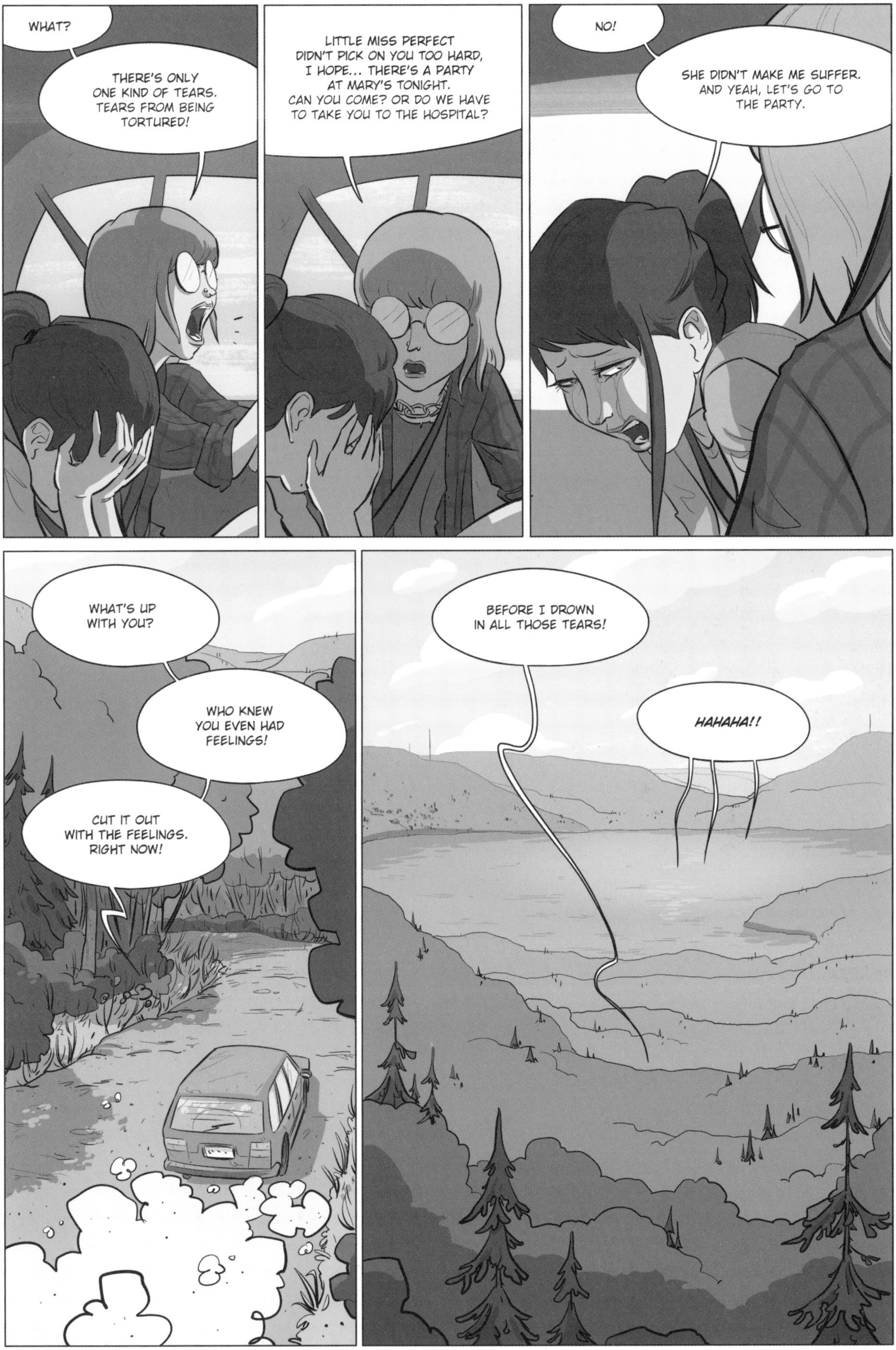
WHAT?
THERE'S ONLY ONE KIND OF TEARS. TEARS FROM BEING TORTURED!
LITTLE MISS PERFECT DIDN'T PICK ON YOU TOO HARD, I HOPE... THERE'S A PARTY AT MARY'S TONIGHT. CAN YOU COME? OR DO WE HAVE TO TAKE YOU TO THE HOSPITAL?
NO!
SHE DIDN'T MAKE ME SUFFER. AND YEAH, LET'S GO TO THE PARTY.
WHAT'S UP WITH YOU?
WHO KNEW YOU EVEN HAD FEELINGS!
CUT IT OUT WITH THE FEELINGS. RIGHT NOW!
BEFORE I DROWN IN ALL THOSE TEARS!
HAHAHA!!

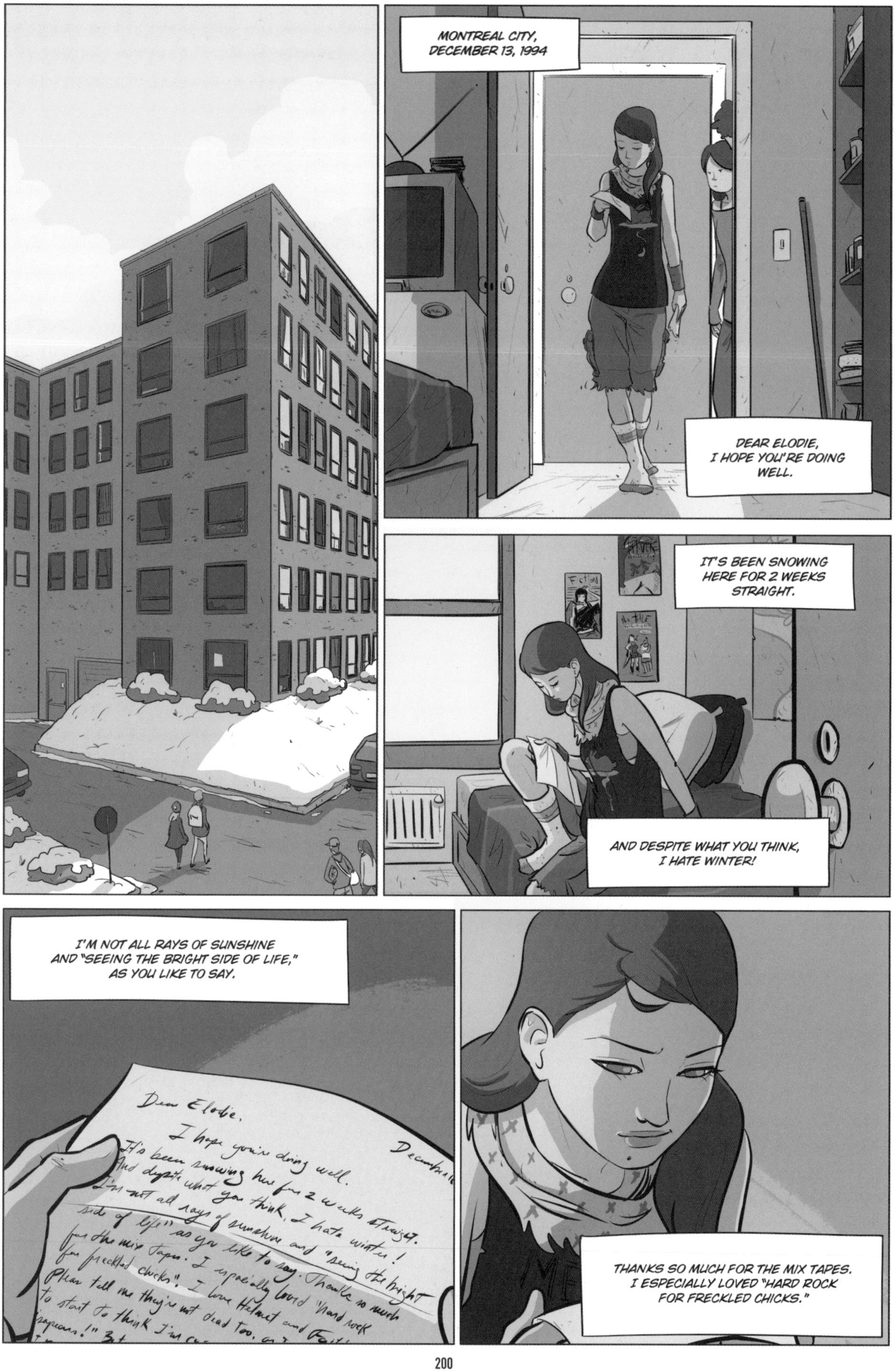
MONTREAL CITY, DECEMBER 13, 1994
DEAR ELODIE, I HOPE YOU'RE DOING WELL.
IT'S BEEN SNOWING HERE FOR 2 WEEKS STRAIGHT.
AND DESPITE WHAT YOU THINK, I HATE WINTER!
I'M NOT ALL RAYS OF SUNSHINE AND "SEEING THE BRIGHT SIDE OF LIFE," AS YOU LIKE TO SAY.
Dear Elodie,
I hope you're doing well.
It's been snowing here for 2 weeks straight.
THANKS SO MUCH FOR THE MIX TAPES. I ESPECIALLY LOVED "HARD ROCK FOR FRECKLED CHICKS."

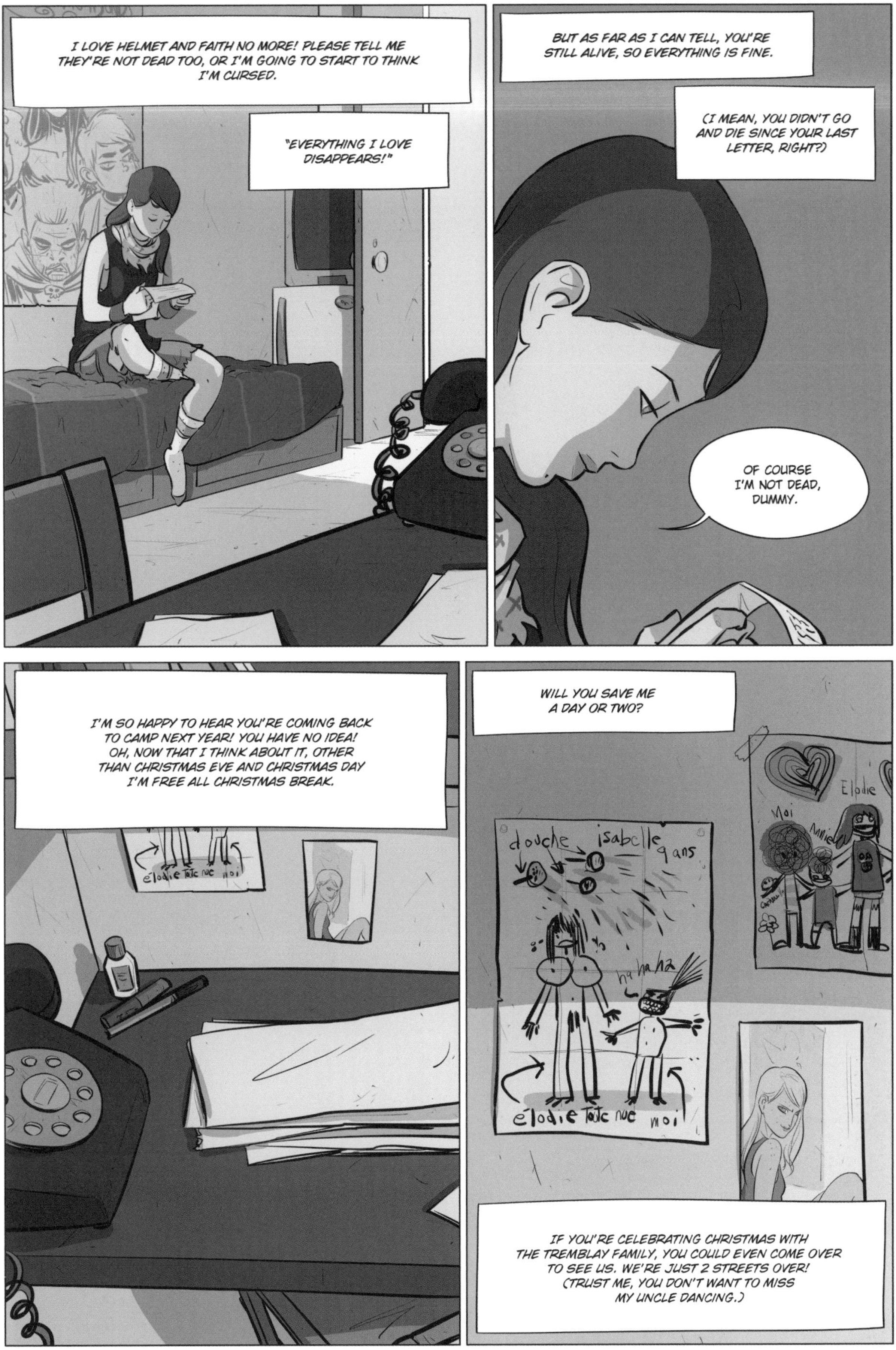
I LOVE HELMET AND FAITH NO MORE! PLEASE TELL ME THEY'RE NOT DEAD TOO, OR I'M GOING TO START TO THINK I'M CURSED.
"EVERYTHING I LOVE DISAPPEARS!"
BUT AS FAR AS I CAN TELL, YOU'RE STILL ALIVE, SO EVERYTHING IS FINE.
(I MEAN, YOU DIDN'T GO AND DIE SINCE YOUR LAST LETTER, RIGHT?)
OF COURSE I'M NOT DEAD, DUMMY.
I'M SO HAPPY TO HEAR YOU'RE COMING BACK TO CAMP NEXT YEAR! YOU HAVE NO IDEA! OH, NOW THAT I THINK ABOUT IT, OTHER THAN CHRISTMAS EVE AND CHRISTMAS DAY I'M FREE ALL CHRISTMAS BREAK.
WILL YOU SAVE ME A DAY OR TWO?
douche
isabelle 9 ans
ha ha ha
moi
Elodie
Moi
IF YOU'RE CELEBRATING CHRISTMAS WITH THE TREMBLAY FAMILY, YOU COULD EVEN COME OVER TO SEE US. WE'RE JUST 2 STREETS OVER! (TRUST ME, YOU DON'T WANT TO MISS MY UNCLE DANCING.)

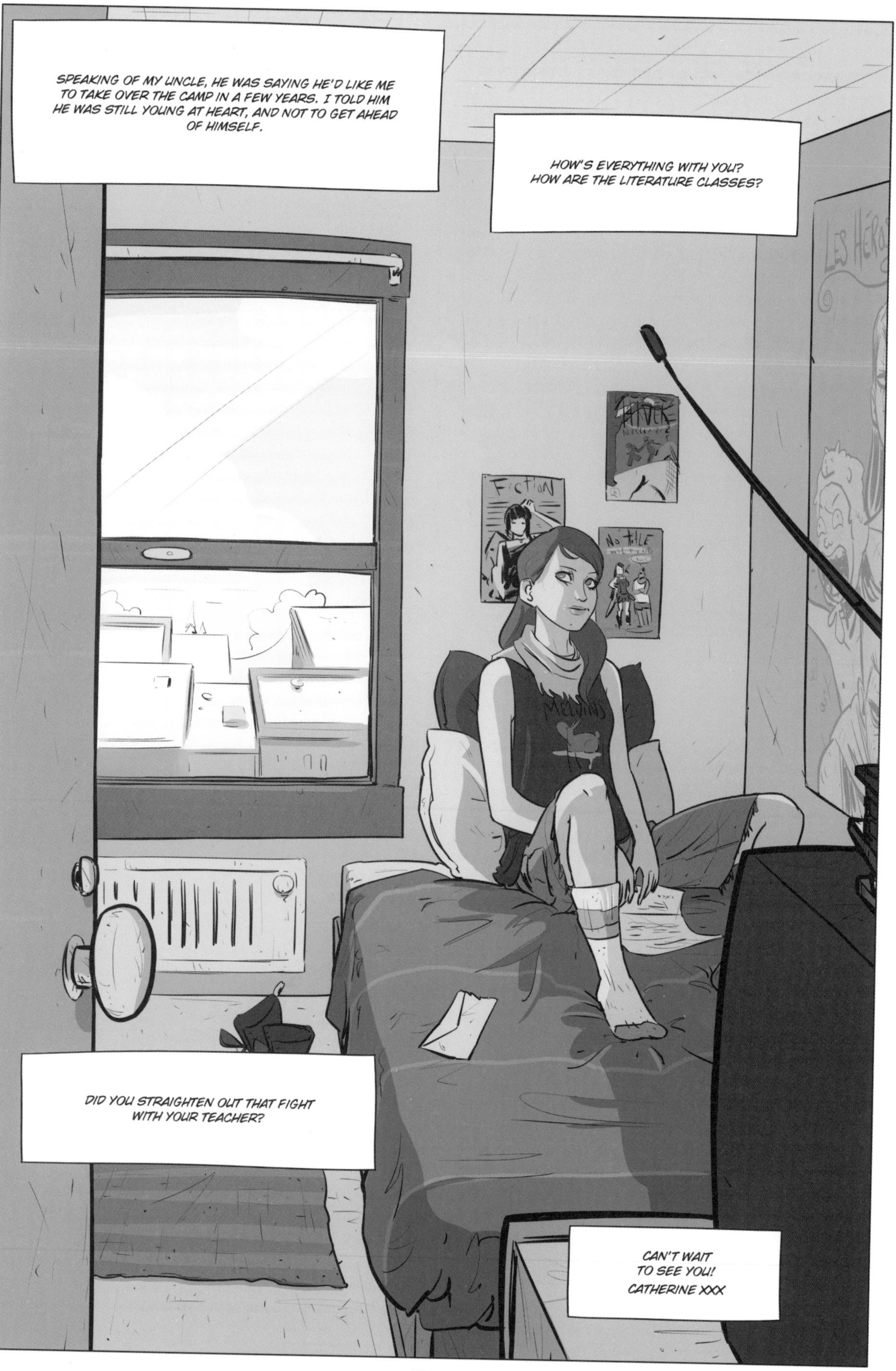
SPEAKING OF MY UNCLE, HE WAS SAYING HE'D LIKE ME TO TAKE OVER THE CAMP IN A FEW YEARS. I TOLD HIM HE WAS STILL YOUNG AT HEART, AND NOT TO GET AHEAD OF HIMSELF.
HOW'S EVERYTHING WITH YOU? HOW ARE THE LITERATURE CLASSES?
FICTION
NO TITLE
MELVINS
DID YOU STRAIGHTEN OUT THAT FIGHT WITH YOUR TEACHER?
CAN'T WAIT TO SEE YOU!
CATHERINE XXX

August 11, 1994
The director is always
in dire need of attention ...

August 13, 1994
Smooch attack: Complete.

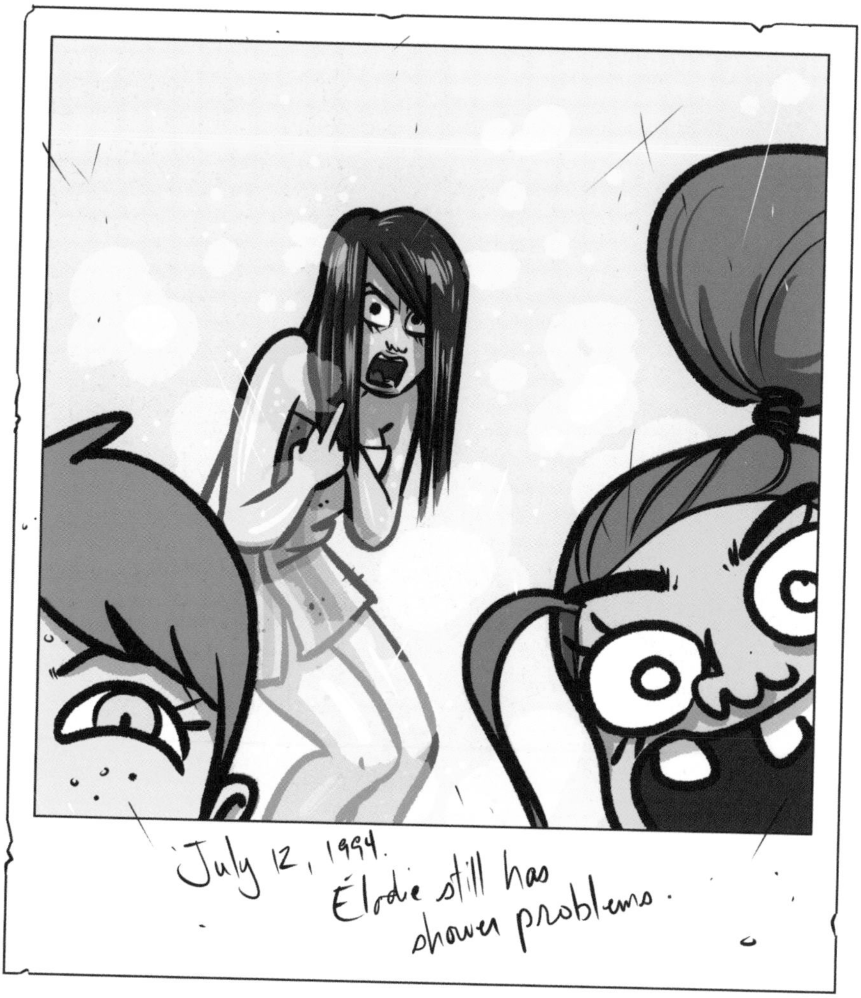
July 12, 1994.
Élodie still has shower problems.

August 4, 1994.

Who knew Magalie had a soft side underneath that demonic aura?